REMARKABLY
ruby

TERRI LIBENSON

BALZER + BRAY
An Imprint of HarperCollins*Publishers*

Balzer + Bray is an imprint of HarperCollins Publishers.

Remarkably Ruby
Copyright © 2022 by Terri Libenson
All rights reserved. Printed in the United States of America.
No part of this book may be used or reproduced in any manner whatsoever without
written permission except in the case of brief quotations embodied in critical articles
and reviews. For information address HarperCollins Children's Books, a division of
HarperCollins Publishers, 195 Broadway, New York, NY 10007.
www.harpercollinschildrens.com

Library of Congress Control Number: 2021950856
ISBN 978-0-06-313919-0 (hardcover) — ISBN 978-0-06-313918-3 (pbk.)

Typography by Terri Libenson and Laura Mock
22 23 24 25 26 PC/WOR 10 9 8 7 6 5 4 3 2 1
❖
First Edition

To my remarkable readers:
I'm always grateful

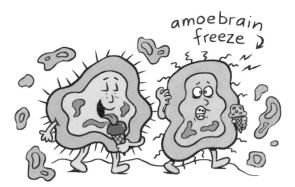

PROLOGUE: RUBY

I'm not what you would call a people person.

Circle the thing that doesn't belong:

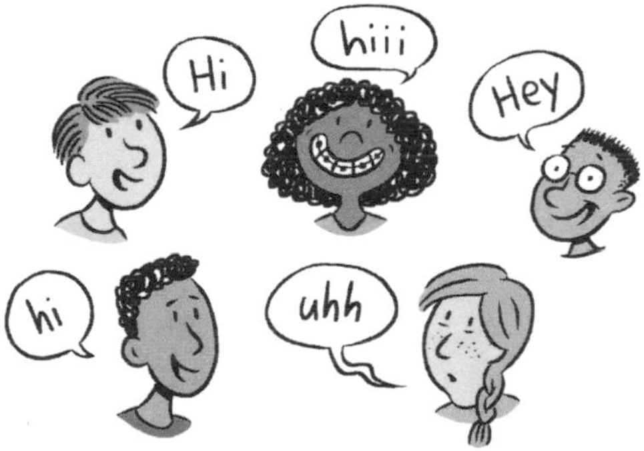
Hi
hiii
Hey
hi
uhh

It's not that I don't try. I do. But most of the time, making friends in middle school is a huge chore. I don't have the greatest social skills.

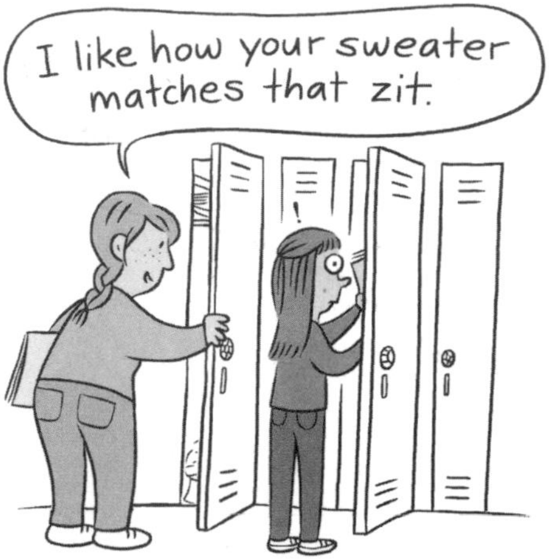
I like how your sweater matches that zit.
!

I also don't have a lot in common with the kids around here. Most of them are into things I'm not, like dances, social media, and sports.

Me?

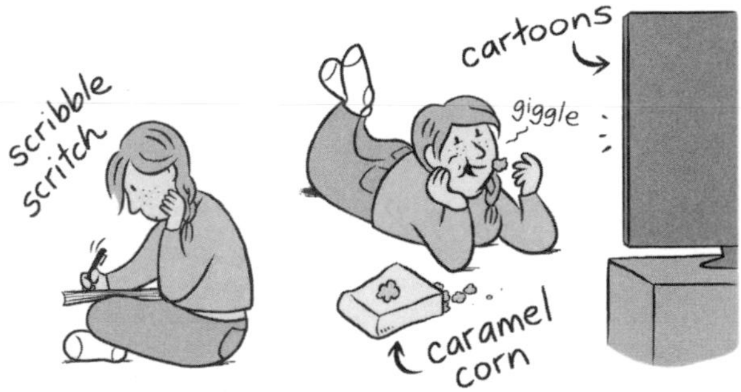
scribble
scritch
cartoons
giggle
caramel corn

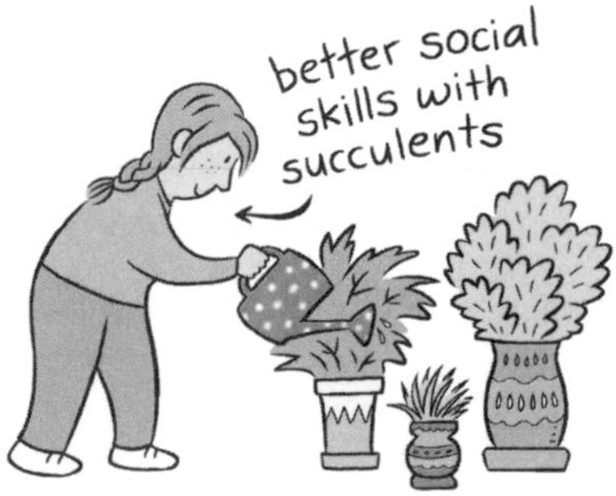
better social skills with succulents

Back in grade school, it was another story. There were a couple kids I was close to. And yep, they were also a little different, which helped.

But one moved away in fifth grade. And since I didn't get a phone until this year, we didn't really stay in touch.

our pen pal agreement
was one-sided

And the other . . . well, we had a falling-out.
I'll get to that later. In the meantime, it's just:

me, myself, and I

Déjà vu

I'm mostly okay with it. People don't pick on me or anything. They leave me alone.

helps that I'm the same height as some of my teachers

Besides, my mom says that the most important thing is to be "a strong, independent person." So that's what I'm attempting to do. And I think I'm succeeding.

scribble scribble scritch

got the "independent" part nailed

On the outside, anyway.

RUBY

It all began in fourth grade. That's when I shot up.
  And by "shot up," I mean "grew to the size of our money tree."

both have braids
and tall trunks

  I love that tree. It's supposed to bring good fortune. (I'm still waiting on that.) My mom keeps it in the corner of the living room* near a window. So that it "thrives."

*If your house is older, you probably have a formal living room—which, in our house, never gets used except at midnight, when our cat gets the "zoomies."

6

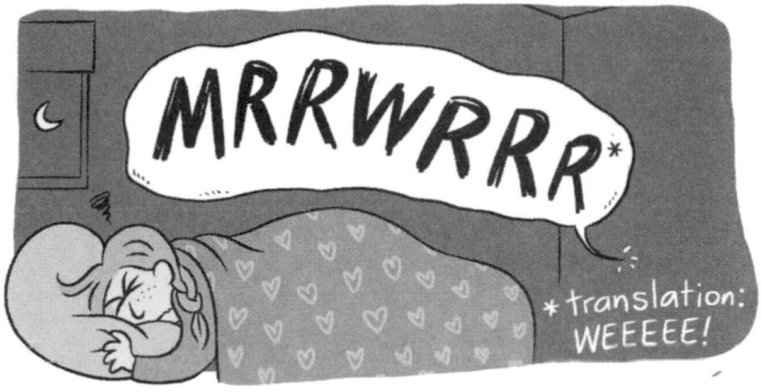
MRRWRRR*
* translation:
WEEEEE!

We have a ton of plants in that living room. Our cat, Buford, likes to hide behind them. He probably imagines he's a jungle tiger, ready to pounce.

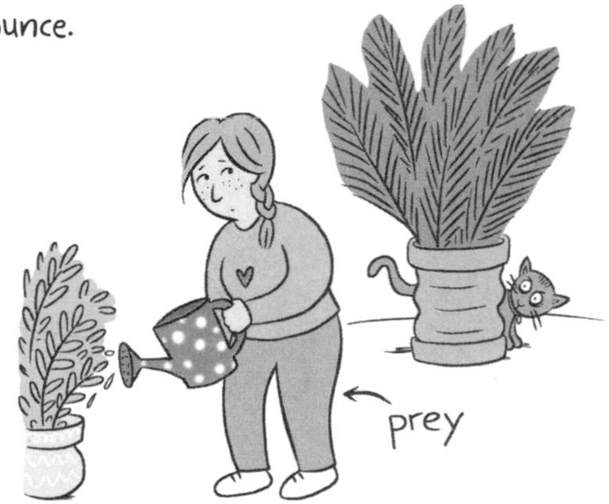
prey

I'm in charge of watering the plants. That's my main chore and I'm good at it.

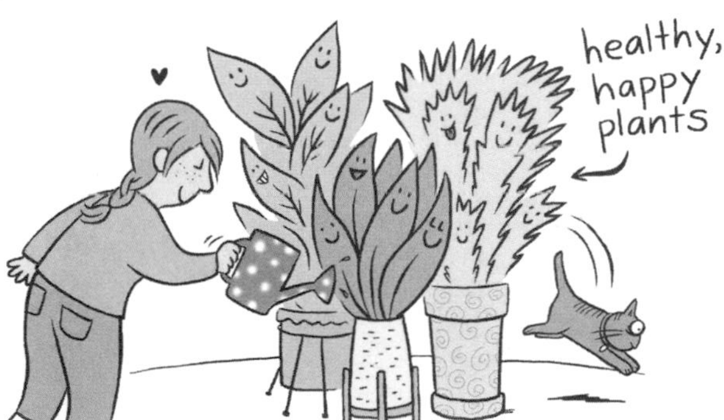
healthy,
happy
plants

I find it kinda funny that when a plant gets nice and big, it's "robust" and "thriving." But when I did . . .

(105th percentile)

self-conscious

sticks out

It makes my "aloneness" more noticeable.

hard not to notice a tree among shrubs

Speaking of alone . . . right now, I'm in the restroom at school by myself. It's early, right before homeroom. My stomach is kind of bugging me. That happens sometimes. I've been to the doctor. She calls it a "nervous stomach," which is a nice way of saying what I really have:

IBS:
Irritable
Bowel
Syndrome

or as I call it, "Irritating
Bathroom Struggles"

I've heard some kids call me "Baked Bean Girl," which is another way of putting it. It's 'cause I once had to rush to the restroom after a lunch of . . . well, you get the idea. I told my mom, who thought it was funny and wanted to make me a T-shirt:

NOTORIOUS

BEANZ

BBG

I didn't think it was that funny.

Anyway, I deal with it. I've stopped announcing my latest meals, anyway. And stopped eating stuff on the doctor's "do not ingest" list, like:

MOVE! Spicy breakfast burrito!

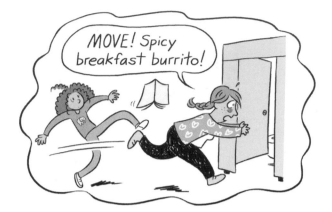

I leave the stall and try to find an open sink. It's not easy. This is the busiest restroom time, other than after lunch. It really bugs me that girls come in and hog the sinks to put on makeup and brush their hair and stuff, when there are people who actually need to wash up. It's not like they can't get ready at their lockers.

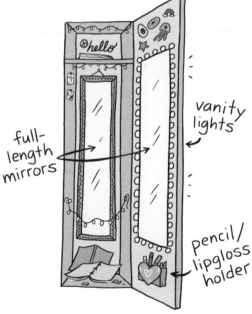

hello
full-length mirrors
vanity lights
pencil/lipgloss holder

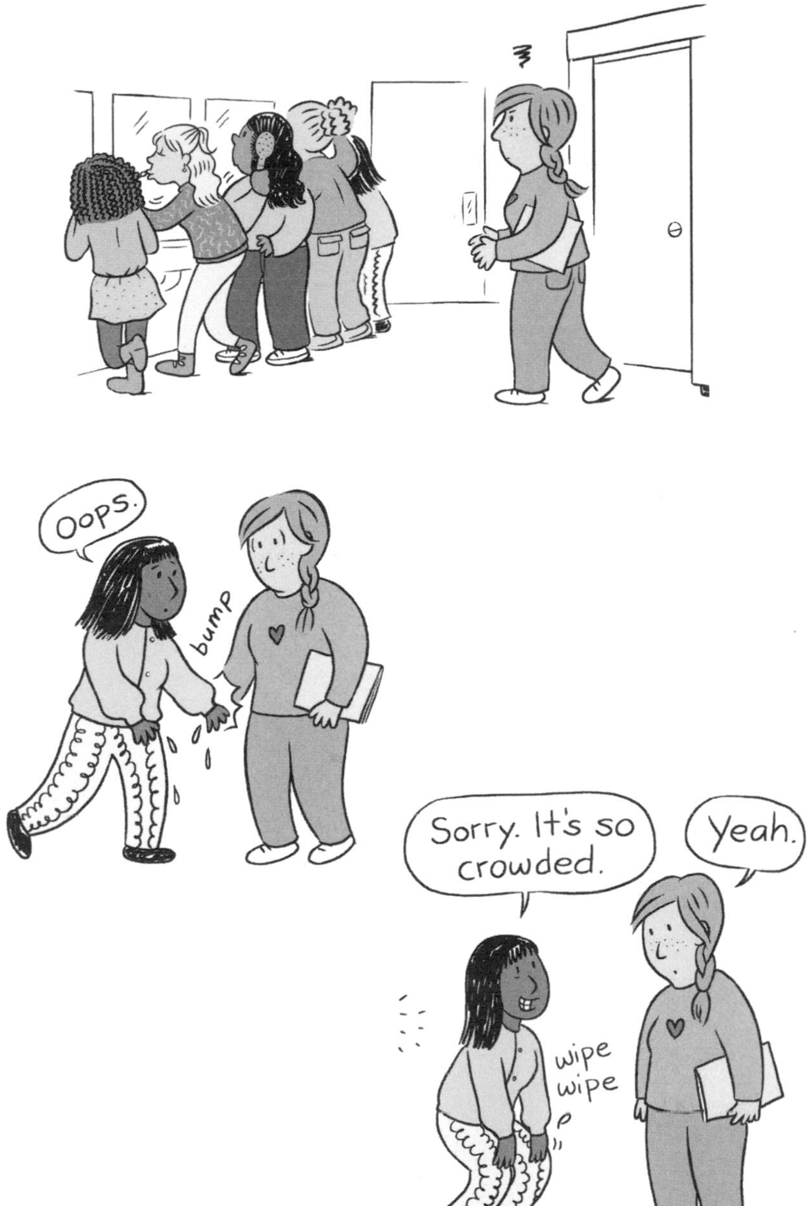
Oops.
bump
Sorry. It's so crowded.
Yeah.
wipe wipe

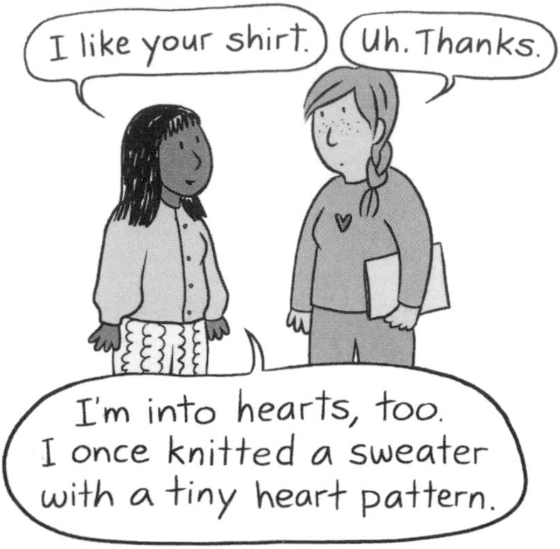
I like your shirt.
Uh. Thanks.
I'm into hearts, too. I once knitted a sweater with a tiny heart pattern.

I don't know what to say to that. Sarah Reyes is really nice—one of the nicer kids in my grade—but it's not like I know anything about making clothes.

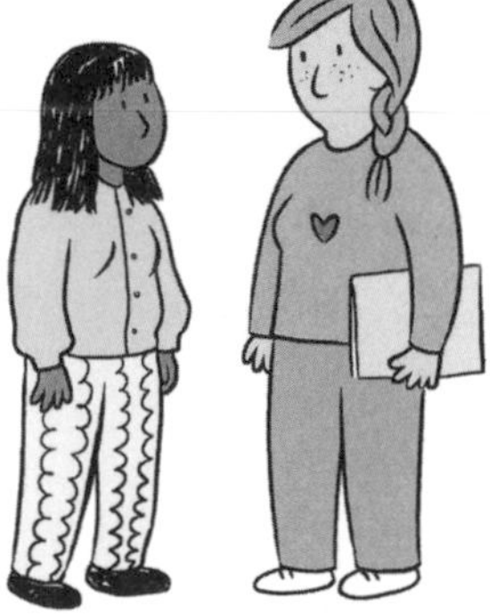

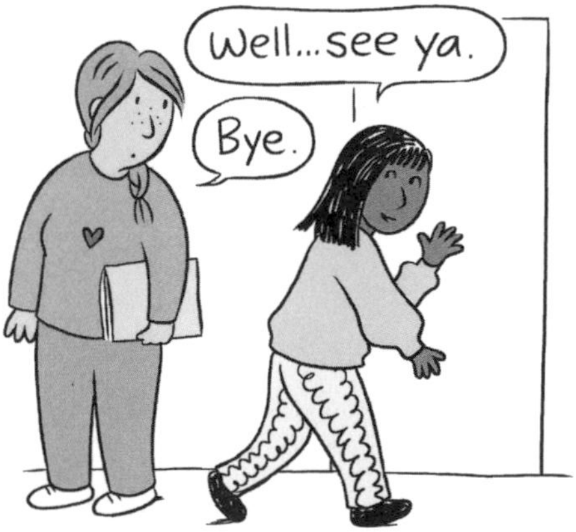
Well...see ya.
Bye.

I finally think of something to say.

Hearts are tool.

She looks confused, smiles awkwardly, and leaves.

I meant to say, "Hearts are totally cool." Ughh!

I finally find a sink. A girl makes room, looking a little scared of me.

Being bigger than most kids sometimes has that effect on people, mainly sixth graders who don't know me. Doesn't help that I've accidentally knocked a few of them down.

SLAM WHACK WOK WOMP

I leave the restroom and head to homeroom. Mrs. Winn, my favorite teacher (English), is walking in my direction.

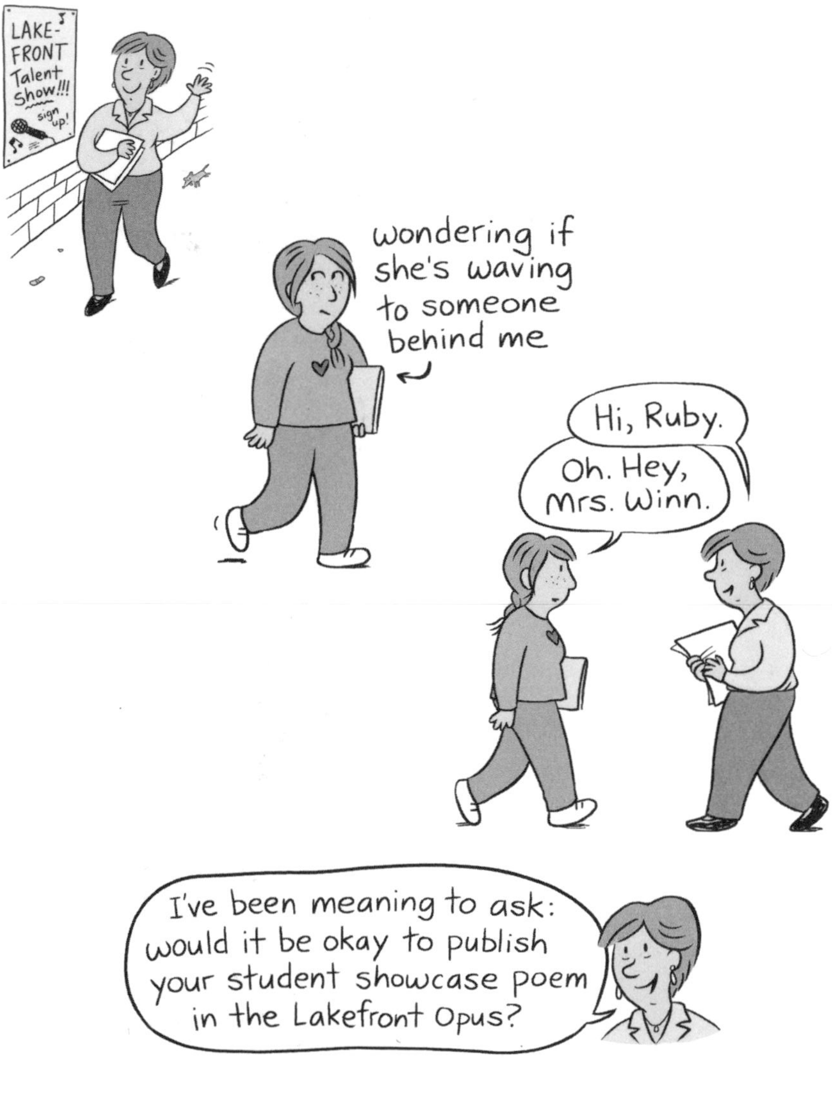
LAKE-FRONT Talent Show!!!
sign up!
wondering if she's waving to someone behind me
Hi, Ruby.
Oh. Hey, Mrs. Winn.
I've been meaning to ask: would it be okay to publish your student showcase poem in the Lakefront Opus?

That's the school's art and literary magazine. Mrs. Winn always asks me and a bunch of other kids to submit.

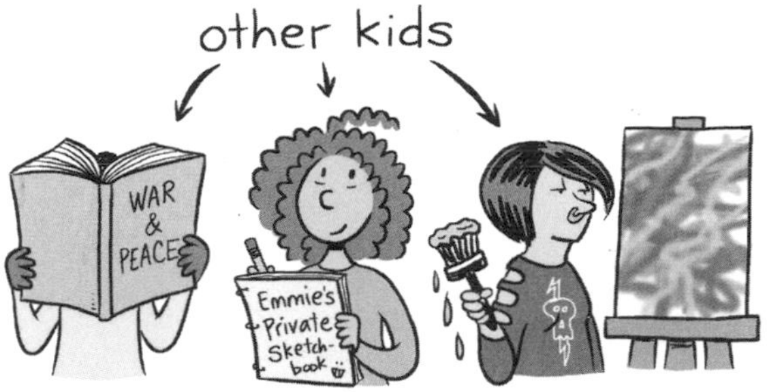
other kids
WAR & PEACE
Emmie's Private Sketch-book

A few months ago, Mrs. Winn encouraged me to enter my poem (an English assignment) in the Student Showcase. That's a big event around here. Kids show off their history and science projects, stories, and artwork. There's a contest for each category.

An' guess what?

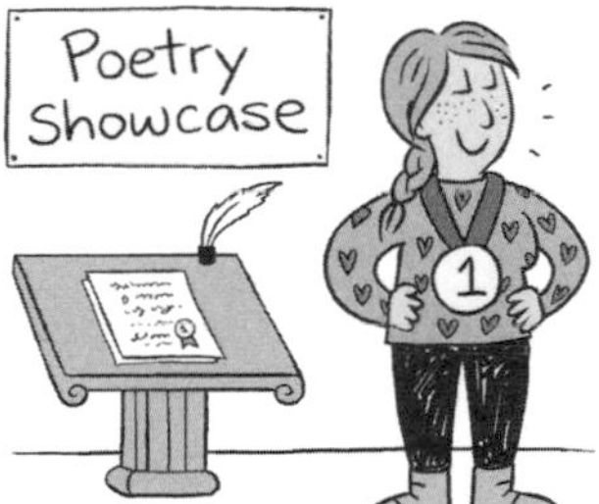
Poetry Showcase
1

Yep! I won the poetry contest. I was totally shocked. I didn't even want to enter in the first place.

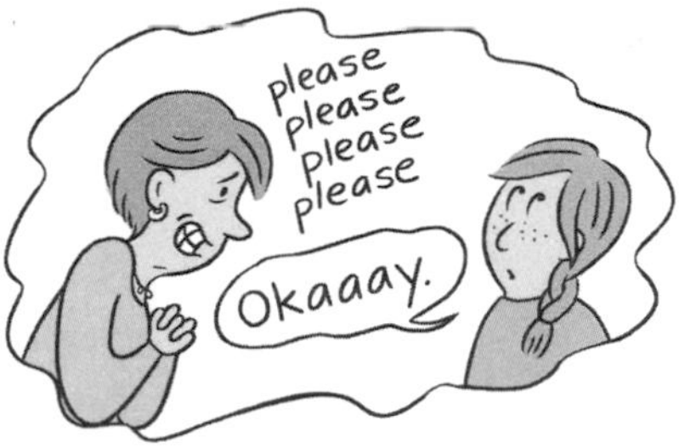
please please please please
Okaaay.

The thing is, I don't like attention. It just makes . . . well, me . . . that much more obvious to everyone.

But now I'm glad she entered it. 'Cause it made me want to write even more.

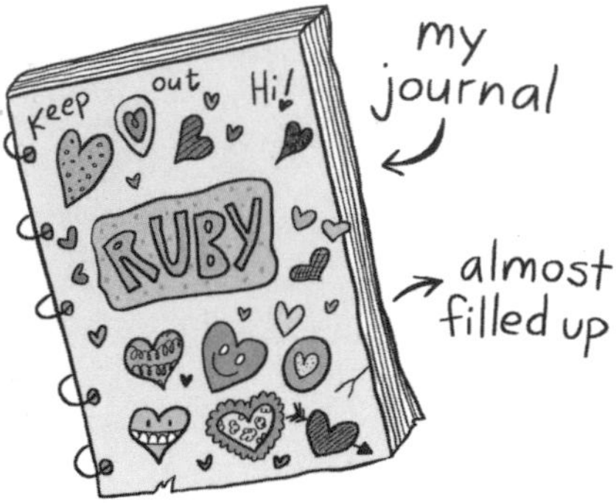
my journal
Keep out
Hi!
RUBY
almost filled up

I write all the time now. I mean, I always wrote in my journal and stuff, but then I started turning some of those journal entries into actual things.

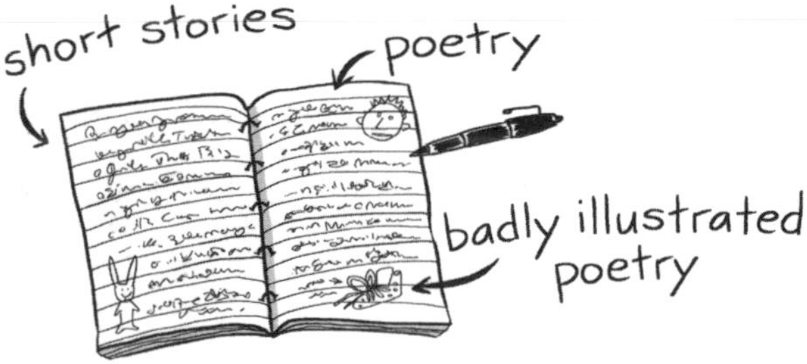
short stories
poetry
badly illustrated poetry

Usually they're about feelings, but sometimes they're also about little things I notice. Things a lot of people don't pay attention to. (When you're alone a lot, that's what happens.)

Like shoelaces.

You can tell a lot about a person by how they tie their shoes.

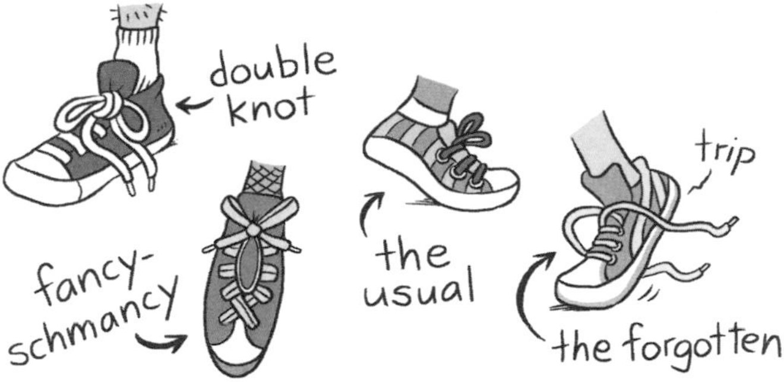
double knot
fancy-schmancy
the usual
trip
the forgotten

I once wrote an entire poem comparing people to shoelaces using what Mrs. Winn calls:

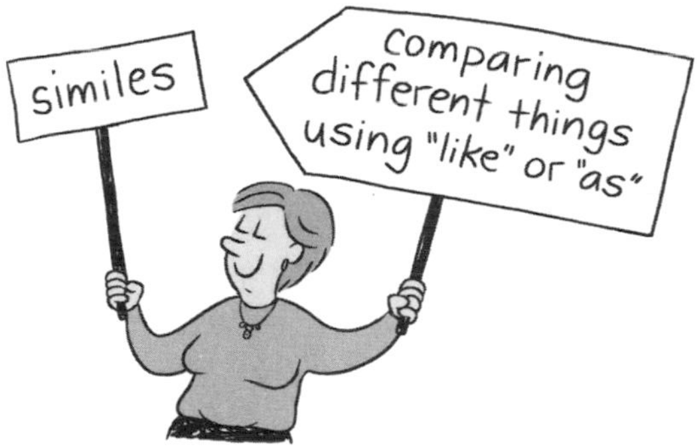
similes
comparing different things using "like" or "as"

As for the Showcase poem—I wrote that about making patterns with my fingers on my fogged-up kitchen window in the morning. I really do that. It kind of calms me.

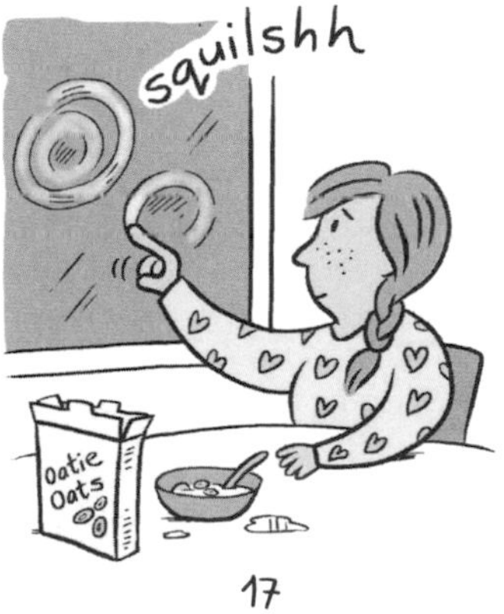
squilshh
Oatie Oats

And as my nervous stomach knows, I could use some calming.

Uh. Sure.

Great, Ruby! That poem will be perfect for the magazine.

She leaves and I head for homeroom.

Hey.
Hey.

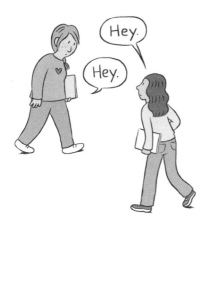

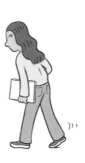

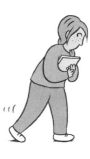

I feel my stomach act up again, but I ignore it.

I walk into homeroom and sit at my usual desk in the second-to-last row. Lindsay Donsky and Kyle Duncan sit in front of me and secretly text each other (as usual). Quiet Girl (Emmie Douglass) sketches away in her notebook. She quickly holds it up to show her best friend, Brianna, who sits across the room. I can't see the drawing, but Brianna giggles and gives her a thumbs-up.

SUPER
DUPER
advanced
MATH

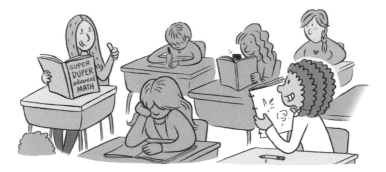

Sometimes I pretend I'm like them.

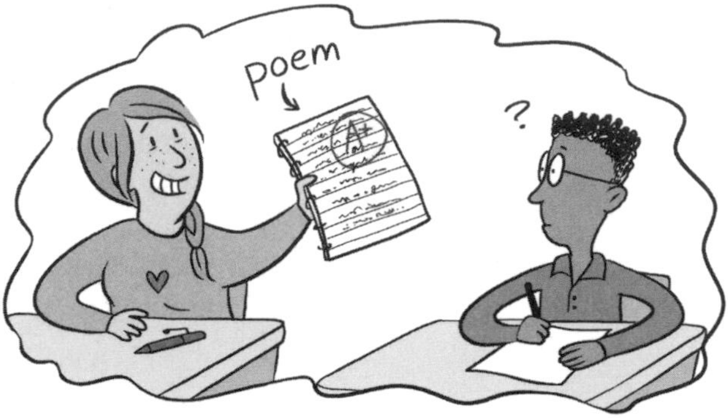
poem
?

But this time I don't. Instead, I take out my social studies notebook so I can finish an assignment, and I tell myself the same thing that I do every morning at this time:

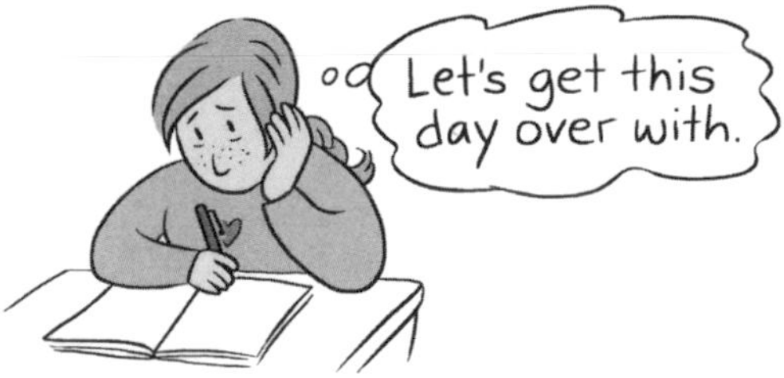
Let's get this day over with.

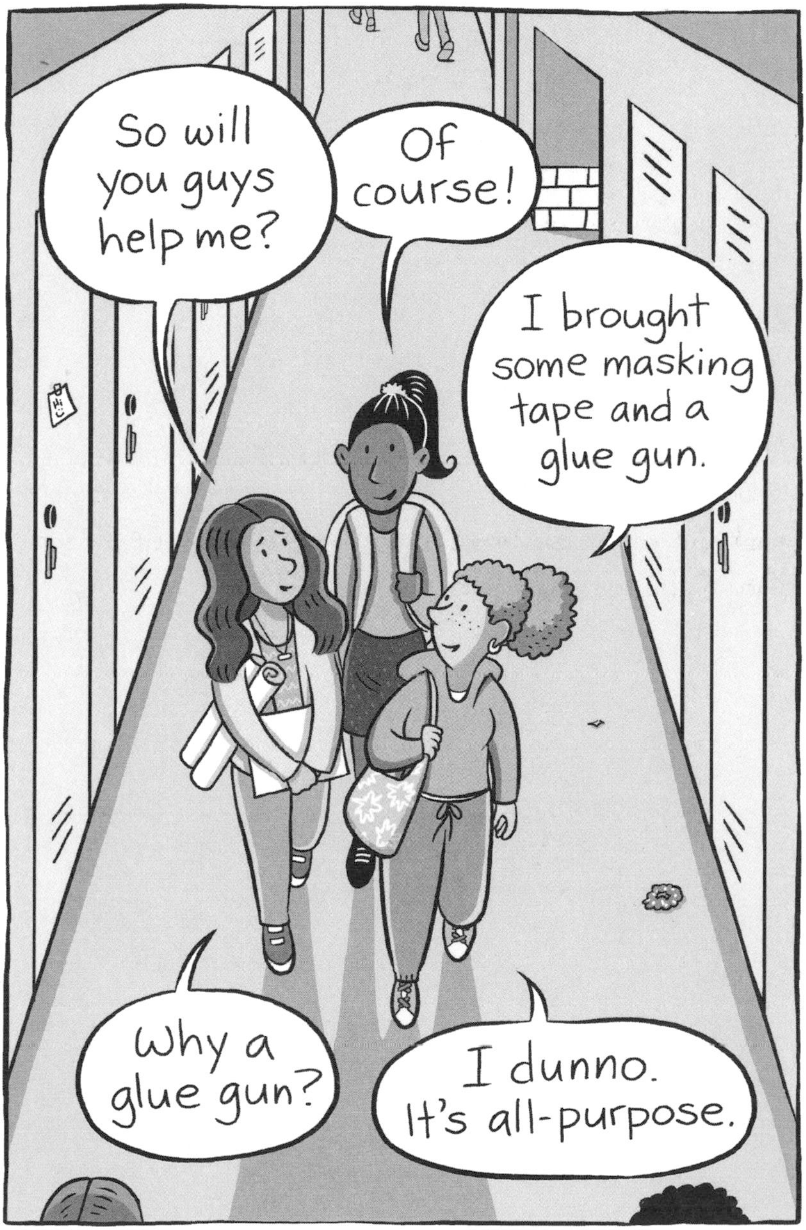
So will you guys help me?
Of course!
I brought some masking tape and a glue gun.
Why a glue gun?
I dunno. It's all-purpose.

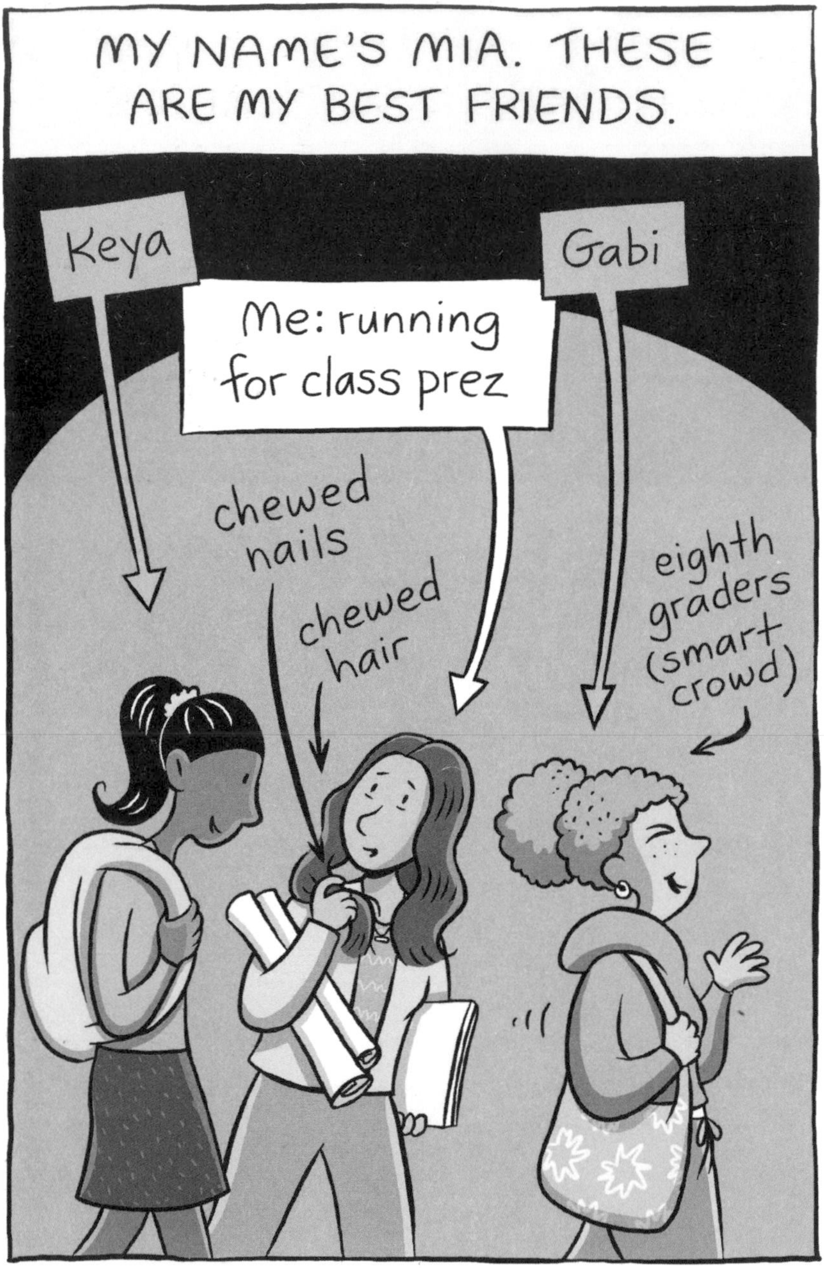
MY NAME'S MIA. THESE ARE MY BEST FRIENDS.
Keya
Gabi
Me: running for class prez
chewed nails
chewed hair
eighth graders (smart crowd)

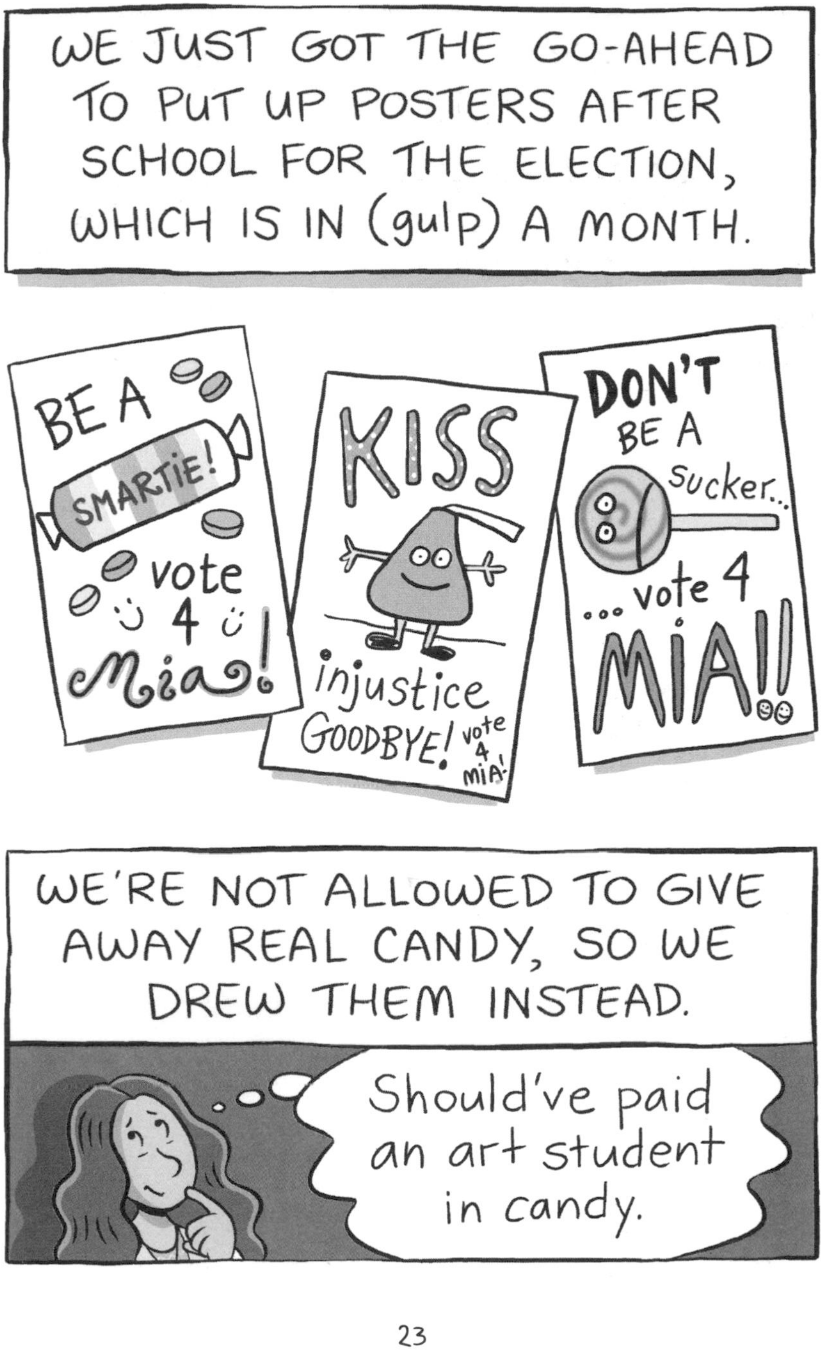
WE JUST GOT THE GO-AHEAD TO PUT UP POSTERS AFTER SCHOOL FOR THE ELECTION, WHICH IS IN (gulp) A MONTH.
BE A SMARTIE! vote 4 Mia!
KISS injustice GOODBYE! vote 4 MIA!
DON'T BE A sucker... ...vote 4 MIA!!
WE'RE NOT ALLOWED TO GIVE AWAY REAL CANDY, SO WE DREW THEM INSTEAD.
Should've paid an art student in candy.

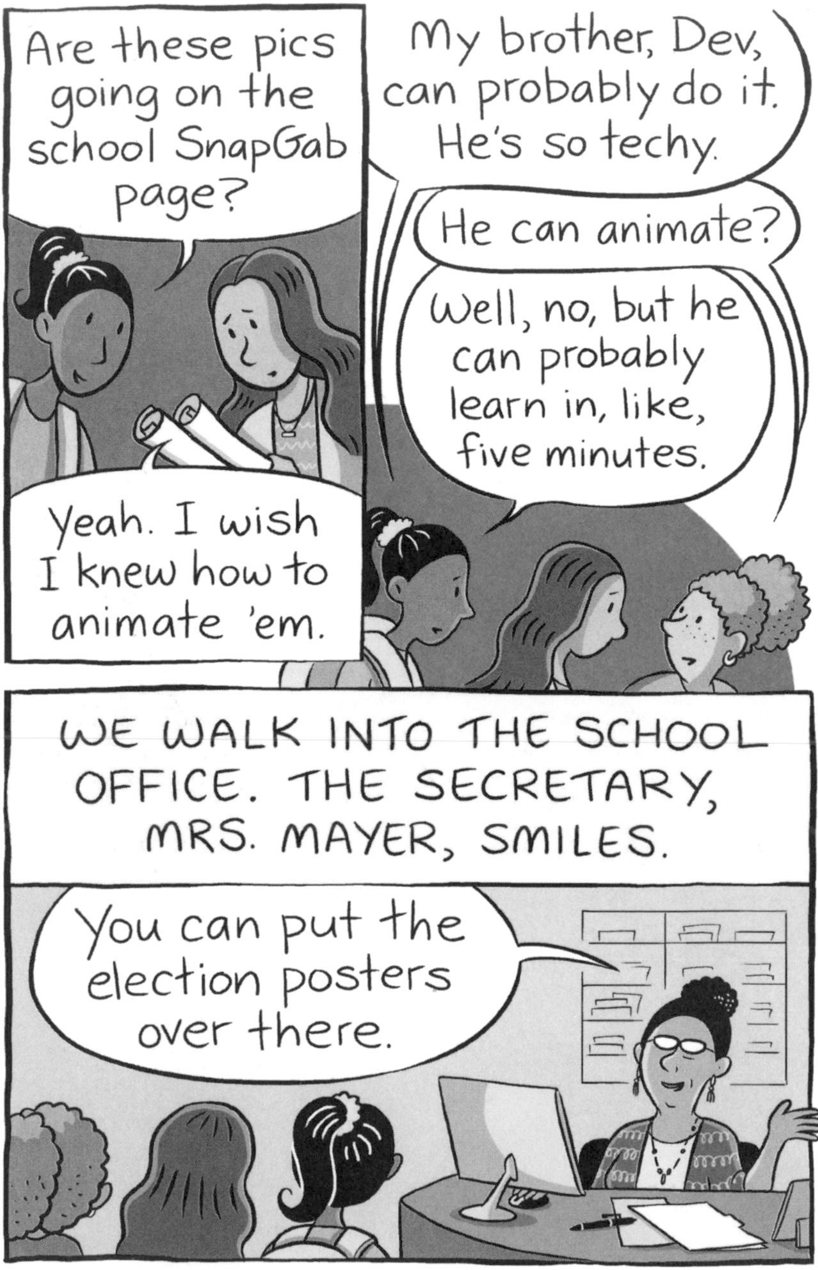
Are these pics going on the school SnapGab page?
Yeah. I wish I knew how to animate 'em.
My brother, Dev, can probably do it. He's so techy.
He can animate?
Well, no, but he can probably learn in, like, five minutes.
WE WALK INTO THE SCHOOL OFFICE. THE SECRETARY, MRS. MAYER, SMILES.
You can put the election posters over there.

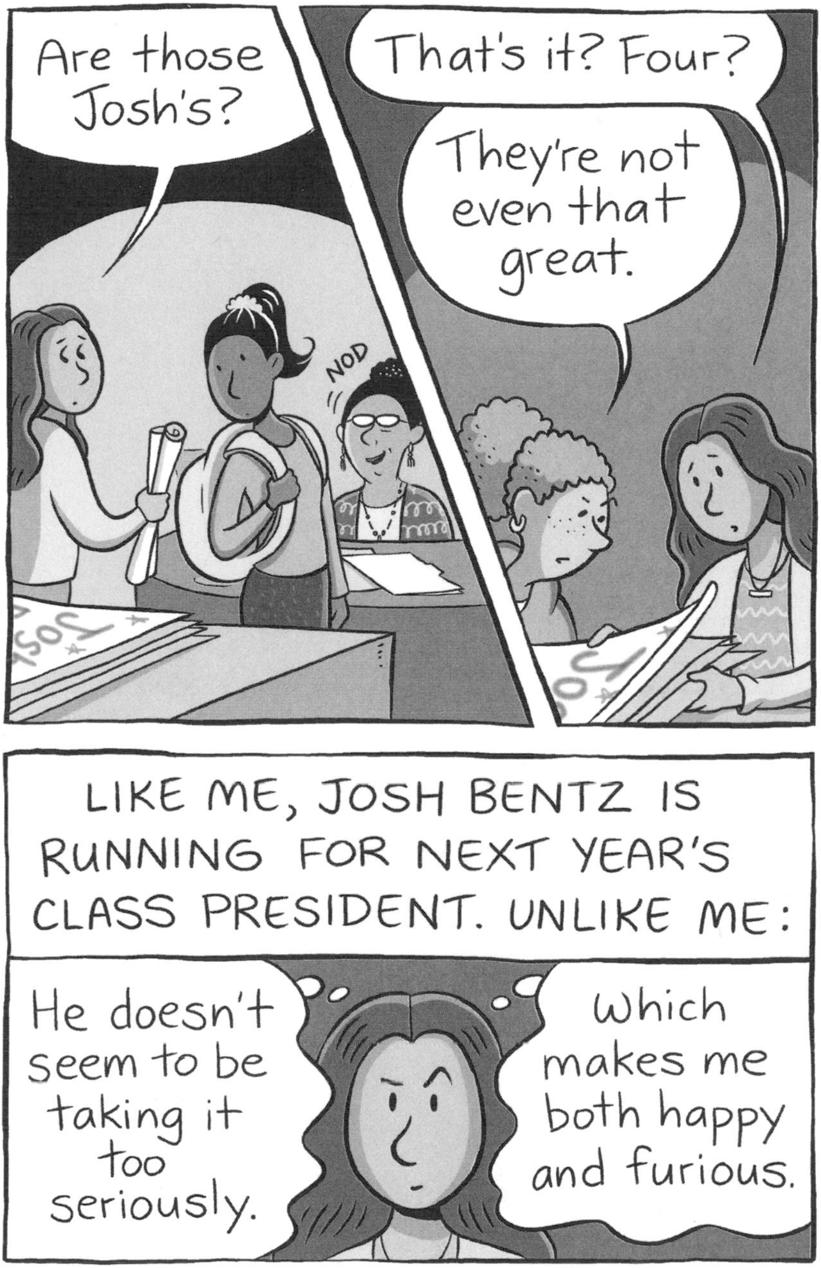
Are those Josh's?
NOD
That's it? Four?
They're not even that great.
LIKE ME, JOSH BENTZ IS RUNNING FOR NEXT YEAR'S CLASS PRESIDENT. UNLIKE ME:
He doesn't seem to be taking it too seriously.
Which makes me both happy and furious.

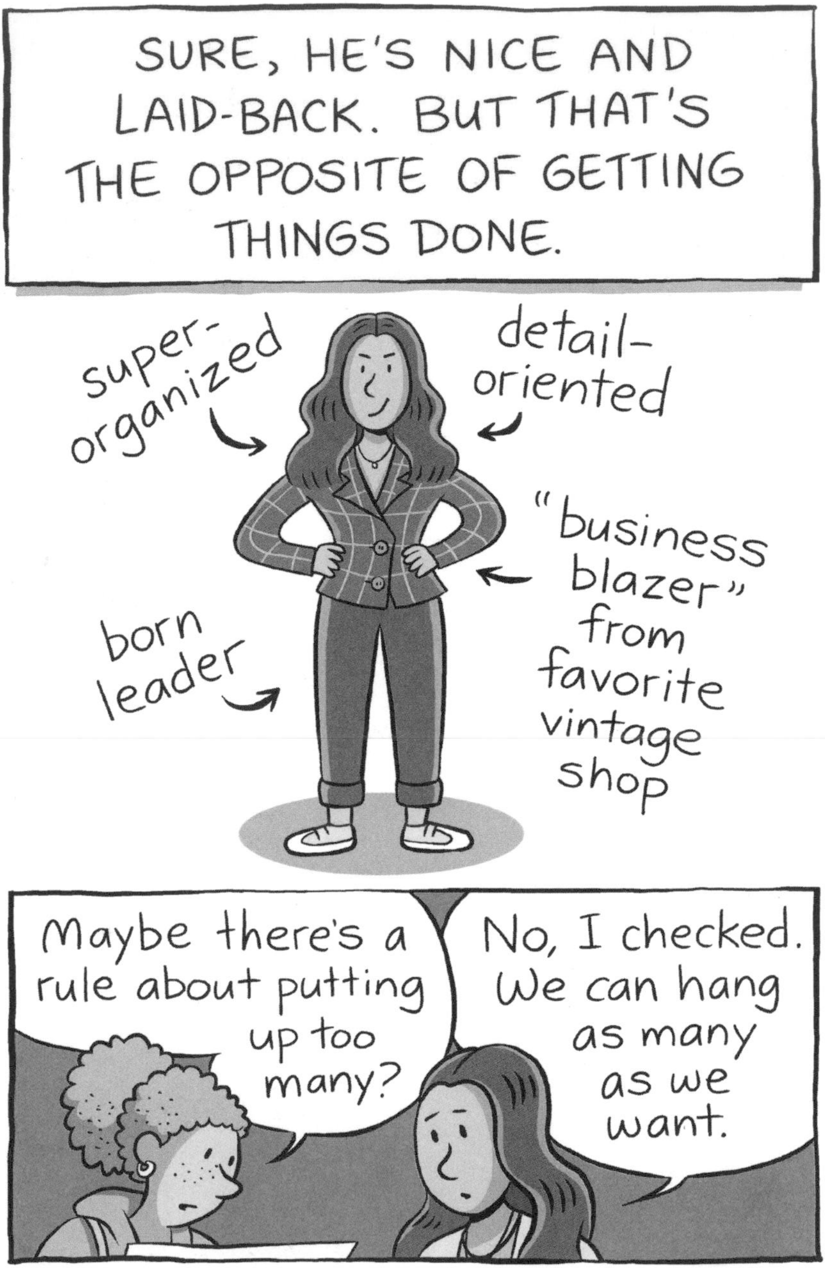
SURE, HE'S NICE AND LAID-BACK. BUT THAT'S THE OPPOSITE OF GETTING THINGS DONE.
super-organized
detail-oriented
"business blazer" from favorite vintage shop
born leader
Maybe there's a rule about putting up too many?
No, I checked. We can hang as many as we want.

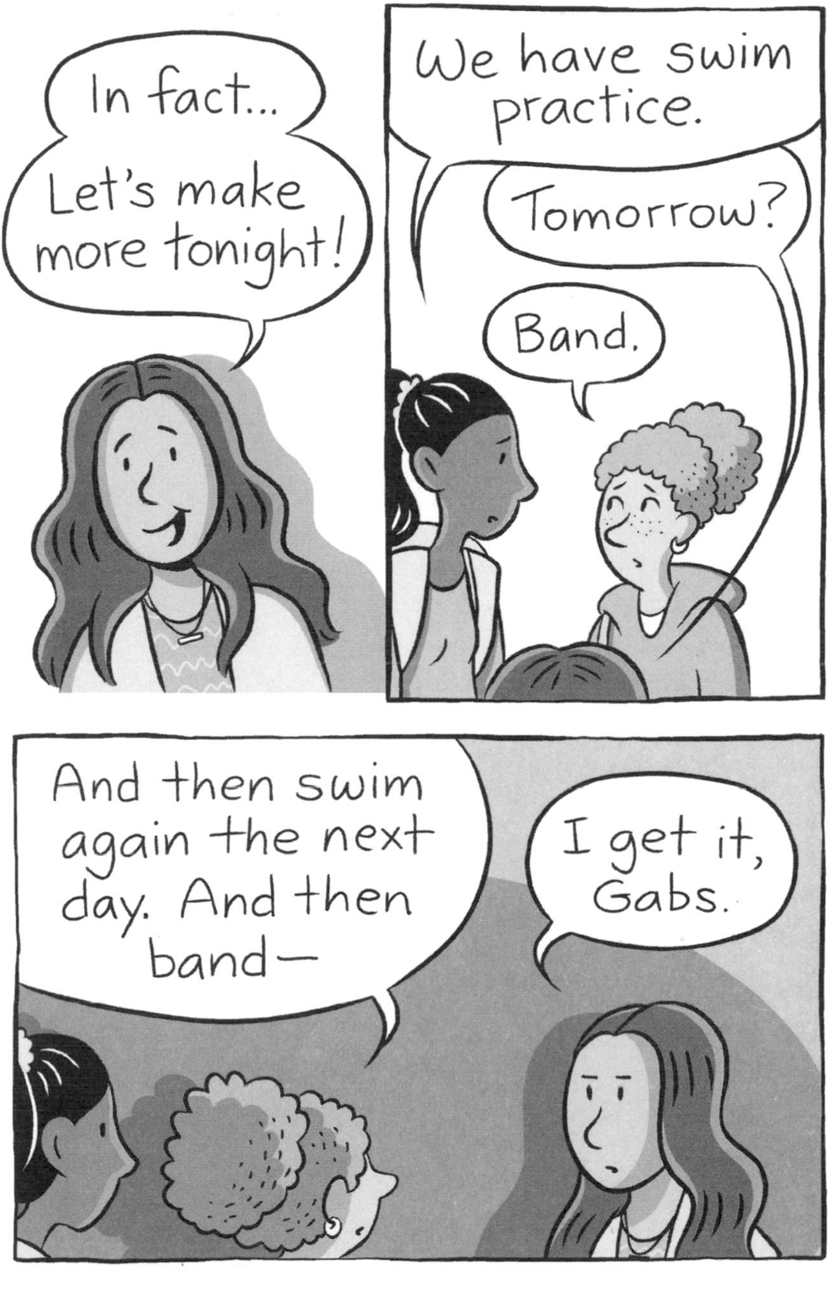
In fact...
Let's make more tonight!
We have swim practice.
Tomorrow?
Band.
And then swim again the next day. And then band—
I get it, Gabs.

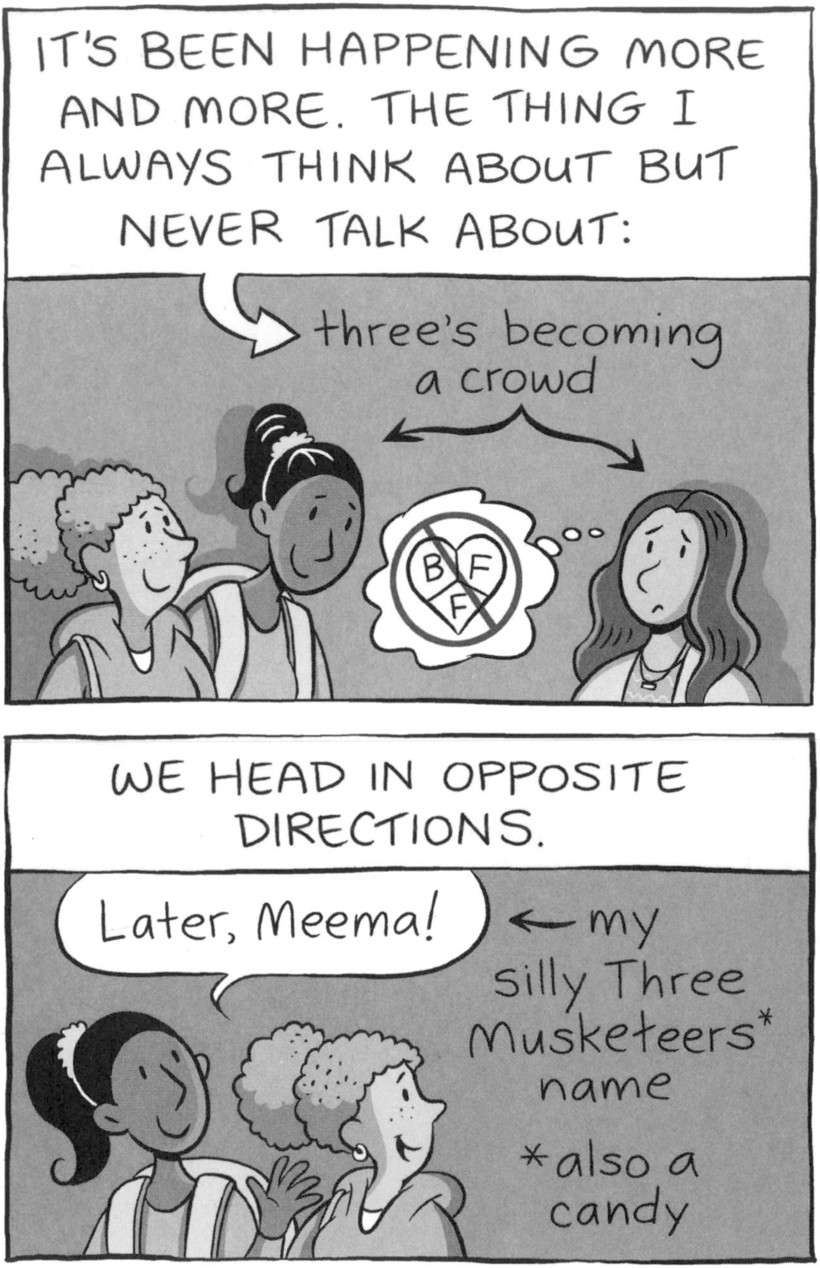
IT'S BEEN HAPPENING MORE AND MORE. THE THING I ALWAYS THINK ABOUT BUT NEVER TALK ABOUT:
three's becoming a crowd
BFF
WE HEAD IN OPPOSITE DIRECTIONS.
Later, Meema!
← my silly Three Musketeers* name
*also a candy

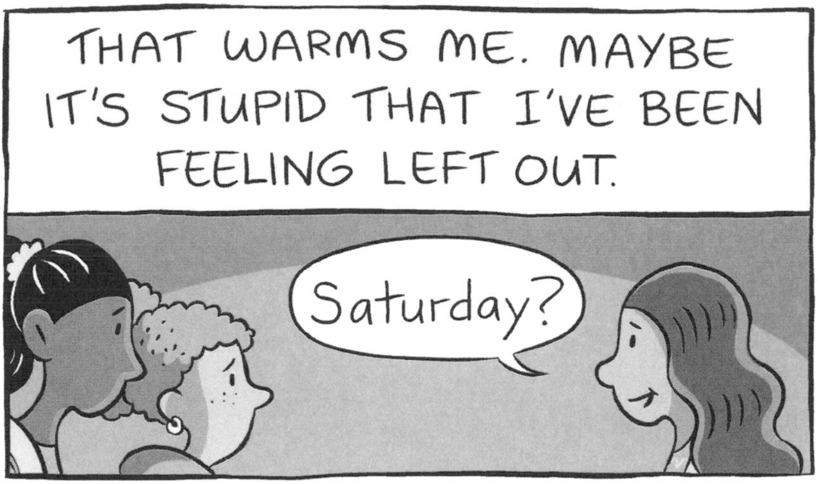
THAT WARMS ME. MAYBE IT'S STUPID THAT I'VE BEEN FEELING LEFT OUT.
Saturday?

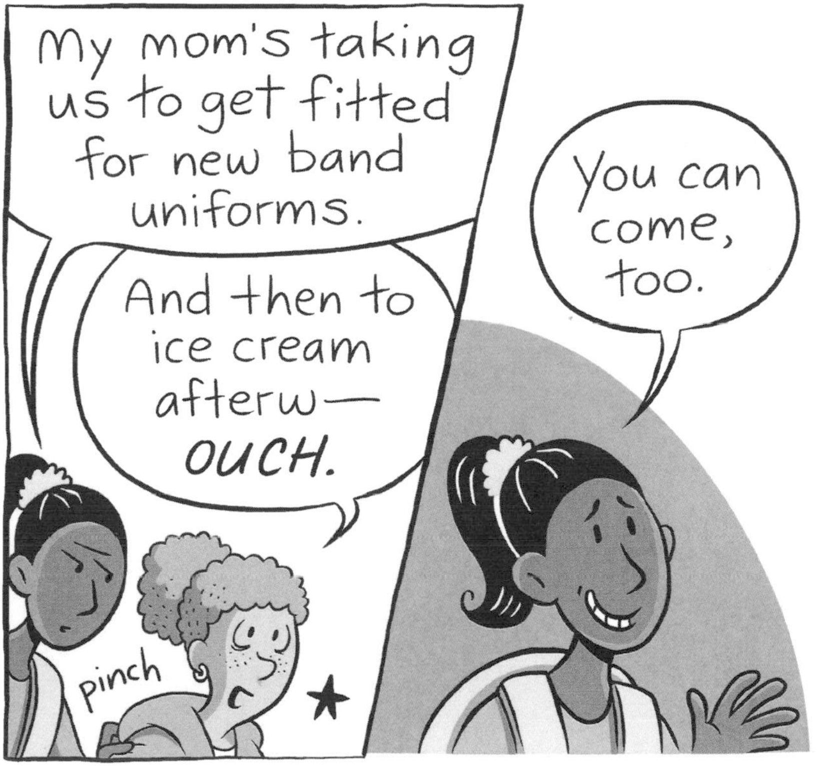
My mom's taking us to get fitted for new band uniforms.
And then to ice cream afterw— OUCH.
pinch
You can come, too.

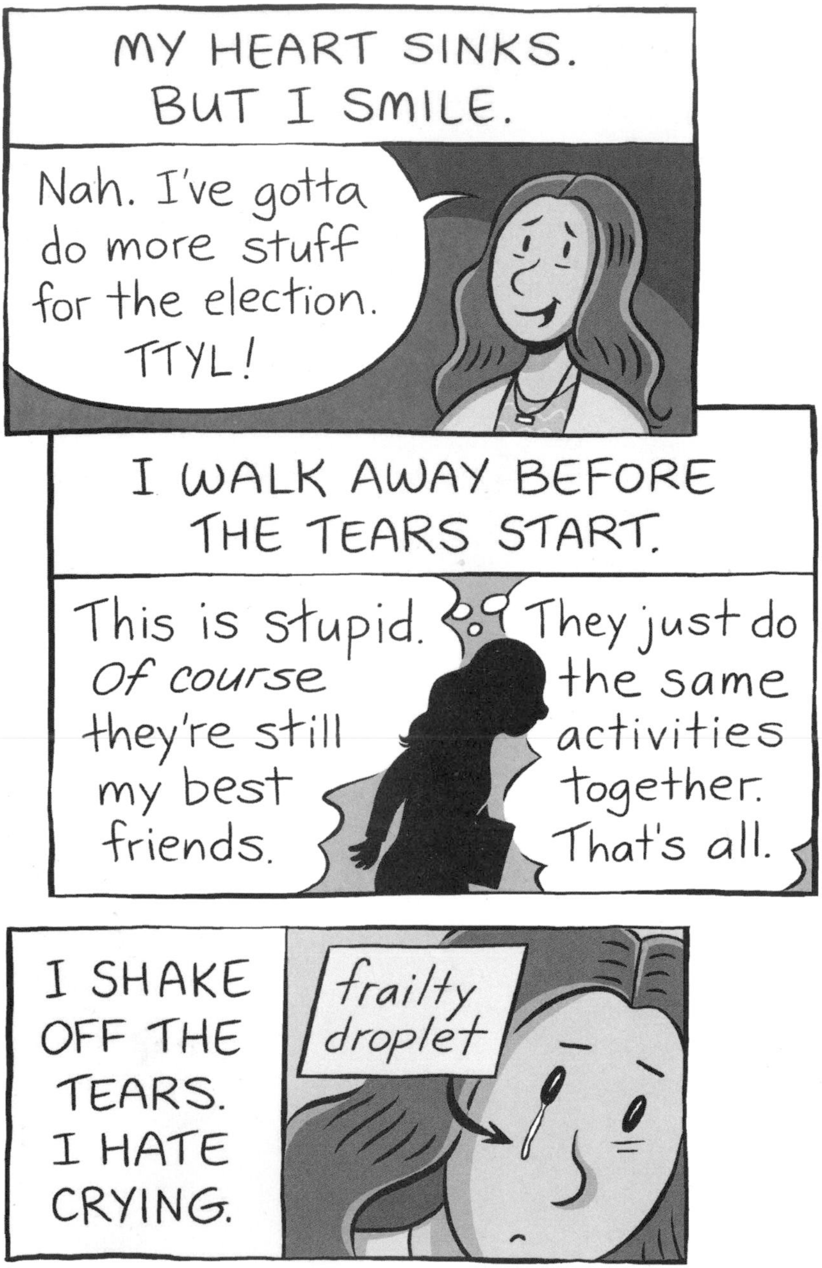

MY HEART SINKS. BUT I SMILE.
Nah. I've gotta do more stuff for the election. TTYL!
I WALK AWAY BEFORE THE TEARS START.
This is stupid. *Of course* they're still my best friends.
They just do the same activities together. That's all.
I SHAKE OFF THE TEARS. I HATE CRYING.
frailty droplet

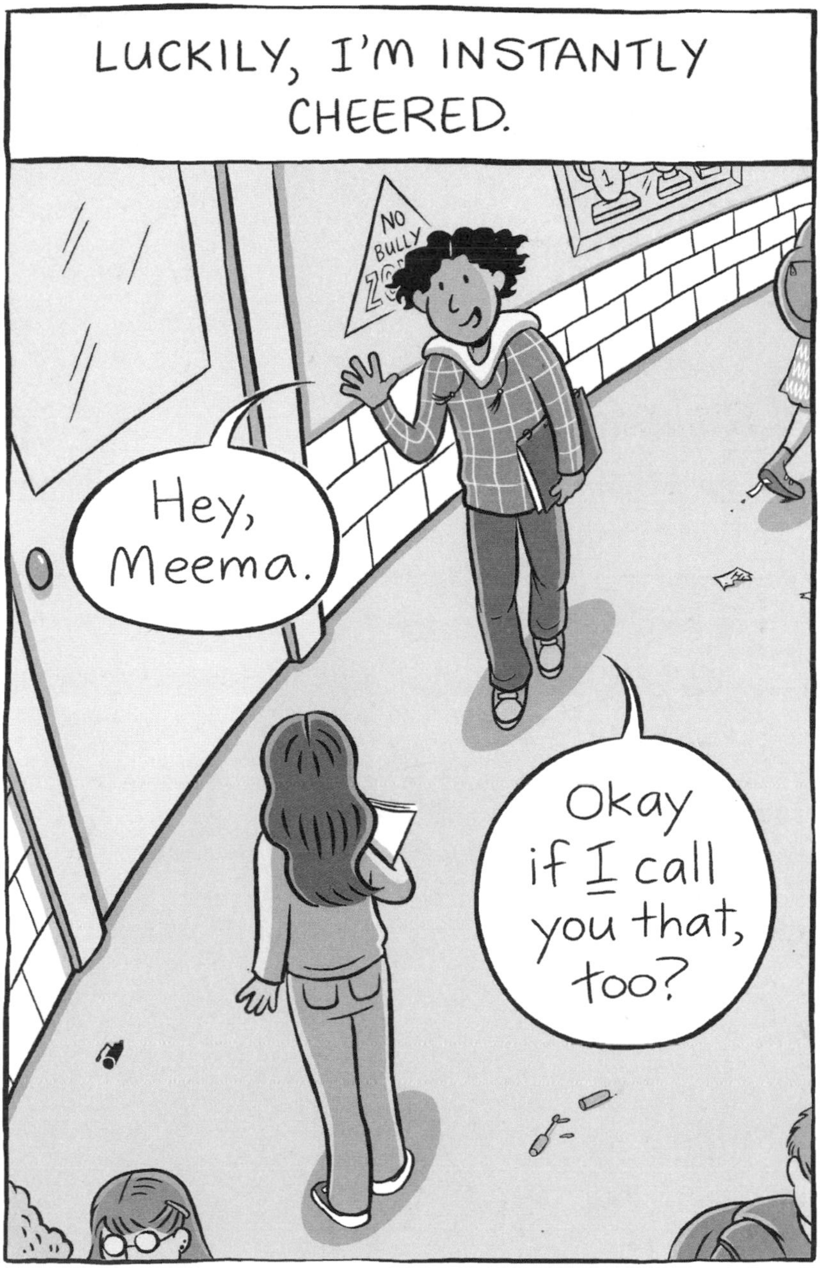
LUCKILY, I'M INSTANTLY CHEERED.
NO BULLY ZO
Hey, Meema.
Okay if I call you that, too?

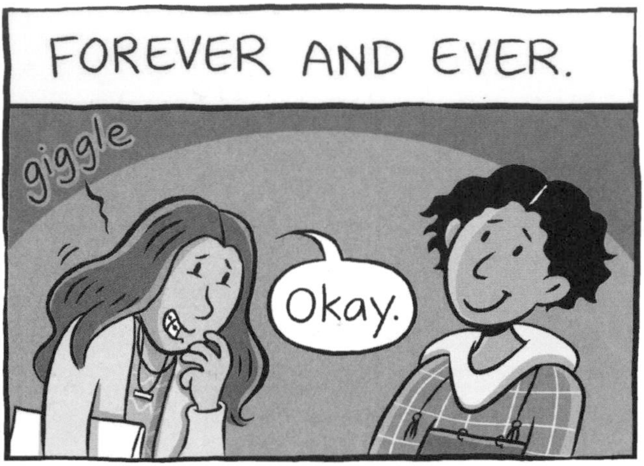
FOREVER AND EVER.
giggle
Okay.

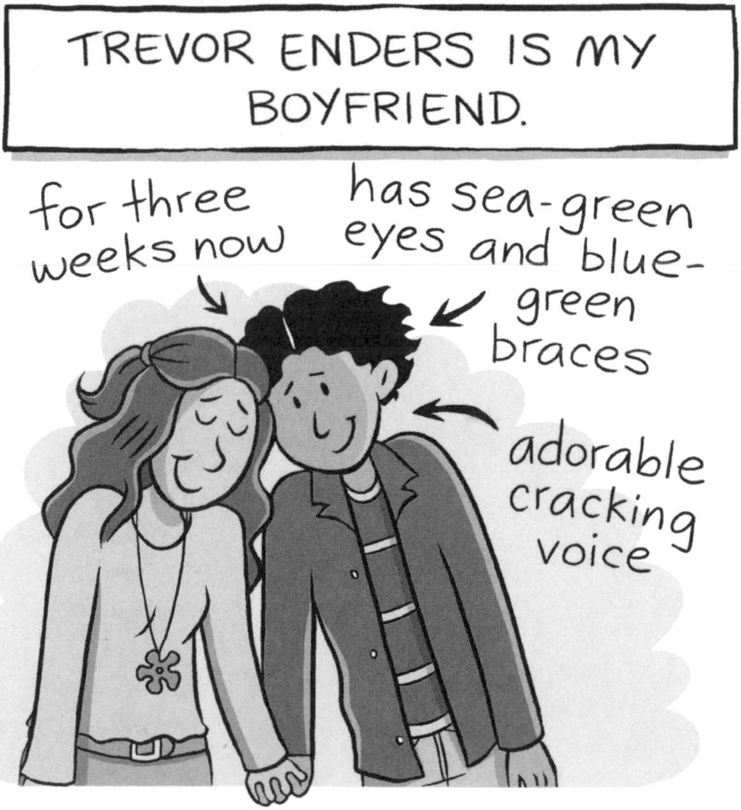
TREVOR ENDERS IS MY BOYFRIEND.
for three weeks now
has sea-green eyes and blue-green braces
adorable cracking voice

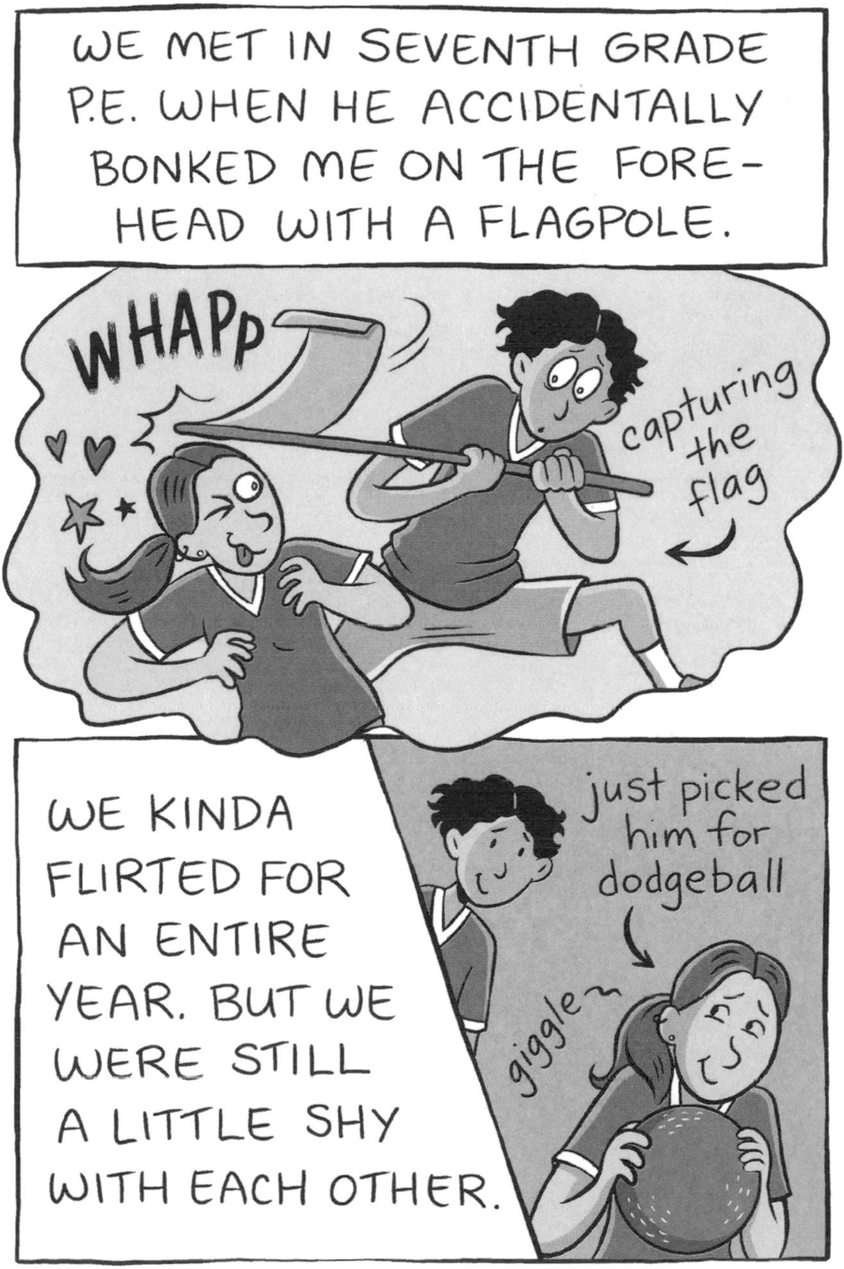
WE MET IN SEVENTH GRADE P.E. WHEN HE ACCIDENTALLY BONKED ME ON THE FORE-HEAD WITH A FLAGPOLE.
WHAPP
capturing the flag
WE KINDA FLIRTED FOR AN ENTIRE YEAR. BUT WE WERE STILL A LITTLE SHY WITH EACH OTHER.
just picked him for dodgeball
giggle~

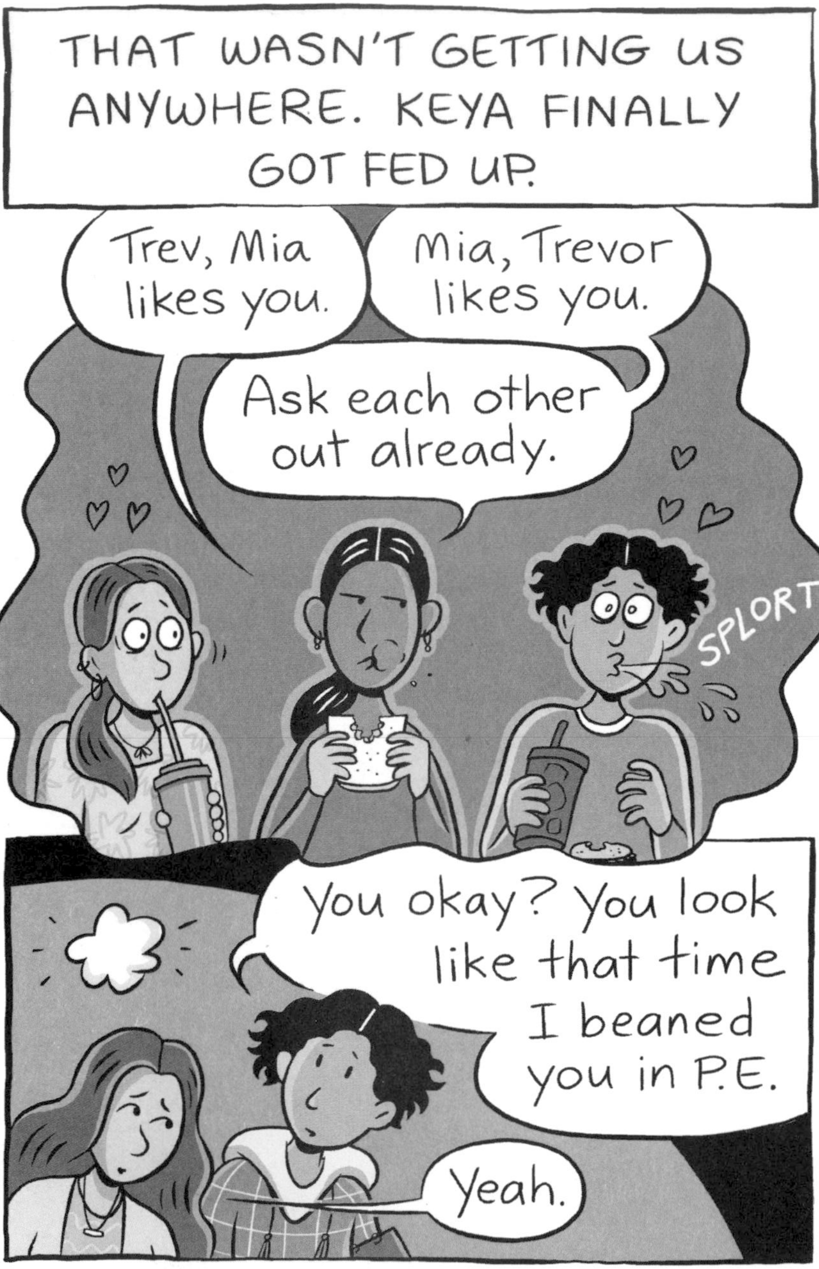
THAT WASN'T GETTING US ANYWHERE. KEYA FINALLY GOT FED UP.
Trev, Mia likes you.
Mia, Trevor likes you.
Ask each other out already.
SPLORT
You okay? You look like that time I beaned you in P.E.
Yeah.

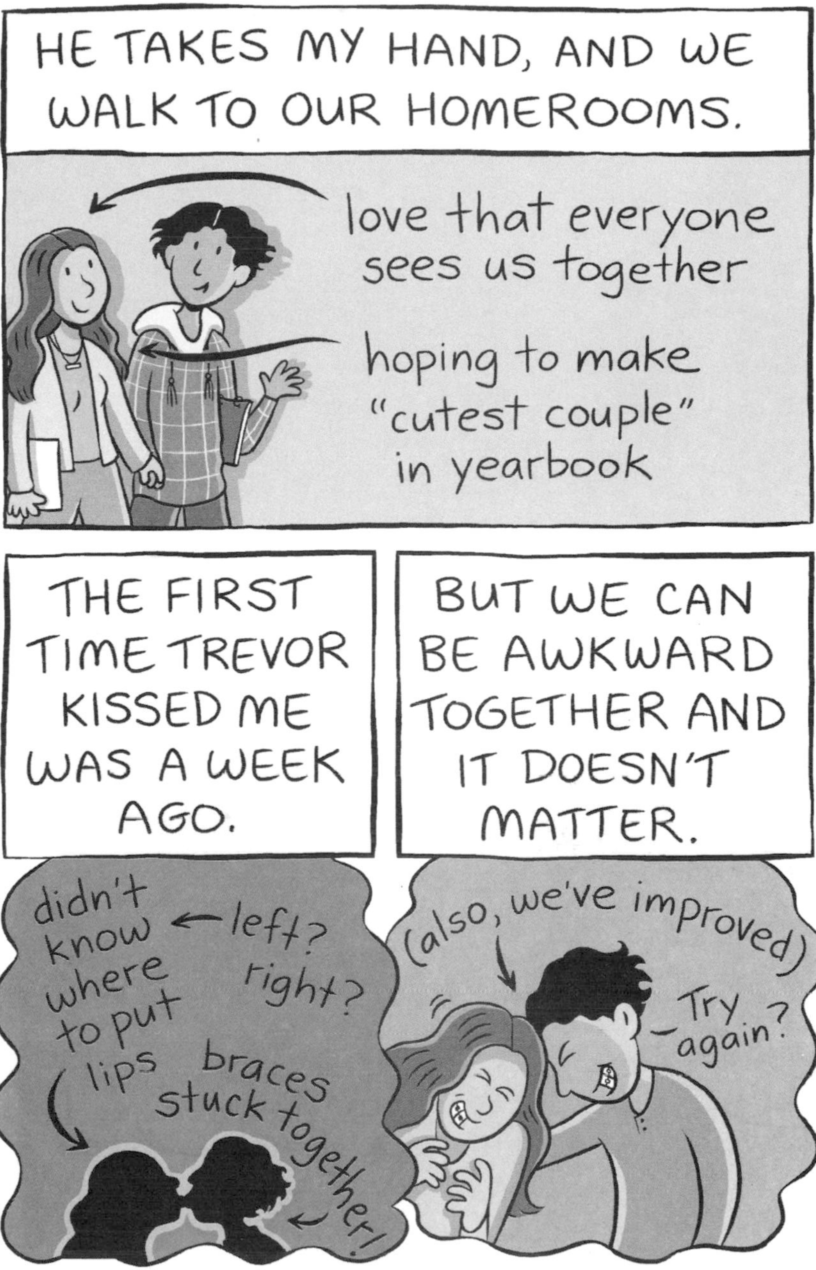
HE TAKES MY HAND, AND WE WALK TO OUR HOMEROOMS.
love that everyone sees us together
hoping to make "cutest couple" in yearbook
THE FIRST TIME TREVOR KISSED ME WAS A WEEK AGO.
didn't know where to put lips
left? right?
braces stuck together!
BUT WE CAN BE AWKWARD TOGETHER AND IT DOESN'T MATTER.
(also, we've improved)
Try again?

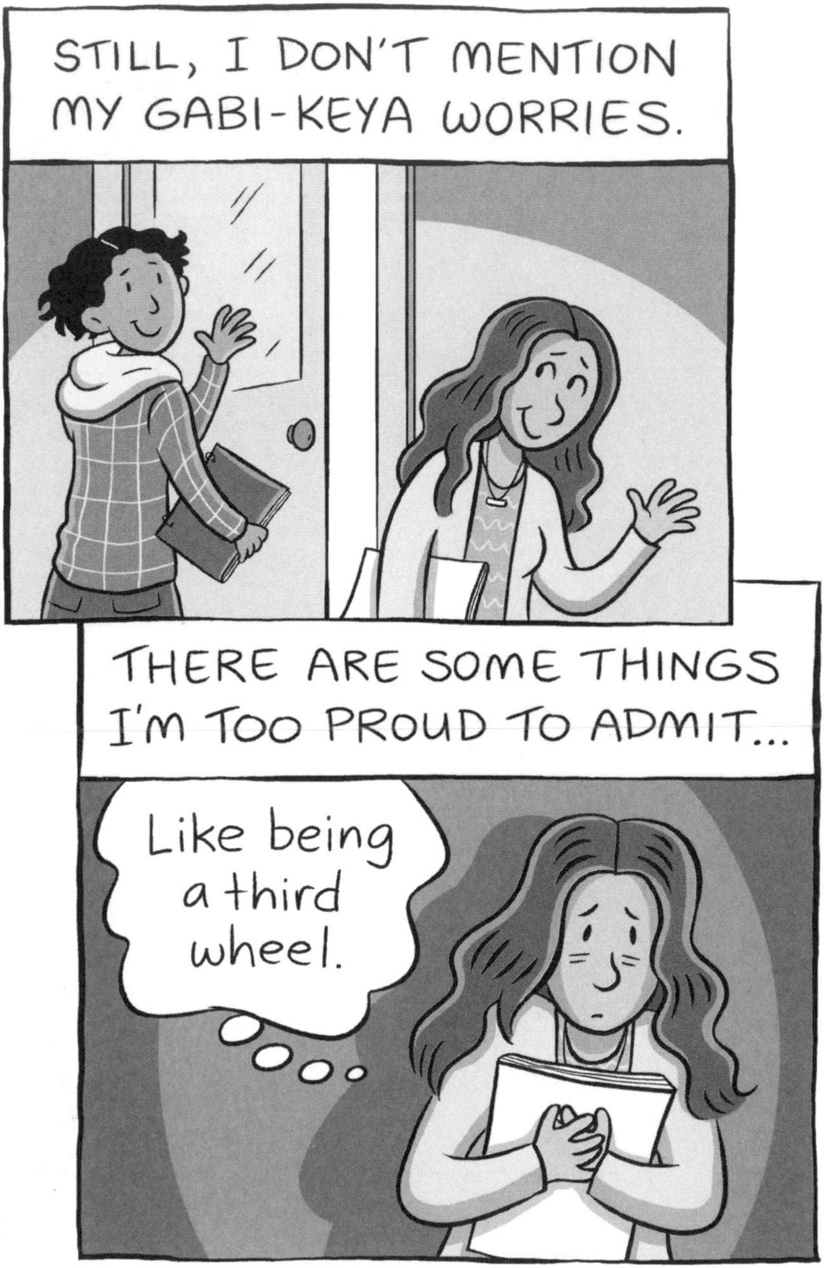
STILL, I DON'T MENTION MY GABI-KEYA WORRIES.
THERE ARE SOME THINGS I'M TOO PROUD TO ADMIT...
Like being a third wheel.

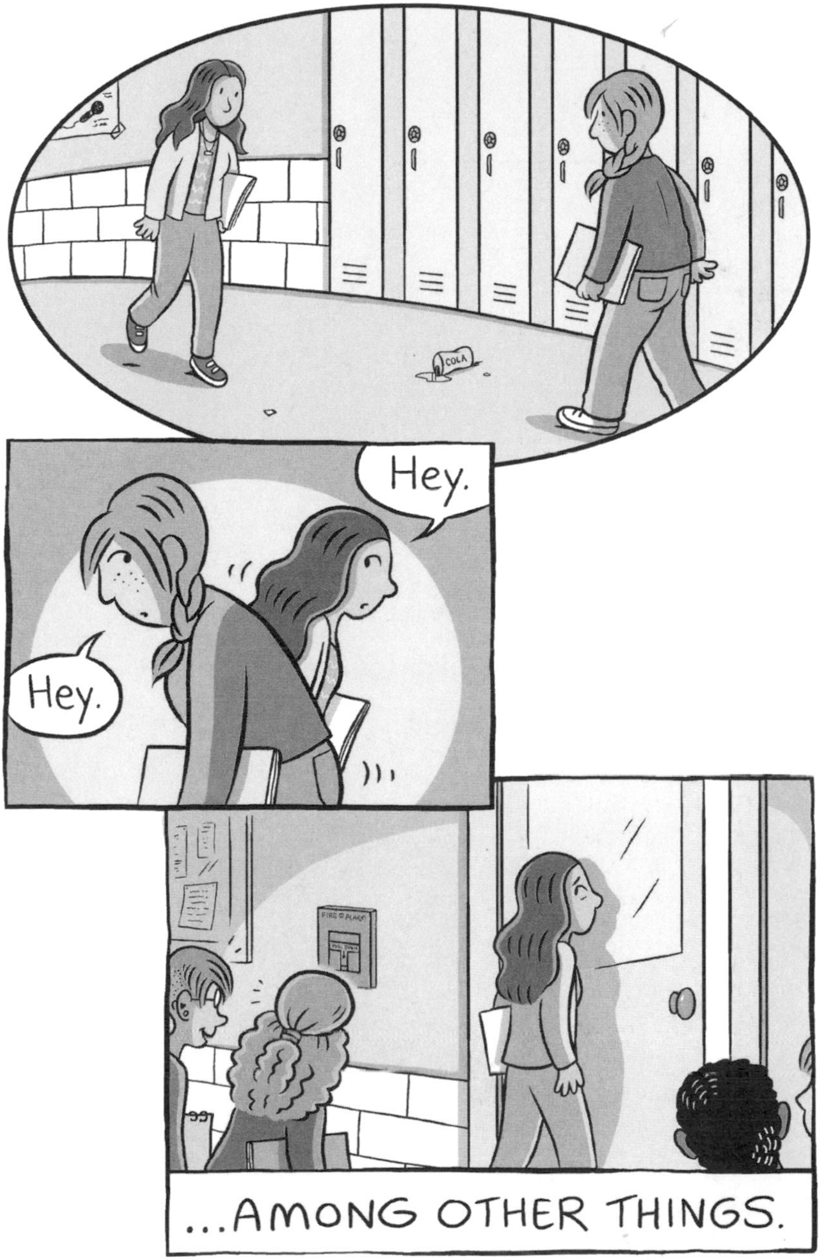
COLA
Hey.
Hey.
FIRE ALARM
...AMONG OTHER THINGS.

RUBY

I'm in Mrs. Winn's second-period English class. My favorite.

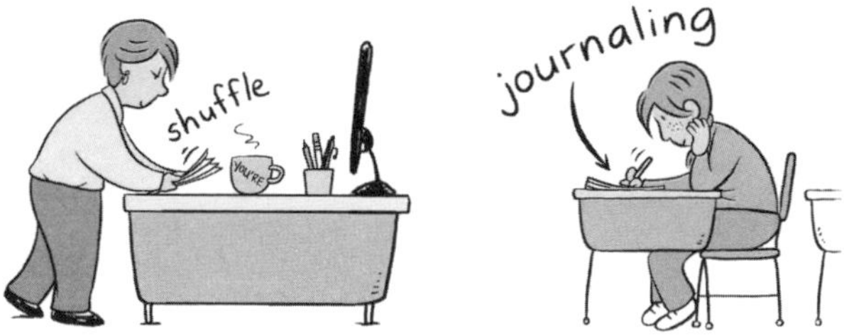
shuffle
YOU'RE
journaling

Well, except for one thing.

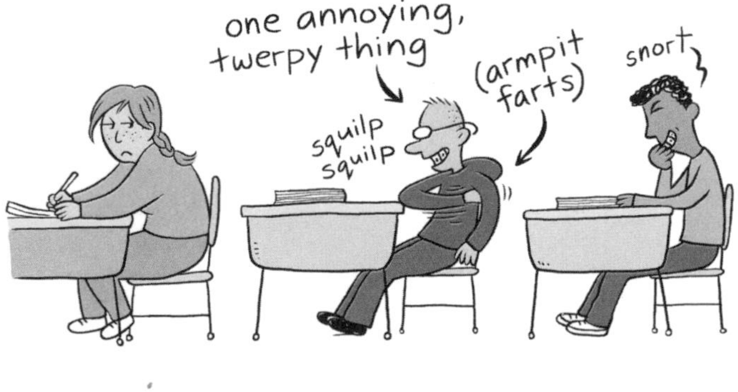
one annoying, twerpy thing
squilp squilp
(armpit farts)
snort

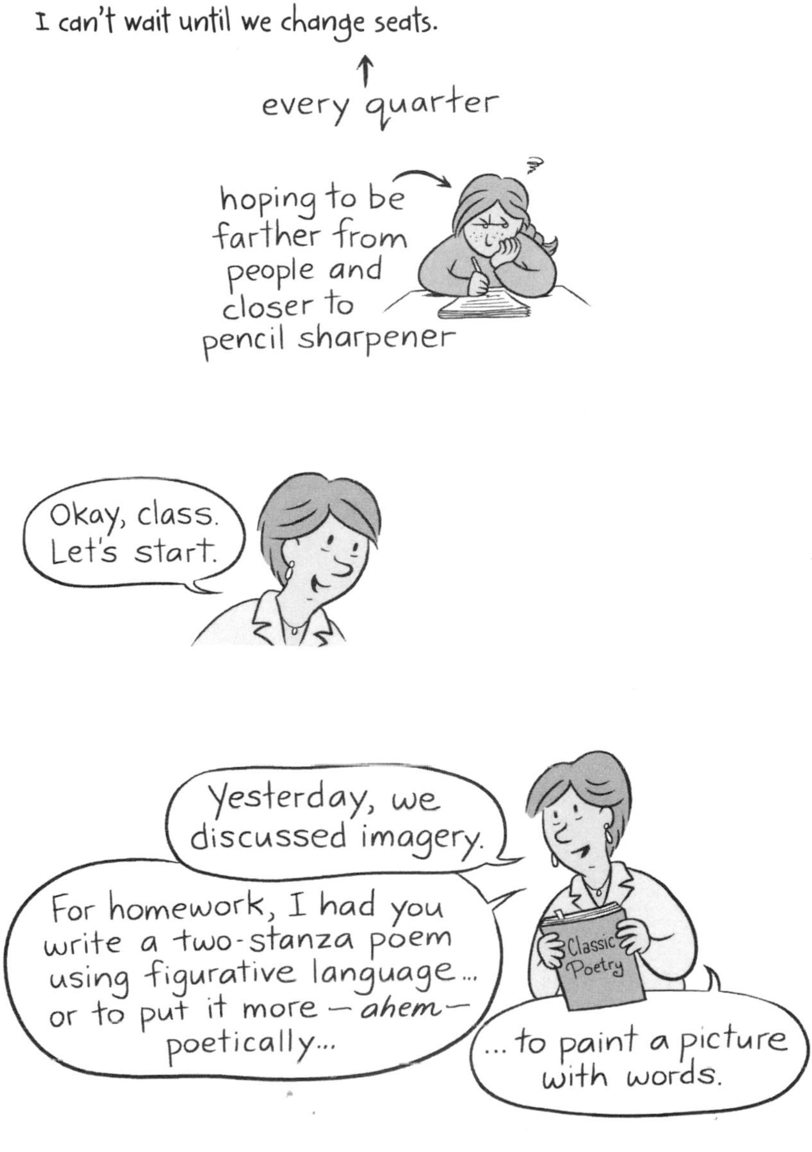
I can't wait until we change seats.
every quarter
hoping to be farther from people and closer to pencil sharpener
Okay, class. Let's start.
Yesterday, we discussed imagery.
For homework, I had you write a two-stanza poem using figurative language... or to put it more —*ahem*— poetically...
...to paint a picture with words.
Classic Poetry

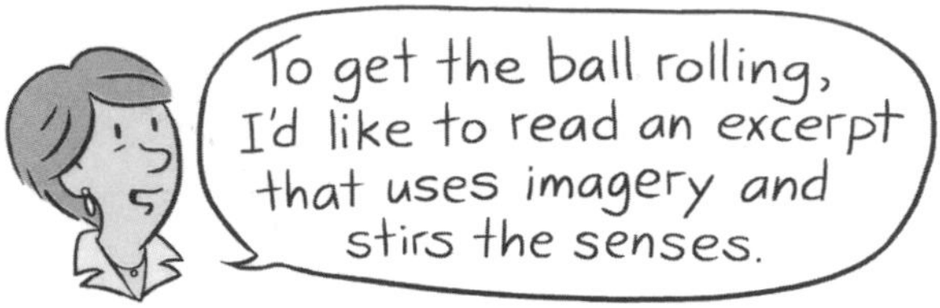
To get the ball rolling, I'd like to read an excerpt that uses imagery and stirs the senses.

"The night was creeping on the ground;
She crept and did not make a sound
Until she reached the tree, and then
She covered it, and sole again

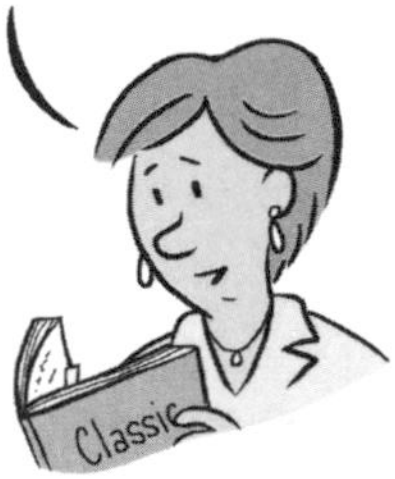
Classic

Along the grass beside the wall.
I heard the rustle of her shawl
As she threw blackness everywhere
Upon the sky and ground and air."

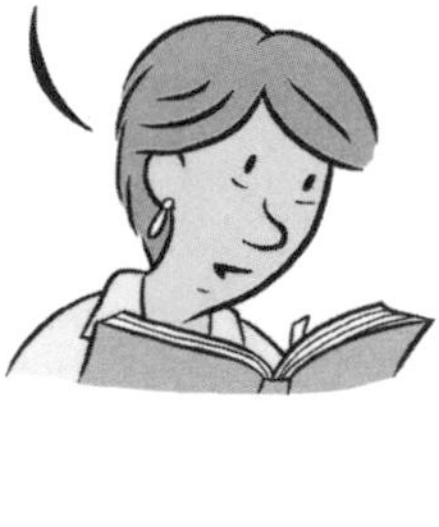

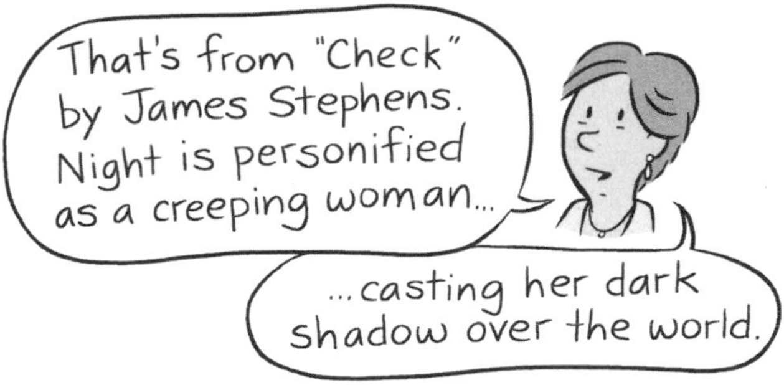

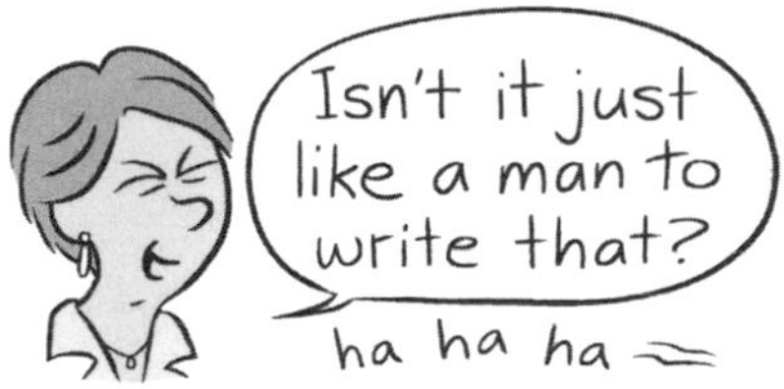

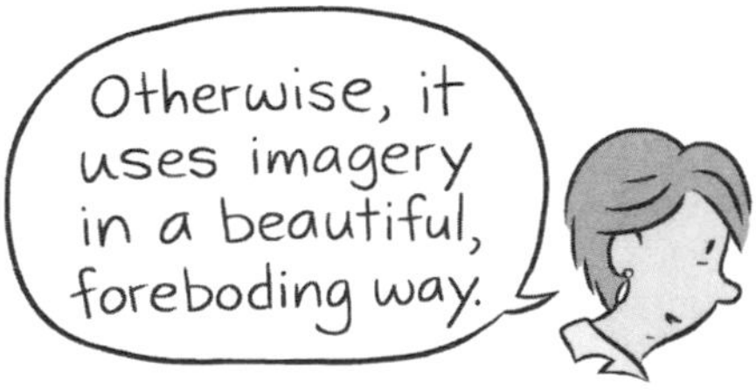

She clears her throat.

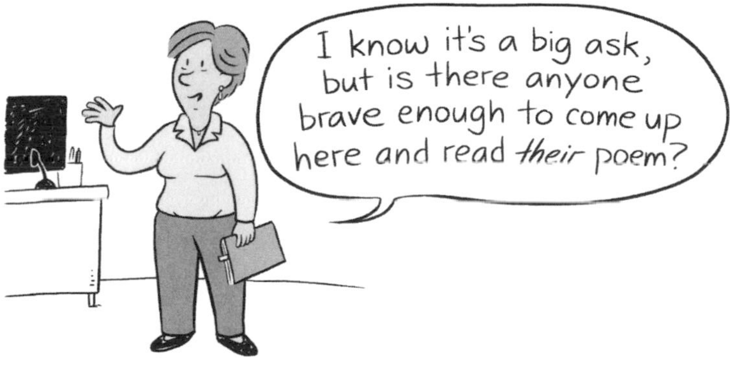

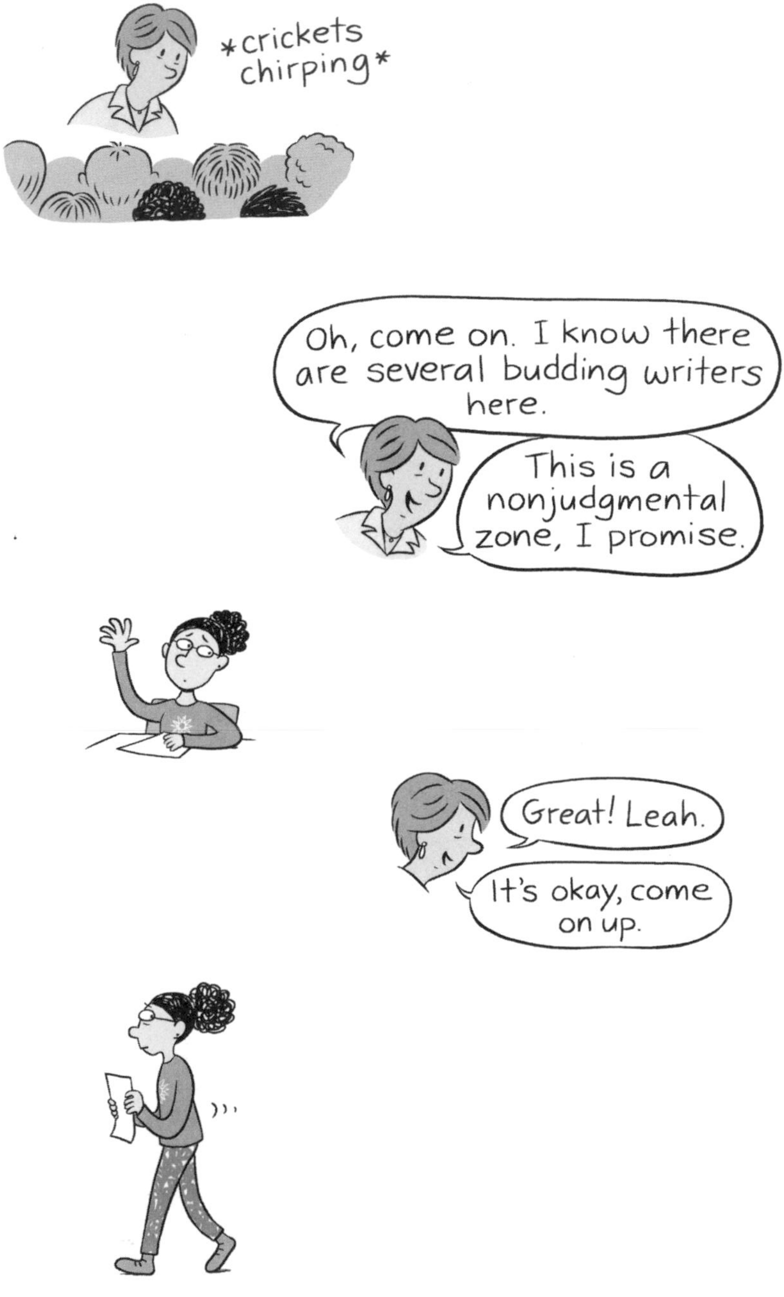
crickets chirping
Oh, come on. I know there are several budding writers here.
This is a nonjudgmental zone, I promise.
Great! Leah.
It's okay, come on up.

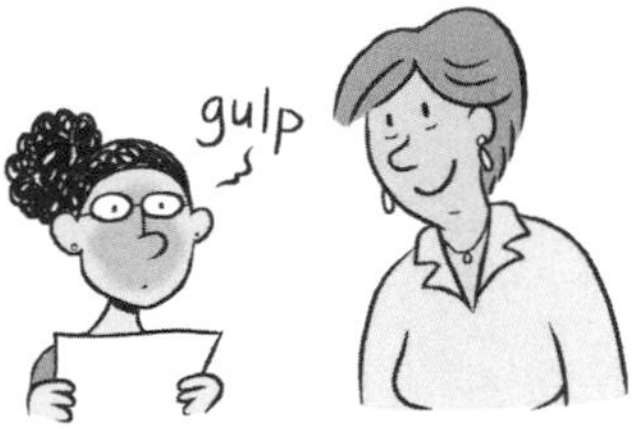
gulp

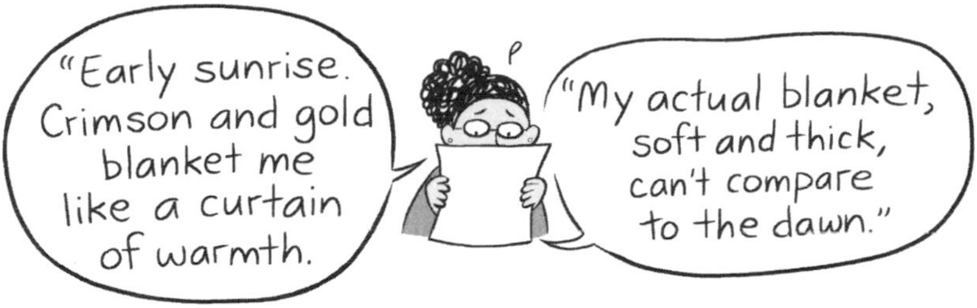
"Early sunrise. Crimson and gold blanket me like a curtain of warmth.
"My actual blanket, soft and thick, can't compare to the dawn."

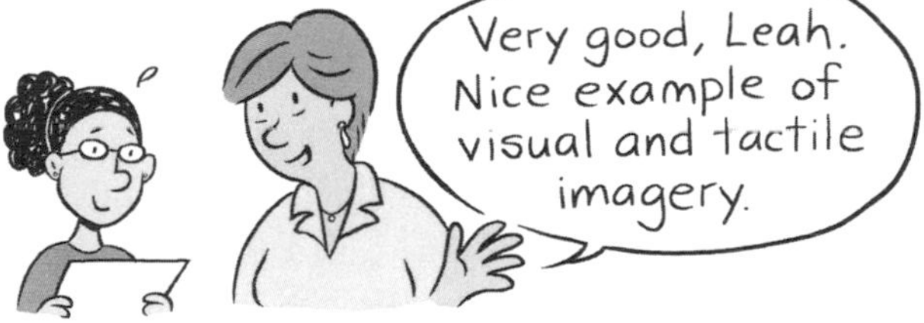
Very good, Leah. Nice example of visual and tactile imagery.

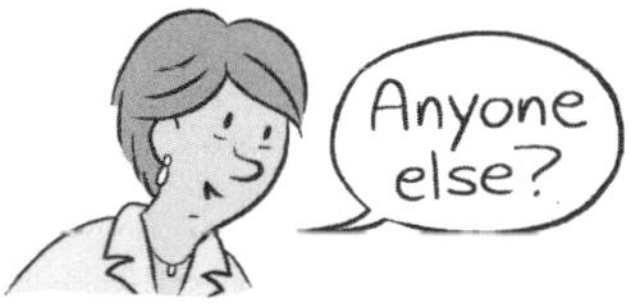
Anyone else?

Her eyes scan the room. Could be my imagination, but I feel like they pause on me for more than a couple seconds.

And I don't know why; maybe it's my showcase prize, and the fact that I kinda like what I wrote, but suddenly . . .

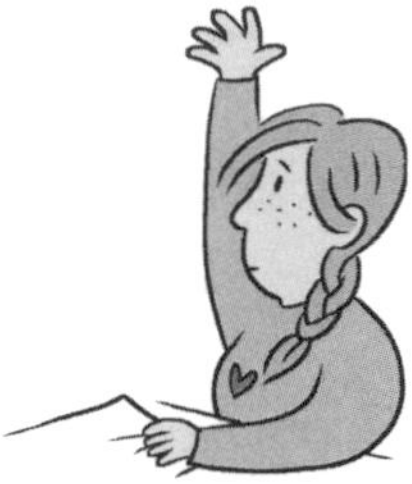

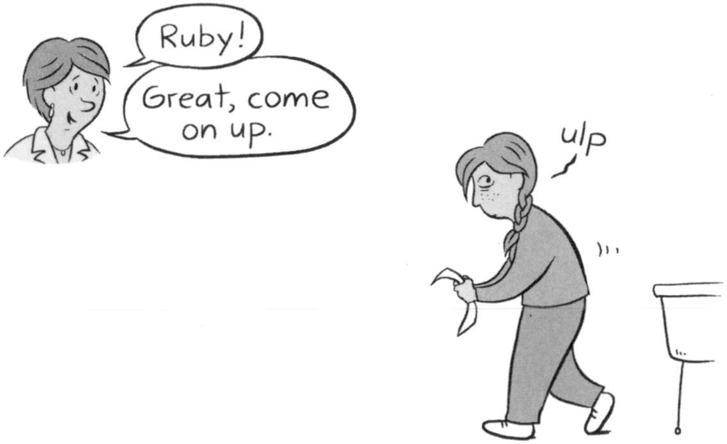
Ruby!
Great, come on up.
ulp

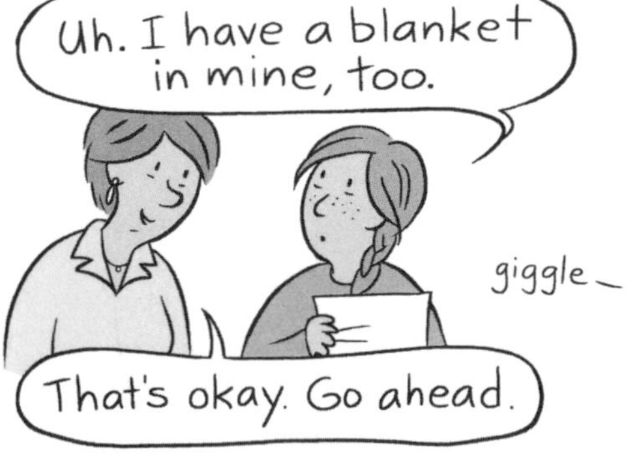
Uh. I have a blanket in mine, too.
giggle
That's okay. Go ahead.

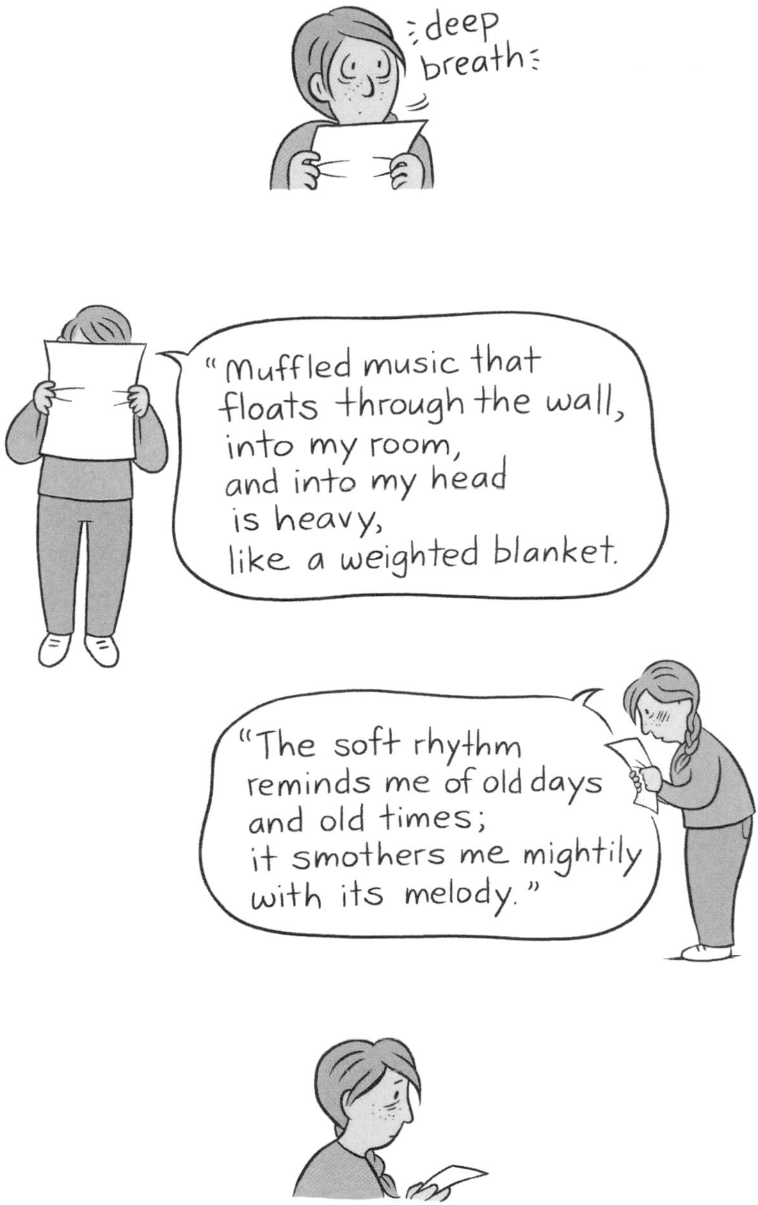
deep breath
"Muffled music that floats through the wall, into my room, and into my head is heavy, like a weighted blanket.
"The soft rhythm reminds me of old days and old times; it smothers me mightily with its melody."

I catch Joe and Anthony whispering to each other, but I can't tell if it's about me.

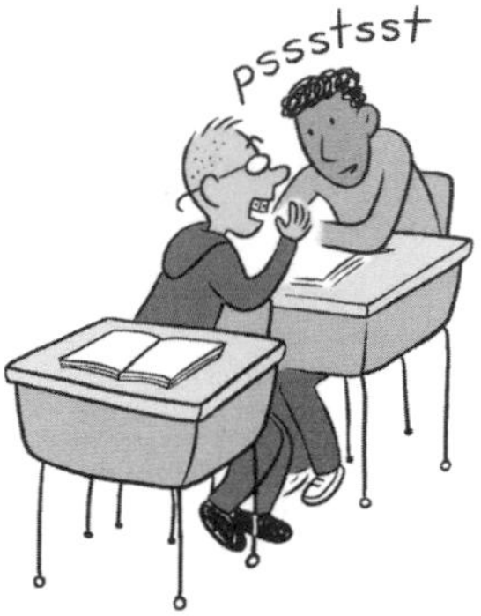
pssstsst

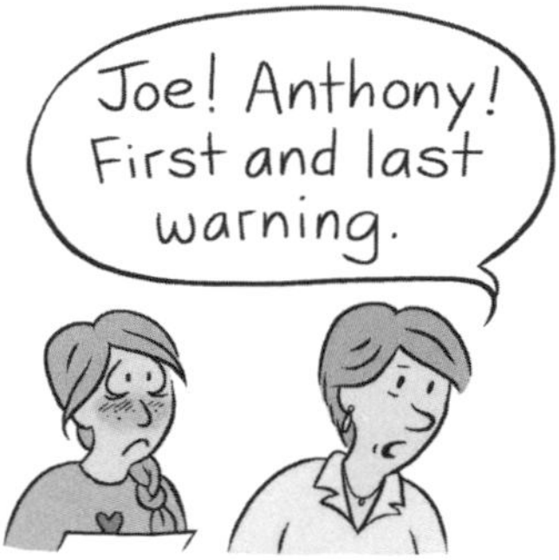
Joe! Anthony! First and last warning.

I want to die. Why did I do this??

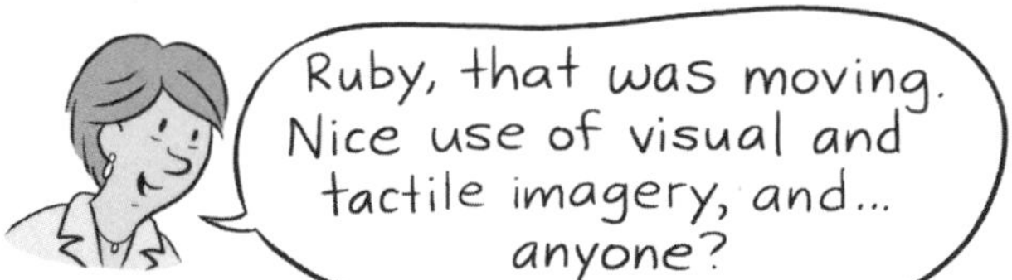
Ruby, that was moving. Nice use of visual and tactile imagery, and... anyone?

A few kids raise their hands. Mrs. Winn calls on one.

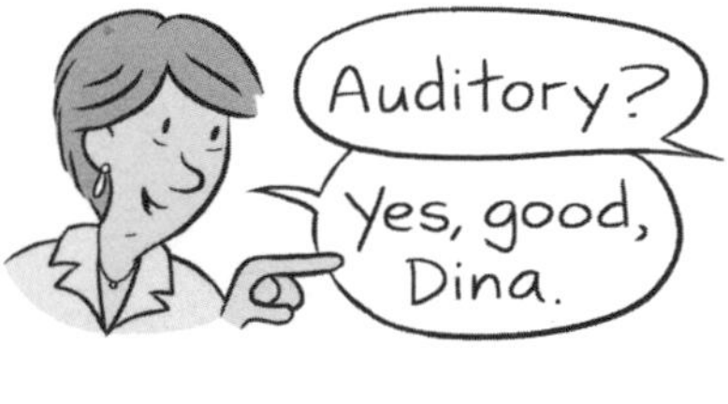
Auditory?
Yes, good, Dina.

Thank you, Ruby. Great job.

That cheers me instantly. I still can't believe I volunteered.

Anyone else?

A couple more kids go up. One recites a poem about a snowy night (which makes me cold). Kyle Duncan reads about a cheese-and-mustard sandwich (which makes me hungry). Imagery sure is powerful.

When the bell rings, Mrs. Winn calls me over.

Ruby, there's something I've been thinking about for a while. Something I think you'd be perfect for.

I wait.

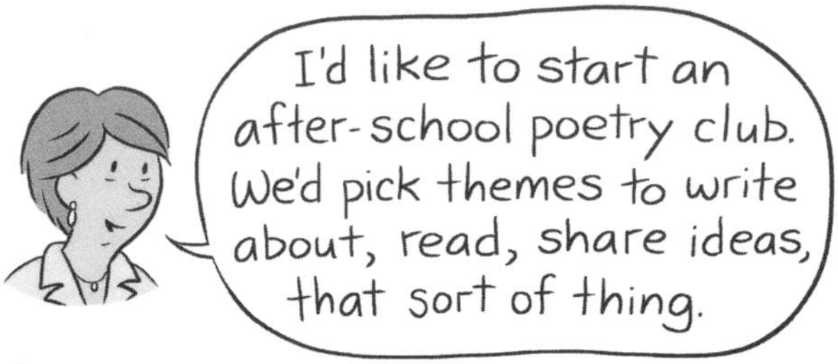
I'd like to start an after-school poetry club. We'd pick themes to write about, read, share ideas, that sort of thing.

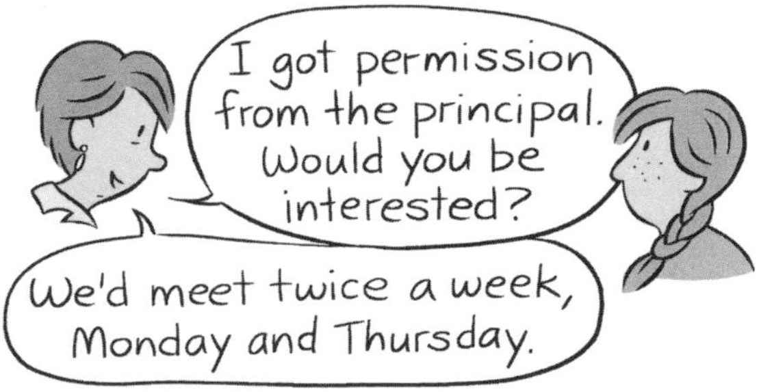
I got permission from the principal. Would you be interested?
We'd meet twice a week, Monday and Thursday.

Huh. A poetry club.

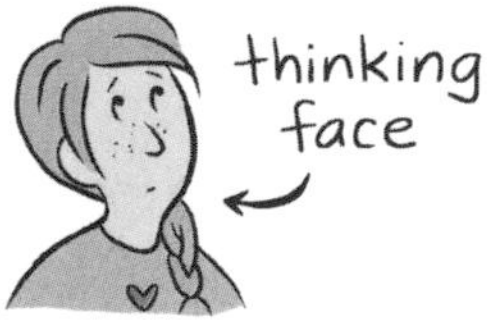
thinking face

It's nice that she asked, but truth is, I've never wanted to try after-school stuff. I just don't fit in anywhere.

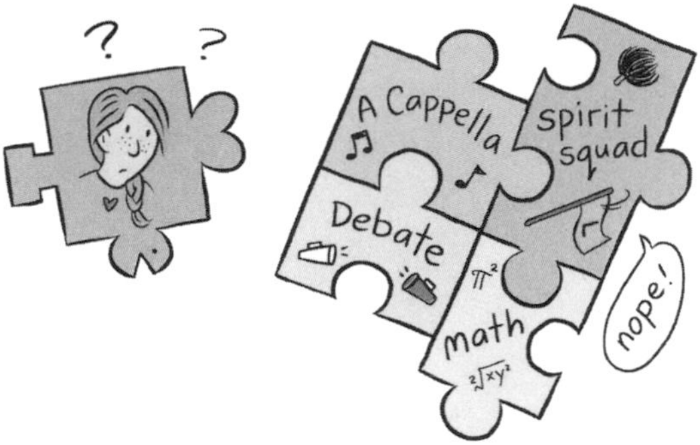
A Cappella
spirit squad
Debate
math
nope!

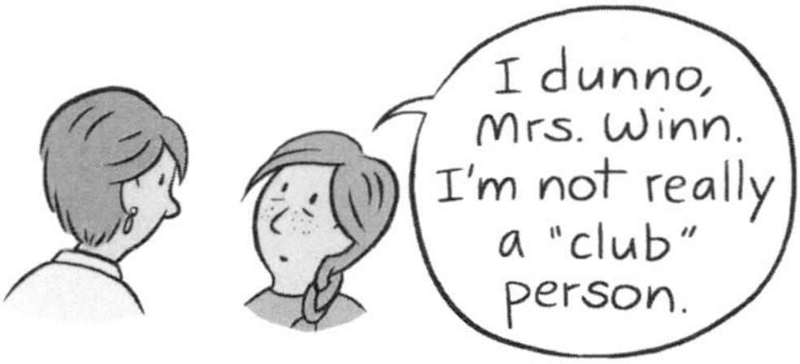
I dunno, Mrs. Winn. I'm not really a "club" person.

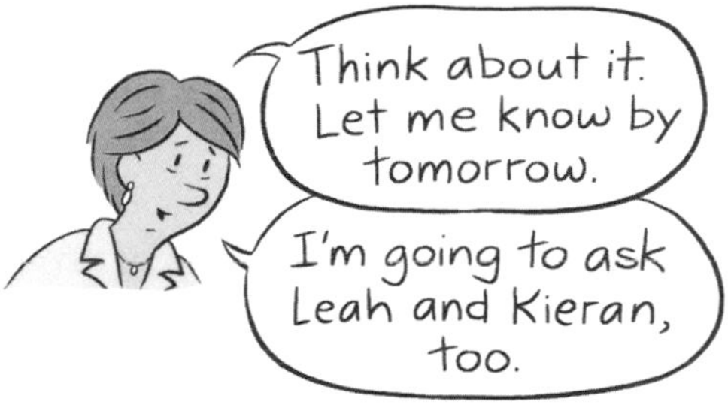
Think about it. Let me know by tomorrow.
I'm going to ask Leah and Kieran, too.

The two shyest (but most talented) kids in our class. I don't know if I'm as good. Maybe my winning poem was just a freak thing.

But . . .

. . . it could be fun. And more exciting than writing in my room.

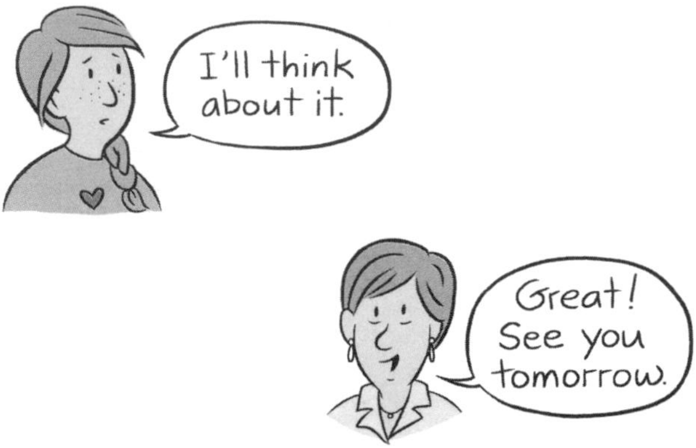
I'll think about it.
Great! See you tomorrow.

I leave and head to third period, thinking, just like I said I'd do.

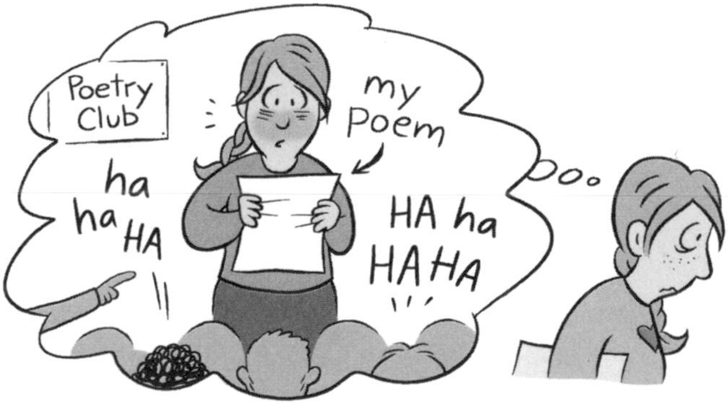
Poetry Club
my Poem
ha ha HA
HA ha HA HA

Maybe I should leave the thinking to later.

Mia

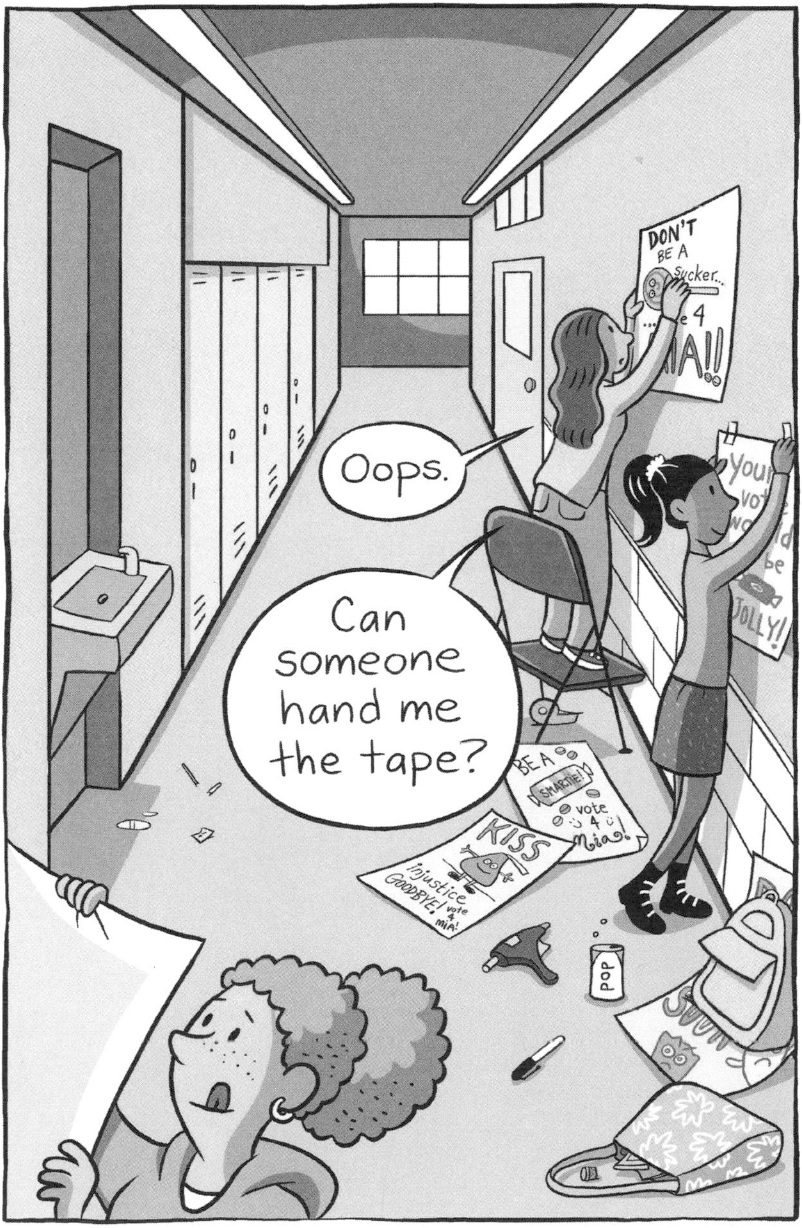
DON'T BE A sucker...
Oops.
Can someone hand me the tape?
BE A SMARTIE! vote 4 Mia!
KISS injustice GOODBYE! vote 4 MIA!
POP

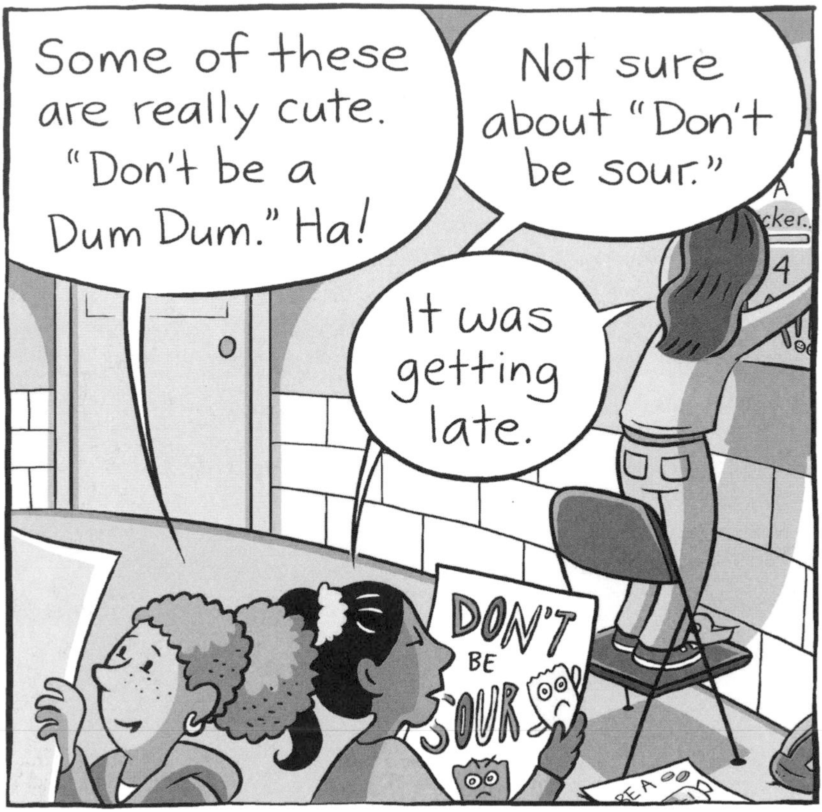
Some of these are really cute. "Don't be a Dum Dum." Ha!
Not sure about "Don't be sour."
It was sure getting late.
DON'T BE SOUR

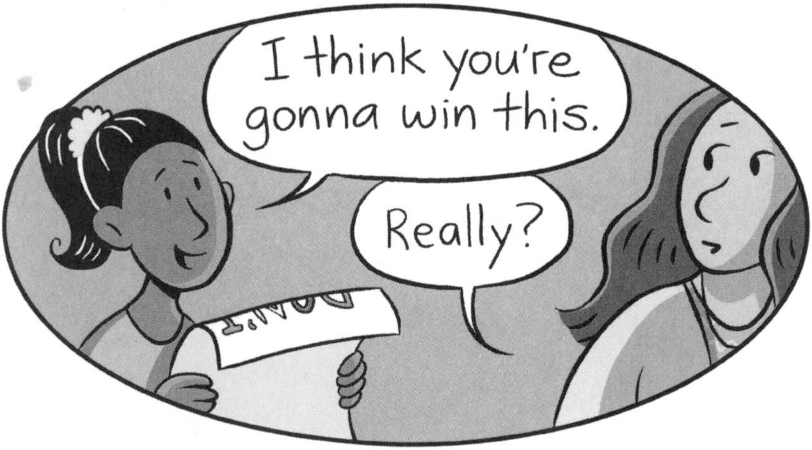
I think you're gonna win this.
Really?

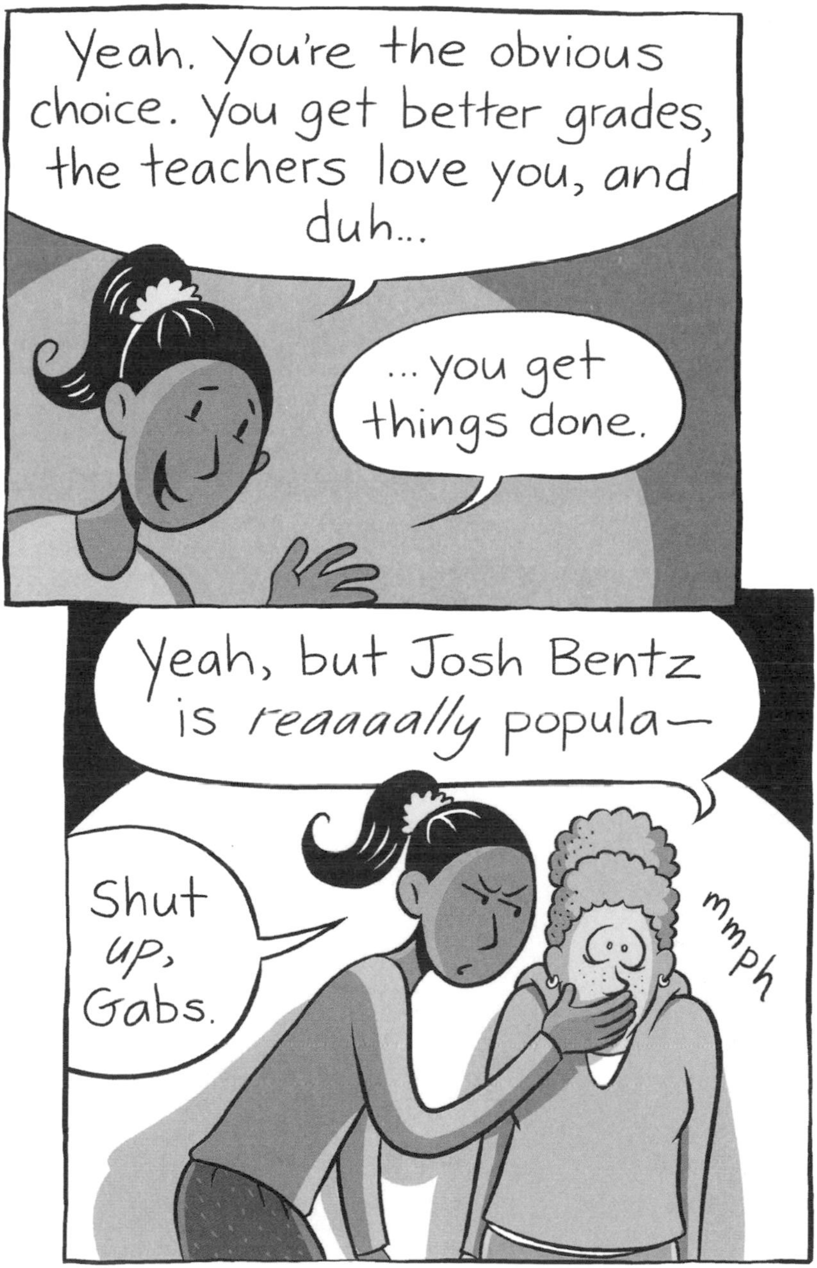
Yeah. You're the obvious choice. You get better grades, the teachers love you, and duh...
...you get things done.
Yeah, but Josh Bentz is *reaaaally* popula—
Shut *up*, Gabs.
mmph

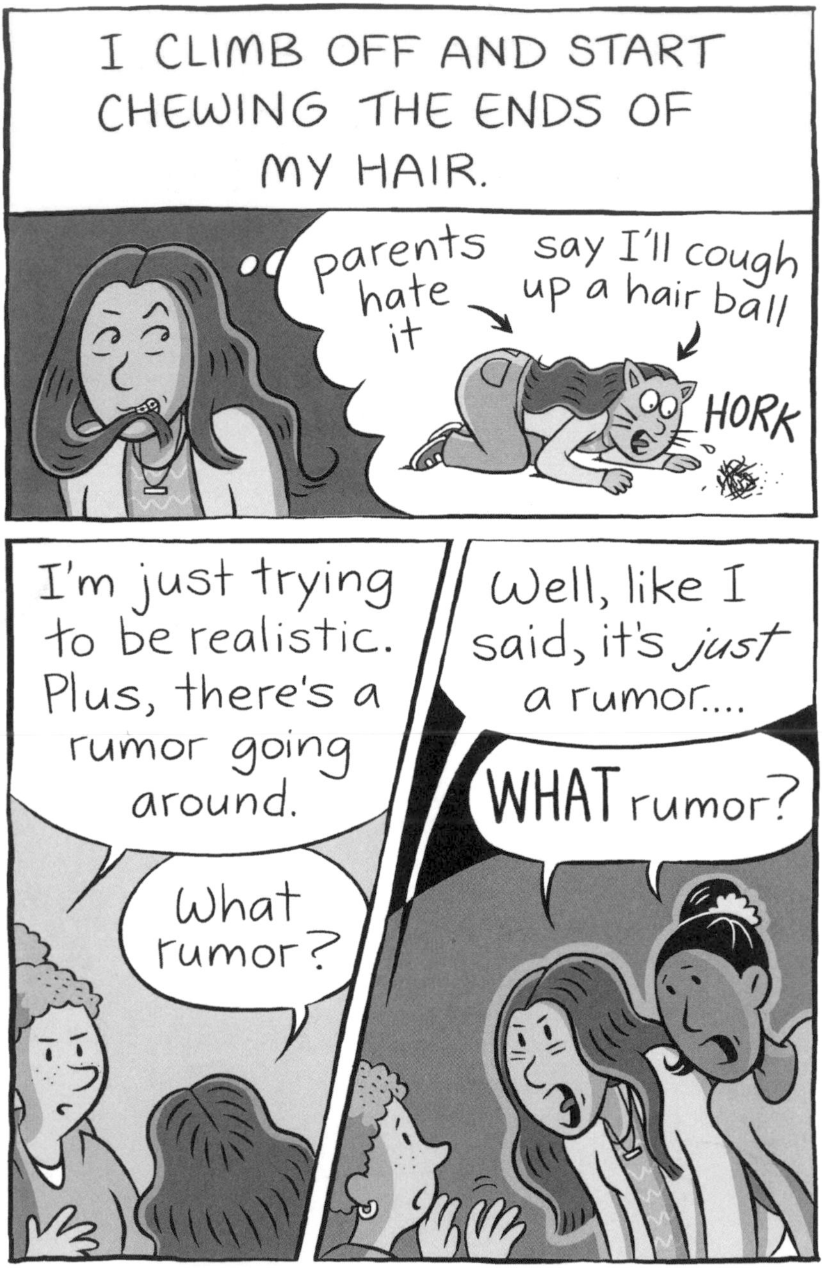
I CLIMB OFF AND START CHEWING THE ENDS OF MY HAIR.
parents hate it
say I'll cough up a hair ball
HORK
I'm just trying to be realistic. Plus, there's a rumor going around.
What rumor?
Well, like I said, it's *just* a rumor....
WHAT rumor?

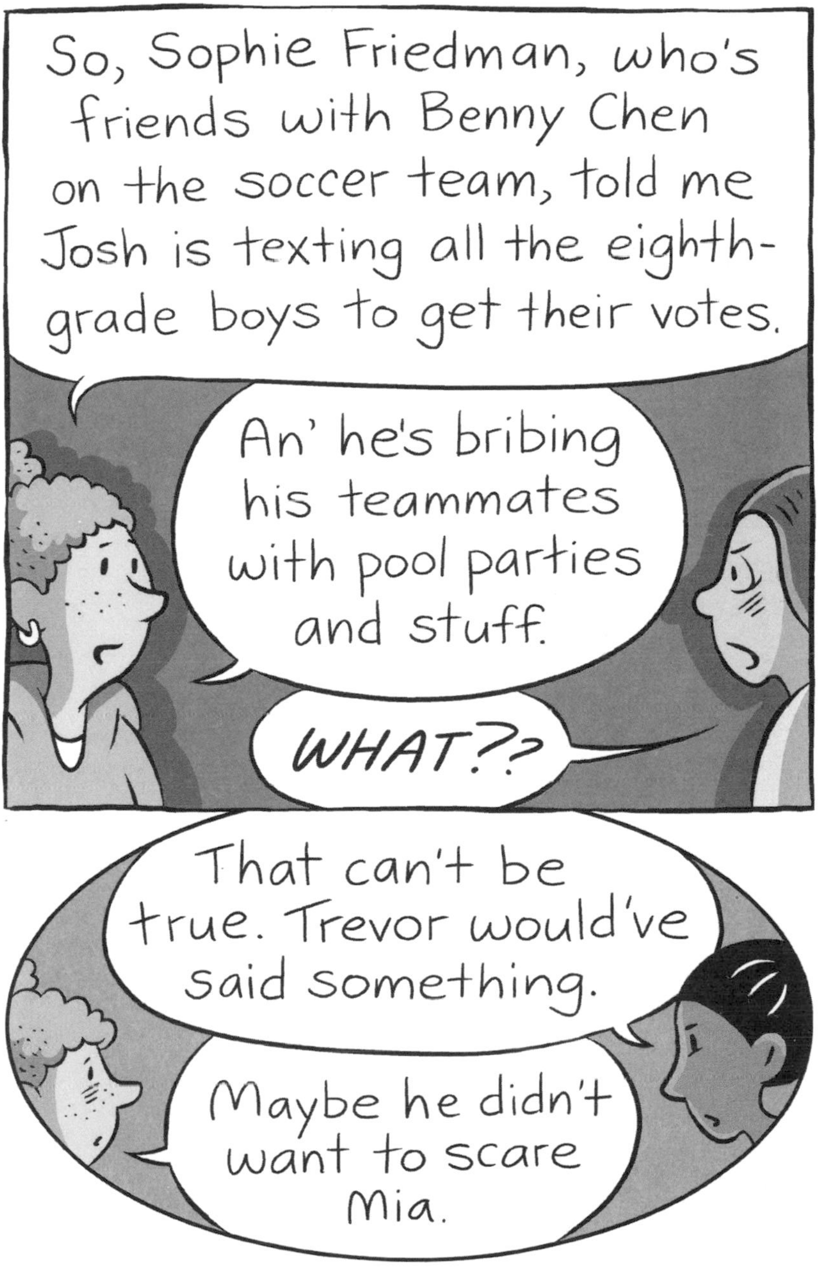
So, Sophie Friedman, who's friends with Benny Chen on the soccer team, told me Josh is texting all the eighth-grade boys to get their votes.
An' he's bribing his teammates with pool parties and stuff.
WHAT??
That can't be true. Trevor would've said something.
Maybe he didn't want to scare Mia.

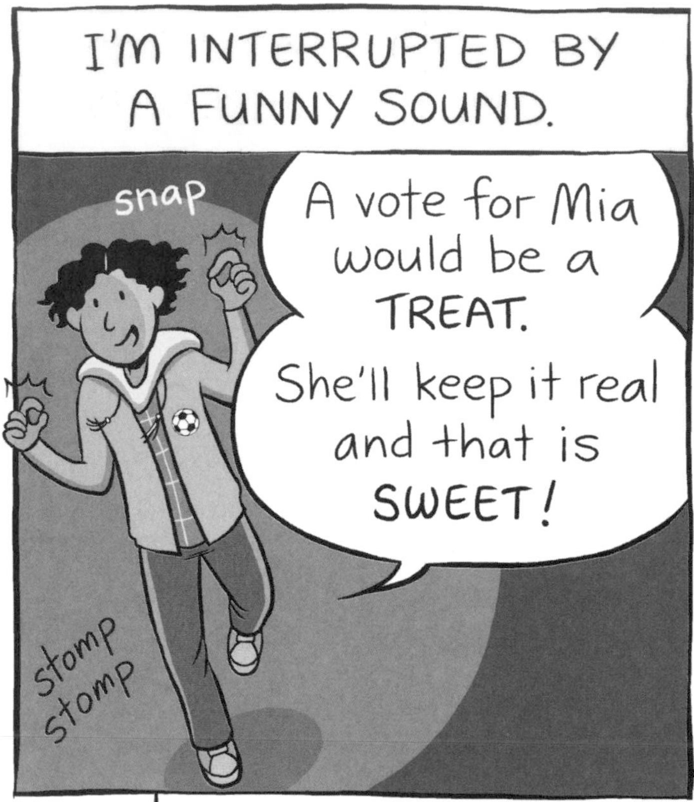
I'M INTERRUPTED BY A FUNNY SOUND.
snap
A vote for Mia would be a TREAT. She'll keep it real and that is SWEET!
stomp stomp

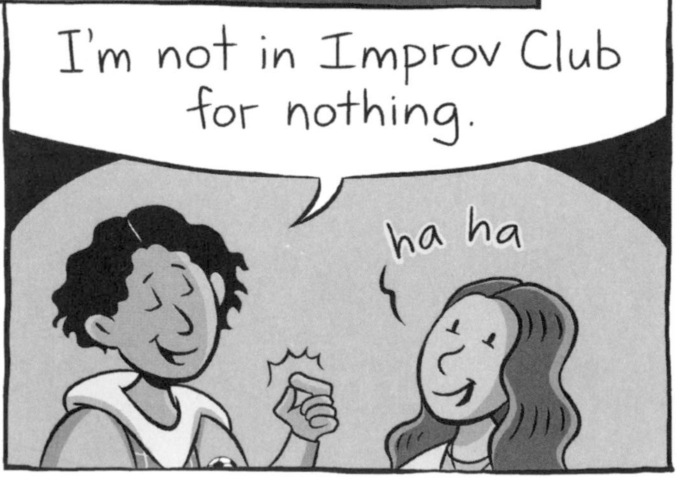
I'm not in Improv Club for nothing.
ha ha

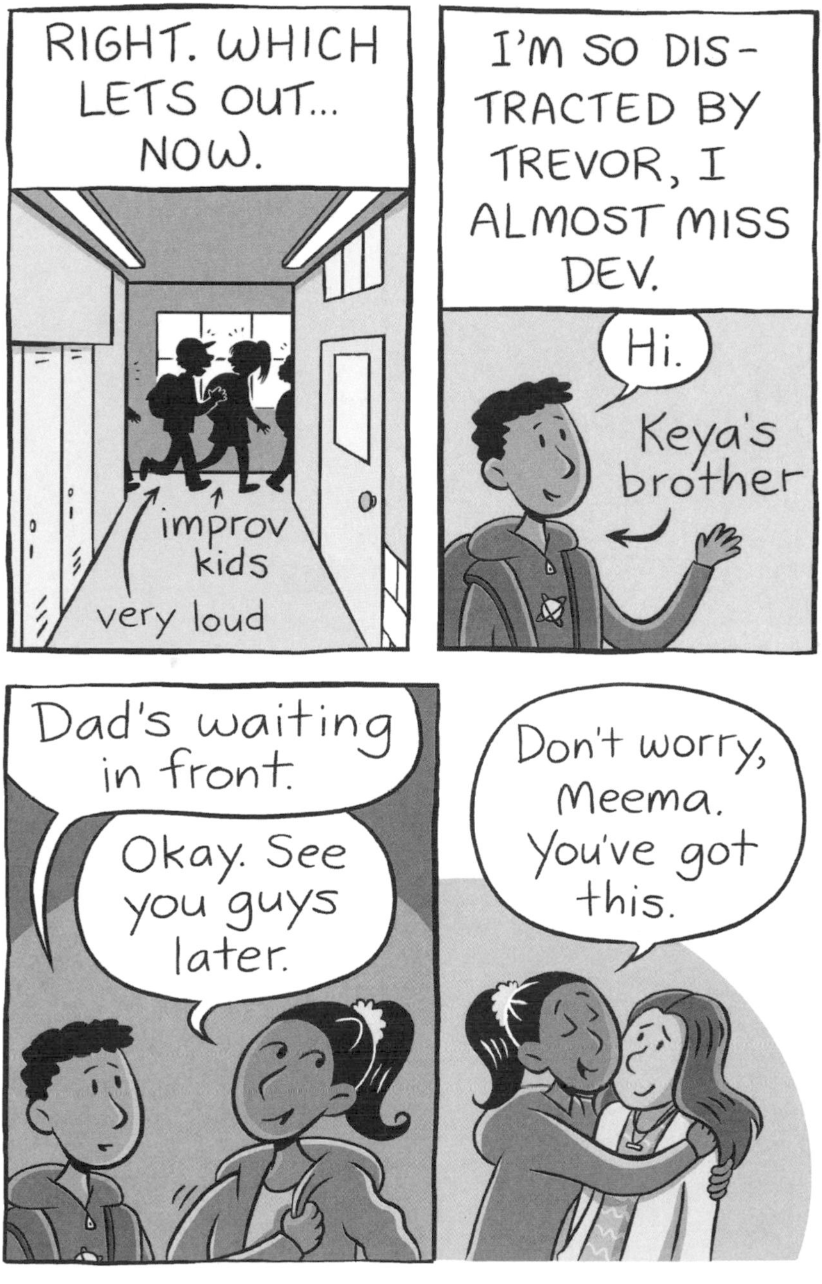
RIGHT. WHICH LETS OUT... NOW.
improv kids
very loud
I'M SO DIS-TRACTED BY TREVOR, I ALMOST MISS DEV.
Hi.
Keya's brother
Dad's waiting in front.
Okay. See you guys later.
Don't worry, Meema. You've got this.

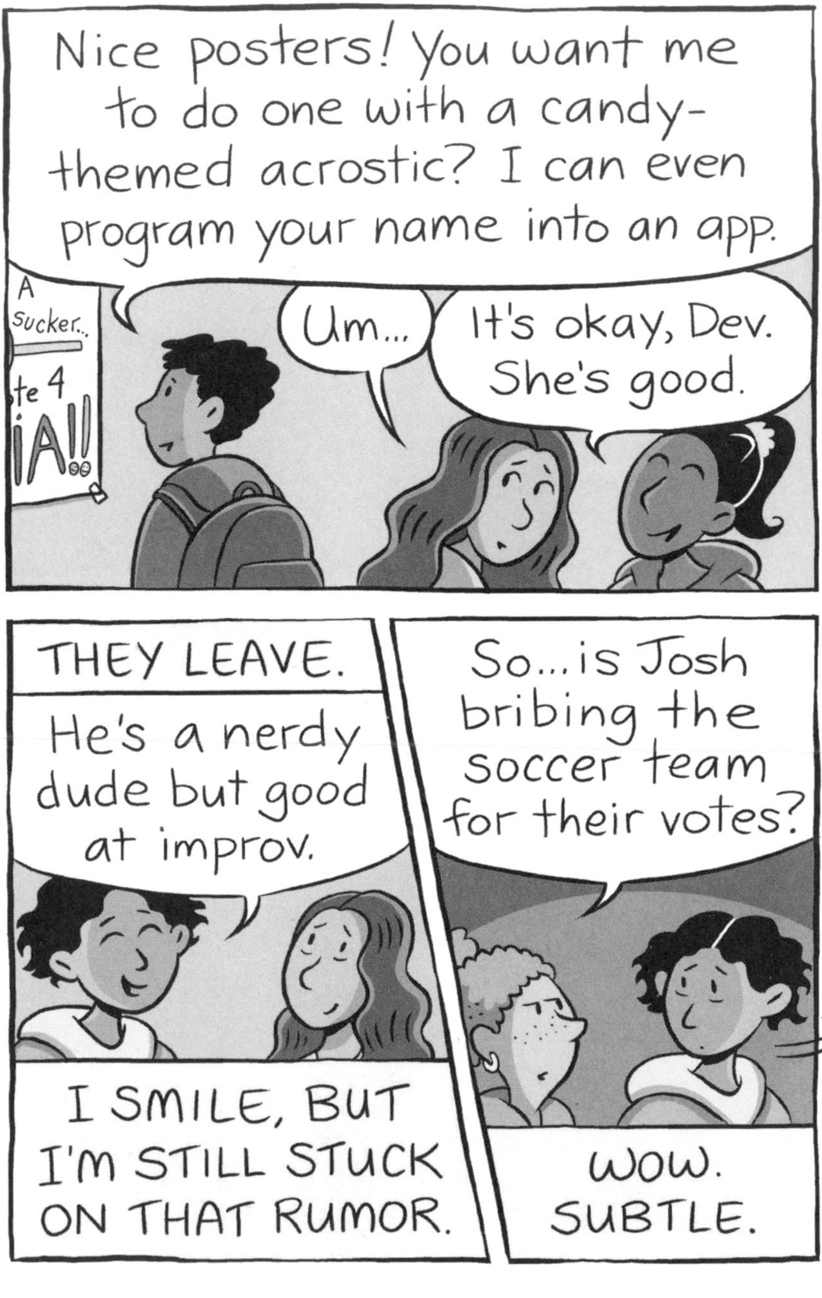
Nice posters! You want me to do one with a candy-themed acrostic? I can even program your name into an app.
A sucker...
te 4
iA!!
Um...
It's okay, Dev. She's good.
THEY LEAVE.
He's a nerdy dude but good at improv.
I SMILE, BUT I'M STILL STUCK ON THAT RUMOR.
So...is Josh bribing the soccer team for their votes?
WOW. SUBTLE.

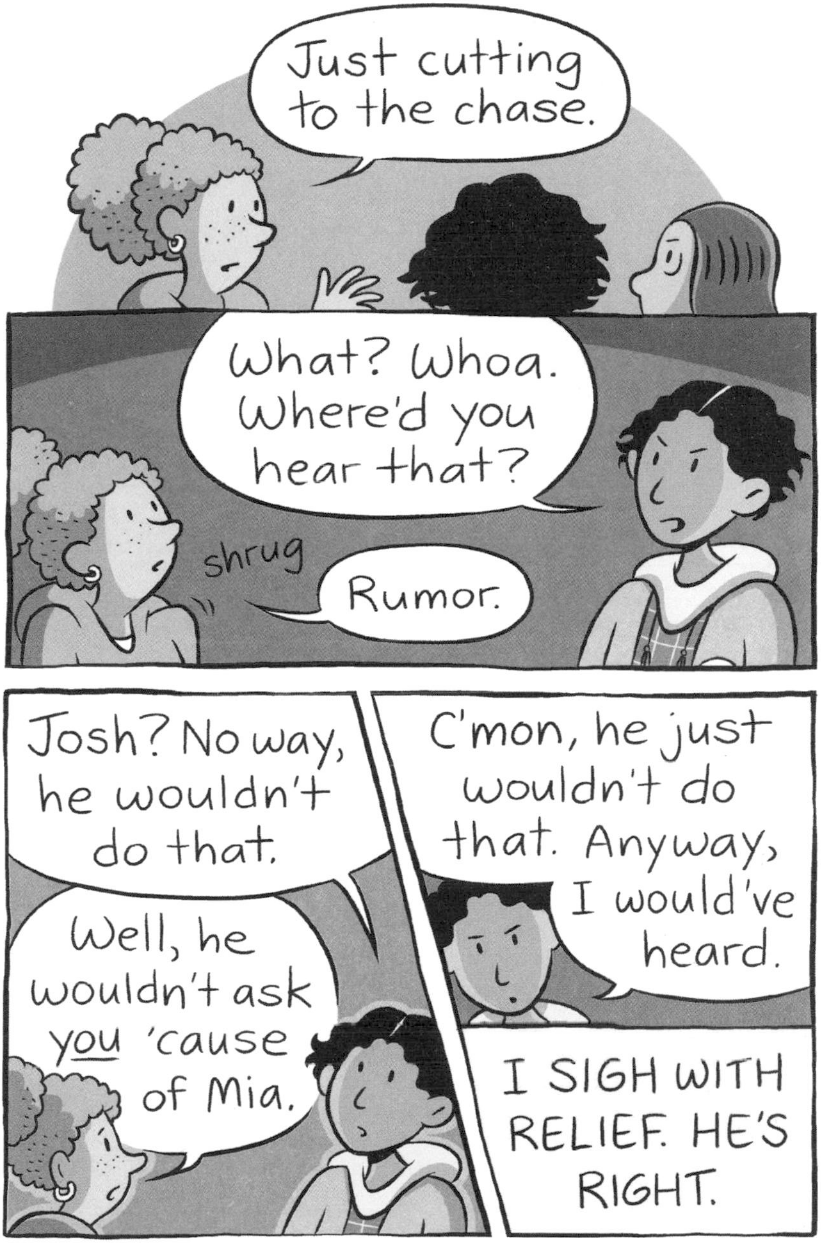
Just cutting to the chase.
What? Whoa. Where'd you hear that?
shrug
Rumor.
Josh? No way, he wouldn't do that.
Well, he wouldn't ask you 'cause of Mia.
C'mon, he just wouldn't do that. Anyway, I would've heard.
I SIGH WITH RELIEF. HE'S RIGHT.

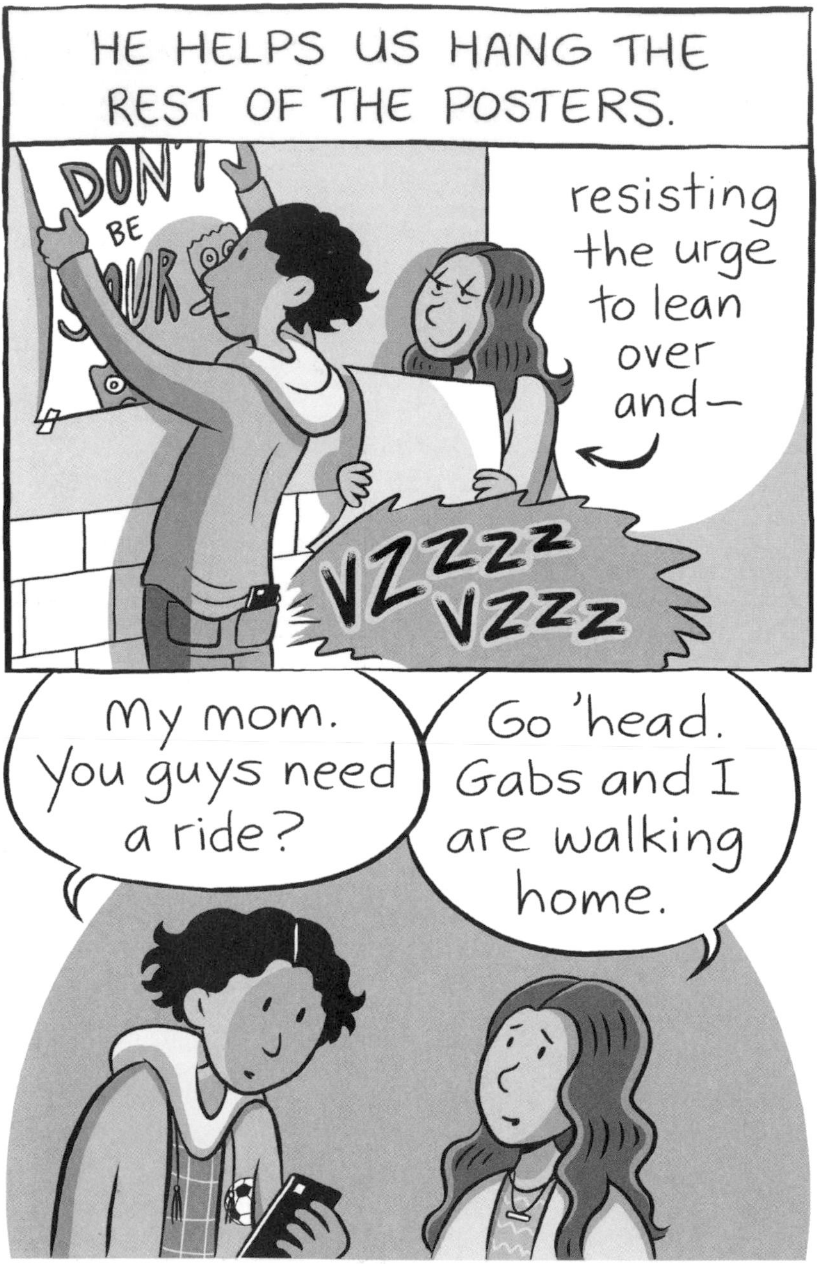
HE HELPS US HANG THE REST OF THE POSTERS.
DON'T BE
resisting the urge to lean over and—
VZZZZ VZZZ
My mom. You guys need a ride?
Go 'head. Gabs and I are walking home.

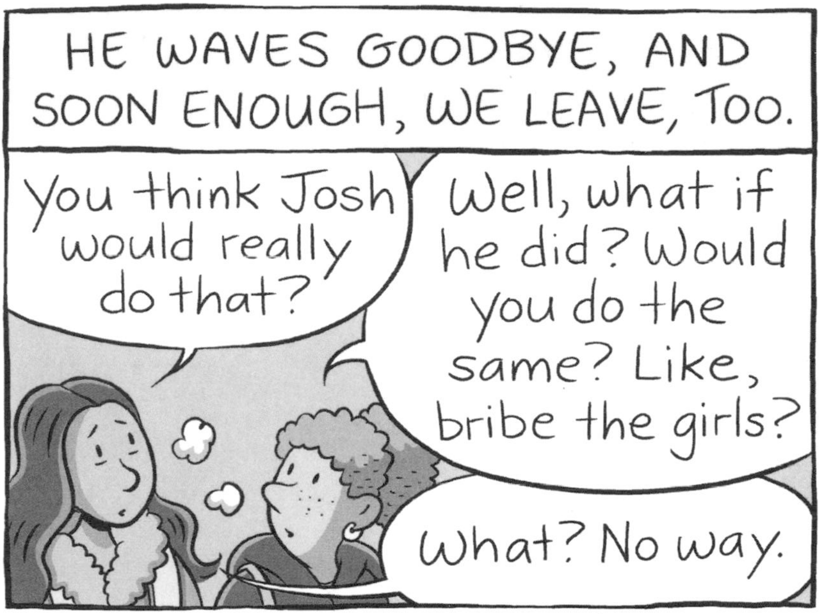
HE WAVES GOODBYE, AND SOON ENOUGH, WE LEAVE, TOO.
You think Josh would really do that?
Well, what if he did? Would you do the same? Like, bribe the girls?
What? No way.

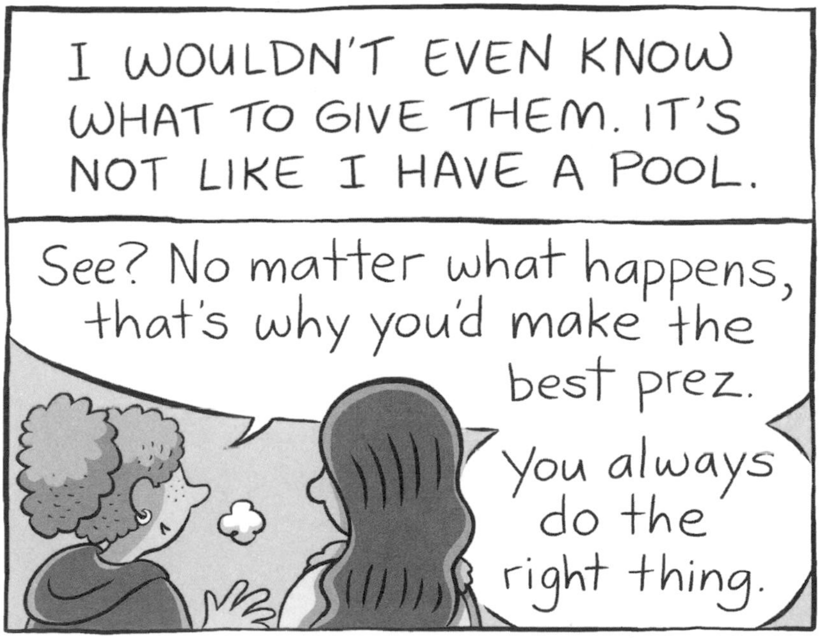
I WOULDN'T EVEN KNOW WHAT TO GIVE THEM. IT'S NOT LIKE I HAVE A POOL.
See? No matter what happens, that's why you'd make the best prez.
You always do the right thing.

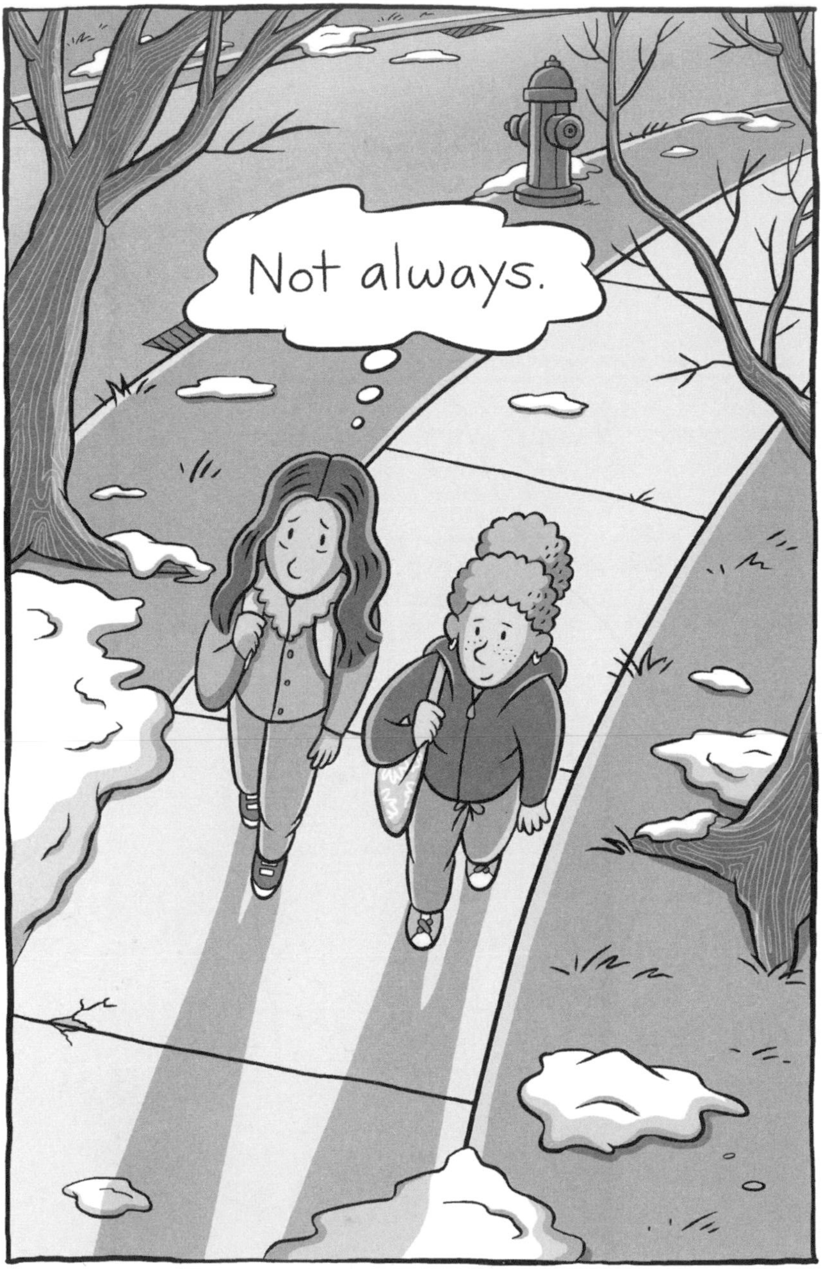
Not always.

RUBY

Back at home, I try to avoid my nosy mom, but she corners me.

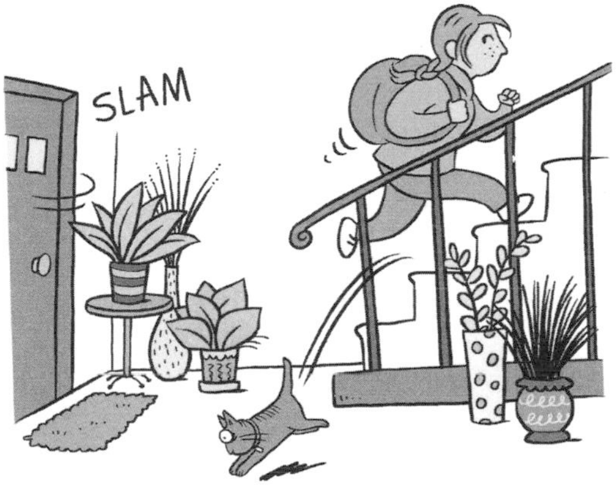
SLAM

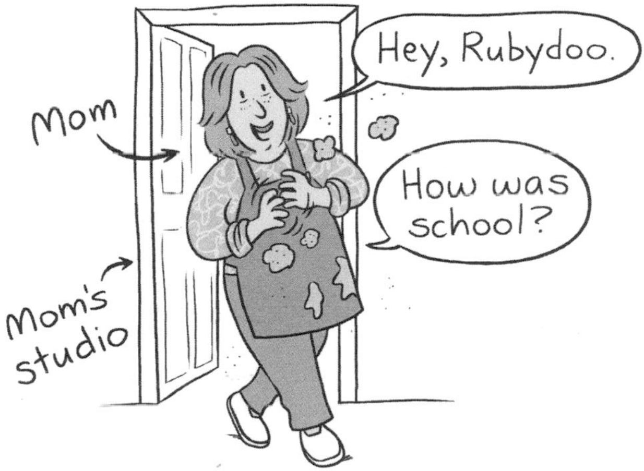
Hey, Rubydoo.
Mom
How was school?
Mom's studio

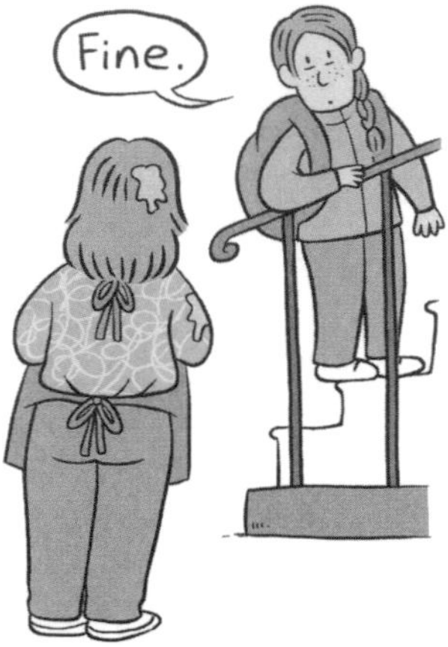
Fine.

My mom is a sculptor. That is, she makes ceramic pots, vases, candlesticks, and her specialty: little figurines. She sells them in local galleries and online. They're pretty nice. But we can't escape them—they're everywhere in our house.

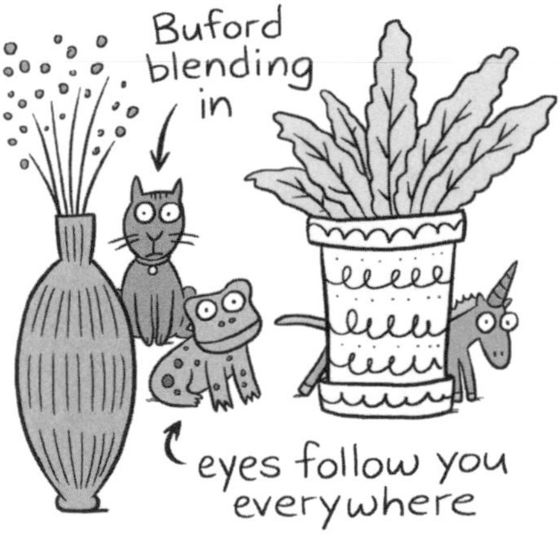
Buford blending in
eyes follow you everywhere

With all her clay creatures, it's like living in the Amazon . . . but with the wrong animal species.

One thing about my mom and me—we look a lot alike.

same build, same hair
color, same freckles...

... in the same places!
(Little Dipper-shaped
constellations across our
cheeks)

But that's where it ends. My mom has a lot more energy. And is kinda high-strung. She calls this her "artistic temperament."

I just think she needs an off button.

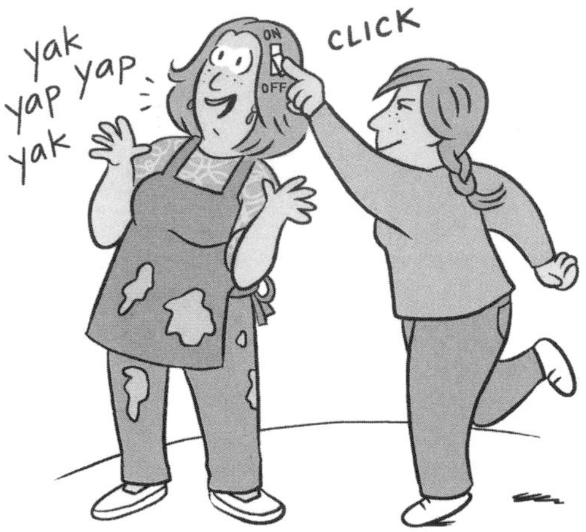
yak
yap yap
yap
yak
ON
OFF
CLICK

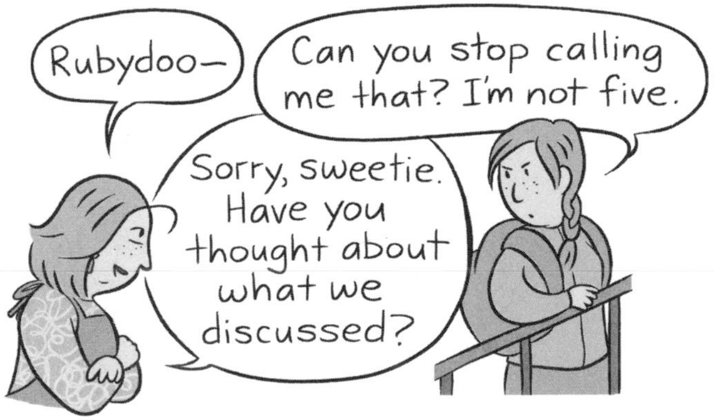
Rubydoo—
Can you stop calling me that? I'm not five.
Sorry, sweetie. Have you thought about what we discussed?

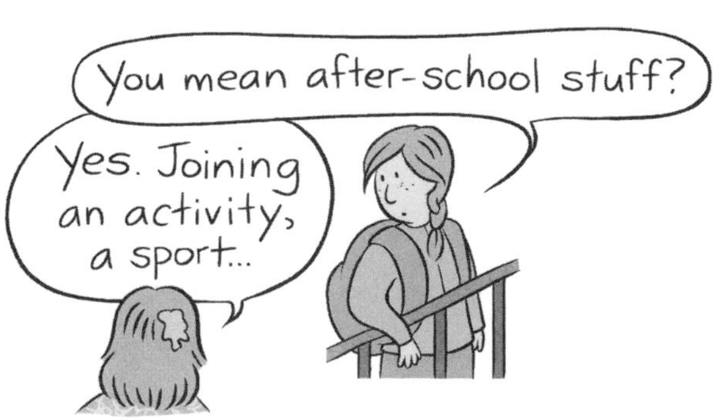
You mean after-school stuff?
Yes. Joining an activity, a sport...

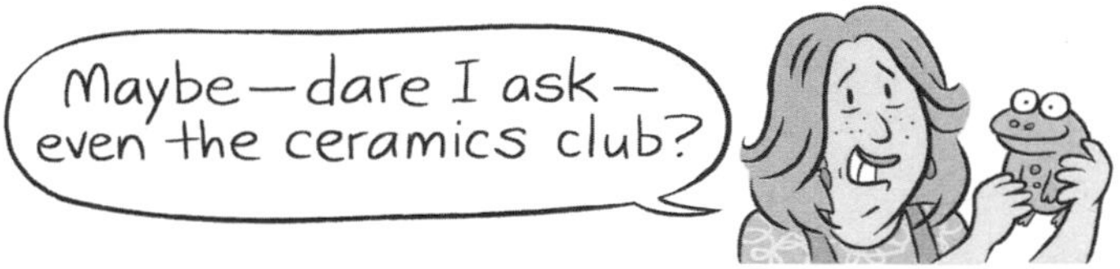
Maybe—dare I ask—even the ceramics club?

Her voice scales up hopefully.

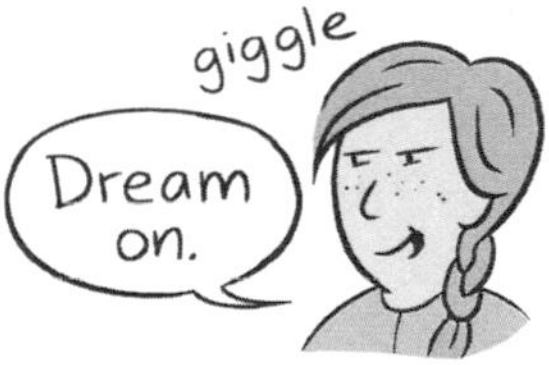
giggle
Dream on.

My mom worries about me . . . a lot. She thinks I'm antisocial and wants me to "get involved." But the last place I want to involve myself any longer than I have to is at school.

Usually, I'd change the subject and say I've gotta do homework or something, but I finally have an answer that'll make her day. Maybe her year.

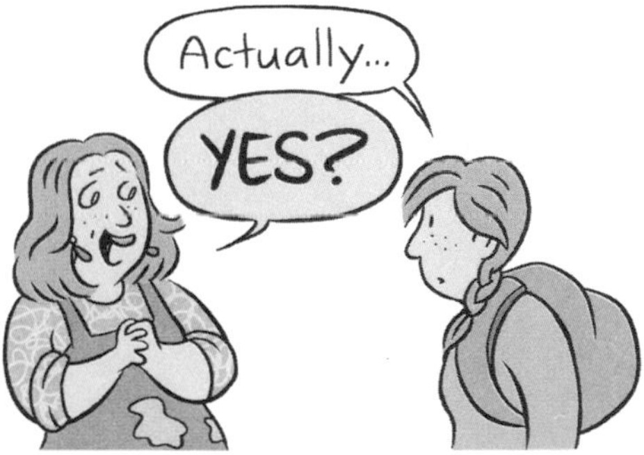
Actually...
YES?

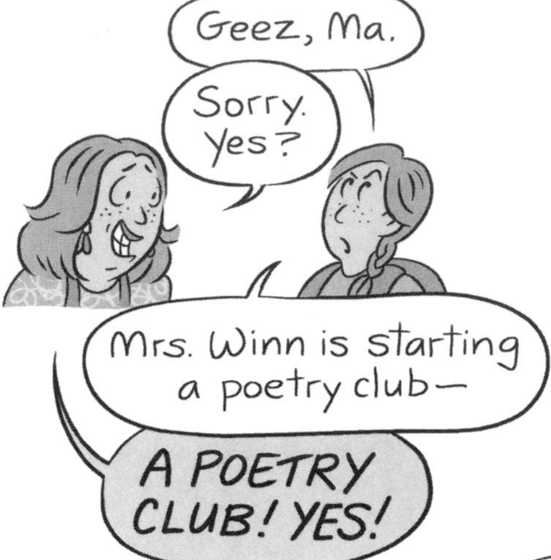
Geez, Ma.
Sorry. Yes?
Mrs. Winn is starting a poetry club—
A POETRY CLUB! YES!

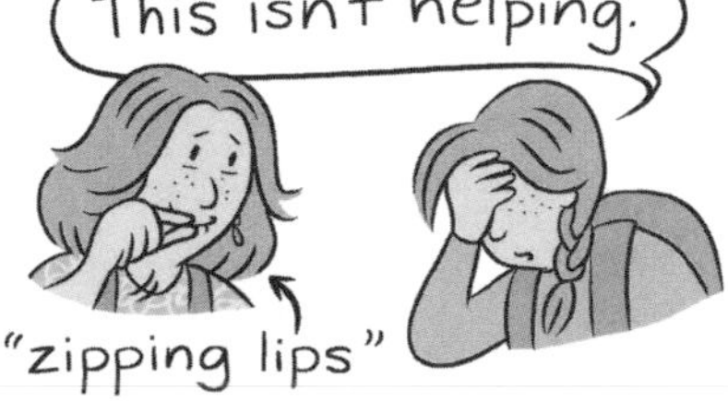
This isn't helping.
"zipping lips"

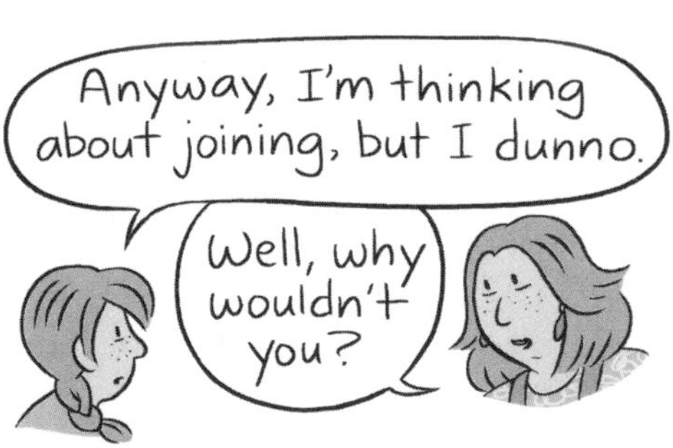
Anyway, I'm thinking about joining, but I dunno.
Well, why wouldn't you?

I think of a million reasons. I'm worried no one will like what I write. Or I won't think of anything good. Or it'll be boring, it'll be awkward, the other kids will hate me, I'll hate them, and so on and so on and—

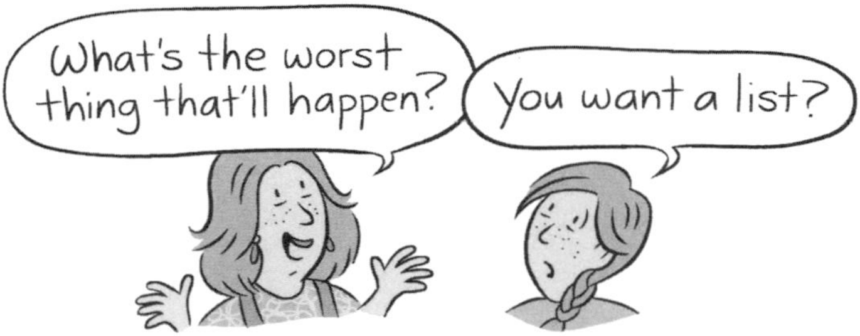
What's the worst thing that'll happen?
You want a list?

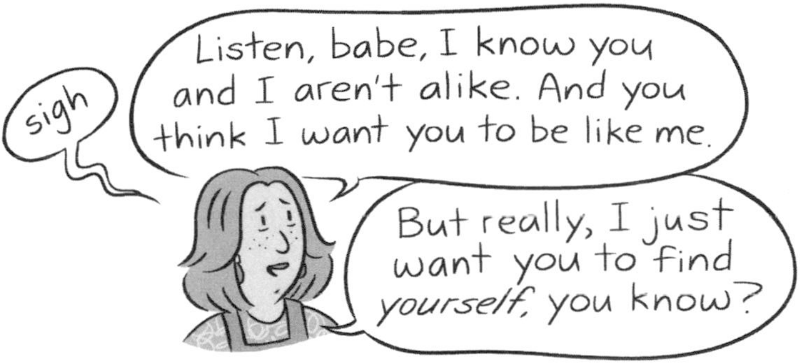
sigh
Listen, babe, I know you and I aren't alike. And you think I want you to be like me.
But really, I just want you to find *yourself*, you know?

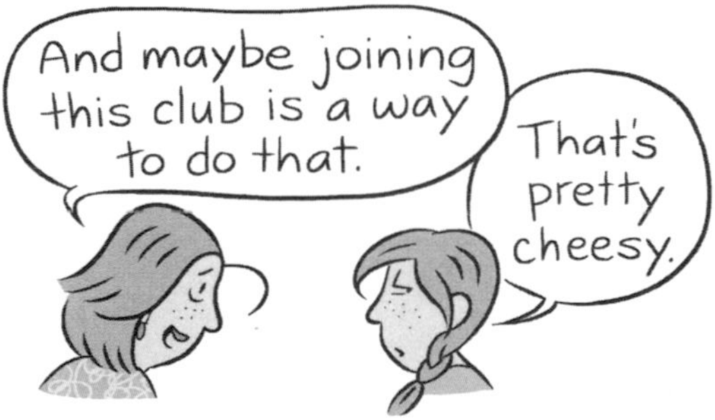
And maybe joining this club is a way to do that.
That's pretty cheesy.

But I smile. A little.

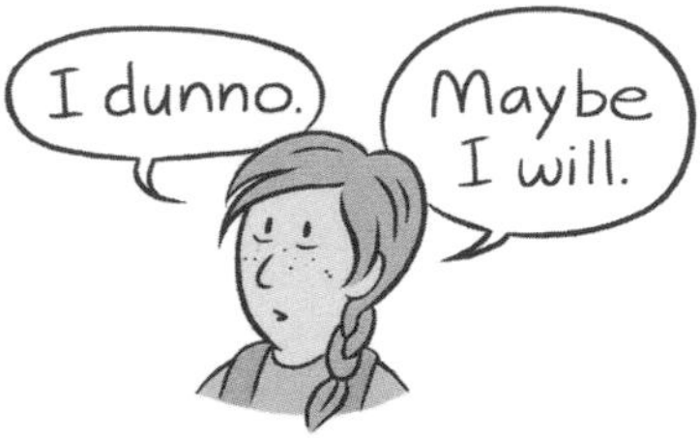
I dunno.
Maybe I will.

I know this sounds mean, but . . . anything to get her off my back.

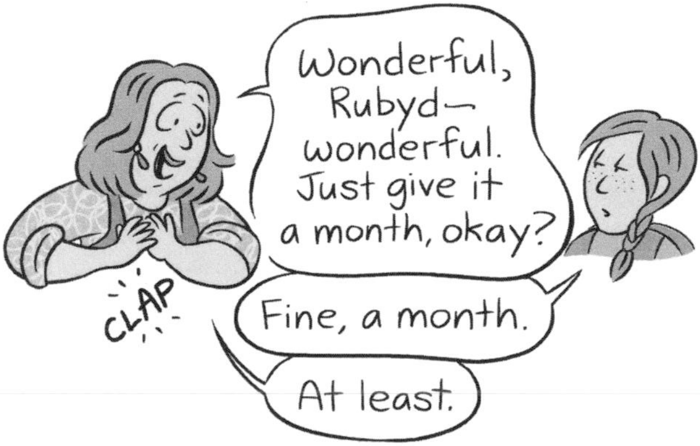
Wonderful, Rubyd— wonderful. Just give it a month, okay?
CLAP
Fine, a month.
At least.

She blows me a kiss and goes back in her studio.

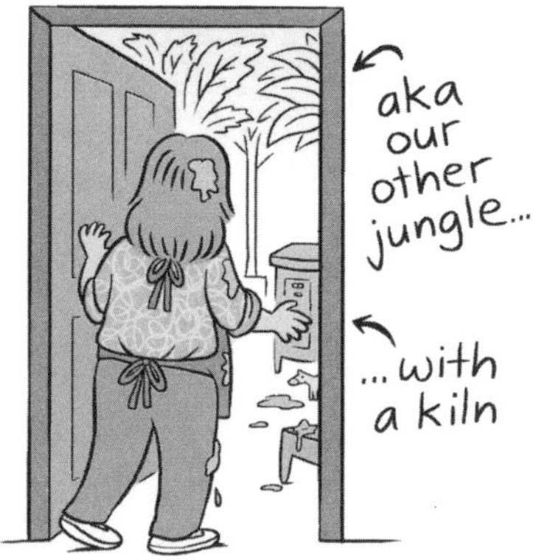
aka our other jungle...
...with a kiln

I stand there for a minute, wondering what I just agreed to.

Yeah, I know in the whole big scheme of things, joining a poetry club is no big deal. It's nothing. But . . .

. . . it's a huge step for me. I haven't joined anything since elementary school. And those weren't exactly wild successes.

frozen →

Ballet class:

THUNK

playing the recorder:

Art class:

I know, I know, this is different. But back then, I thought I'd be good at that stuff, too.

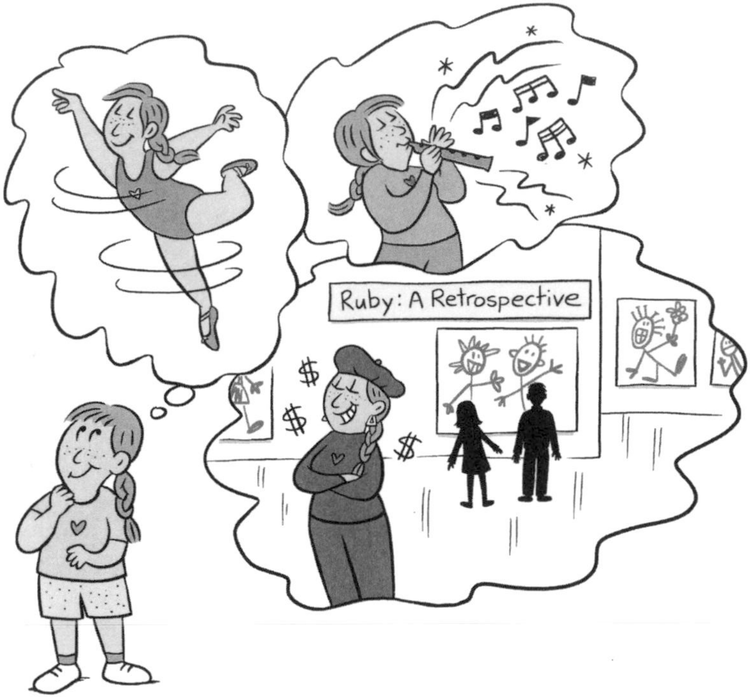
Ruby: A Retrospective

So how can I be sure?

Mia

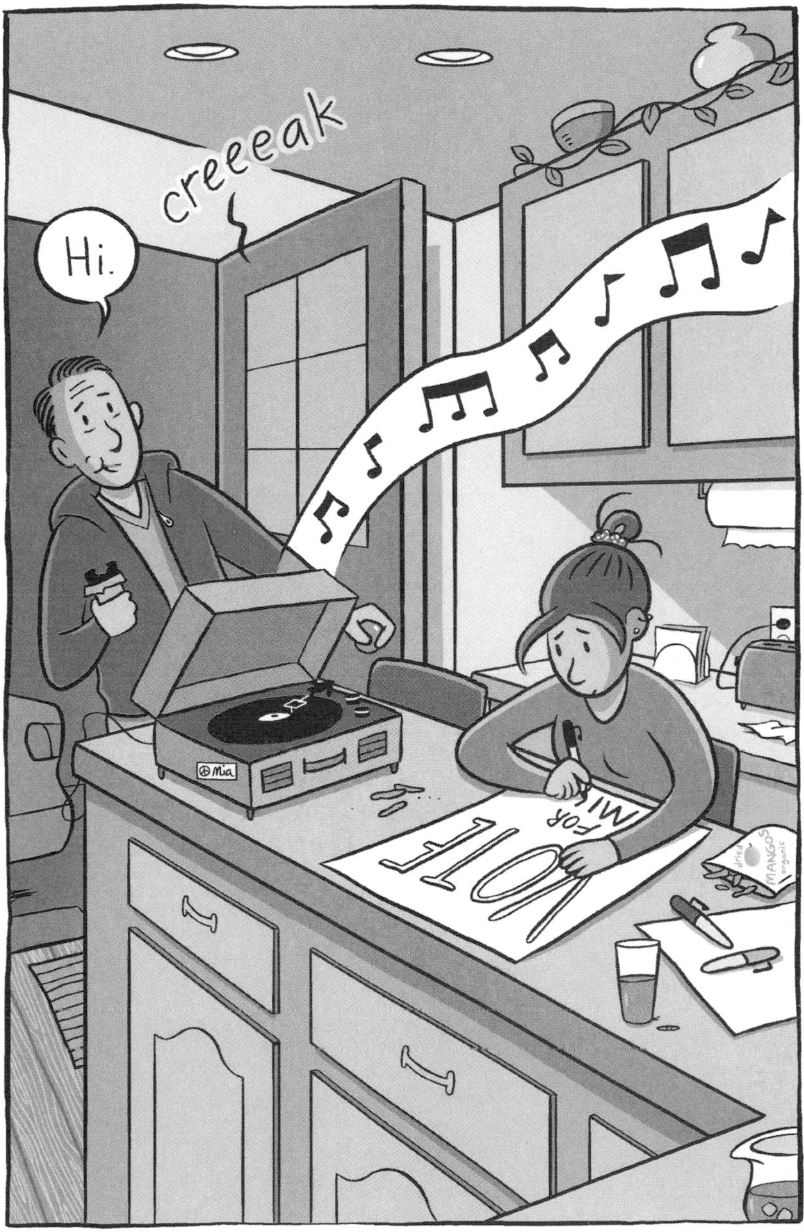
Hi.
creeeak
Mia
VOTE
FOR
dried MANGOS organic

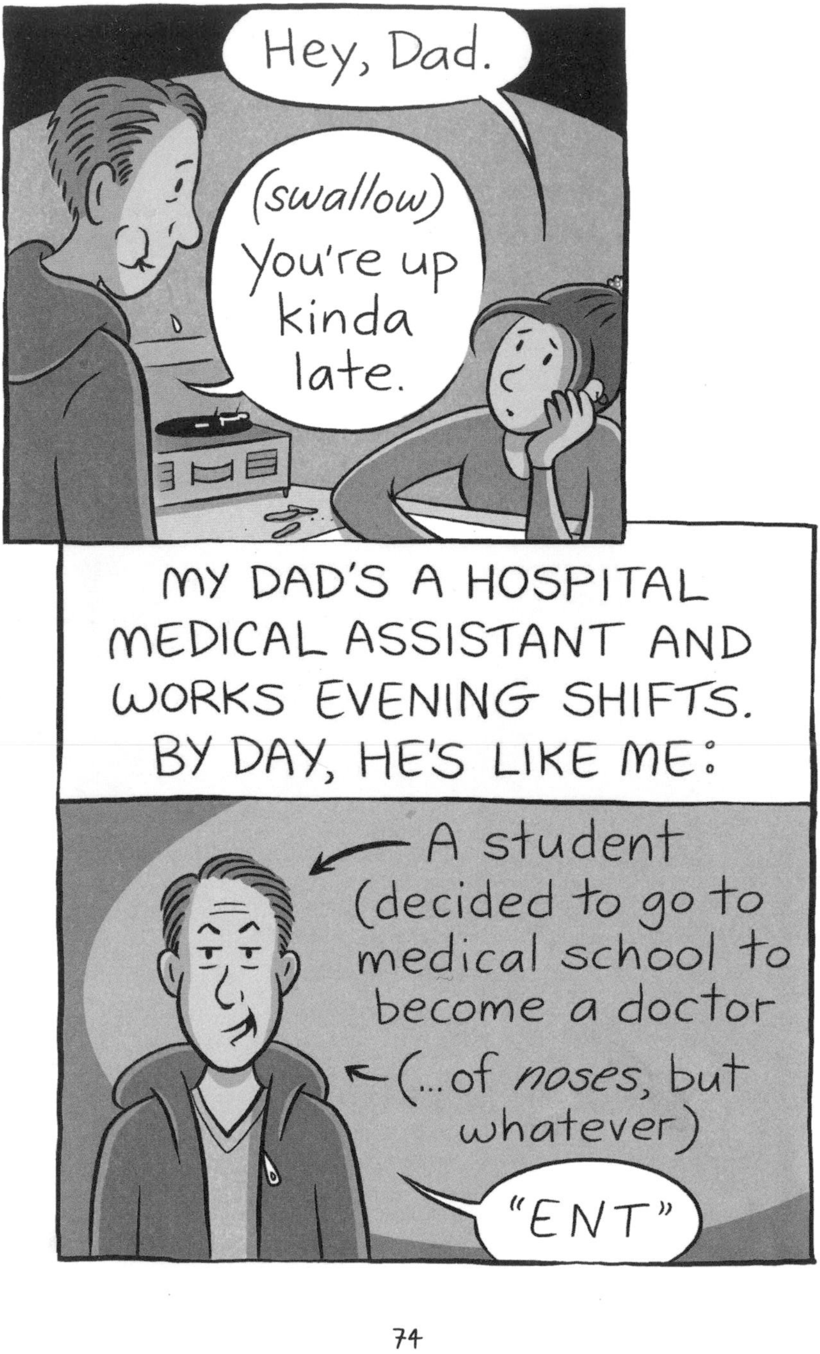
Hey, Dad.
(swallow) You're up kinda late.
MY DAD'S A HOSPITAL MEDICAL ASSISTANT AND WORKS EVENING SHIFTS. BY DAY, HE'S LIKE ME:
A student (decided to go to medical school to become a doctor
(...of *noses*, but whatever)
"ENT"

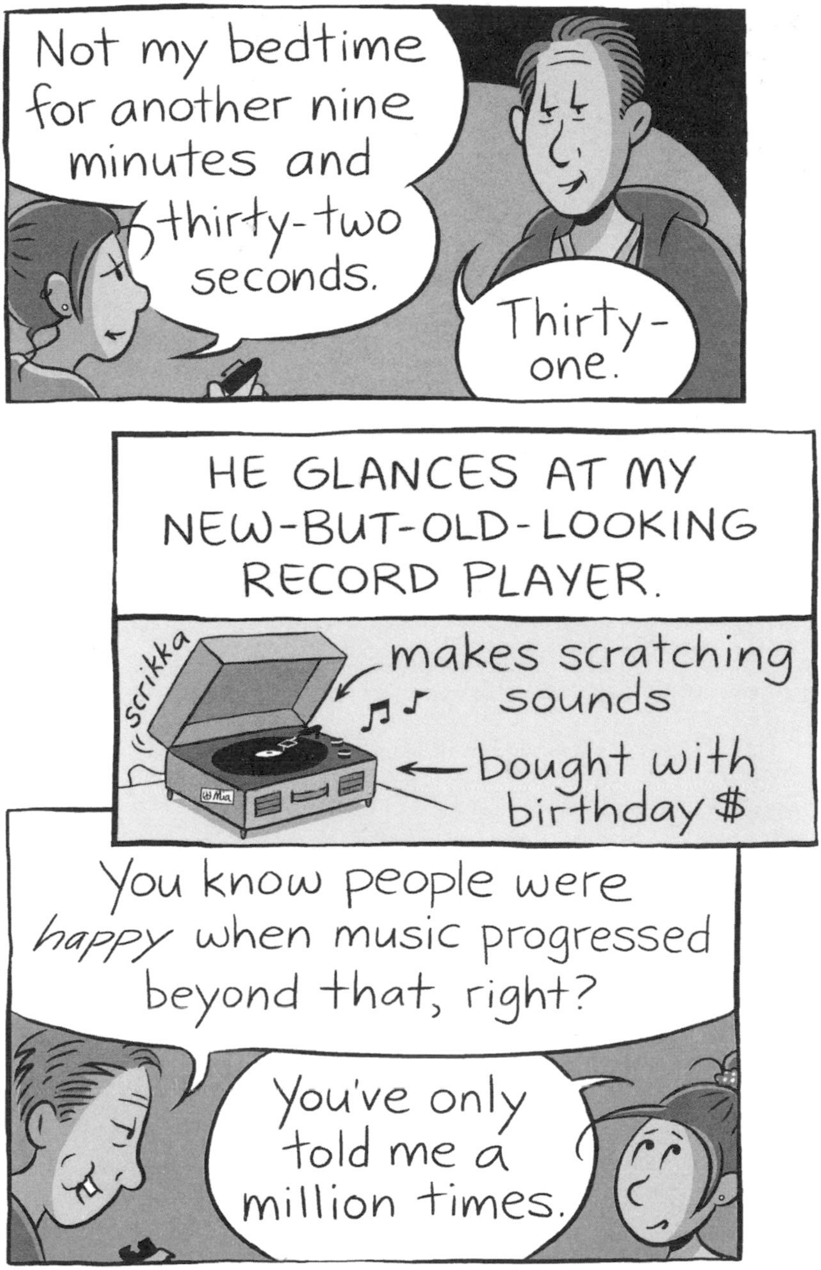
Not my bedtime for another nine minutes and thirty-two seconds.
Thirty-one.
HE GLANCES AT MY NEW-BUT-OLD-LOOKING RECORD PLAYER.
scrikka
makes scratching sounds
bought with birthday $
You know people were *happy* when music progressed beyond that, right?
You've only told me a million times.

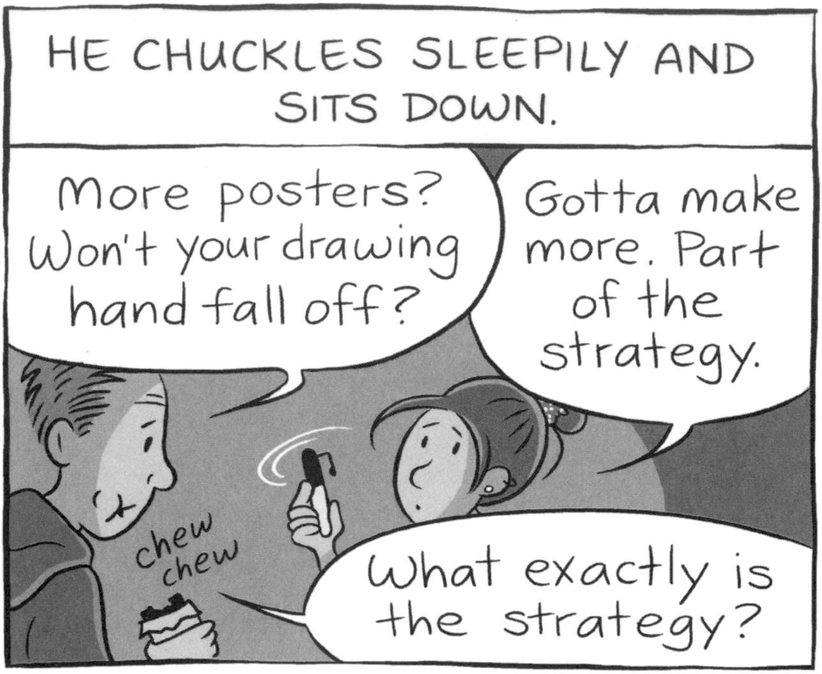
HE CHUCKLES SLEEPILY AND SITS DOWN.
More posters? Won't your drawing hand fall off?
Gotta make more. Part of the strategy.
chew chew
What exactly is the strategy?

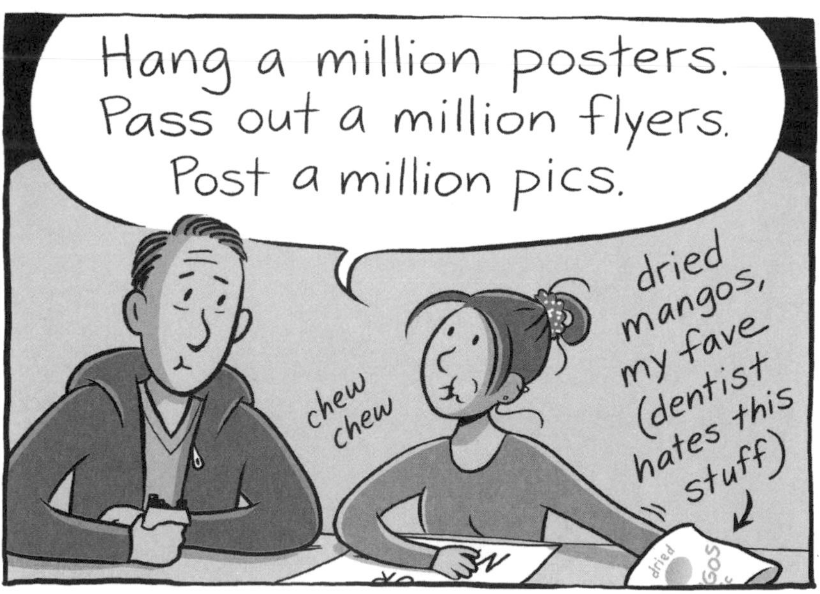
Hang a million posters. Pass out a million flyers. Post a million pics.
chew chew
dried mangos, my fave (dentist hates this stuff)
dried

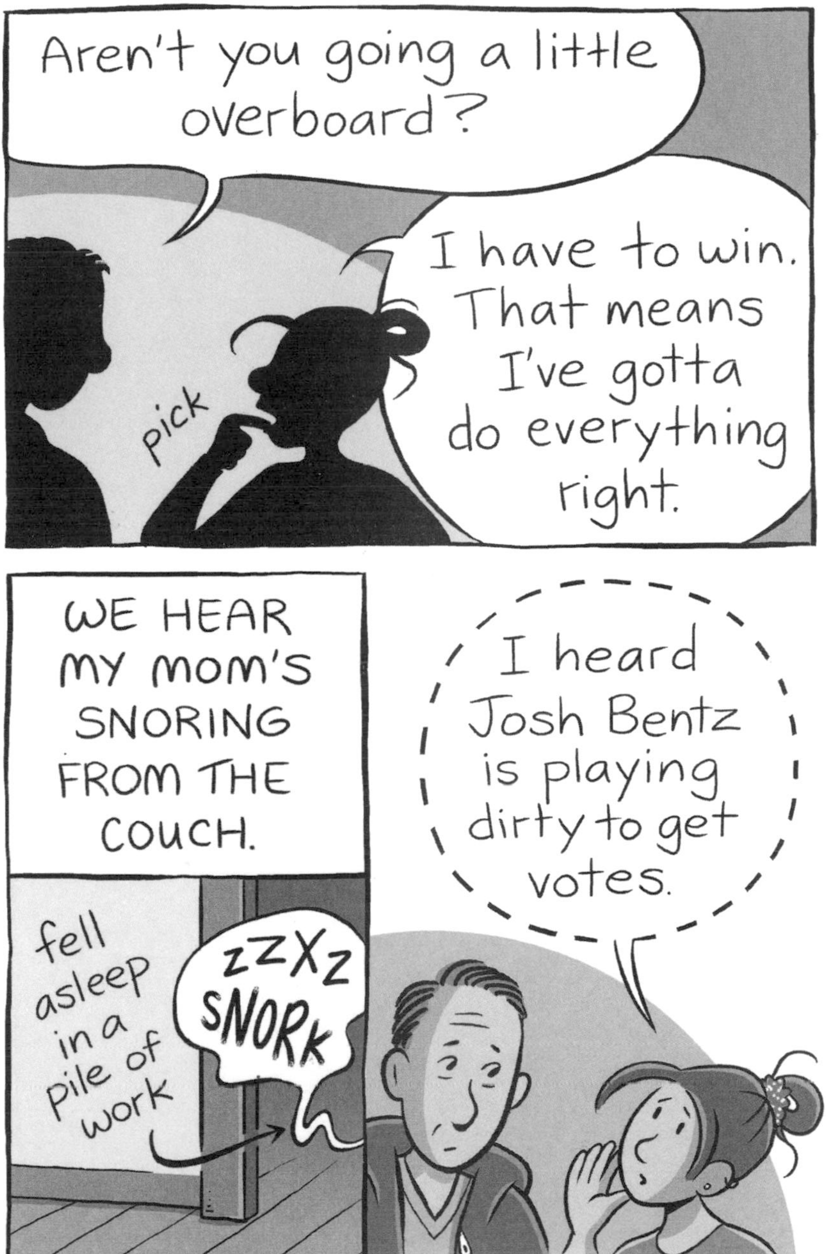
Aren't you going a little overboard?
I have to win. That means I've gotta do everything right.
pick
WE HEAR MY MOM'S SNORING FROM THE COUCH.
fell asleep in a pile of work
zZXz SNORK
I heard Josh Bentz is playing dirty to get votes.

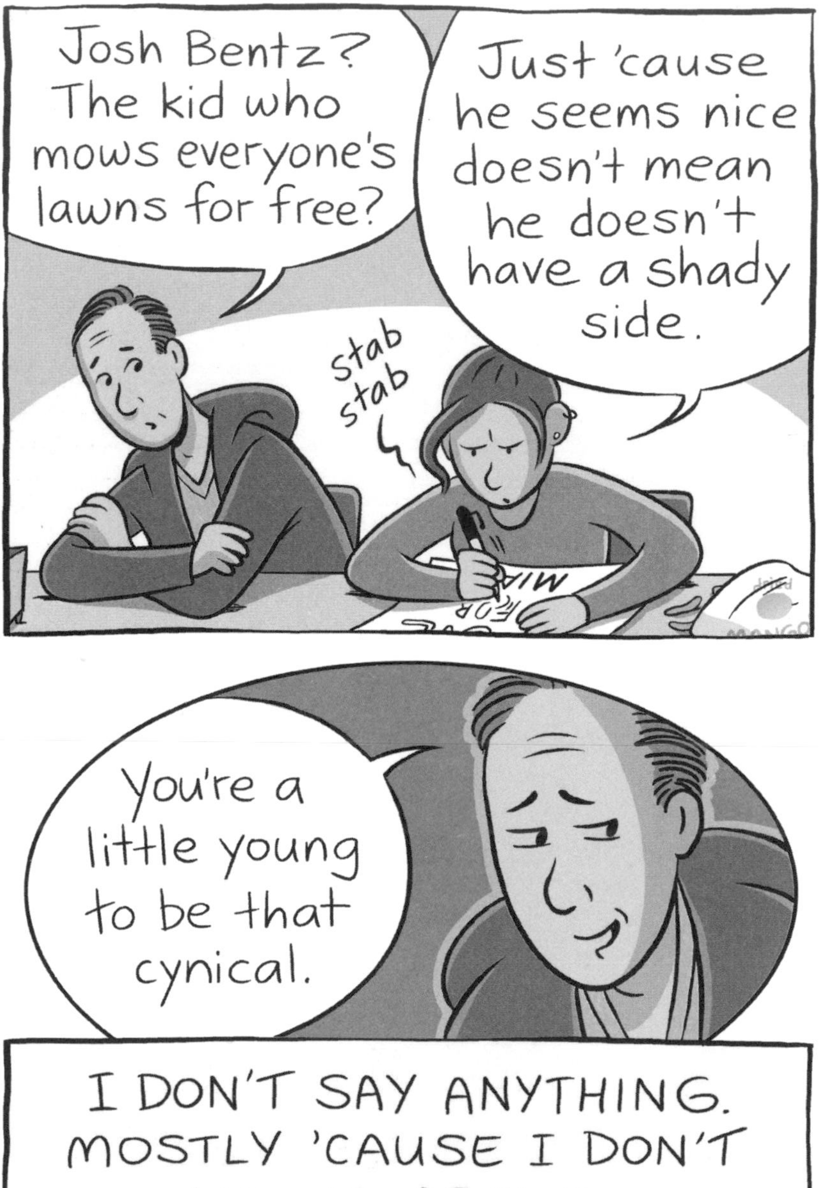
Josh Bentz? The kid who mows everyone's lawns for free?
Just 'cause he seems nice doesn't mean he doesn't have a shady side.
stab stab
You're a little young to be that cynical.
I DON'T SAY ANYTHING. MOSTLY 'CAUSE I DON'T WANNA ARGUE.

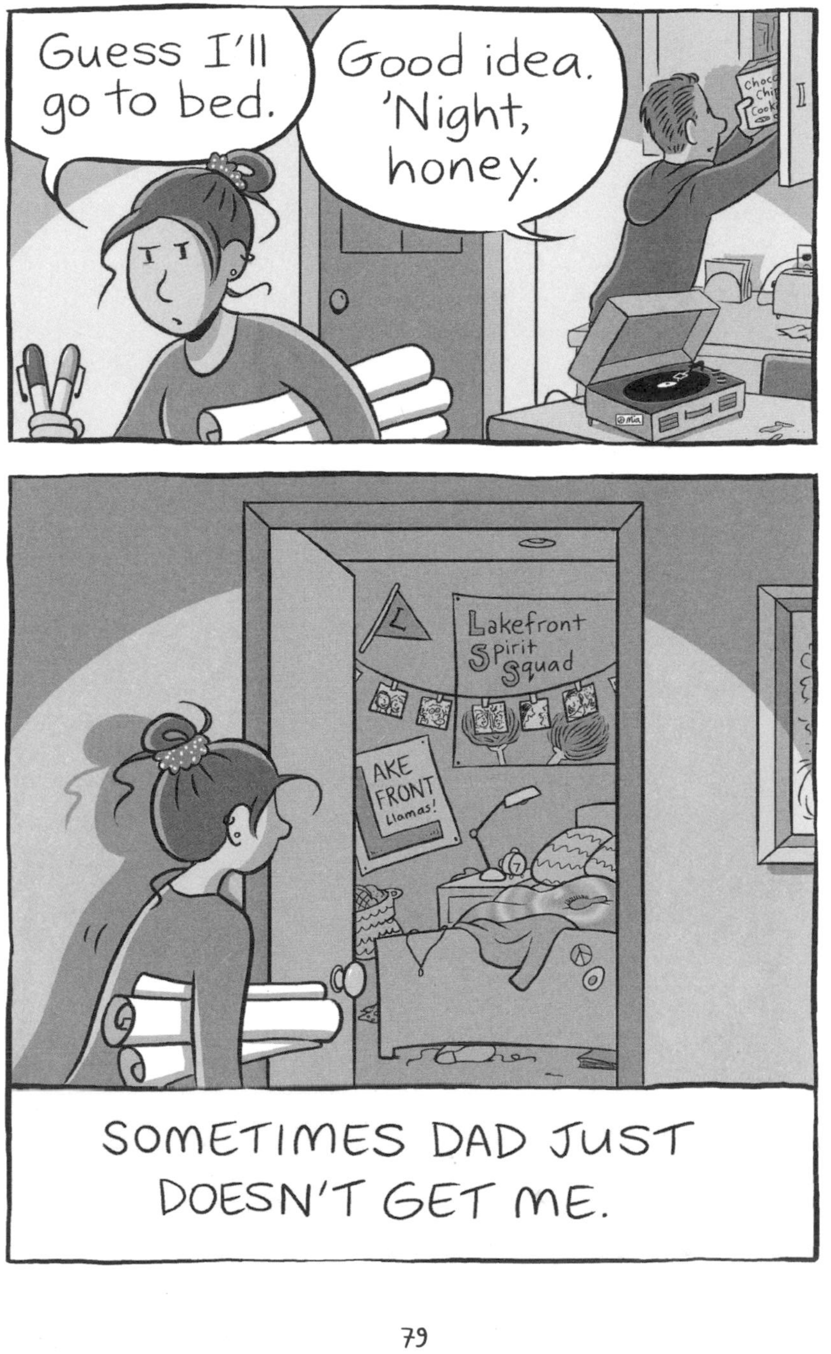
Guess I'll go to bed.
Good idea. 'Night, honey.
Lakefront Spirit Squad
AKE FRONT Llamas!
SOMETIMES DAD JUST DOESN'T GET ME.

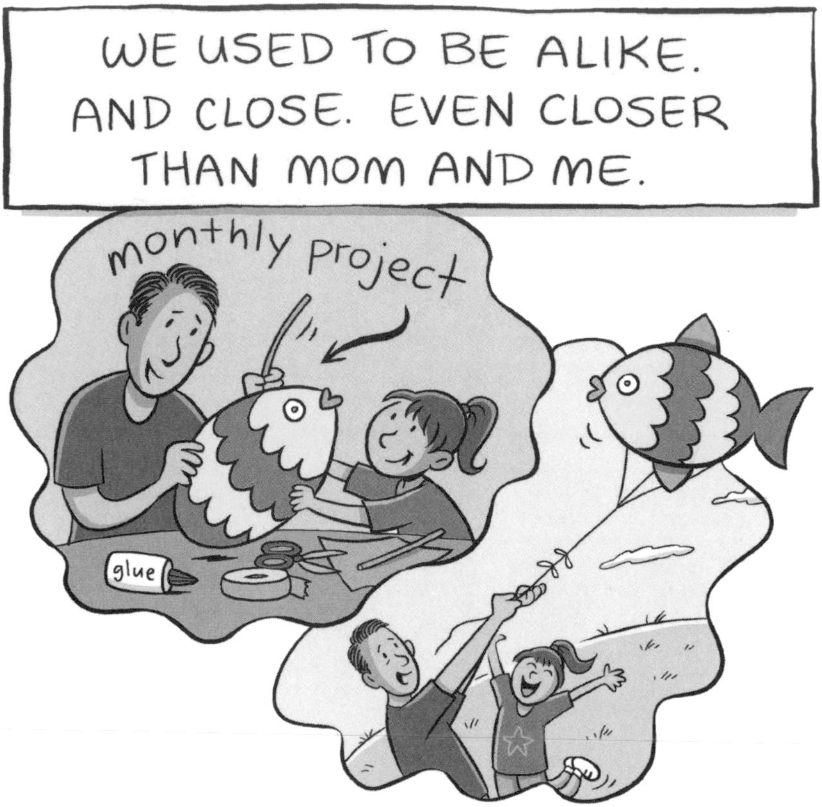
WE USED TO BE ALIKE. AND CLOSE. EVEN CLOSER THAN MOM AND ME.
monthly project
glue

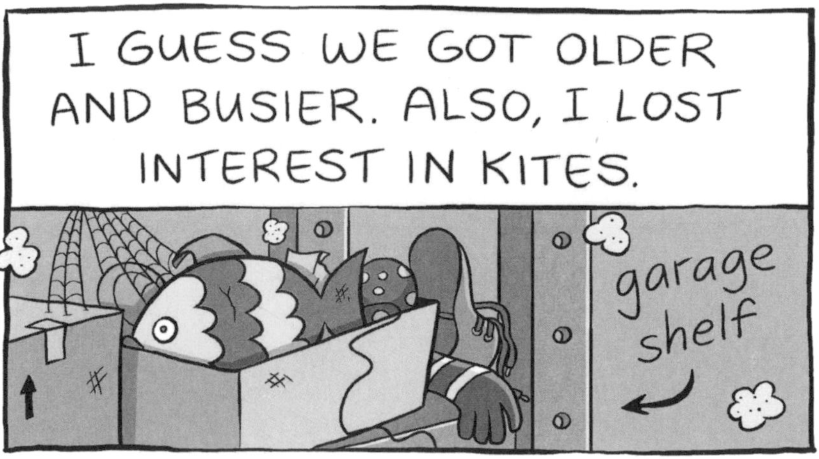
I GUESS WE GOT OLDER AND BUSIER. ALSO, I LOST INTEREST IN KITES.
garage shelf

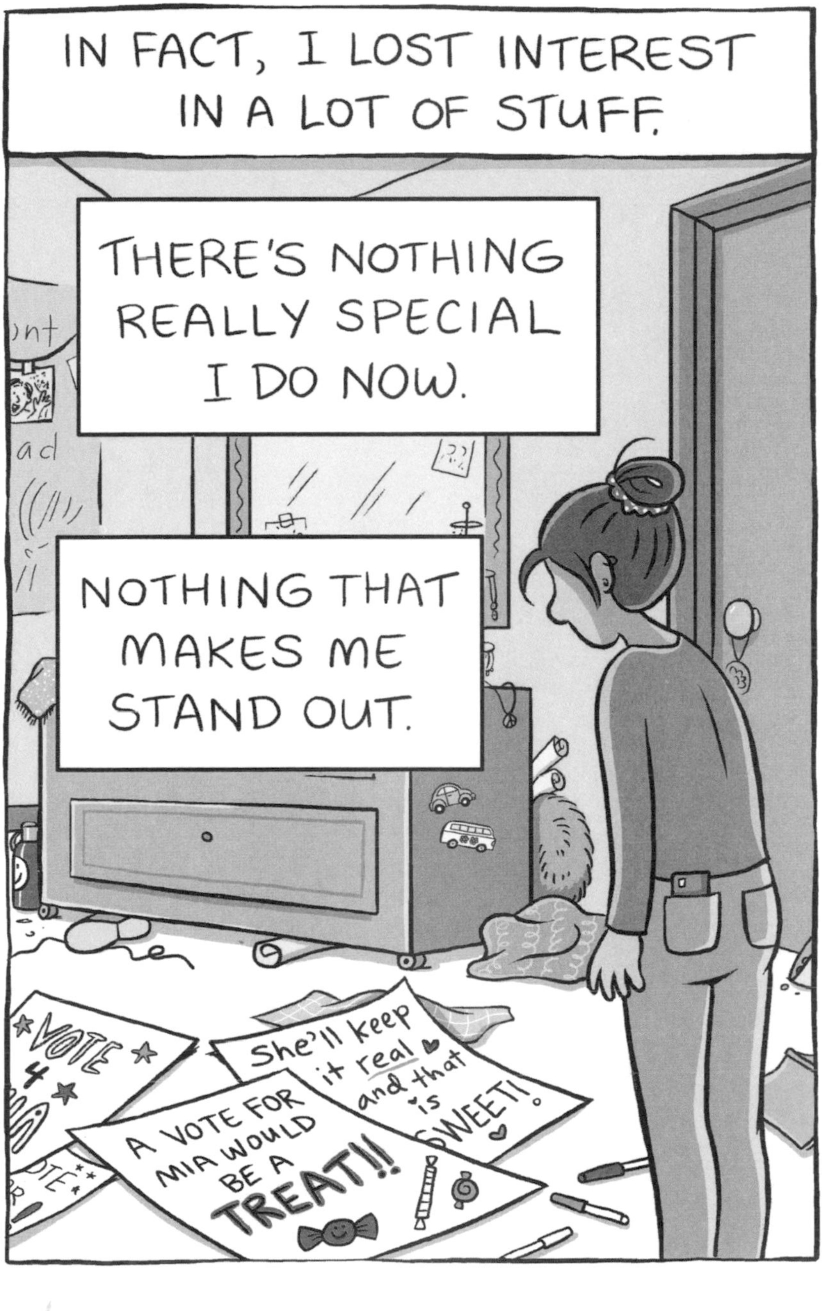
IN FACT, I LOST INTEREST IN A LOT OF STUFF.
THERE'S NOTHING REALLY SPECIAL I DO NOW.
NOTHING THAT MAKES ME STAND OUT.
VOTE 4
She'll keep it real and that is SWEET!
A VOTE FOR MIA WOULD BE A TREAT!!

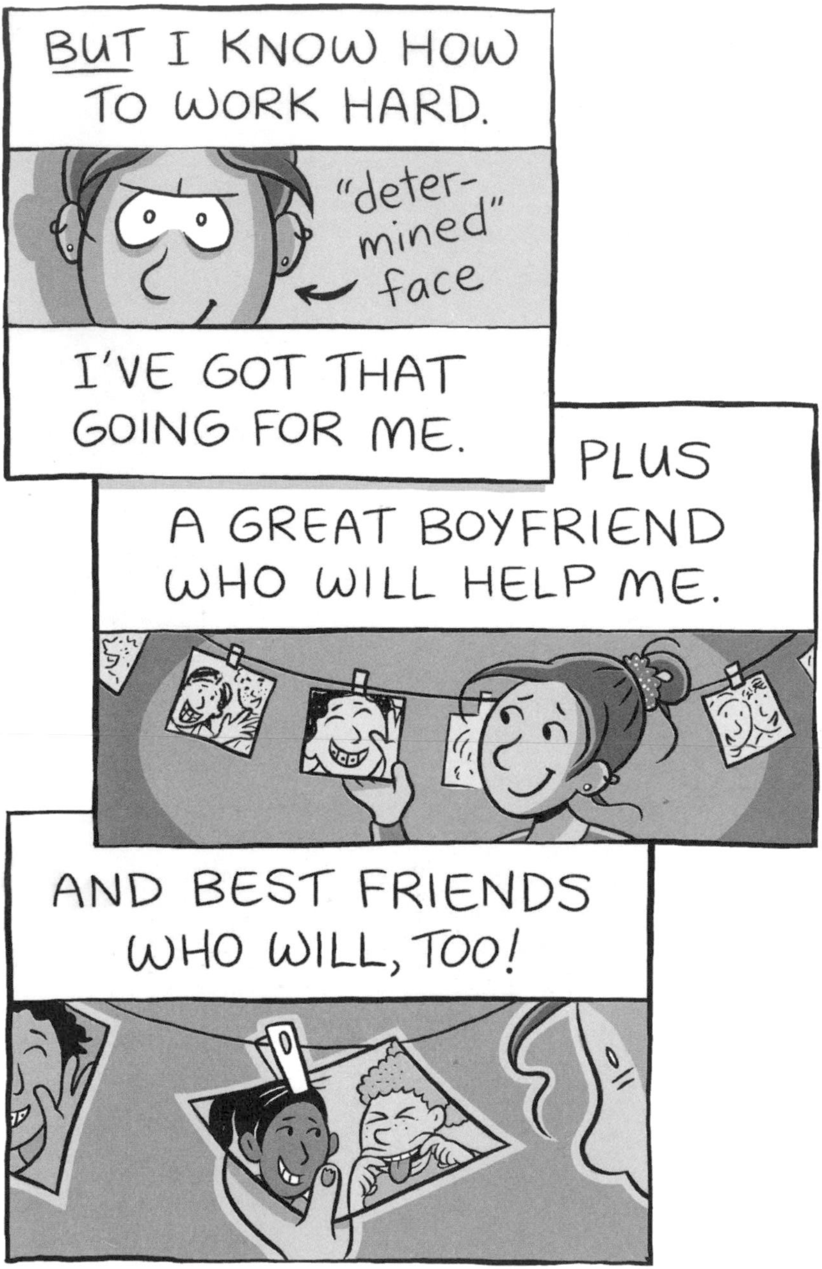
BUT I KNOW HOW TO WORK HARD.
"deter-mined" face
I'VE GOT THAT GOING FOR ME.
PLUS A GREAT BOYFRIEND WHO WILL HELP ME.
AND BEST FRIENDS WHO WILL, TOO!

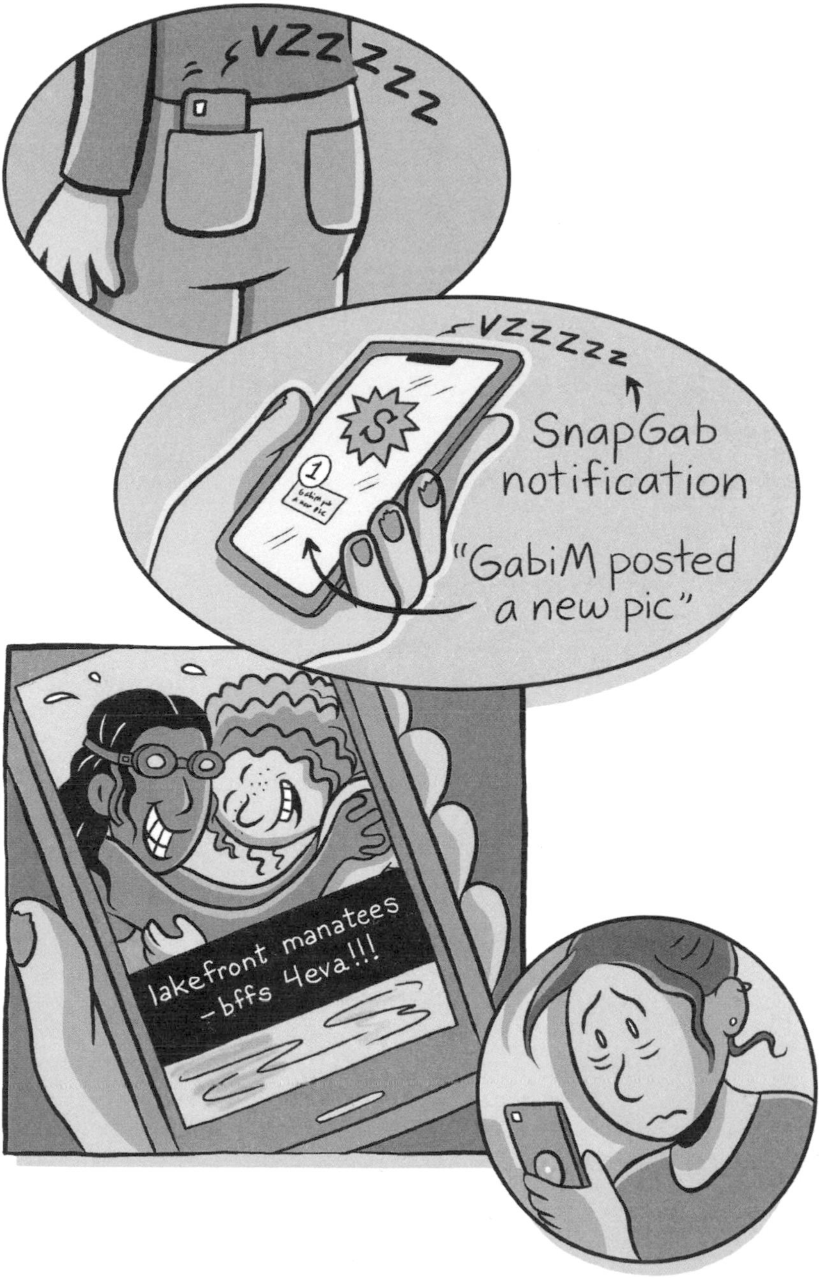
VZZZZZZZ
VZZZZZZ
SnapGab notification
"GabiM posted a new pic"
lakefront manatees
-bffs 4eva!!!

RUBY

Me and my big mouth.

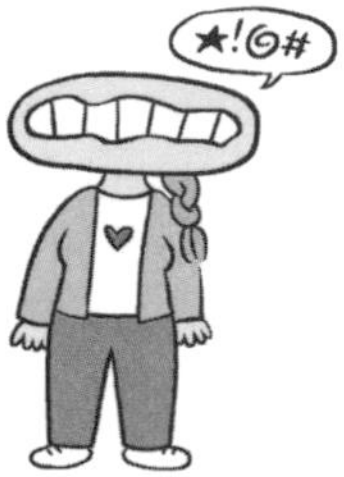
★!@#

I'm in Mrs. Winn's room, right before first period. It's on my way. Thought I'd pop in and tell her the good news.

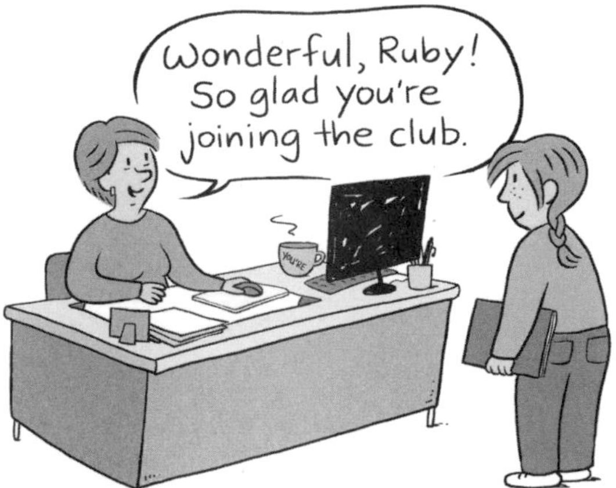
Wonderful, Ruby! So glad you're joining the club.
YOU'RE

And as part of your new membership responsibilities...

... I'd like you to help recruit other students.

What?

I don't... get it. Don't you already have members?

Mrs. Winn gets a funny look on her face.

Well...

Right now it's just you and Leah. Kieran has violin lessons and swim practice, so he's out.

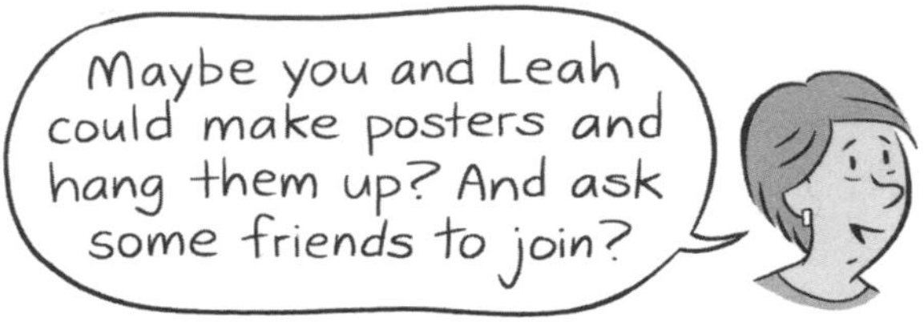
Maybe you and Leah could make posters and hang them up? And ask some friends to join?

Uh. Friends?

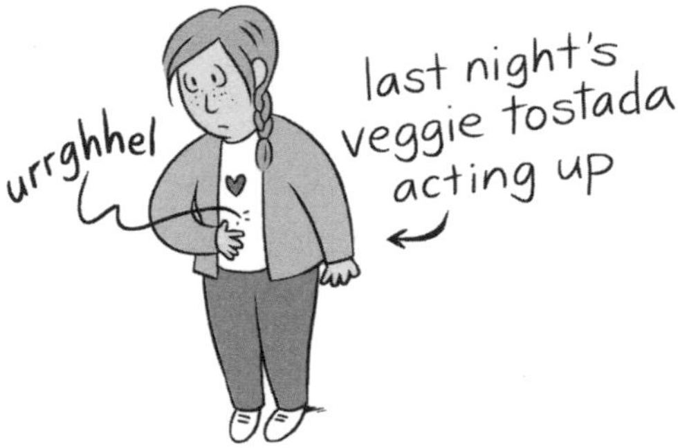
urrghhel
last night's veggie tostada acting up

Mrs. Winn grins in that pleading way that reminds me too much of my mom.

But it's one thing to say no to a parent. It's another to say no to your favorite teacher.

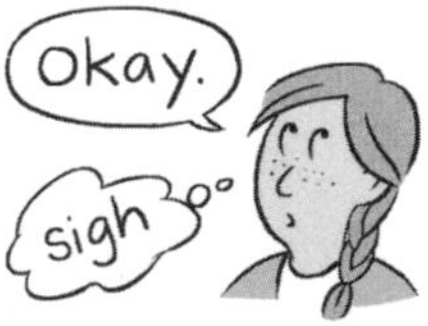
Okay.
sigh

Great, Ruby! Thank you!
I'll get some poster board and markers from the art room. You and Leah have special permission to make them during class. You can use the library.

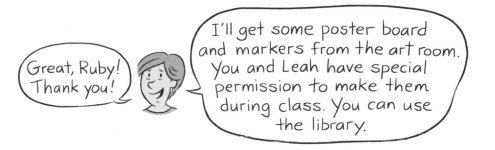

Little Leah who's even quieter than me?

AWKWARD

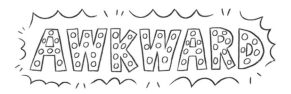

I'm regretting this already.

I head to first period. It's the only time that history class flies.

yakka yak yakkity
z
drool
tick tick tick
Slow down

BRNNG

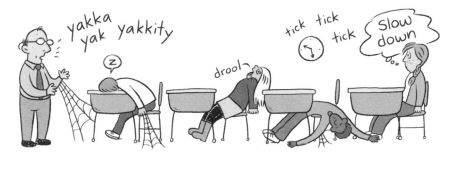

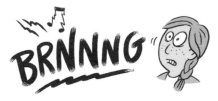

I return to Mrs. Winn's to collect our supplies. Leah is already there, holding a stack of poster board bigger than she is. Mrs. Winn gives me a set of markers. Leah and I head to the library—which, luckily, is right down the hall. That means we don't have to do anything awful like:

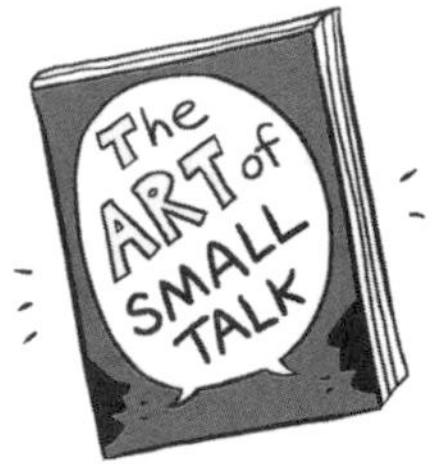
The ART of SMALL TALK

In the library, Ms. Regas points us to a table in back. We sit down silently. But then Leah smiles kinda shyly at me and holds up a notebook.

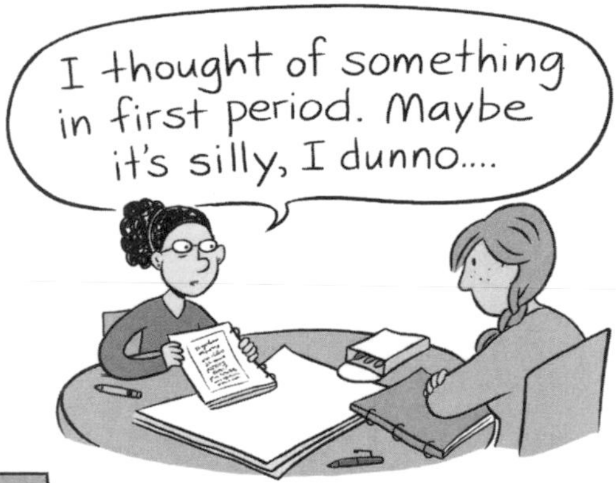
I thought of something in first period. Maybe it's silly, I dunno....

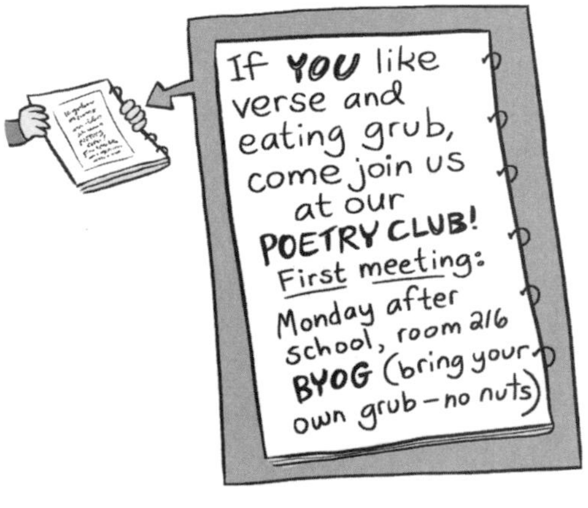
If YOU like verse and eating grub, come join us at our POETRY CLUB!
First meeting: Monday after school, room 216
BYOG (bring your own grub—no nuts)

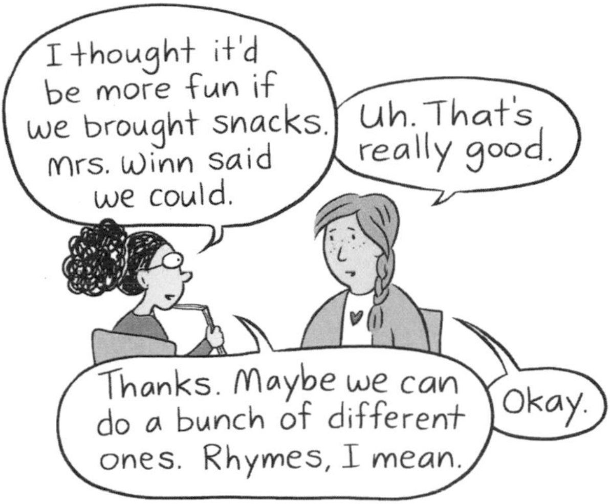
I thought it'd be more fun if we brought snacks. Mrs. Winn said we could.
Uh. That's really good.
Thanks. Maybe we can do a bunch of different ones. Rhymes, I mean.
Okay.

We sit and think. After a minute or two, I come up with some ideas.

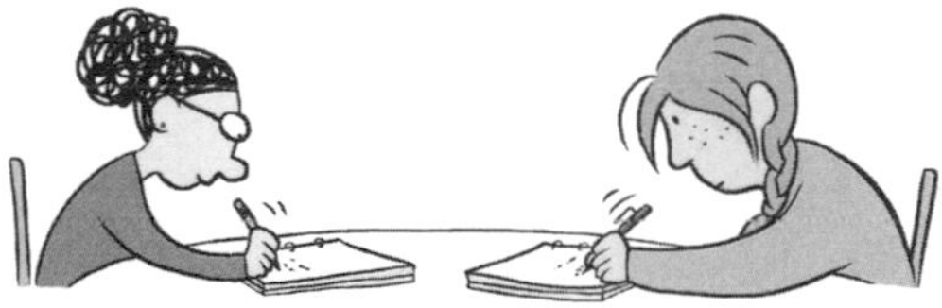

Huh. This isn't so bad.

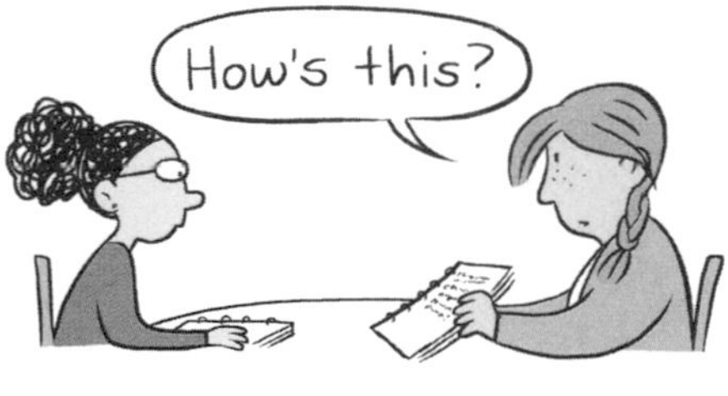
How's this?

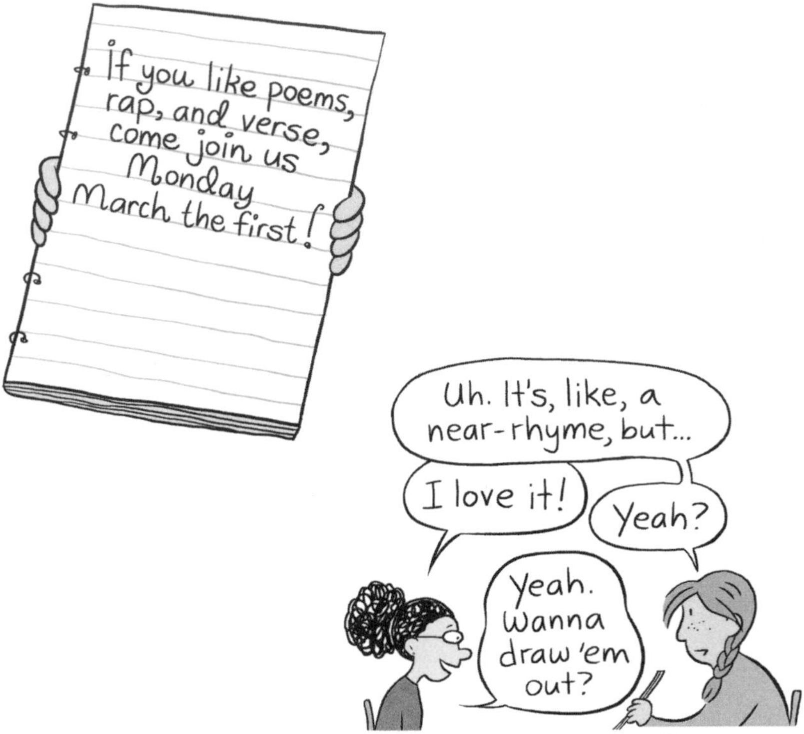
If you like poems,
rap, and verse,
come join us
Monday
March the first!
Uh. It's, like, a
near-rhyme, but...
I love it!
Yeah?
Yeah.
Wanna
draw 'em
out?

We do. We use markers in every color. I even illustrate a poster in my famous block letters (perfected in third grade). Soon, I'm not worrying about small talk and stuff. We bounce more ideas off each other.

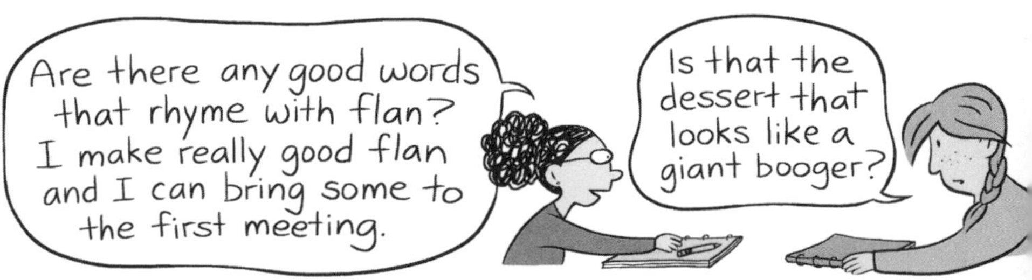
Are there any good words
that rhyme with flan?
I make really good flan
and I can bring some to
the first meeting.
Is that the
dessert that
looks like a
giant booger?

She gets this stunned look, like I just dumped flan in her lap. Oh no, me and my big mouth. I'm such a—

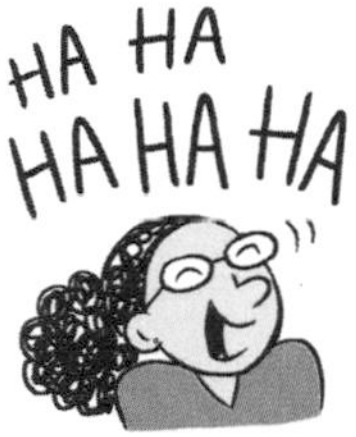
HA HA
HA HA HA

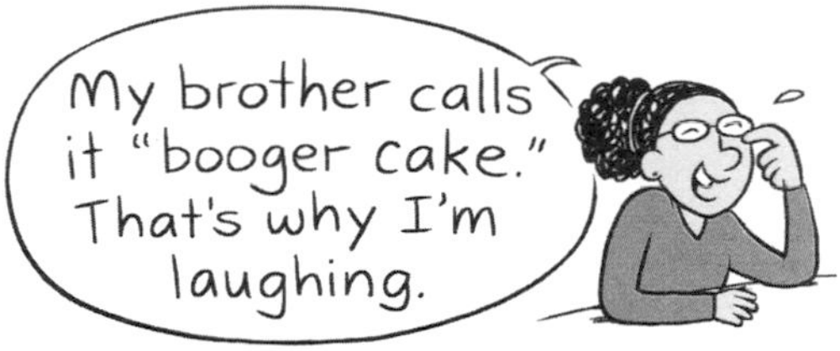
My brother calls it "booger cake." That's why I'm laughing.

I laugh, too.

Before we know it, we have a stack of finished posters . . . including one with flan (rhymed with "spawn"—don't ask). And no time to spare. The bell's about to ring.

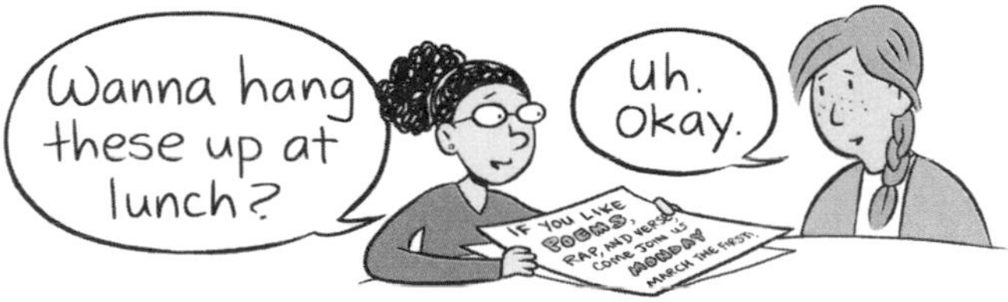
Wanna hang these up at lunch?
Uh. Okay.
IF YOU LIKE POEMS, RAP, AND VERSE, COME JOIN US MONDAY MARCH THE FIRST.

The bell rings. We take the posters back to Mrs. Winn's and separate for third period.

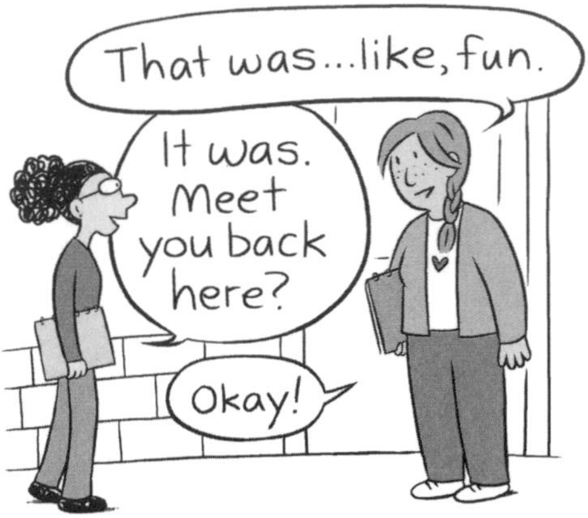
That was...like, fun.
It was. Meet you back here?
Okay!

I head to gym. Not my favorite class.

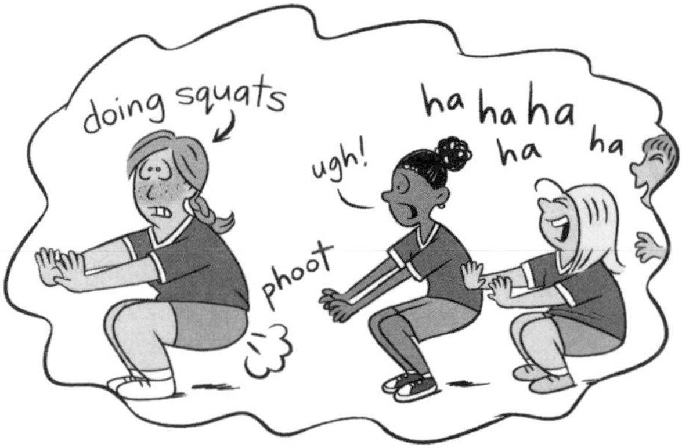
doing squats
ugh!
ha ha ha
ha
ha
phoot

But for the first time walking there . . .

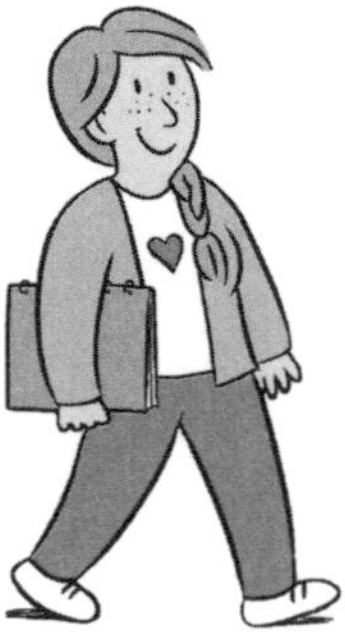

. . . I'm smiling.

Mia

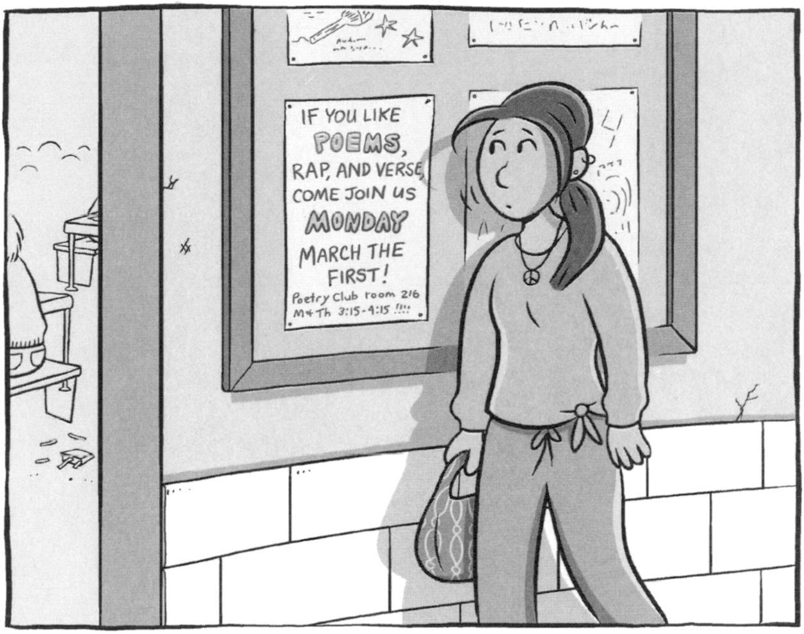
IF YOU LIKE
POEMS,
RAP, AND VERSE,
COME JOIN US
MONDAY
MARCH THE
FIRST!
Poetry Club room 216
M&Th 3:15-4:15 !!!!

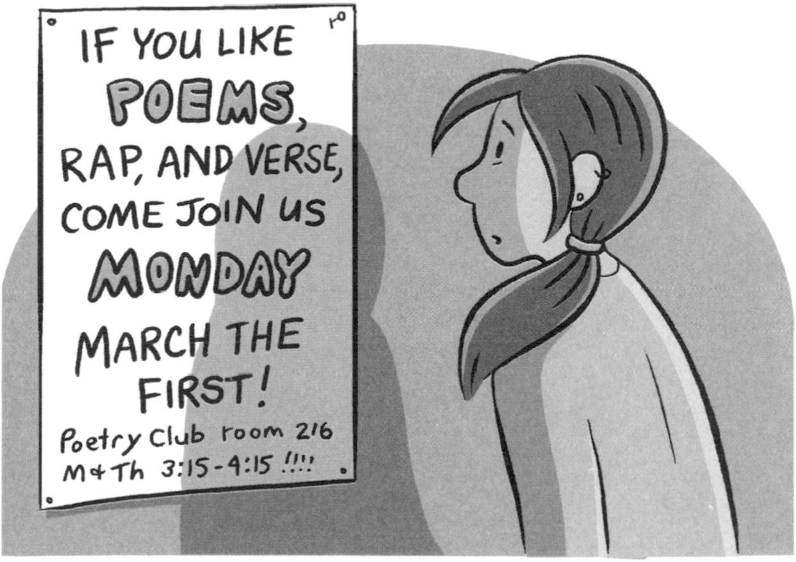
IF YOU LIKE
POEMS,
RAP, AND VERSE,
COME JOIN US
MONDAY
MARCH THE
FIRST!
Poetry Club room 216
M&Th 3:15-4:15 !!!!

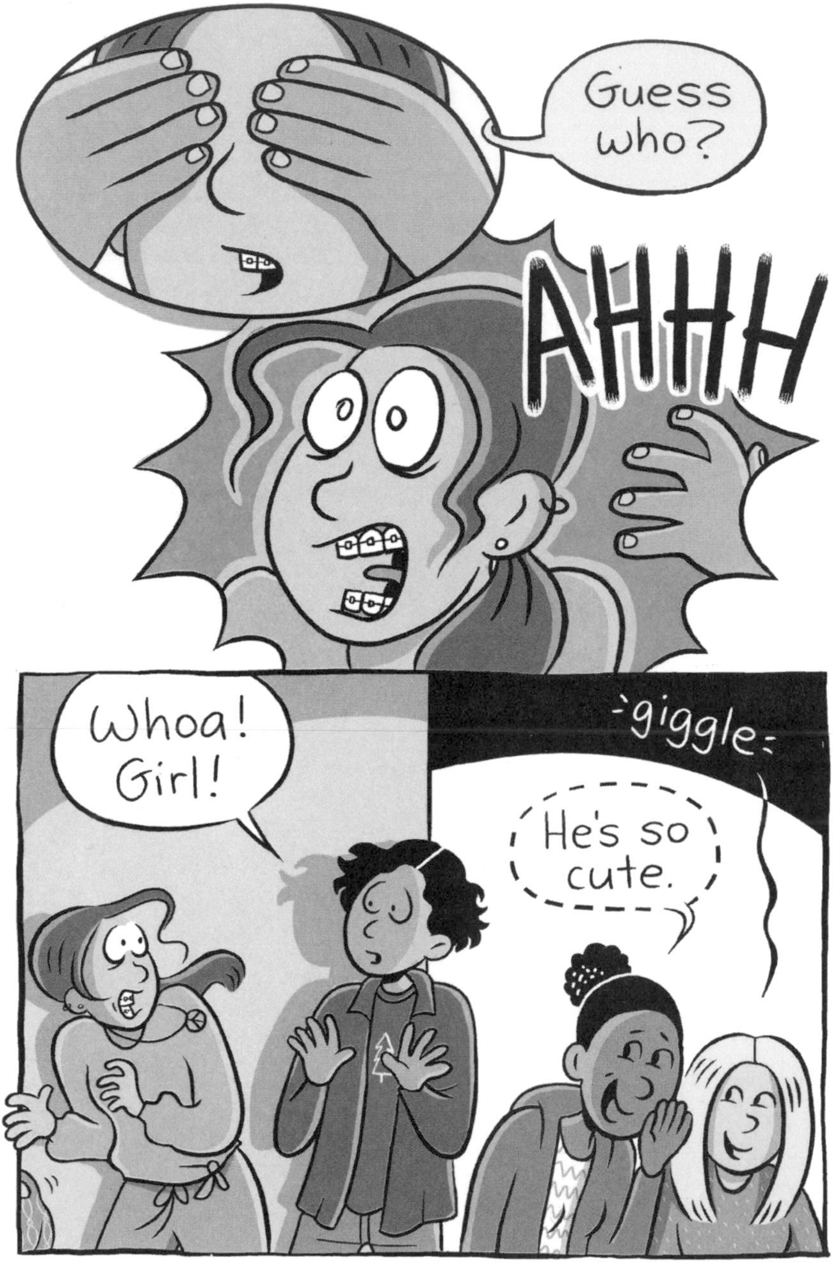
Guess who?
AHHH
Whoa! Girl!
-giggle-
He's so cute.

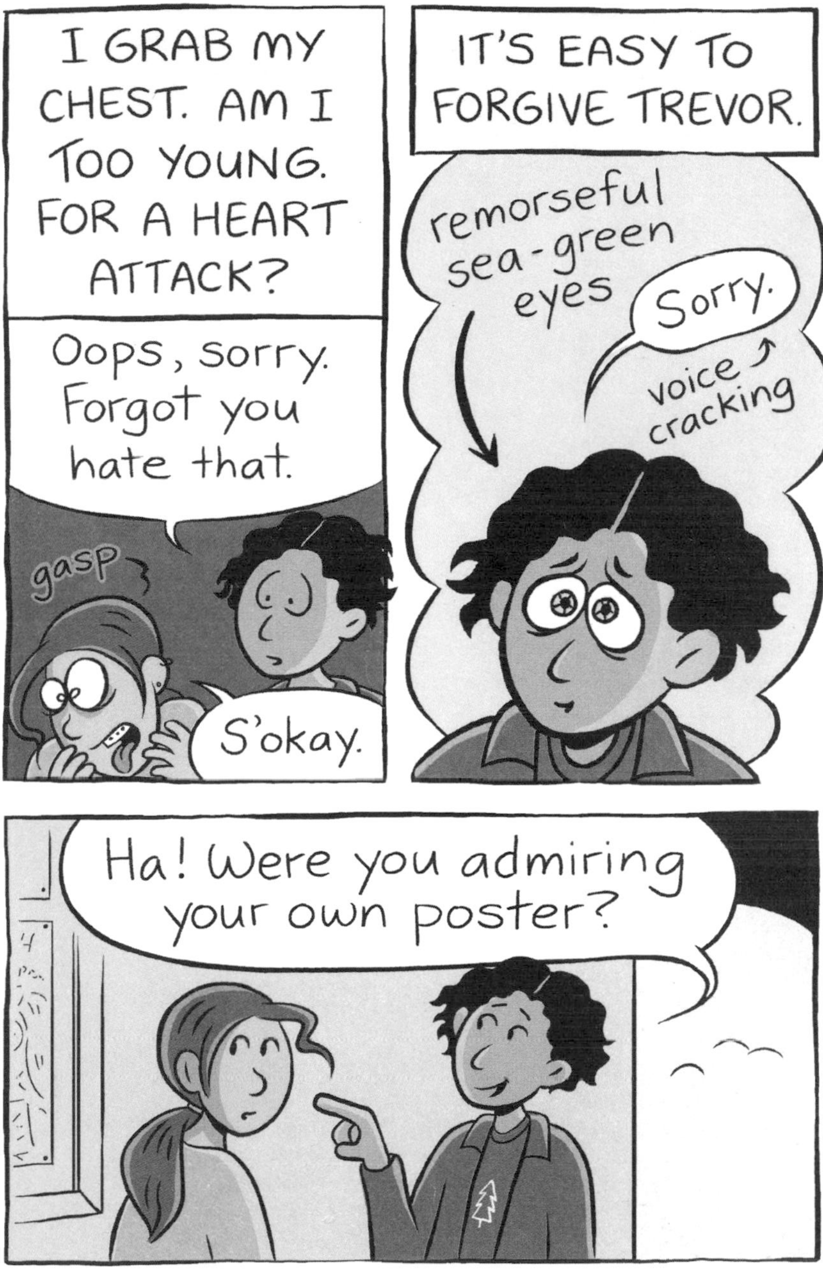
I GRAB MY CHEST. AM I TOO YOUNG. FOR A HEART ATTACK?
Oops, sorry. Forgot you hate that.
gasp
S'okay.
IT'S EASY TO FORGIVE TREVOR.
remorseful sea-green eyes
Sorry.
voice cracking
Ha! Were you admiring your own poster?

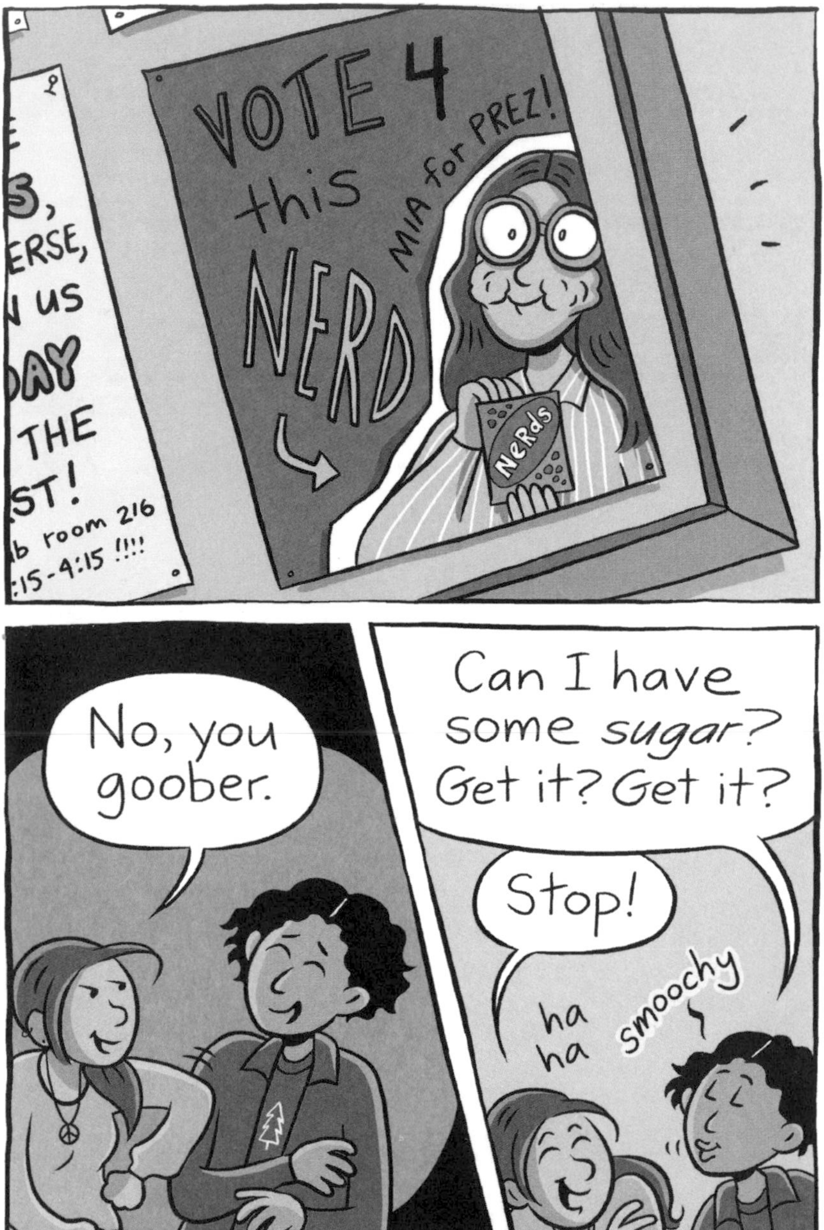
VOTE 4
this
NERD
MIA for PREZ!
NeRds
ERSE,
US
DAY
THE
ST!
b room 216
:15-4:15 !!!!
No, you goober.
Can I have some *sugar*? Get it? Get it?
Stop!
ha
ha
smoochy

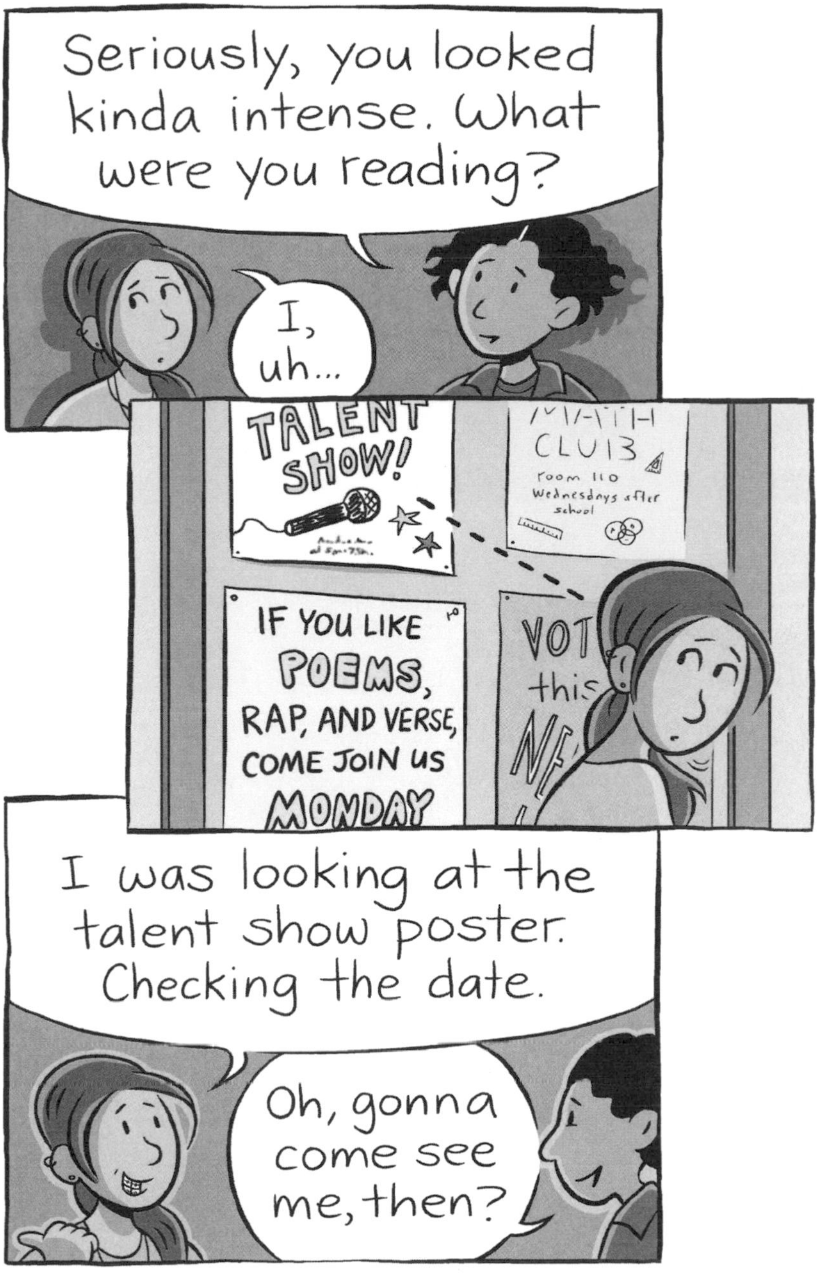
Seriously, you looked kinda intense. What were you reading?
I, uh...
TALENT SHOW!
CLUB
room 110
Wednesdays after school
IF YOU LIKE POEMS, RAP, AND VERSE, COME JOIN US MONDAY
I was looking at the talent show poster. Checking the date.
Oh, gonna come see me, then?

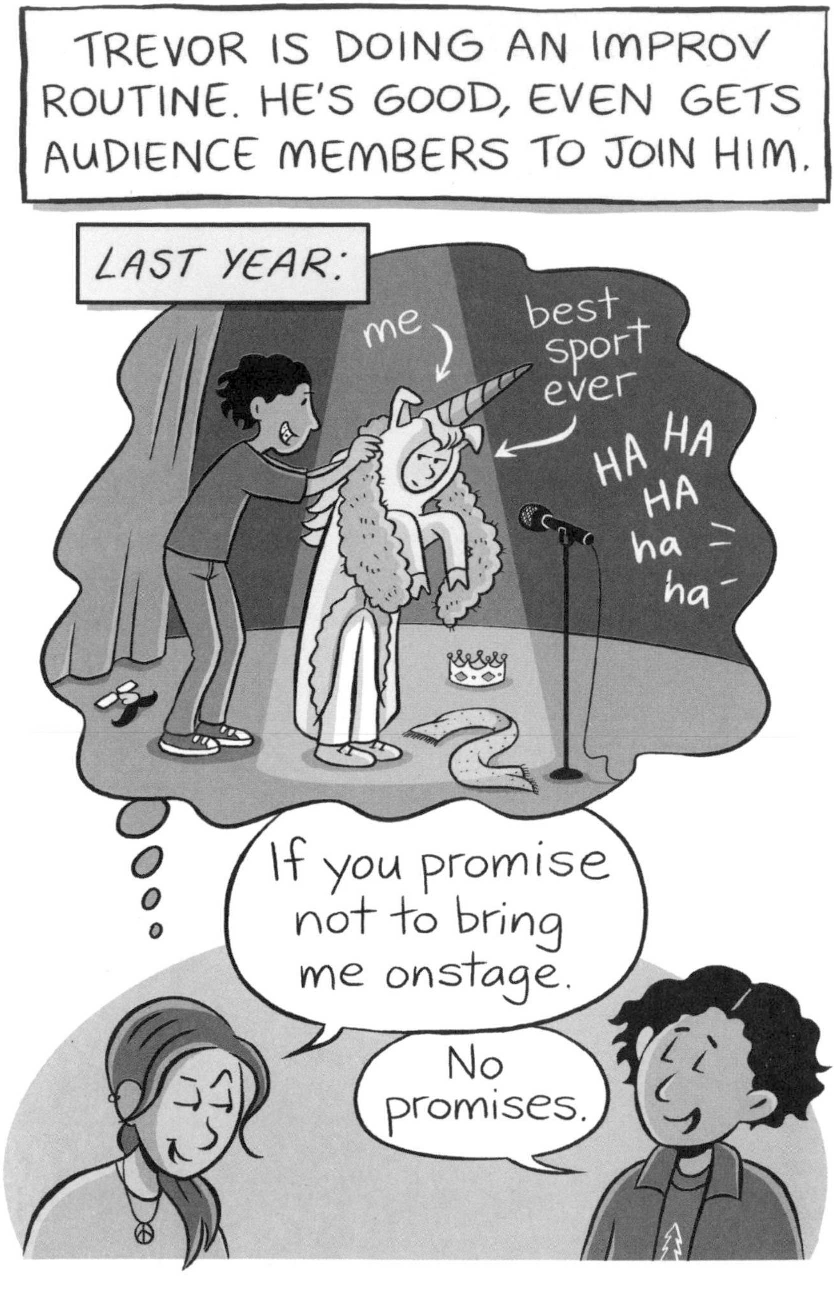
TREVOR IS DOING AN IMPROV ROUTINE. HE'S GOOD, EVEN GETS AUDIENCE MEMBERS TO JOIN HIM.
LAST YEAR:
me
best sport ever
HA HA HA ha ha
If you promise not to bring me onstage.
No promises.

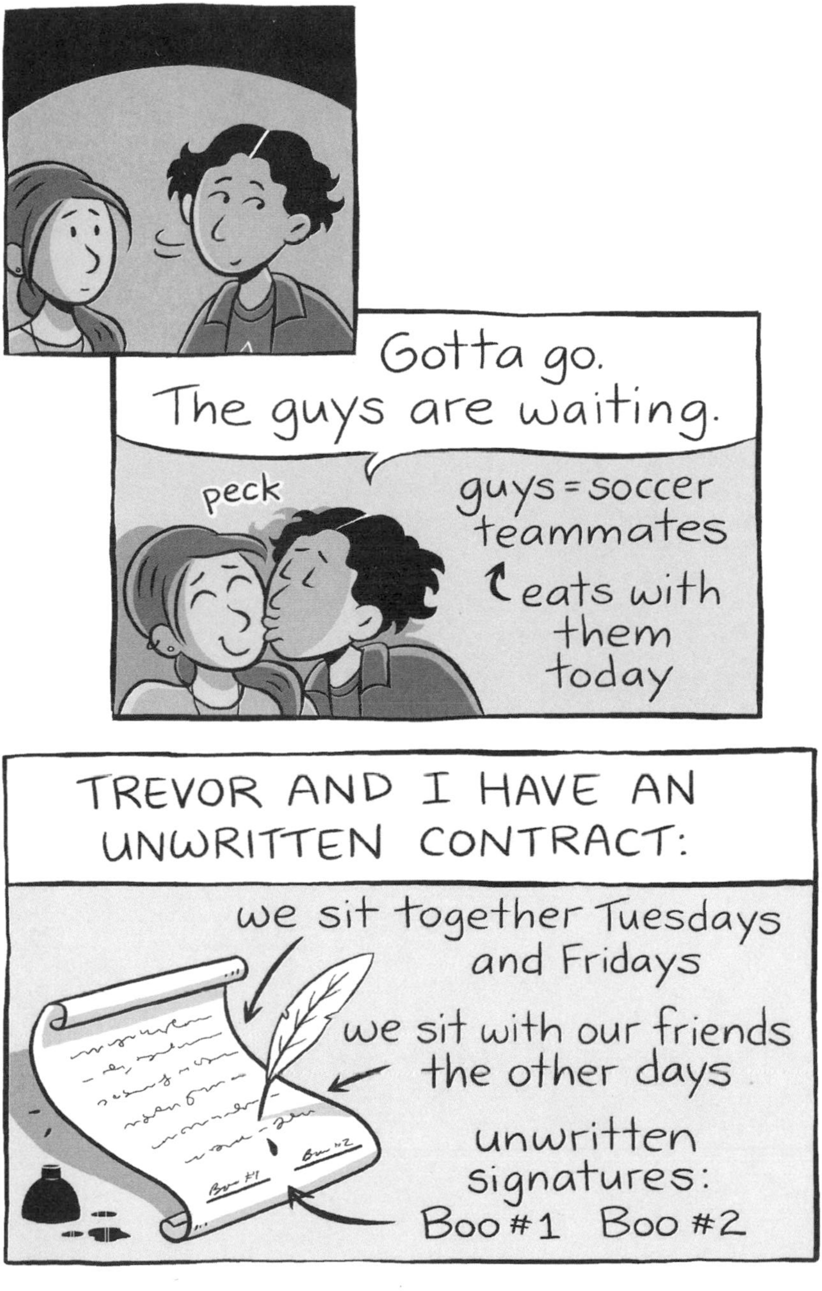
Gotta go. The guys are waiting.
peck
guys = soccer teammates
eats with them today
TREVOR AND I HAVE AN UNWRITTEN CONTRACT:
we sit together Tuesdays and Fridays
we sit with our friends the other days
unwritten signatures: Boo #1 Boo #2

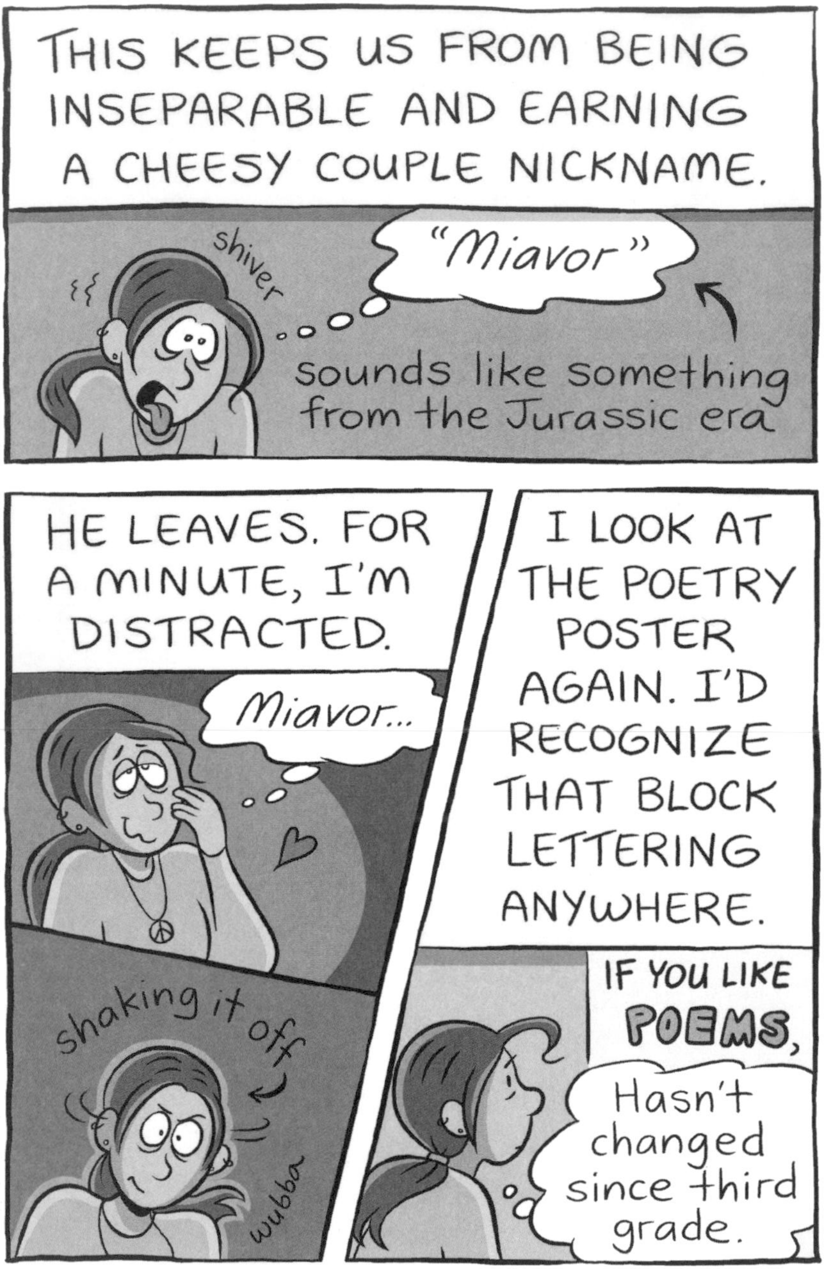
THIS KEEPS US FROM BEING INSEPARABLE AND EARNING A CHEESY COUPLE NICKNAME.
shiver
"Miavor"
sounds like something from the Jurassic era
HE LEAVES. FOR A MINUTE, I'M DISTRACTED.
Miavor...
shaking it off
wubba
I LOOK AT THE POETRY POSTER AGAIN. I'D RECOGNIZE THAT BLOCK LETTERING ANYWHERE.
IF YOU LIKE POEMS,
Hasn't changed since third grade.

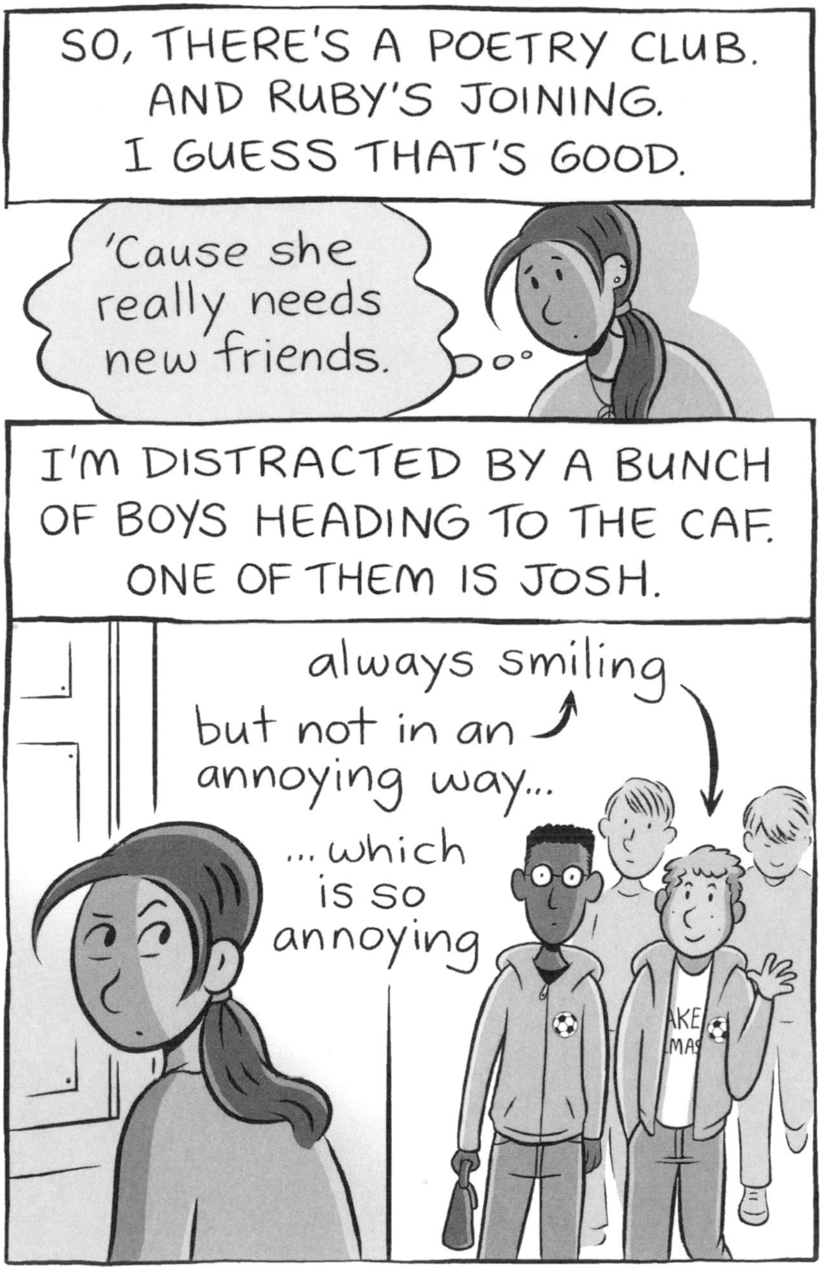
SO, THERE'S A POETRY CLUB. AND RUBY'S JOINING. I GUESS THAT'S GOOD.
'Cause she really needs new friends.
I'M DISTRACTED BY A BUNCH OF BOYS HEADING TO THE CAF. ONE OF THEM IS JOSH.
always smiling
but not in an annoying way...
...which is so annoying

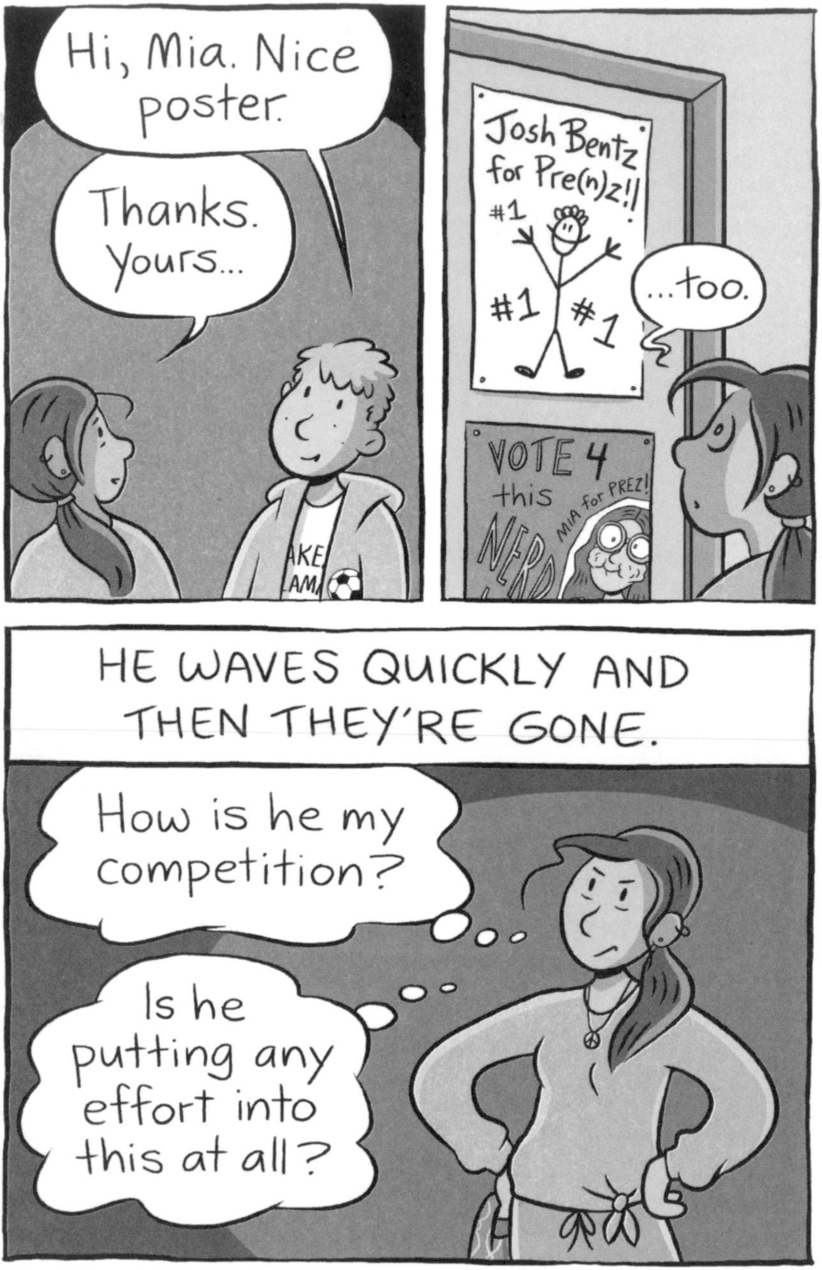
Hi, Mia. Nice poster.
Thanks. Yours...
Josh Bentz for Pre(n)z!! #1 #1 #1
VOTE 4 this NERD
MIA for PREZ!
...too.
HE WAVES QUICKLY AND THEN THEY'RE GONE.
How is he my competition?
Is he putting any effort into this at all?

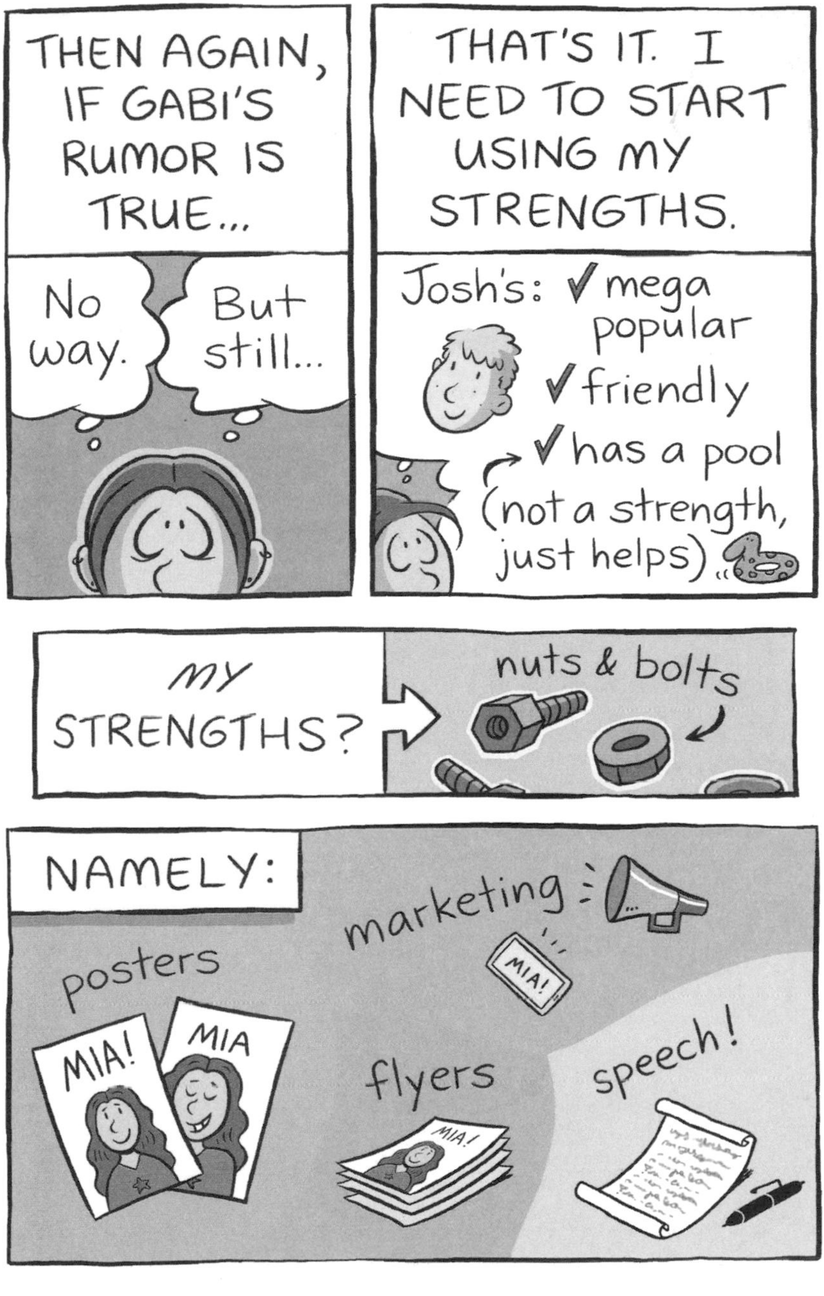
THEN AGAIN, IF GABI'S RUMOR IS TRUE...
No way.
But still...
THAT'S IT. I NEED TO START USING MY STRENGTHS.
Josh's: ✓mega popular
✓friendly
✓has a pool
(not a strength, just helps)
MY STRENGTHS?
nuts & bolts
NAMELY:
marketing
MIA!
posters
MIA!
MIA
flyers
MIA!
speech!

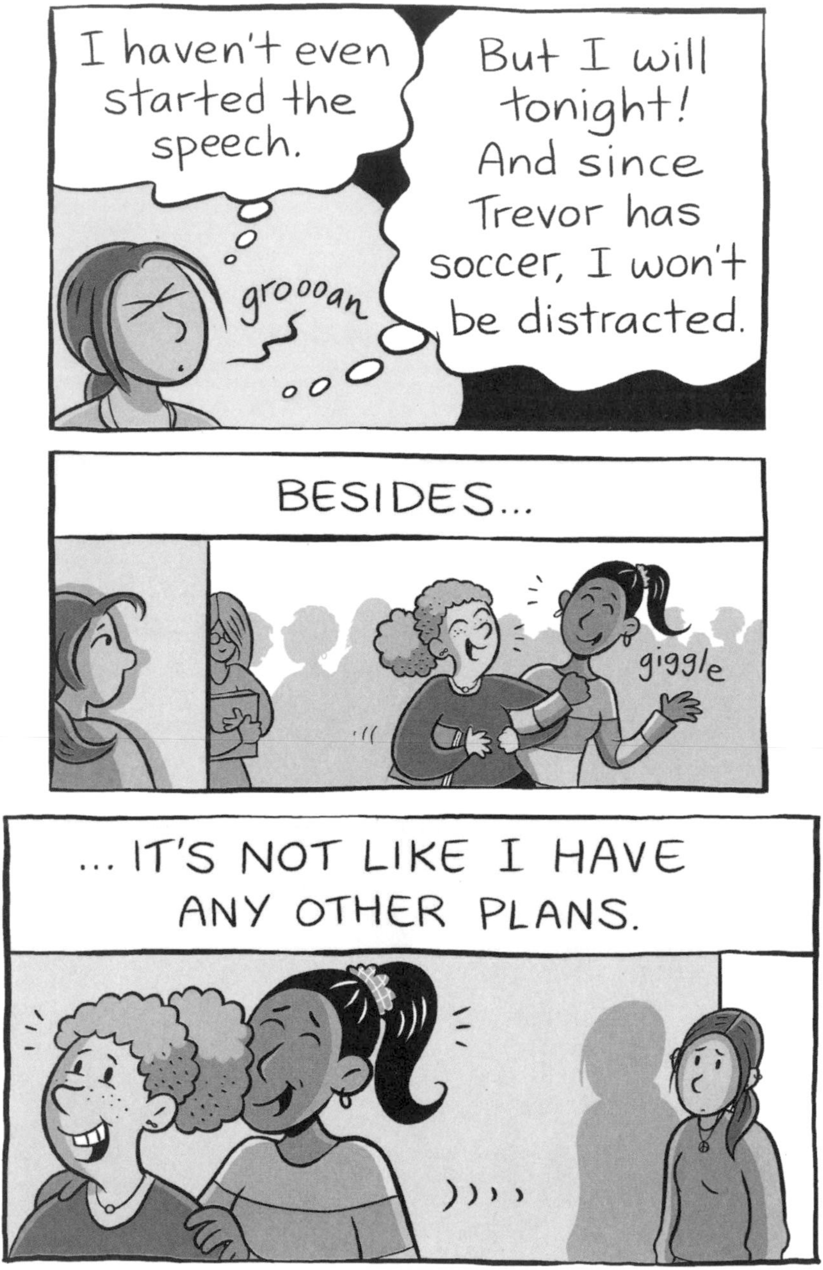
I haven't even started the speech.
groooan
But I will tonight! And since Trevor has soccer, I won't be distracted.
BESIDES...
giggle
... IT'S NOT LIKE I HAVE ANY OTHER PLANS.

RUBY

Just spotted Mia outside the cafeteria, checking out my poster.

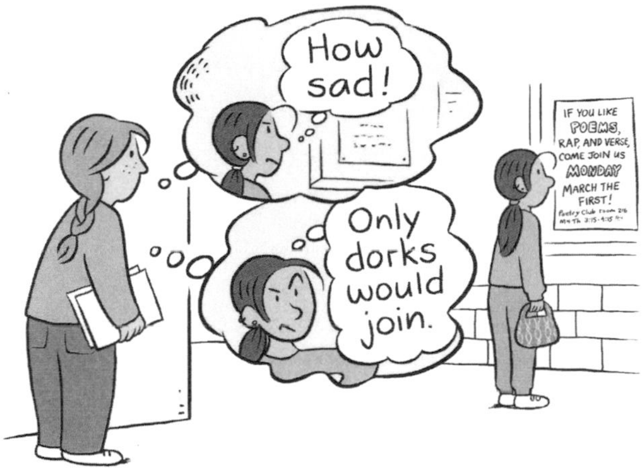
How sad!
Only dorks would join.
IF YOU LIKE POEMS, RAP, AND VERSE, COME JOIN US MONDAY MARCH THE FIRST!

I remember when she was a fellow dork. Seems like a zillion years ago.

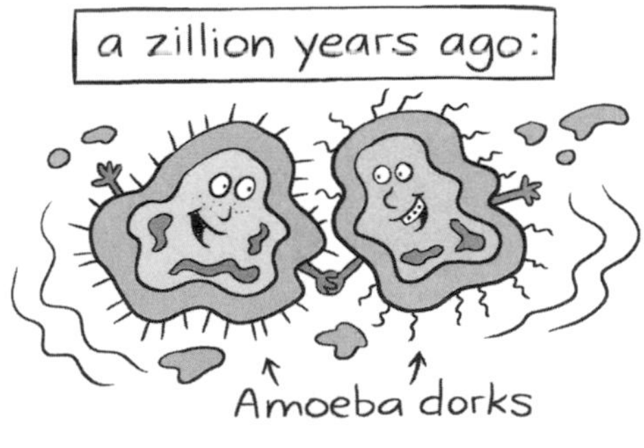
a zillion years ago:
Amoeba dorks

Okay, never mind that. It's time to start recruiting members. Glad I'm not doing it alone.

one shy girl + one loner girl = twice the bravery

We made a flyer from one of the posters and photocopied it. Leah's idea, not Mrs. Winn's. I'm already impressed.

← ~~shy~~ resourceful

Second lunch period is crowded with seventh and eighth graders. Kinda intimidating, but that's where we can find more kids at once. My idea this time. Don't know if it's a good or bad idea, but it's someplace to start. We agree to avoid:

jocks and other popular people

chomp chomp

And hit up:

bookish and artsy types

chew chew

They aren't hard to find since the cafeteria is divided into obvious cliques.

Second Lunch Period (a handy blueprint):*

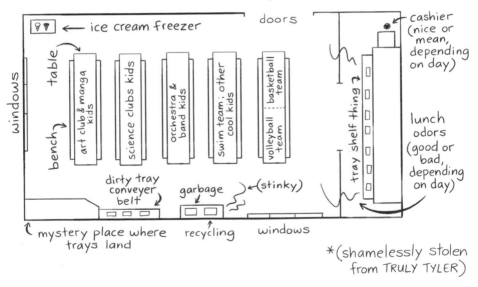

ice cream freezer

doors

cashier (nice or mean, depending on day)

windows

table

bench

art club & manga kids

science clubs kids

orchestra & band kids

swim team; other cool kids

volleyball team | basketball team

tray shelf thing

lunch odors (good or bad, depending on day)

dirty tray conveyer belt

garbage

(stinky)

mystery place where trays land

recycling

windows

*(shamelessly stolen from TRULY TYLER)

We spot some harmless-looking seventh graders at a table near the back and approach them.

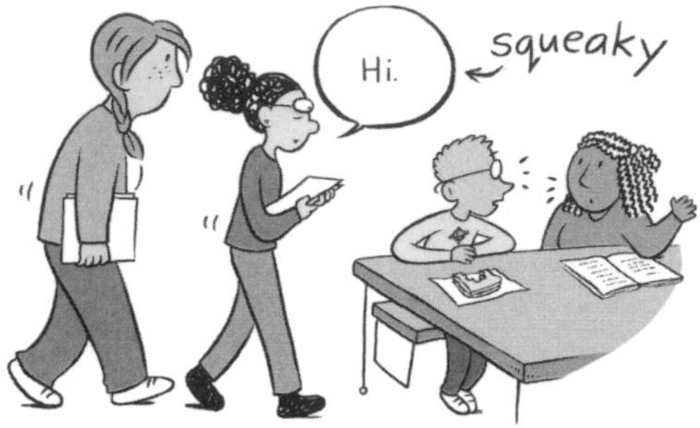
Hi.
squeaky

They don't hear her.

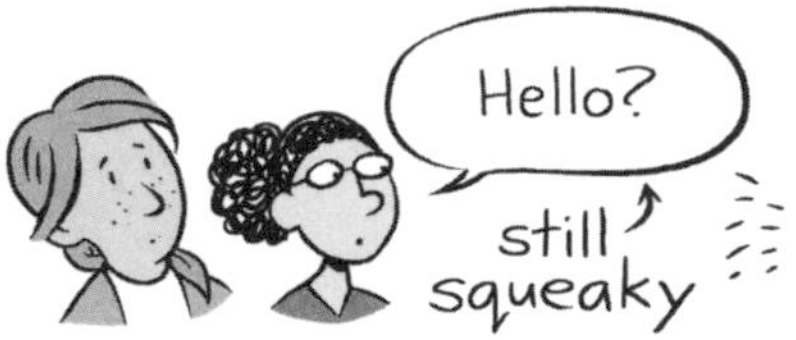
Hello?
still squeaky

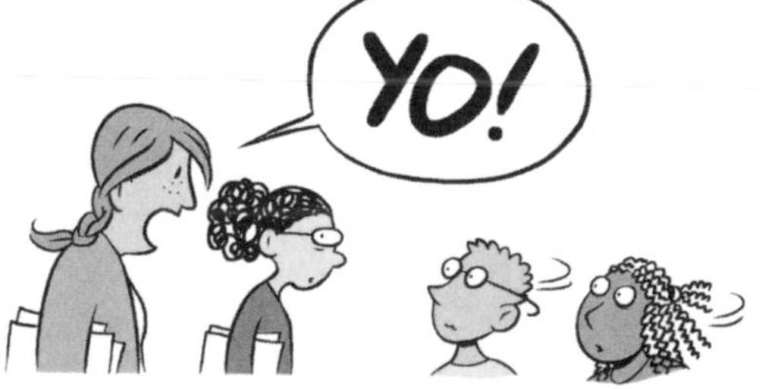
YO!

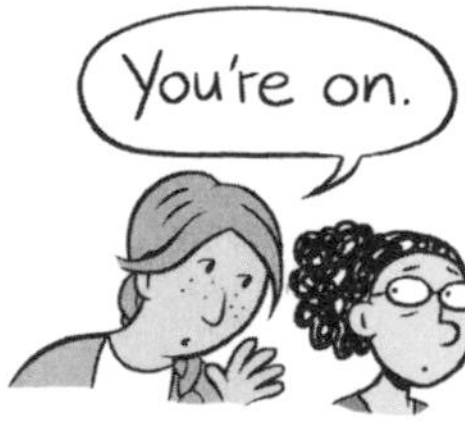
You're on.

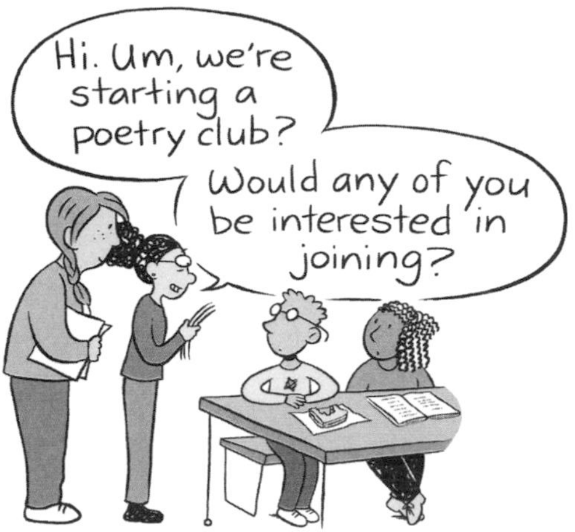
Hi. Um, we're starting a poetry club?
Would any of you be interested in joining?

I plop a stack of flyers in front of them. A little too hard.

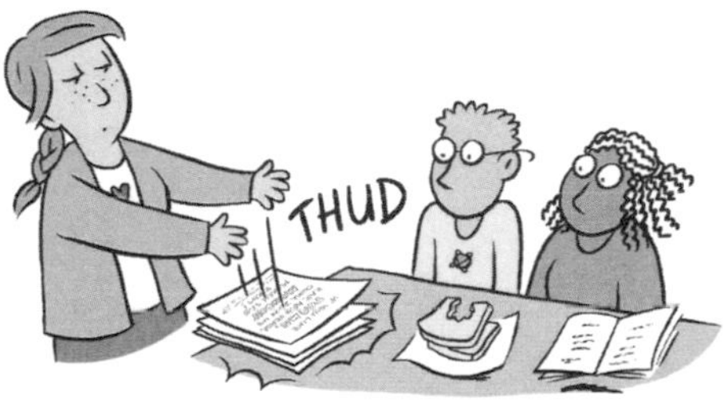
THUD

After giving me a weird look, they each pick one up.

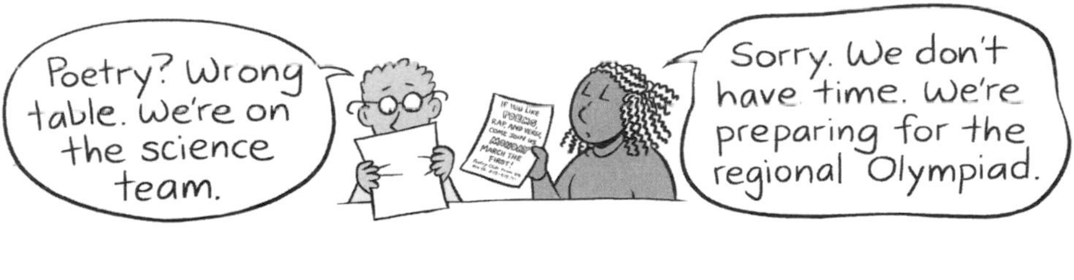
Poetry? Wrong table. We're on the science team.
Sorry. We don't have time. We're preparing for the regional Olympiad.

A skinny kid walks over holding a cafeteria tray. On it are chicken nuggets that are supposed to be shaped like stars but look like bloated frogs.

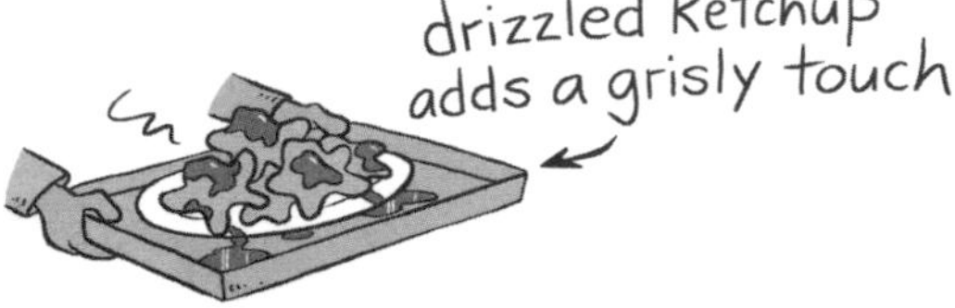
drizzled ketchup
adds a grisly touch

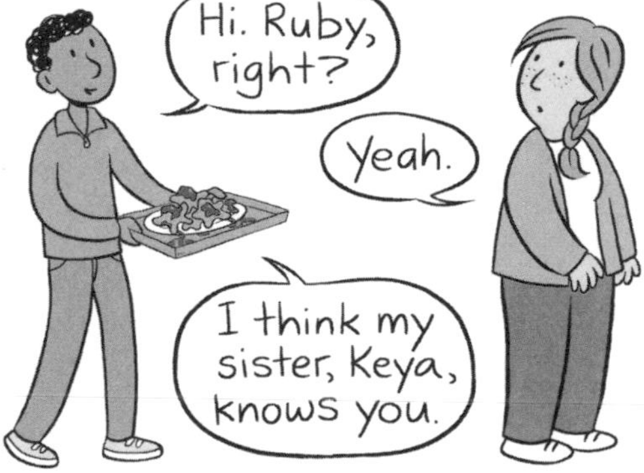
Hi. Ruby, right?
Yeah.
I think my sister, Keya, knows you.

I nod.

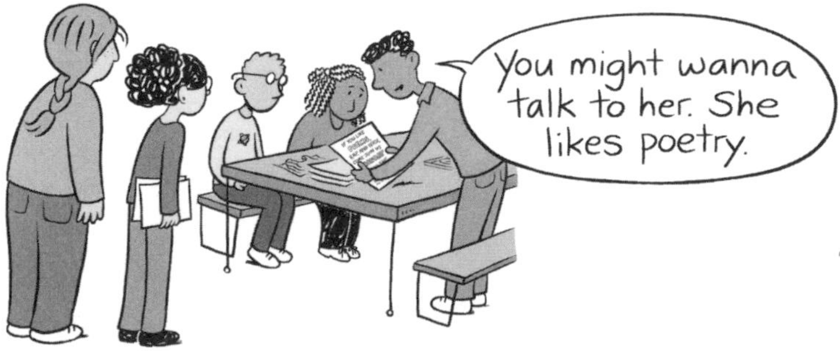
You might wanna talk to her. She likes poetry.

I don't say anything.

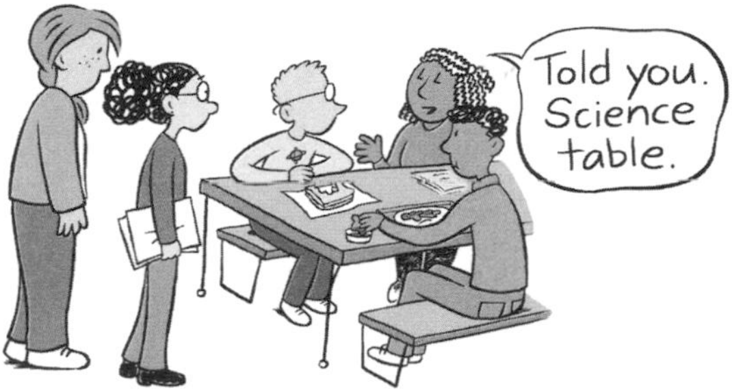
Told you. Science table.

Helpful.

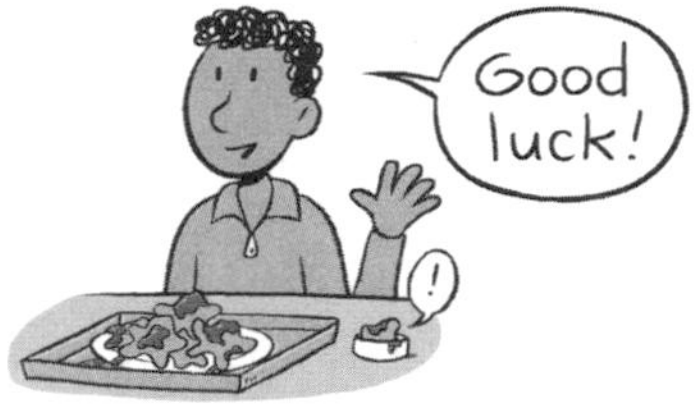
Good luck!
!

Leah and I look at each other. We grab the stack and leave. Leah points to a quiet corner, and we head over.

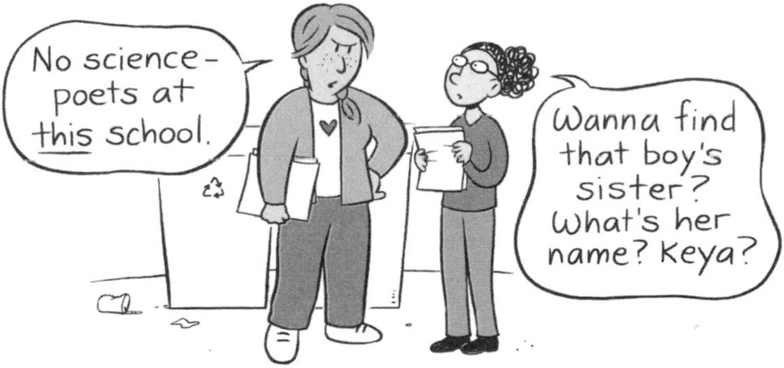
No science-poets at this school.
Wanna find that boy's sister? What's her name? Keya?

I glance to my right.

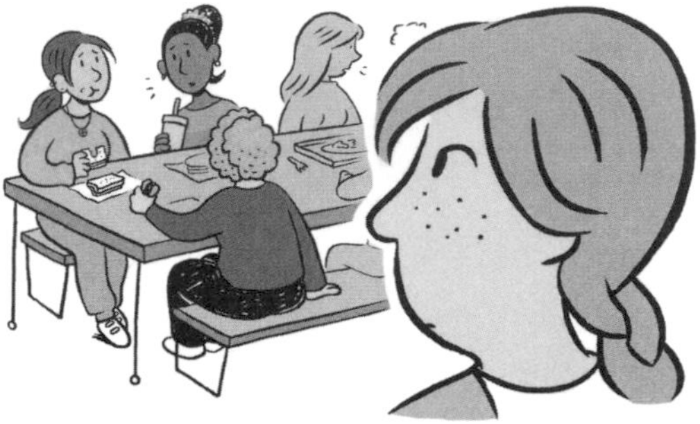

I shake my head.

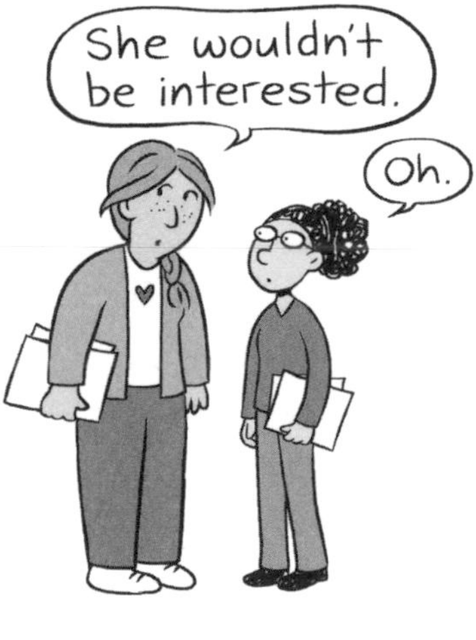
She wouldn't be interested.
Oh.

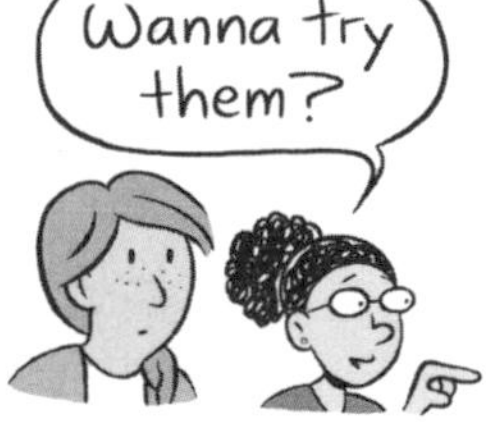
Wanna try them?

She points to a more "eclectic" (Winn Word of the Week!) table near the windows.

I nod. We head over.

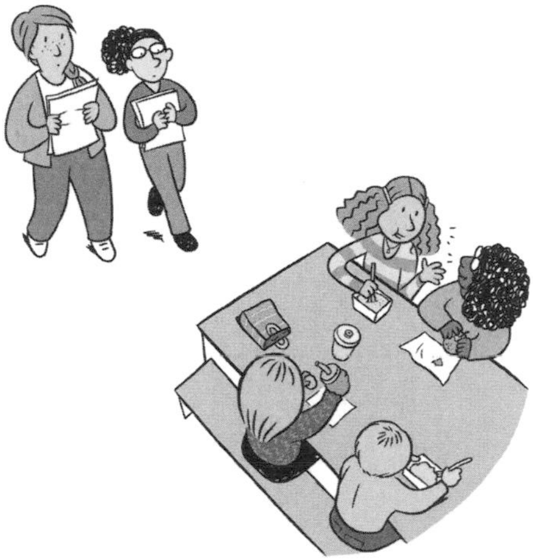

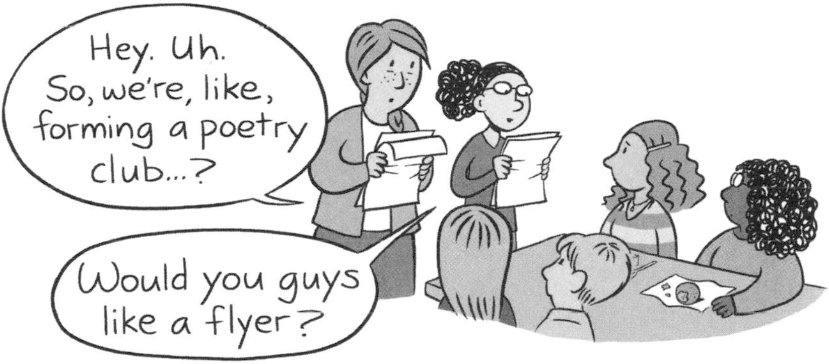
Hey. Uh.
So, we're, like, forming a poetry club...?
Would you guys like a flyer?

After a moment of hesitation, they all shake their heads. A couple girls give us the up-and-down look, which at first makes me mad and then makes me wanna hide behind the tray conveyor belt.

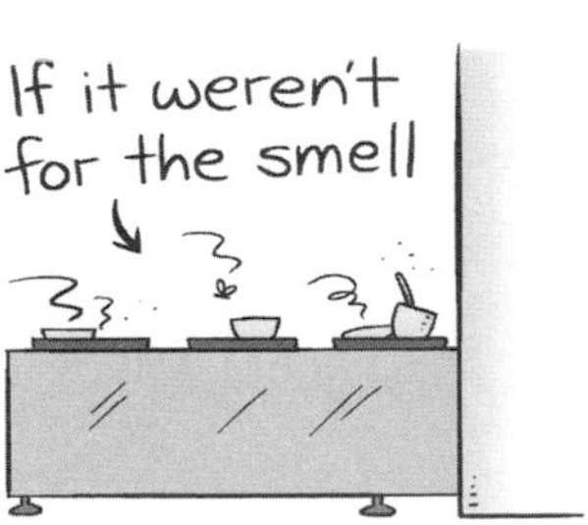
If it weren't for the smell

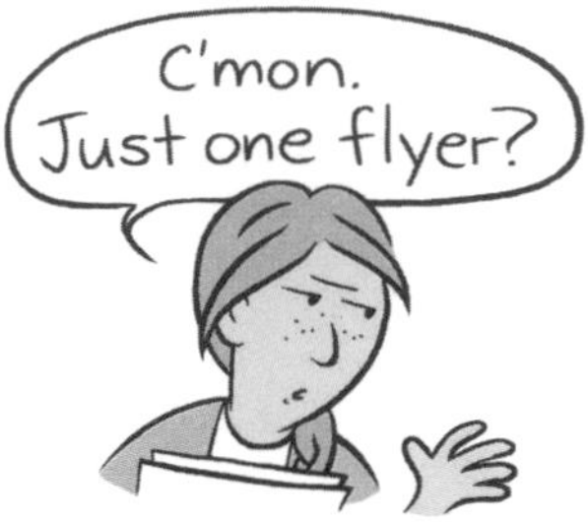
C'mon. Just one flyer?

That doesn't come out as nice as I'd hoped.

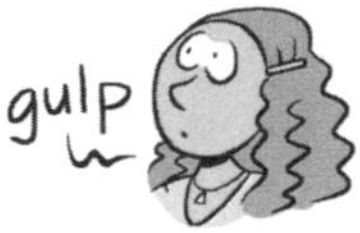
gulp

A girl takes one, and we walk away. Quickly.

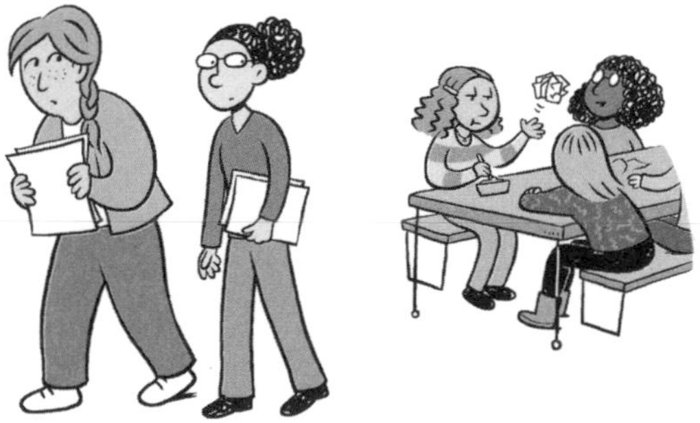

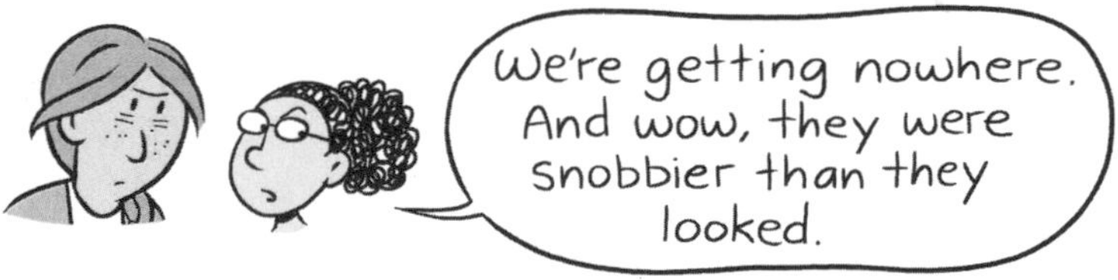
We're getting nowhere. And wow, they were snobbier than they looked.

I'm ready to give up. I might just quit myself. I mean, what kind of club has only two members?

other than the short-lived Goldfish Appreciation Club:

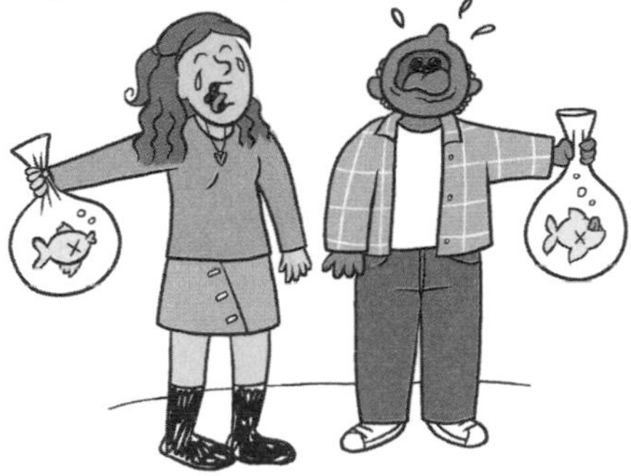

But I remember Mrs. Winn, who really wants to get this going.

I rack my brain, trying to think. I notice a bunch of rowdy kids playing Frisbee with a dirty plate (Joe and his friends, ew). Then I spot someone.

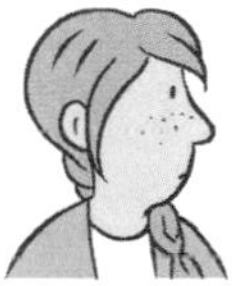

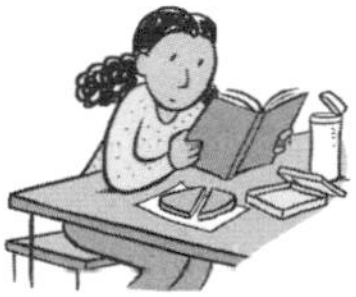

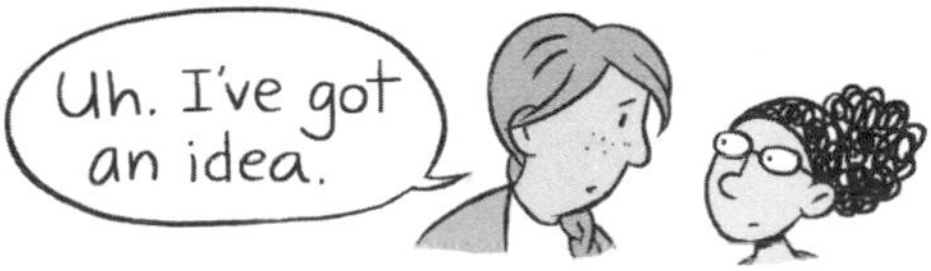
Uh. I've got an idea.

I tell Leah my plan. Her eyes get really big and she nods in agreement. We head out.

Leah and I stop in the hallway. The bell rings.

Meet you after school, then?

I nod.

I know that was a total flop, but I still had fun. If you wanna do homework together sometime and hang out, that'd be fun, too.

Really?

Sure. If...you want.

I don't think Leah has many friends, either. She probably worked up all her nerve to ask me.

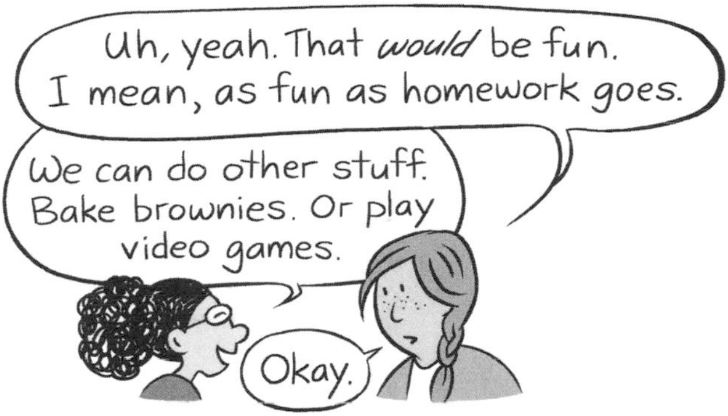
Uh, yeah. That *would* be fun. I mean, as fun as homework goes.
We can do other stuff. Bake brownies. Or play video games.
Okay.

The second bell's about to ring. I leave quickly, not wanting to be late for health. Not that Mr. Bauman's mean or anything, but I've already gotten a few tardy slips. And I hate, hate, hate everyone staring at me when I come in late.

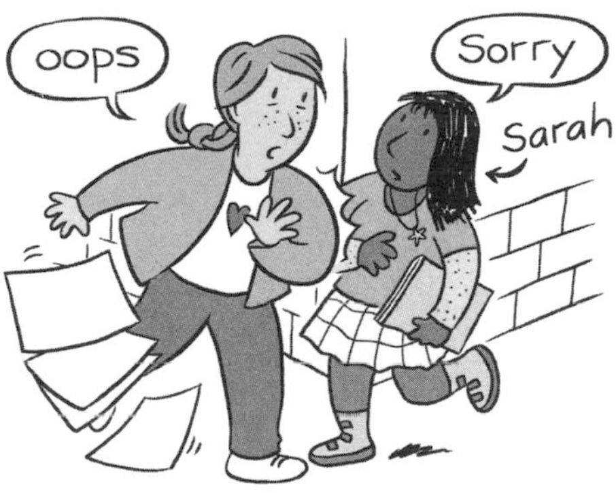
oops
Sorry
Sarah

She helps me pick up the papers.

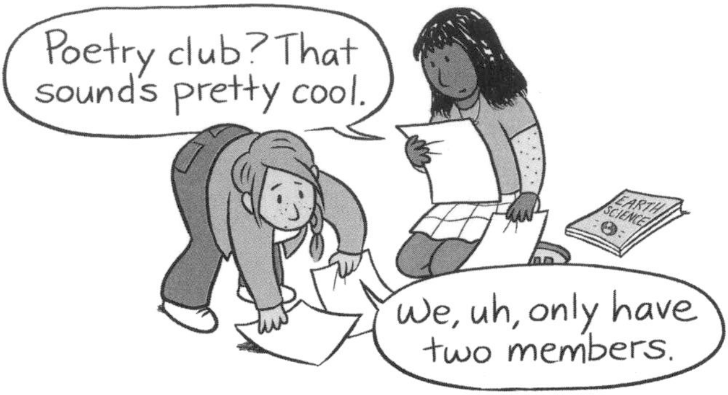
Poetry club? That sounds pretty cool.
EARTH SCIENCE
We, uh, only have two members.

Why did I say that?

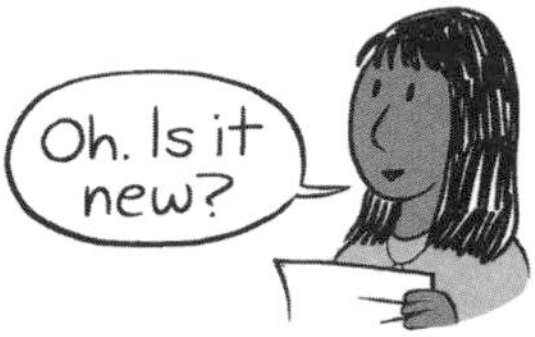
Oh. Is it new?

I nod rapidly.

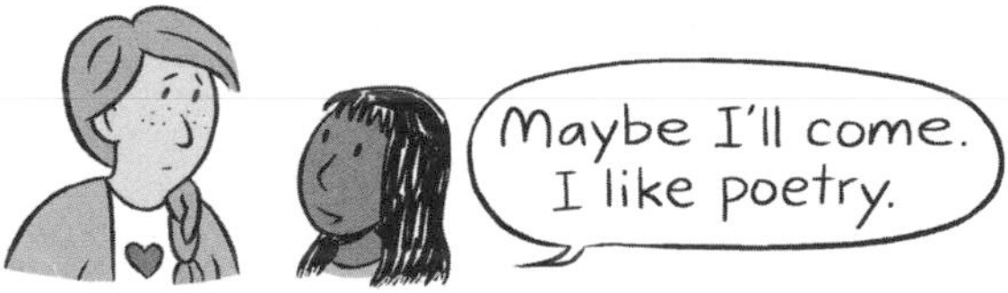
Maybe I'll come. I like poetry.

Really? We might get **three** members?

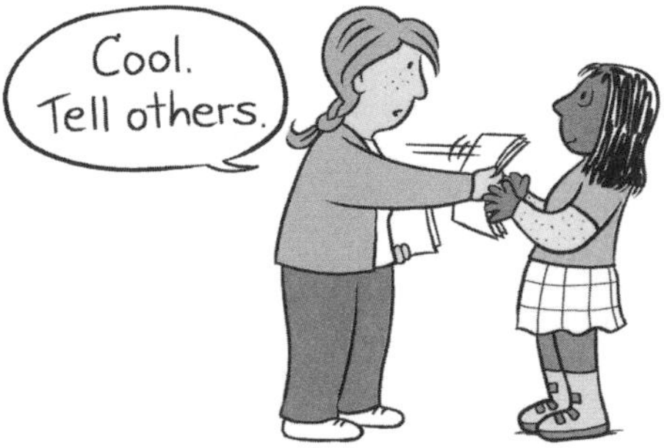
Cool. Tell others.

Sarah waves and leaves.
Just when I started to think this was a total waste of time.

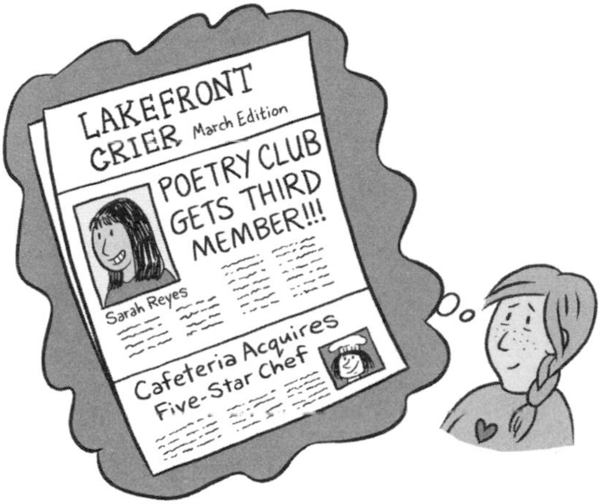
LAKEFRONT CRIER
March Edition
POETRY CLUB GETS THIRD MEMBER!!!
Sarah Reyes
Cafeteria Acquires Five-Star Chef

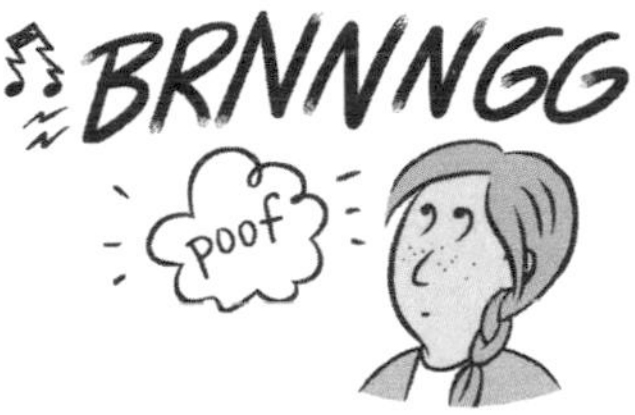
BRNNNGG
poof

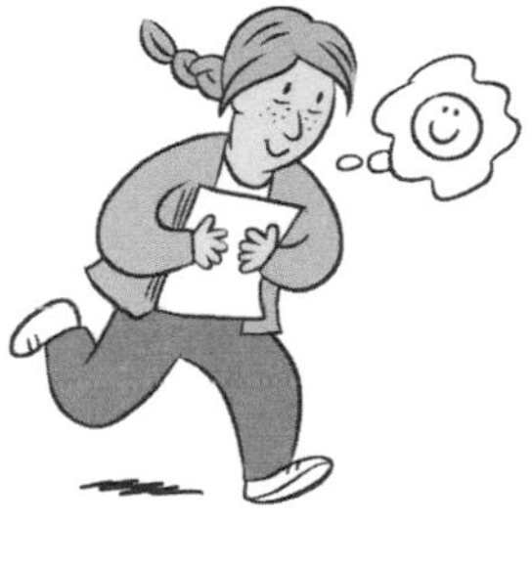

Maybe that was worth the tardy bell.

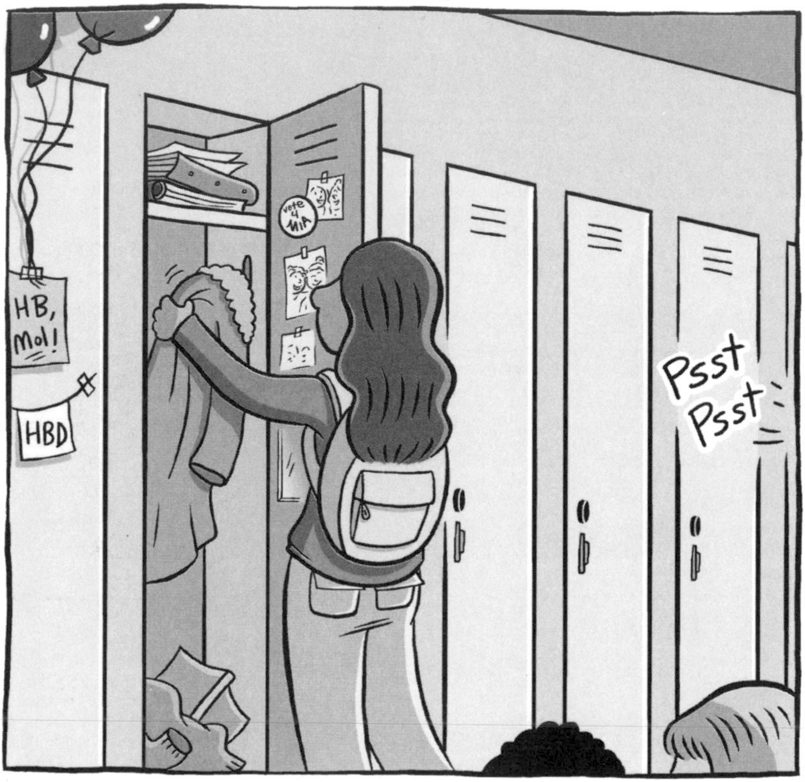
vote 4 MIA
HB, Mol!
HBD
Psst
Psst

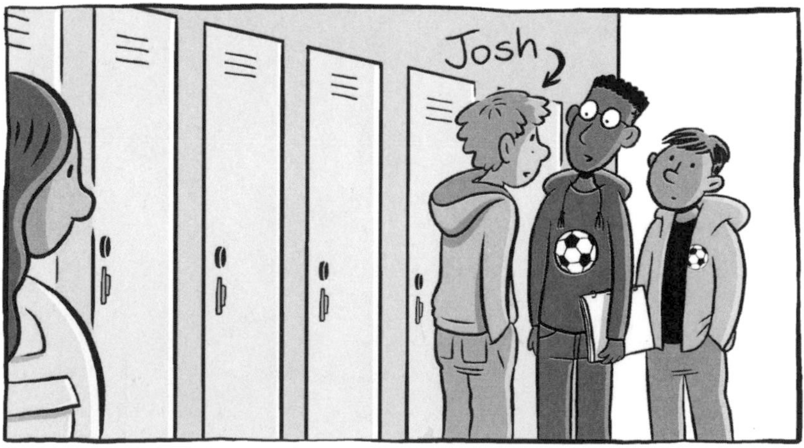
Josh

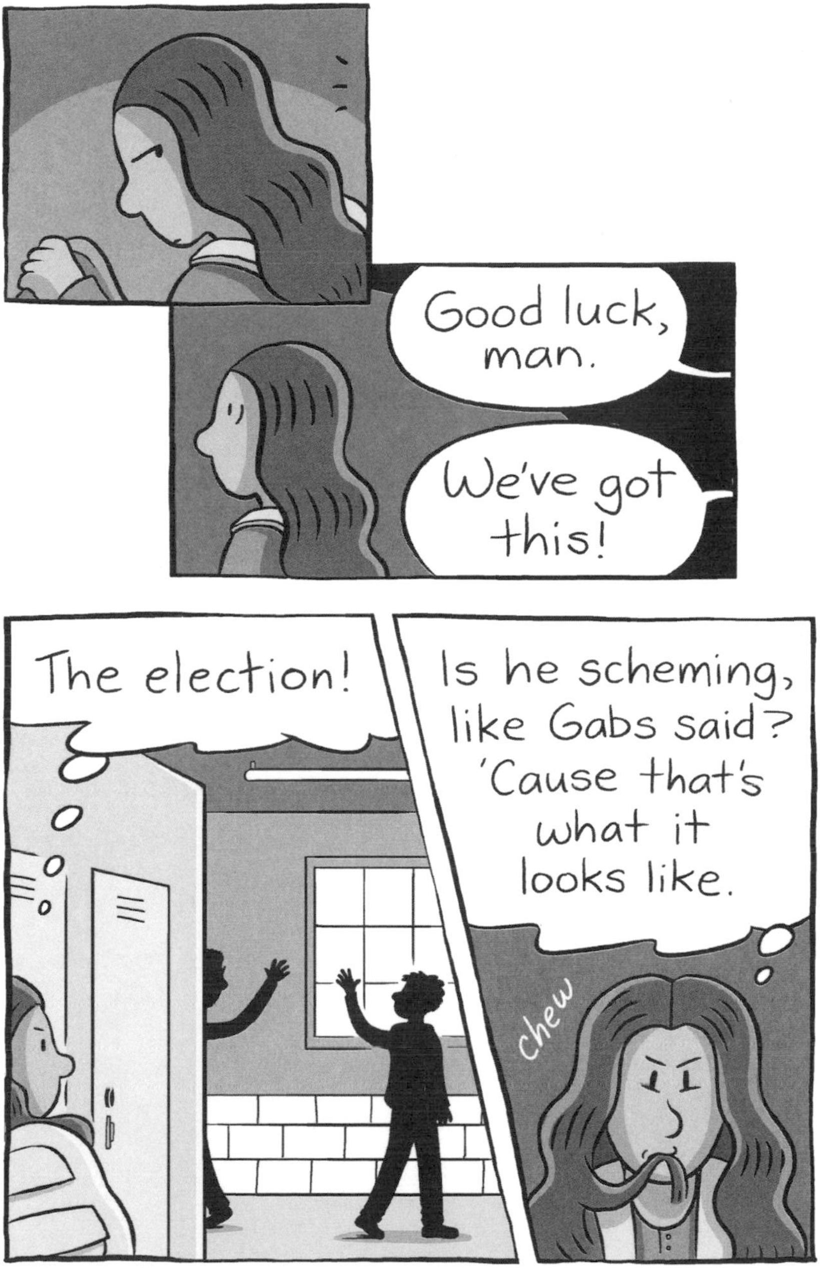
Good luck, man.
We've got this!
The election!
Is he scheming, like Gabs said? 'Cause that's what it looks like.
chew

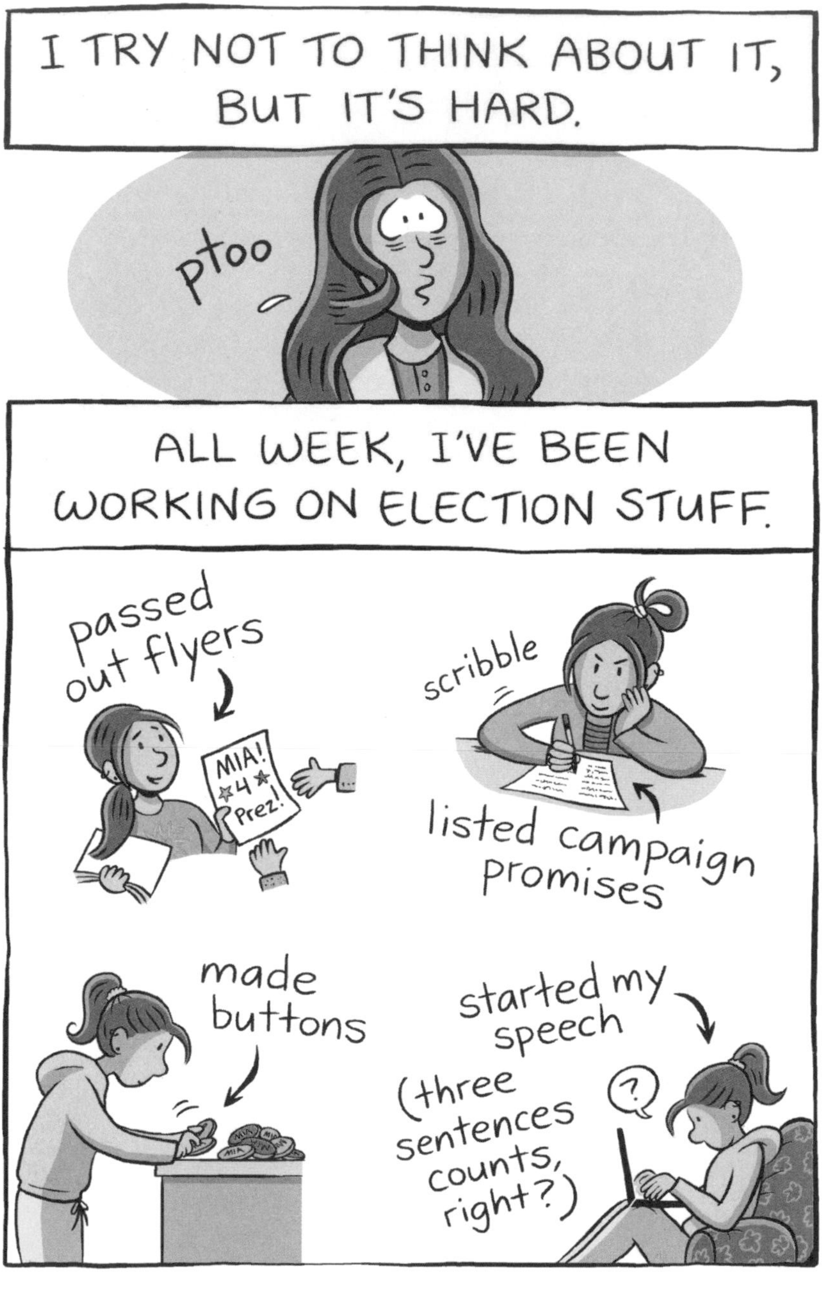
I TRY NOT TO THINK ABOUT IT, BUT IT'S HARD.
ptoo
ALL WEEK, I'VE BEEN WORKING ON ELECTION STUFF.
passed out flyers
MIA! 4 Prez!
scribble
listed campaign promises
made buttons
MIA
started my speech
(three sentences counts, right?)
?

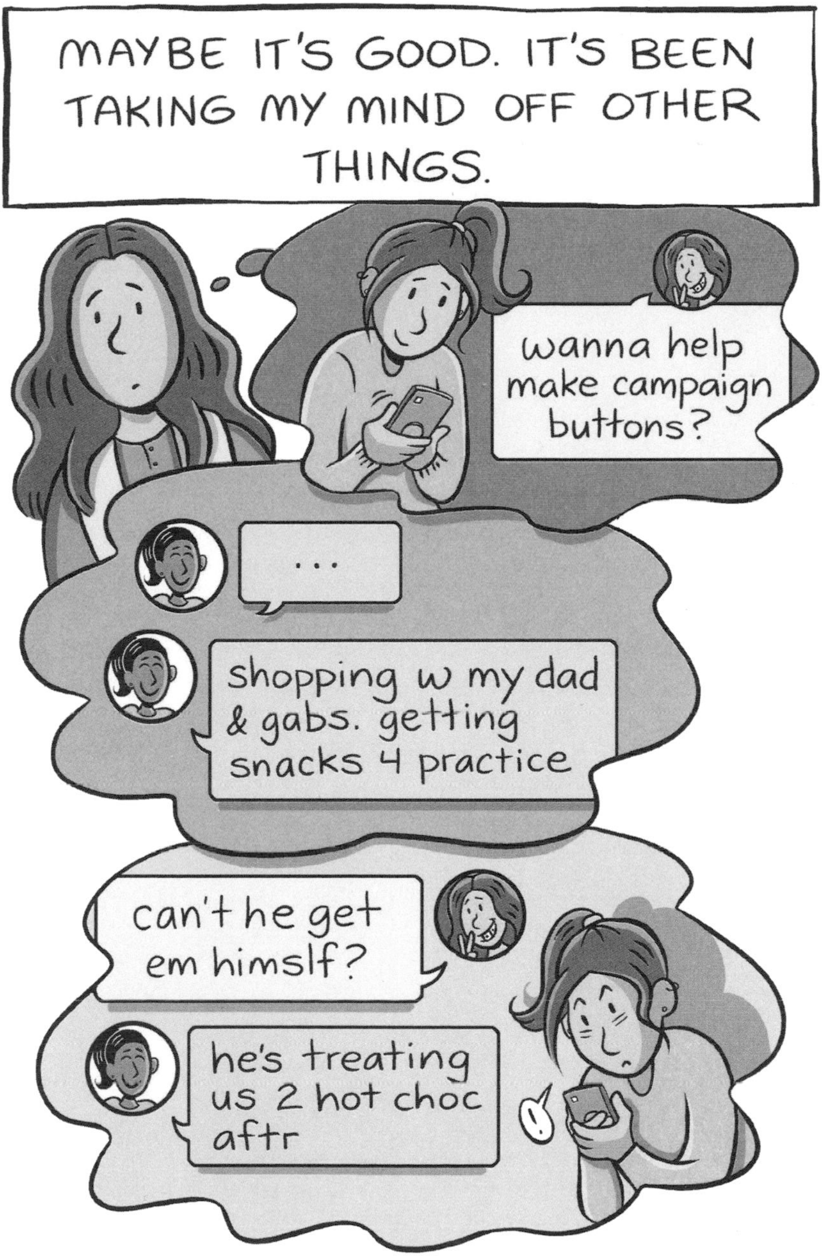
MAYBE IT'S GOOD. IT'S BEEN TAKING MY MIND OFF OTHER THINGS.
wanna help make campaign buttons?
...
shopping w my dad & gabs. getting snacks 4 practice
can't he get em himslf?
he's treating us 2 hot choc aftr
!

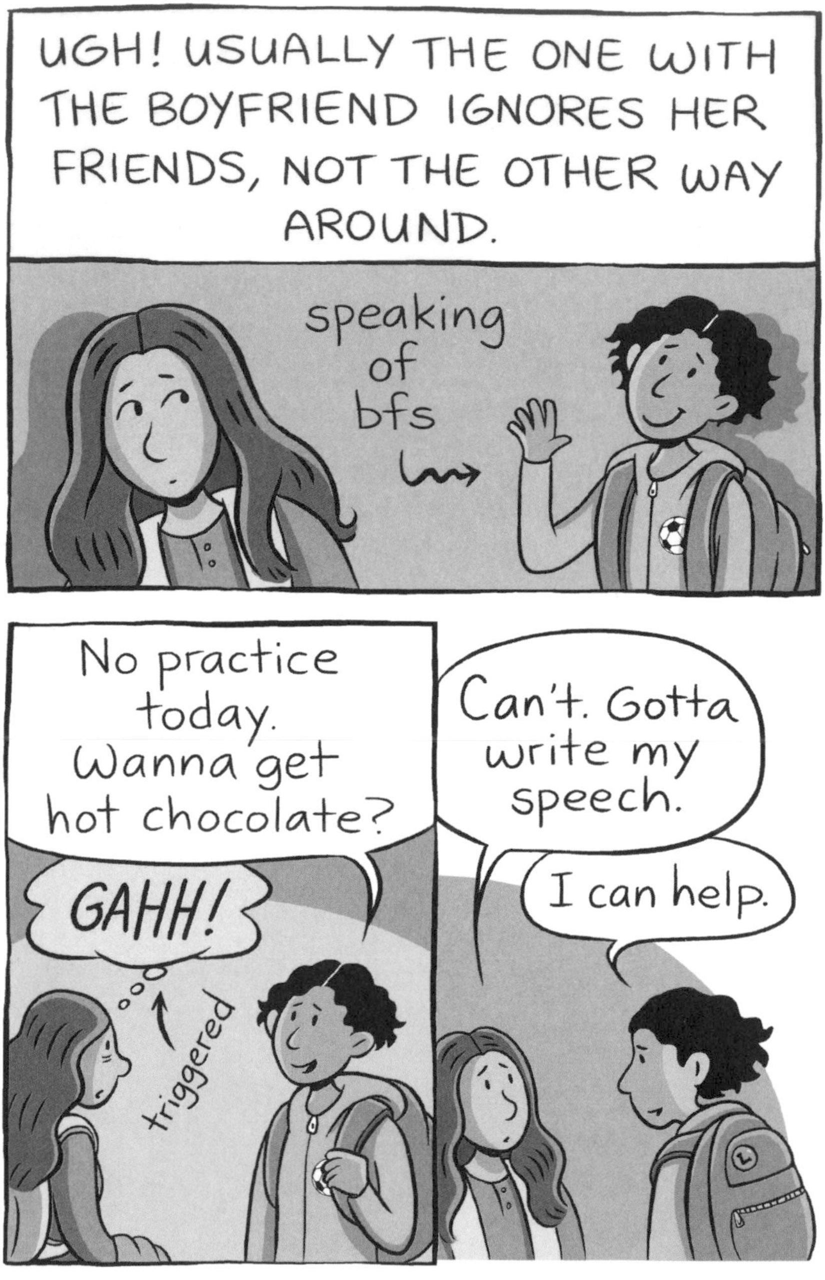
UGH! USUALLY THE ONE WITH THE BOYFRIEND IGNORES HER FRIENDS, NOT THE OTHER WAY AROUND.
speaking of bfs
No practice today. Wanna get hot chocolate?
GAHH!
triggered
Can't. Gotta write my speech.
I can help.

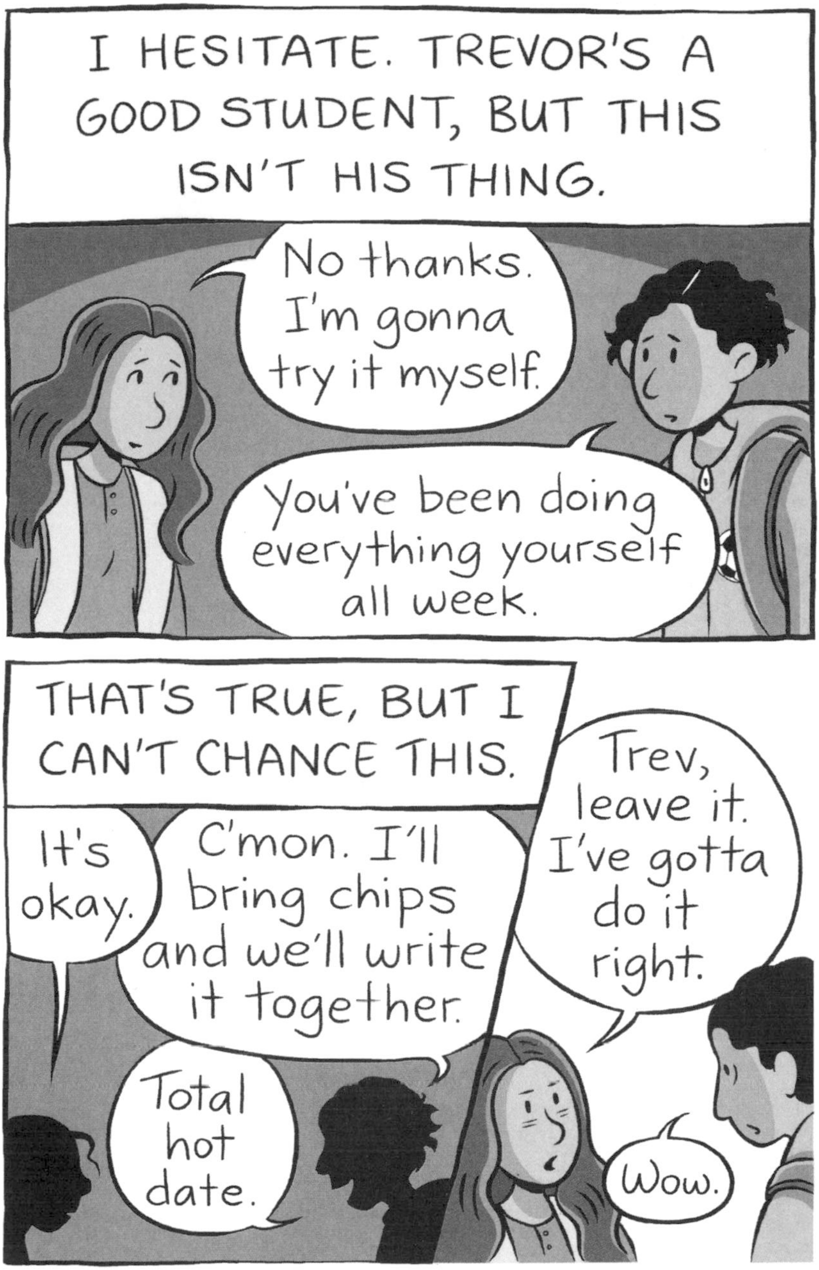
I HESITATE. TREVOR'S A GOOD STUDENT, BUT THIS ISN'T HIS THING.
No thanks. I'm gonna try it myself.
You've been doing everything yourself all week.
THAT'S TRUE, BUT I CAN'T CHANCE THIS.
It's okay.
C'mon. I'll bring chips and we'll write it together.
Total hot date.
Trev, leave it. I've gotta do it right.
Wow.

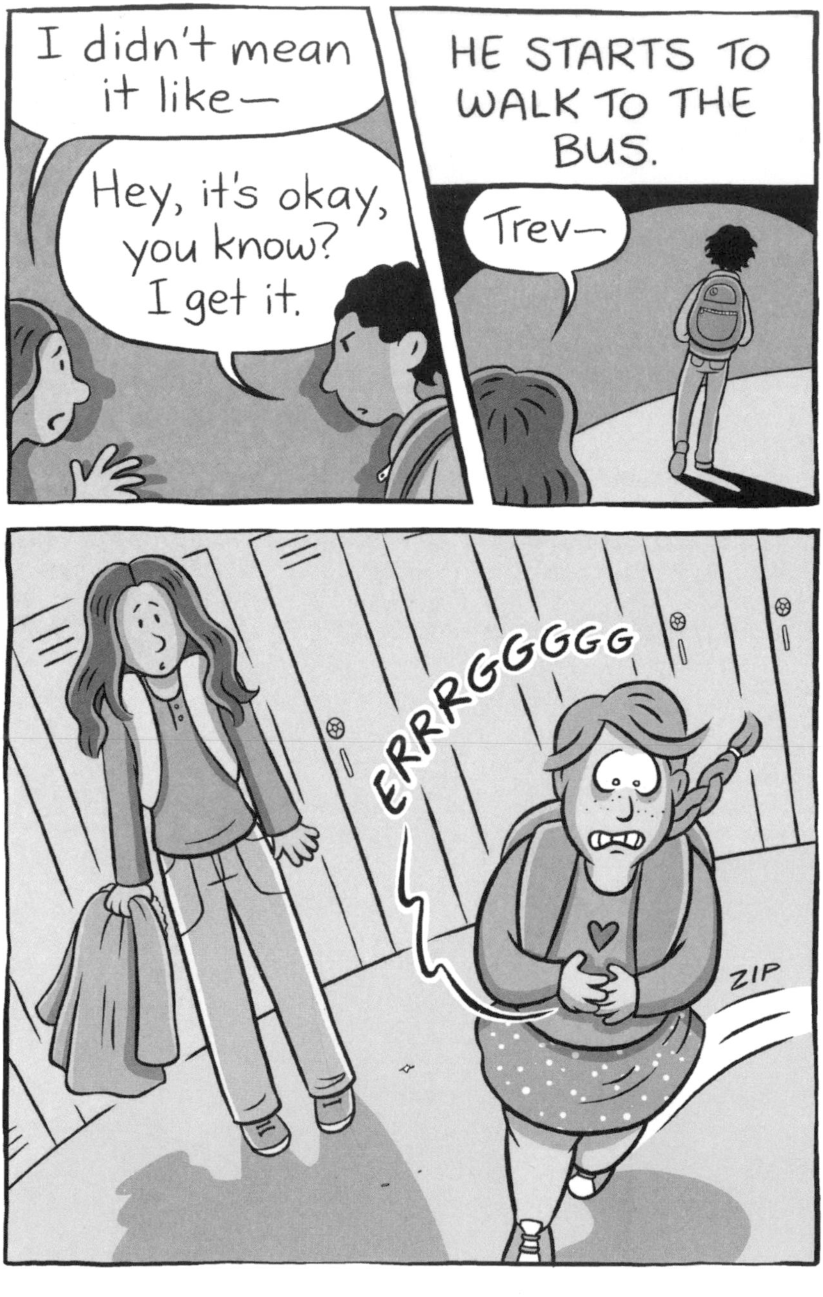
I didn't mean it like—
Hey, it's okay, you know? I get it.
HE STARTS TO WALK TO THE BUS.
Trev—
ERRRGGGGGG
ZIP

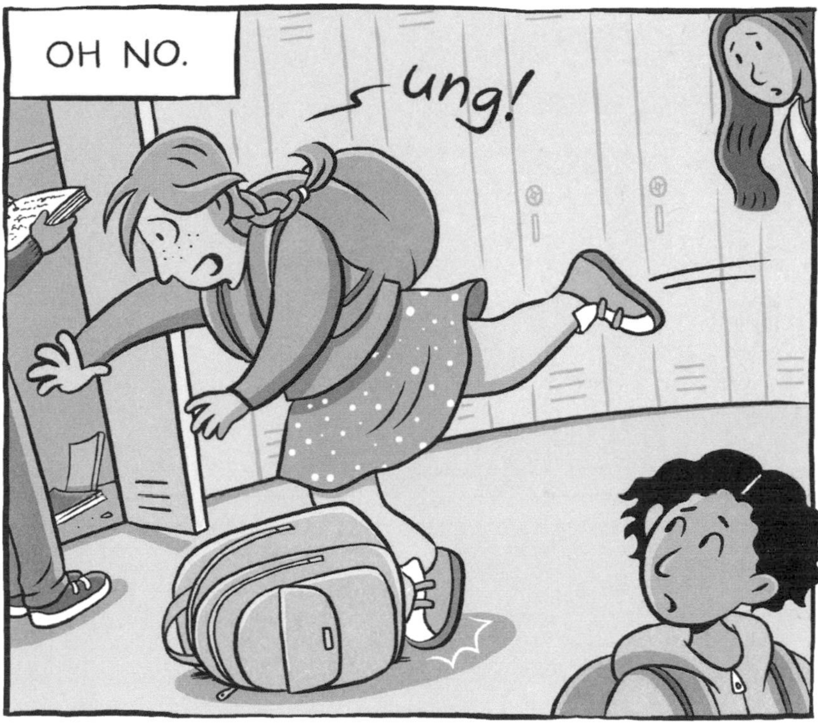
OH NO.
ung!

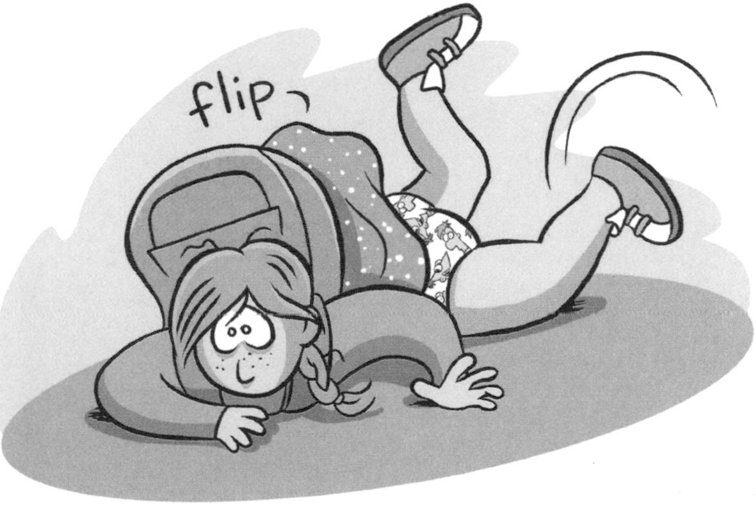
flip

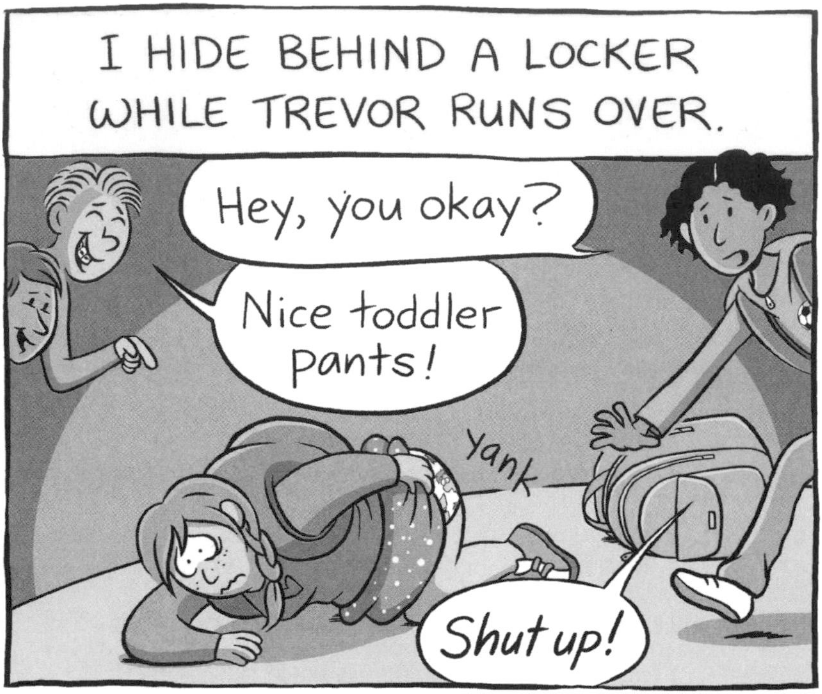
I HIDE BEHIND A LOCKER WHILE TREVOR RUNS OVER.
Hey, you okay?
Nice toddler pants!
yank
Shut up!

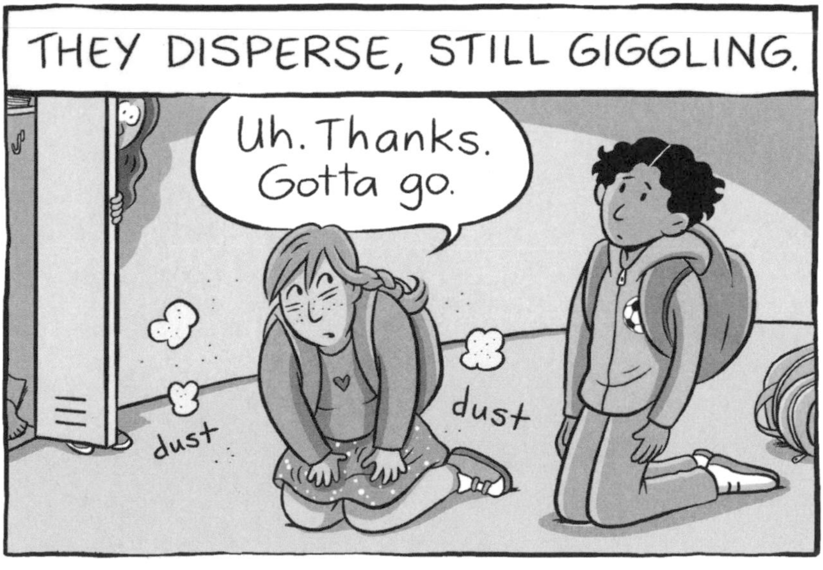
THEY DISPERSE, STILL GIGGLING.
Uh. Thanks. Gotta go.
dust
dust

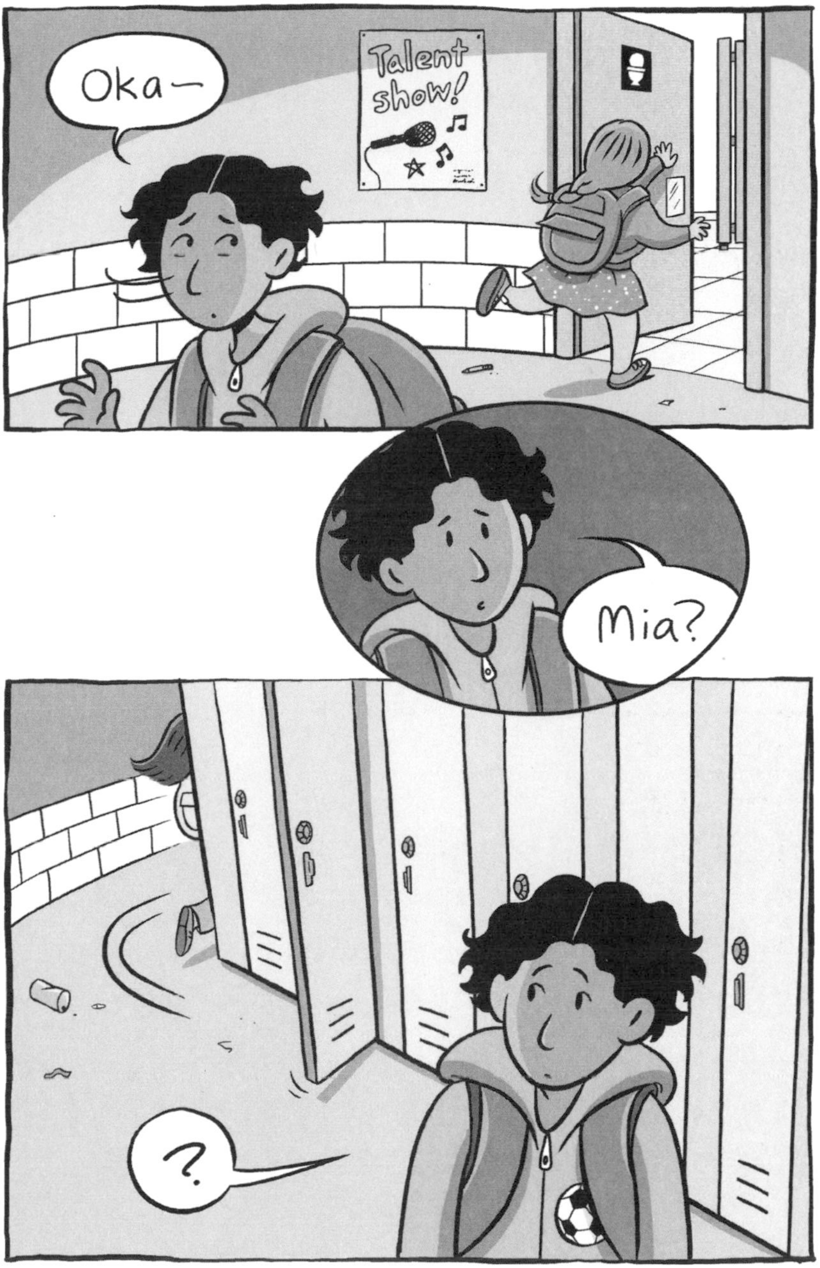
Oka—
Talent show!
Mia?
?

RUBY

I'm such a dweebert!

↳ word that Mia and I used back when we were still talking

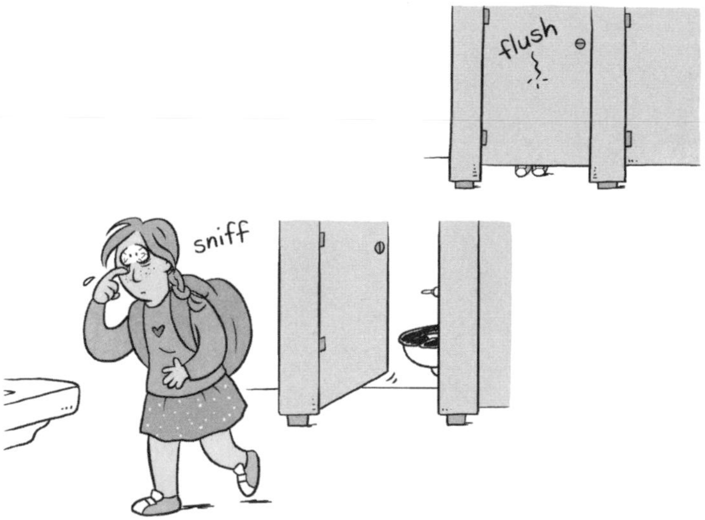
flush
sniff

I haven't had a stomach attack in ages. But I started thinking about poetry club and got super nervous. Tomorrow is the first meeting. I've never been in a club. I don't know what to expect, and I'm one of the recruiters!

And then there's Mia.

She didn't even help me after I fell in front of everyone.

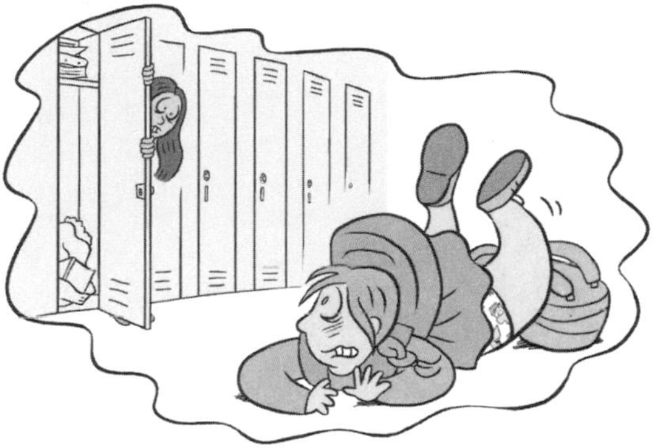

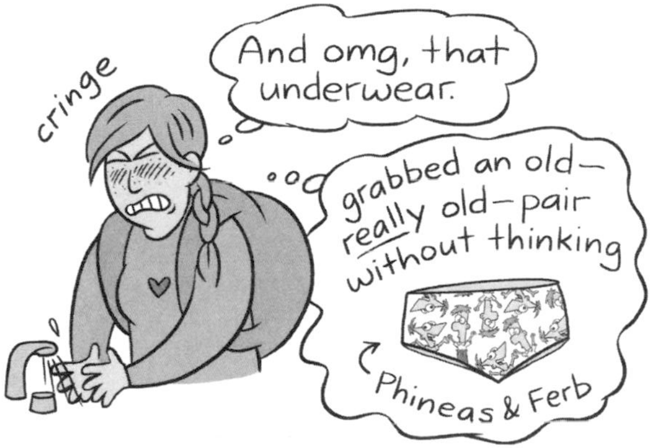

cringe
And omg, that underwear.
grabbed an old—really old—pair without thinking
Phineas & Ferb

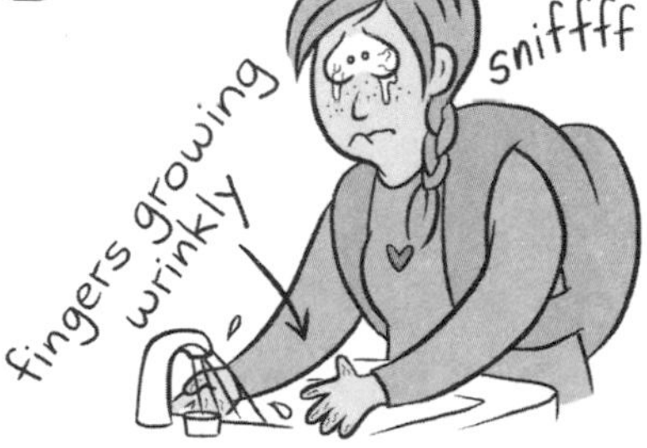

fingers growing wrinkly
sniffff

The door opens slowly.

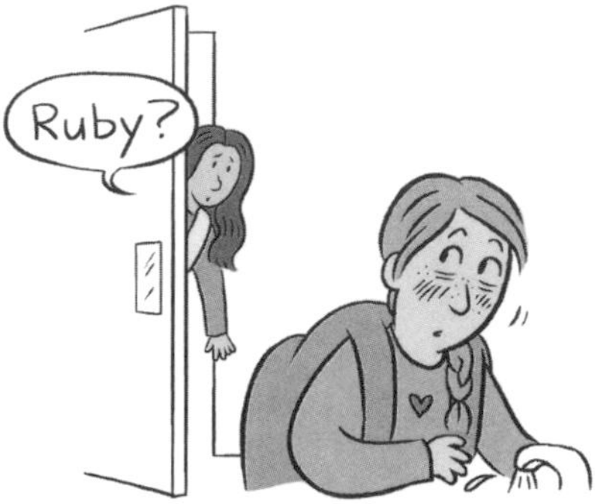
Ruby?

I wipe my eyes again.

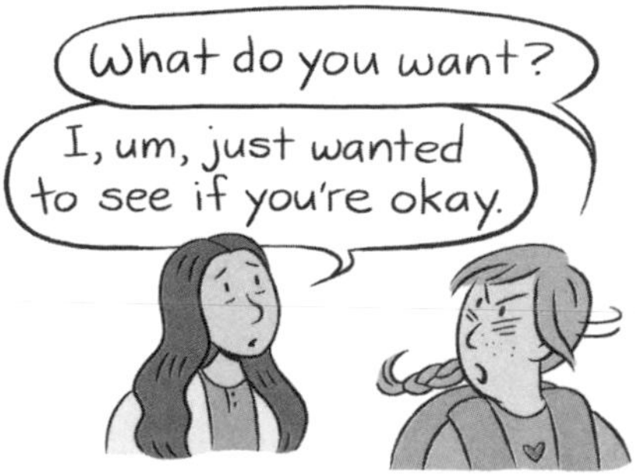
What do you want?
I, um, just wanted to see if you're okay.

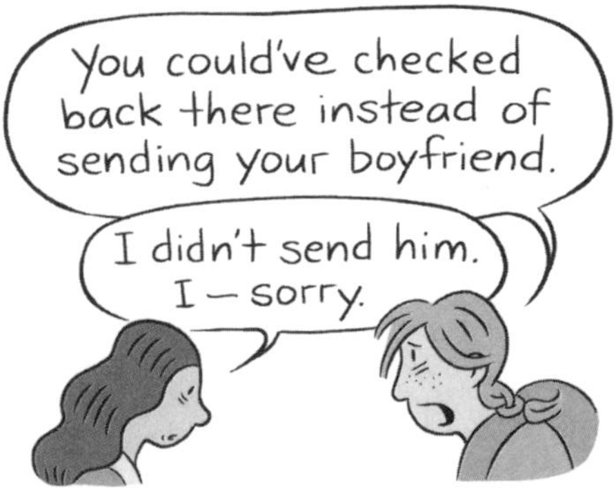
You could've checked back there instead of sending your boyfriend.
I didn't send him. I — sorry.

Whatever.

I, uh, have to go. Election stuff.

Yeah. I wouldn't want to <u>embarrass</u> you before the big day.

She throws me an awkward look and leaves, closing the door. I wait while my eyes turn from red to pink. Glad I walk home instead of taking the bus. I can stay here till my eyes are dry.

Waiting gives me time to notice stuff:

fake nail clippings — fake eye- lashes — real dead rodent

This isn't the first time I've done something like that in front of Mia. I don't know why it keeps happening. Worst part is, I know she's Miss Perfect and I know we have nothing in common anymore and that she's embarrassed to be around me.

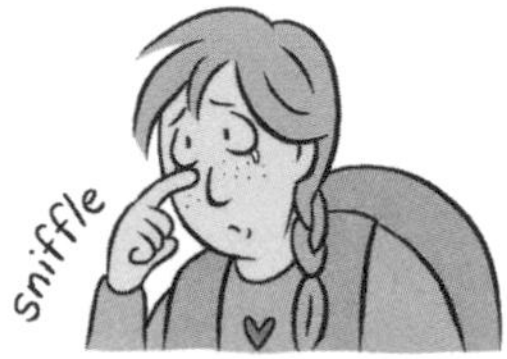
sniffle

Which is why I'm not just mad at her. I'm also mad at:

Me, myself, and I

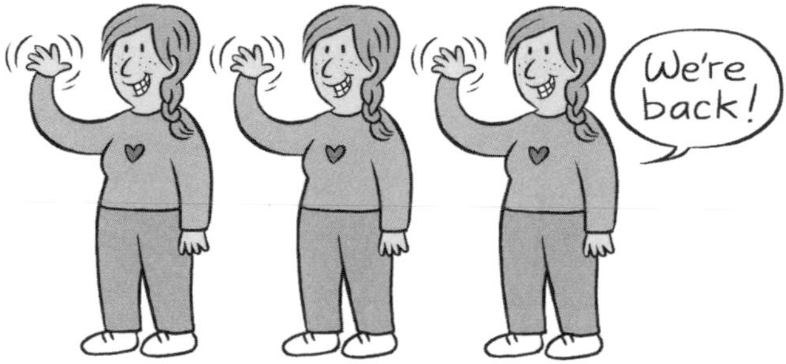
We're back!

'Cause if I had a perfect life, with perfect friends and a perfect bf with a good chance of becoming class prez . . .

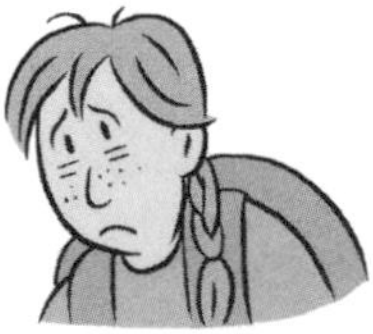

. . . I wouldn't want a klutzo dork ruining it for me, either.

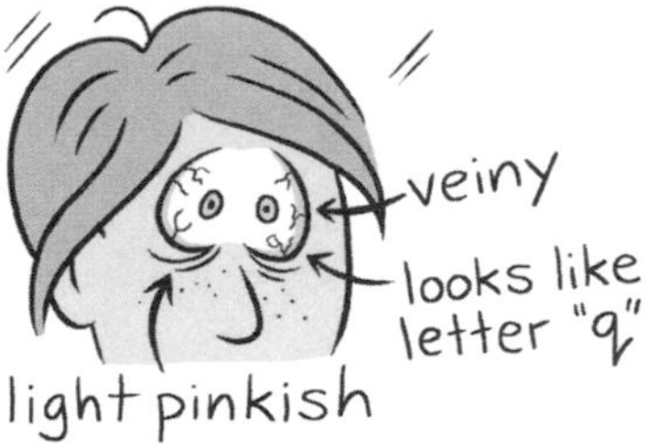
veiny
looks like letter "q"
light pinkish

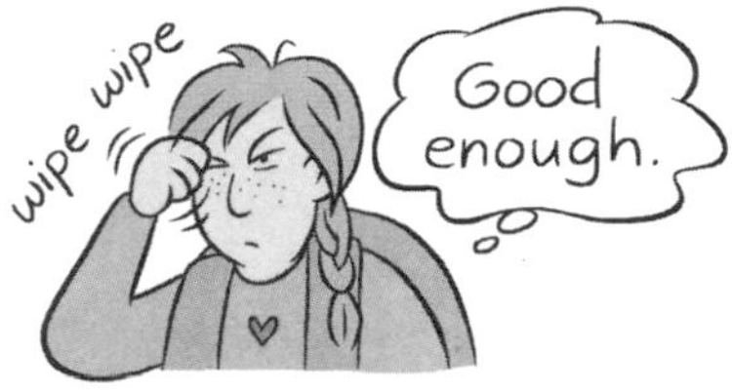
wipe wipe
Good enough.

I open the door, make sure the hall is empty . . .

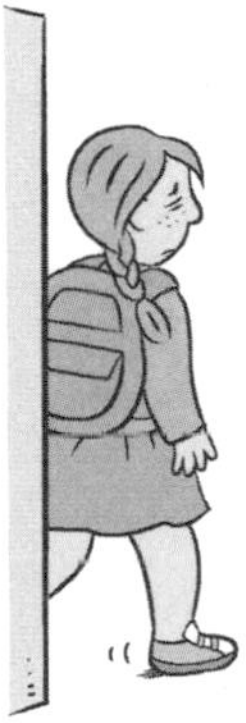

. . . and pray no one sees me.

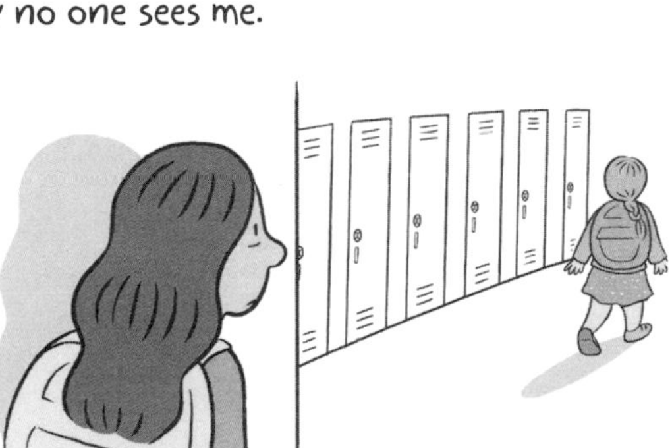

Mia

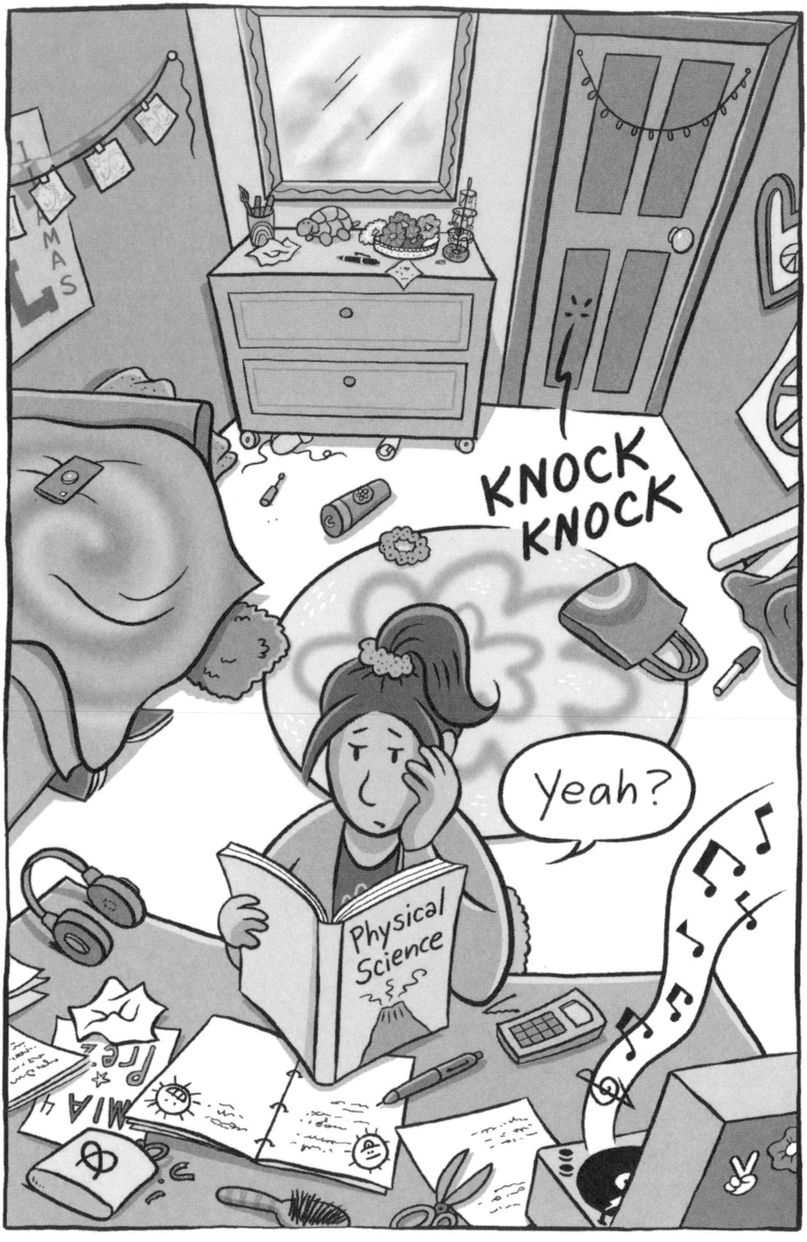
KNOCK
KNOCK
Yeah?
Physical Science

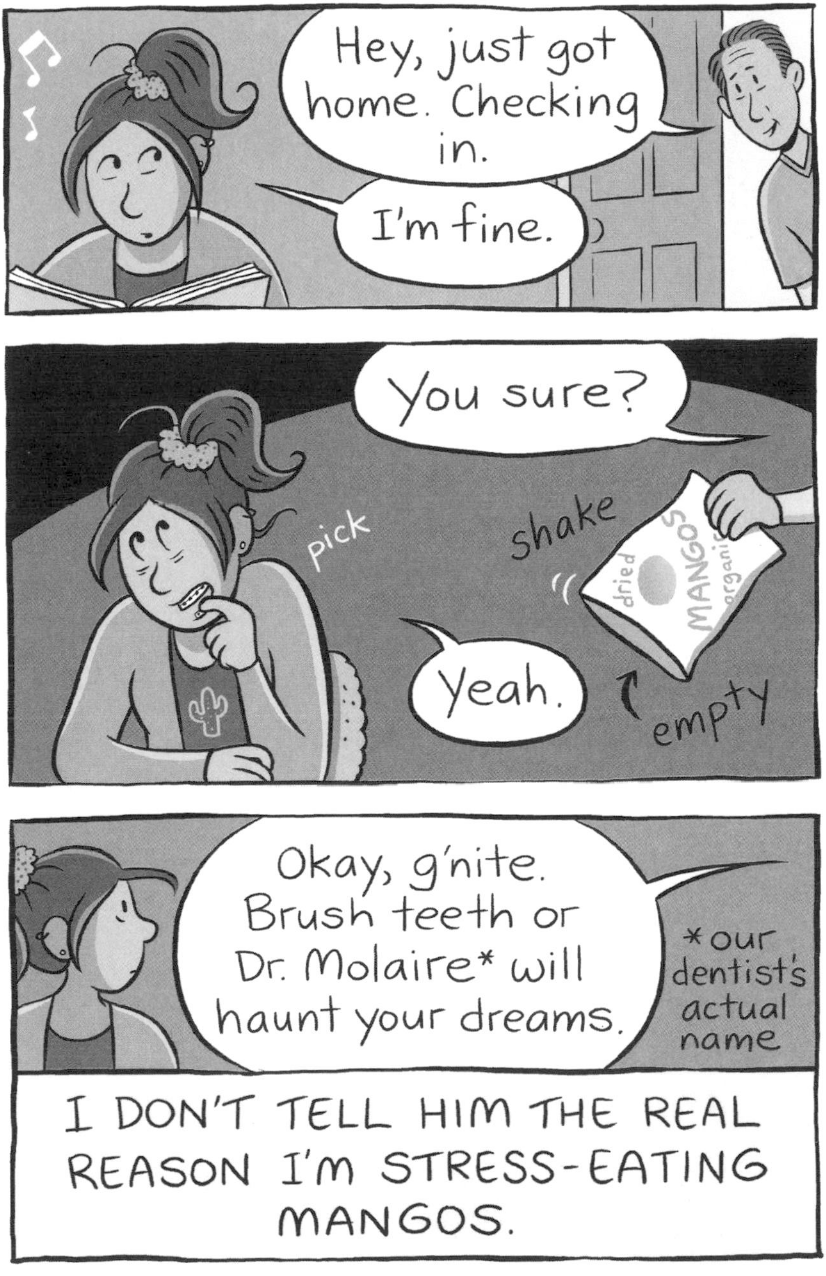
Hey, just got home. Checking in.
I'm fine.
You sure?
pick
shake
dried MANGOS organic
Yeah.
empty
Okay, g'nite. Brush teeth or Dr. Molaire* will haunt your dreams.
*our dentist's actual name
I DON'T TELL HIM THE REAL REASON I'M STRESS-EATING MANGOS.

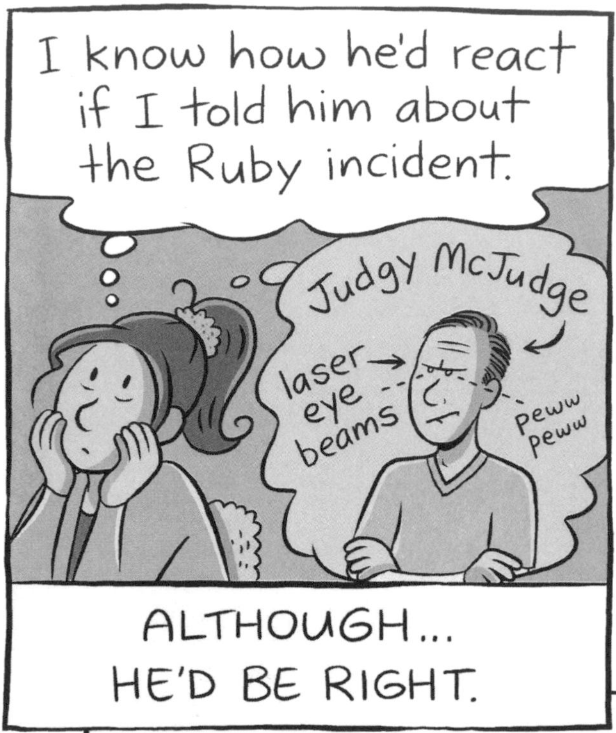
I know how he'd react if I told him about the Ruby incident.
Judgy McJudge
laser eye beams
peww peww
ALTHOUGH... HE'D BE RIGHT.

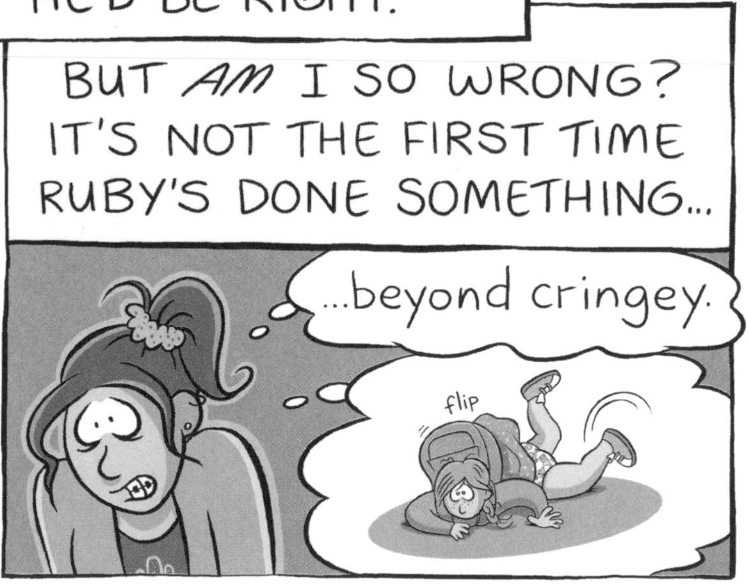
BUT *AM* I SO WRONG? IT'S NOT THE FIRST TIME RUBY'S DONE SOMETHING...
...beyond cringey.
flip

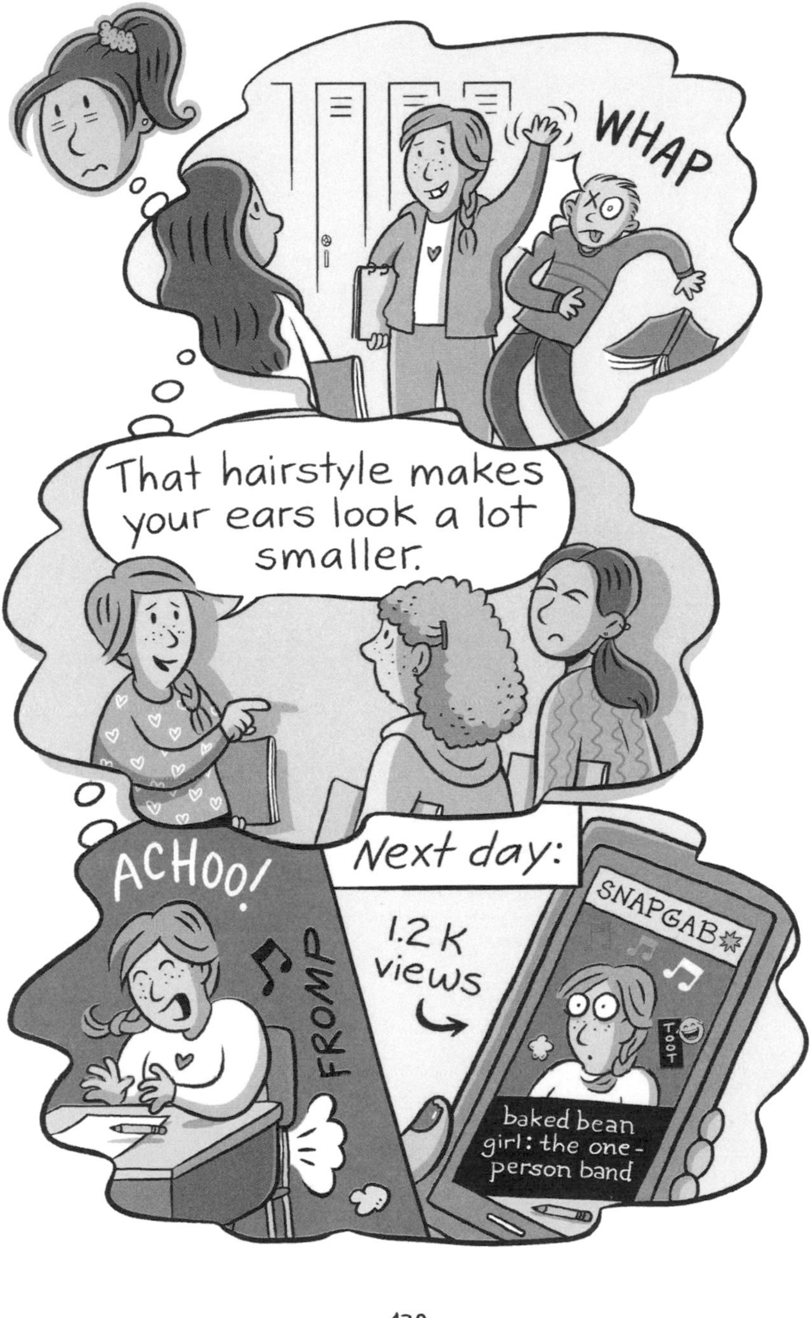
WHAP
That hairstyle makes your ears look a lot smaller.
ACHOO!
FROMP
Next day:
1.2 K views
SNAPGAB
TOOT
baked bean girl: the one-person band

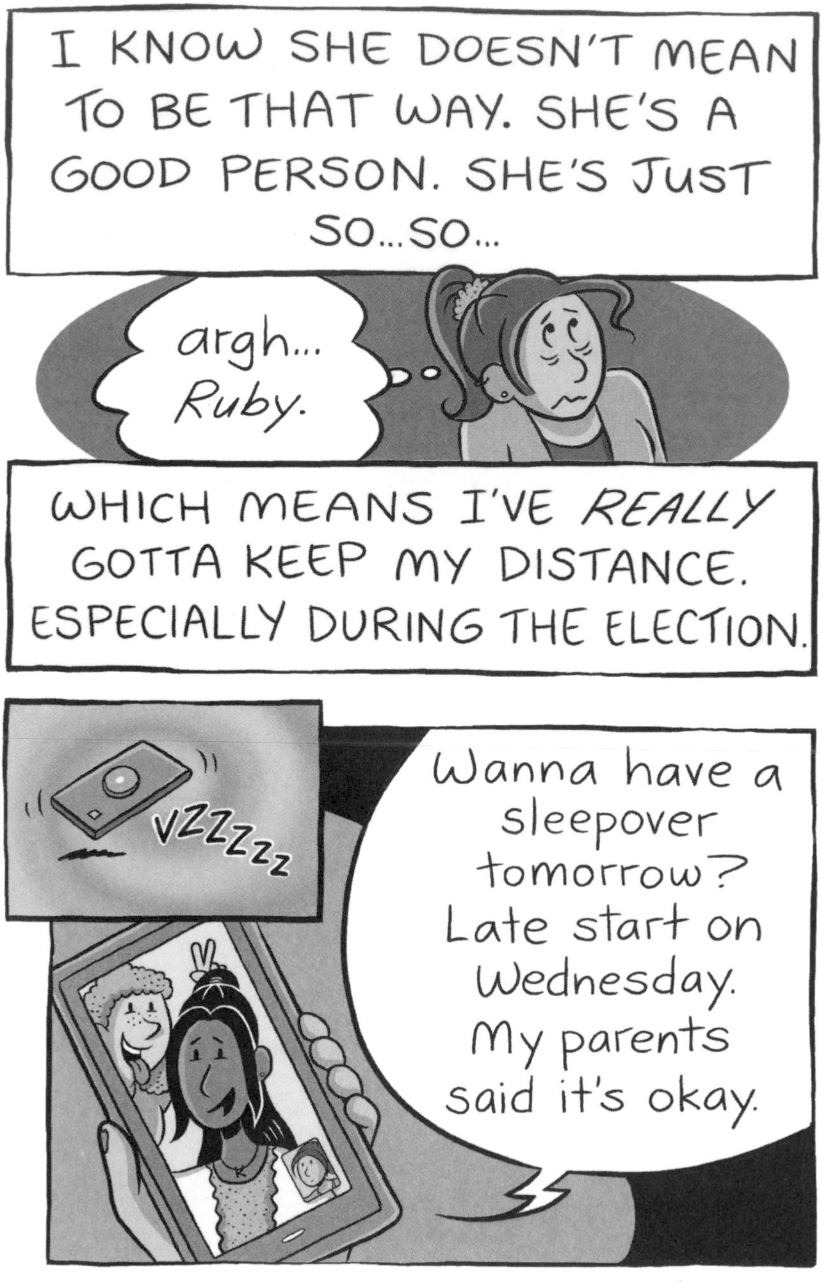
I KNOW SHE DOESN'T MEAN TO BE THAT WAY. SHE'S A GOOD PERSON. SHE'S JUST SO...SO...
argh... *Ruby.*
WHICH MEANS I'VE *REALLY* GOTTA KEEP MY DISTANCE. ESPECIALLY DURING THE ELECTION.
VZZZZZ
Wanna have a sleepover tomorrow? Late start on Wednesday. My parents said it's okay.

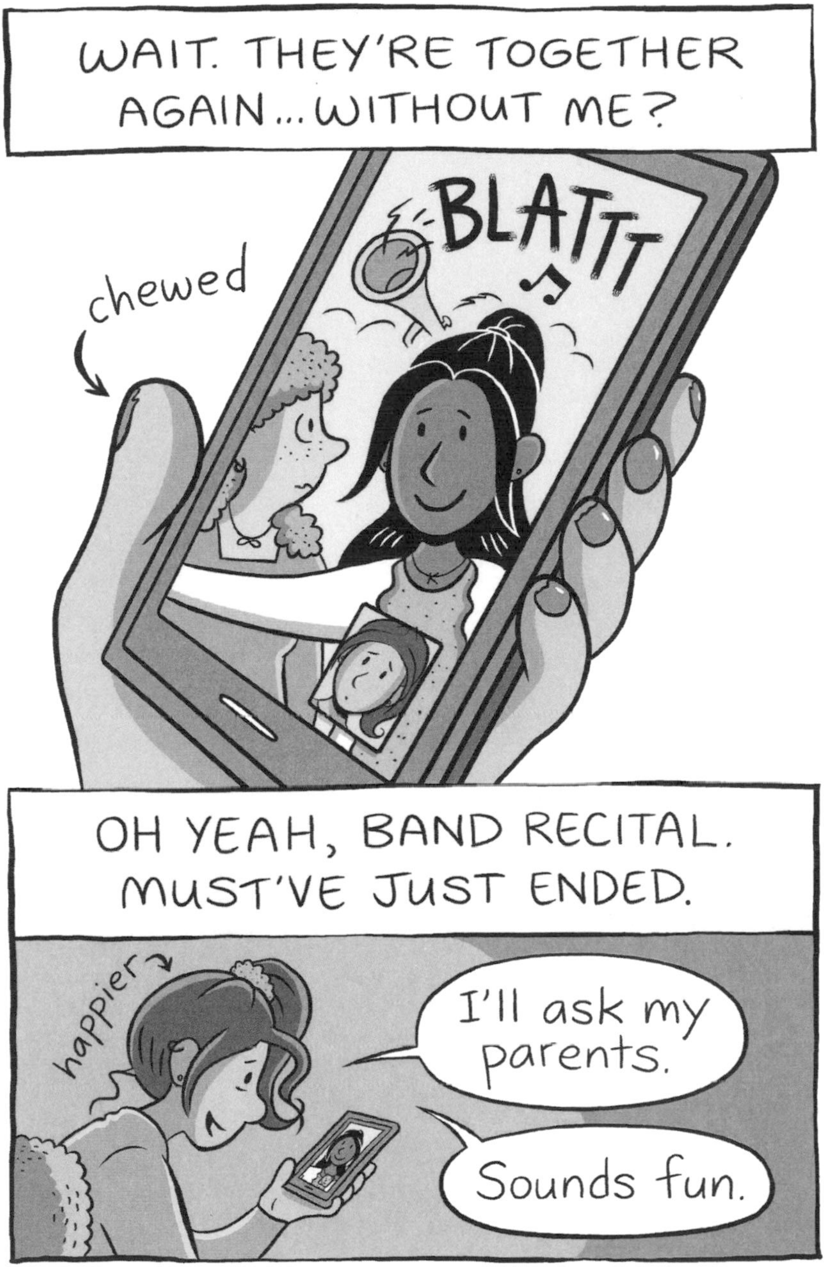
WAIT. THEY'RE TOGETHER AGAIN...WITHOUT ME?
BLATTT
chewed
OH YEAH, BAND RECITAL. MUST'VE JUST ENDED.
happier
I'll ask my parents.
Sounds fun.

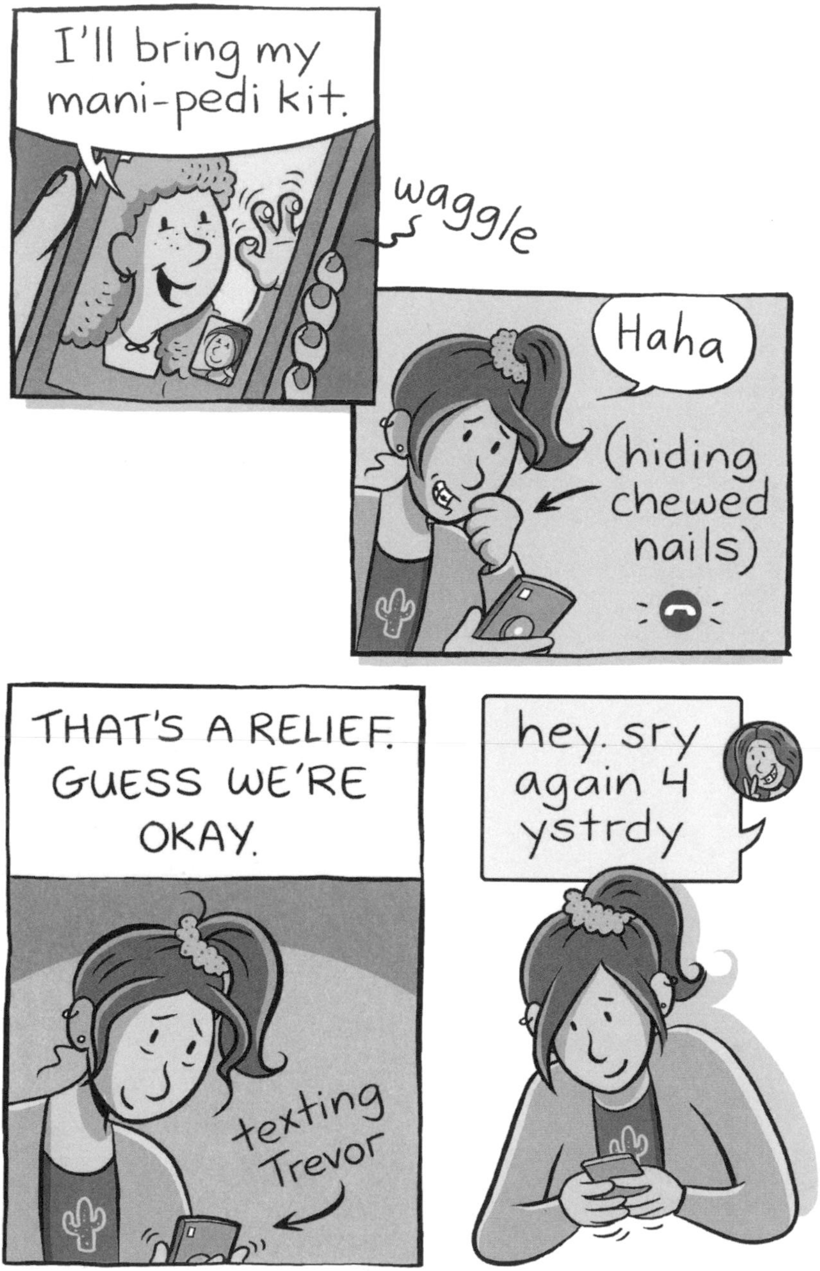
I'll bring my mani-pedi kit.
waggle
Haha
(hiding chewed nails)
THAT'S A RELIEF. GUESS WE'RE OKAY.
texting Trevor
hey. sry again 4 ystrdy

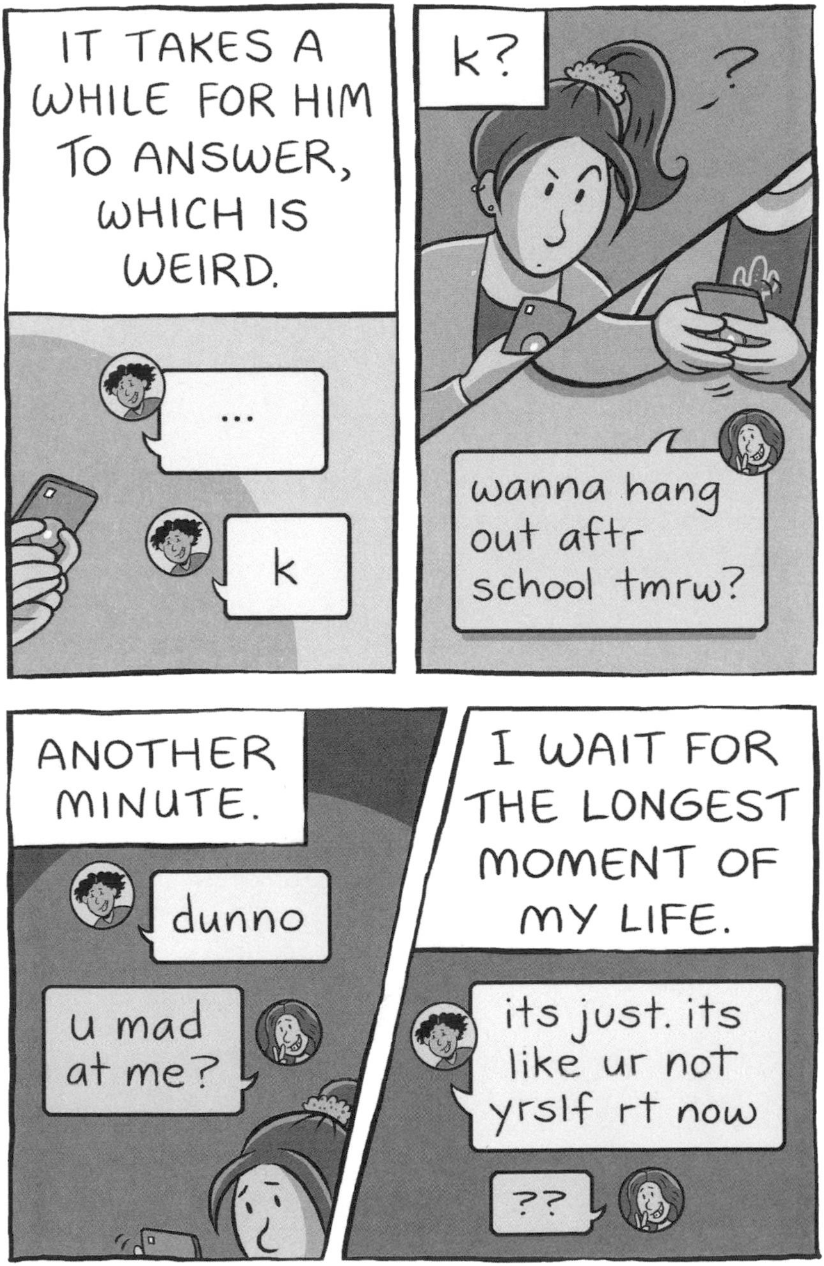
IT TAKES A WHILE FOR HIM TO ANSWER, WHICH IS WEIRD.
...
k
k?
?
wanna hang out aftr school tmrw?
ANOTHER MINUTE.
dunno
u mad at me?
I WAIT FOR THE LONGEST MOMENT OF MY LIFE.
its just. its like ur not yrslf rt now
??

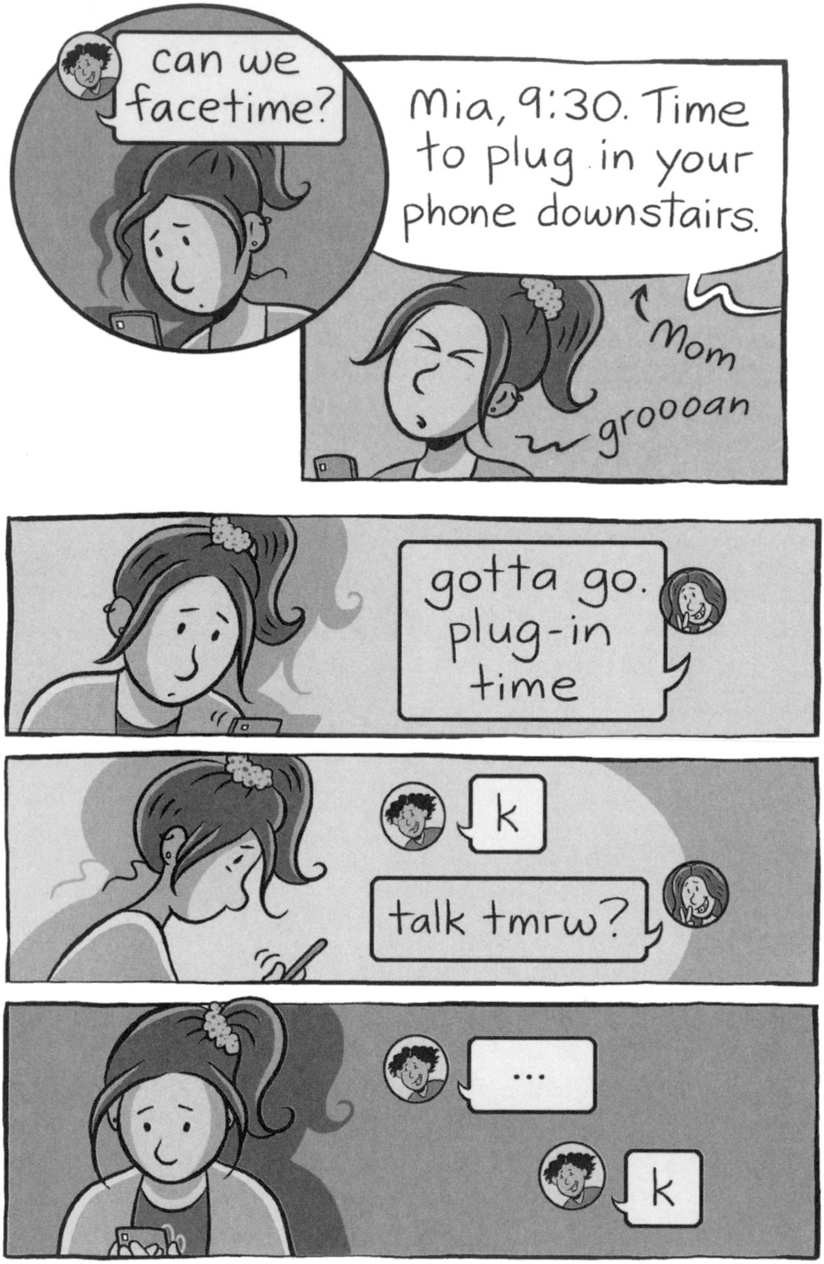
can we facetime?
Mia, 9:30. Time to plug in your phone downstairs.
Mom
groooan
gotta go. plug-in time
k
talk tmrw?
...
k

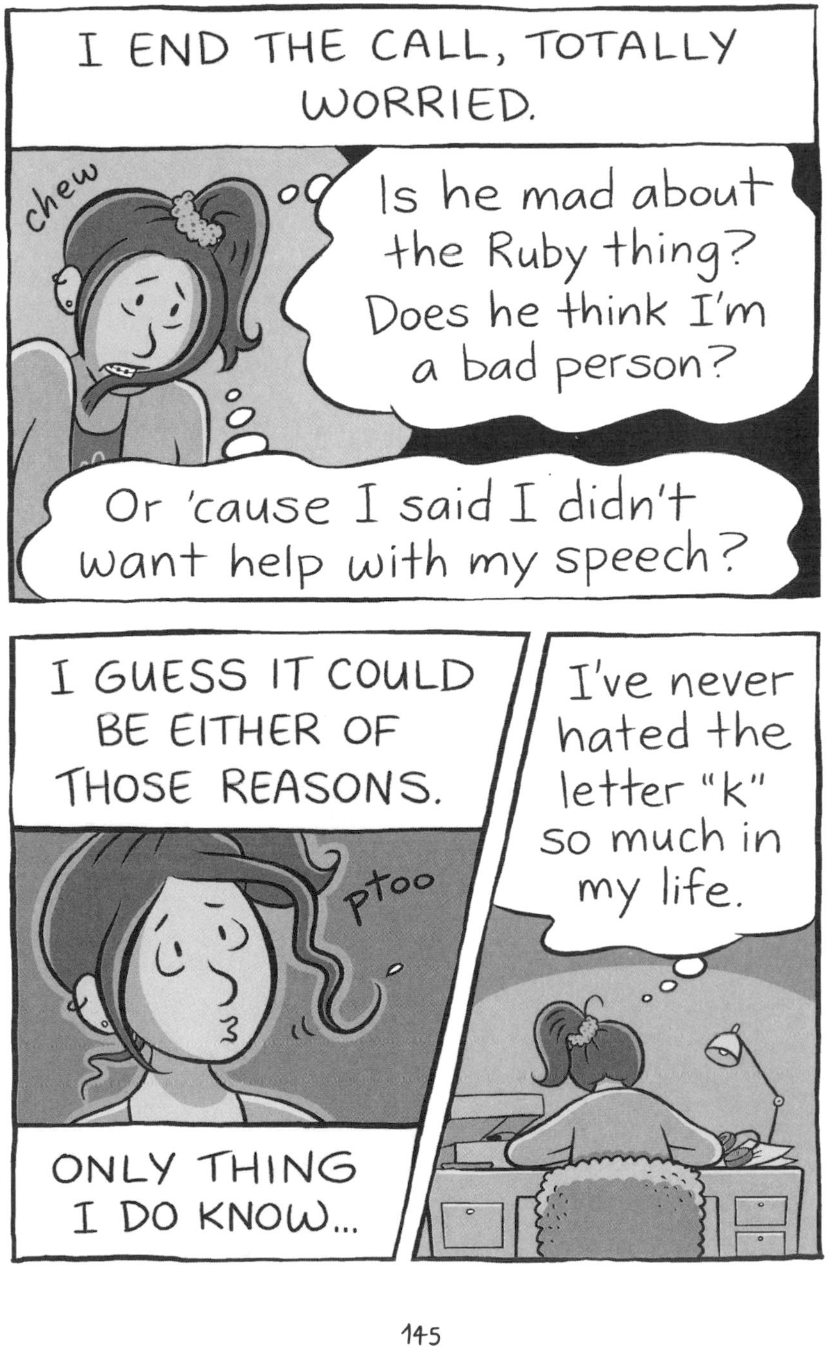
I END THE CALL, TOTALLY WORRIED.
chew
Is he mad about the Ruby thing? Does he think I'm a bad person?
Or 'cause I said I didn't want help with my speech?
I GUESS IT COULD BE EITHER OF THOSE REASONS.
ptoo
ONLY THING I DO KNOW...
I've never hated the letter "k" so much in my life.

RUBY

First poetry club meeting.

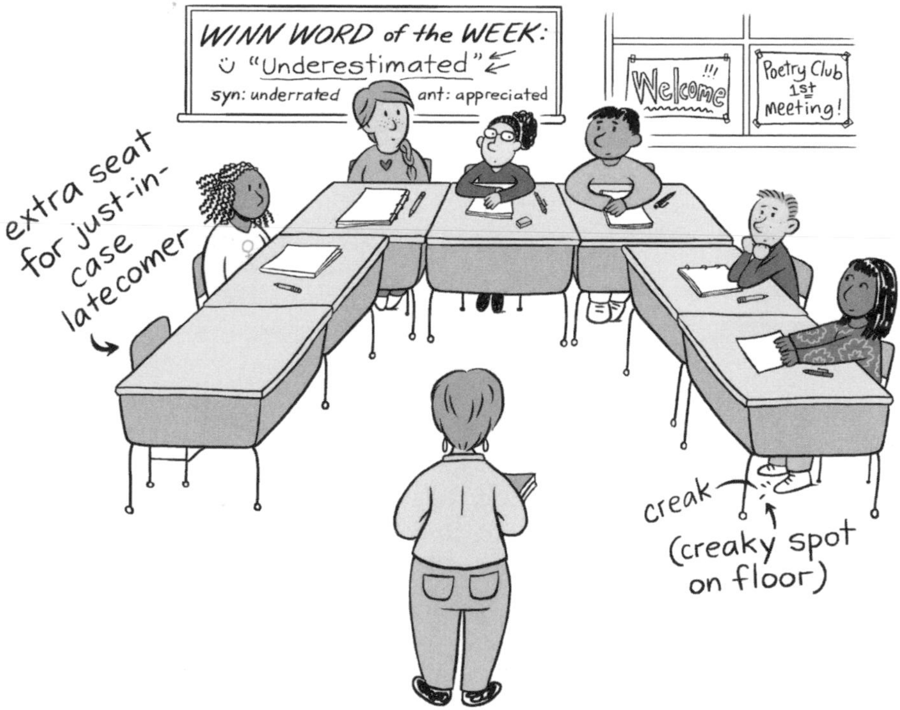
WINN WORD of the WEEK:
"Underestimated"
syn: underrated
ant: appreciated
Welcome !!!
Poetry Club 1st meeting!
extra seat for just-in-case latecomer
creak
(creaky spot on floor)

I'm pretty happy with the turnout. A few days ago, Leah and I went to Mr. Taleb's room. He's the eighth-grade English teacher in charge of the school's book club.

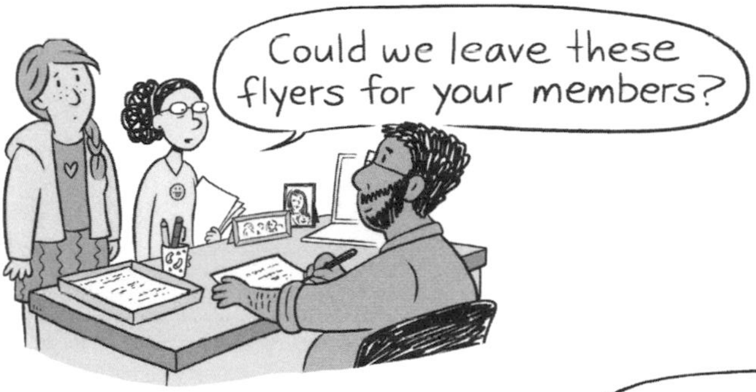
Could we leave these flyers for your members?

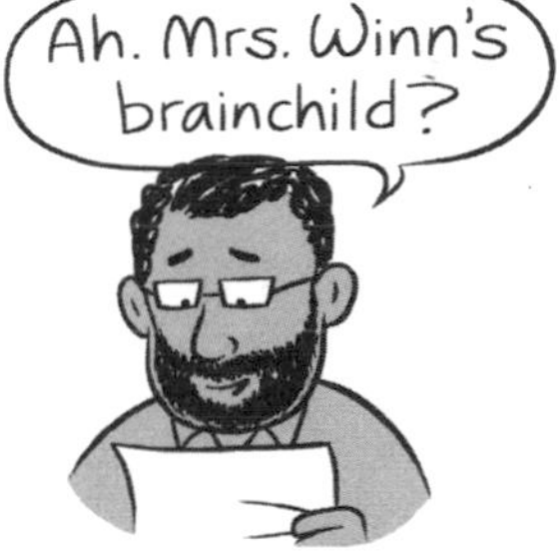
Ah. Mrs. Winn's brainchild?

We nodded.

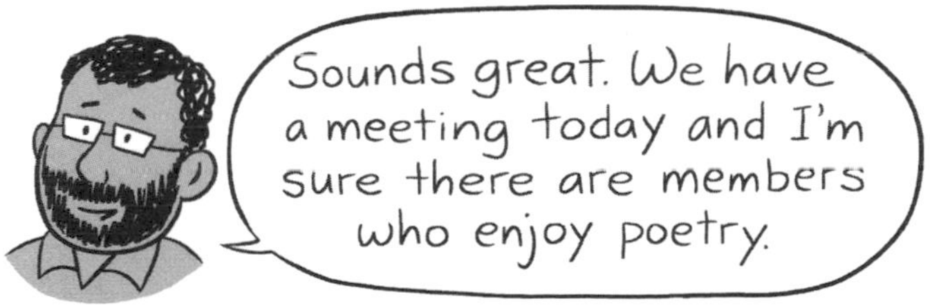
Sounds great. We have a meeting today and I'm sure there are members who enjoy poetry.

Guess Mr. Taleb came through. There are some kids here we don't recognize.

Also, one of the science kids from the cafeteria.

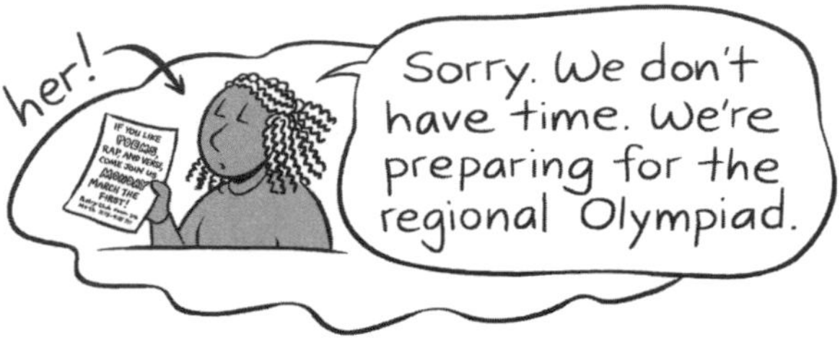
her!
Sorry. We don't have time. We're preparing for the regional Olympiad.

Go figure.

When we first arrived, Mrs. Winn had us do introductions and share our other interests.

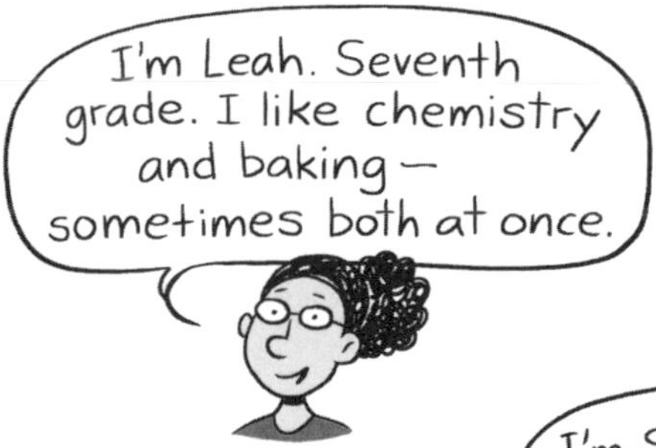
I'm Leah. Seventh grade. I like chemistry and baking — sometimes both at once.

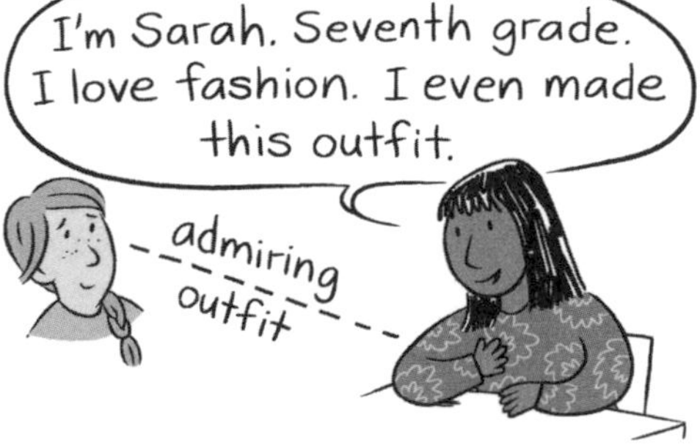
I'm Sarah. Seventh grade. I love fashion. I even made this outfit.
admiring outfit

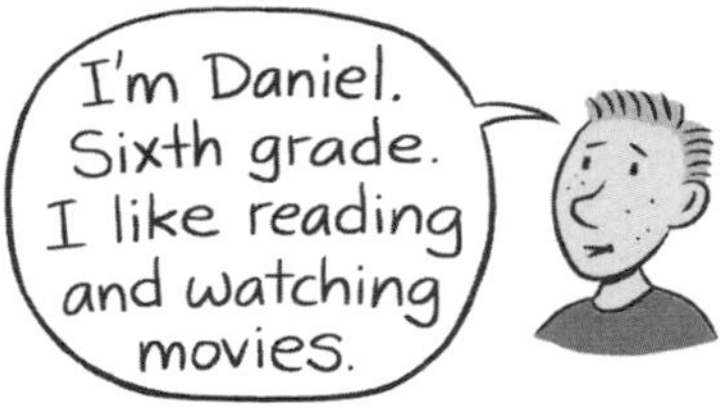
I'm Daniel. Sixth grade. I like reading and watching movies.

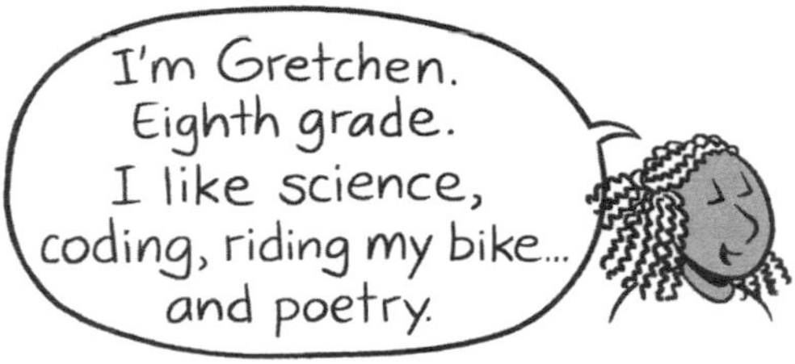
I'm Gretchen. Eighth grade. I like science, coding, riding my bike... and poetry.

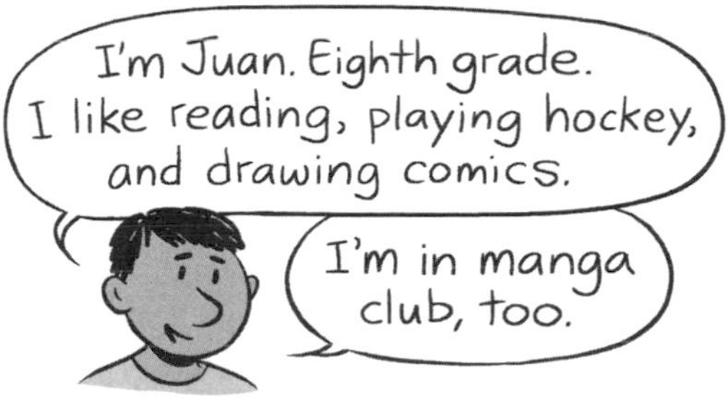
I'm Juan. Eighth grade. I like reading, playing hockey, and drawing comics.
I'm in manga club, too.

Everyone has a lot of hobbies.

Except me.

All eyes look my way.

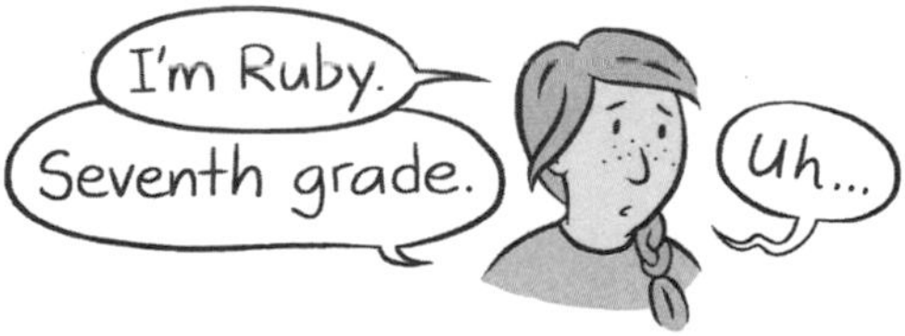
I'm Ruby.
Seventh grade.
Uh...

I glance down in panic. I can't think of anything I like to do except watch TV, water plants, and . . .

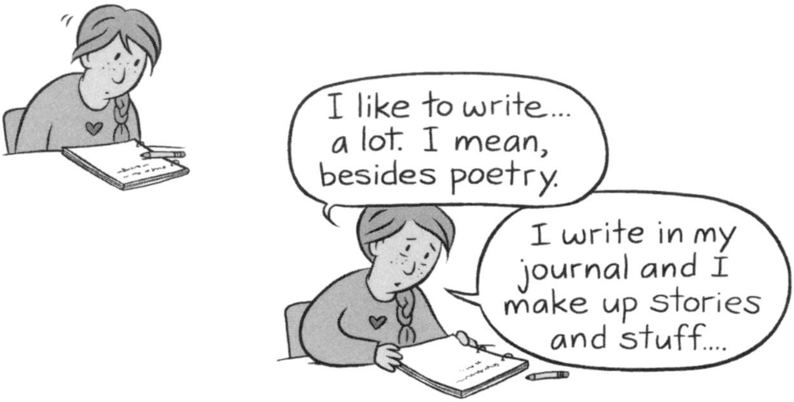
I like to write... a lot. I mean, besides poetry.
I write in my journal and I make up stories and stuff....

My voice trails off.

When I look up, I'm surprised to see that they all seem kinda interested.

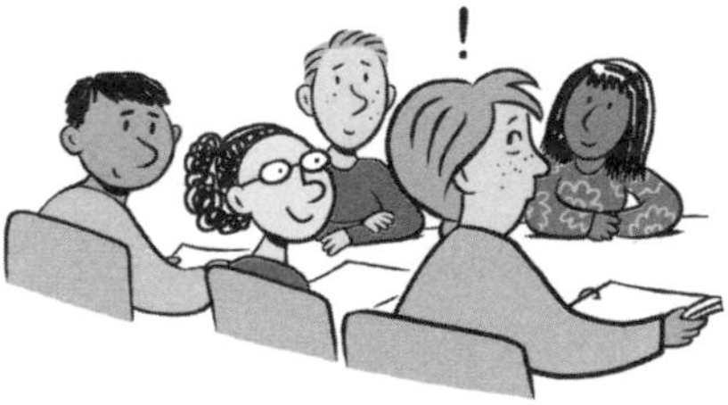
!

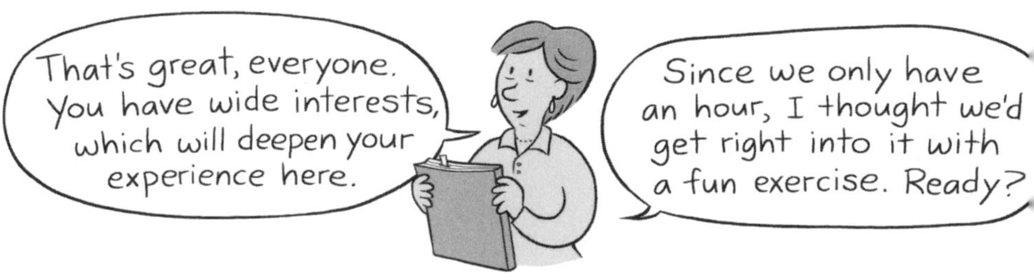
That's great, everyone. You have wide interests, which will deepen your experience here.
Since we only have an hour, I thought we'd get right into it with a fun exercise. Ready?

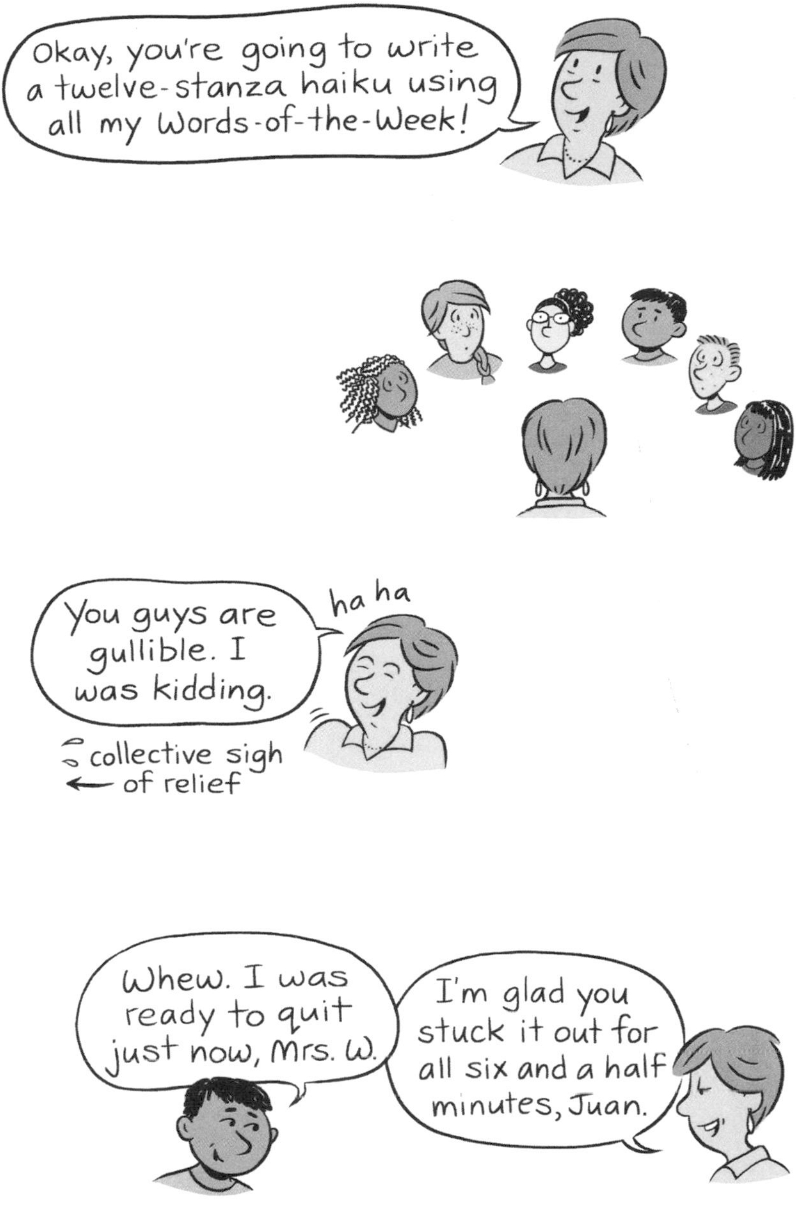
Okay, you're going to write a twelve-stanza haiku using all my Words-of-the-Week!
You guys are gullible. I was kidding.
ha ha
collective sigh of relief
Whew. I was ready to quit just now, Mrs. W.
I'm glad you stuck it out for all six and a half minutes, Juan.

Okay, seriously. First exercise.
Let's think outside the box. Literally.

The box is yourself. Your perspective.
Let's think—not just from another person's perspective—but another *thing's* point of view.

I'll give you an example. I'm going to read a poem by H.W. Longfellow.

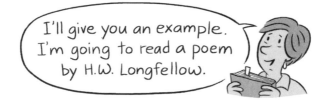

"Behold! a giant am I!
Aloft here in my tower,
With my granite jaws I devour
The maize, and the wheat, and the rye,
And grind them into flour."

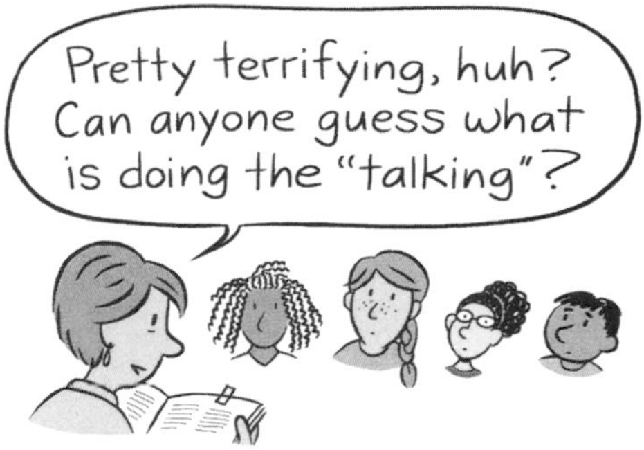
Pretty terrifying, huh? Can anyone guess what is doing the "talking"?

No one answers.

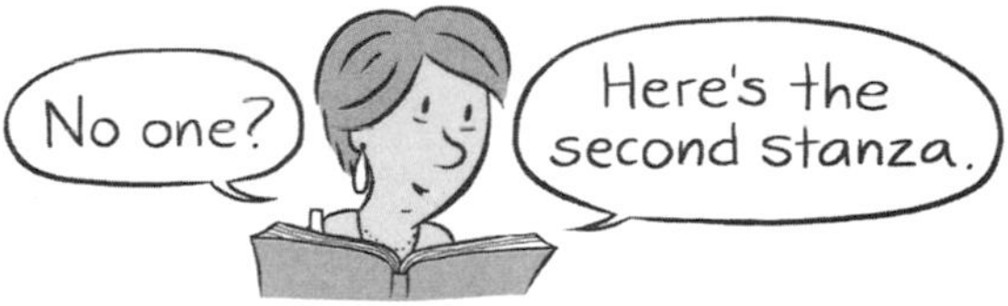
No one?
Here's the second stanza.

"I look down over the farms;
In the fields of grain I see
The harvest that is to be,
And I fling to the air my arms,
For I know it is all for me."

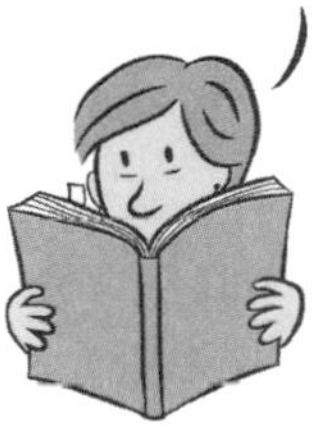

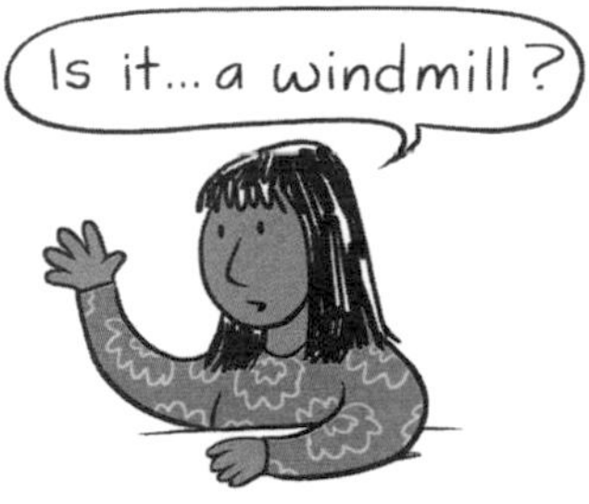
Is it... a windmill?

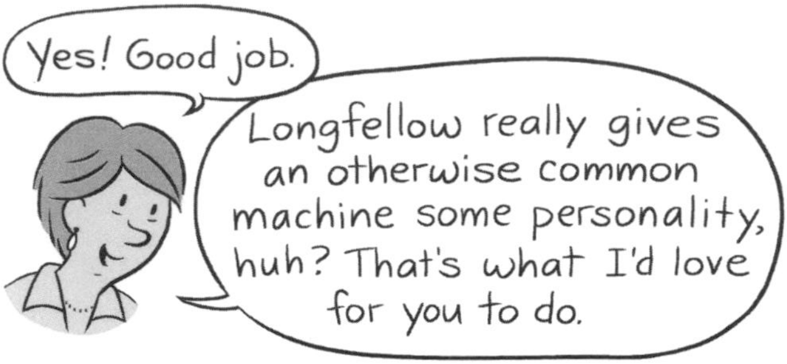
Yes! Good job.
Longfellow really gives an otherwise common machine some personality, huh? That's what I'd love for you to do.

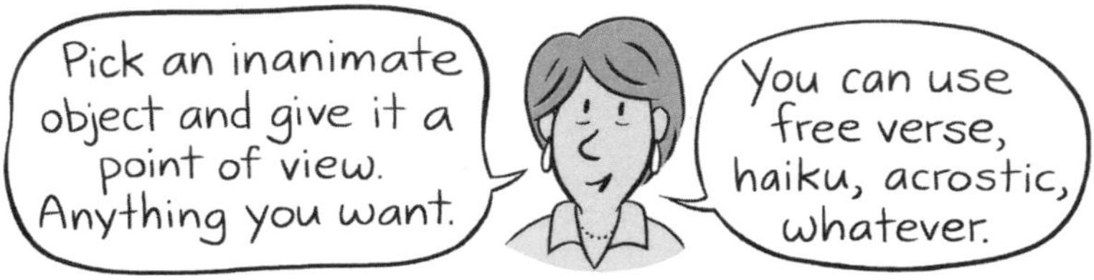
Pick an inanimate object and give it a point of view. Anything you want.
You can use free verse, haiku, acrostic, whatever.

I try to think of something. At first, I can't.

But then . . .

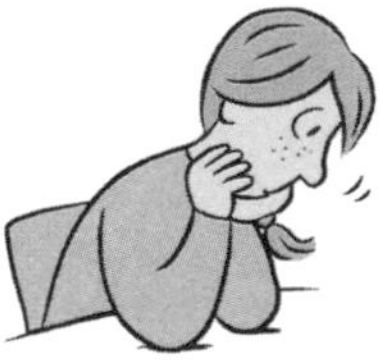

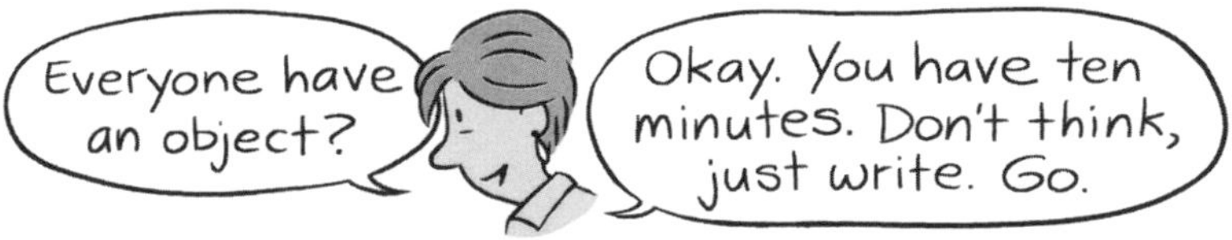
Everyone have an object?
Okay. You have ten minutes. Don't think, just write. Go.

I do what she says.

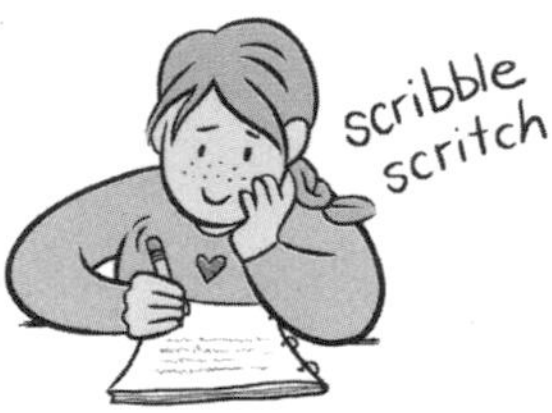
scribble
scritch

The time goes by so fast. No chance to double-check myself or see if I messed up.

I just write.

I hear the scratches of everyone's pencils and pens. No other sound. It's kinda nice.

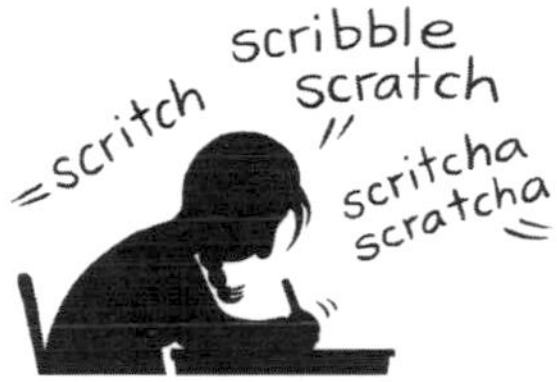
scritch
scribble
scratch
scritcha
scratcha

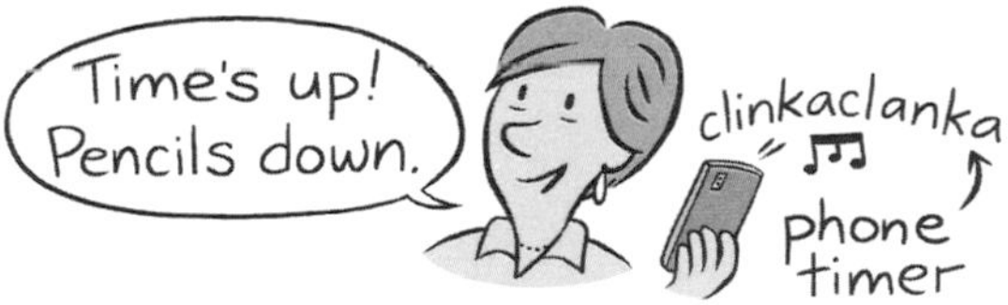
Time's up! Pencils down.
clinkaclanka
phone timer

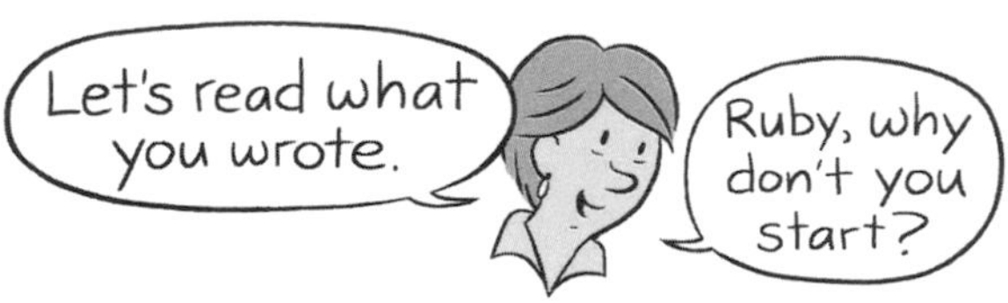
Let's read what you wrote.
Ruby, why don't you start?

Is she serious?? My stomach lurches. Not again.

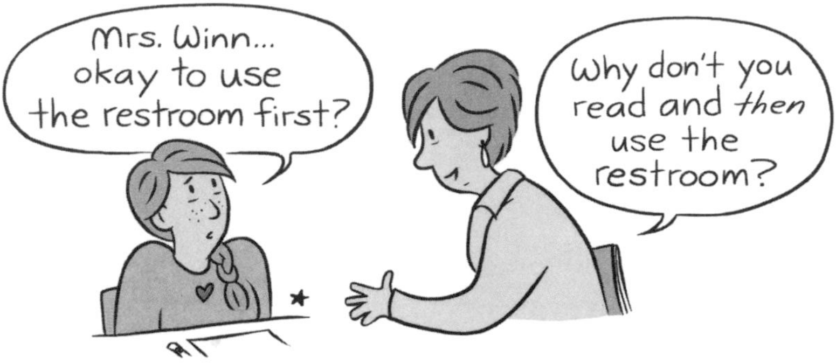
Mrs. Winn...
okay to use
the restroom first?
Why don't you
read and *then*
use the
restroom?

She gives me this encouraging smile; I wonder if she understands my nervous stomach.

I take a deep, shuddery breath and try not to think about anyone judging my poem.

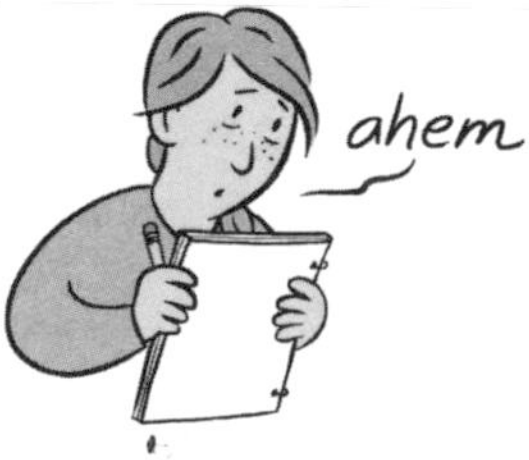
ahem

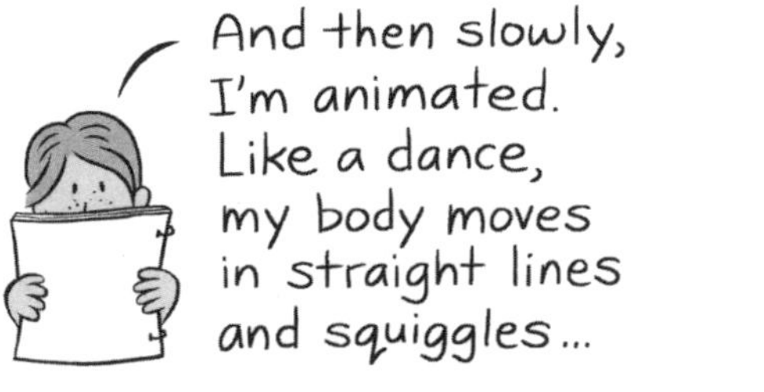
At the start, I'm stiff.
And then slowly,
I'm animated.
Like a dance,
my body moves
in straight lines
and squiggles...

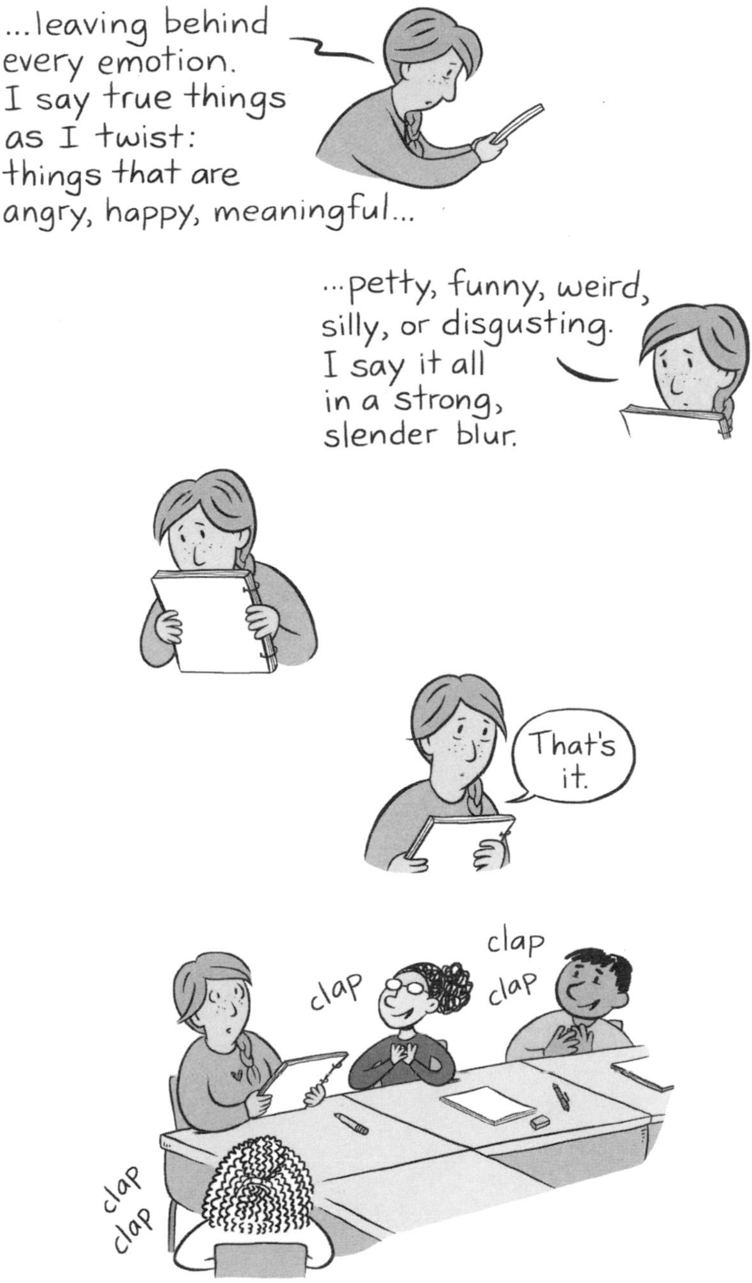
...leaving behind every emotion. I say true things as I twist: things that are angry, happy, meaningful...
...petty, funny, weird, silly, or disgusting. I say it all in a strong, slender blur.
That's it.
clap
clap
clap
clap
clap

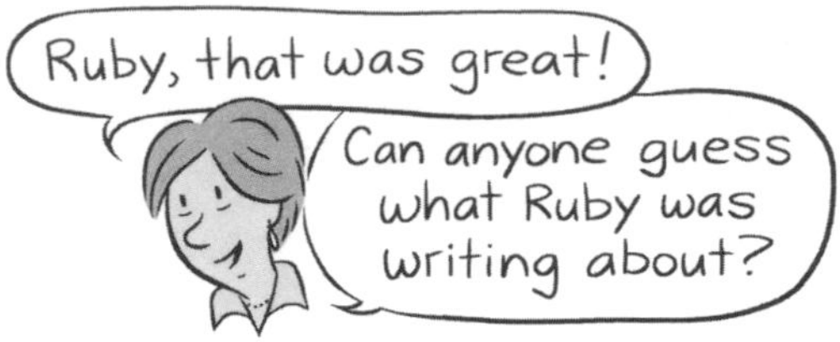
Ruby, that was great!
Can anyone guess what Ruby was writing about?

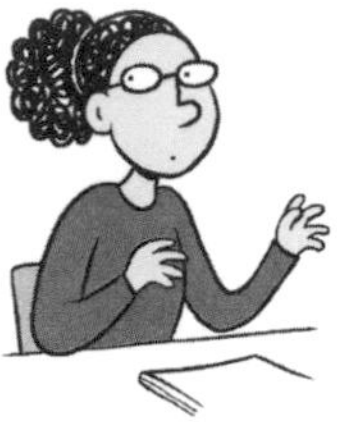

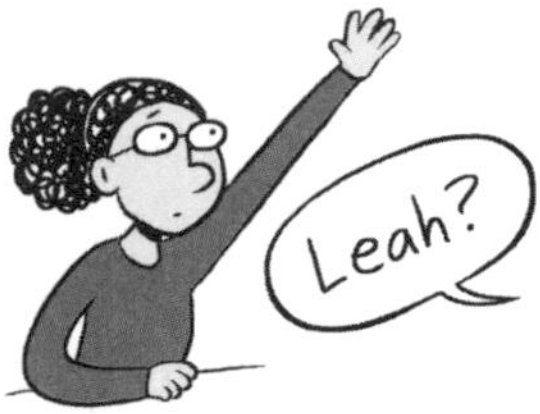
Leah?

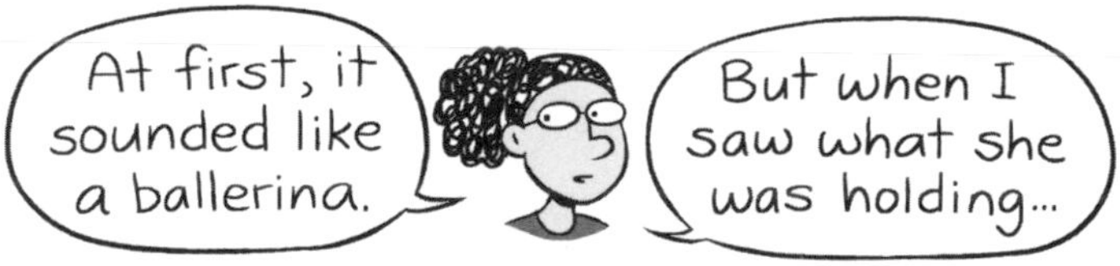
At first, it sounded like a ballerina.
But when I saw what she was holding...

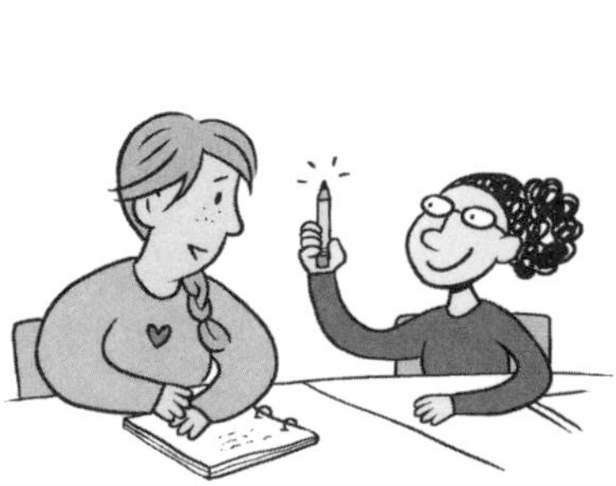

I smile, too.

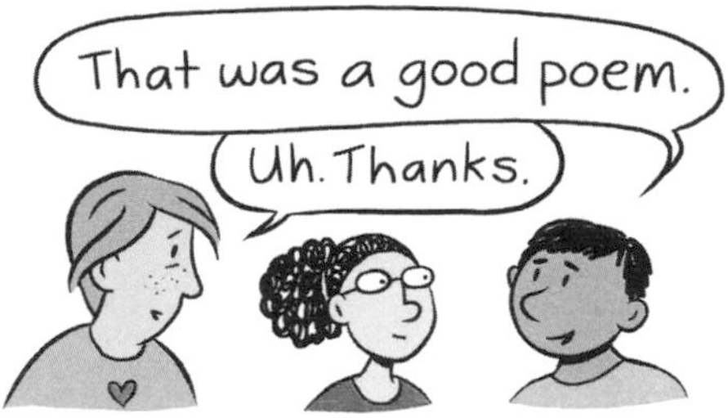
That was a good poem.
Uh. Thanks.

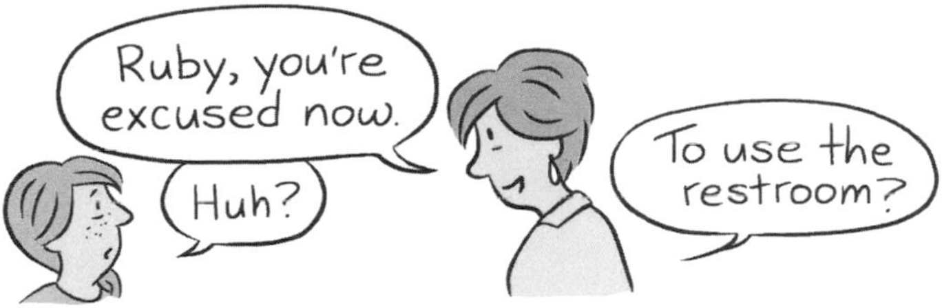
Ruby, you're excused now.
Huh?
To use the restroom?

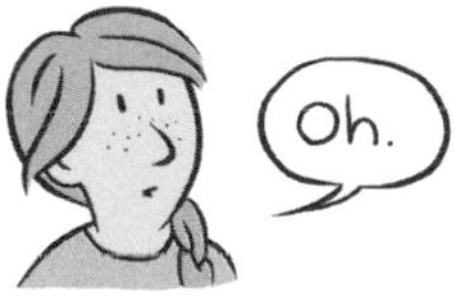
Oh.

I get up, but then change my mind and sit down. I realize I don't need to go anymore.

Also, I wanna hear the other poems.

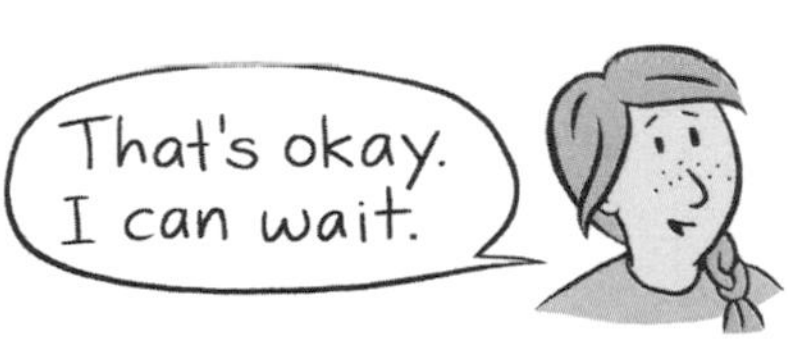
That's okay. I can wait.

Mrs. Winn calls on the others, one at a time. All the poems are pretty good. Daniel's is about a falling leaf. Leah's is about a blender. Sarah's is about a rickety chair.

And Juan's is flat-out clever.

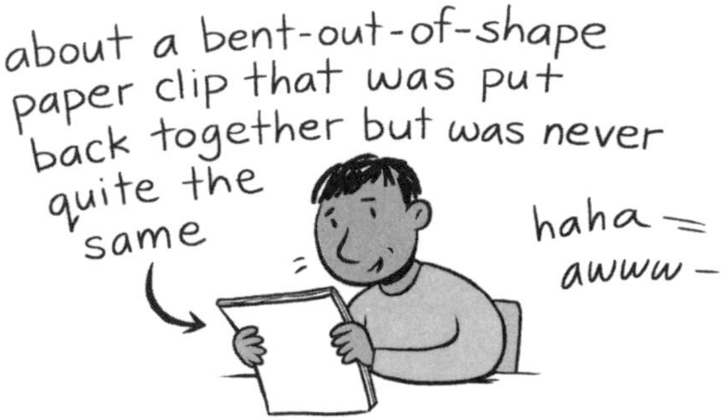
about a bent-out-of-shape paper clip that was put back together but was never quite the same
haha
awww

We do another exercise: Mrs. Winn has us write freestyle poems from the perspective of . . .

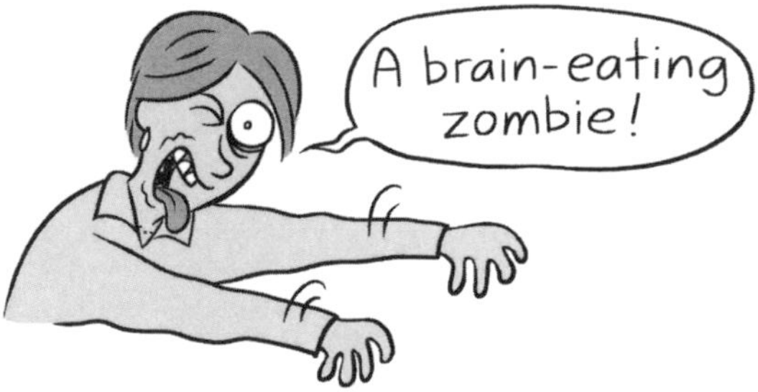
A brain-eating zombie!

We have fun with that. Juan even illustrates his poem.

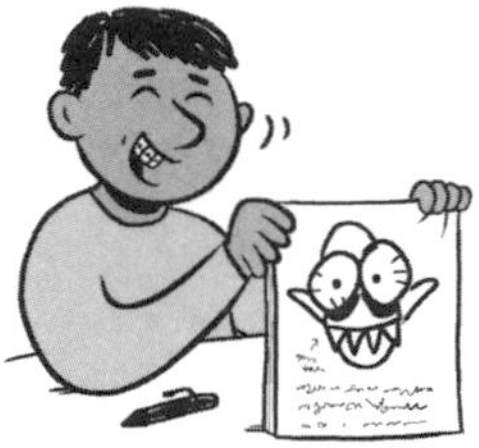

And then . . .

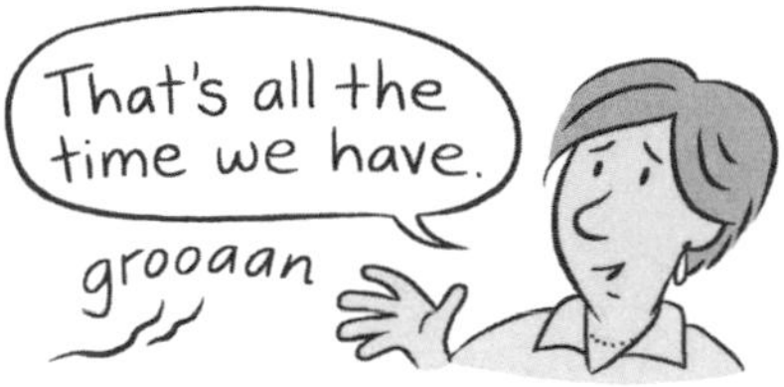
That's all the time we have.
grooaan

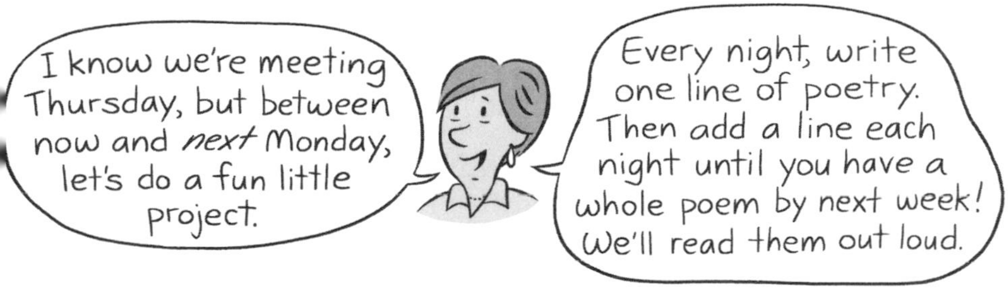
I know we're meeting Thursday, but between now and *next* Monday, let's do a fun little project.
Every night, write one line of poetry. Then add a line each night until you have a whole poem by next week! We'll read them out loud.

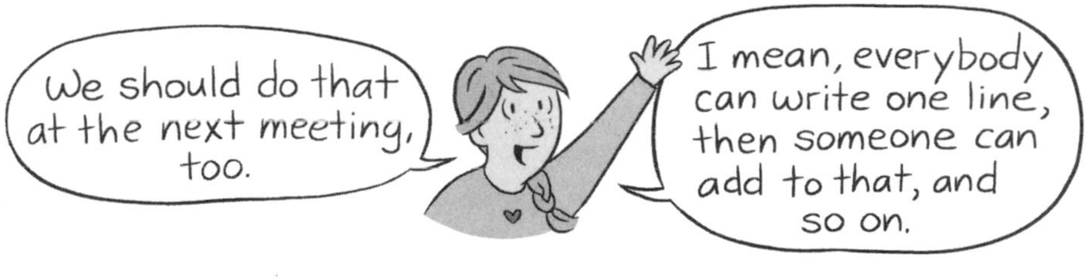
We should do that at the next meeting, too.
I mean, everybody can write one line, then someone can add to that, and so on.

I really said that out loud?

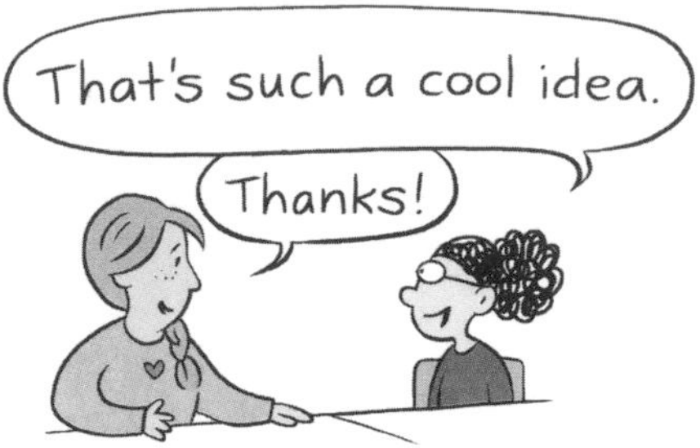
That's such a cool idea.
Thanks!

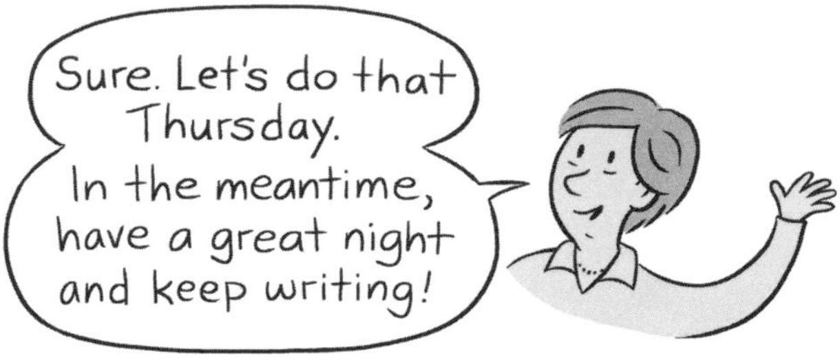
Sure. Let's do that Thursday. In the meantime, have a great night and keep writing!

We all leave. But I don't leave alone.

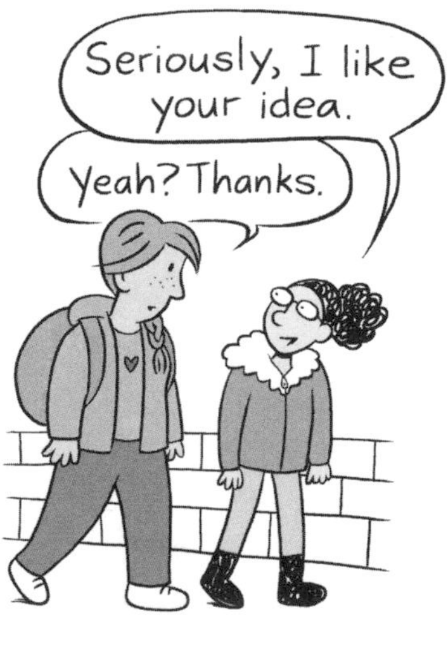
Seriously, I like your idea.
Yeah? Thanks.

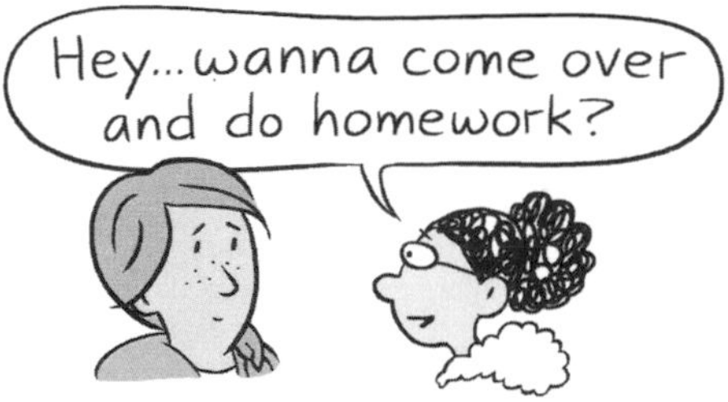
Hey...wanna come over and do homework?

We had talked about that the other day, but nothing ever came out of it. I thought maybe she'd changed her mind.

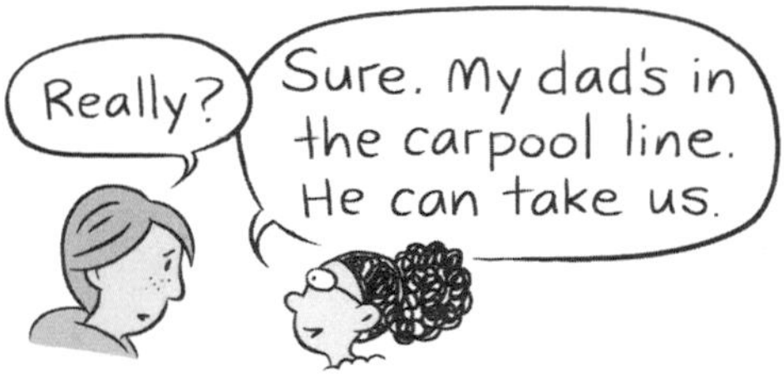
Really?
Sure. My dad's in the carpool line. He can take us.

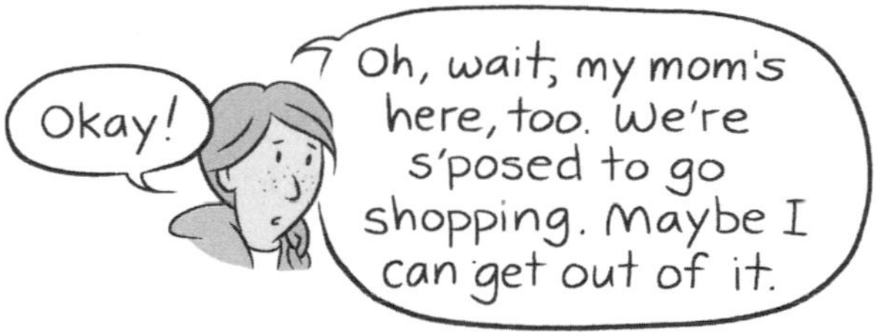
Okay!
Oh, wait, my mom's here, too. We're s'posed to go shopping. Maybe I can get out of it.

We walk out of the building. My mom waits in her parked car, earbuds in. Probably listening to her new-agey playlist.

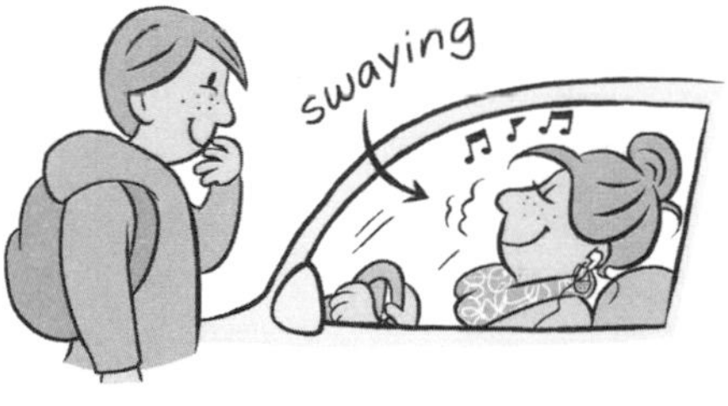
swaying

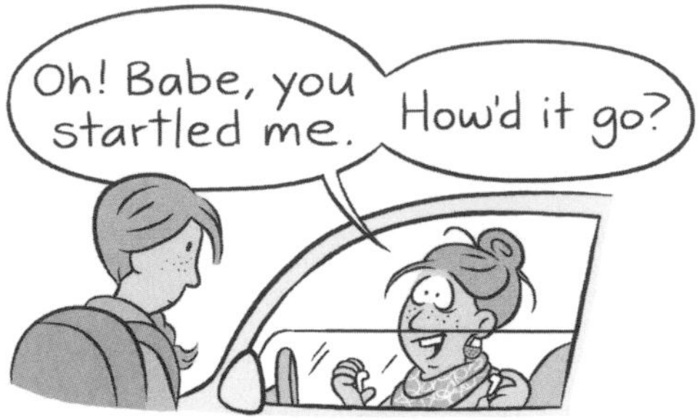
Oh! Babe, you startled me.
How'd it go?

She looks at me eagerly—which is sooo annoying. But also kinda . . . sweet.

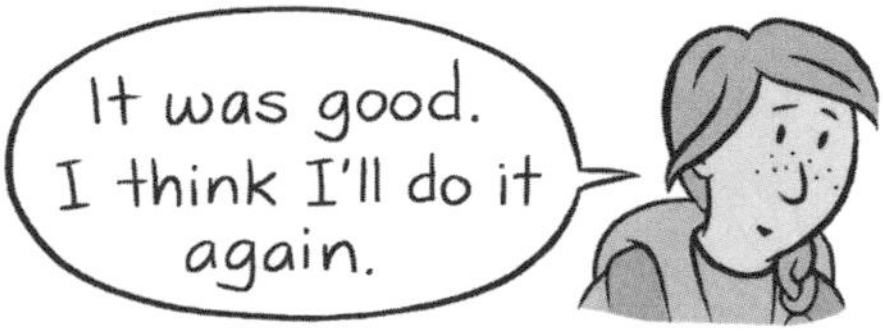
It was good. I think I'll do it again.

I might as well have told her I won the lottery or a genie granted me three wishes.

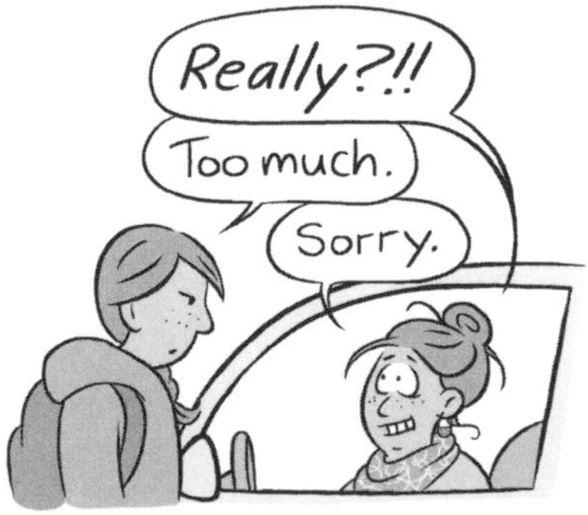
Really?!!
Too much.
Sorry.

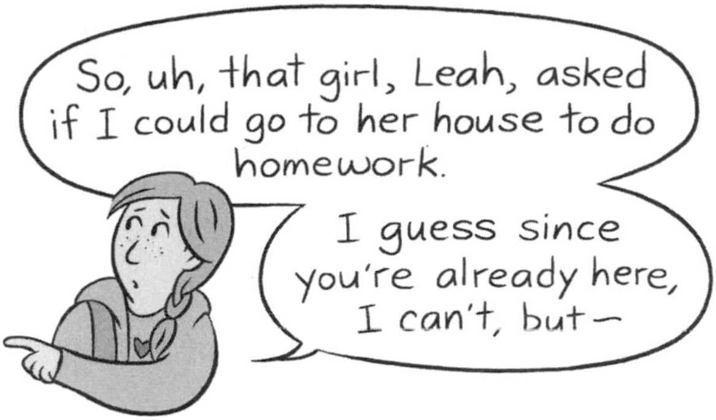
So, uh, that girl, Leah, asked if I could go to her house to do homework.
I guess since you're already here, I can't, but—

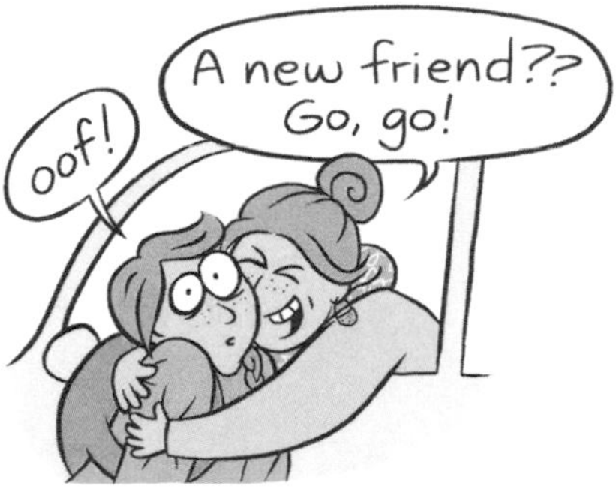
oof!
A new friend?? Go, go!

She realizes what she's doing, midhug, and drops her arms.

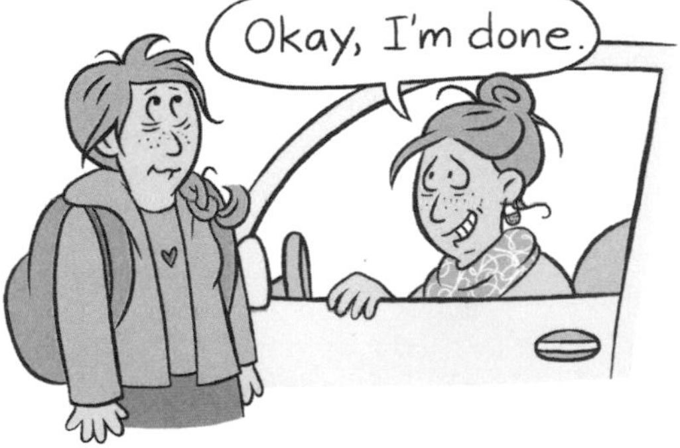
Okay, I'm done.

With a grateful snort, I leave and go catch up with Leah.

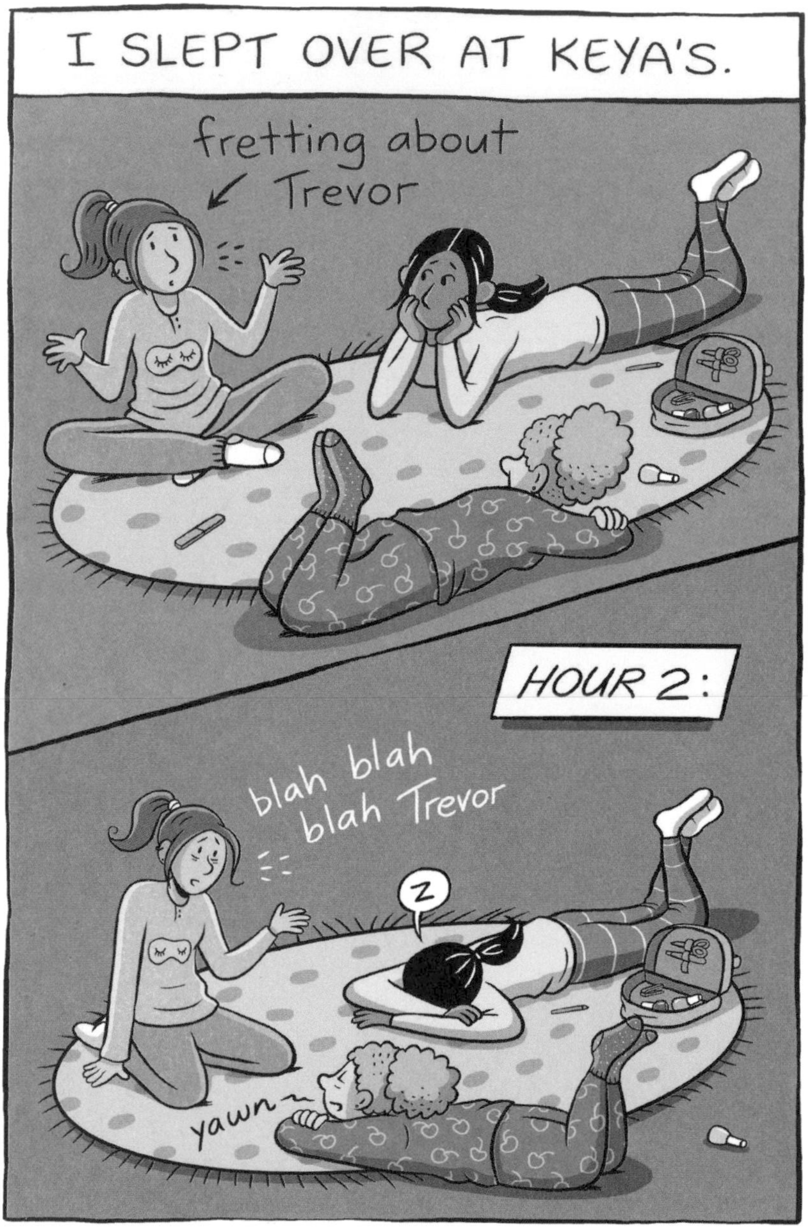
I SLEPT OVER AT KEYA'S.
fretting about Trevor
HOUR 2:
blah blah blah Trevor
Z
yawn~

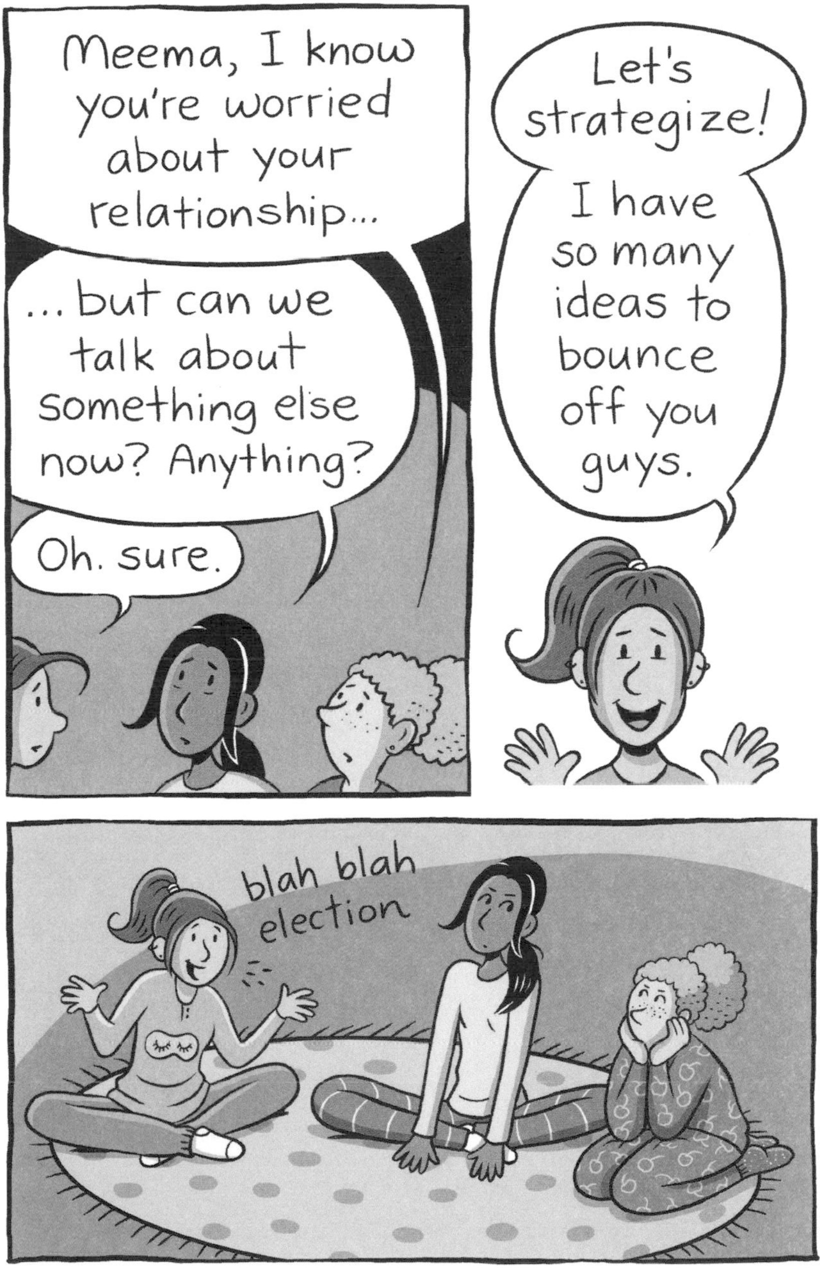
Meema, I know you're worried about your relationship...
... but can we talk about something else now? Anything?
Oh. sure.
Let's strategize!
I have so many ideas to bounce off you guys.
blah blah election

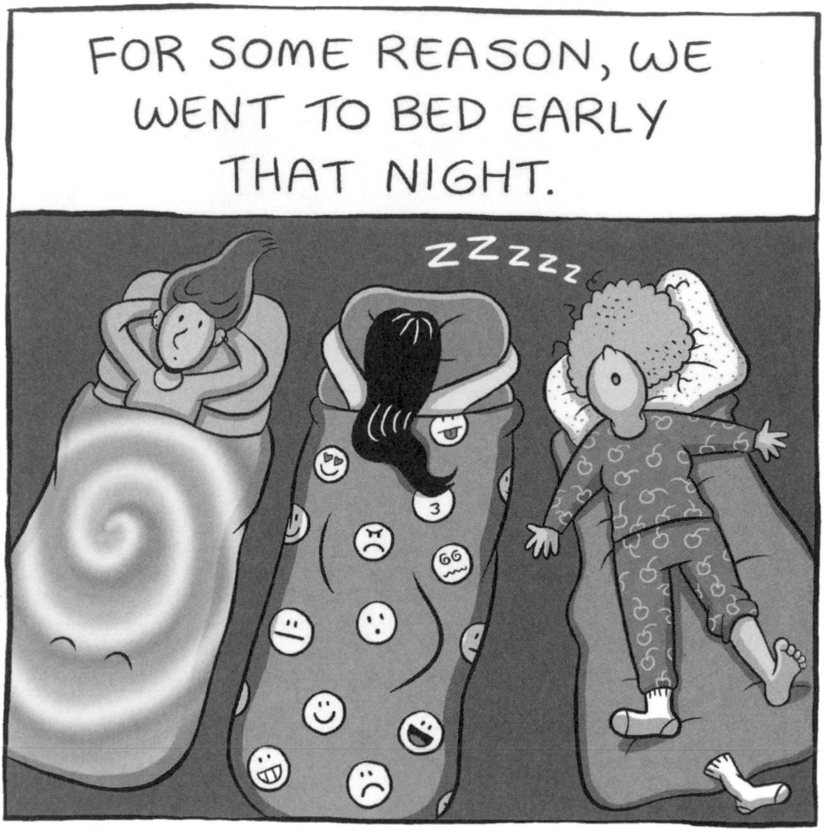
FOR SOME REASON, WE WENT TO BED EARLY THAT NIGHT.
ZZZZZZ

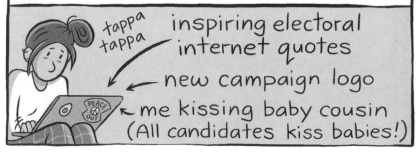

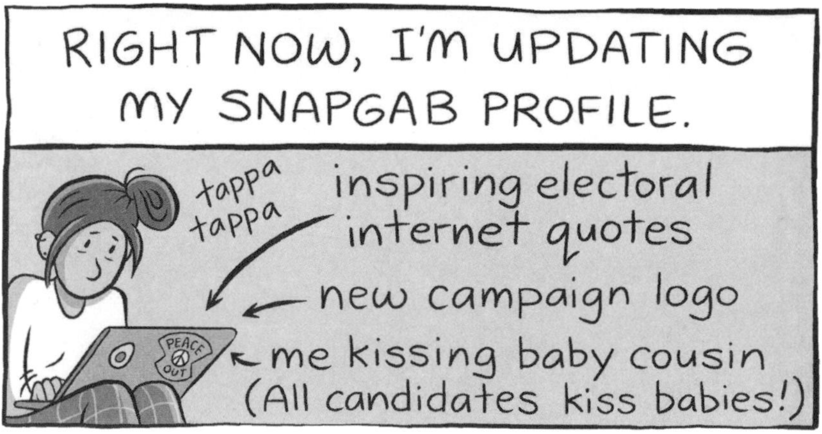
RIGHT NOW, I'M UPDATING MY SNAPGAB PROFILE.
tappa tappa
inspiring electoral internet quotes
new campaign logo
me kissing baby cousin (All candidates kiss babies!)
PEACE OUT

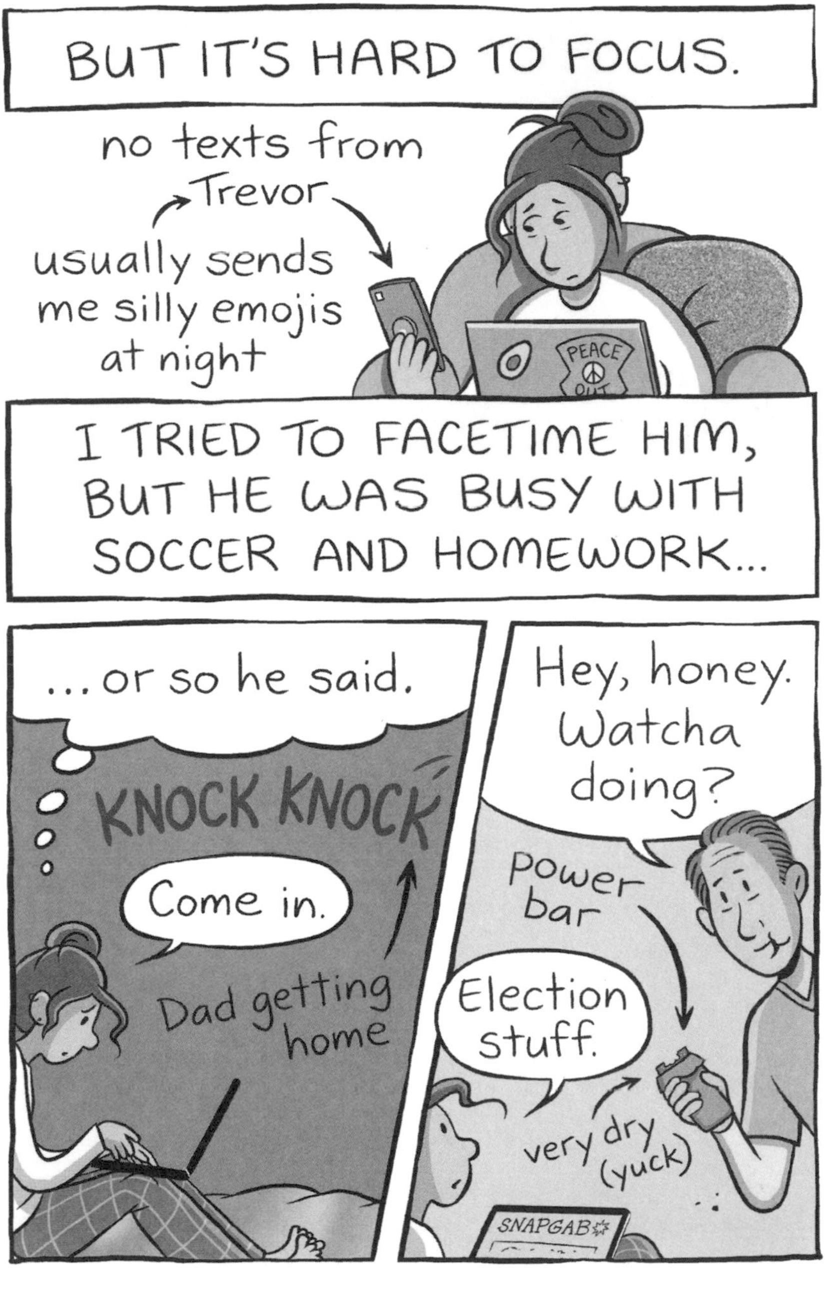
BUT IT'S HARD TO FOCUS.
no texts from Trevor
usually sends me silly emojis at night
PEACE
I TRIED TO FACETIME HIM, BUT HE WAS BUSY WITH SOCCER AND HOMEWORK...
...or so he said.
KNOCK KNOCK
Come in.
Dad getting home
Hey, honey. Watcha doing?
Power bar
Election stuff.
very dry (yuck)
SNAPGAB

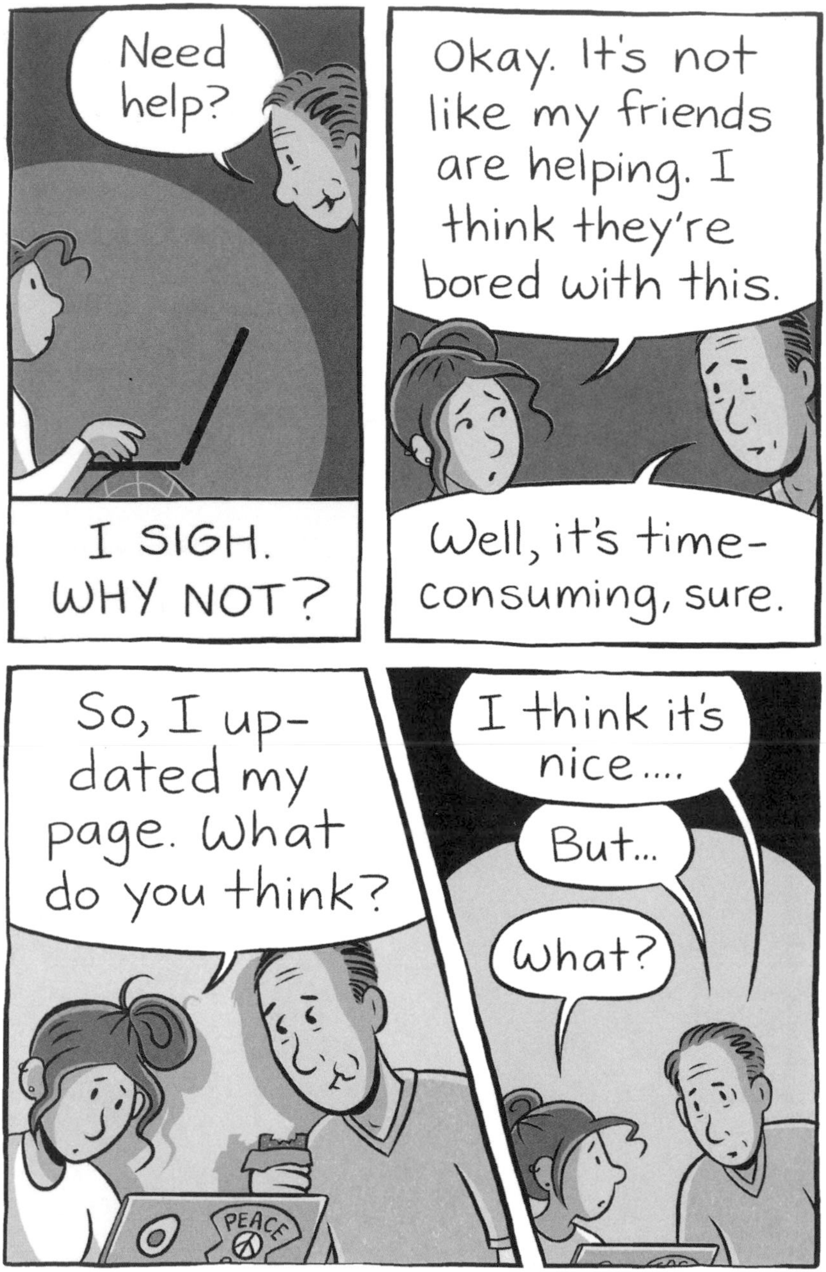
Need help?
I SIGH. WHY NOT?
Okay. It's not like my friends are helping. I think they're bored with this.
Well, it's time-consuming, sure.
So, I updated my page. What do you think?
PEACE
I think it's nice....
But...
What?

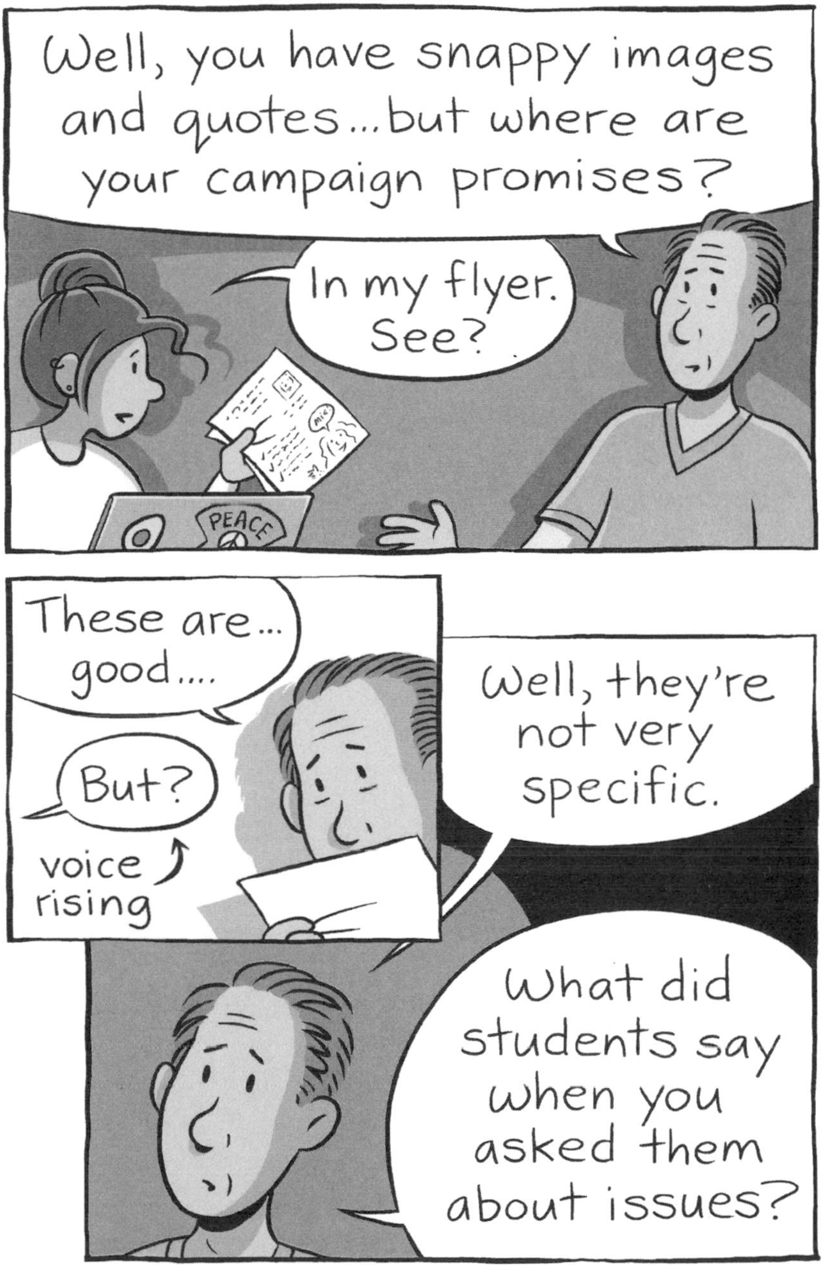
Well, you have snappy images and quotes...but where are your campaign promises?
In my flyer. See?
PEACE
These are... good....
But?
voice rising
Well, they're not very specific.
What did students say when you asked them about issues?

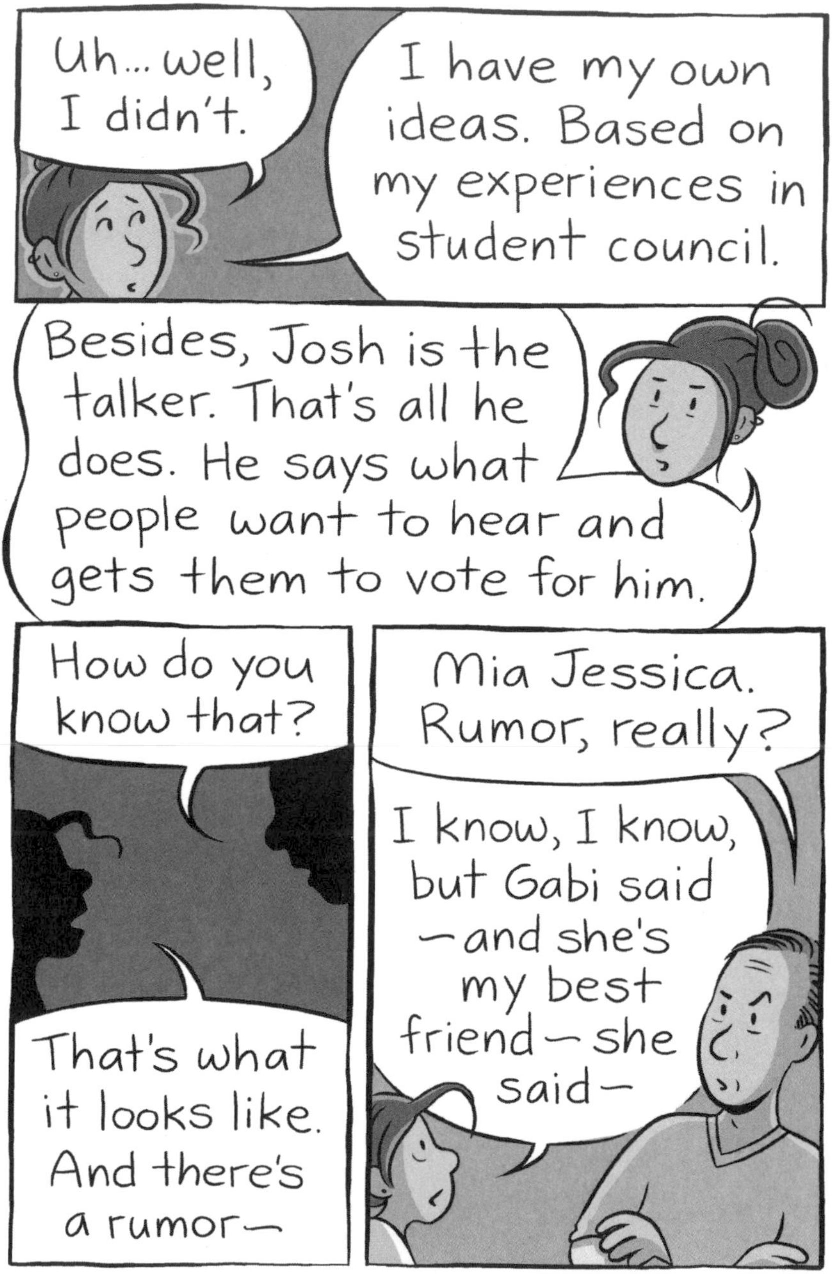
Uh... well, I didn't.
I have my own ideas. Based on my experiences in student council.
Besides, Josh is the talker. That's all he does. He says what people want to hear and gets them to vote for him.
How do you know that?
That's what it looks like. And there's a rumor—
Mia Jessica. Rumor, really?
I know, I know, but Gabi said —and she's my best friend—she said—

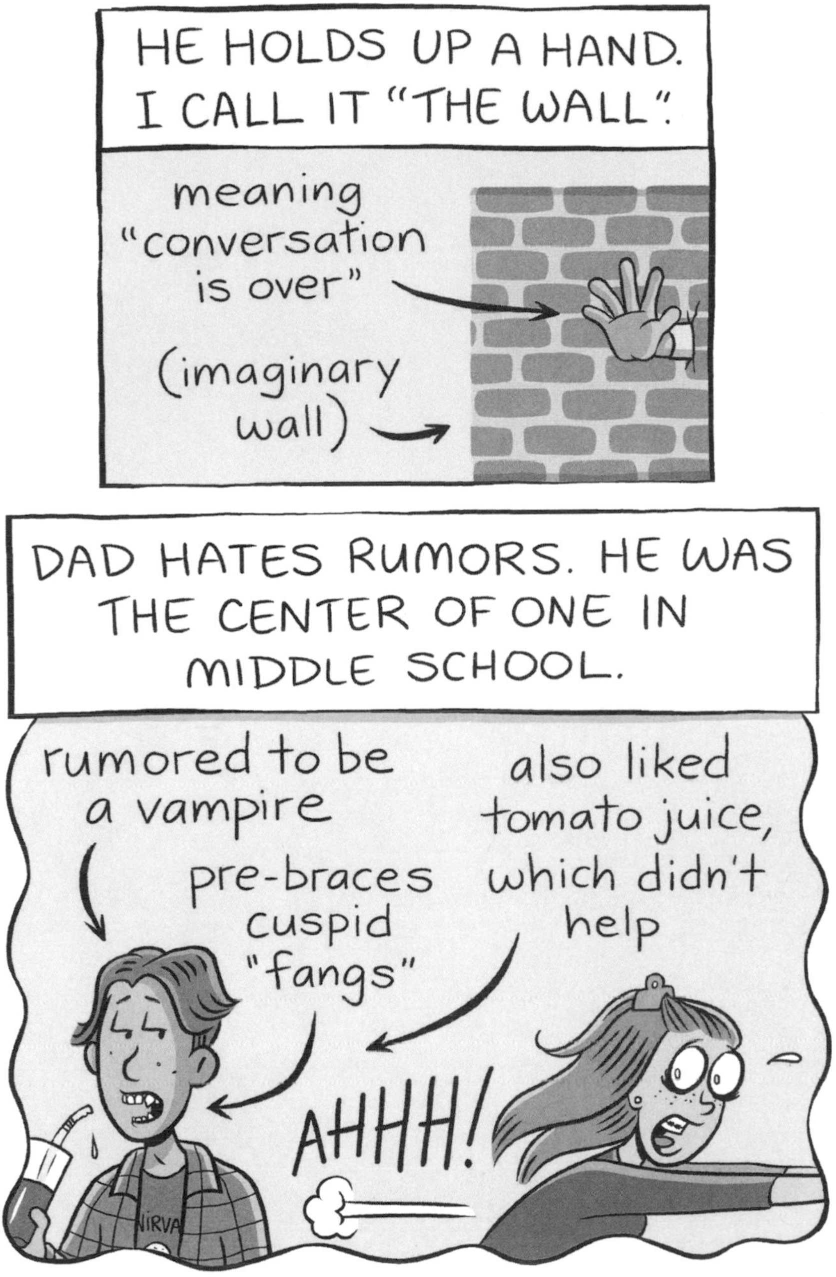
HE HOLDS UP A HAND. I CALL IT "THE WALL".
meaning "conversation is over"
(imaginary wall)
DAD HATES RUMORS. HE WAS THE CENTER OF ONE IN MIDDLE SCHOOL.
rumored to be a vampire
pre-braces cuspid "fangs"
also liked tomato juice, which didn't help
AHHH!
NIRVA

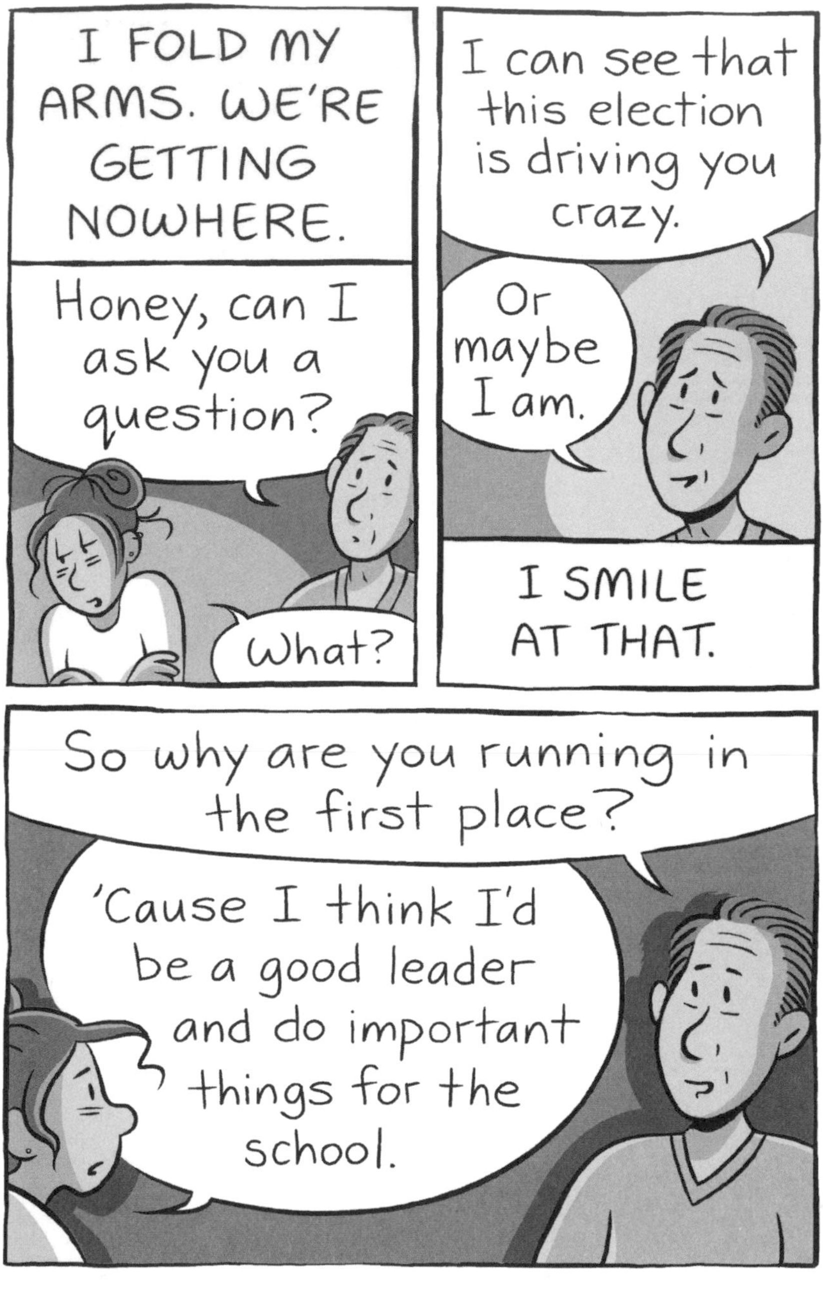
I FOLD MY ARMS. WE'RE GETTING NOWHERE.
Honey, can I ask you a question?
What?
I can see that this election is driving you crazy.
Or maybe I am.
I SMILE AT THAT.
So why are you running in the first place?
'Cause I think I'd be a good leader and do important things for the school.

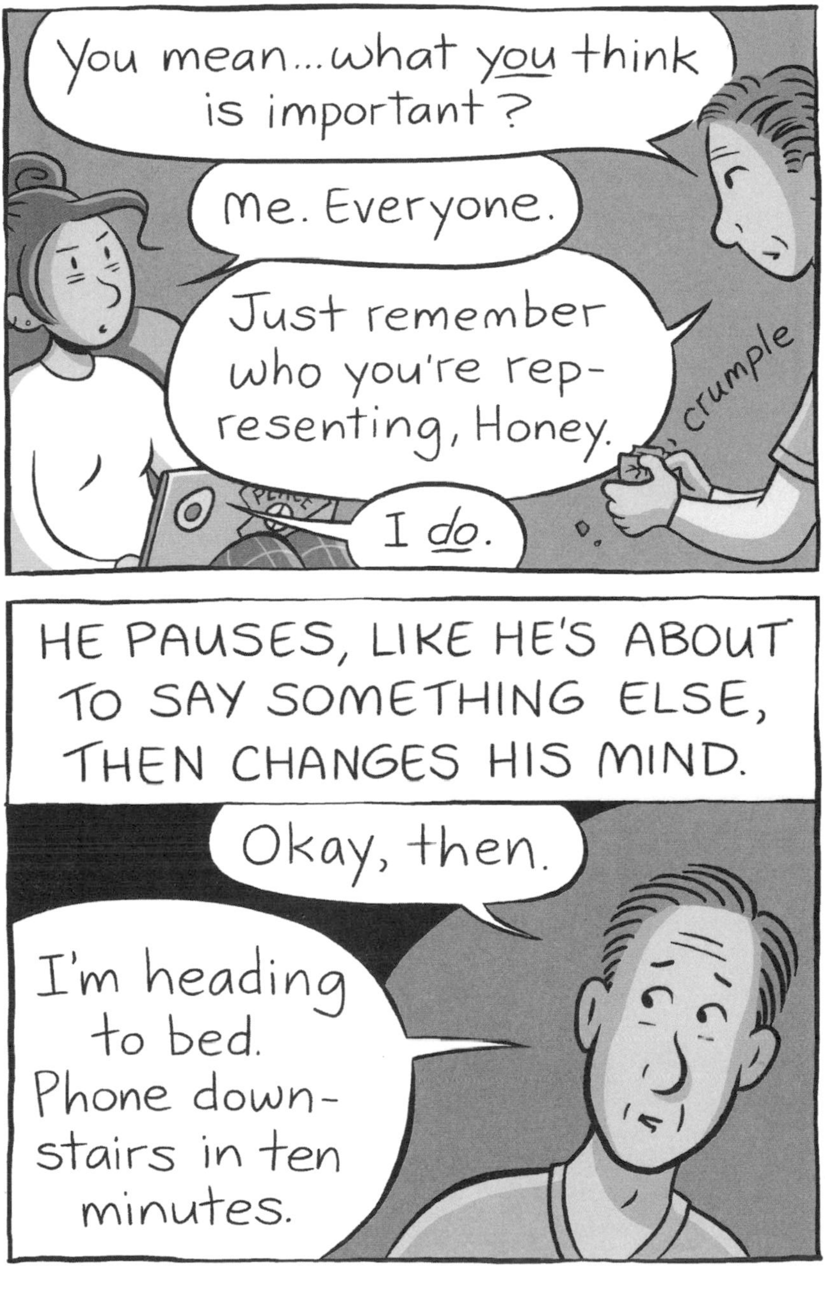
You mean...what you think is important?
Me. Everyone.
Just remember who you're representing, Honey.
crumple
PEACE
I do.
HE PAUSES, LIKE HE'S ABOUT TO SAY SOMETHING ELSE, THEN CHANGES HIS MIND.
Okay, then.
I'm heading to bed. Phone downstairs in ten minutes.

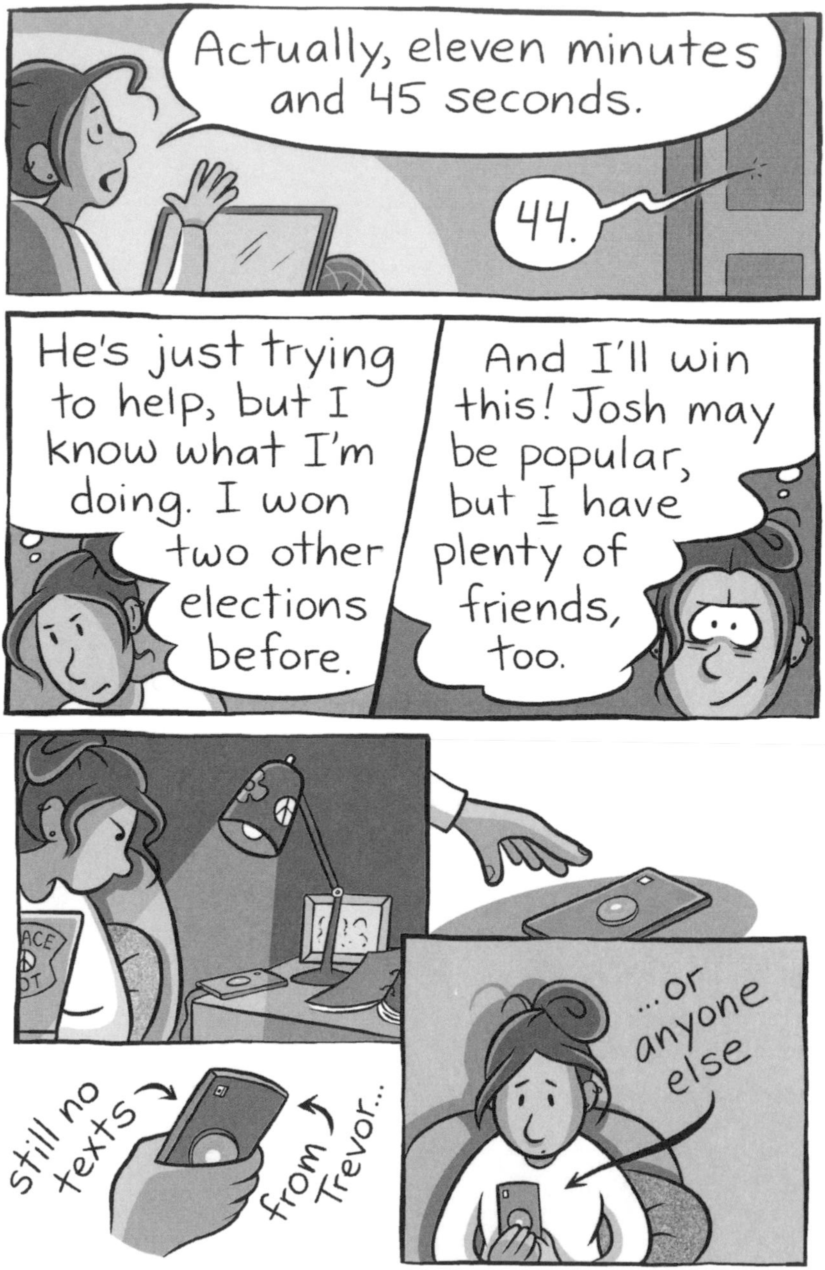
Actually, eleven minutes and 45 seconds.
44.
He's just trying to help, but I know what I'm doing. I won two other elections before.
And I'll win this! Josh may be popular, but I have plenty of friends, too.
still no texts
from Trevor...
...or anyone else

RUBY

We've met three times now.

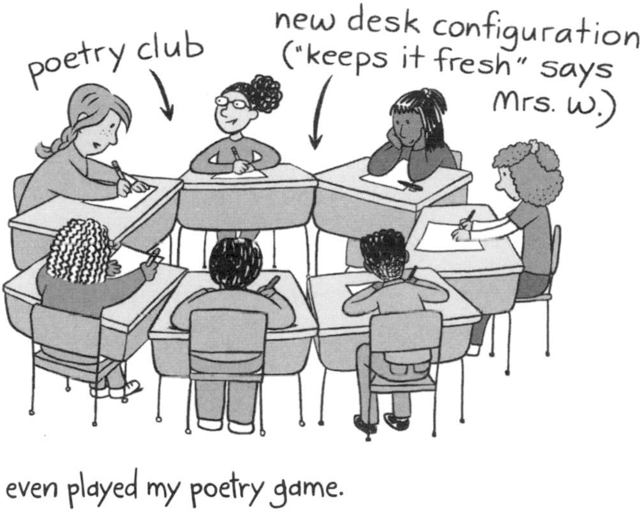
poetry club
new desk configuration ("keeps it fresh" says Mrs. W.)

We even played my poetry game.

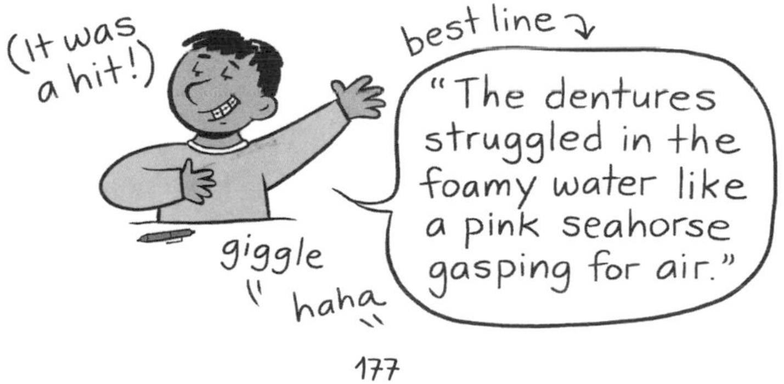
(It was a hit!)
best line
"The dentures struggled in the foamy water like a pink seahorse gasping for air."
giggle
haha

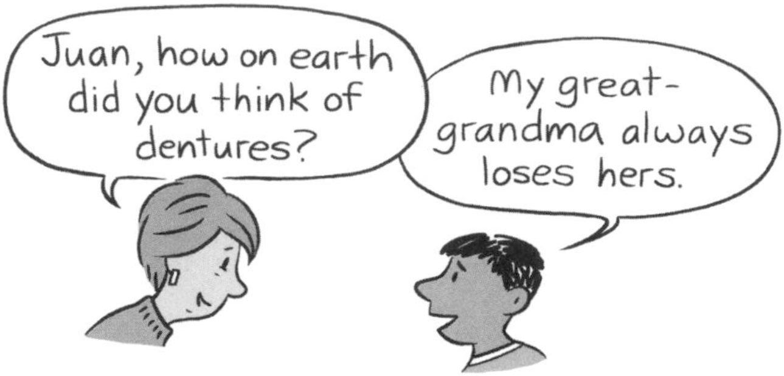
Juan, how on earth did you think of dentures?
My great-grandma always loses hers.

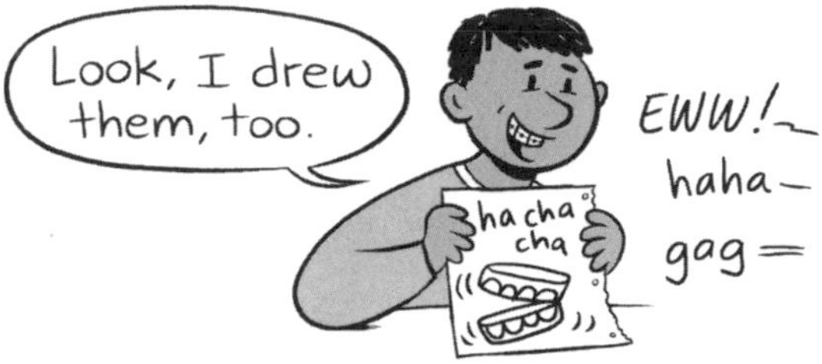
Look, I drew them, too.
ha cha cha
EWW!
haha
gag

Daniel dropped out, but a new boy and girl joined.

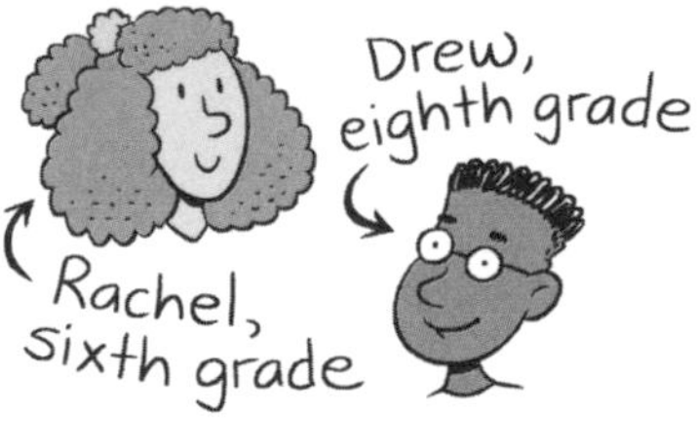
Drew, eighth grade
Rachel, sixth grade

Not everyone shows up each time, but we've had a few regulars: me, Juan, and Leah. Speaking of Leah, I did go to her house last week. And I've gotta admit . . .

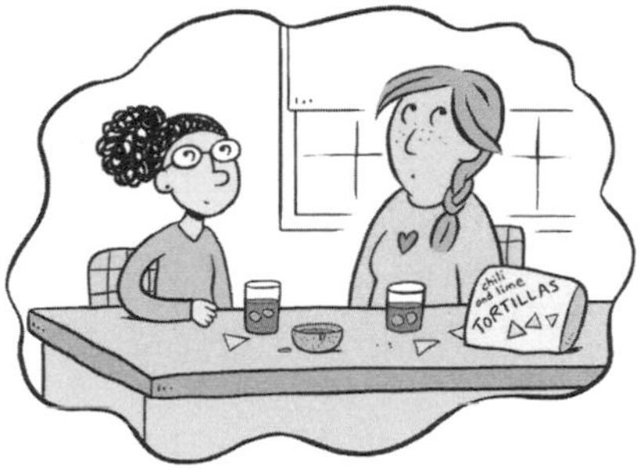
chili and lime TORTILLAS

. . . it was weird.

But once we started talking about school, teachers, and poetry club, it became fun.

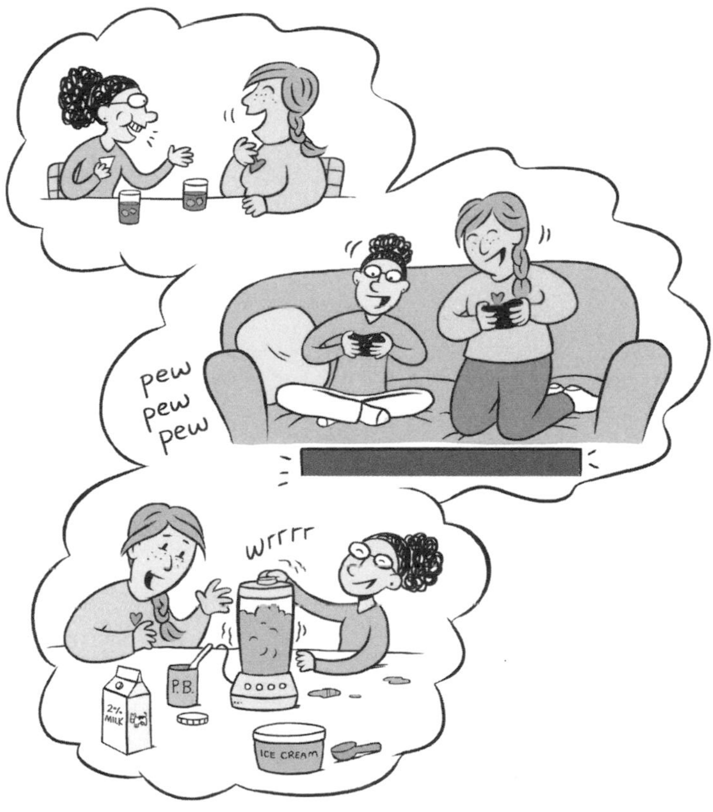
pew
pew
pew
wrrrr
P.B.
2%
MILK
ICE CREAM

We had so much fun, we forgot to do homework. So I was up pretty late that night.

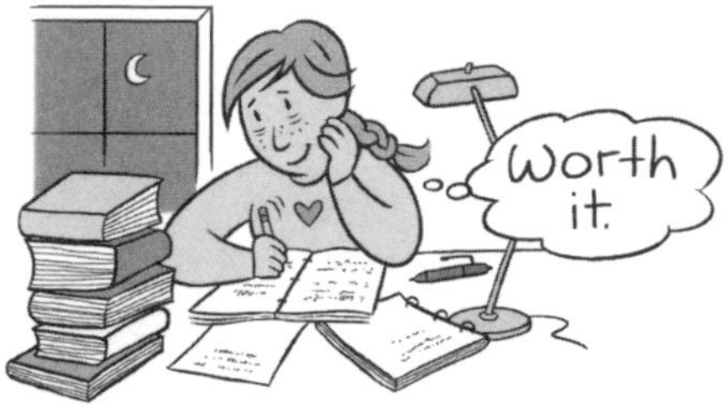
Worth it.

Turns out we have lots in common.

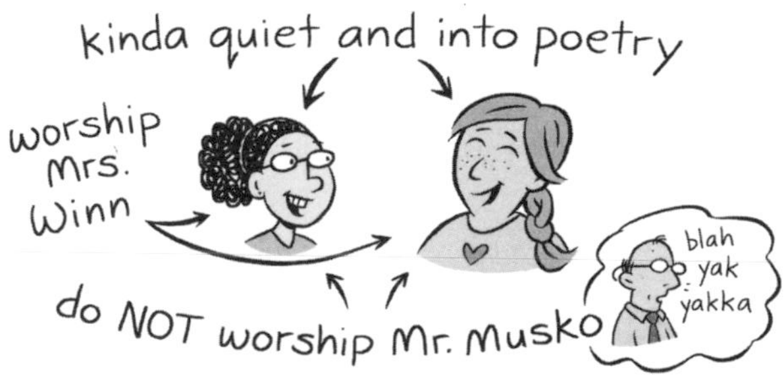
kinda quiet and into poetry
worship Mrs. Winn
do NOT worship Mr. Musko
blah yak yakka

Also, there's stuff she does that I didn't even know I liked until I tried it with her. Like kitchen experiments.

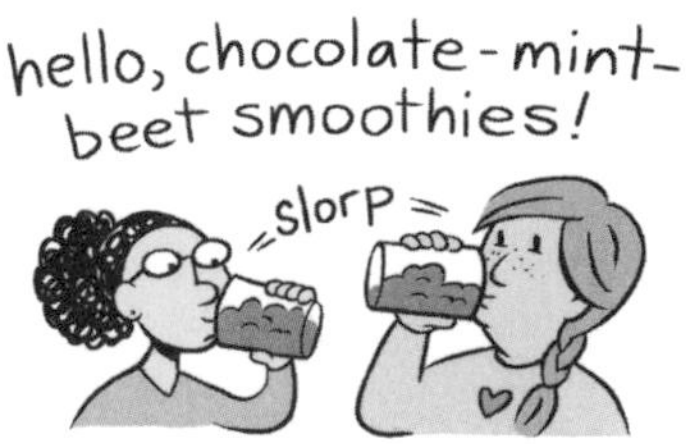
hello, chocolate-mint-beet smoothies!
slorp

She has lots of collections, too. So many, I couldn't help looking at all of them.

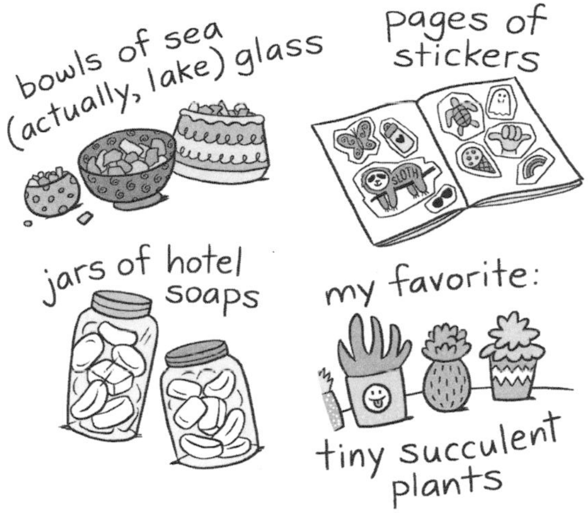
bowls of sea
(actually, lake) glass
pages of
stickers
SLOTH
jars of hotel
soaps
my favorite:
tiny succulent
plants

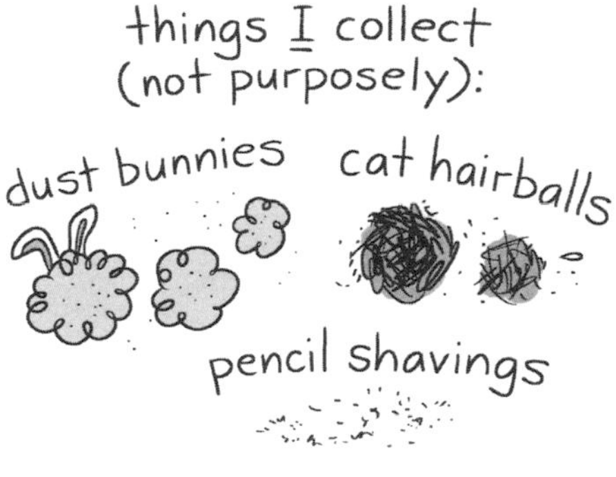
things I collect
(not purposely):
dust bunnies
cat hairballs
pencil shavings

We've been hanging out at school ever since. It's so cool to have a new friend. The best part is she doesn't care about my bad social skills (probably 'cause of her shyness). Anyway, around her, that issue has sort of . . . disappeared.

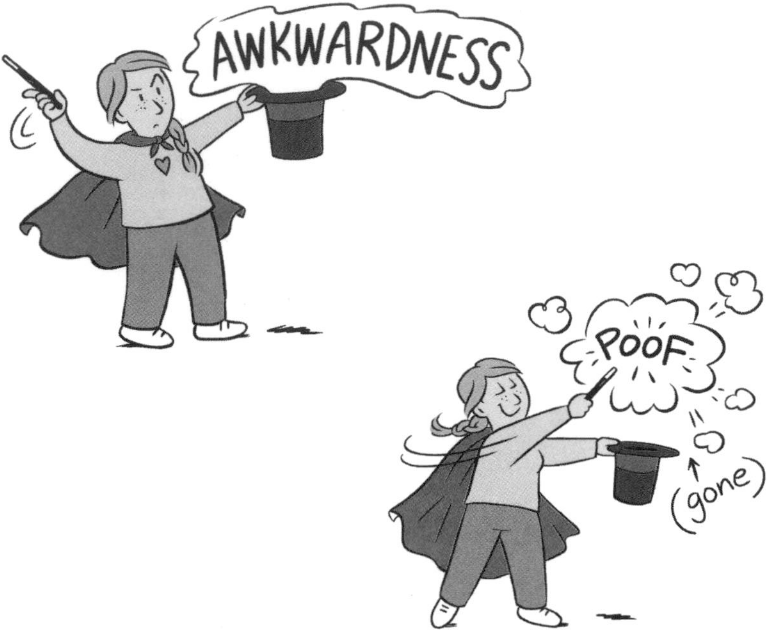
AWKWARDNESS
POOF
(gone)

Leah told me she and her sixth-grade friends drifted apart—just like Mia and me.

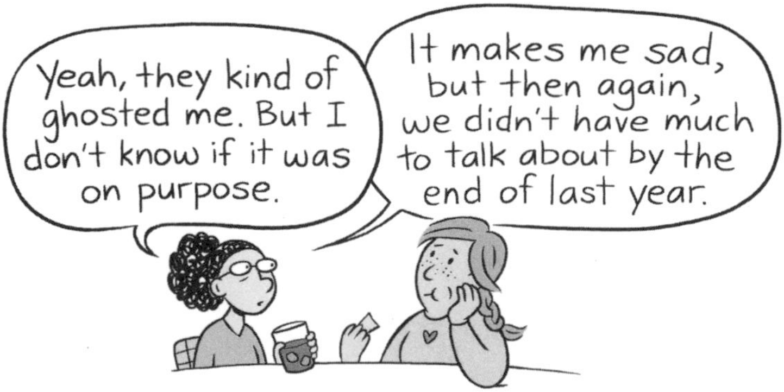
Yeah, they kind of ghosted me. But I don't know if it was on purpose.
It makes me sad, but then again, we didn't have much to talk about by the end of last year.

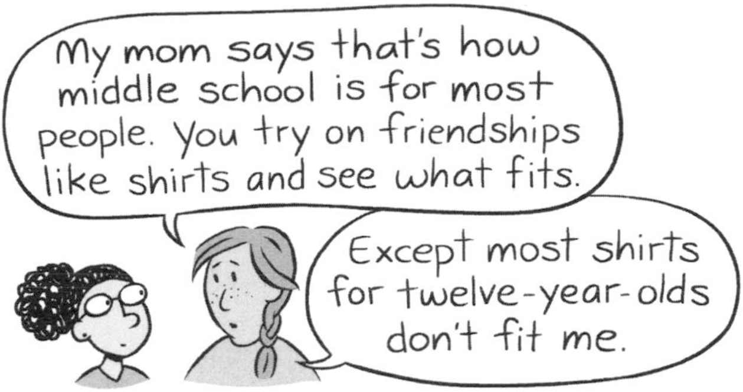
My mom says that's how middle school is for most people. You try on friendships like shirts and see what fits.
Except most shirts for twelve-year-olds don't fit me.

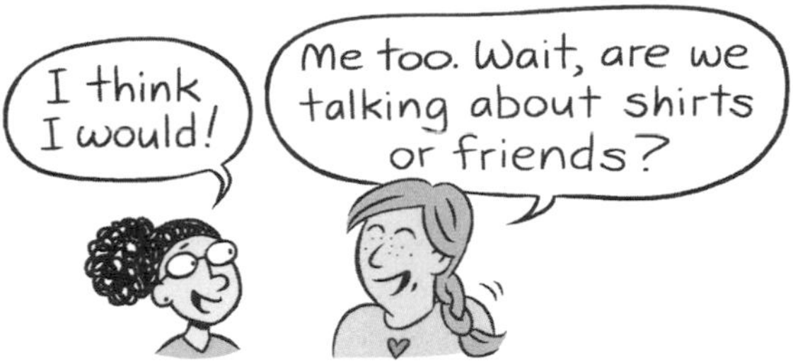
I think I would!
Me too. Wait, are we talking about shirts or friends?

We both laugh.

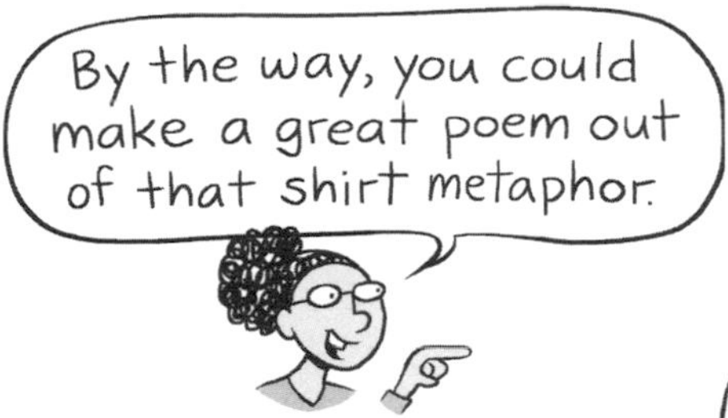
By the way, you could make a great poem out of that shirt metaphor.

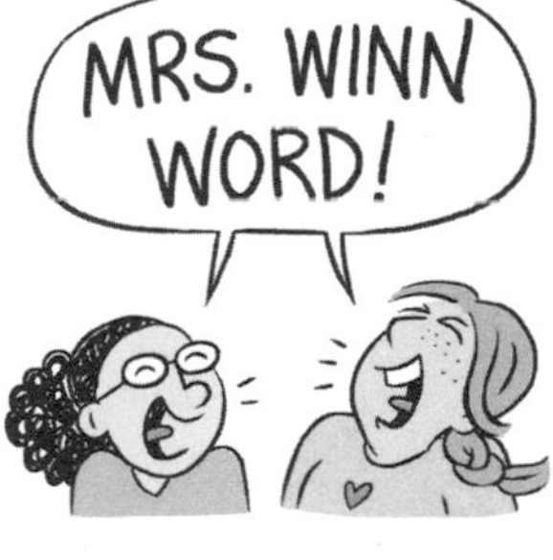
MRS. WINN WORD!

Today, I've worked up the nerve to tell her about my stomach problems. Except for Mia, she's the only other kid I've ever shared that with.

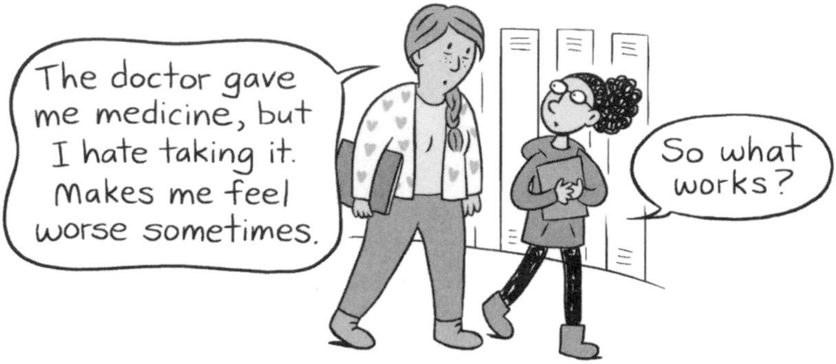
The doctor gave me medicine, but I hate taking it. Makes me feel worse sometimes.
So what works?

I think for a minute.

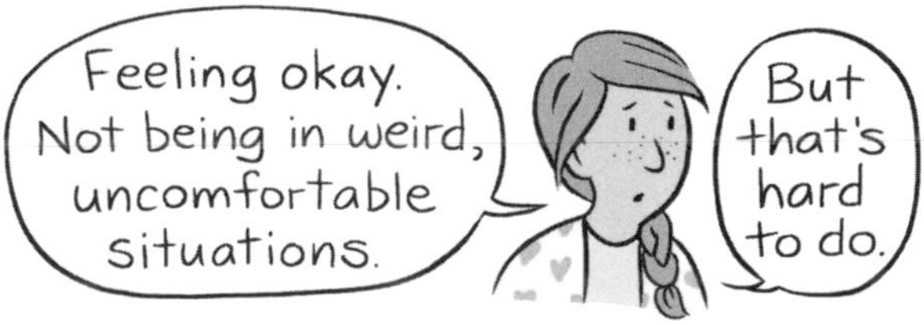
Feeling okay. Not being in weird, uncomfortable situations.
But that's hard to do.

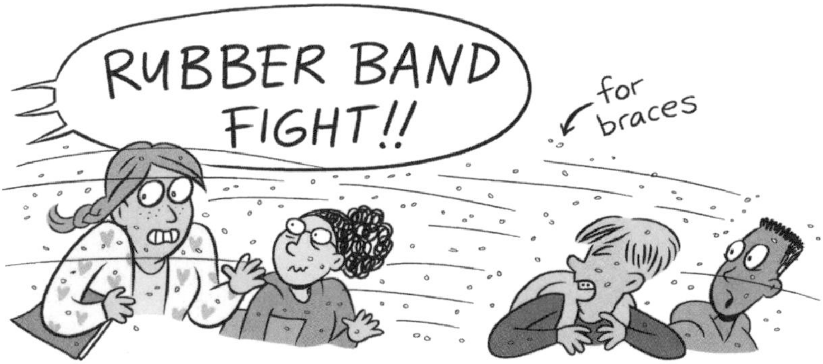
RUBBER BAND FIGHT!!
for braces

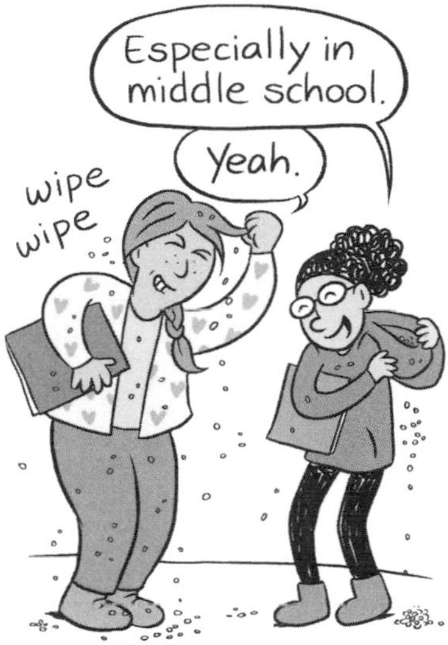
Especially in middle school.
Yeah.
wipe wipe

We separate at the stairwell to go to our classes. As I wave bye, I see Mia at her locker down the hall.

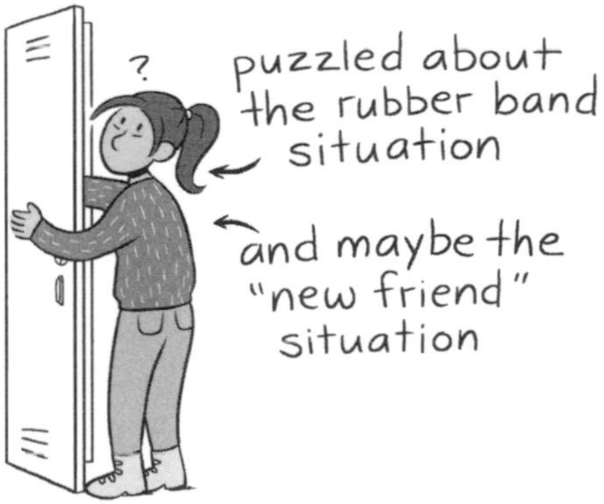
?
puzzled about the rubber band situation
and maybe the "new friend" situation

Yeah, it's cool to have a new friend. And I can't help feeling kinda smug in front of someone who thinks I'm a loser.

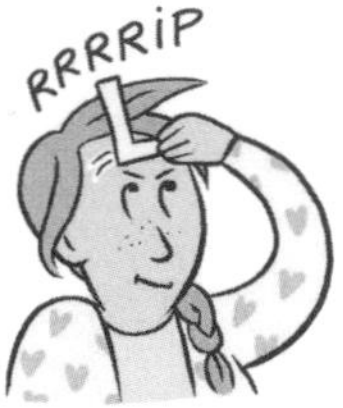
RRRRIP

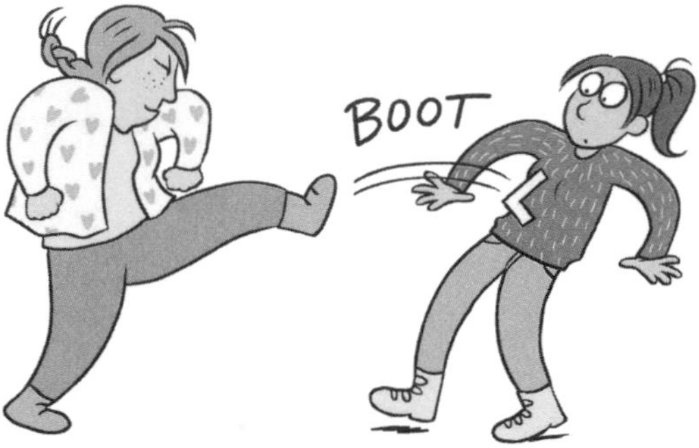
BOOT

But . . . I'm still a little sad.

'Cause even though Leah and I are getting tight doesn't mean I don't miss Mia. We used to laugh about stuff, too. We had a lot of inside jokes. We'd fight and make up. We just . . . got each other. And the weirdest thing about all that is . . .

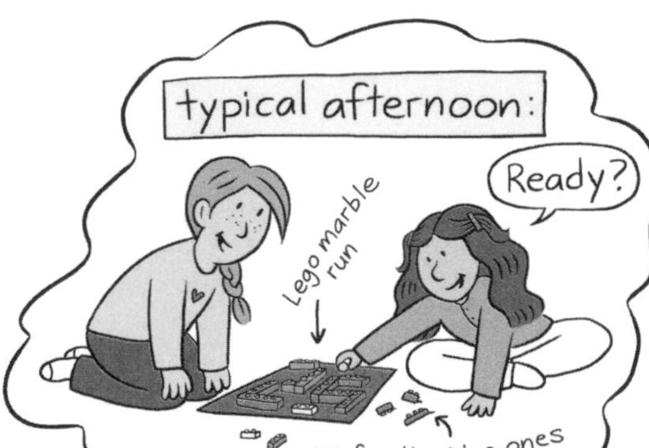
typical afternoon:
Ready?
Lego marble run
prefer the blue ones

. . . it wasn't that long ago.

Mia

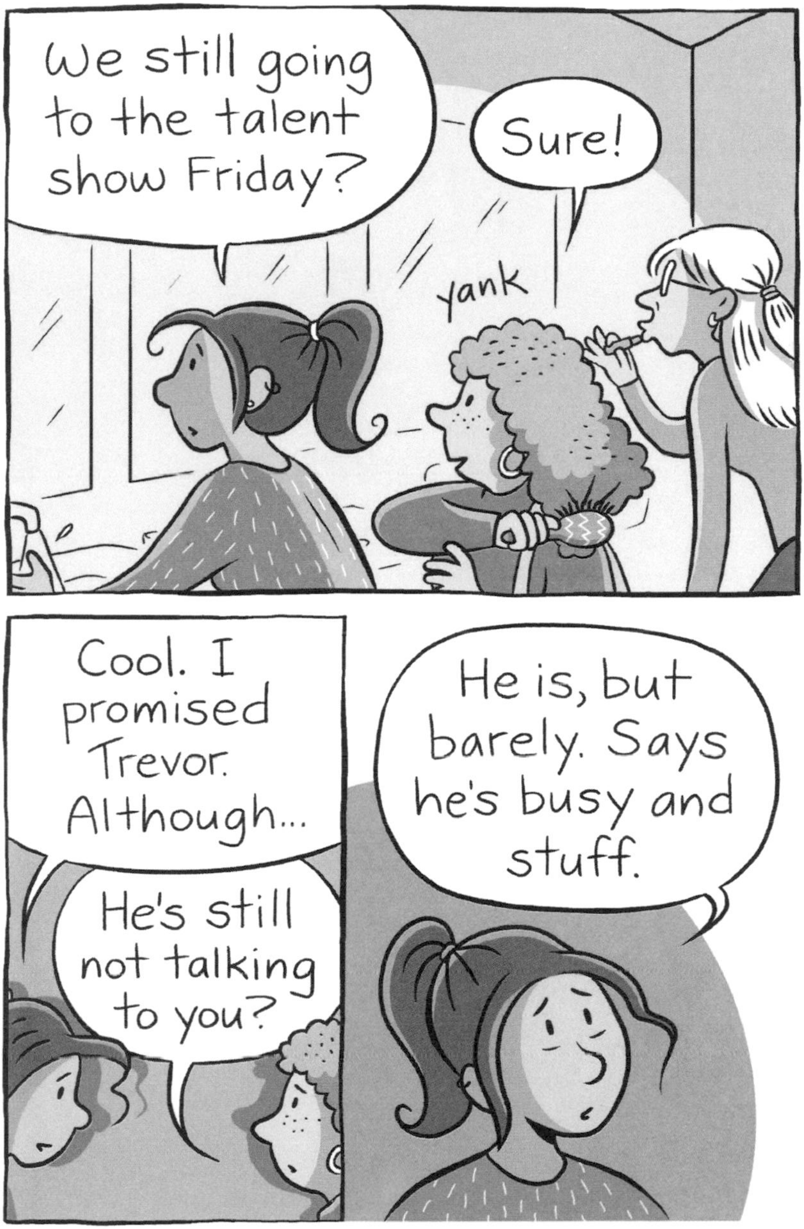
We still going to the talent show Friday?
Sure!
yank
Cool. I promised Trevor. Although...
He's still not talking to you?
He is, but barely. Says he's busy and stuff.

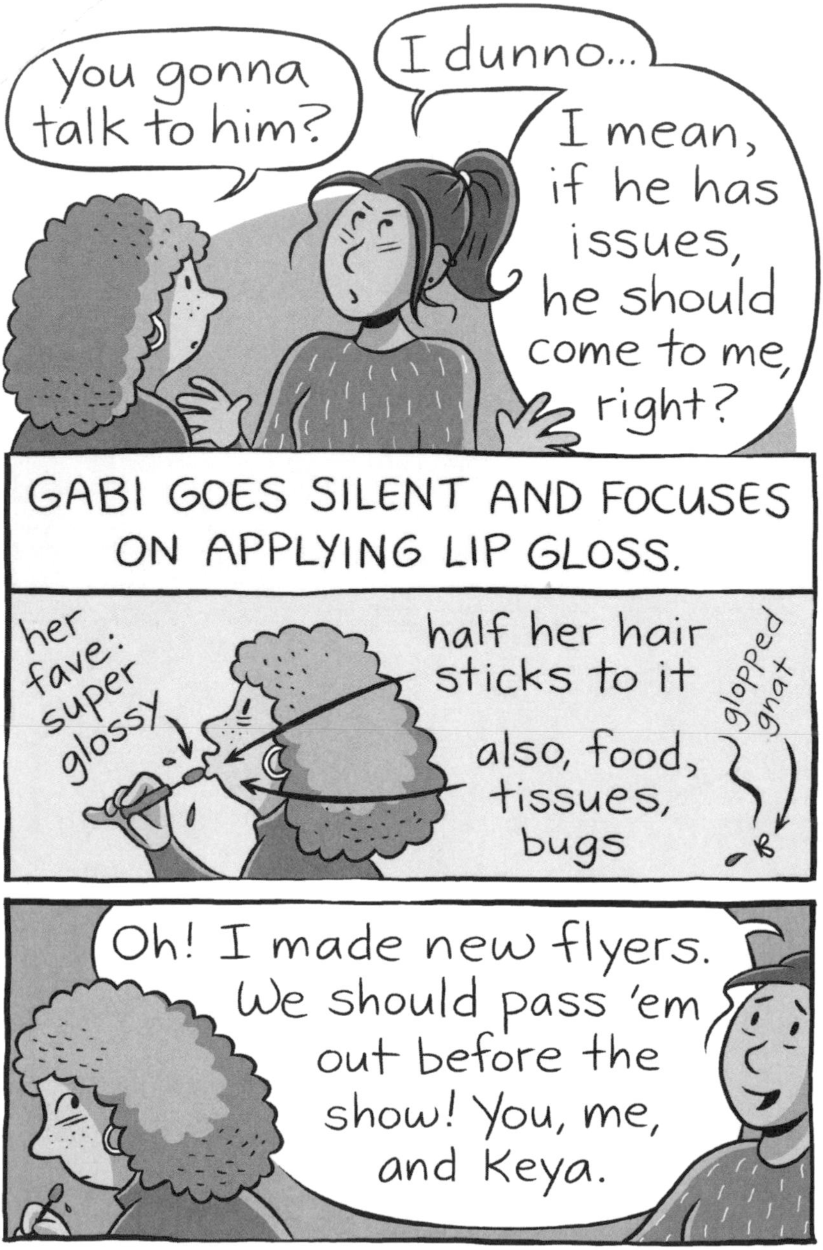
You gonna talk to him?
I dunno...
I mean, if he has issues, he should come to me, right?
GABI GOES SILENT AND FOCUSES ON APPLYING LIP GLOSS.
her fave: super glossy
half her hair sticks to it
also, food, tissues, bugs
glopped gnat
Oh! I made new flyers. We should pass 'em out before the show! You, me, and Keya.

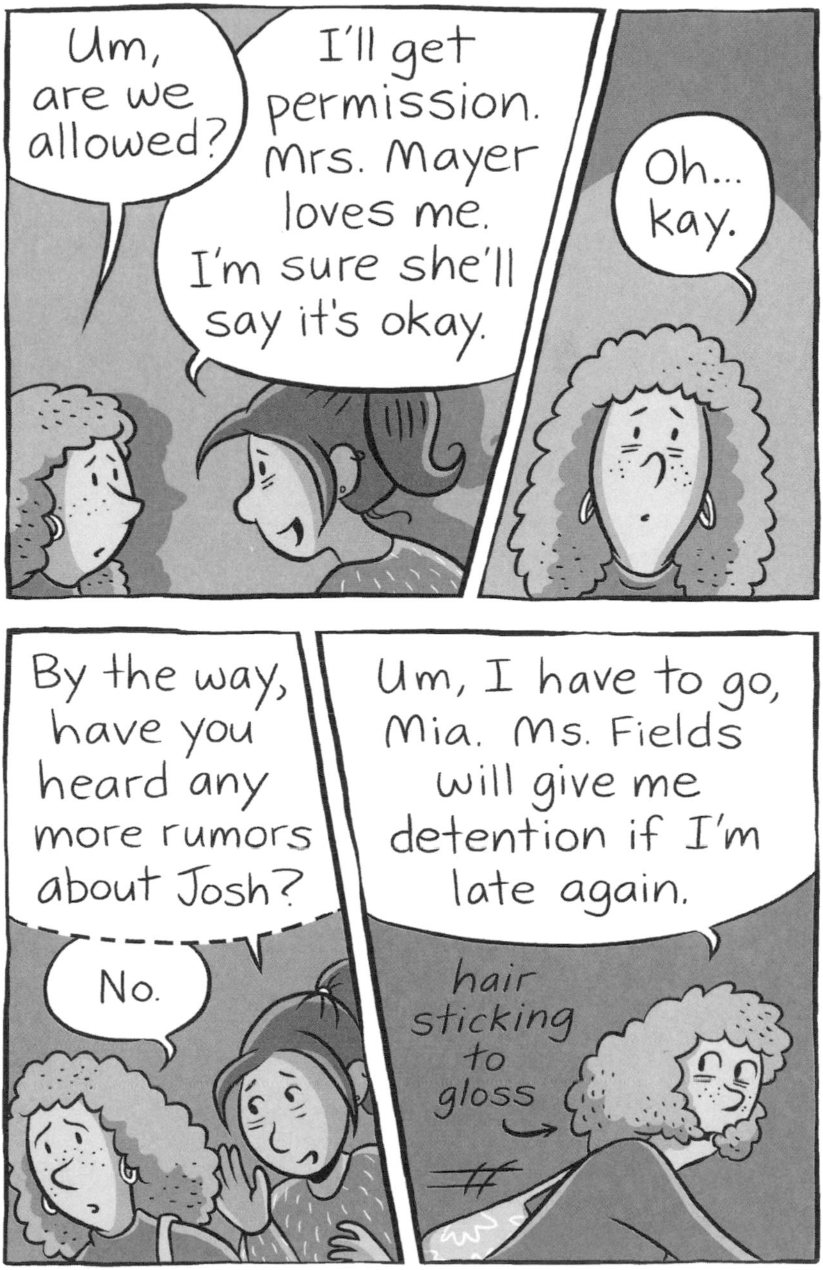
Um, are we allowed?
I'll get permission. Mrs. Mayer loves me. I'm sure she'll say it's okay.
Oh... kay.
By the way, have you heard any more rumors about Josh?
No.
Um, I have to go, Mia. Ms. Fields will give me detention if I'm late again.
hair sticking to gloss

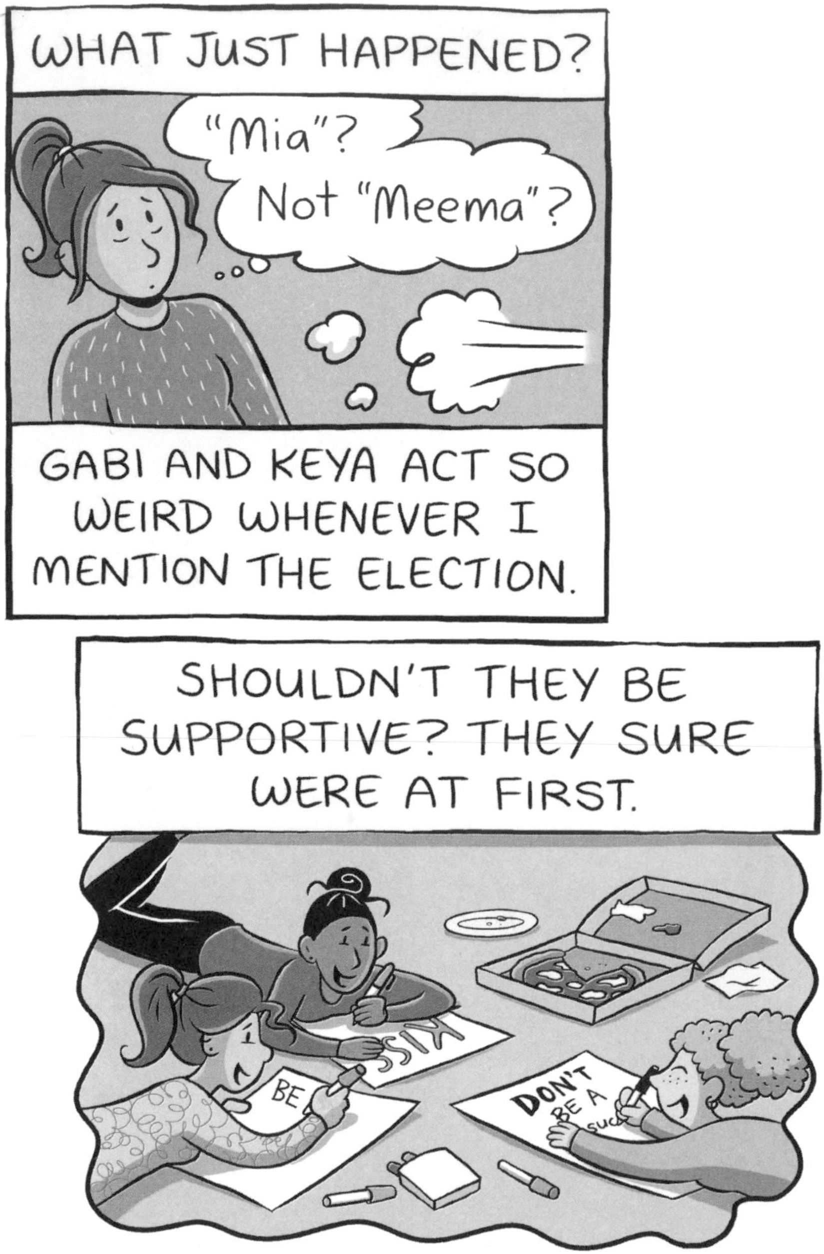
WHAT JUST HAPPENED?
"Mia"? Not "Meema"?
GABI AND KEYA ACT SO WEIRD WHENEVER I MENTION THE ELECTION.
SHOULDN'T THEY BE SUPPORTIVE? THEY SURE WERE AT FIRST.
BE
DON'T BE A

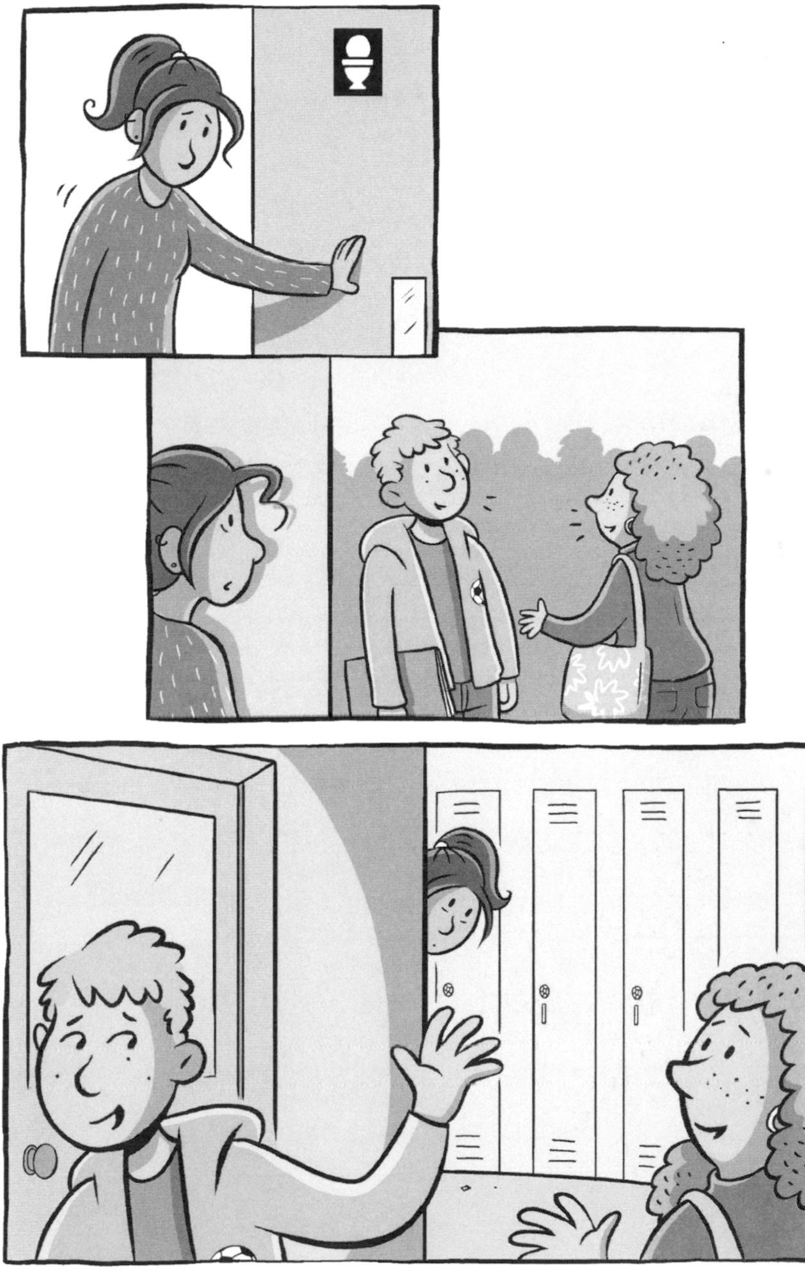

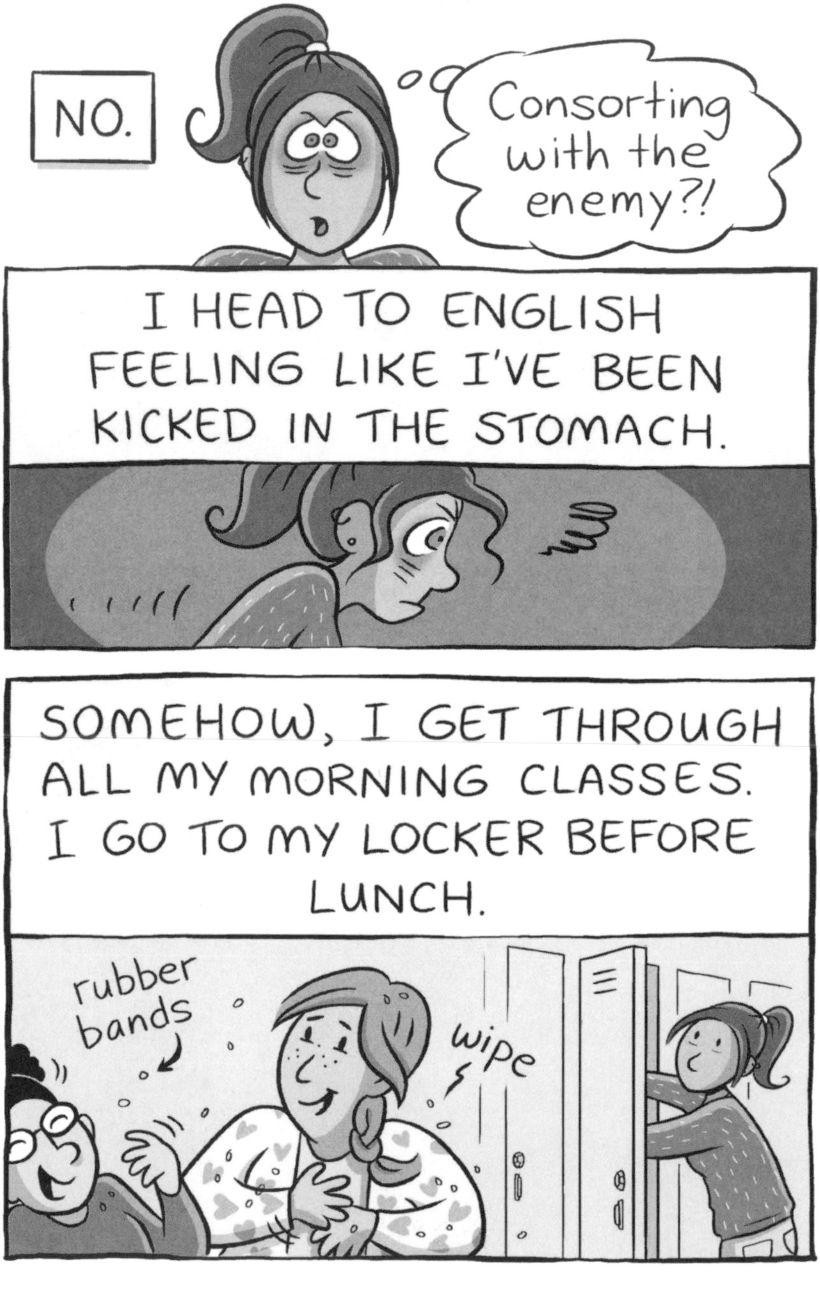
NO.
Consorting with the enemy?!
I HEAD TO ENGLISH FEELING LIKE I'VE BEEN KICKED IN THE STOMACH.
SOMEHOW, I GET THROUGH ALL MY MORNING CLASSES. I GO TO MY LOCKER BEFORE LUNCH.
rubber bands
wipe

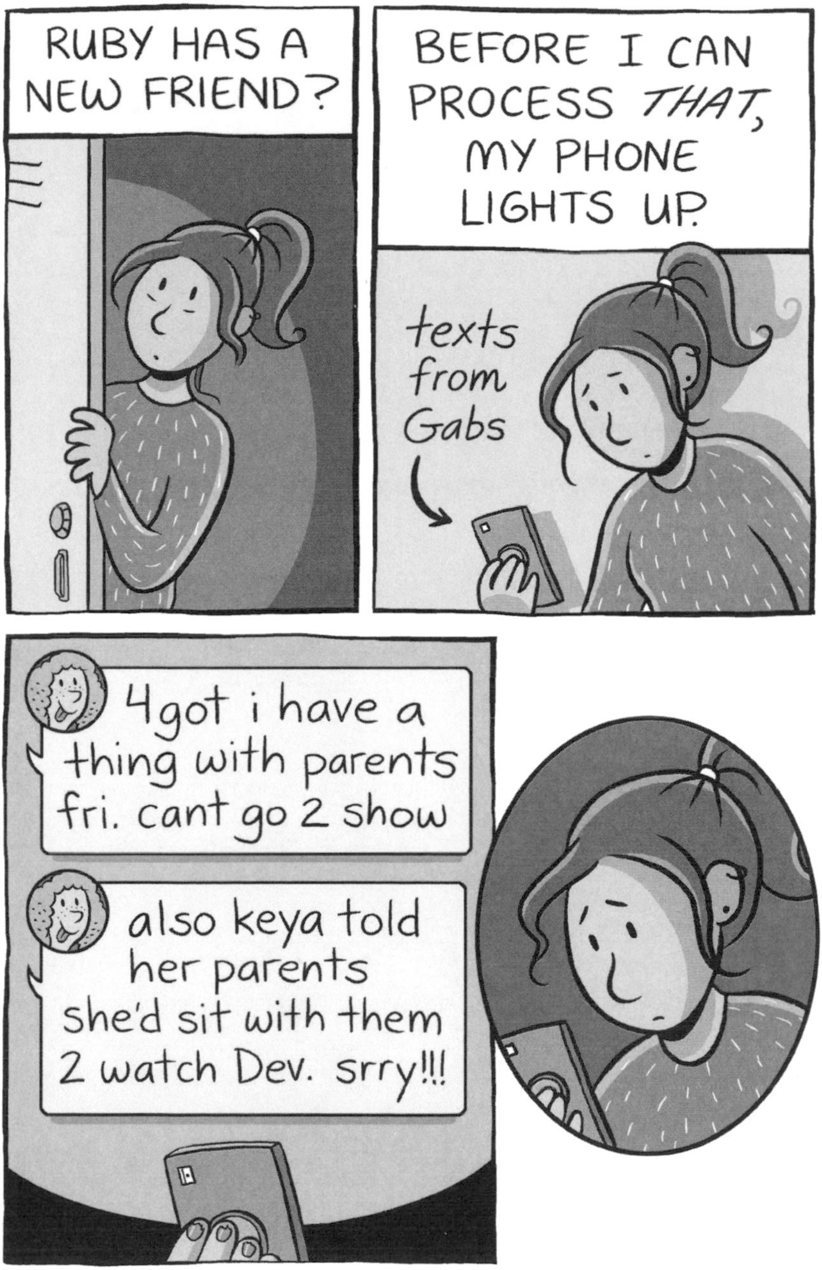
RUBY HAS A NEW FRIEND?
BEFORE I CAN PROCESS *THAT*, MY PHONE LIGHTS UP.
texts from Gabs
4got i have a thing with parents fri. cant go 2 show
also keya told her parents she'd sit with them 2 watch Dev. srry!!!

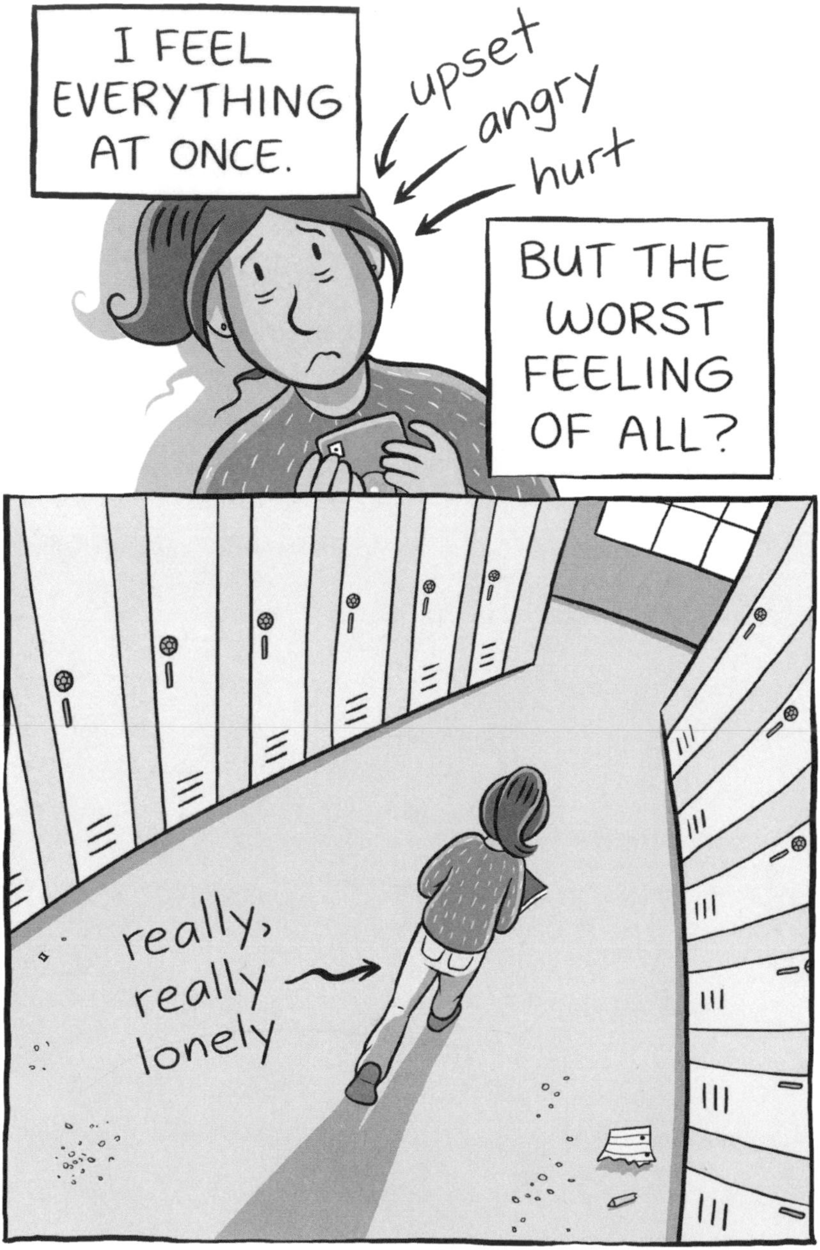
I FEEL EVERYTHING AT ONCE.
upset
angry
hurt
BUT THE WORST FEELING OF ALL?
really, really lonely

RUBY

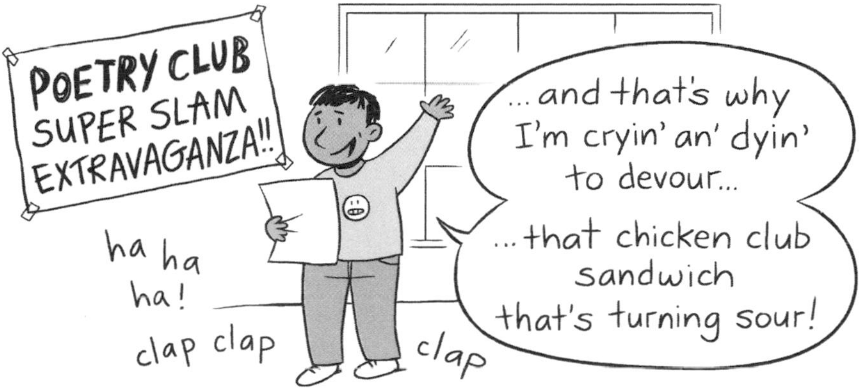
POETRY CLUB SUPER SLAM EXTRAVAGANZA!!
...and that's why I'm cryin' an' dyin' to devour...
...that chicken club sandwich that's turning sour!
ha ha ha!
clap clap
clap

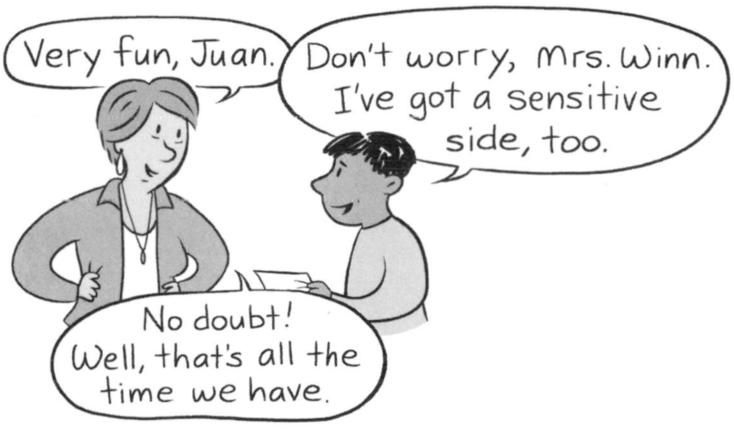
Very fun, Juan.
Don't worry, Mrs. Winn. I've got a sensitive side, too.
No doubt! Well, that's all the time we have.

Before we go, I'd like to remind you about the talent show coming up.

Poetry can be included!

In fact, I highly encourage it. What you did here today is a great example.

Everyone starts murmuring as we get up to leave.

I might do it. I love performing.

Uh. No kidding.

Not me. I'd die up there.

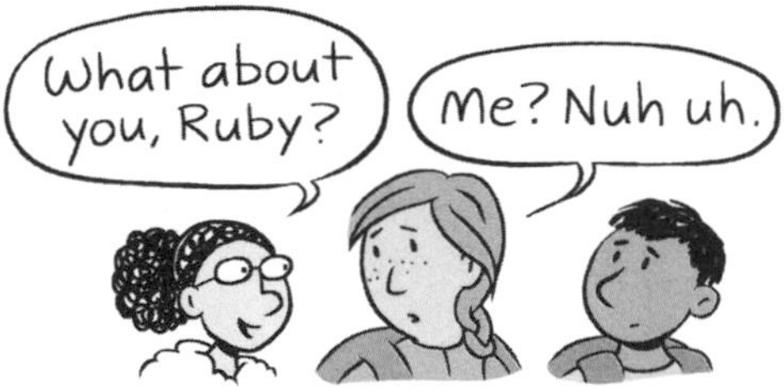
What about you, Ruby?
Me? Nuh uh.

It's one thing to stand up in front of people you're pretty comfortable with, like at poetry club. I mean, that's where I feel most like myself now.

But it's another thing to get up in front of the whole school and be . . .

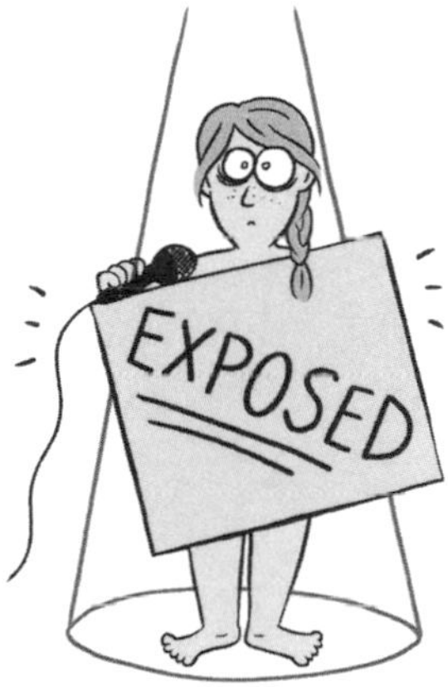
EXPOSED

Still . . .

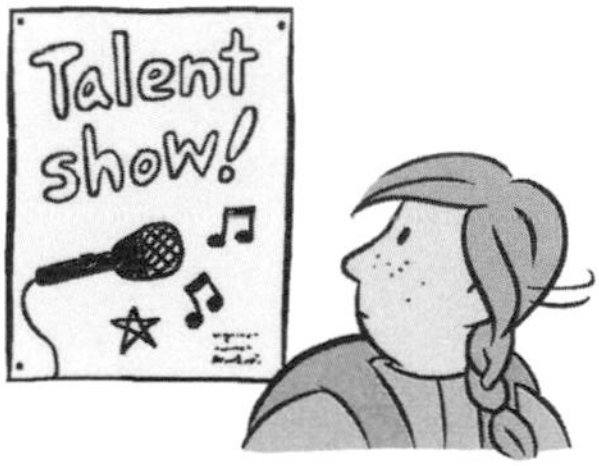
Talent show!

Nah.

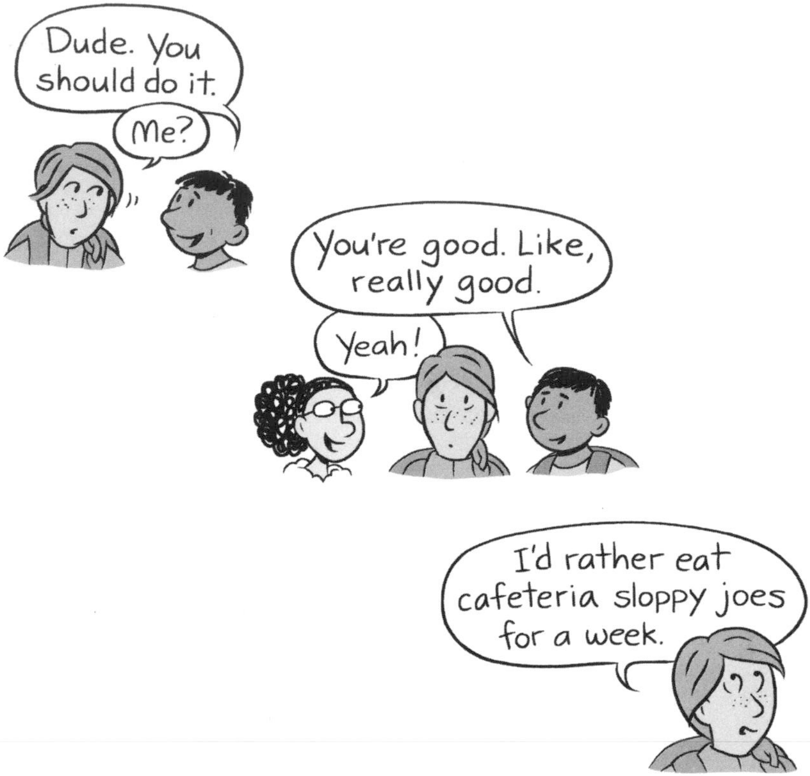
Dude. You should do it.
Me?
You're good. Like, really good.
Yeah!
I'd rather eat cafeteria sloppy joes for a week.

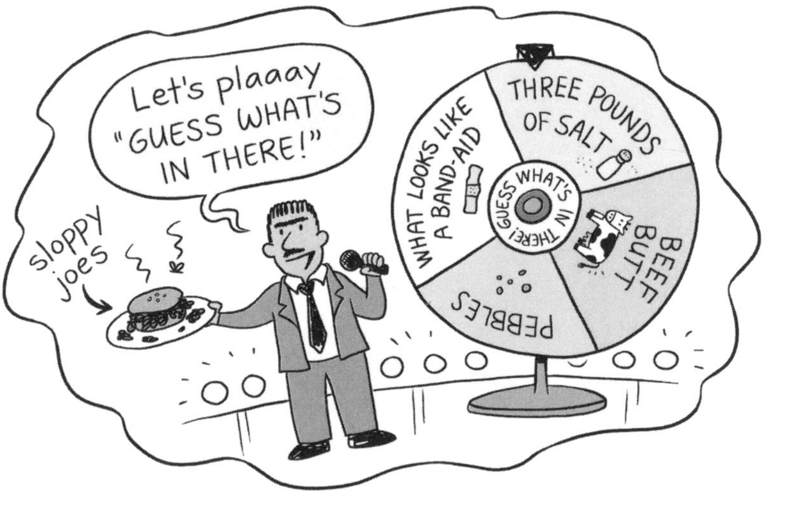
Let's plaaay "GUESS WHAT'S IN THERE!"
sloppy joes
THREE POUNDS OF SALT
BEEF BUTT
PEBBLES
WHAT LOOKS LIKE A BAND-AID
GUESS WHAT'S IN THERE!

But when I get home, I think about it (the talent show, not sloppy joes).

I don't think anyone's read a poem before.

Ruby♥

So it'd be cool to try it.

I glance at the journal on my nightstand. It's not really a journal—more like a thick notebook that I got discounted and decorated with heart stickers. It's filled with two years of entries, stories, and poetry.

falling apart

keep out

Hi!

RUBY

stickers peeling off

"well loved," as our librarian, Ms. Regas, calls beat-up books

clawed by Buford

I grab it. Maybe there's something in here . . . ?

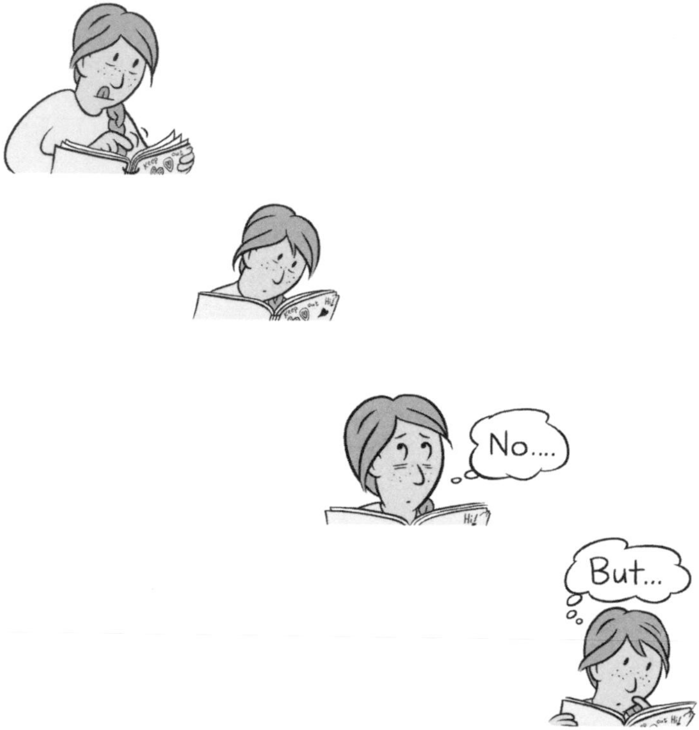
No....
But...

I'm the kind of person who, when I decide to do something, just does it. Mom says that runs in the family. That's good for some things, like homework and chores and stuff. But bad for other things . . .

. . . like deciding to recite a poem for the talent show.

But when I see it, I realize I have to. Well, not have to, but want to. Which is pretty much the same thing.

Because it's a poem that might help things.

Things that are broken.

Okay, it's a last-ditch effort, but why not? I'll just change the poem a little. So no one knows who it's about except me . . .

scritcha
scritcha

. . . and her.

Mia

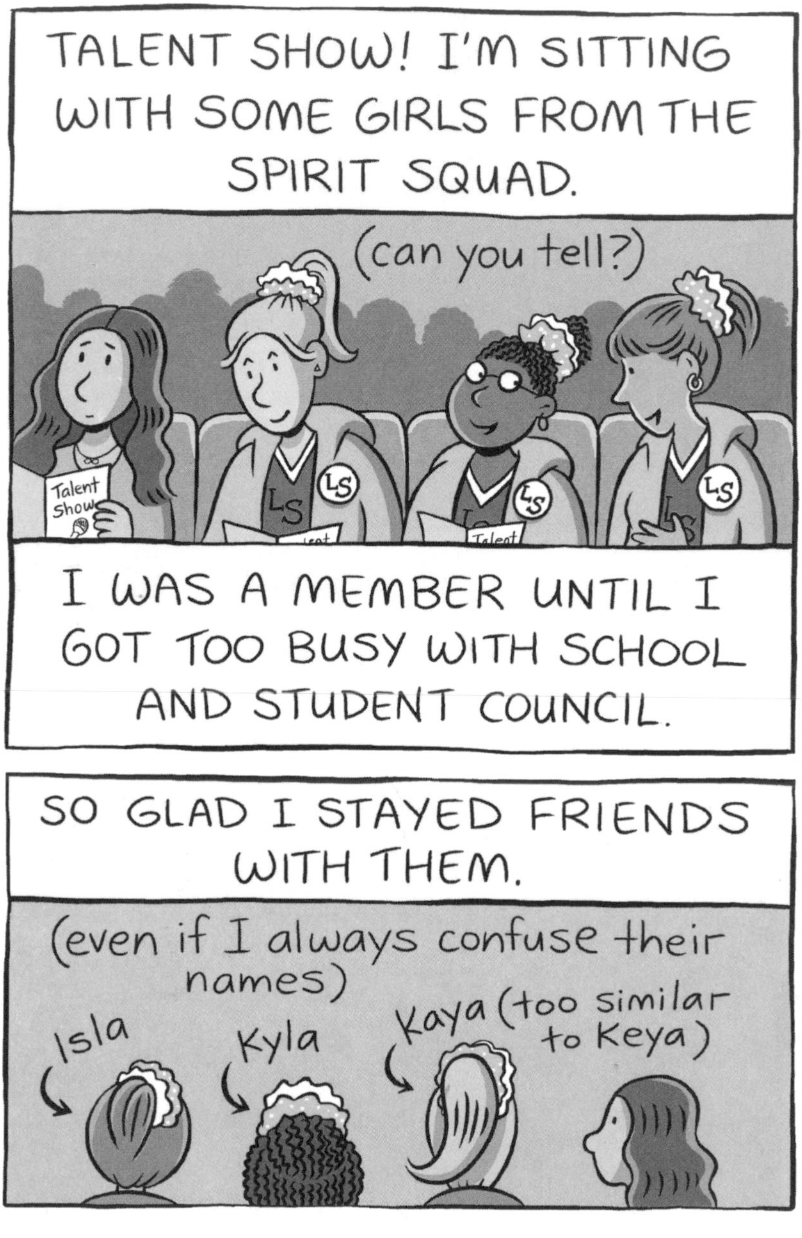
TALENT SHOW! I'M SITTING WITH SOME GIRLS FROM THE SPIRIT SQUAD.
(can you tell?)
Talent Show
LS
I WAS A MEMBER UNTIL I GOT TOO BUSY WITH SCHOOL AND STUDENT COUNCIL.
SO GLAD I STAYED FRIENDS WITH THEM.
(even if I always confuse their names)
Isla
Kyla
Kaya (too similar to Keya)

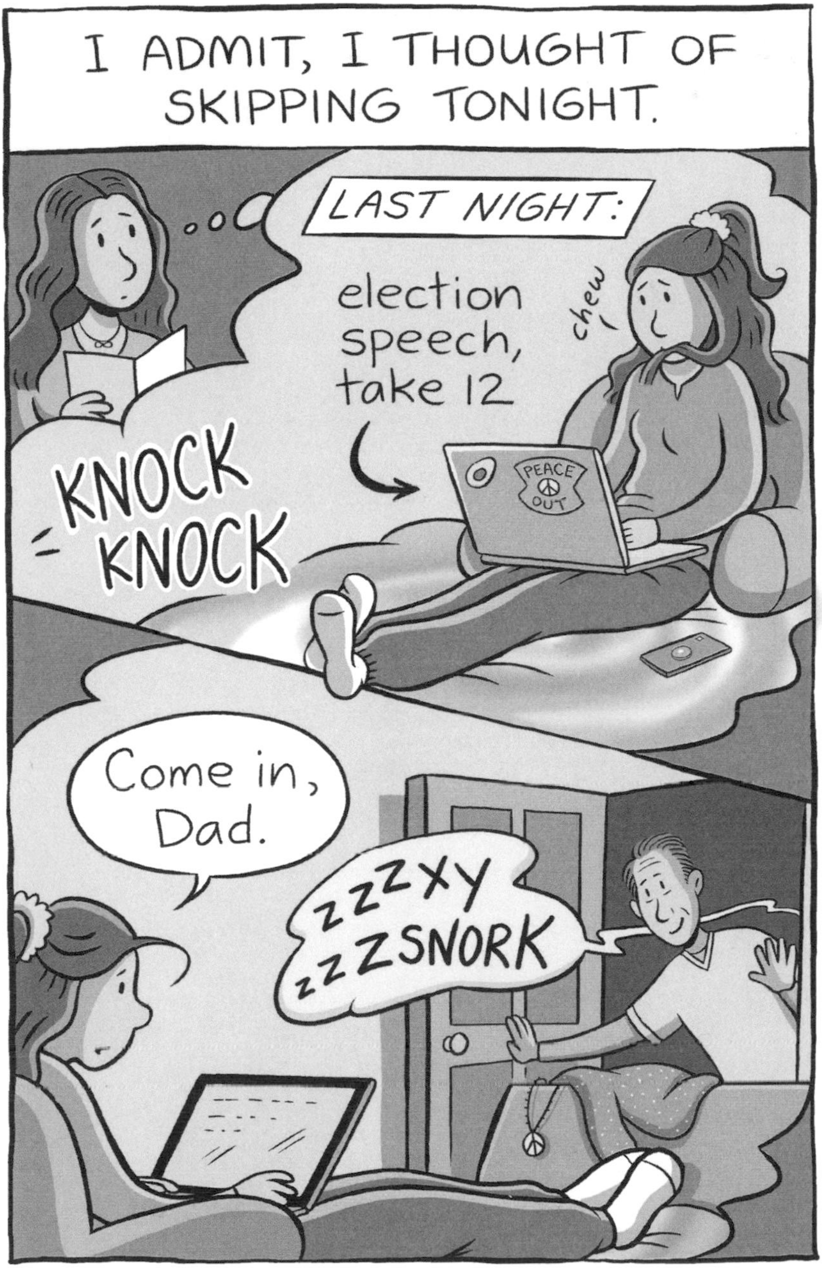
I ADMIT, I THOUGHT OF SKIPPING TONIGHT.
LAST NIGHT:
election speech, take 12
chew
PEACE OUT
KNOCK KNOCK
Come in, Dad.
zzzzxy zzzSNORK

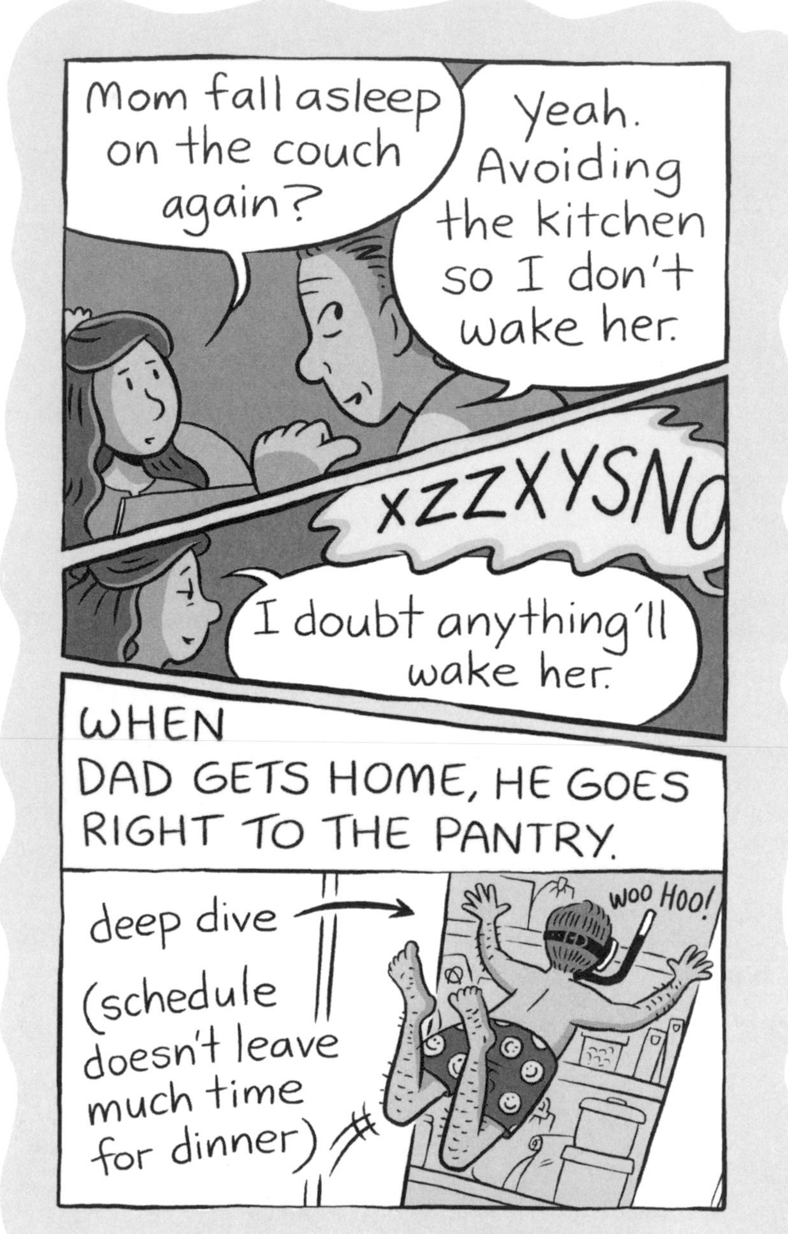
Mom fall asleep on the couch again?
Yeah. Avoiding the kitchen so I don't wake her.
XZZXYSNO
I doubt anything'll wake her.
WHEN DAD GETS HOME, HE GOES RIGHT TO THE PANTRY.
deep dive
(schedule doesn't leave much time for dinner)
WOO HOO!

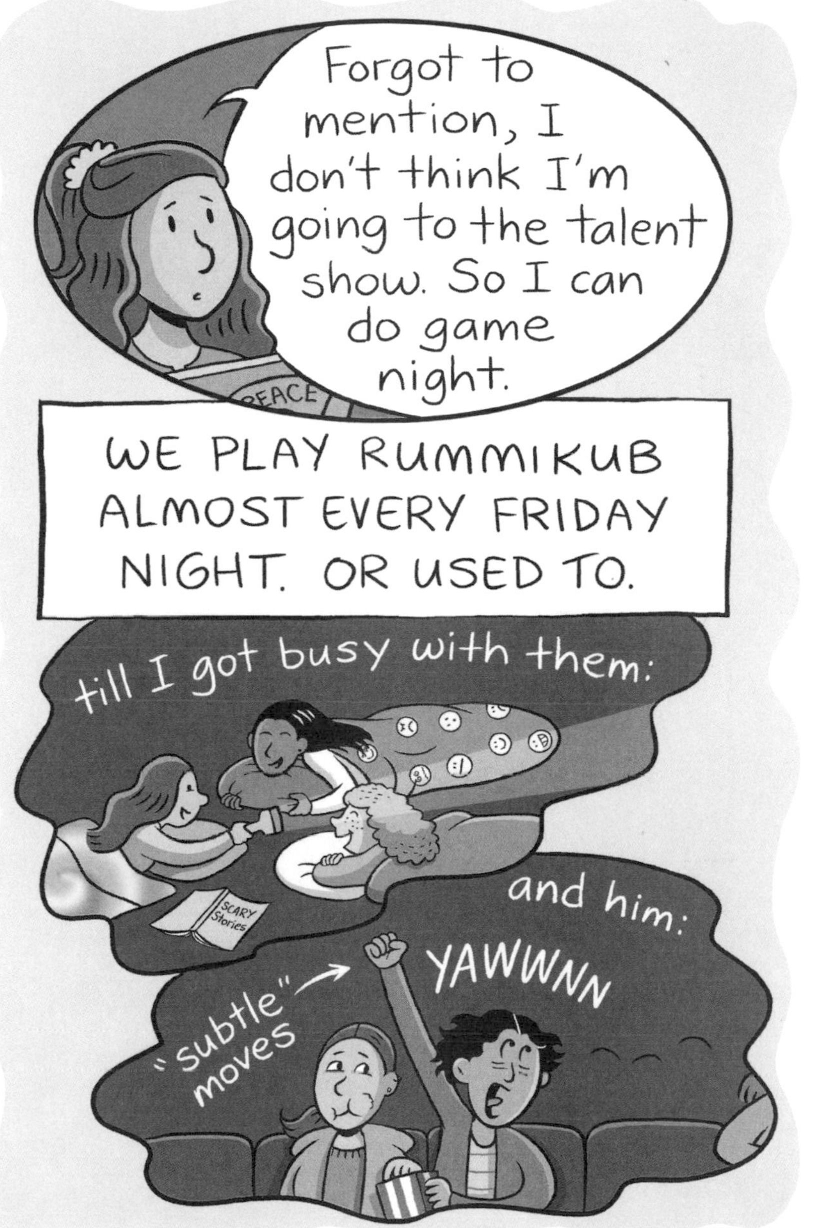
Forgot to mention, I don't think I'm going to the talent show. So I can do game night.
PEACE
WE PLAY RUMMIKUB ALMOST EVERY FRIDAY NIGHT. OR USED TO.
till I got busy with them:
SCARY Stories
and him:
"subtle" moves
YAWWNN

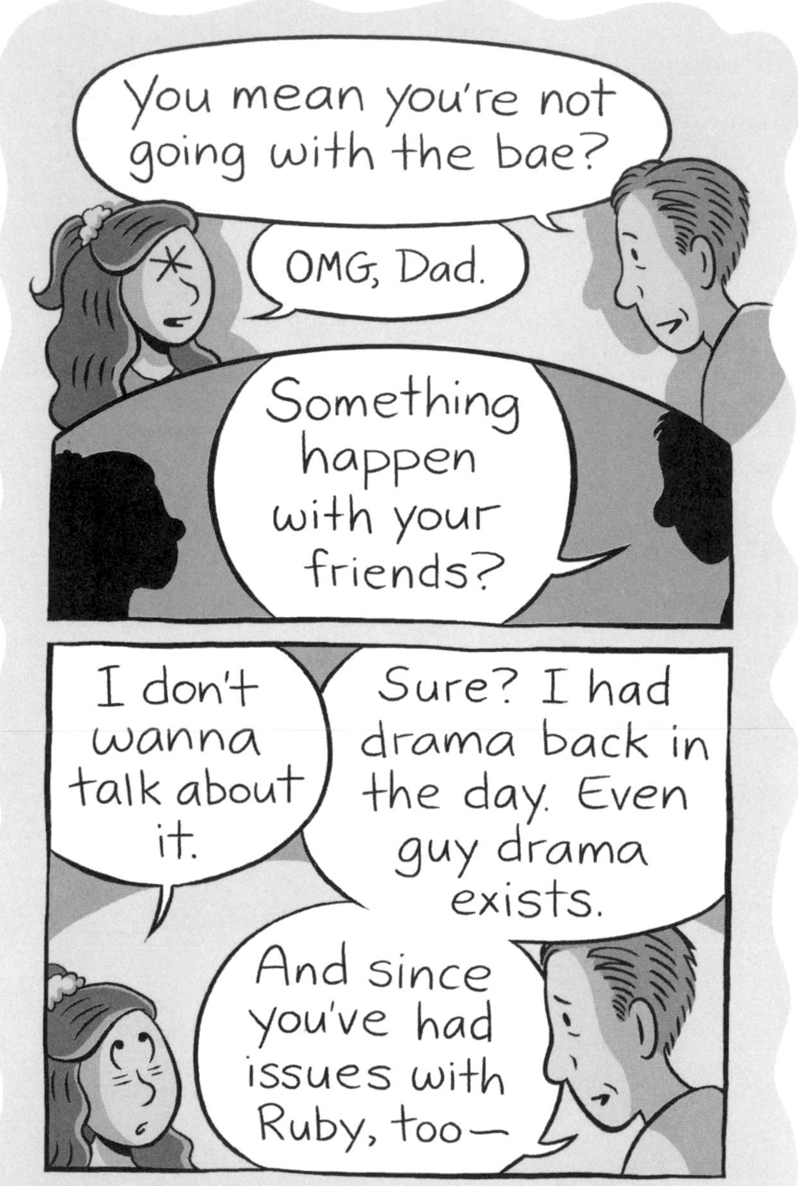
You mean you're not going with the bae?
OMG, Dad.
Something happen with your friends?
I don't wanna talk about it.
Sure? I had drama back in the day. Even guy drama exists.
And since you've had issues with Ruby, too—

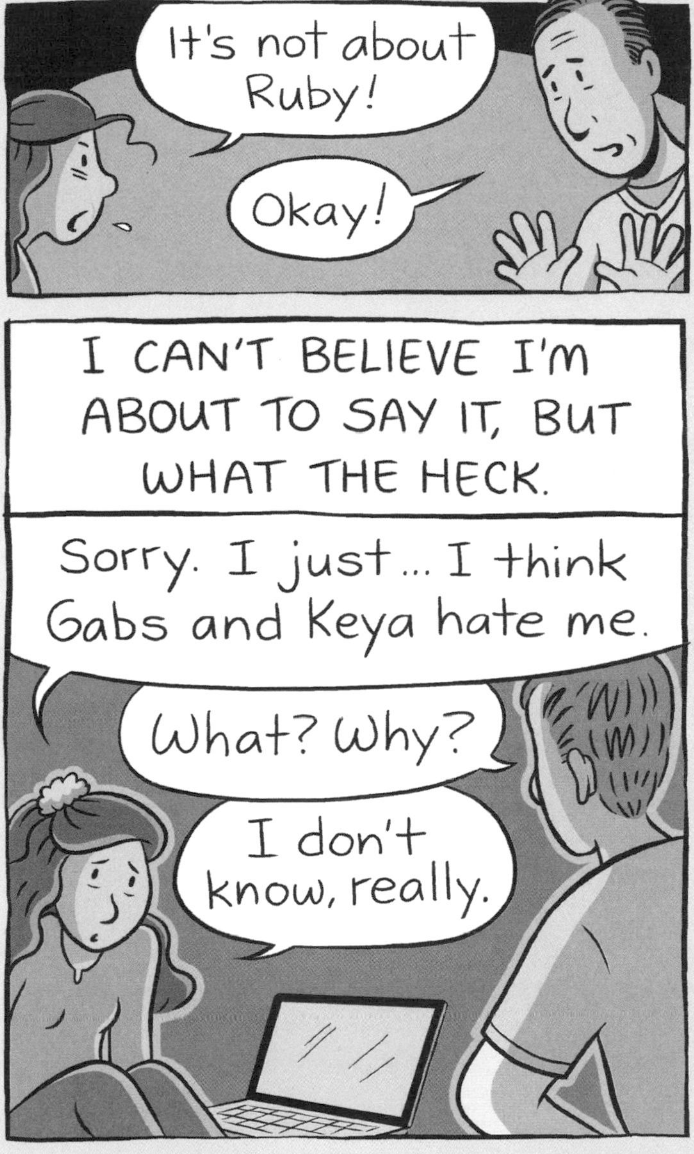
It's not about Ruby!
Okay!
I CAN'T BELIEVE I'M ABOUT TO SAY IT, BUT WHAT THE HECK.
Sorry. I just... I think Gabs and Keya hate me.
What? Why?
I don't know, really.

Is it jealousy? Because that often leads to fear. Fear leads to anger. Anger leads to hate, and—
Sorry. Just realized I'm quoting Yoda.
I CRACK UP.
Not jealousy.
It's okay, Dad. I'll go. I'll just sit with the Squad.

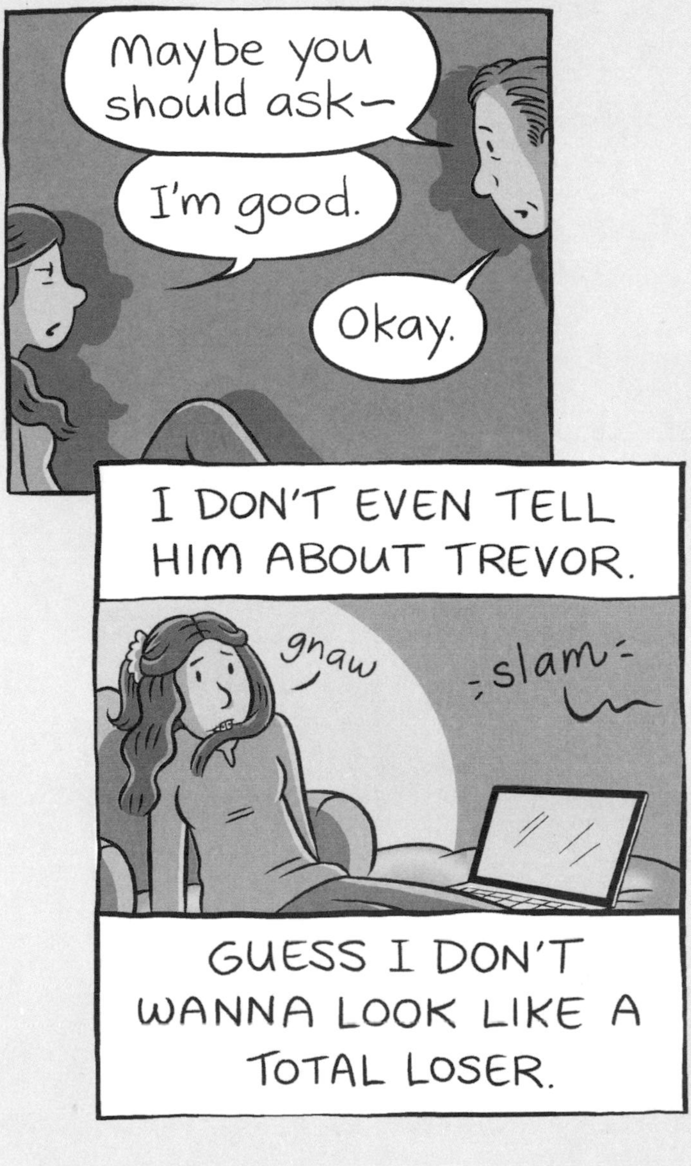

Maybe you should ask—
I'm good.
Okay.
I DON'T EVEN TELL HIM ABOUT TREVOR.
gnaw
slam
GUESS I DON'T WANNA LOOK LIKE A TOTAL LOSER.

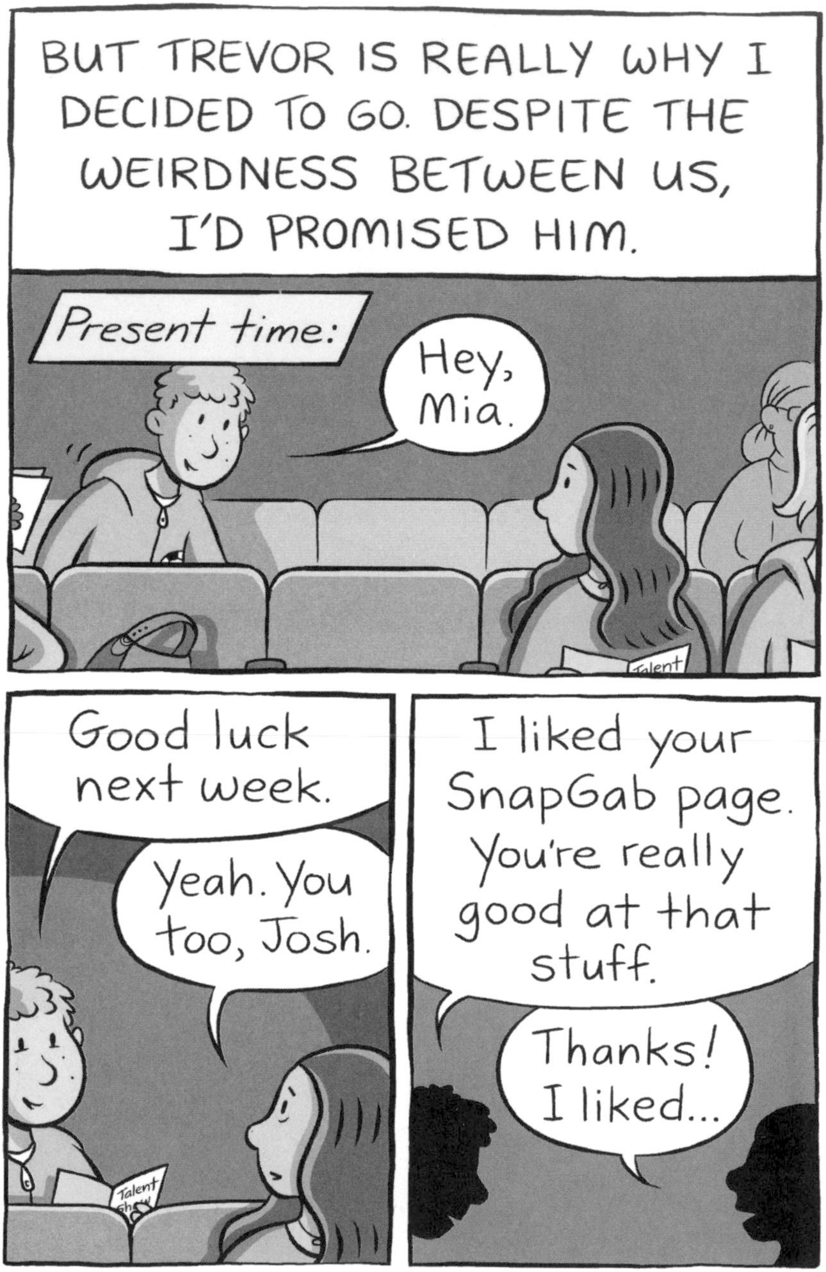
BUT TREVOR IS REALLY WHY I DECIDED TO GO. DESPITE THE WEIRDNESS BETWEEN US, I'D PROMISED HIM.
Present time:
Hey, Mia.
Talent
Good luck next week.
Yeah. You too, Josh.
Talent Show
I liked your SnapGab page. You're really good at that stuff.
Thanks! I liked...

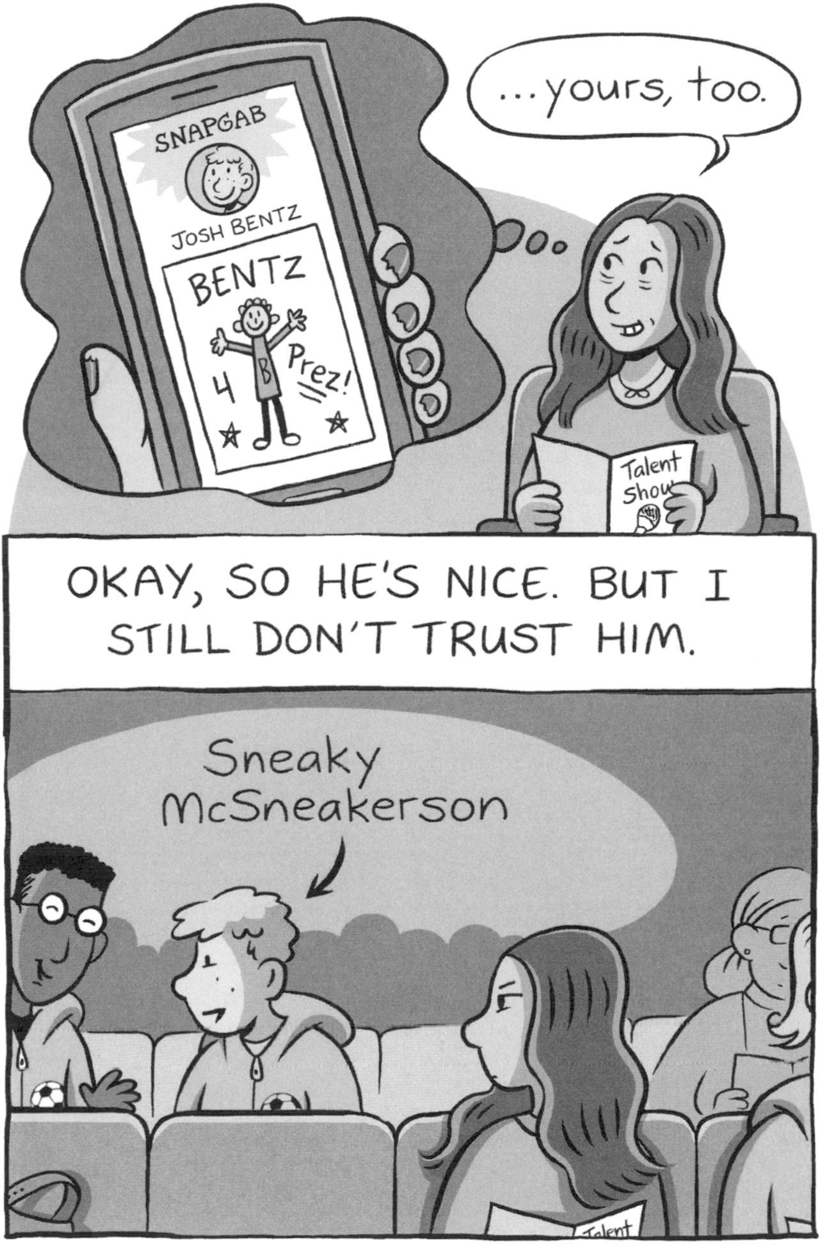
...yours, too.
SNAPGAB
JOSH BENTZ
BENTZ
4 B Prez!
Talent Show
OKAY, SO HE'S NICE. BUT I STILL DON'T TRUST HIM.
Sneaky McSneakerson

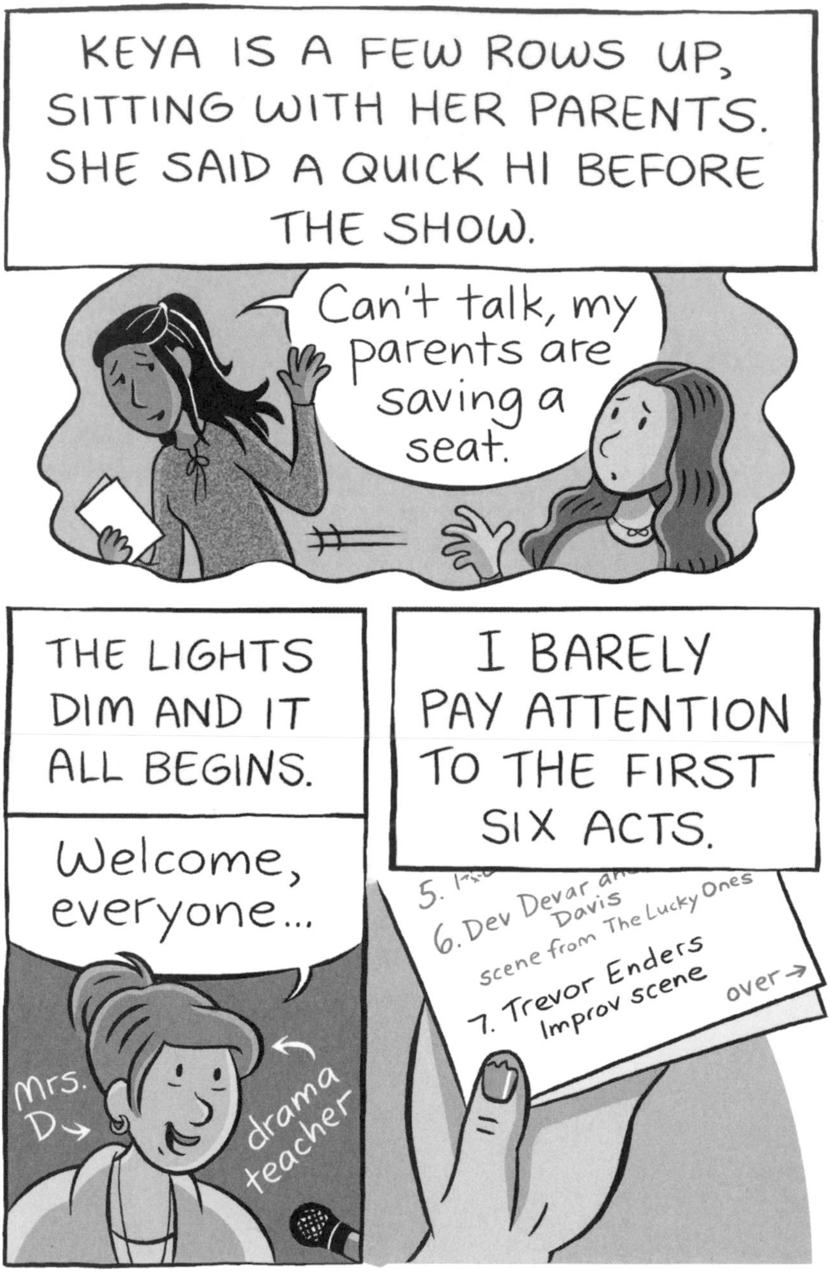
KEYA IS A FEW ROWS UP, SITTING WITH HER PARENTS. SHE SAID A QUICK HI BEFORE THE SHOW.
Can't talk, my parents are saving a seat.
THE LIGHTS DIM AND IT ALL BEGINS.
Welcome, everyone...
Mrs. D
drama teacher
I BARELY PAY ATTENTION TO THE FIRST SIX ACTS.
6. Dev Devar
Davis
scene from The Lucky Ones
7. Trevor Enders
Improv scene
over

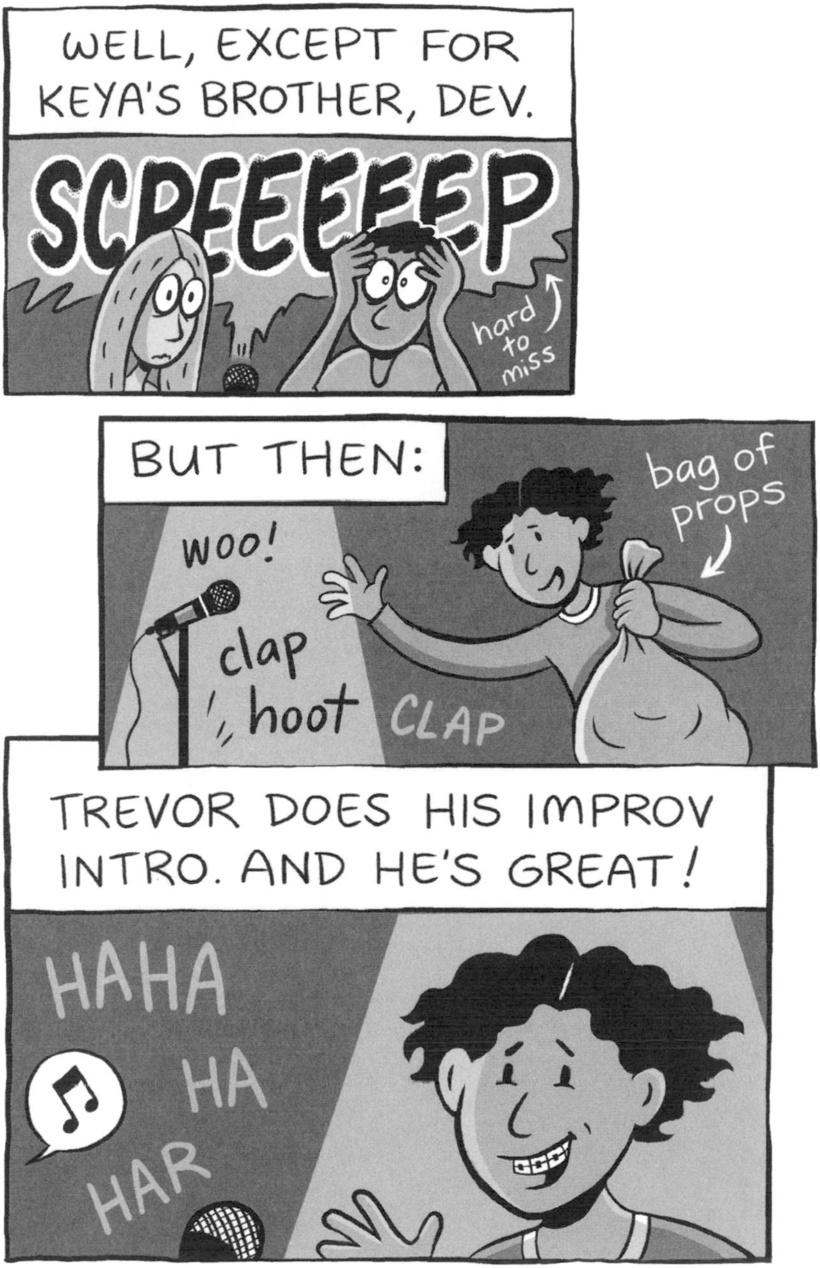
WELL, EXCEPT FOR KEYA'S BROTHER, DEV.
SCREEEEEP
hard to miss
BUT THEN:
bag of props
woo!
clap
hoot
CLAP
TREVOR DOES HIS IMPROV INTRO. AND HE'S GREAT!
HAHA
HA
HAR

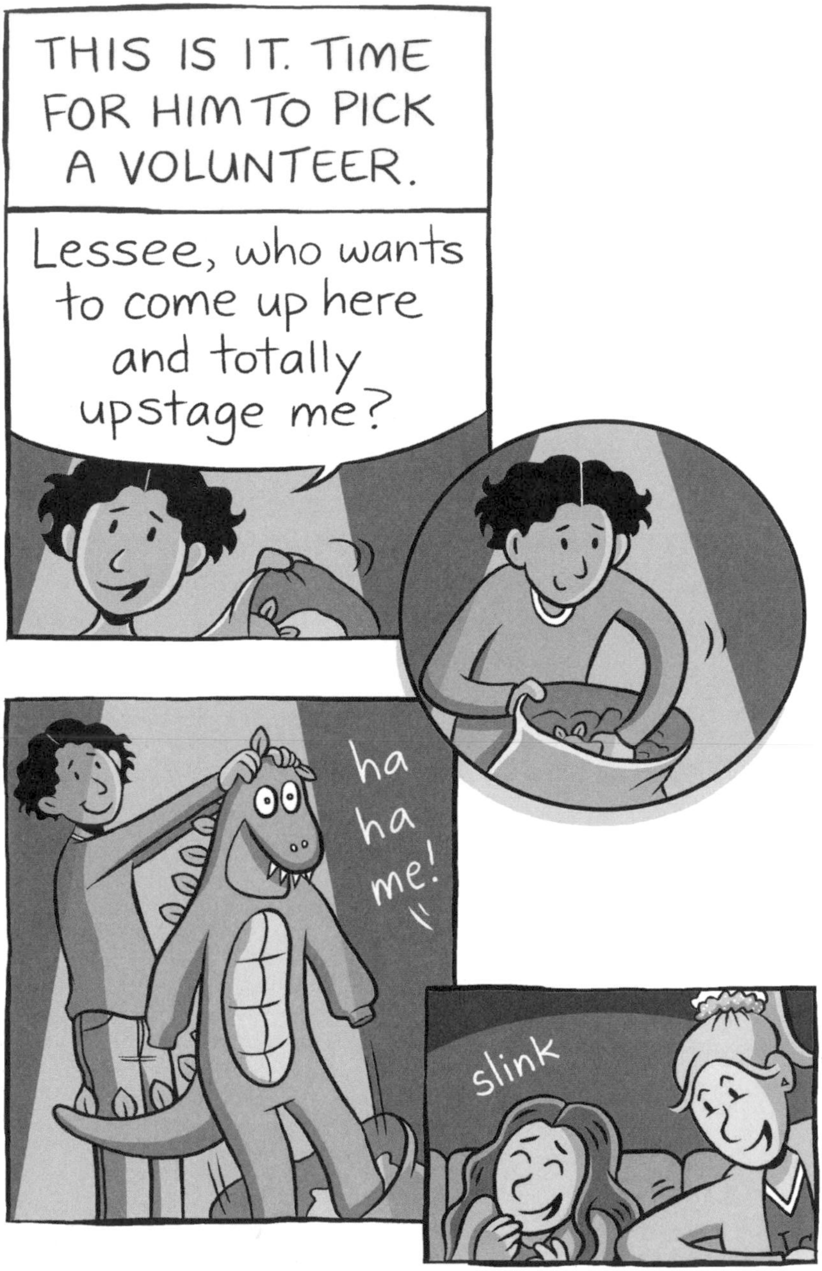
THIS IS IT. TIME FOR HIM TO PICK A VOLUNTEER.
Lessee, who wants to come up here and totally upstage me?
ha ha me!
slink

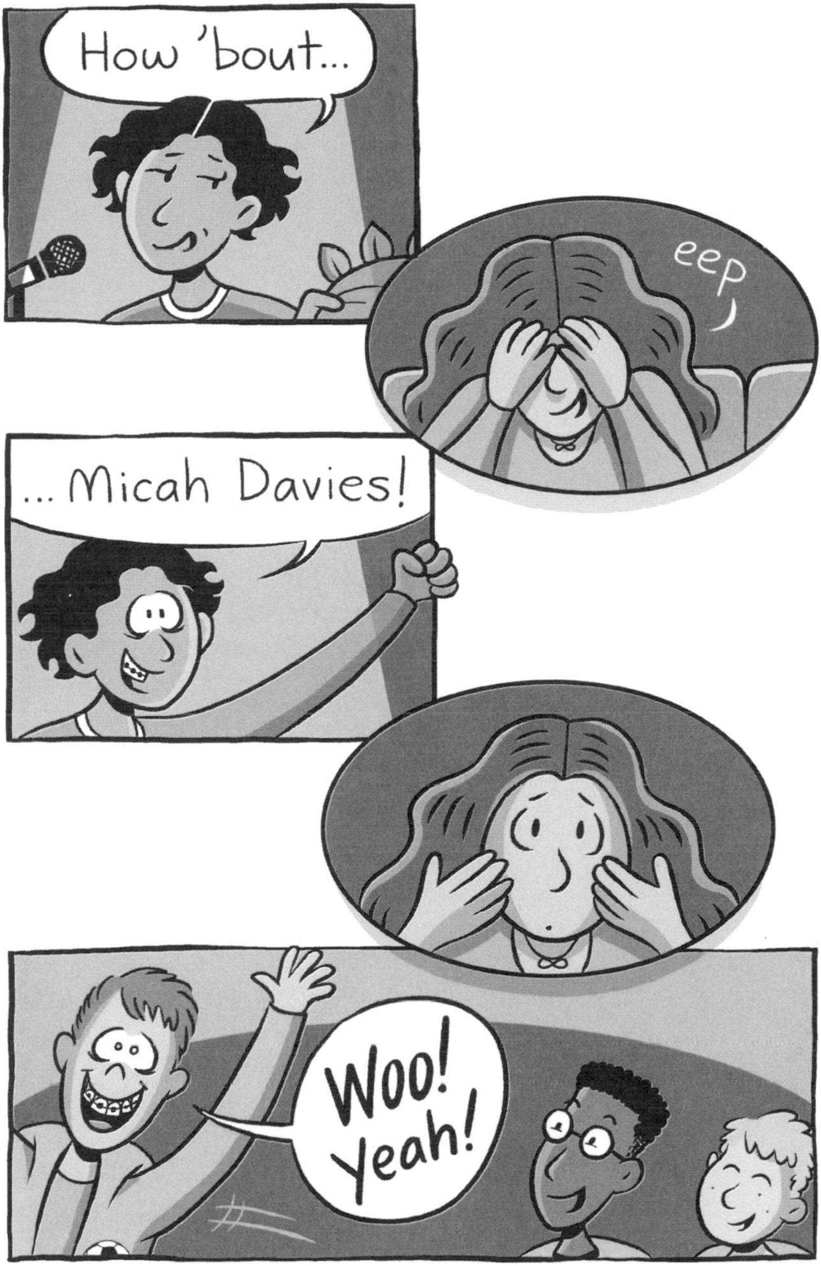
How 'bout...
eep
...Micah Davies!
Woo! Yeah!

WELL... HE KNEW I DIDN'T WANNA GO UP THERE. THAT'S THE REASON HE DIDN'T PICK ME...

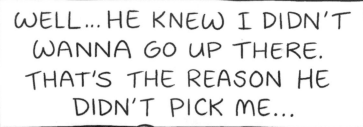

...ISN'T IT?

RUBY

Gulp.

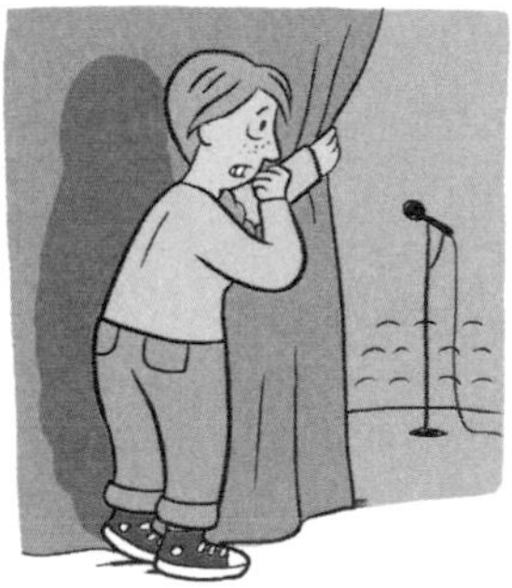

I can't believe I'm doing this.

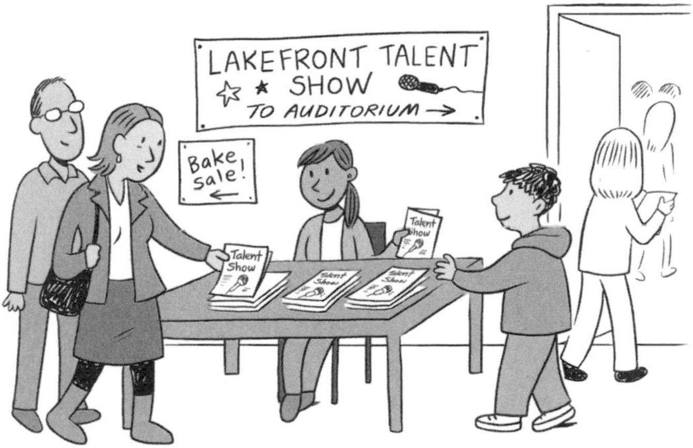
LAKEFRONT TALENT SHOW
TO AUDITORIUM →
Bake sale! ←
Talent Show
Talent Show
Talent Show
Talent Show

The place is packed. Am I the only nervous one?

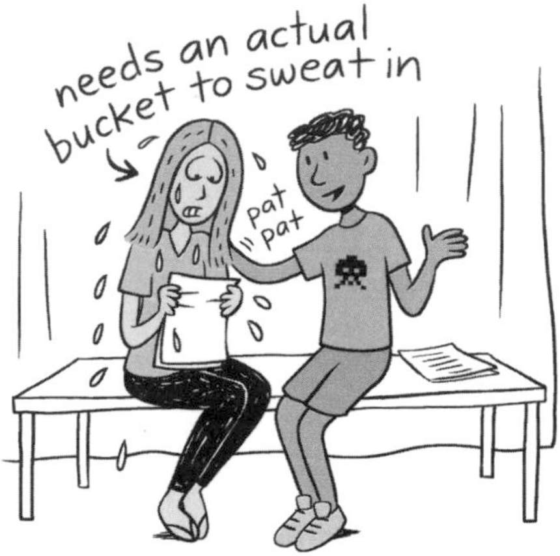
needs an actual bucket to sweat in
pat pat

Guess not.

I skipped rehearsal. I don't know why. I guess I was too scared, and it seemed like the right thing to do at the time. I kinda regret it now.

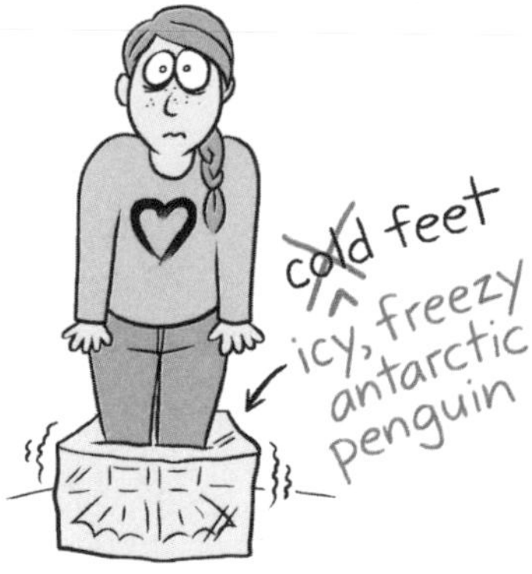
~~cold~~ feet
icy, freezy antarctic penguin

When Leah and Juan suggested doing the talent show, it was like they planted a bug in my ear. It buzzed around until I put a stop to it—by signing up.

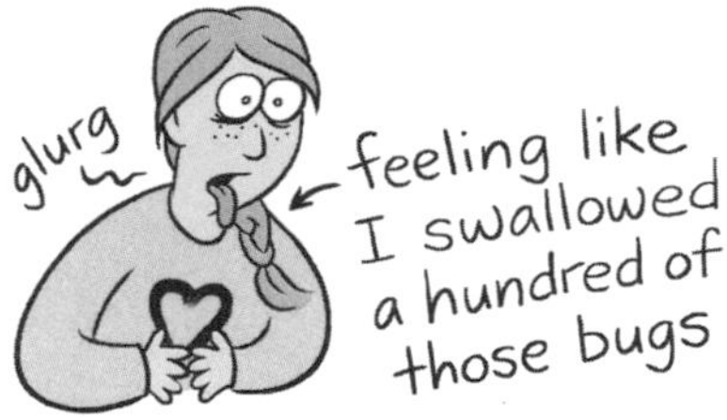
glurg
feeling like I swallowed a hundred of those bugs

I hope it was the right thing to do.

Brianna is still sweating. I hate to admit it but seeing that makes me feel better.

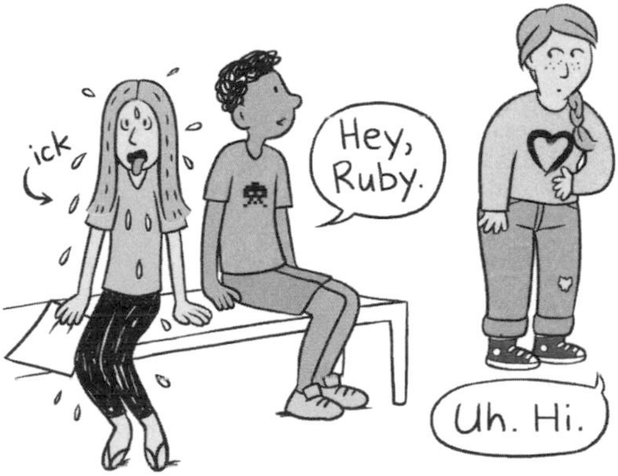
ick
Hey, Ruby.
Uh. Hi.

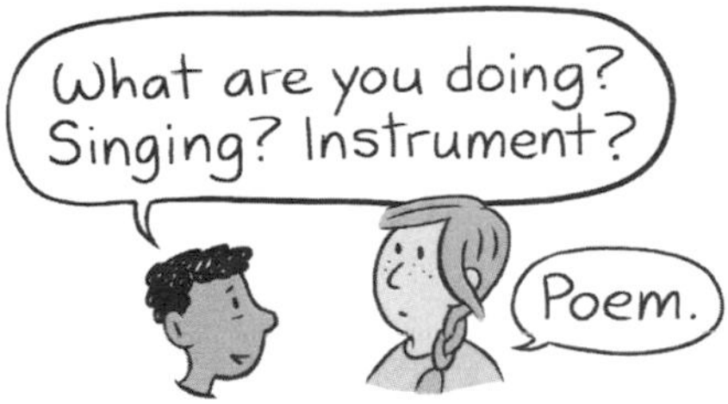
What are you doing? Singing? Instrument?
Poem.

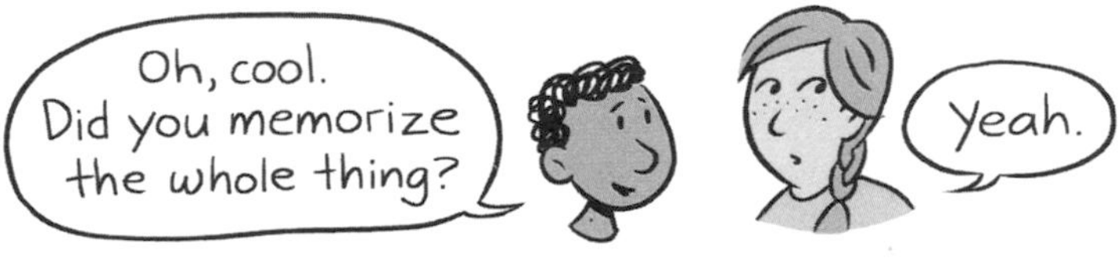
Oh, cool. Did you memorize the whole thing?
Yeah.

eye roll
snap
Well, if you need a mnemonic device, I can make 'em up like that.

Uh.
That's okay.

I want to tell him that all his talking is making me more nervous, but I don't. I'm trying to "use my filter," as adults say. It's hard, but I've gotten better.

1
STOP BABBLING!
filter
2.
filter
POP
(polite silence)

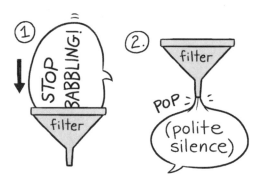

Now I wonder if he's babbling because **he's** nervous. Some people are like that.

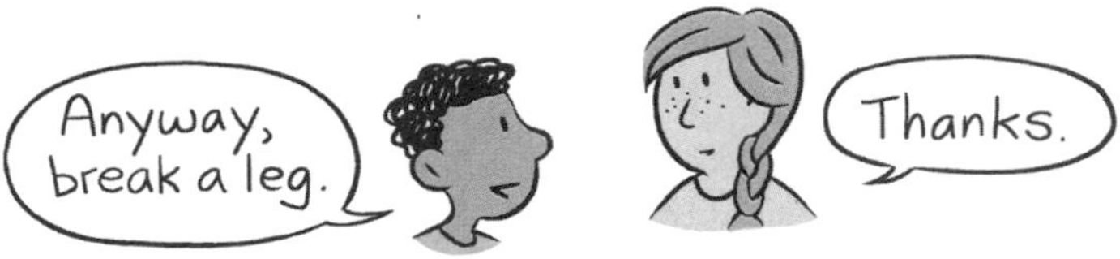
Anyway, break a leg.
Thanks.

Despite all the talking, he's nice. I wonder if we could be friends.

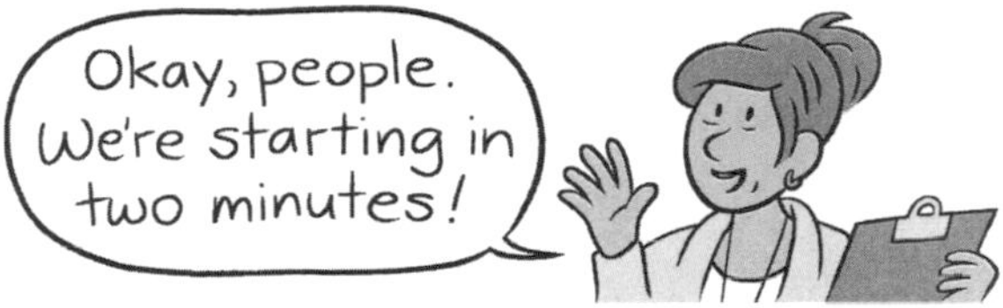
Okay, people. We're starting in two minutes!

The bugs start eating my insides.

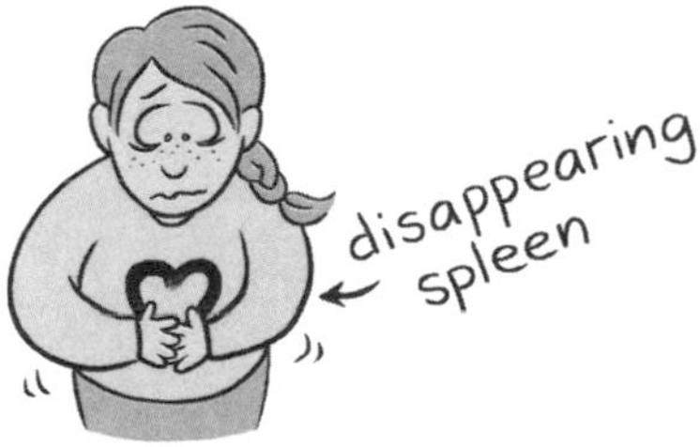
disappearing spleen

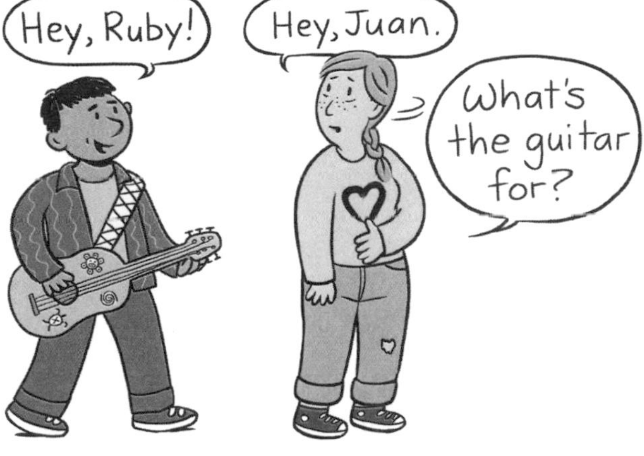
Hey, Ruby!
Hey, Juan.
What's the guitar for?

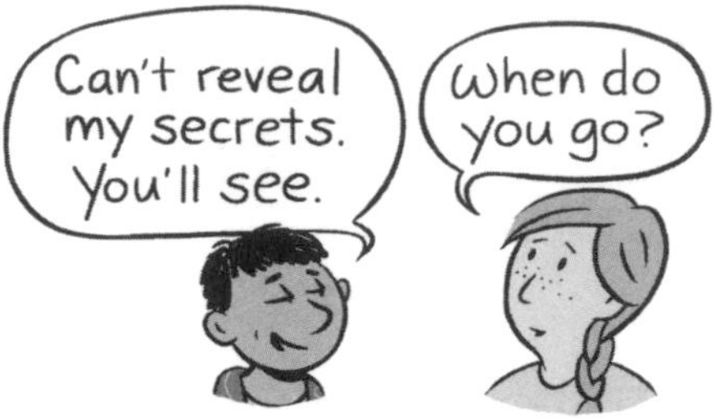
Can't reveal my secrets. You'll see.
When do you go?

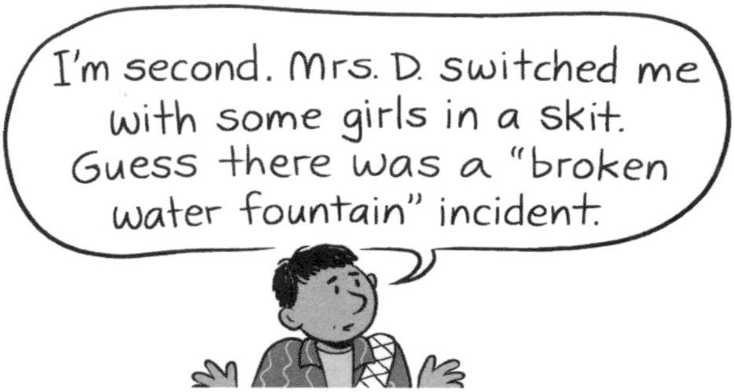
I'm second. Mrs. D. switched me with some girls in a skit. Guess there was a "broken water fountain" incident.

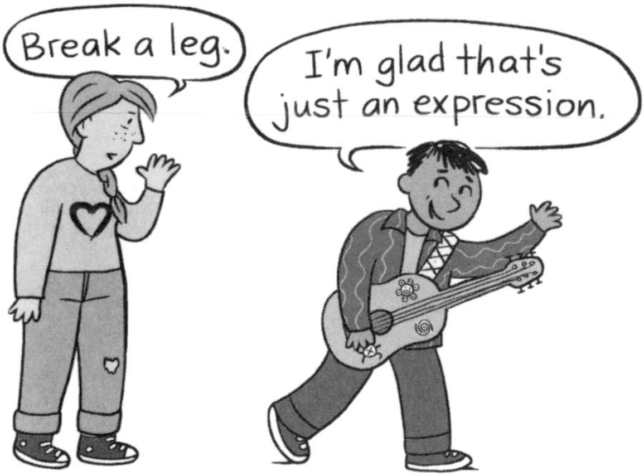
Break a leg.
I'm glad that's just an expression.

I'm both relieved and jealous that he goes on soon. Relieved 'cause I can check the audience's reaction to him. Jealous 'cause he's getting it over with.

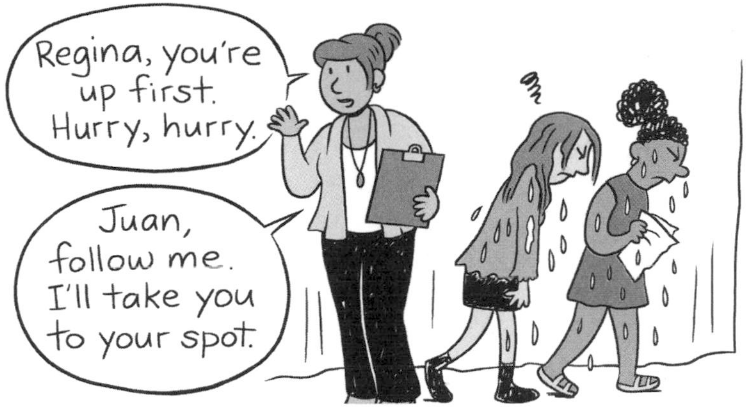
Regina, you're up first. Hurry, hurry.
Juan, follow me. I'll take you to your spot.

He follows Mrs. D. A tiny sixth grader in huge platform shoes, holding a flute, follows, too.

In a few minutes, Mrs. D. goes onstage and welcomes everyone. Then she introduces the first act.

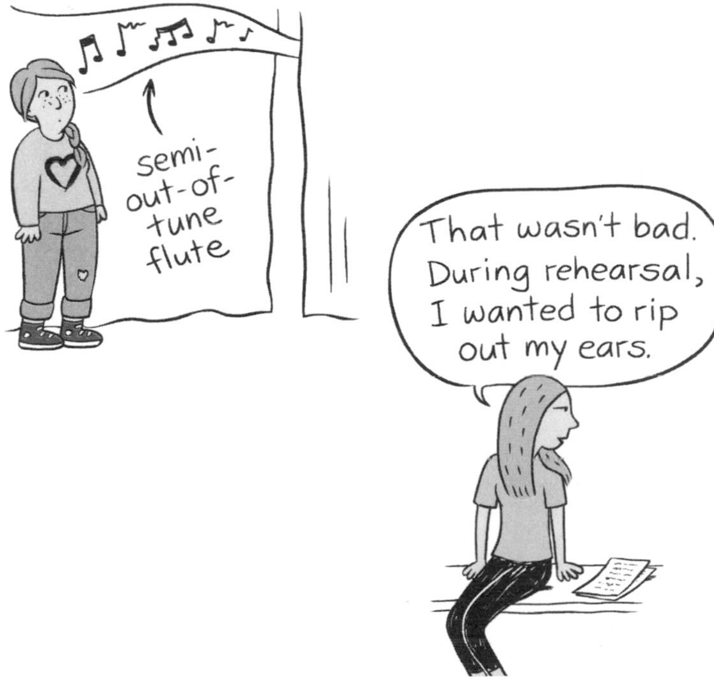
semi-out-of-tune flute
That wasn't bad. During rehearsal, I wanted to rip out my ears.

I laugh. Smart Girl is sassy.

When the flute player is done, there's a lot of clapping.

Thank you, Regina. Next up, we have a guitar solo from Juan Alvarez.

Guitar solo? I thought he was reciting a poem, like me. I can't help it. I slink over to the curtain to peek out.

BONK

I ...

...um...

Whoa. I've never seen Juan nervous before. He's usually so confident.

He kinda gathers himself and stands straighter.

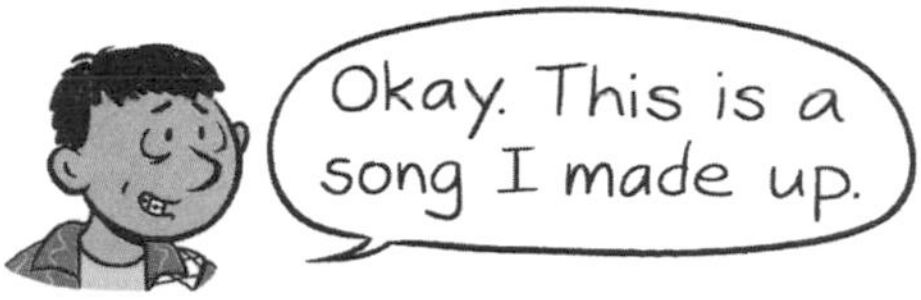
Okay. This is a song I made up.

He strums the guitar, playing a sad, soulful tune for a minute. He must be really comfortable playing; I think it helps him get over his nervousness. Soon—there's no other word for it—he starts to croon.*

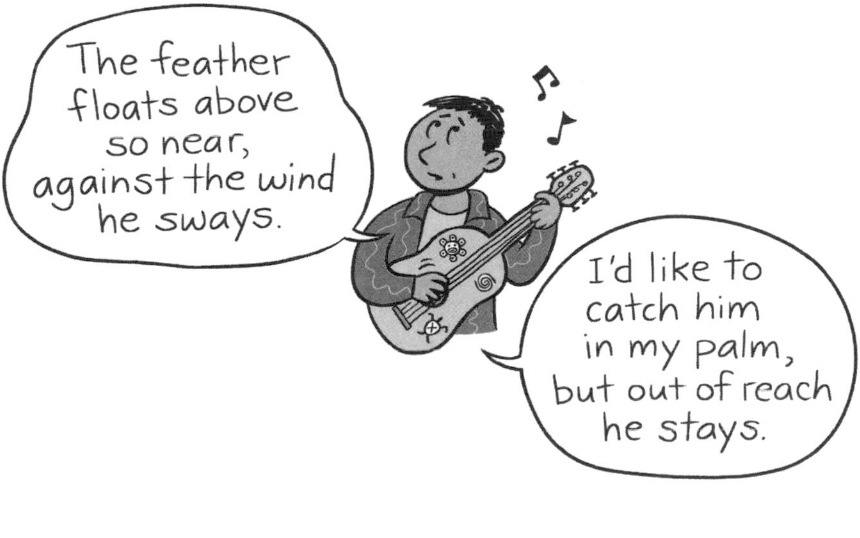
The feather floats above so near, against the wind he sways.
I'd like to catch him in my palm, but out of reach he stays.

*my nana's word for what her favorite old-timey singers do

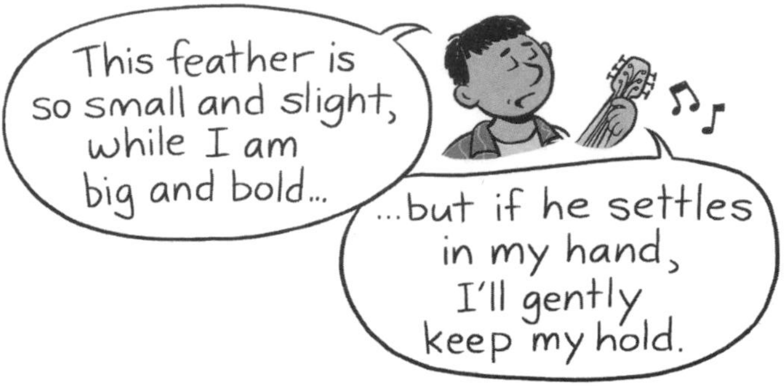
This feather is so small and slight, while I am big and bold...
...but if he settles in my hand, I'll gently keep my hold.

He stops singing but keeps playing the guitar. I wonder why Juan calls the feather "he." Then I remember Mrs. Winn teaching us about personification.

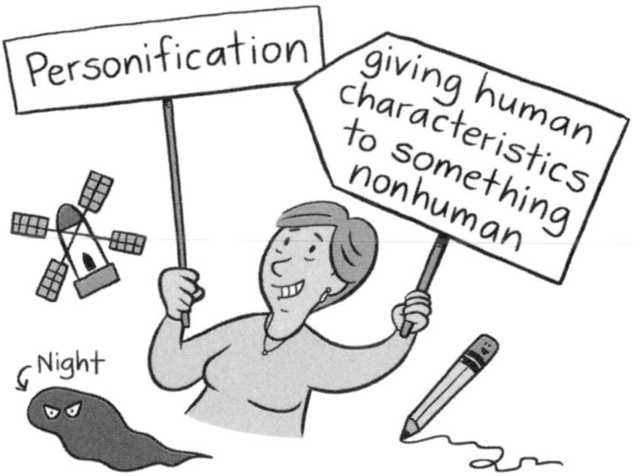
Personification
giving human characteristics to something nonhuman
Night

My mind drifts a little. Then the melody gets softer and softer until it ends.

Juan takes a bow and everyone claps. A few people whistle. I'm just shocked he didn't sing about a farting dog or something.

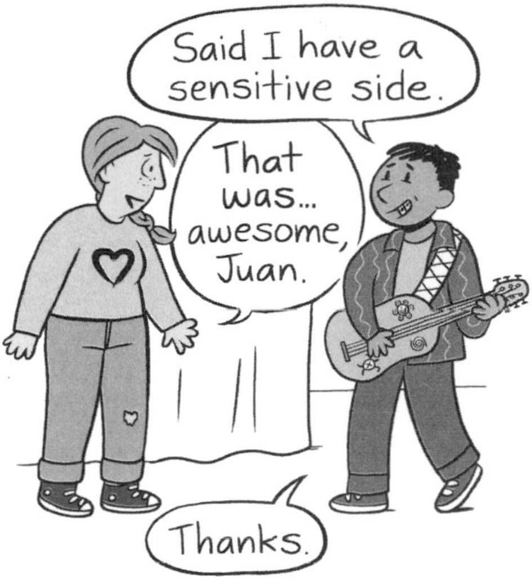
Said I have a sensitive side.
That was... awesome, Juan.
Thanks.

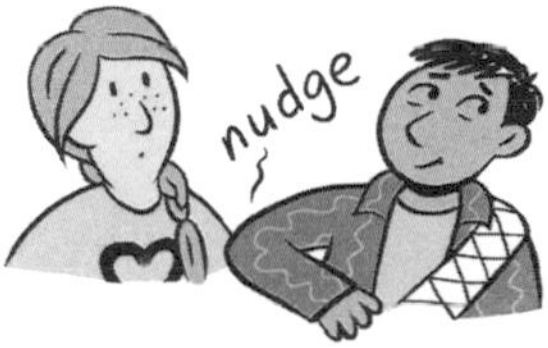
nudge

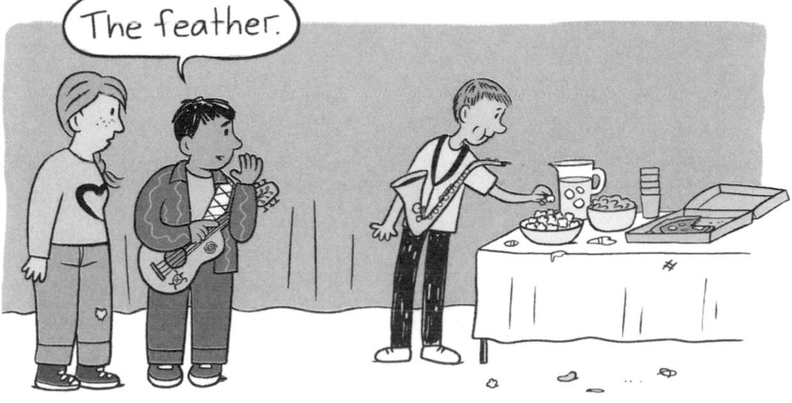
The feather.

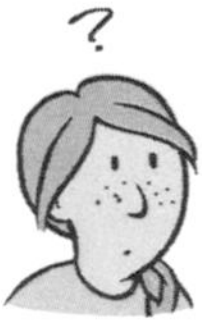
?

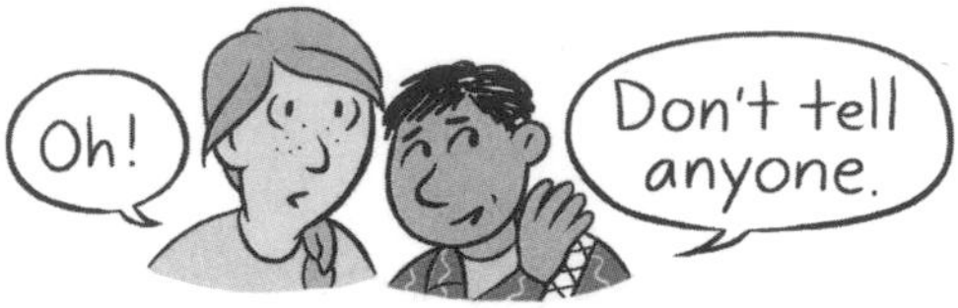
Oh!
Don't tell anyone.

He waves and leaves, making a beeline to the snack table.
I'm even more shocked.

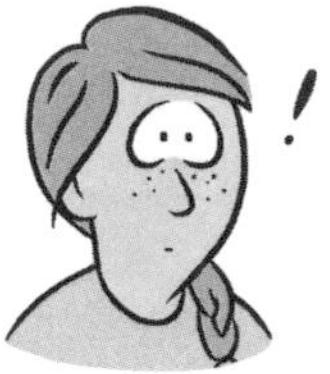
!

He trusted me with that secret. Which means . . .

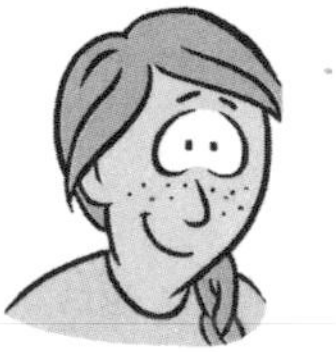

. . . we're friends, too?
Suddenly I forget to be nervous. That lasts about a second.

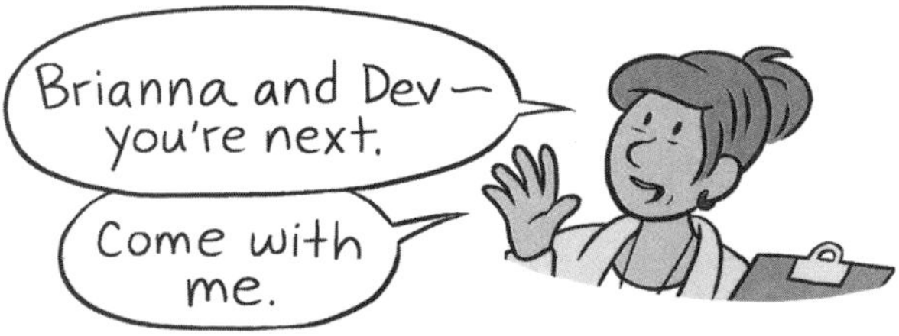
Brianna and Dev— you're next.
Come with me.

They follow Mrs. D. Dev looks kinda scared, and Brianna looks like she's seen ghost.

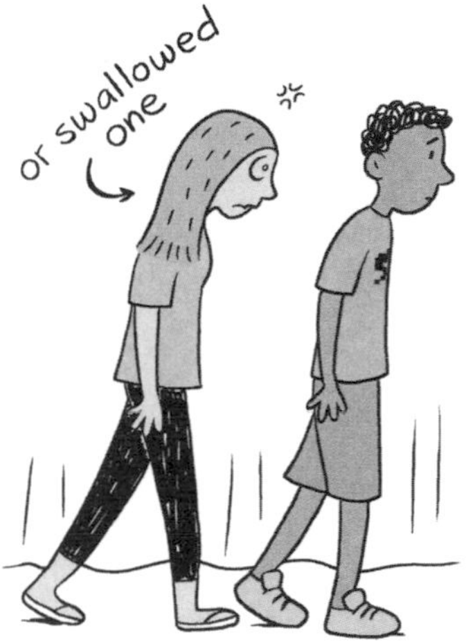
or swallowed one

I wait and listen backstage, feeling tense for them. After an unlucky start (ugh, mic feedback!), it sounds like they're doing okay. Before I know it, they're back.

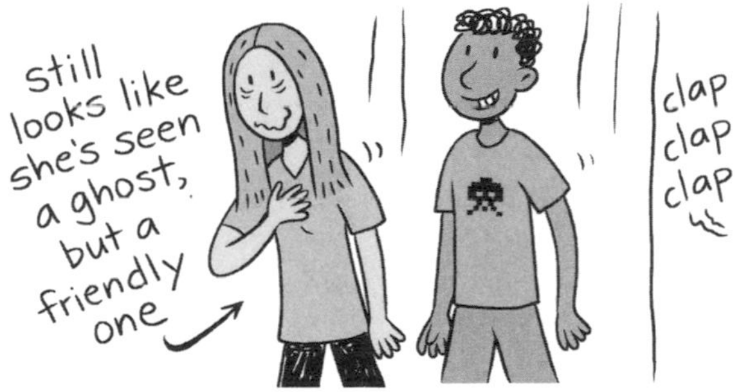
still looks like she's seen a ghost, but a friendly one
clap clap clap

I try not to be terrified, but then . . .

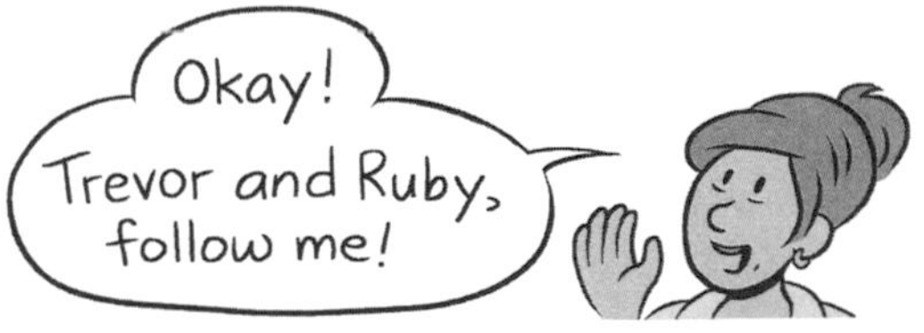
Okay!
Trevor and Ruby, follow me!

Trevor rushes over, looking antsy, as though he wants to run a couple laps. He kinda jumps up and down, like he's warming up. I want to grab his shoulders and hold him in place.

Mrs. D. leads us to an area in between backstage and onstage. It's really dark and we're butted against tall curtains. She walks to the microphone and introduces Trevor, who practically runs onstage. Then Mrs. D. comes back and waits with me.

She must sense I'm nervous.

wonder how she knows

It'll be okay. Just remember to breathe. If you got through rehearsal, you'll get through this!

I guess she forgot I wasn't there.

I hear the audience clap. Trevor rushes past me, looking pumped, sweaty, and holding a bunch of props. He fist-bumps some other kids backstage.

Mrs. D. gestures for me.
OMG. My turn.

OMGOMGOMG.

After waiting in the dark, it's so bright, I can't even see the audience. Which is good, I guess. That might make me turn and run. I hear some coughs, a few whispers, and one person in the middle of a sneezing fit.

I'm so glad I didn't tell anyone I was doing this.

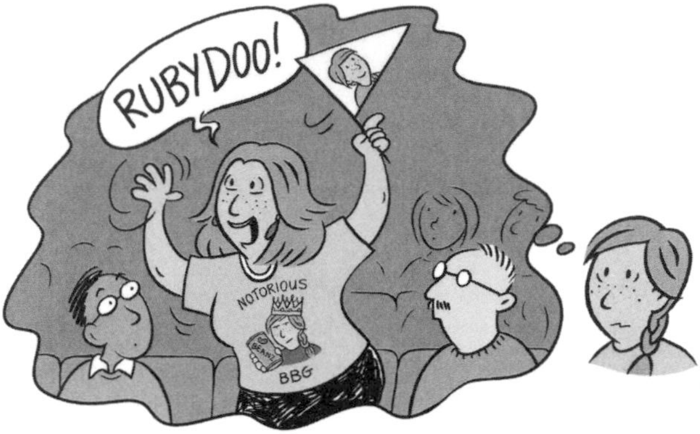
RUBYDOO!
NOTORIOUS
BEANS
BBG

I'm supposed to be "doing homework" at Leah's. My mom's so thrilled I have a new friend, she didn't bother to check in with Leah's parents.

I take a deep breath and try to remember Mrs. Winn's words:

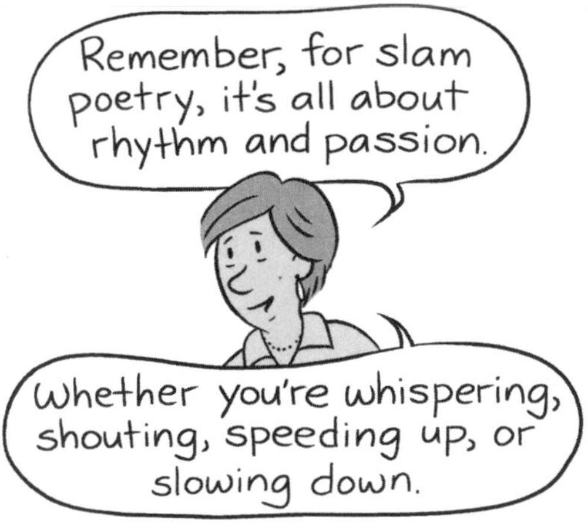
Remember, for slam poetry, it's all about rhythm and passion.
Whether you're whispering, shouting, speeding up, or slowing down.

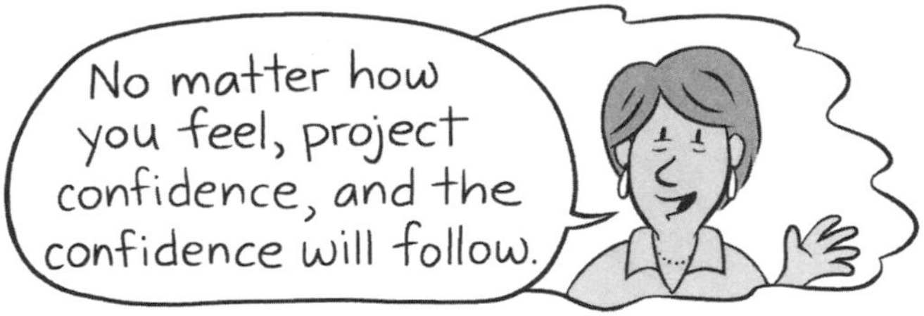
No matter how you feel, project confidence, and the confidence will follow.

I take a deep breath. I'm going all in. I've seen enough YouTube videos to know I can't do it halfway.

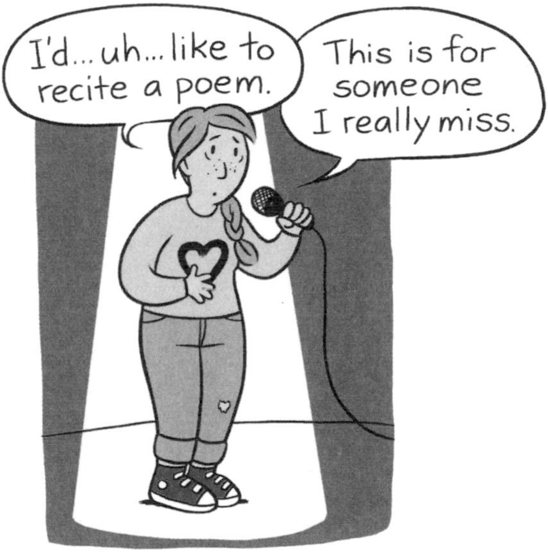
I'd... uh... like to recite a poem.
This is for someone I really miss.

Here goes nothing.

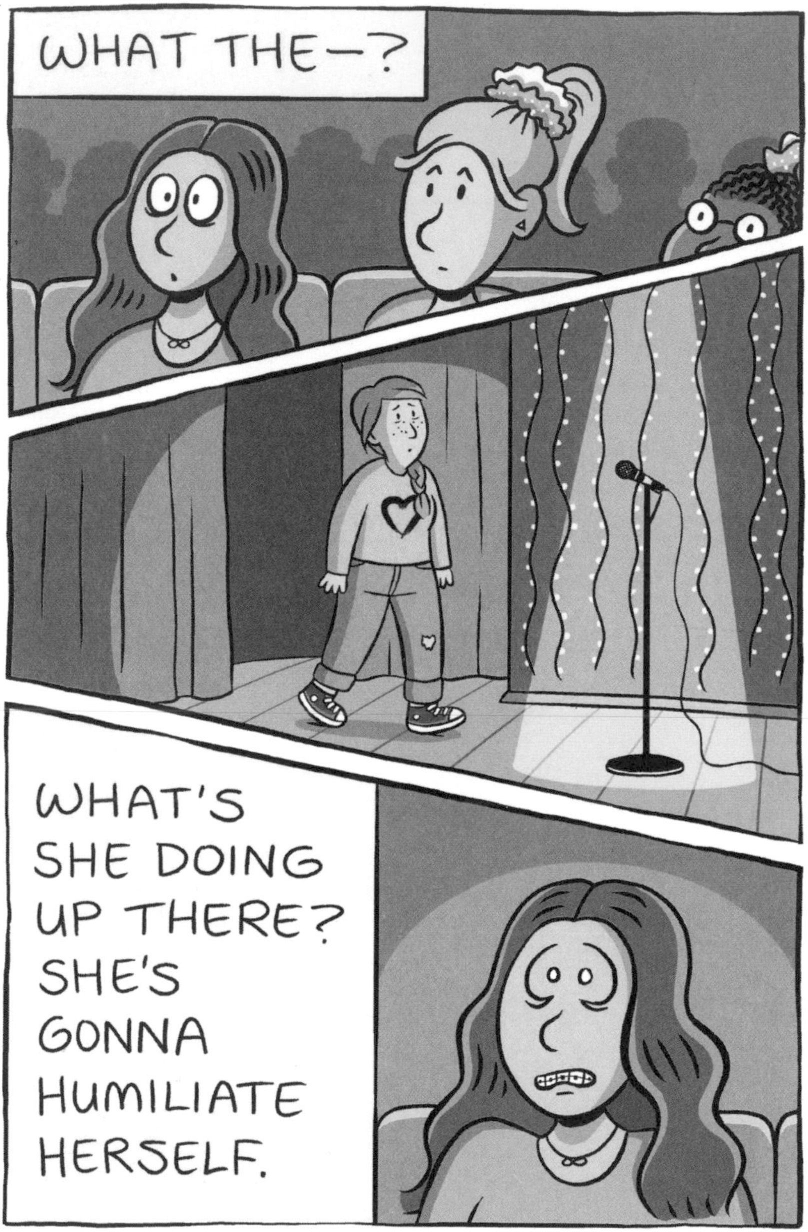
WHAT THE—?
WHAT'S SHE DOING UP THERE? SHE'S GONNA HUMILIATE HERSELF.

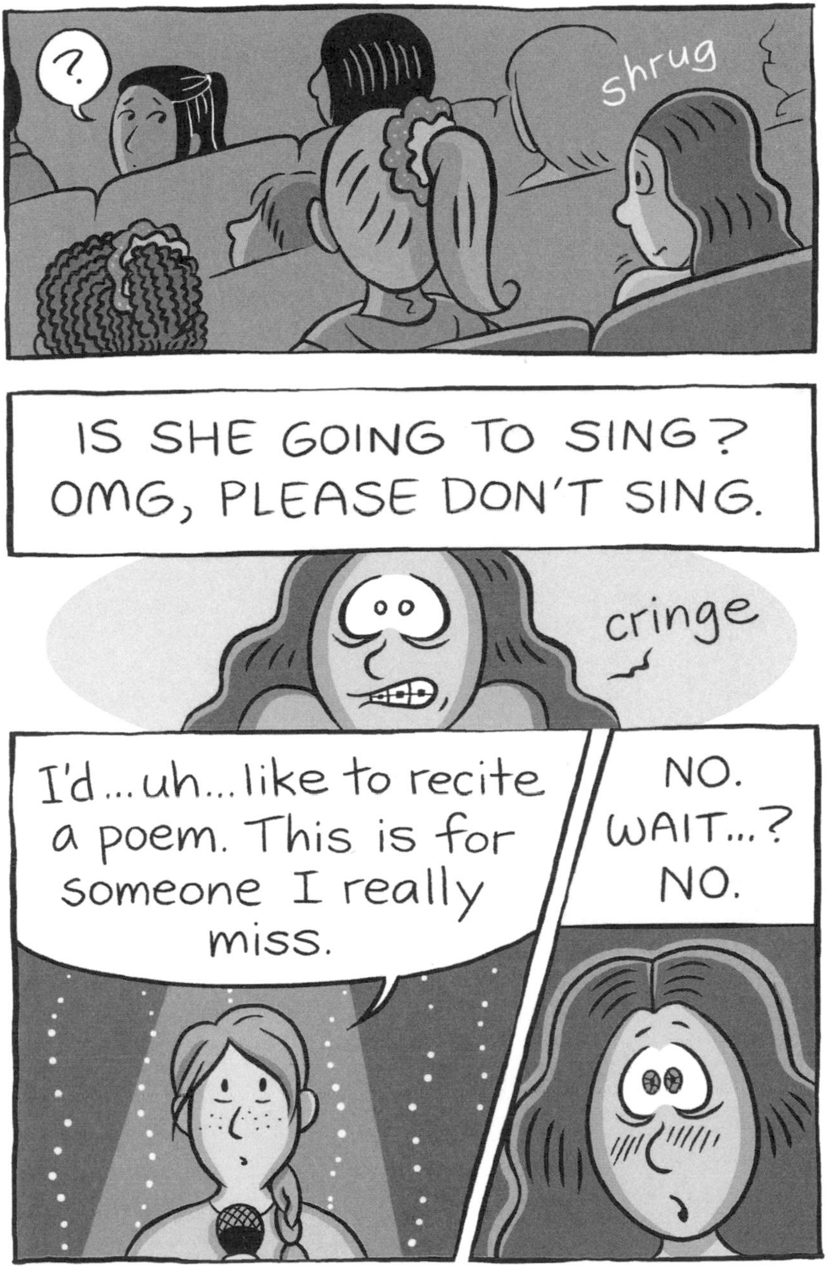
?
shrug
IS SHE GOING TO SING? OMG, PLEASE DON'T SING.
cringe
I'd...uh...like to recite a poem. This is for someone I really miss.
NO. WAIT...? NO.

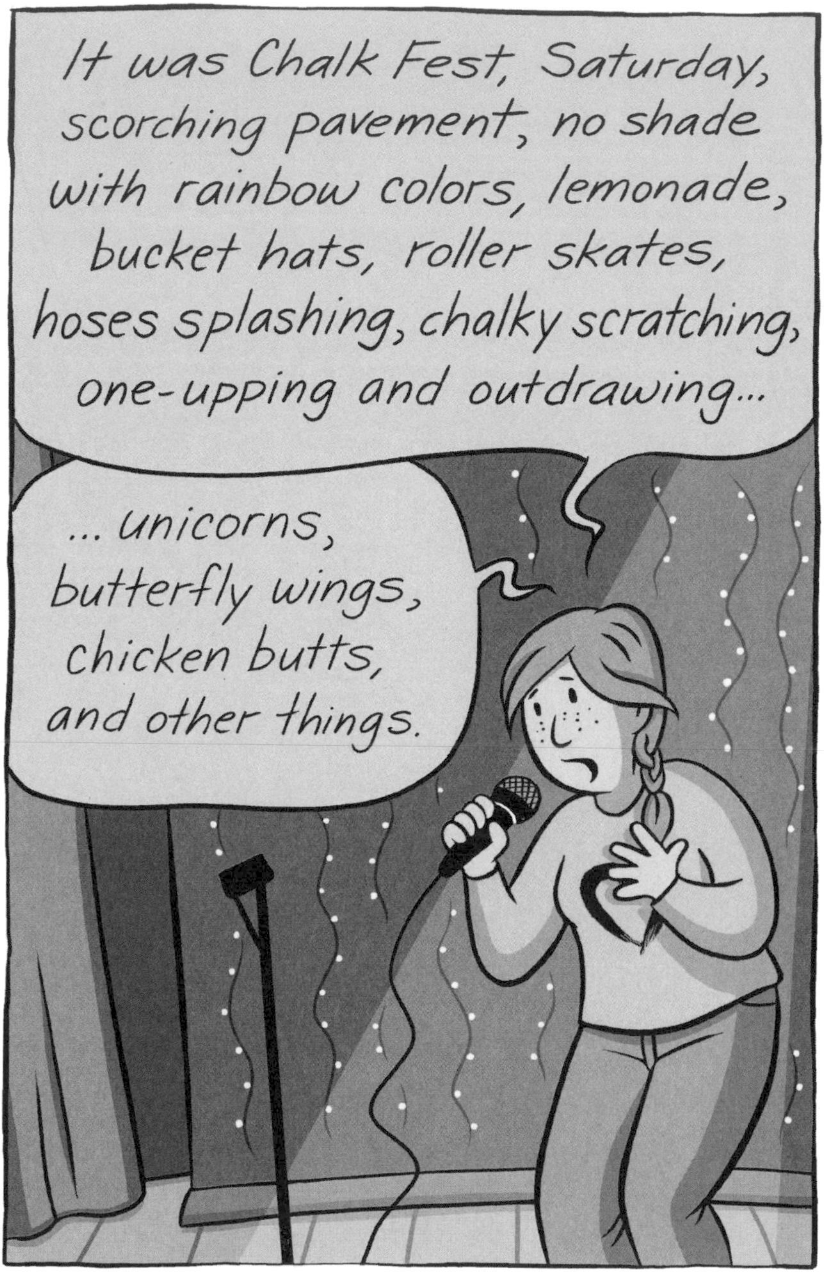
It was Chalk Fest, Saturday, scorching pavement, no shade with rainbow colors, lemonade, bucket hats, roller skates, hoses splashing, chalky scratching, one-upping and outdrawing...
... unicorns, butterfly wings, chicken butts, and other things.

It was Lakefront Kite Days on a field, in the heat, with pretzel bites, funnel cakes, flying our taped-up mistakes, dusty breezes, icy freezes, tails streaming, children screaming...
... soaring visions, sky collisions, tugs, hugs, and other things.

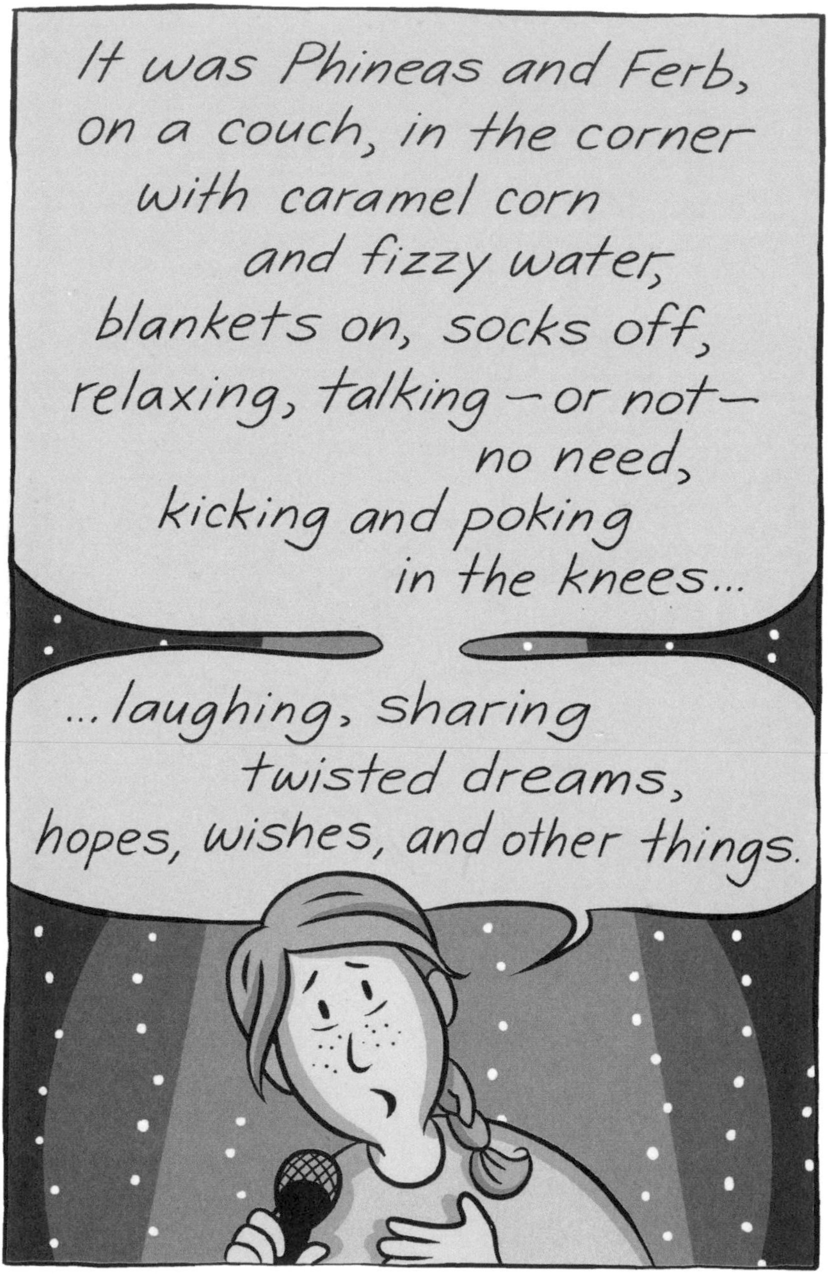
It was Phineas and Ferb, on a couch, in the corner with caramel corn and fizzy water, blankets on, socks off, relaxing, talking—or not—no need, kicking and poking in the knees...
...laughing, sharing twisted dreams, hopes, wishes, and other things.

It's days and nights of these memories, that flat-out refuse to leave, that remind me of safety, of friendship and family, of little things and big moments...
...that are all wrapped up in what used to be.

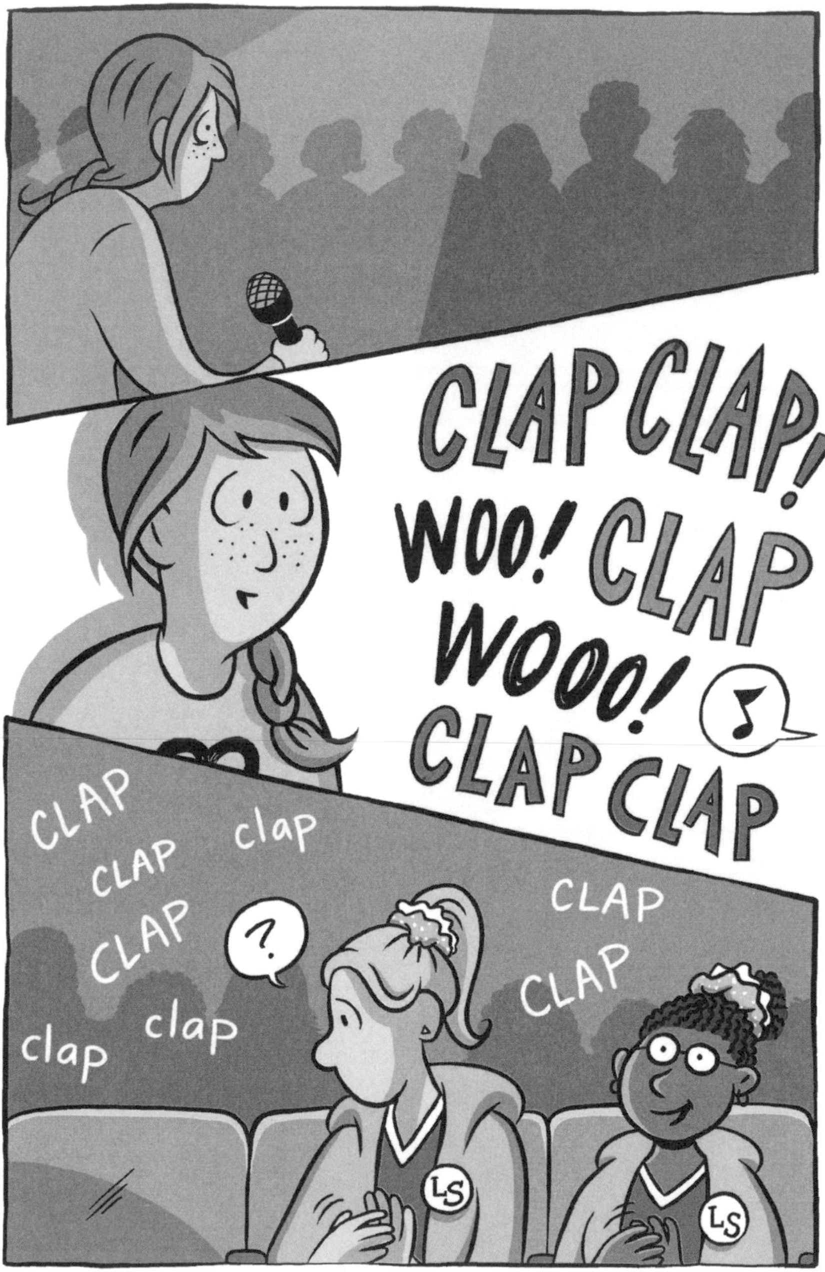
CLAP CLAP!
WOO! CLAP
WOOO!
CLAP CLAP
CLAP
CLAP
clap
CLAP
?
clap
clap
CLAP
CLAP
LS
LS

RUBY

They liked it!

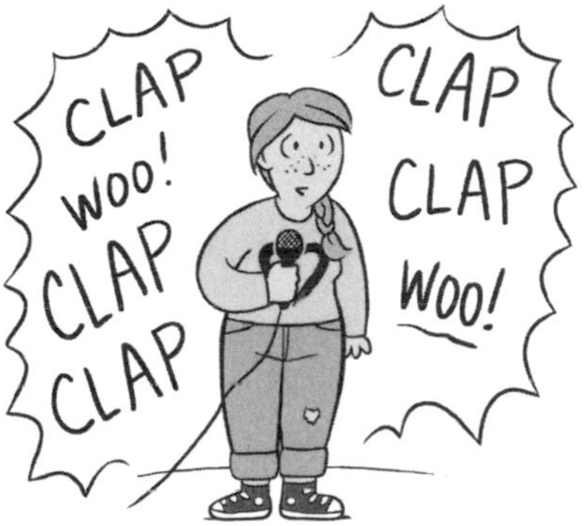
CLAP
WOO!
CLAP
CLAP
CLAP
CLAP
CLAP
WOO!

I smile. Sort of. It's not something I'm used to doing much of. Usually, I feel like I'm trying too hard.

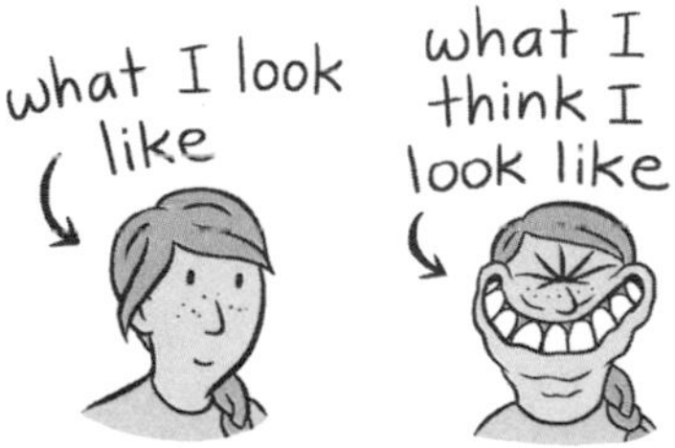
what I look like
what I think I look like

I give a little wave and head backstage. A few people rush over.

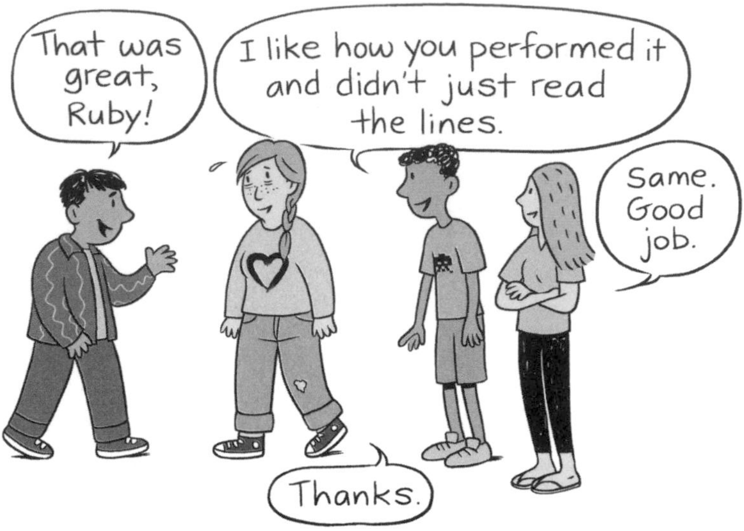
That was great, Ruby!
I like how you performed it and didn't just read the lines.
Same. Good job.
Thanks.

If I wasn't such a klutz, I'd be jumping for joy!

There are a bunch of acts left. I stick around and wait backstage. Juan sits next to me on the dusty floor and shares a bag of honey-mustard pretzels.

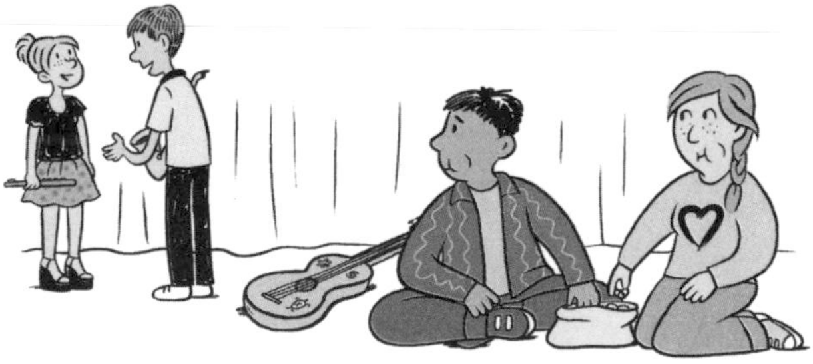

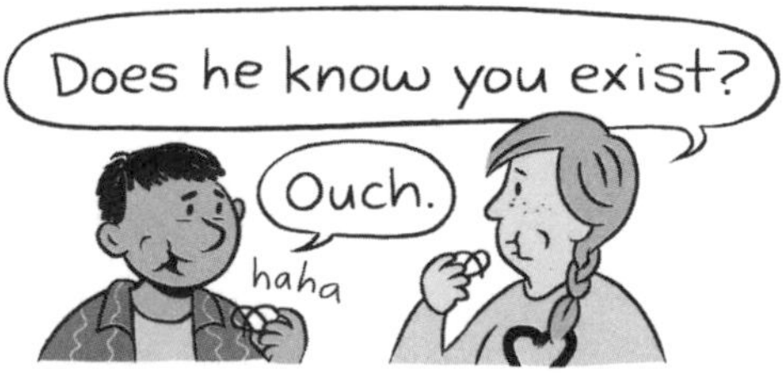
Does he know you exist?
Ouch.
haha

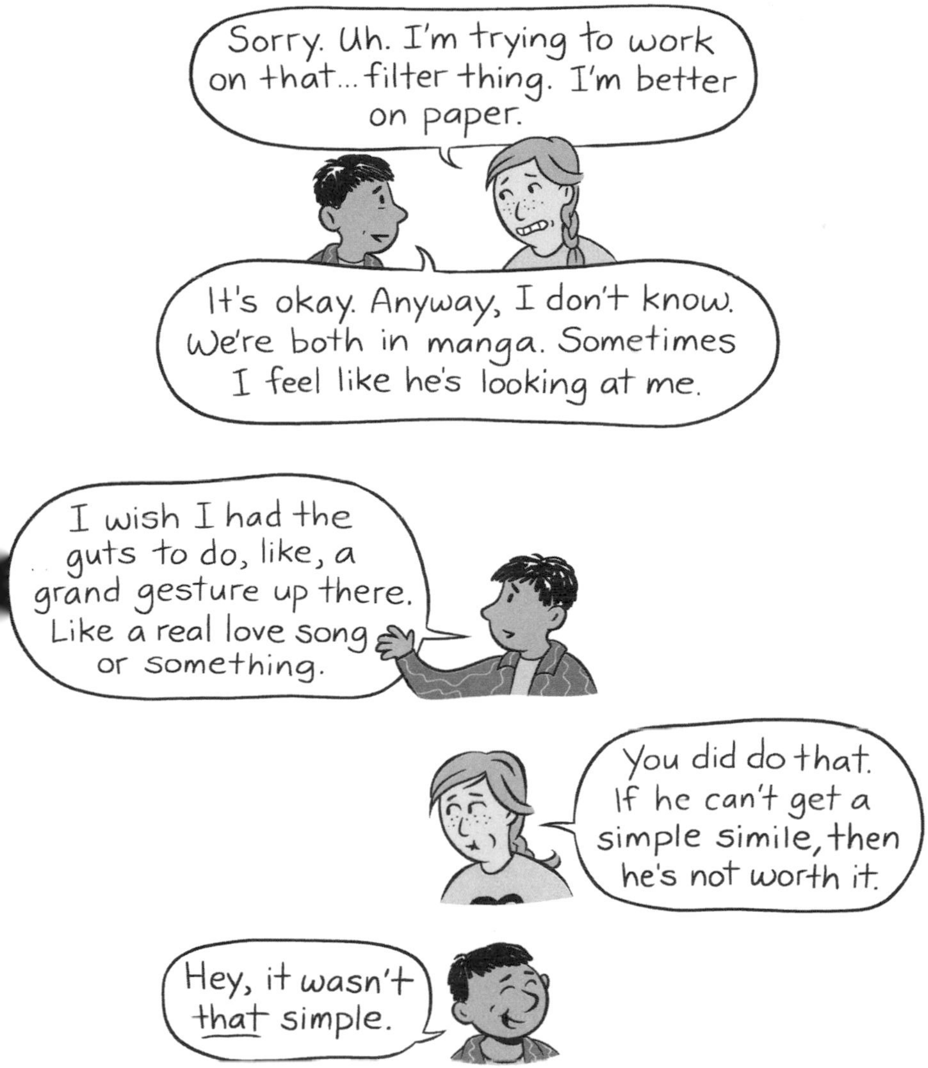
Sorry. Uh. I'm trying to work on that... filter thing. I'm better on paper.
It's okay. Anyway, I don't know. We're both in manga. Sometimes I feel like he's looking at me.
I wish I had the guts to do, like, a grand gesture up there. Like a real love song or something.
You did do that. If he can't get a simple simile, then he's not worth it.
Hey, it wasn't that simple.

We laugh.

I wonder if I'll ever crush on somebody. I haven't yet. I may be tall for my age, but I still feel like I'm back in elementary school compared to a lot of seventh graders.

LIKES:

← cartoons (or silly TV shows)

riding my bike →

DISLIKES:

smooch

→ romantic movies

"grown-up" food like asparagus and lentils ↘

smooch

↑ sappy couples

Well, except for writing. Mrs. Winn tells me my writing style is:

mature

After the show, we all head out. I wave bye to Juan. I live only a block away, so I start to walk home.

Hey, Ruby! Wait up.

What the heck? What does she want?

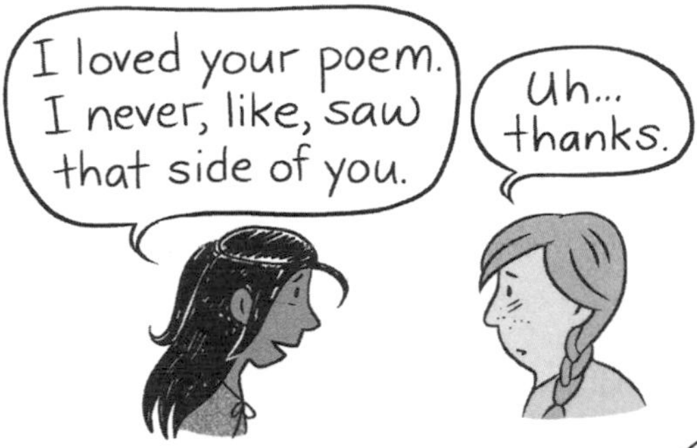
I loved your poem. I never, like, saw that side of you.
Uh... thanks.

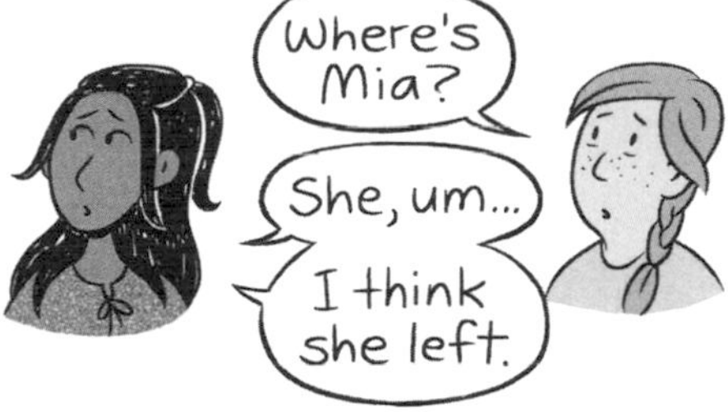
Where's Mia?
She, um...
I think she left.

Her voice trails off.

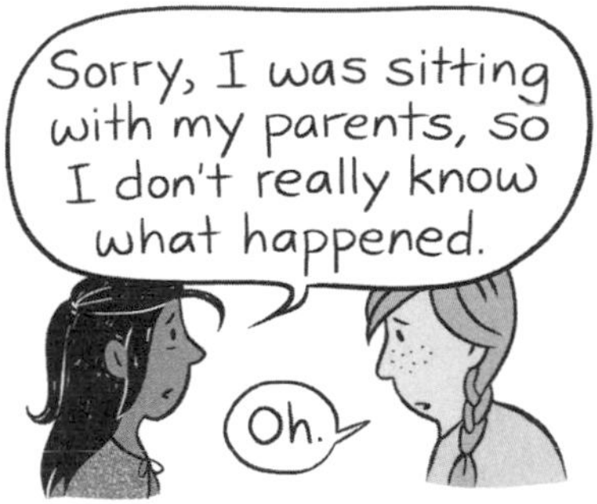
Sorry, I was sitting with my parents, so I don't really know what happened.
Oh.

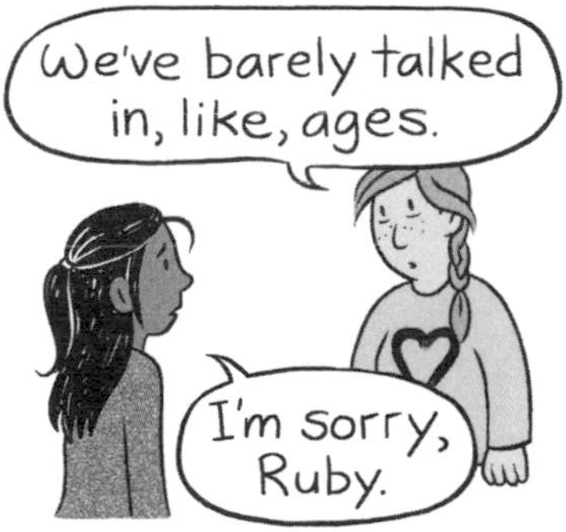
We've barely talked in, like, ages.
I'm sorry, Ruby.

There's kind of an uncomfortable silence.

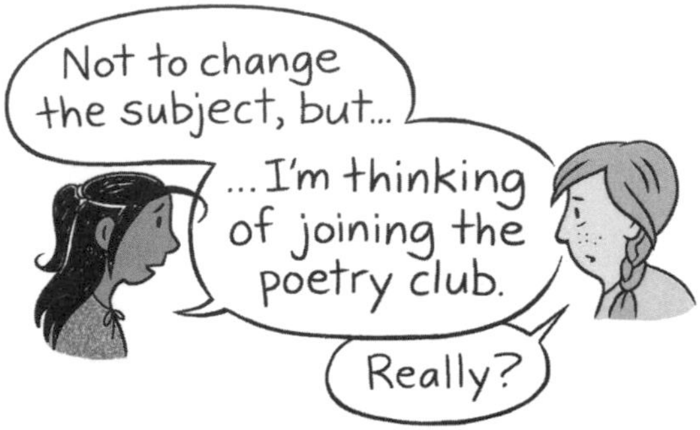
Not to change the subject, but...
...I'm thinking of joining the poetry club.
Really?

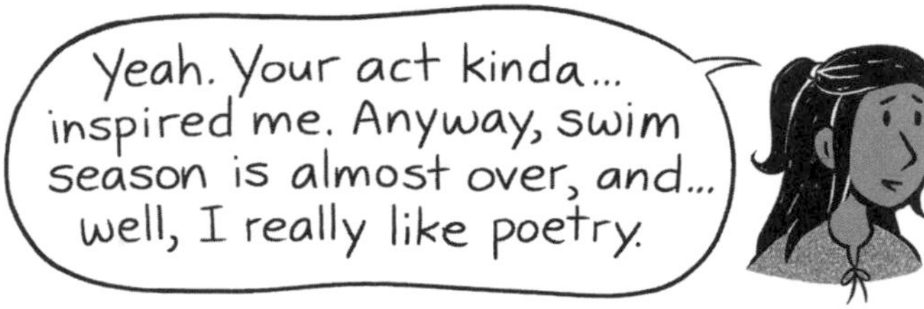
Yeah. Your act kinda... inspired me. Anyway, swim season is almost over, and... well, I really like poetry.

I remember Dev saying that. If I had been brave enough to ask her to join that day in the cafeteria, she might already be a member. But there was no way I was gonna approach her with Mia there (and all their friends).

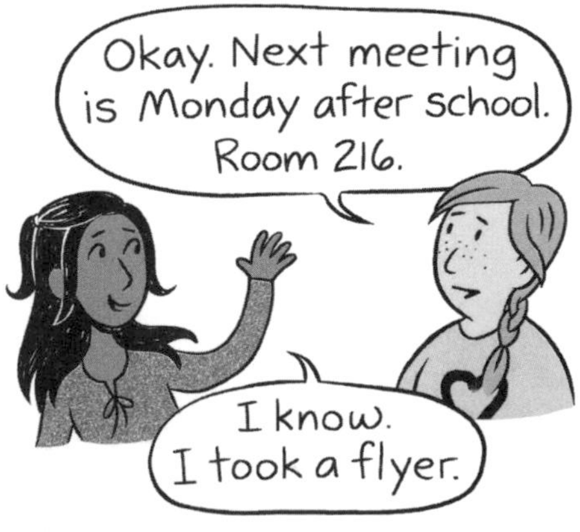
Okay. Next meeting is Monday after school. Room 216.
I know. I took a flyer.

She waves and heads back to the school.

I continue walking home, kinda sad and confused. Now I don't know if reciting that poem was worth it or not. I mean, on one hand it was, 'cause it proved that I'm good at slam poetry! It also got Keya to join the club.

But the main reason I did it was to try to . . . well . . . reach out and make things right, I guess. And that didn't work.

In fact . . .

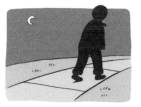

. . . I think it made everything worse.

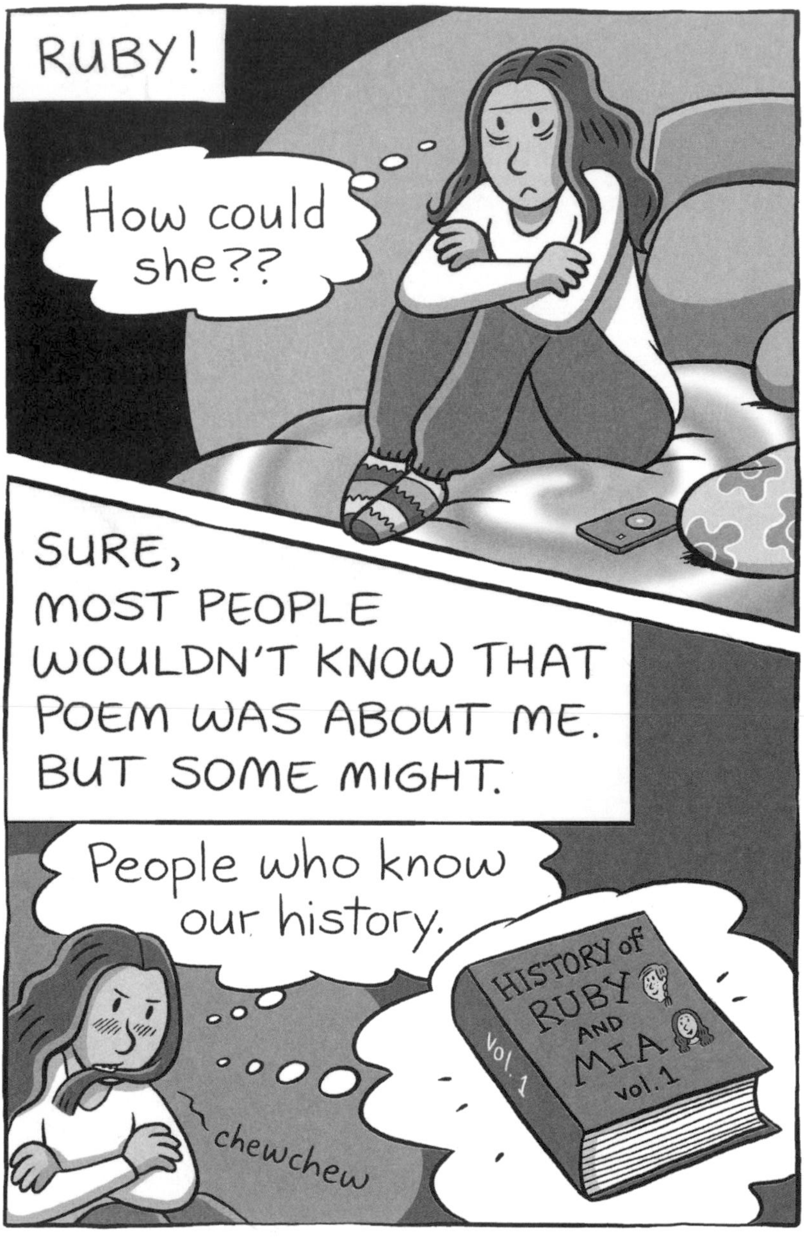
RUBY!
How could she??
SURE, MOST PEOPLE WOULDN'T KNOW THAT POEM WAS ABOUT ME. BUT SOME MIGHT.
People who know our history.
HISTORY of RUBY AND MIA vol. 1
Vol. 1
chewchew

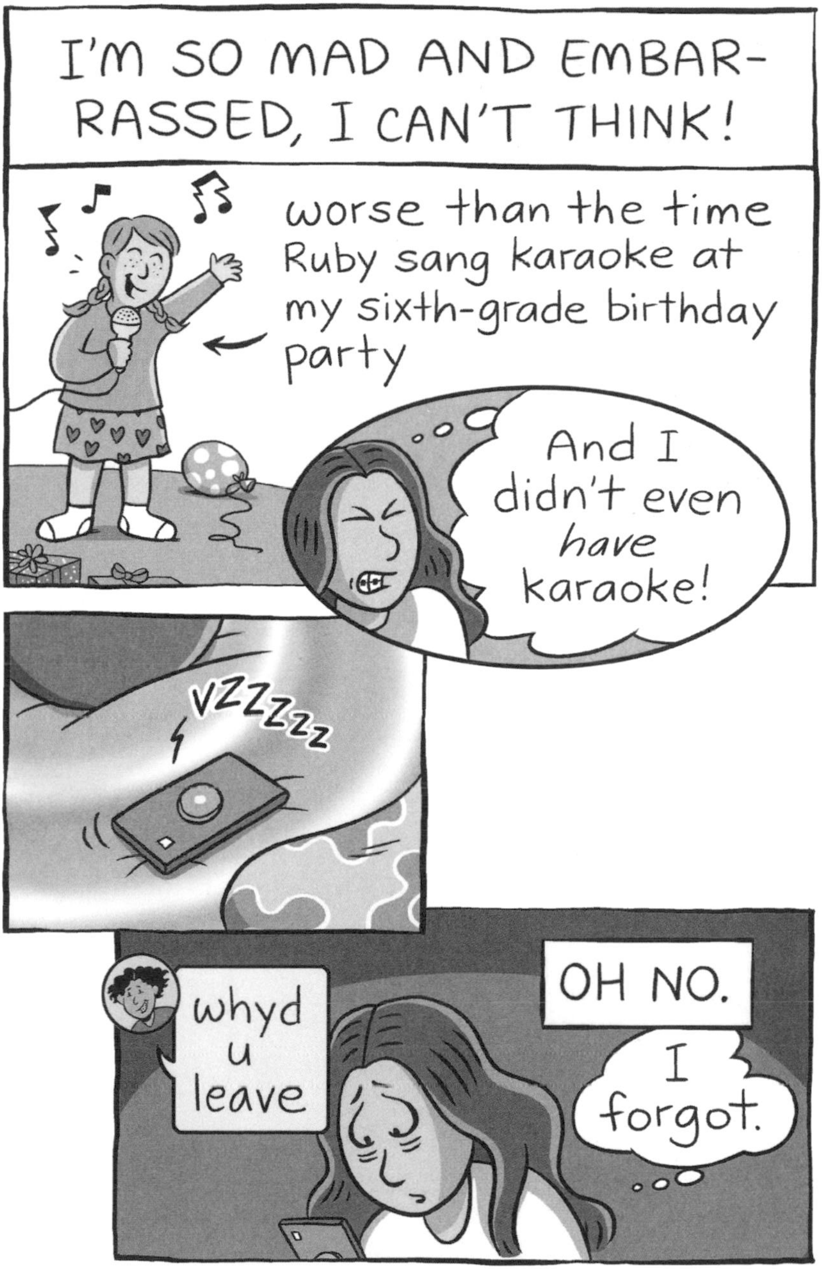
I'M SO MAD AND EMBARRASSED, I CAN'T THINK!
worse than the time Ruby sang karaoke at my sixth-grade birthday party
And I didn't even *have* karaoke!
VZZZzzz
whyd u leave
OH NO.
I forgot.

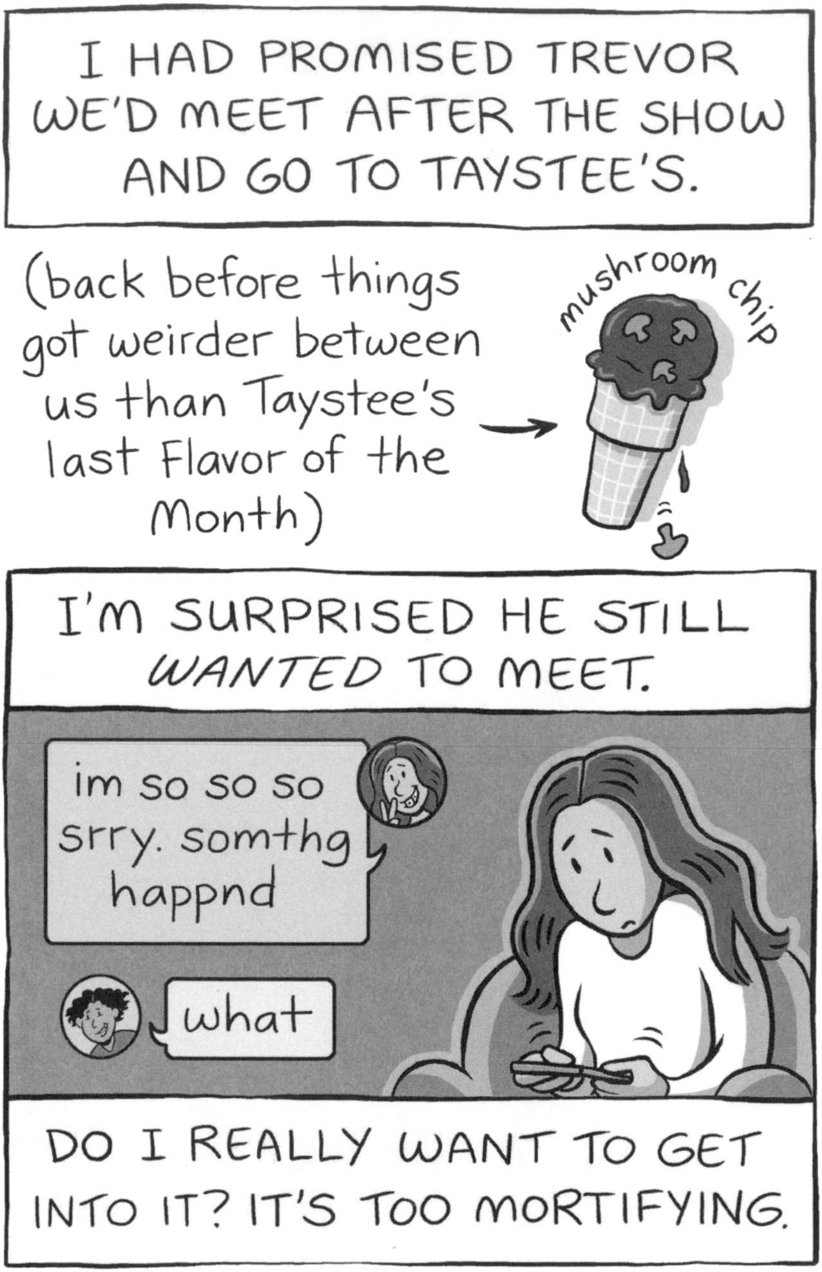
I HAD PROMISED TREVOR WE'D MEET AFTER THE SHOW AND GO TO TAYSTEE'S.
(back before things got weirder between us than Taystee's last Flavor of the Month)
mushroom chip
I'M SURPRISED HE STILL *WANTED* TO MEET.
im so so so srry. somthg happnd
what
DO I REALLY WANT TO GET INTO IT? IT'S TOO MORTIFYING.

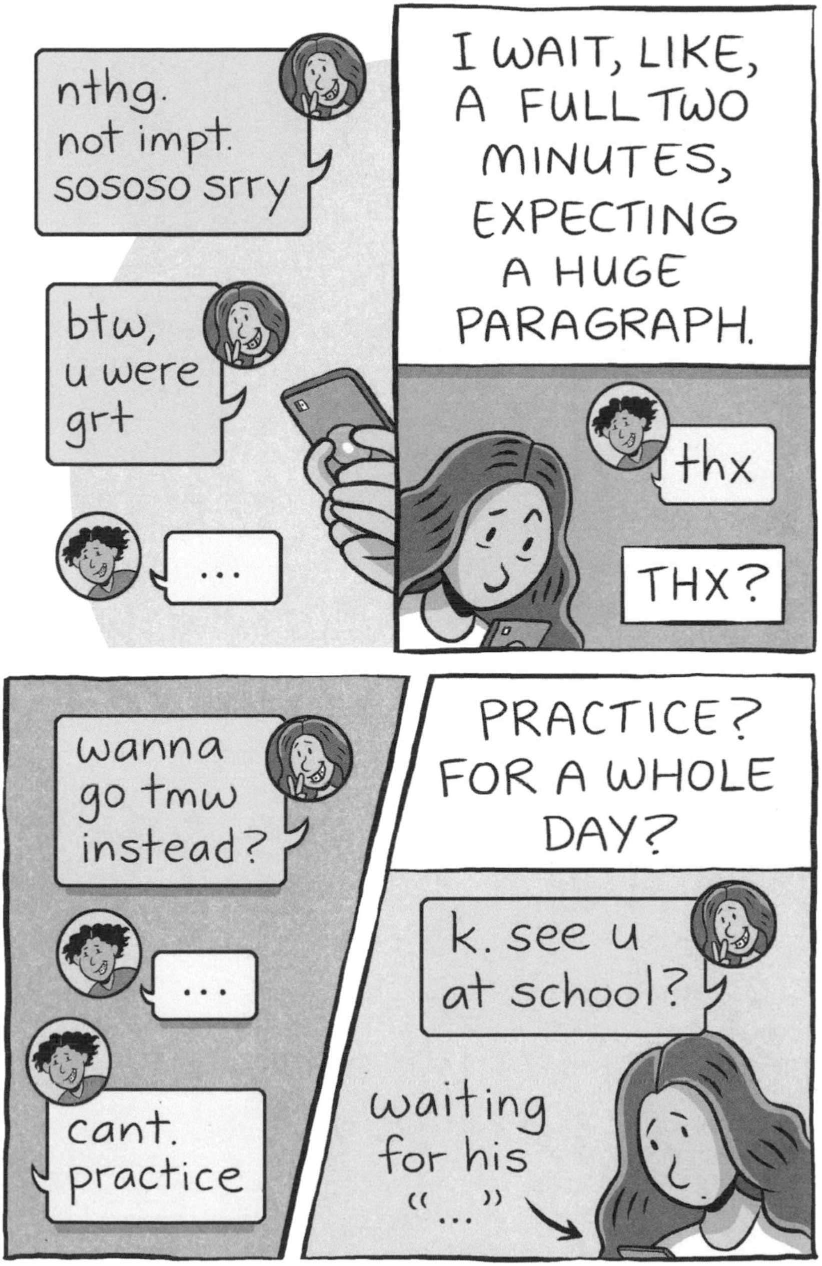
nthg.
not impt.
sososo srry
btw,
u were
grt
...
I WAIT, LIKE, A FULL TWO MINUTES, EXPECTING A HUGE PARAGRAPH.
thx
THX?
wanna
go tmw
instead?
...
cant.
practice
PRACTICE? FOR A WHOLE DAY?
k. see u
at school?
waiting
for his
"..."

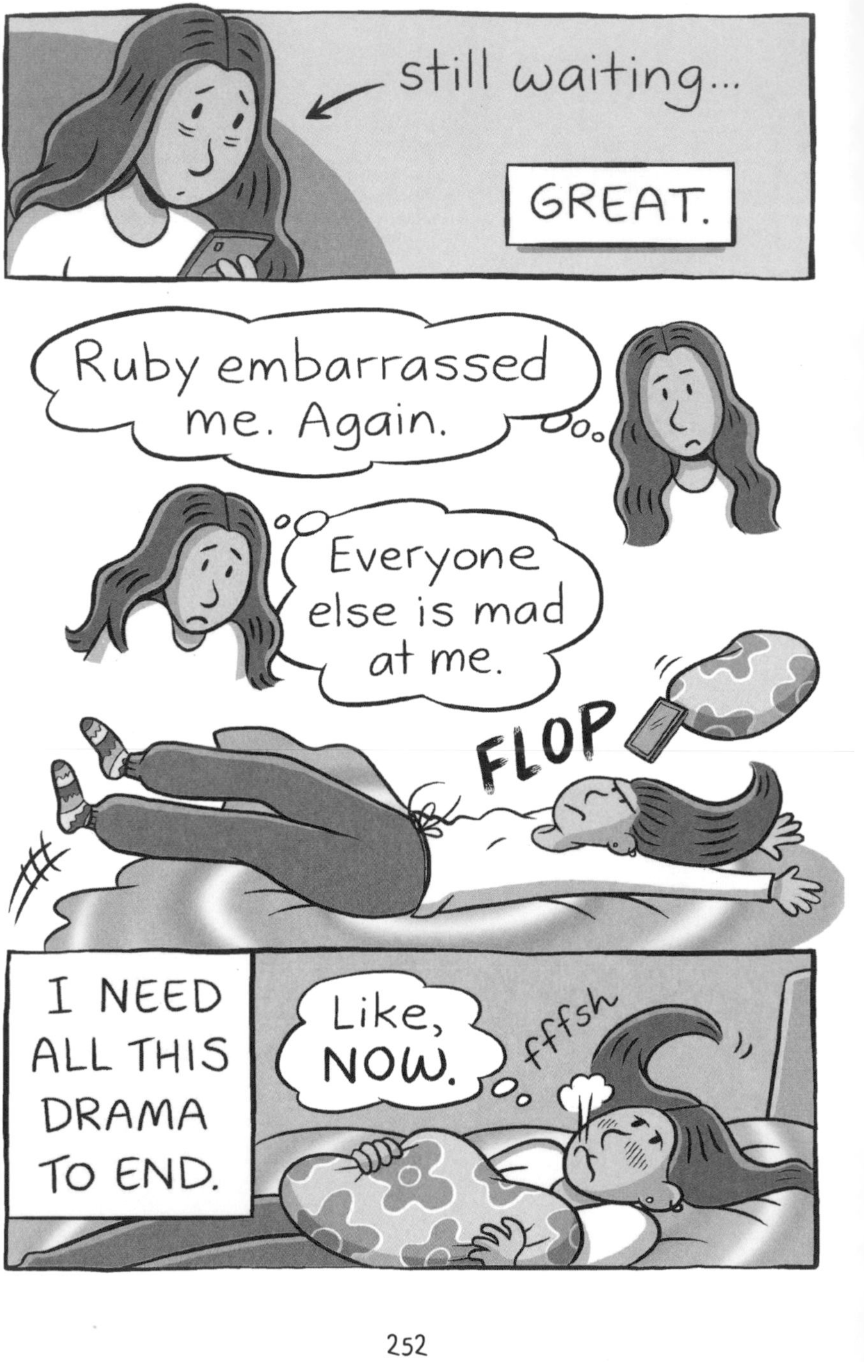
still waiting...
GREAT.
Ruby embarrassed me. Again.
Everyone else is mad at me.
FLOP
I NEED ALL THIS DRAMA TO END.
Like, NOW.
fffsh

RUBY

It all began when Mia started middle school.

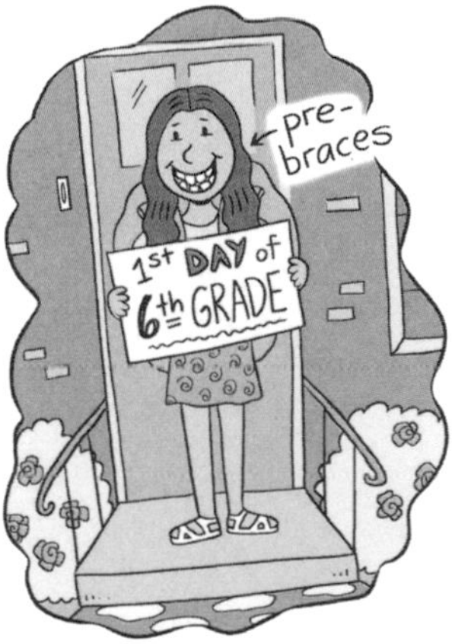
pre-
braces
1st DAY of
6th GRADE

I was in fifth grade—even though I looked about three grades older. (I'm really a year and a half younger, if you wanna get technical.) We were inseparable.

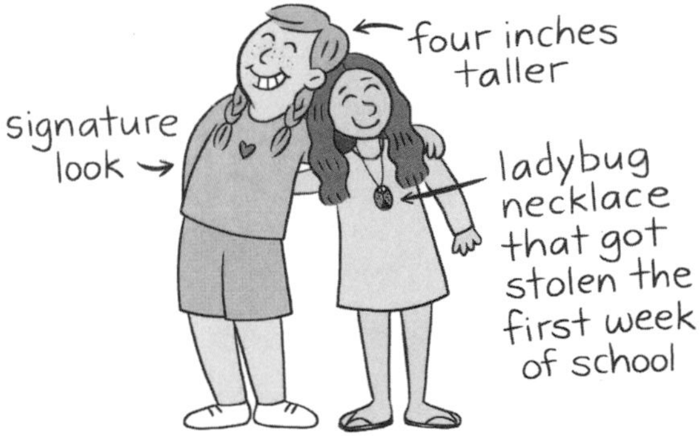
four inches
taller
signature
look
ladybug
necklace
that got
stolen the
first week
of school

She was a little nerdy but outgoing. And back then, she wasn't wound so tightly. Soon, she started making new friends and trying every activity known to humankind.

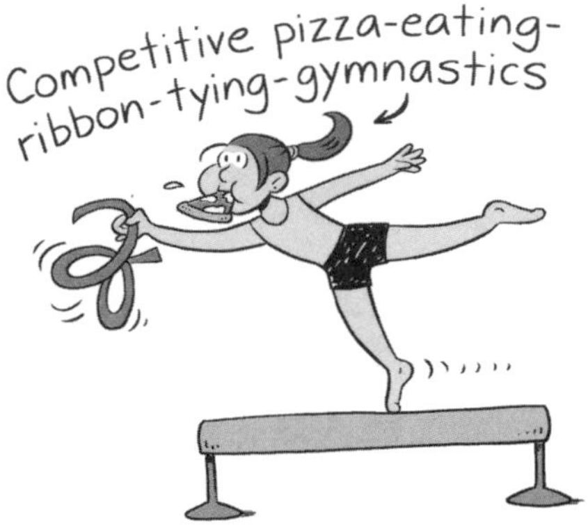
Competitive pizza-eating-ribbon-tying-gymnastics

She stuck it out with student council. She made "Citizenship Czar"* in seventh grade. Then she was elected treasurer for eighth.

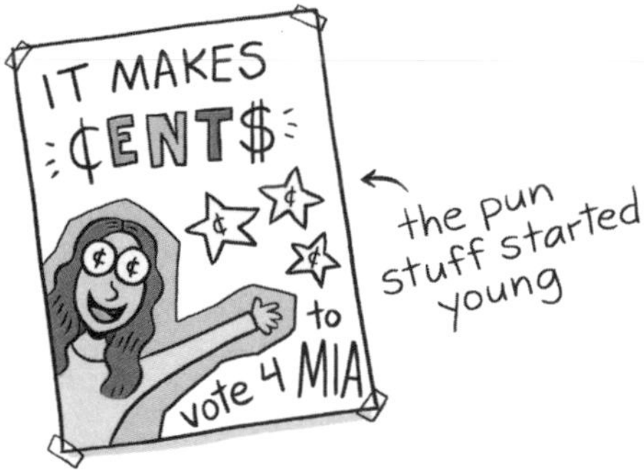
IT MAKES
¢ENT$
to
vote 4 MIA
the pun stuff started young

The hard part: her new friends were (way) more exciting, smarter, and popular than me.

*since changed to "Citizenship Champ" after Benji Sokolov's family complained

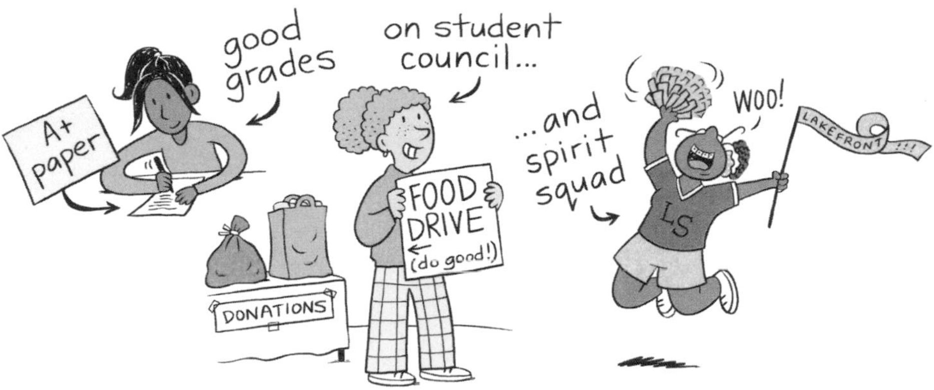
A+ paper
good grades
on student council...
FOOD DRIVE
(do good!)
DONATIONS
...and spirit squad
WOO!
LAKEFRONT !!!
LS

And they weren't . . . well, misfits.

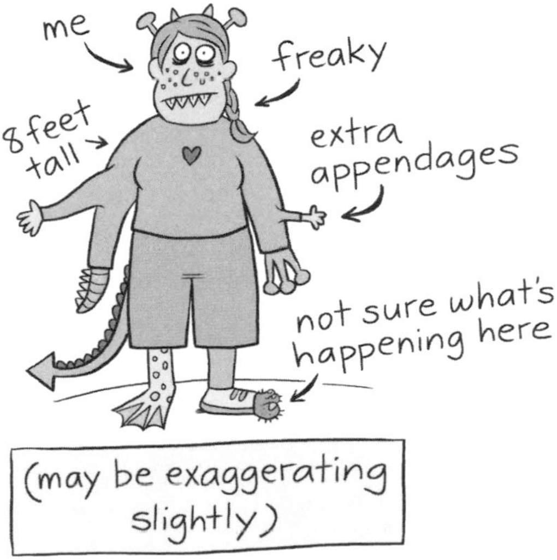
me
freaky
8 feet tall
extra appendages
not sure what's happening here
(may be exaggerating slightly)

Not that Mia ever said anything about that. Not to my face, anyway. But I knew I was holding her back. Especially once I got to middle school.

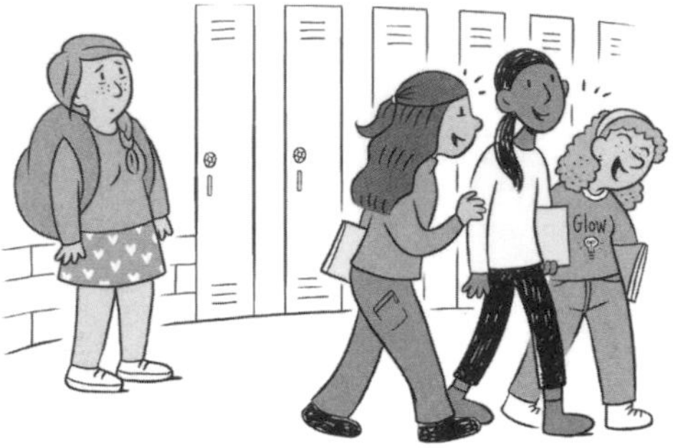
Glow

At first, she didn't totally ignore me or anything. We still hung out after school.

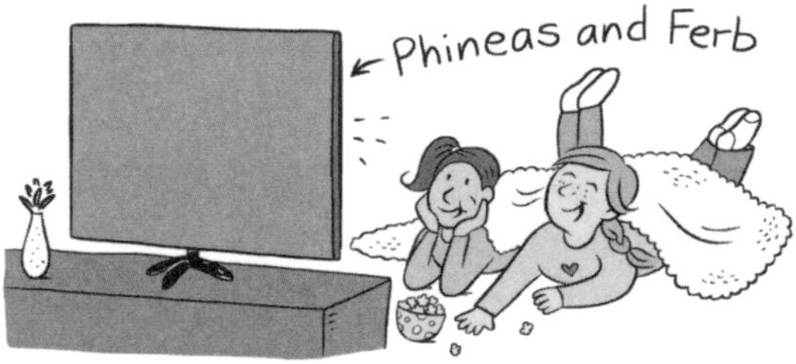
Phineas and Ferb

But I knew she was starting to get uncomfortable. And embarrassed. I didn't fit in with her idea of "popular" and "perfect."

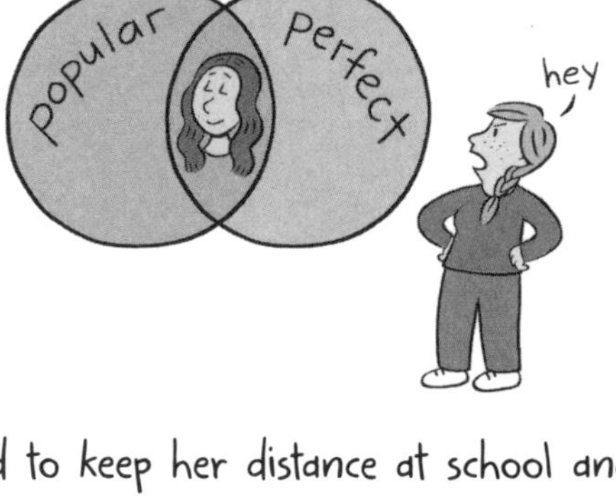
popular
perfect
hey

She started to keep her distance at school and pretend she didn't see me. Stuff like that. Later, if we were in public together, she'd make up these rules about what "we" should or shouldn't say.

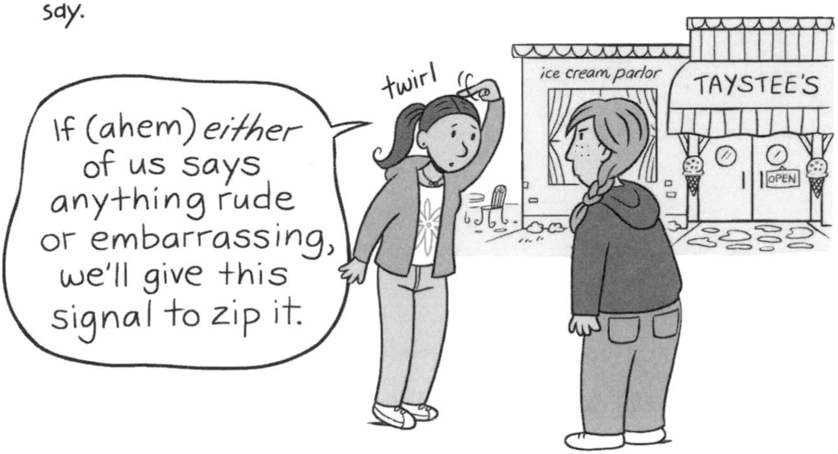

twirl
If (ahem) *either* of us says anything rude or embarrassing, we'll give this signal to zip it.
ice cream parlor
TAYSTEE'S
OPEN

The more uncomfortable she got, the madder I got.

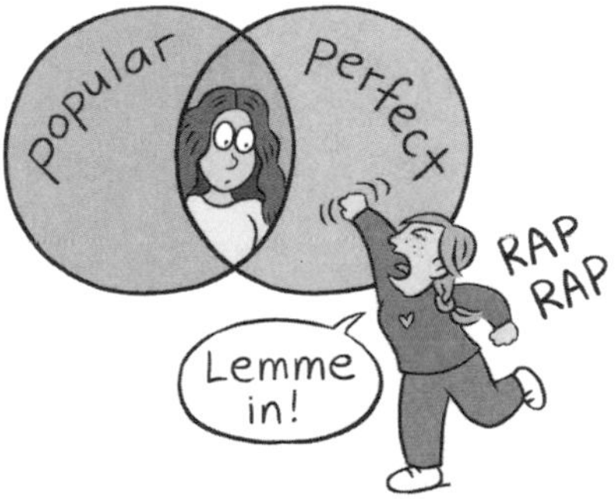

popular
perfect
RAP RAP
Lemme in!

Eventually, I started taking the hint and stopped hanging around her.

But somehow, even now, I don't wanna let go. Even though I do things to upset her. And even though she can seem so self-absorbed and shallow.

Maybe 'cause I know who she still is underneath. I know her

biggest secrets. I know that she kissed Rahul Patel in fourth grade (after he ate pepperoni pizza, yuck). I know that she once wore shredded jeans to camp and the director made her cover the holes with duct tape. I know she secretly did Minecraft until seventh grade. I know she once tried a cheap self-tanner, and when it turned her orange, she faked a cold and stayed home till it faded.

I know how she loves dried mangos, and old *Phineas and Ferb* cartoons, and holding her breath in the pool as long as she can (I had to call for the lifeguard once!), and old songs, and thrift stores, and Taystee's weirdest flavors (jalapeño, really?).

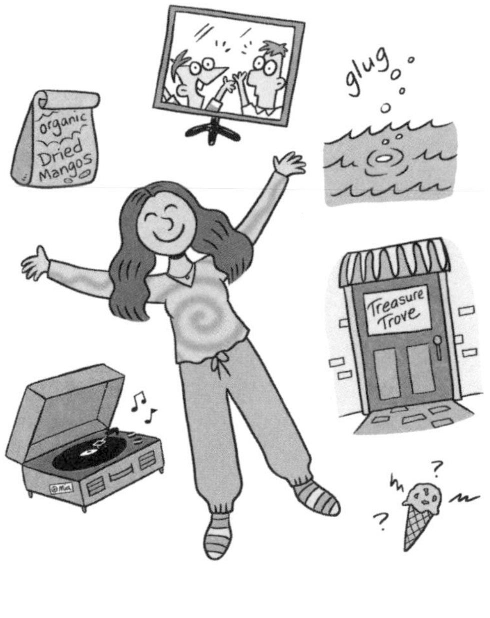
organic
Dried
Mangos
glug
Treasure
Trove

Maybe that's why I don't wanna let go.
Maybe that's why I did what I did at the talent show.

But . . . I'm finally realizing that even a personal poem I wrote and performed in front of everyone won't sway her.

That was my last-ditch effort.

It's really over.

Mia

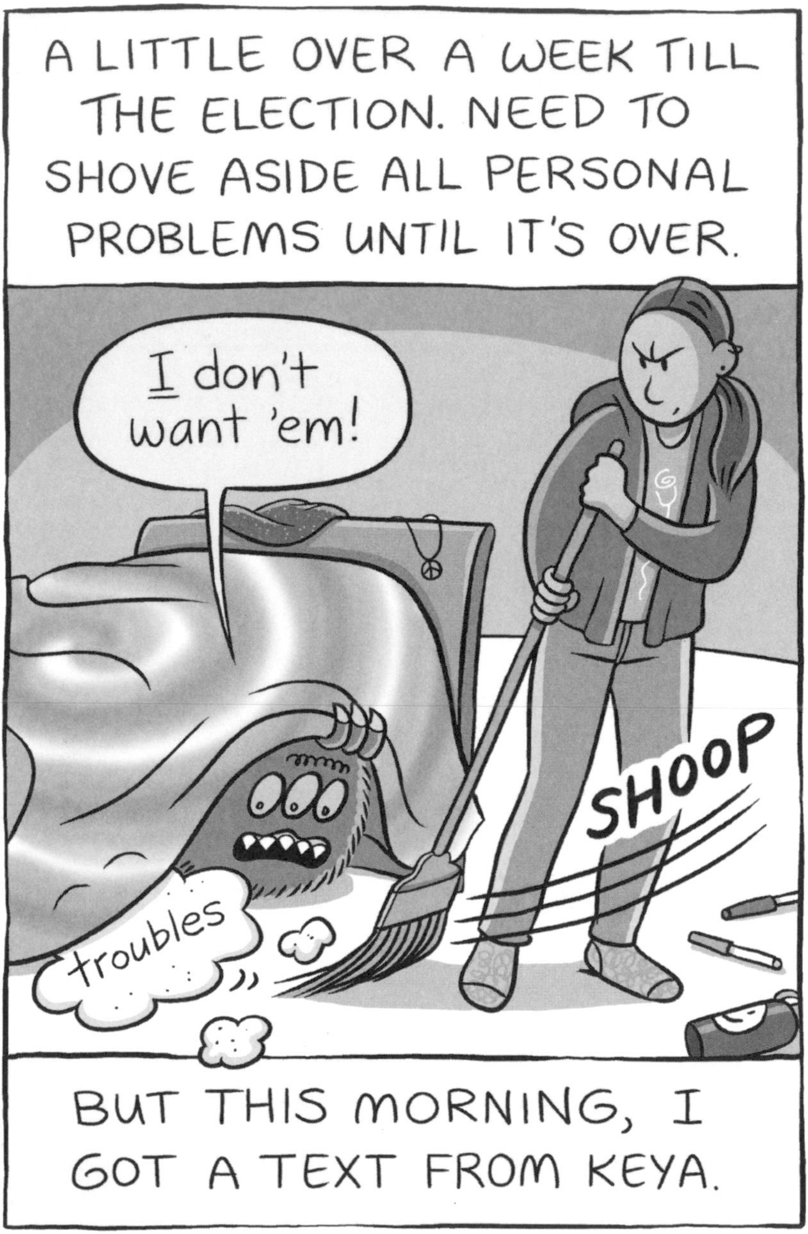
A LITTLE OVER A WEEK TILL THE ELECTION. NEED TO SHOVE ASIDE ALL PERSONAL PROBLEMS UNTIL IT'S OVER.
I don't want 'em!
SHOOP
troubles
BUT THIS MORNING, I GOT A TEXT FROM KEYA.

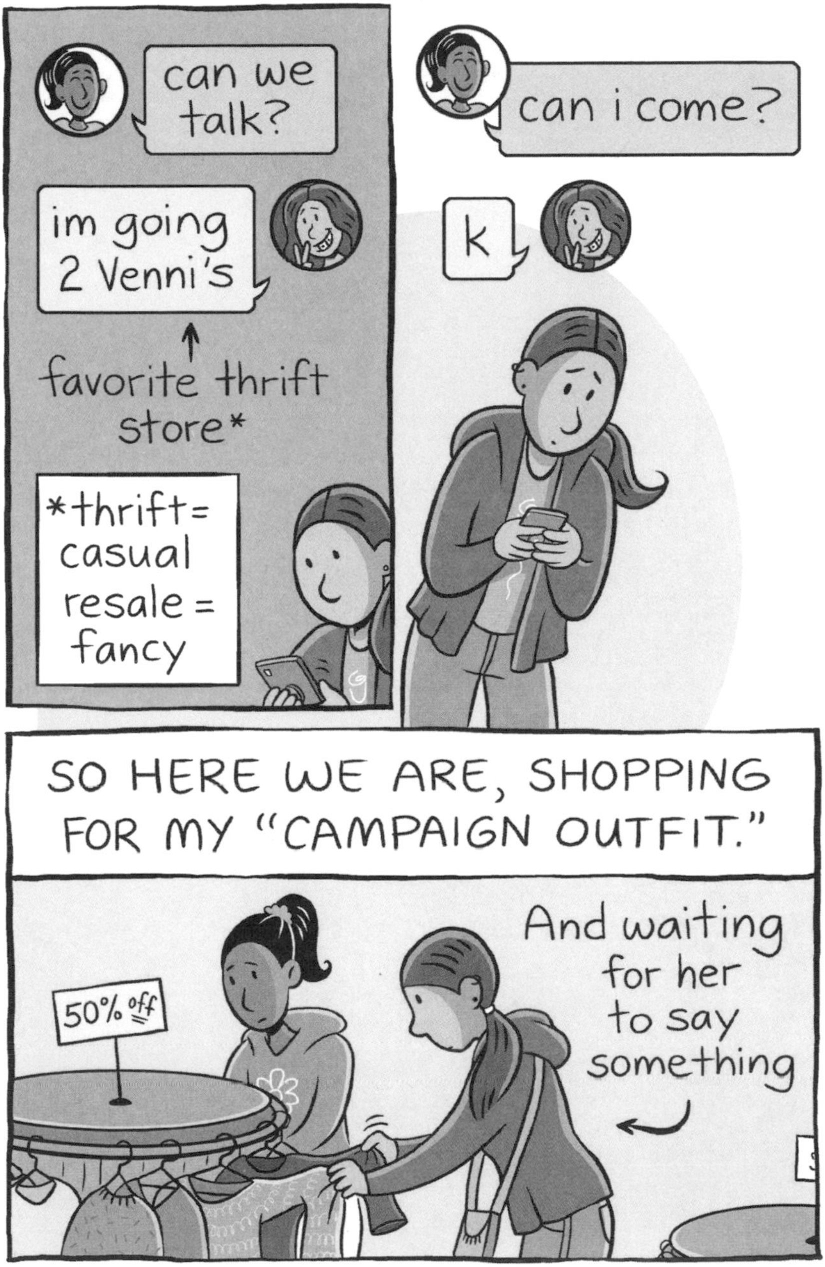
can we talk?
im going 2 Venni's
favorite thrift store*
*thrift= casual resale = fancy
can i come?
k
SO HERE WE ARE, SHOPPING FOR MY "CAMPAIGN OUTFIT."
50% off
And waiting for her to say something

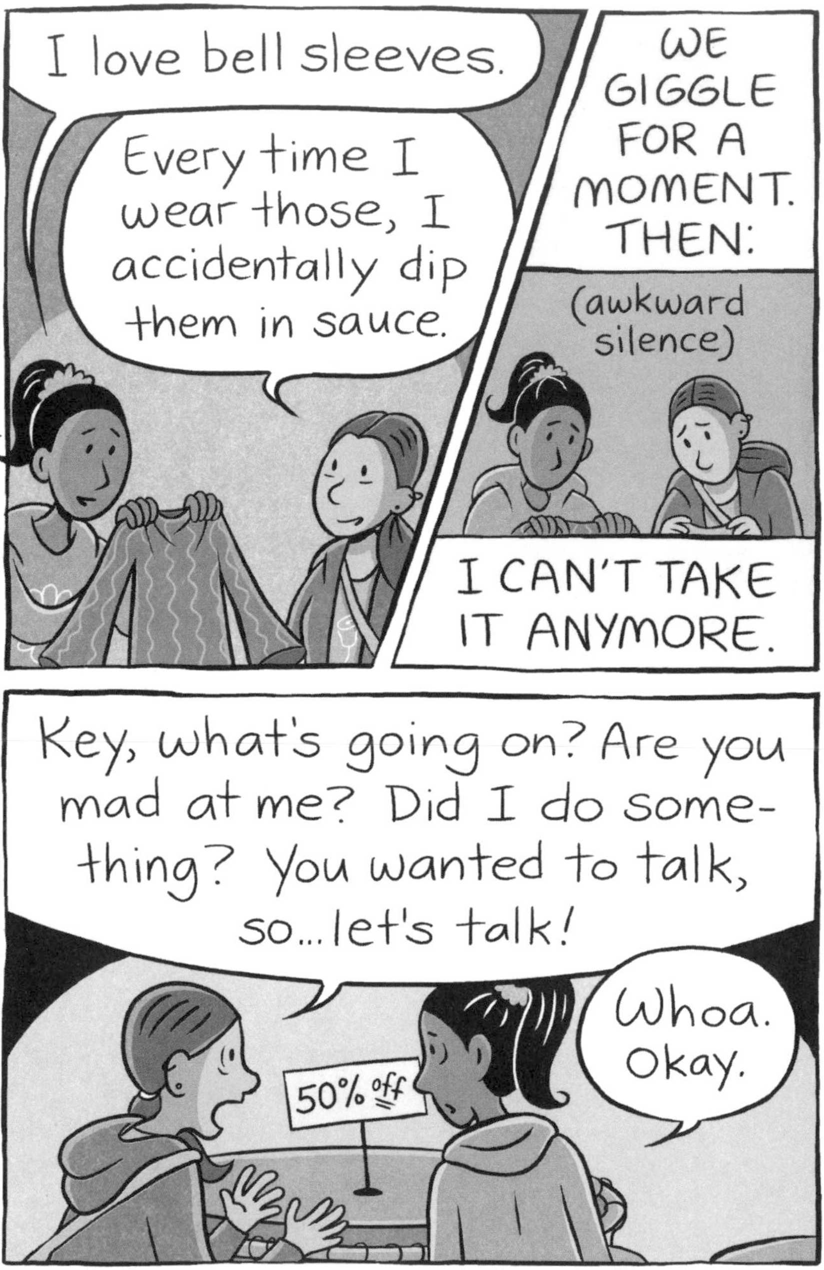
I love bell sleeves.
Every time I wear those, I accidentally dip them in sauce.
WE GIGGLE FOR A MOMENT. THEN:
(awkward silence)
I CAN'T TAKE IT ANYMORE.
Key, what's going on? Are you mad at me? Did I do something? You wanted to talk, so...let's talk!
50% off
Whoa. Okay.

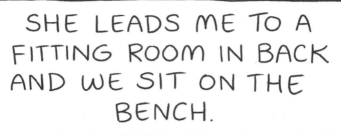

SHE LEADS ME TO A FITTING ROOM IN BACK AND WE SIT ON THE BENCH.

curtains that never fully close

(smells like old shoes and scented candles)

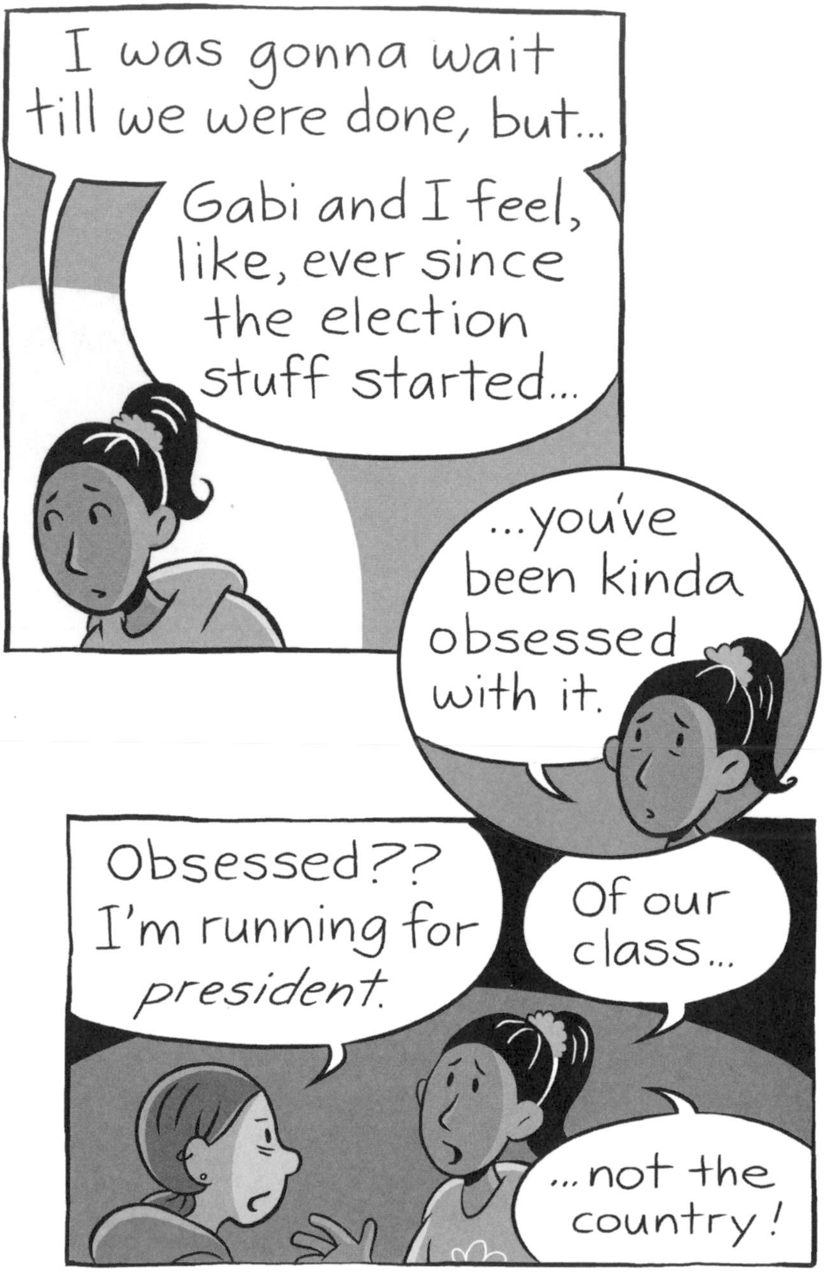
I was gonna wait till we were done, but...
Gabi and I feel, like, ever since the election stuff started...
...you've been kinda obsessed with it.
Obsessed?? I'm running for *president*.
Of our class...
...not the country!

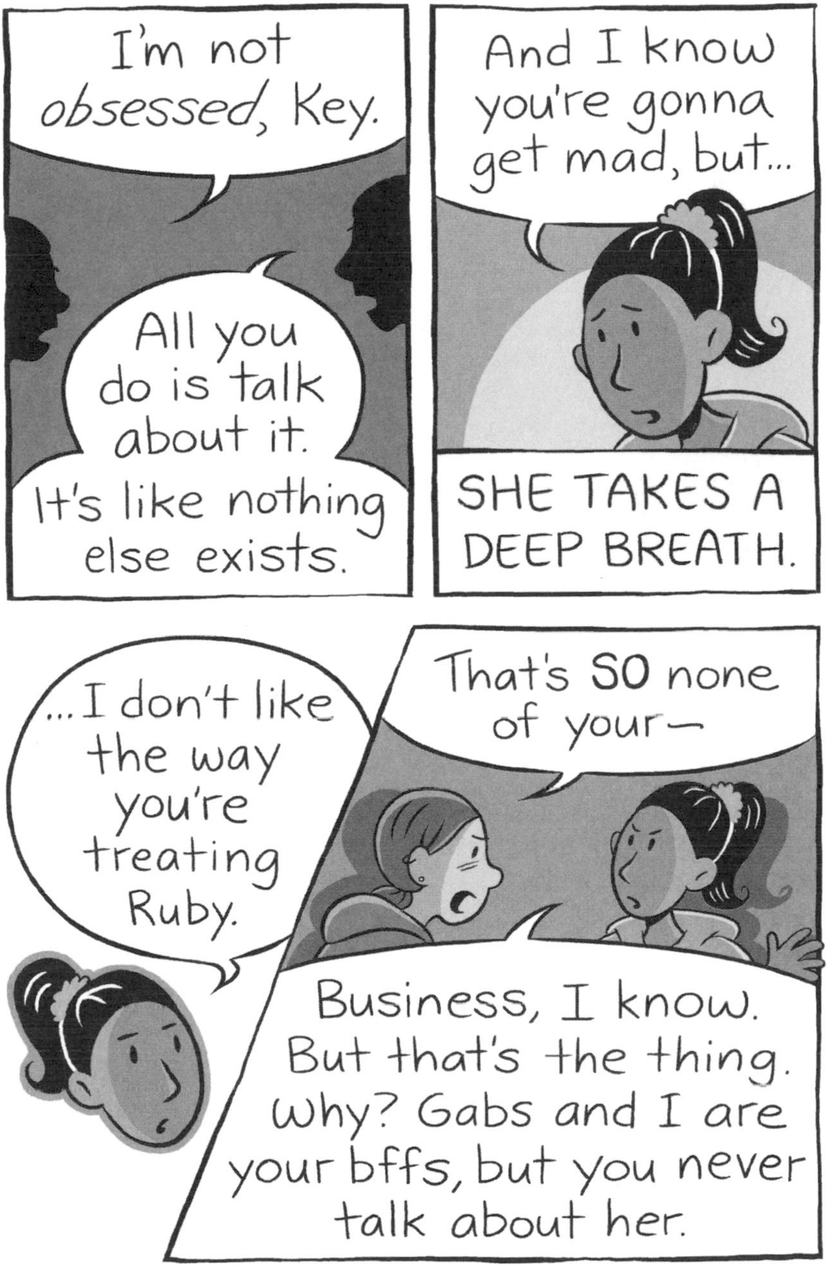
I'm not *obsessed*, Key.
All you do is talk about it.
It's like nothing else exists.
And I know you're gonna get mad, but...
SHE TAKES A DEEP BREATH.
...I don't like the way you're treating Ruby.
That's **SO** none of your—
Business, I know. But that's the thing. Why? Gabs and I are your bffs, but you never talk about her.

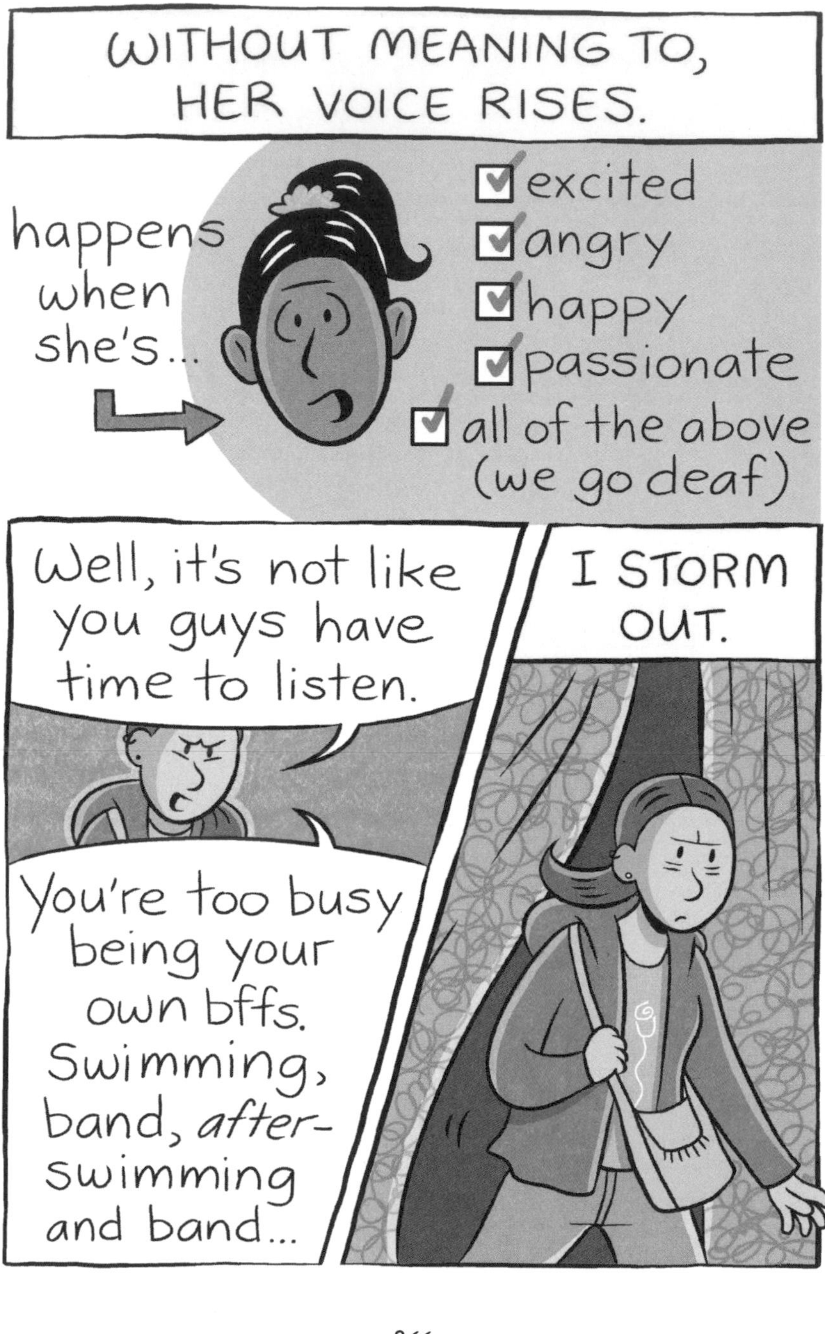
WITHOUT MEANING TO, HER VOICE RISES.
happens when she's...
excited
angry
happy
passionate
all of the above (we go deaf)
Well, it's not like you guys have time to listen.
You're too busy being your own bffs. Swimming, band, *after*-swimming and band...
I STORM OUT.

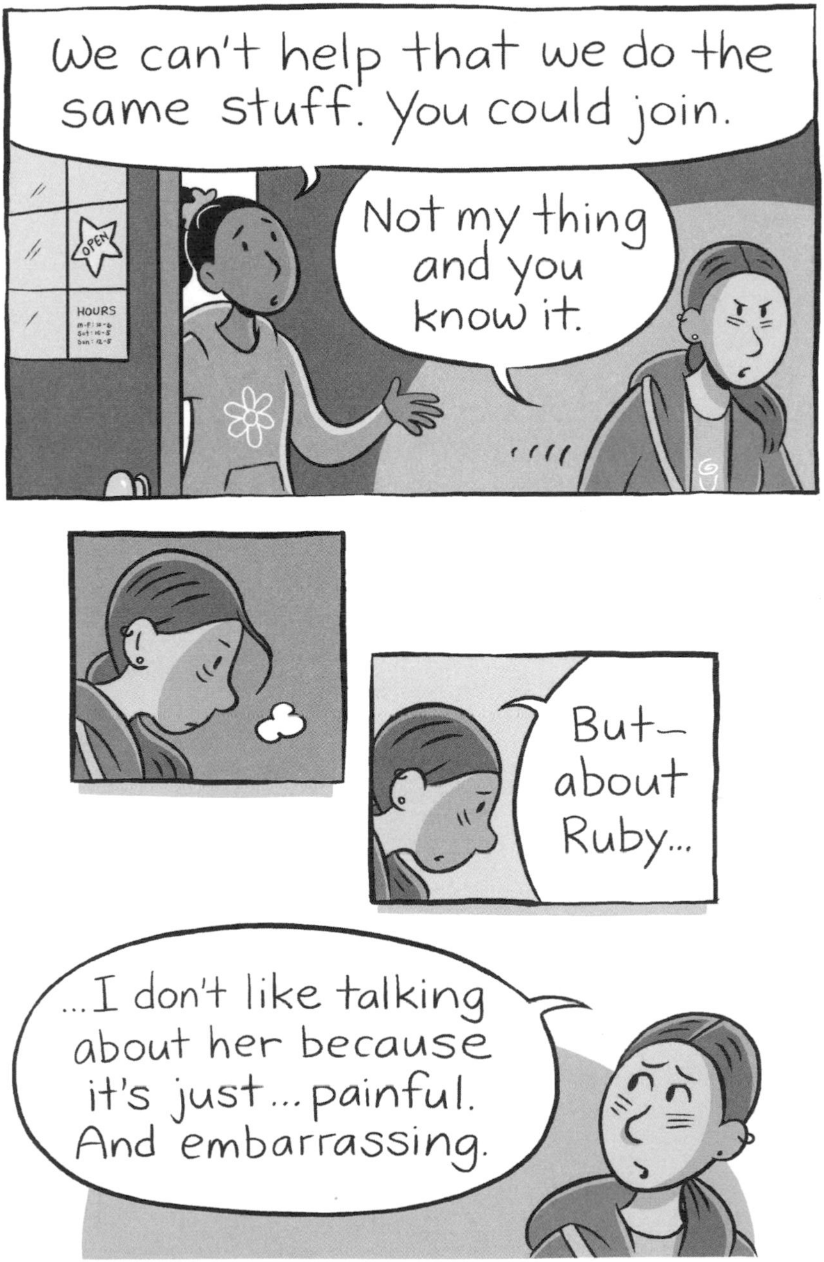
We can't help that we do the same stuff. You could join.
OPEN
HOURS
Not my thing and you know it.
But— about Ruby...
...I don't like talking about her because it's just... painful. And embarrassing.

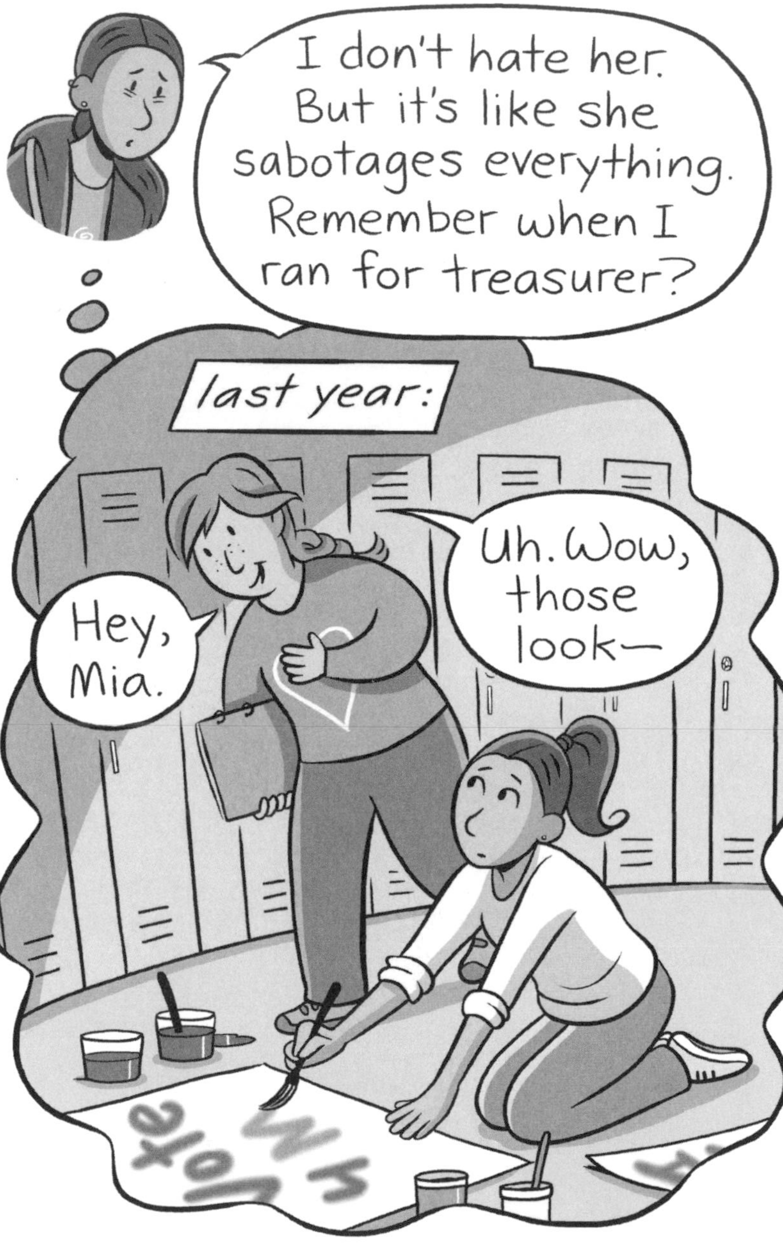
I don't hate her. But it's like she sabotages everything. Remember when I ran for treasurer?
last year:
Hey, Mia.
Uh. Wow, those look—

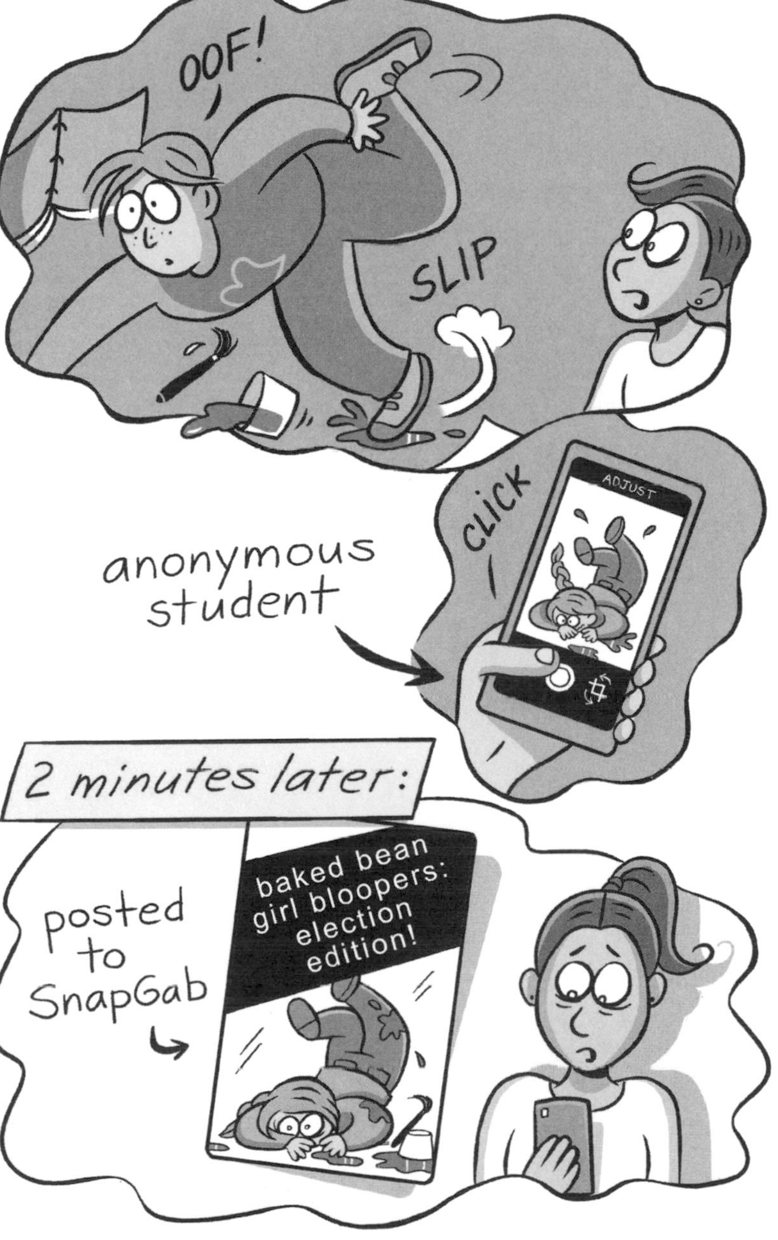
OOF!
SLIP
CLICK
ADJUST
anonymous student
2 minutes later:
posted to SnapGab
baked bean girl bloopers: election edition!

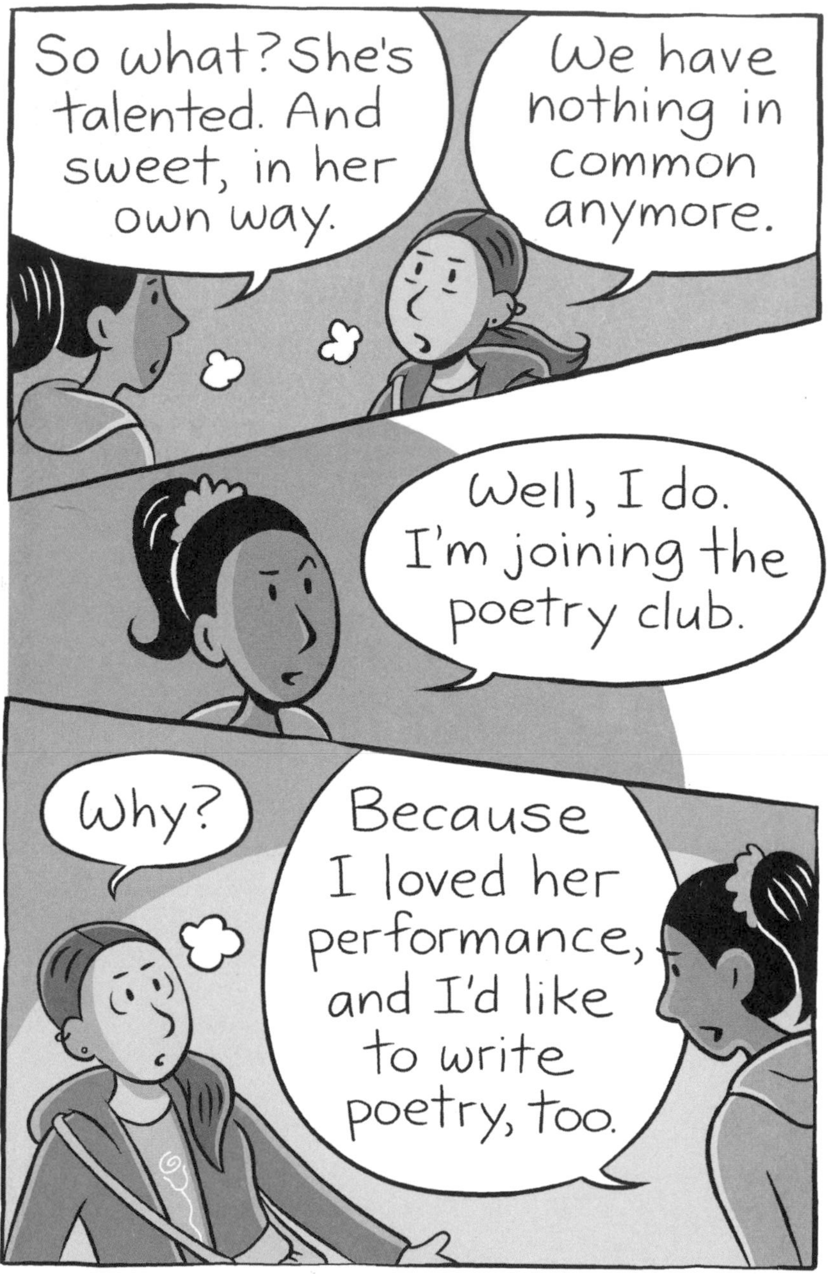

So what? She's talented. And sweet, in her own way.
We have nothing in common anymore.
Well, I do. I'm joining the poetry club.
Why?
Because I loved her performance, and I'd like to write poetry, too.

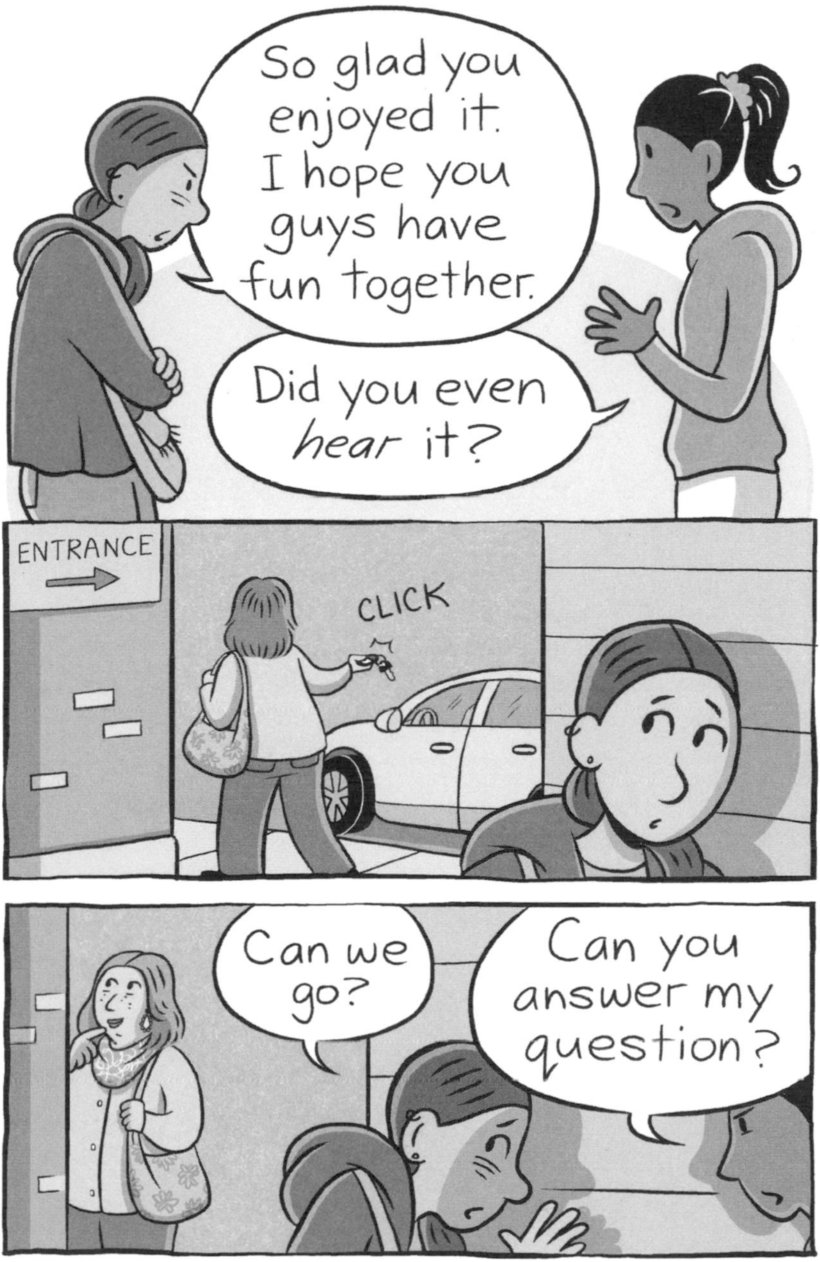
So glad you enjoyed it. I hope you guys have fun together.
Did you even *hear* it?
ENTRANCE
CLICK
Can we go?
Can you answer my question?

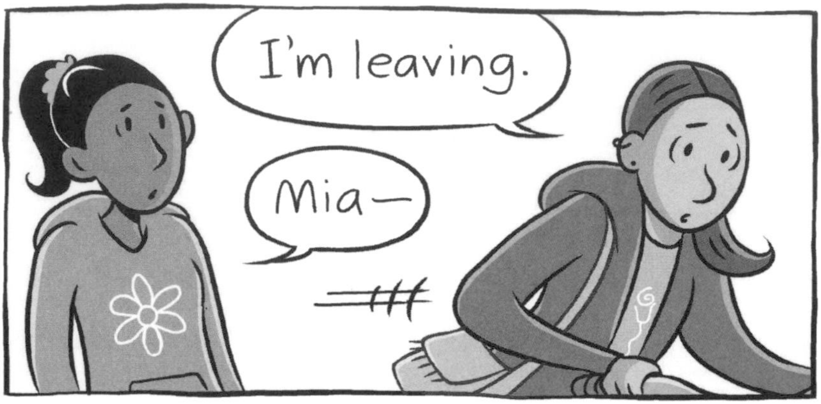
I'm leaving.
Mia—

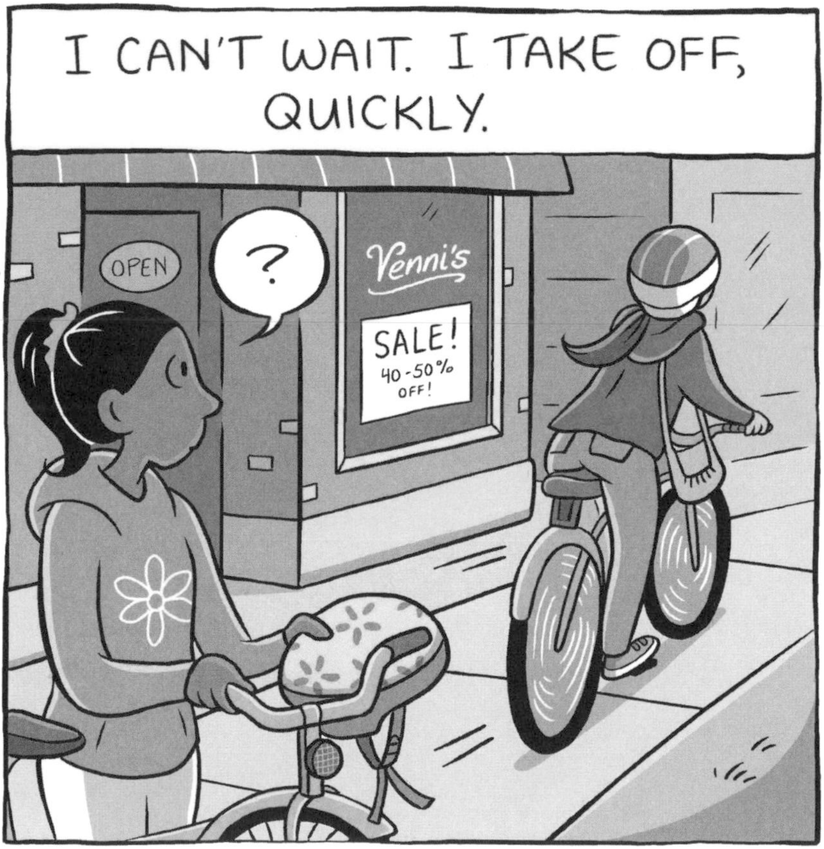
I CAN'T WAIT. I TAKE OFF, QUICKLY.
OPEN
?
Venni's
SALE!
40-50% OFF!

RUBY

Monday. Poetry club.

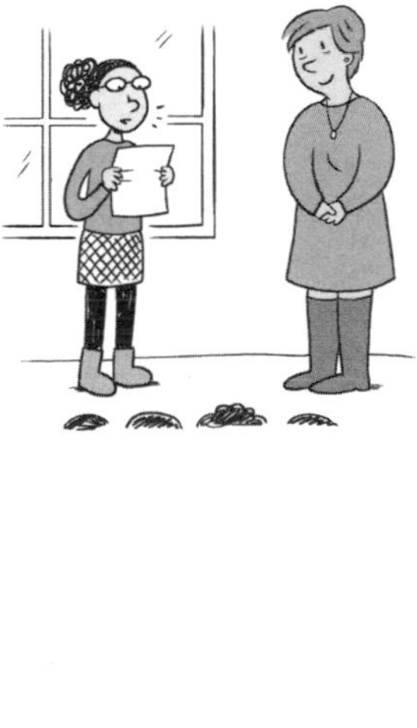

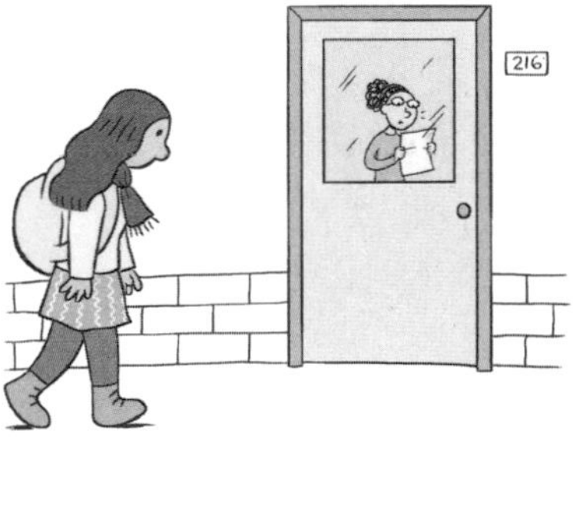
216

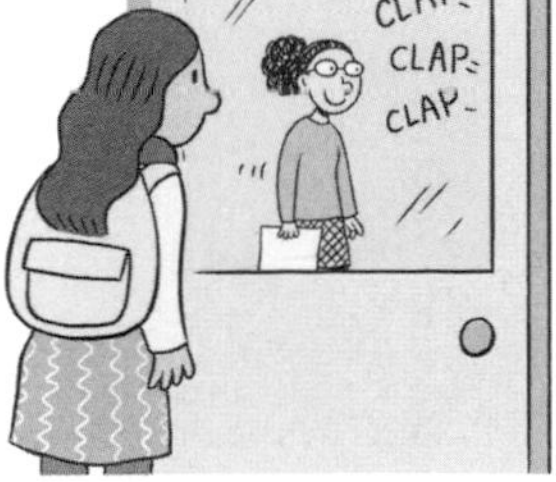
CLAP
CLAP
CLAP

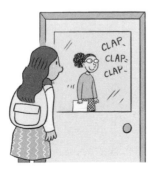

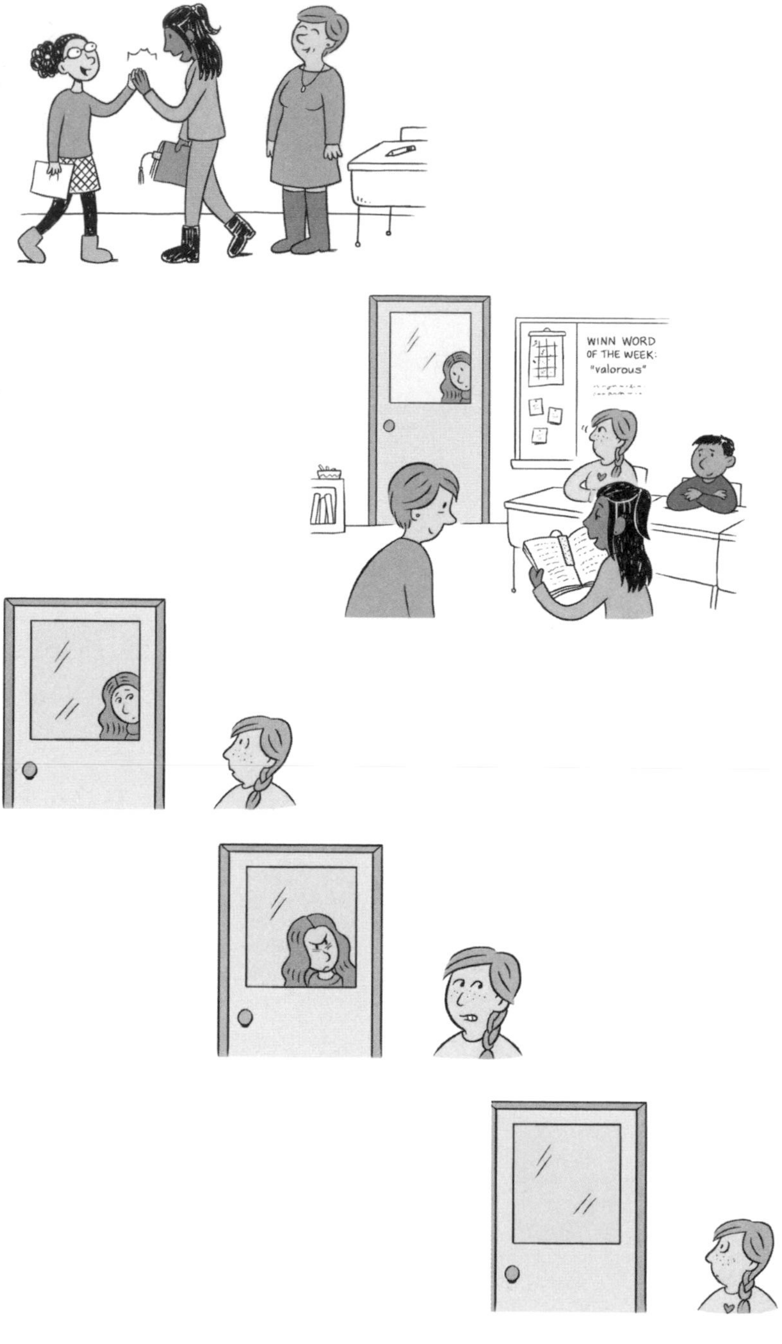
WINN WORD
OF THE WEEK:
"valorous"

There it is.

Proof that Mia is mad at me. More than "silent treatment" mad. She hates me.

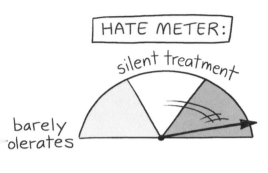

HATE METER:

silent treatment

barely tolerates

wants me banished to a desert island— surrounded by jellyfish and sharks

I try to get her out of my mind. I go back to listening to Keya. Since it's her first meeting, I don't know how good she is at writing poetry, but she sure loves reading it. And listening to ours. She laughed at a funny rap Juan and I made up about smelly armpits. Mrs. Winn laughed, too, even though she looked like she wanted to throw up.

glurgh

This month of poetry club has been, like, the best month of my middle school life. I can't believe I didn't want to do it at first. It seems like a thousand years since I felt like I belonged anywhere.

But now Mia is making me feel bad about it.

Not only is she mad about the talent show, but it's obvious she's mad that Keya joined poetry. As if I stole her friend.

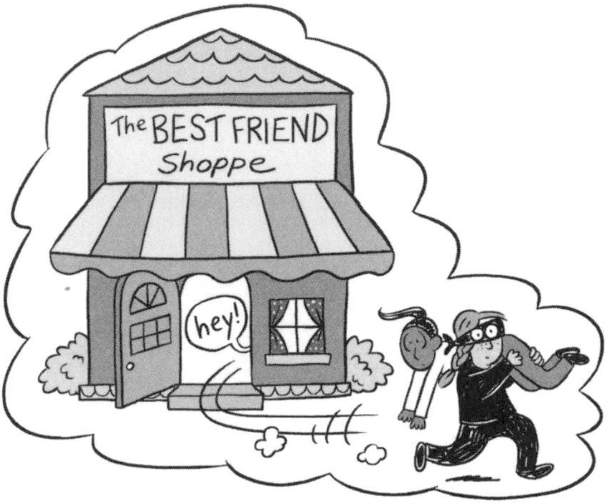
The BEST FRIEND Shoppe
hey!

Well, she can be that way. But I'm not giving up any friends. She's gonna have to share.

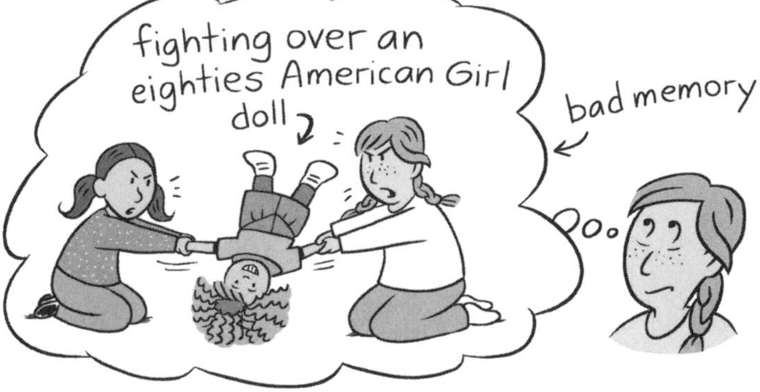
fighting over an eighties American Girl doll
bad memory

We'll see how that goes.

Mia

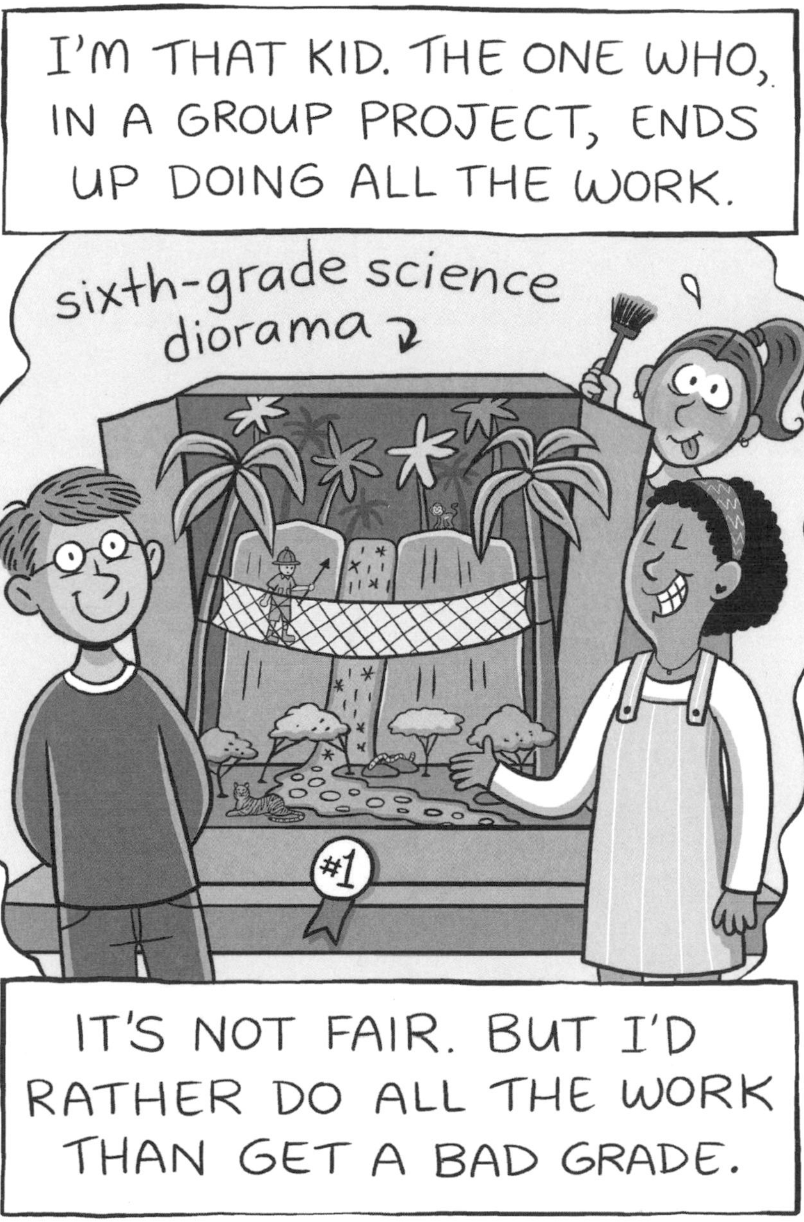
I'M THAT KID. THE ONE WHO, IN A GROUP PROJECT, ENDS UP DOING ALL THE WORK.
sixth-grade science diorama
#1
IT'S NOT FAIR. BUT I'D RATHER DO ALL THE WORK THAN GET A BAD GRADE.

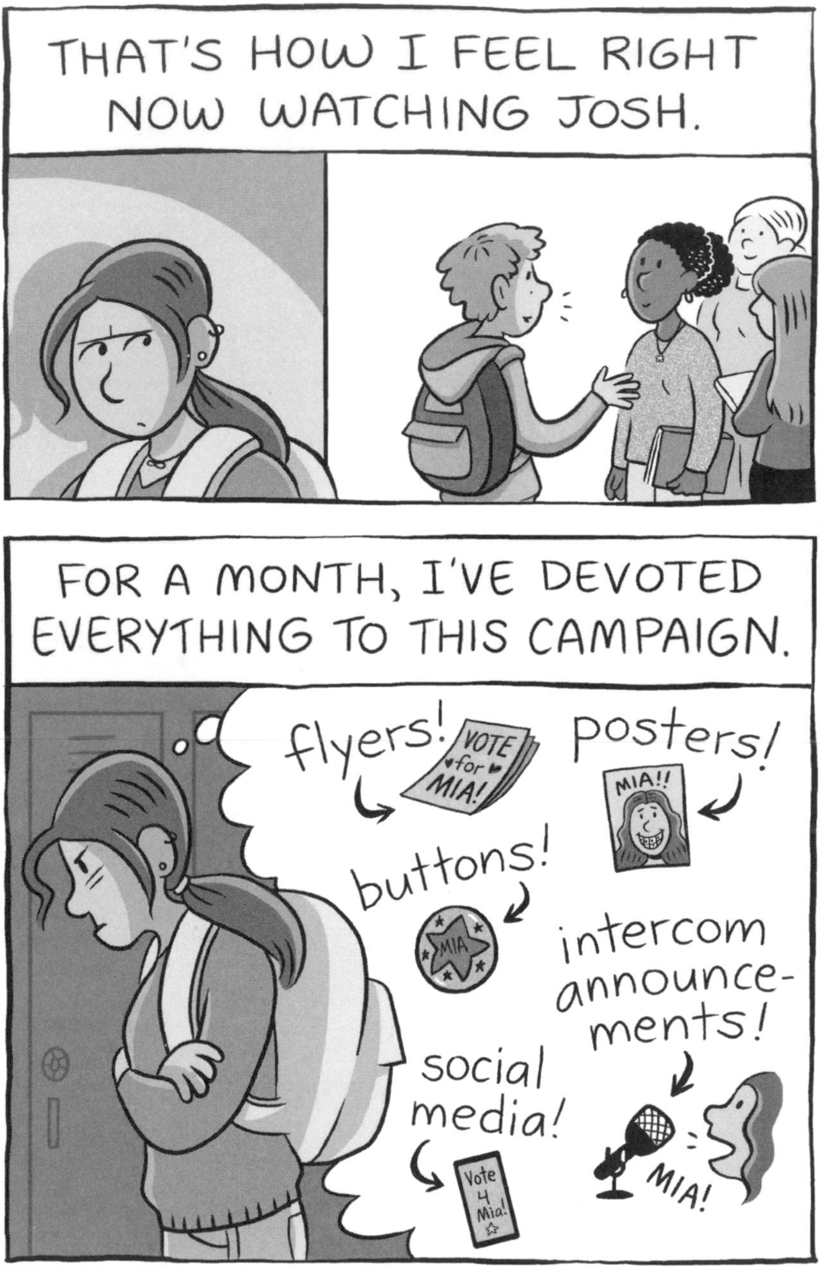
THAT'S HOW I FEEL RIGHT NOW WATCHING JOSH.
FOR A MONTH, I'VE DEVOTED EVERYTHING TO THIS CAMPAIGN.
flyers!
VOTE for MIA!
posters!
MIA!!
buttons!
MIA
intercom announce-ments!
social media!
Vote 4 Mia!
MIA!

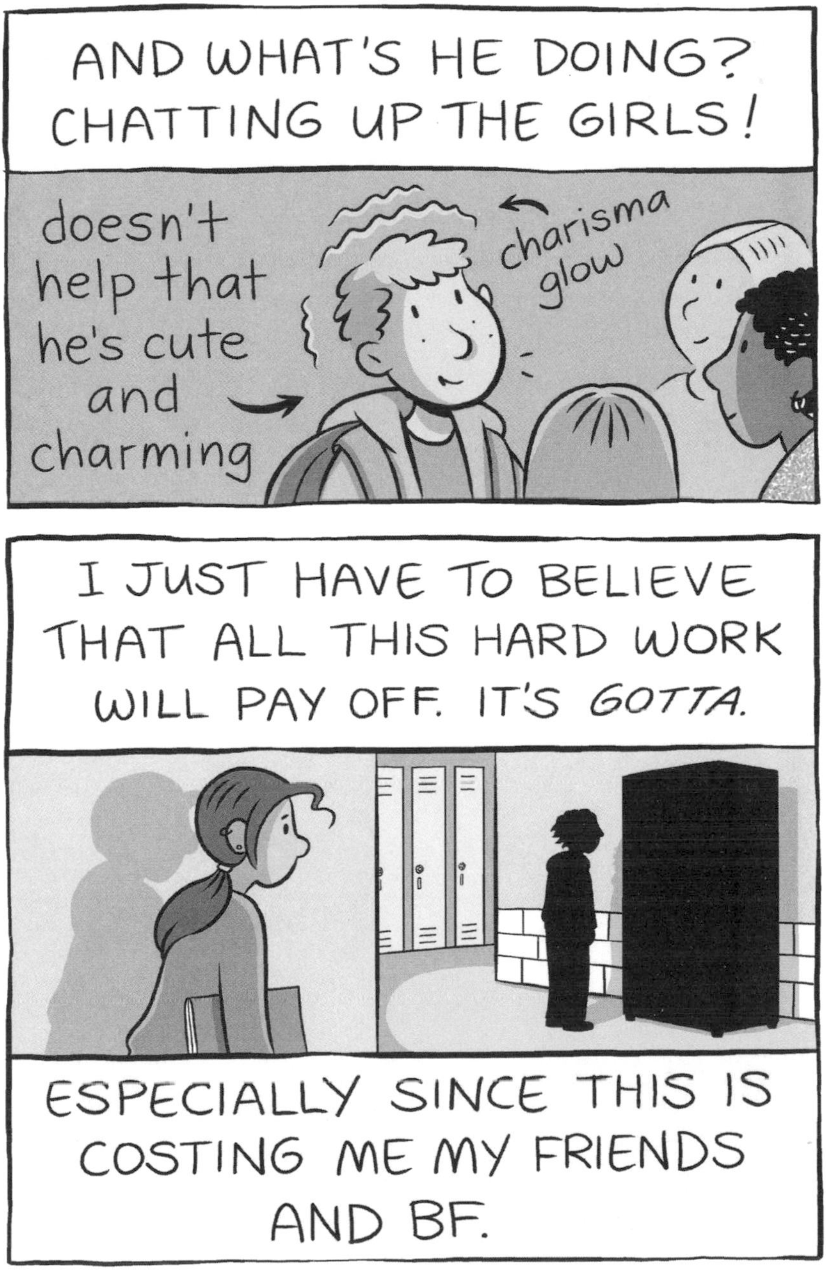
AND WHAT'S HE DOING? CHATTING UP THE GIRLS!
doesn't help that he's cute and charming
charisma glow
I JUST HAVE TO BELIEVE THAT ALL THIS HARD WORK WILL PAY OFF. IT'S *GOTTA*.
ESPECIALLY SINCE THIS IS COSTING ME MY FRIENDS AND BF.

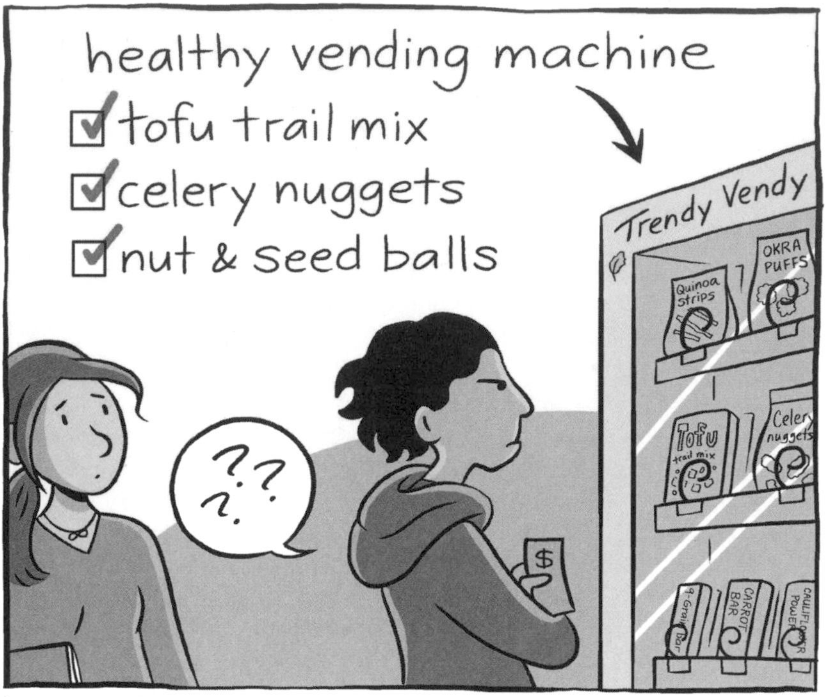
healthy vending machine
tofu trail mix
celery nuggets
nut & seed balls
Trendy Vendy
Quinoa strips
OKRA PUFFS
Tofu trail mix
Celery nuggets
9-Grain Bar
CARROT BAR
CAULIFLOWER POWER
??
??

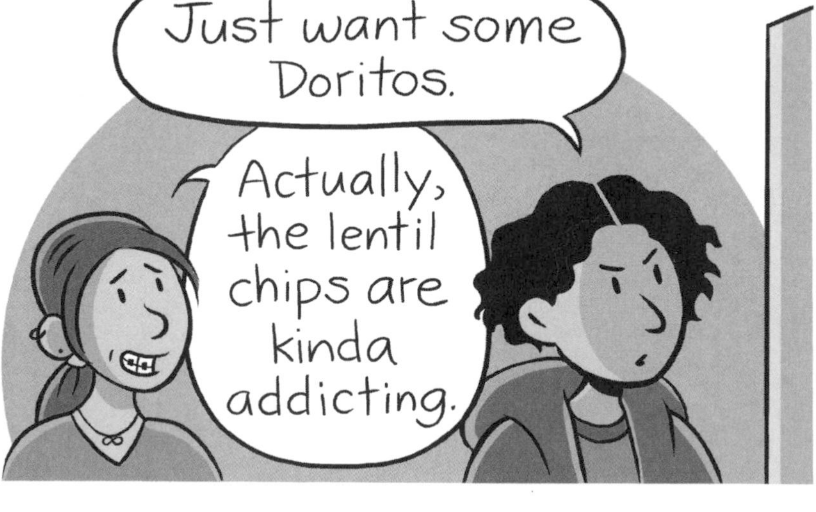
Just want some Doritos.
Actually, the lentil chips are kinda addicting.

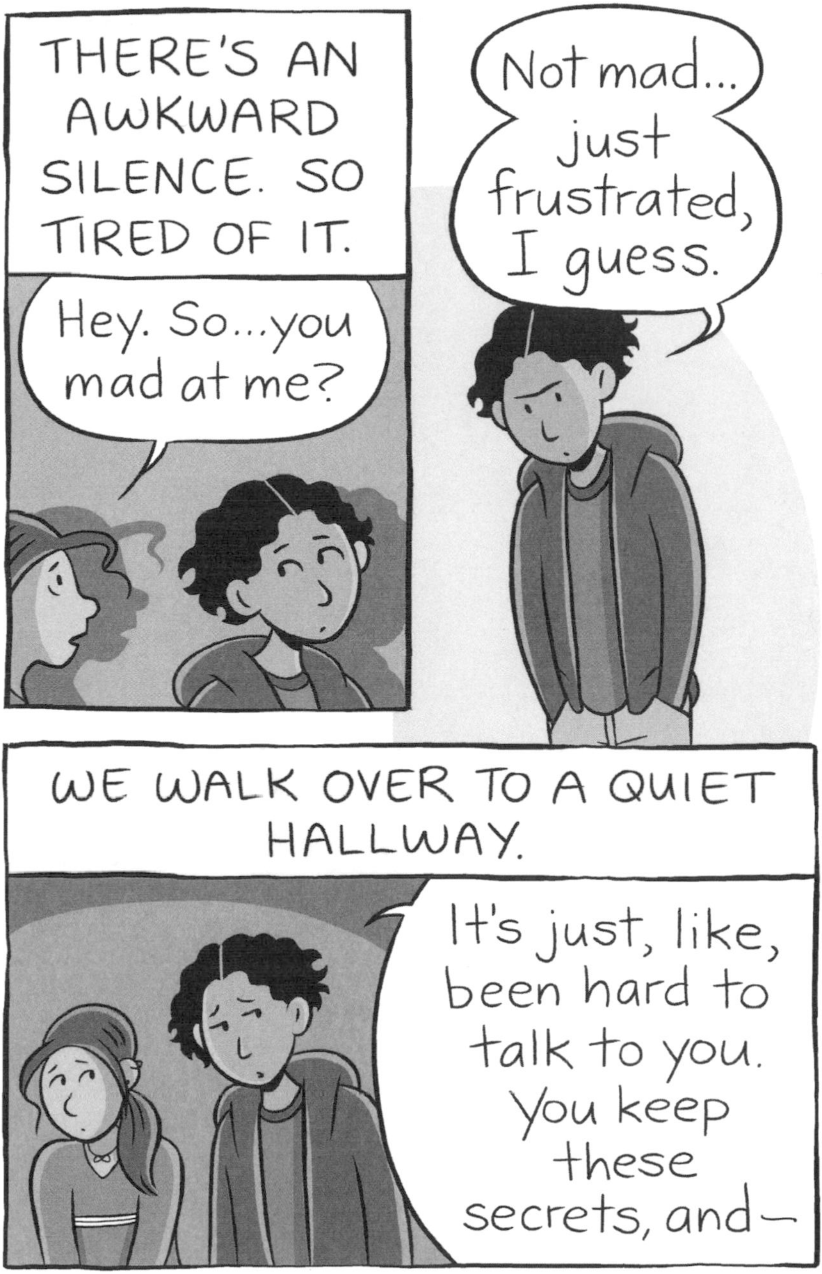
THERE'S AN AWKWARD SILENCE. SO TIRED OF IT.
Hey. So...you mad at me?
Not mad... just frustrated, I guess.
WE WALK OVER TO A QUIET HALLWAY.
It's just, like, been hard to talk to you. You keep these secrets, and—

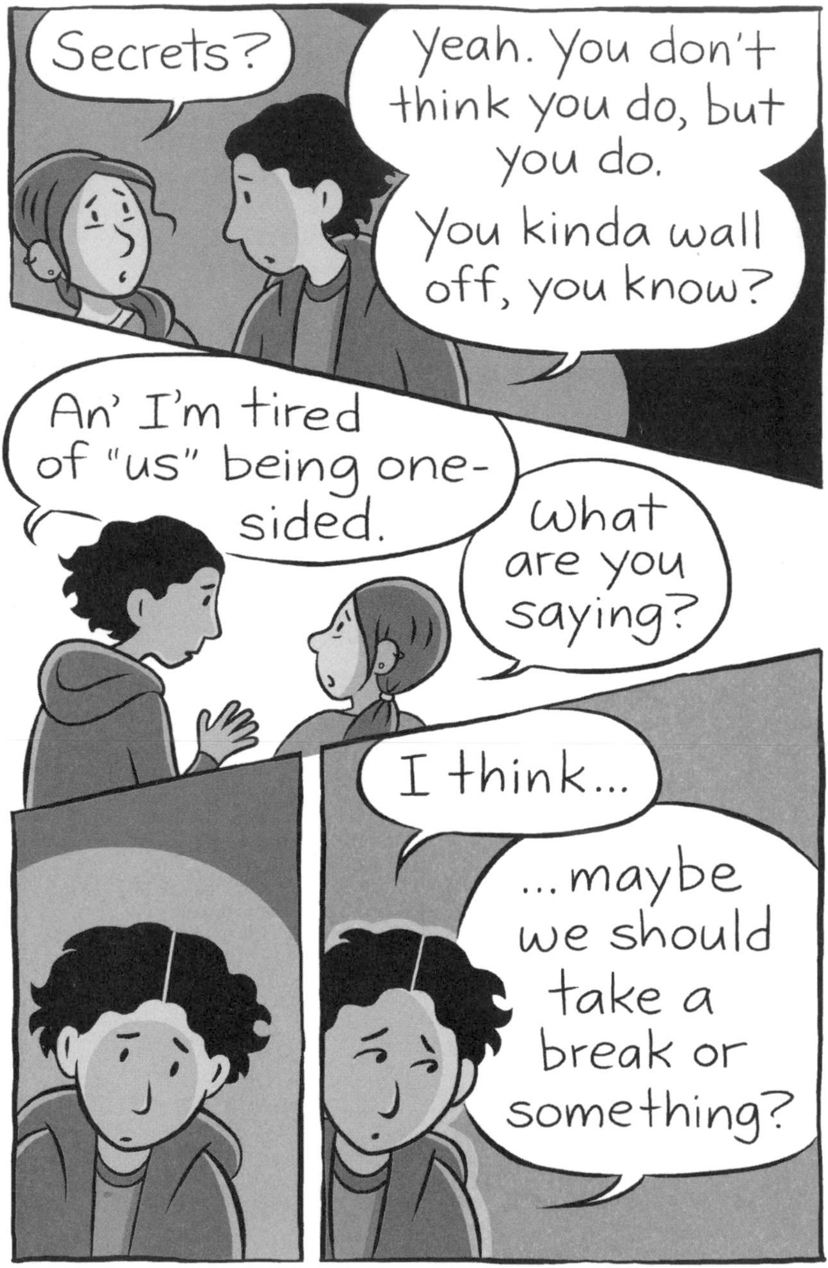
Secrets?
Yeah. You don't think you do, but you do.
You kinda wall off, you know?
An' I'm tired of "us" being one-sided.
What are you saying?
I think...
...maybe we should take a break or something?

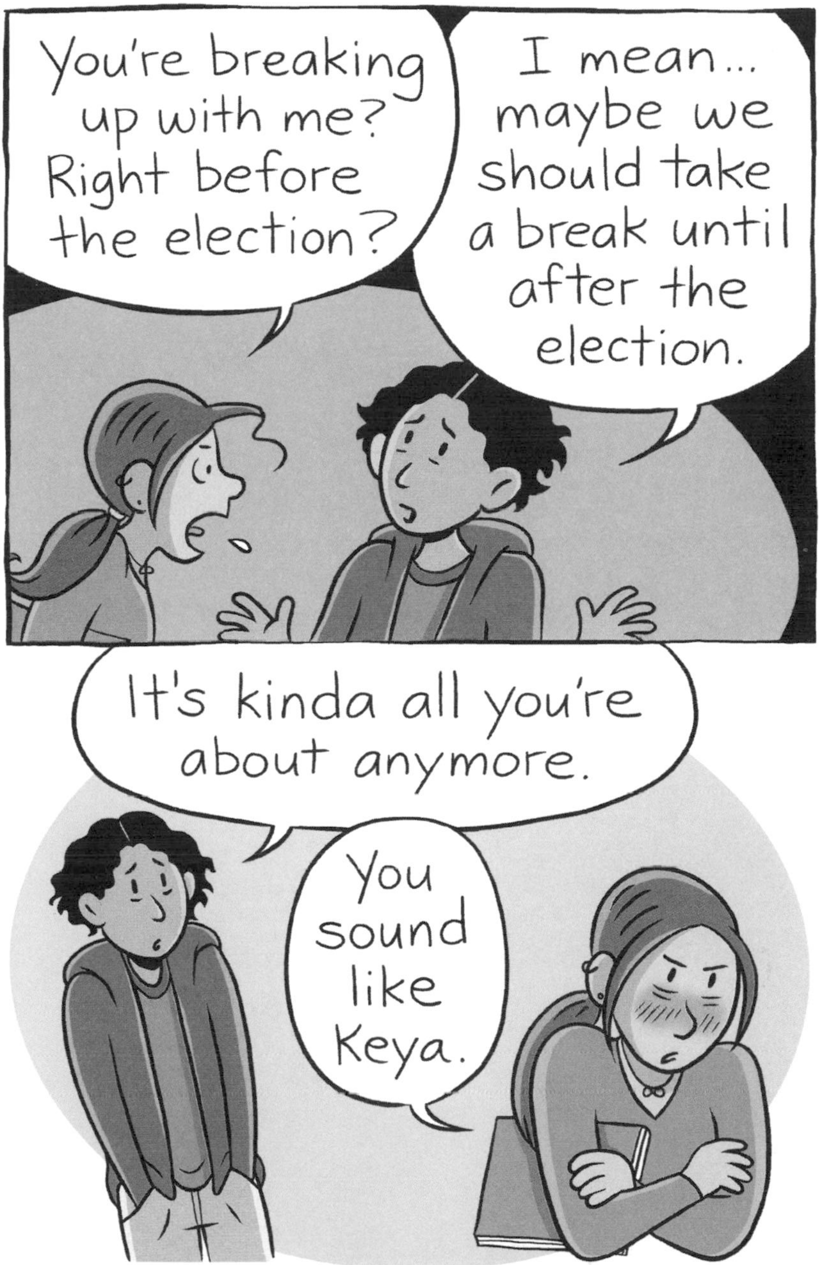
You're breaking up with me? Right before the election?
I mean... maybe we should take a break until after the election.
It's kinda all you're about anymore.
You sound like Keya.

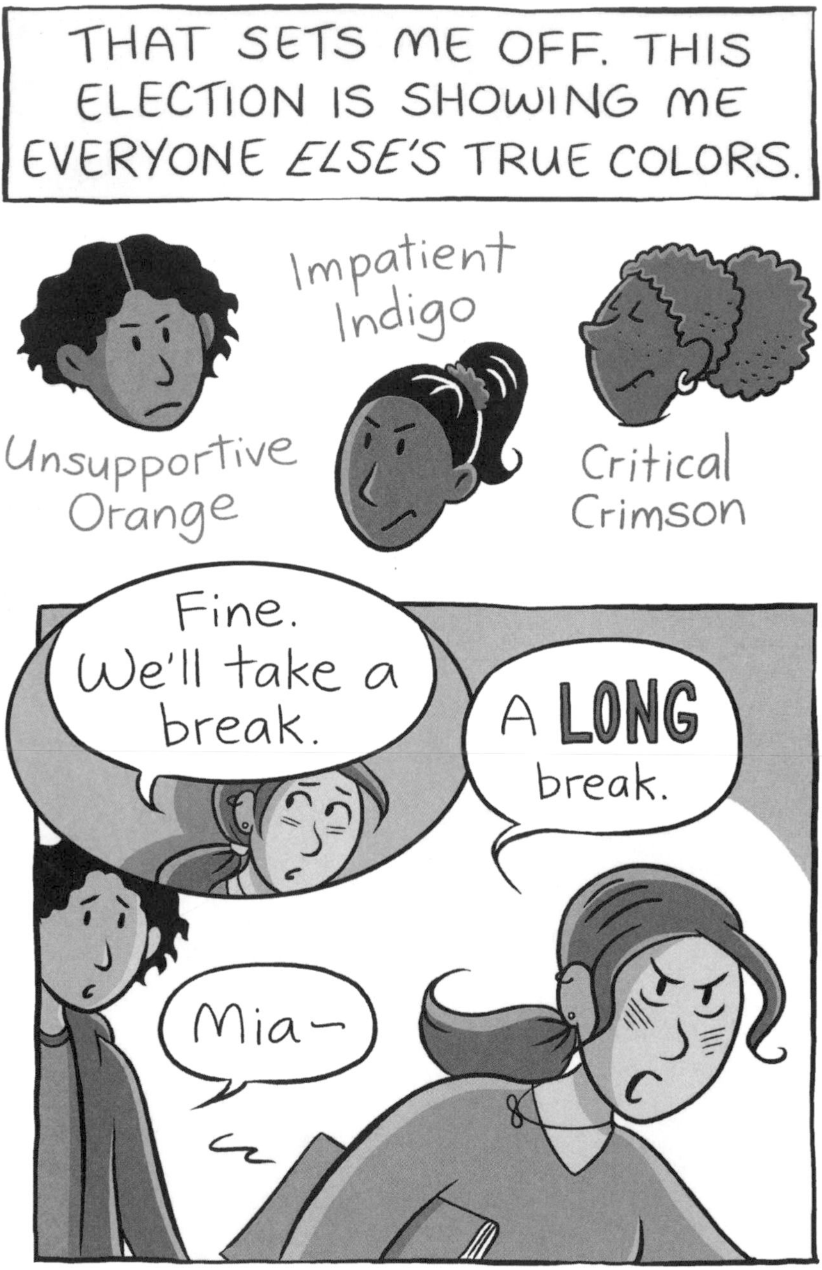
THAT SETS ME OFF. THIS ELECTION IS SHOWING ME EVERYONE *ELSE'S* TRUE COLORS.
Unsupportive Orange
Impatient Indigo
Critical Crimson
Fine. We'll take a break.
A **LONG** break.
Mia—

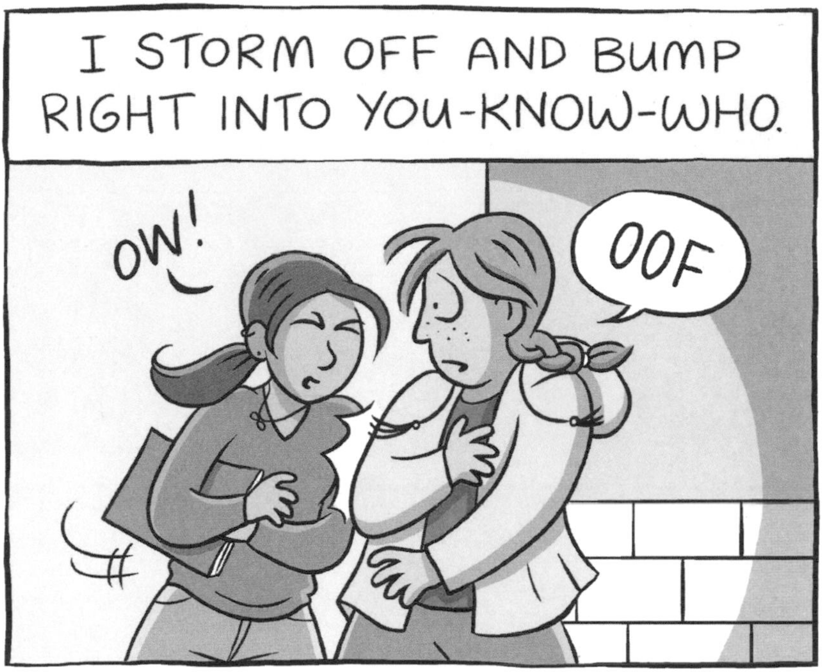
I STORM OFF AND BUMP RIGHT INTO YOU-KNOW-WHO.
OW!
OOF

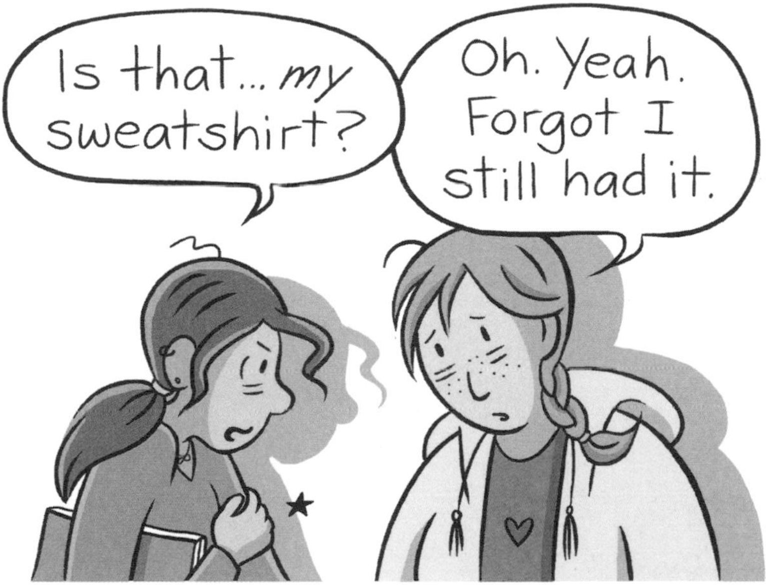
Is that... *my* sweatshirt?
Oh. Yeah. Forgot I still had it.

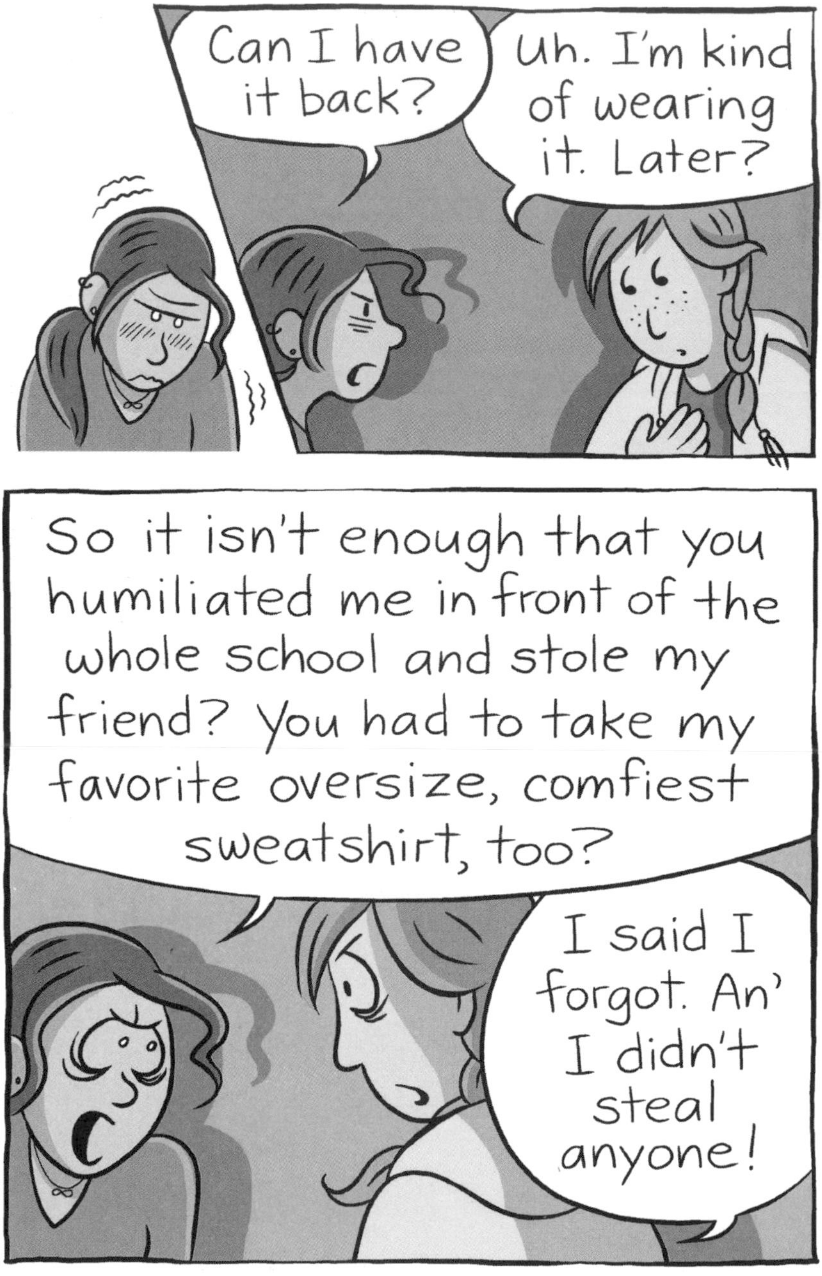
Can I have it back?
Uh. I'm kind of wearing it. Later?
So it isn't enough that you humiliated me in front of the whole school and stole my friend? You had to take my favorite oversize, comfiest sweatshirt, too?
I said I forgot. An' I didn't steal anyone!

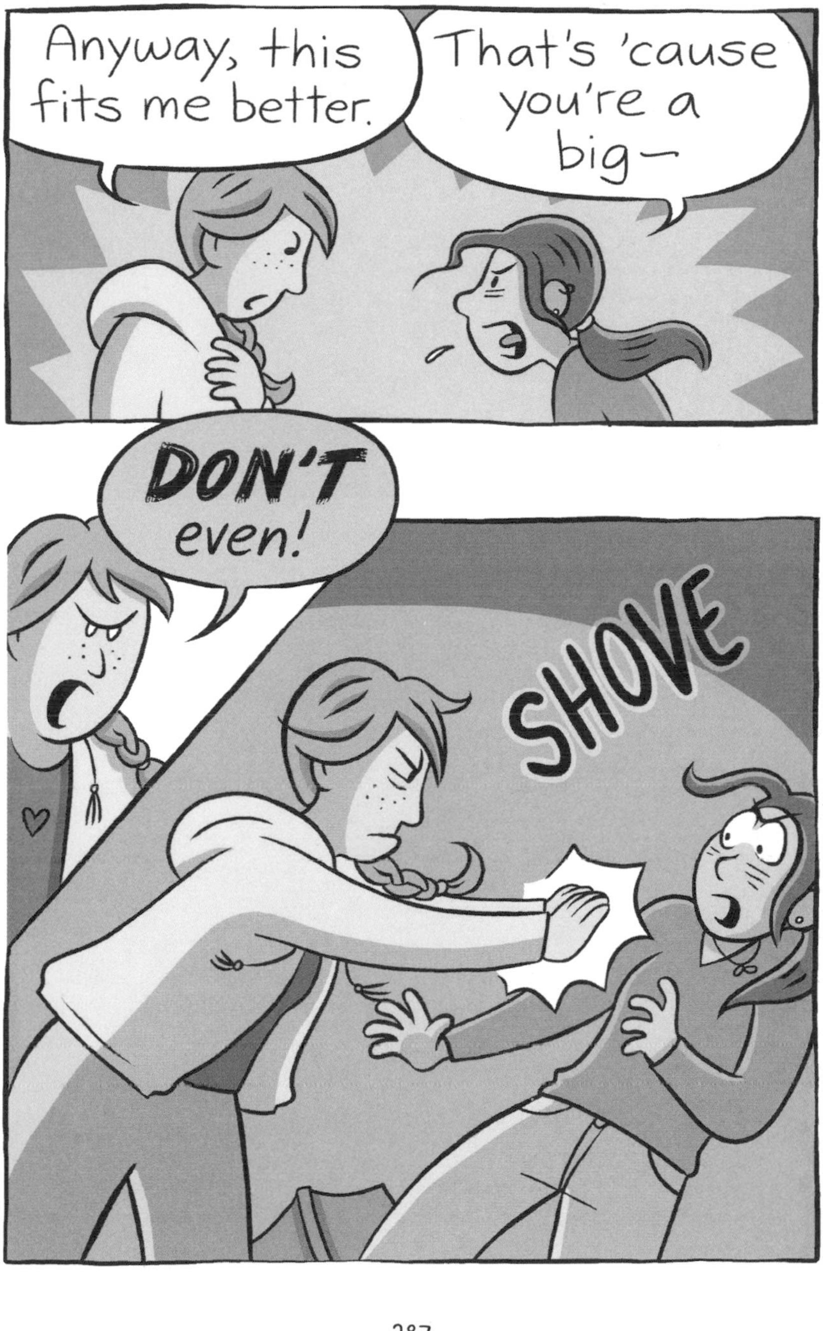
Anyway, this fits me better.
That's 'cause you're a big—
DON'T even!
SHOVE

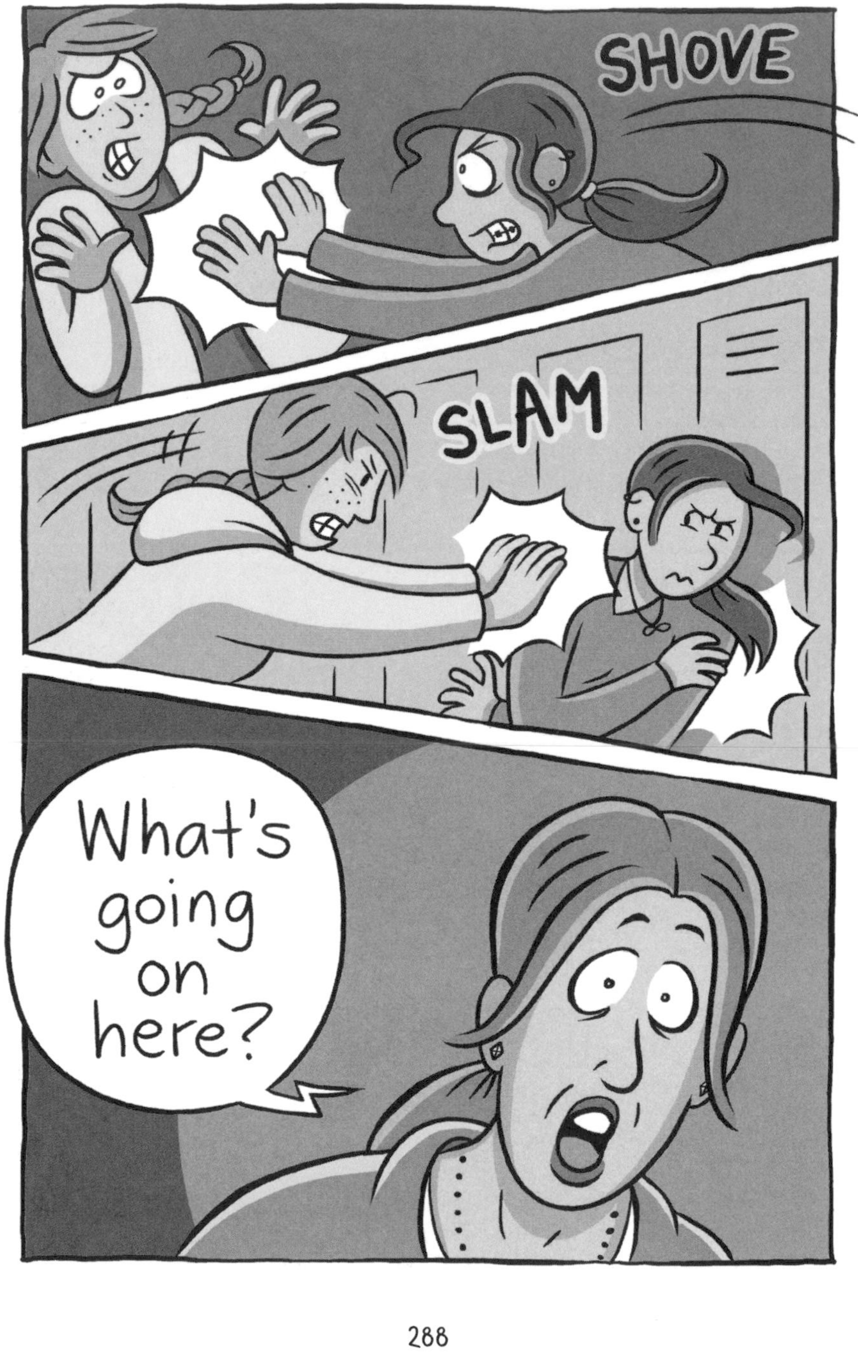
SHOVE
SLAM
What's going on here?

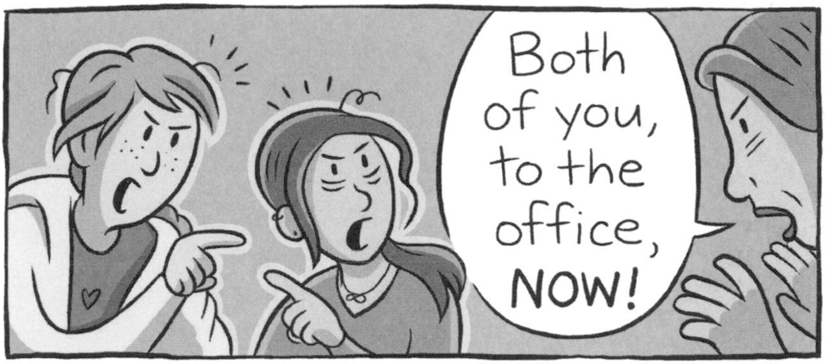
Both of you, to the office, NOW!

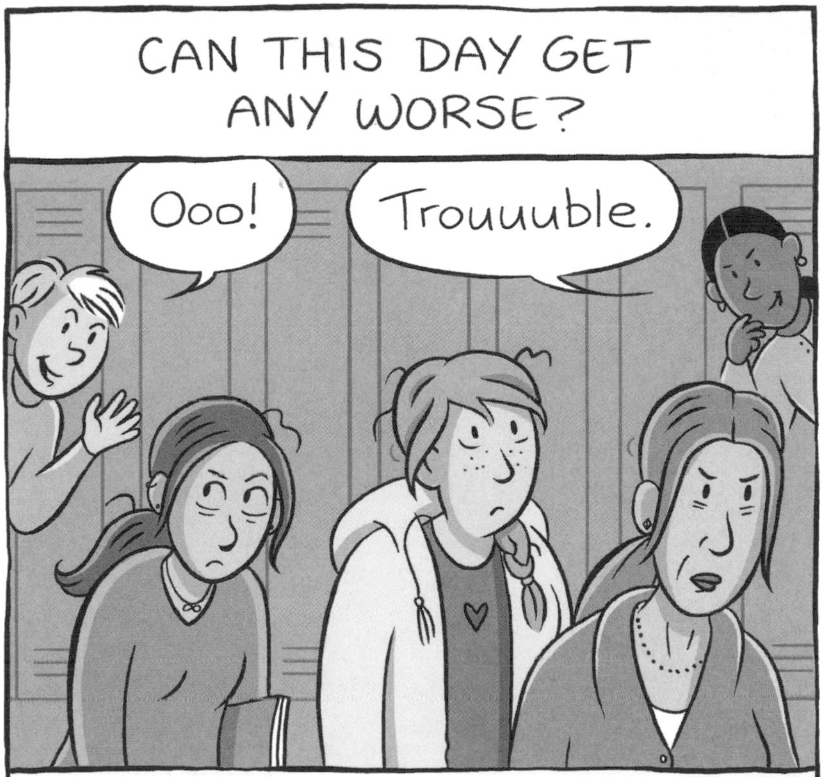
CAN THIS DAY GET ANY WORSE?
Ooo!
Trouuuble.
DON'T ANSWER THAT.

RUBY

Mrs. Langer stares at us without blinking. I start to wonder if she has eyelids.

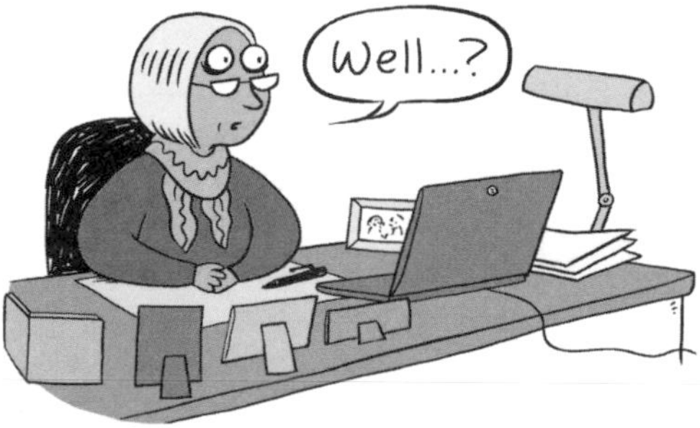
Well...?

I look at Mia and she looks at me.

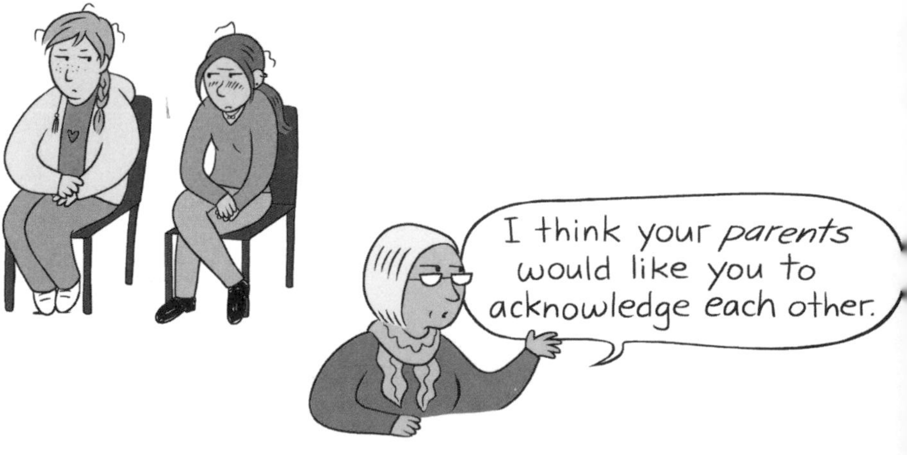
I think your *parents* would like you to acknowledge each other.

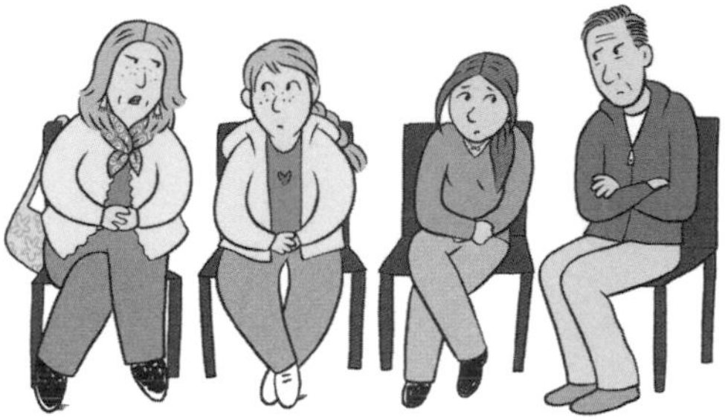

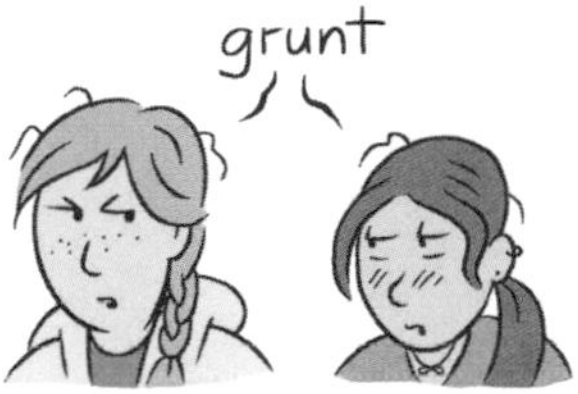
grunt

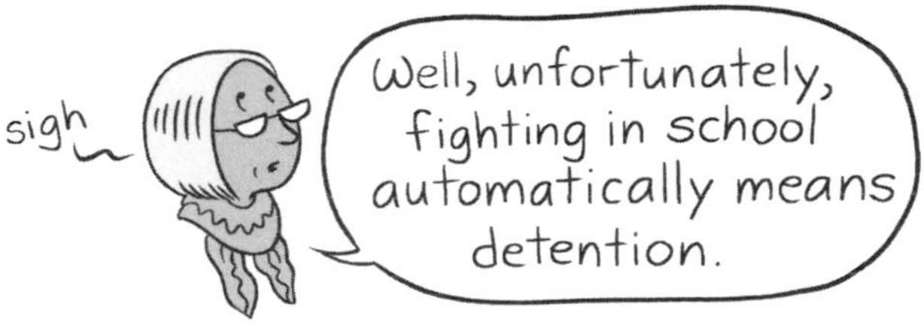
sigh
Well, unfortunately, fighting in school automatically means detention.

I groan. I got detention once, in sixth grade, after accidentally knocking down a hall monitor on my way to the restroom. (The hall monitor was drinking hot tea, so . . .) I've been trying to avoid it ever since. There goes my record.

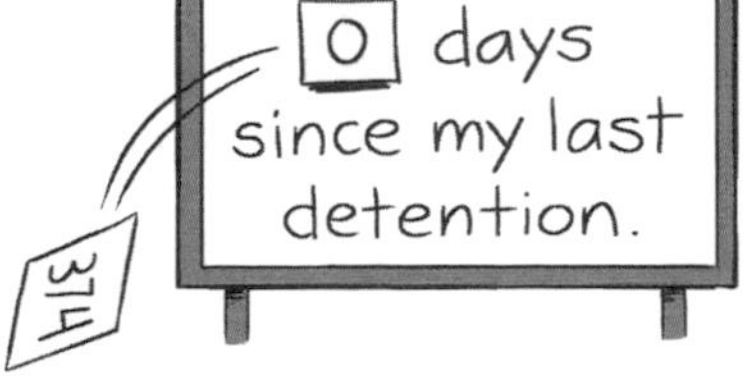
It's been
0 days
since my last
detention.
374

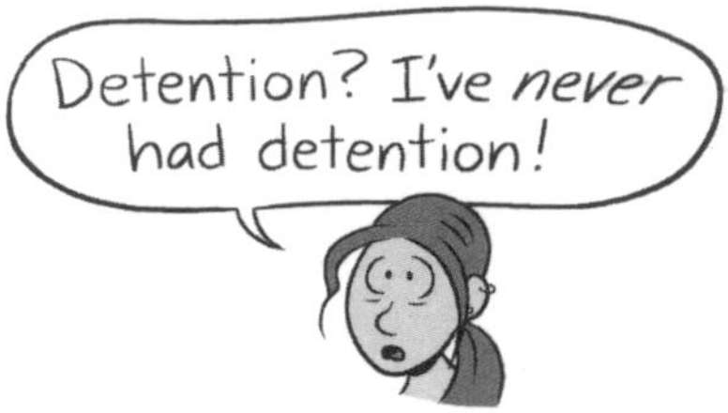
Detention? I've *never* had detention!

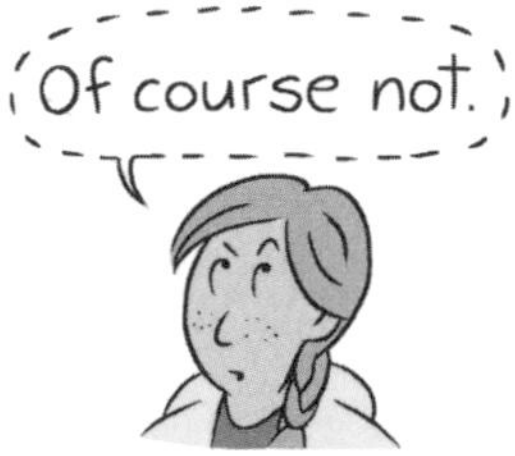
Of course not.

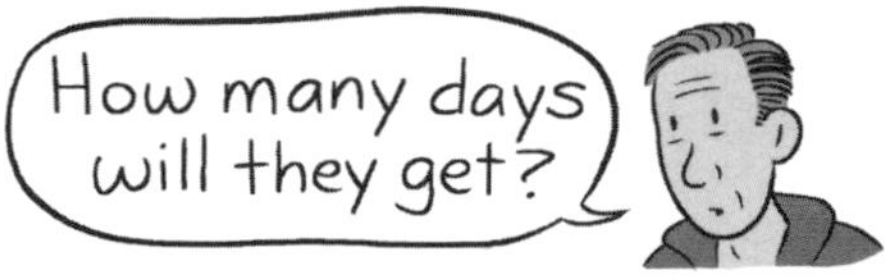
How many days will they get?

Mom is channeling all her nervous energy into bouncing her crossed leg. Augh, make it stop!

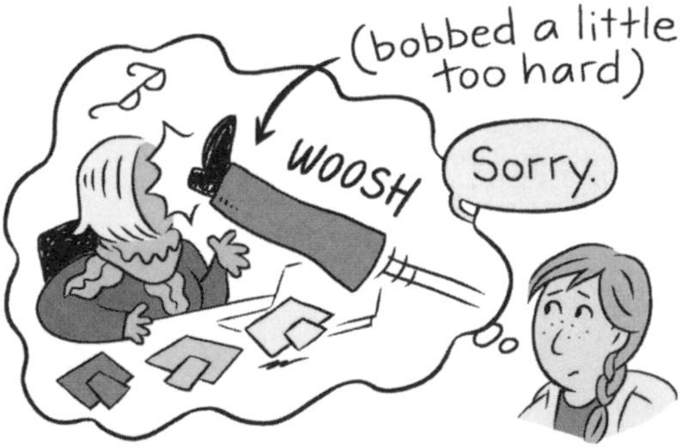
(bobbed a little too hard)
WOOSH
Sorry.

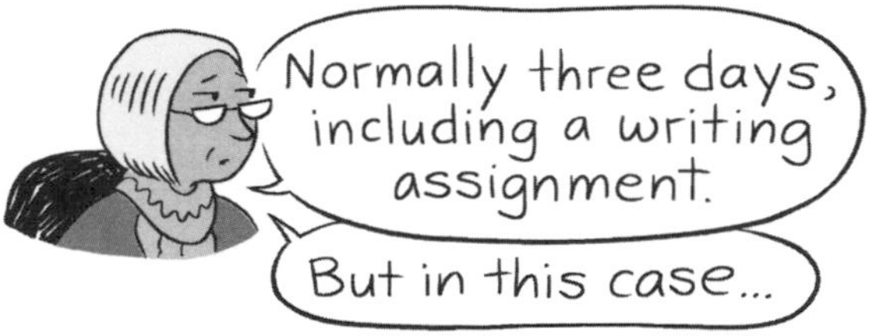
Normally three days, including a writing assignment.
But in this case...

Mia and I both look hopeful.

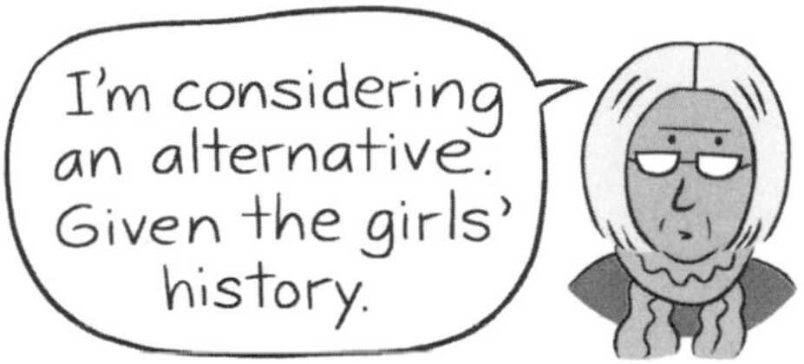
I'm considering an alternative. Given the girls' history.

Mrs. Langer looks down at her desktop, thinking. Her desk is covered with framed photos. She must have a huge family. Sometimes I forget that teachers have actual lives. I think Mrs. Langer is in her sixties, so she probably has grandkids.

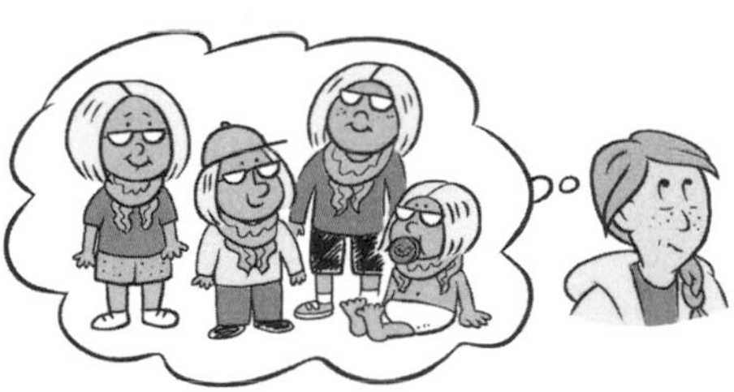

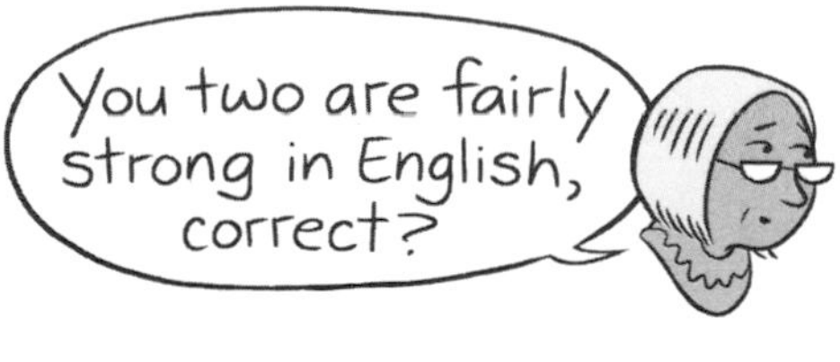
You two are fairly strong in English, correct?

We nod.

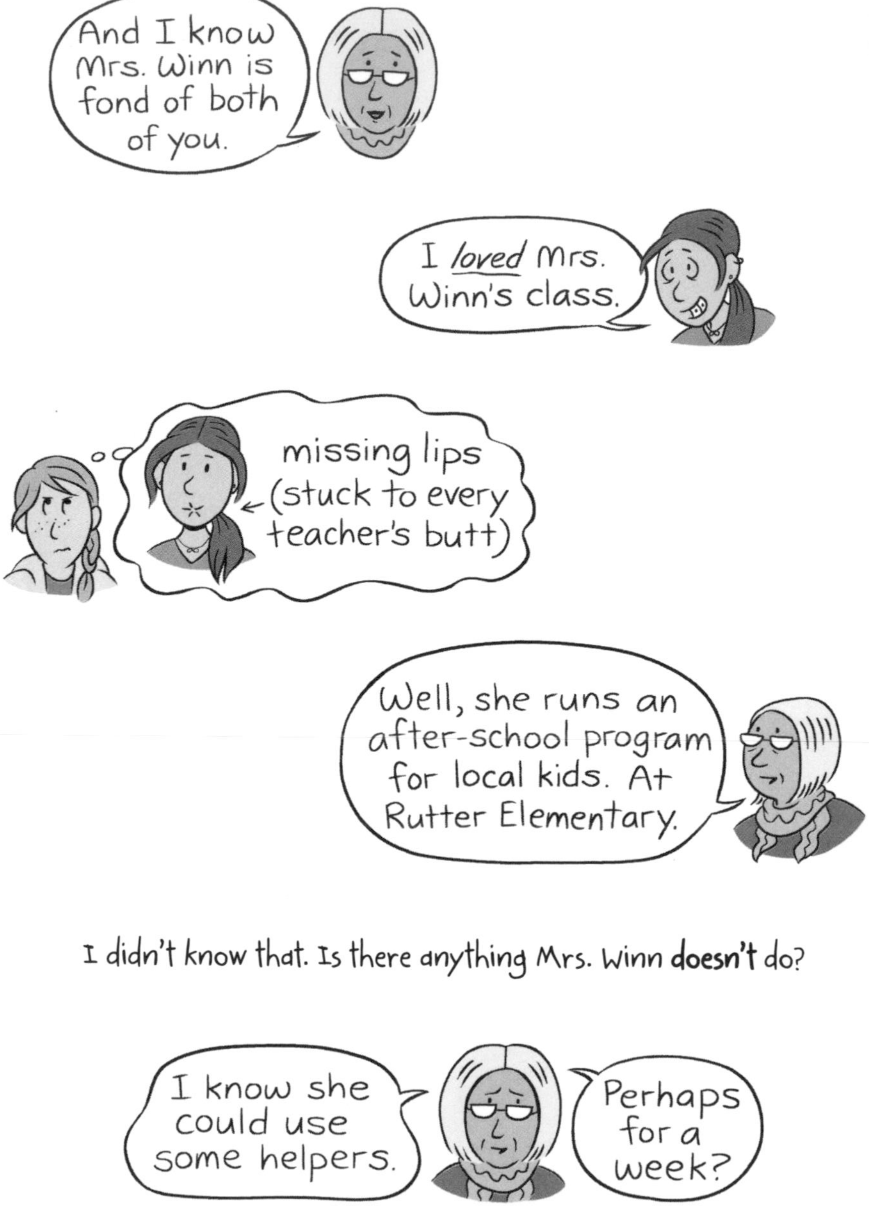
And I know Mrs. Winn is fond of both of you.
I loved Mrs. Winn's class.
missing lips (stuck to every teacher's butt)
Well, she runs an after-school program for local kids. At Rutter Elementary.
I didn't know that. Is there anything Mrs. Winn **doesn't** do?
I know she could use some helpers.
Perhaps for a week?

I don't say it out loud: that working together means we might kill each other.

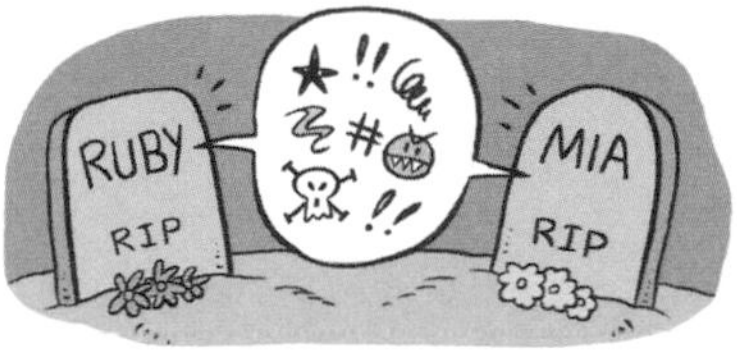
RUBY
RIP
MIA
RIP

But between detention and that . . .

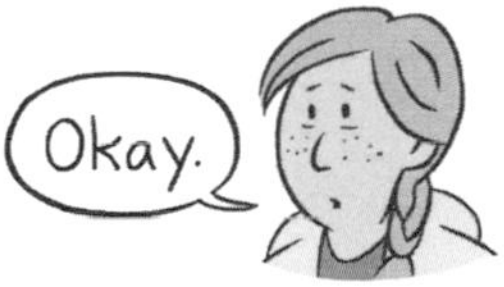
Okay.

We all look at Mia.

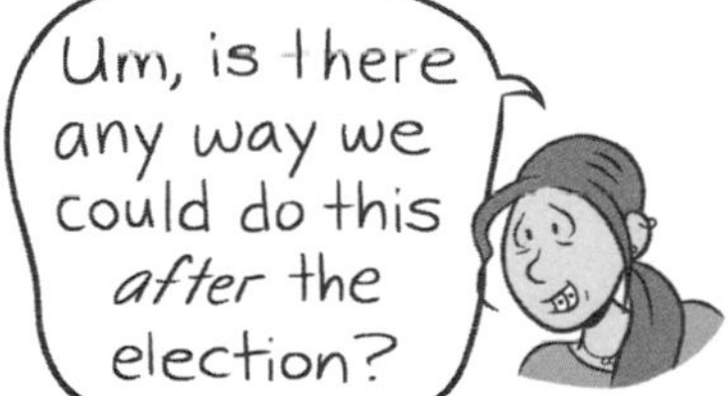
Um, is there any way we could do this *after* the election?

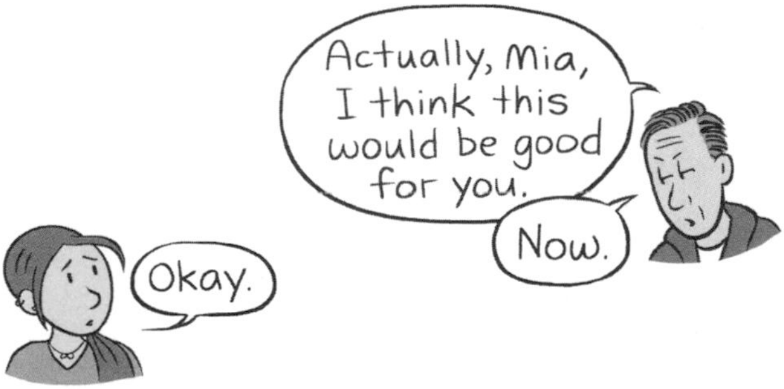
Actually, Mia, I think this would be good for you.
Now.
Okay.

Everyone looks relieved.

It's settled. I'll talk to Mrs. Winn.

We get up and leave, the grown-ups chatting softly (as if we can't hear) while Mia and I trail behind, not talking to each other.

...so unlike them. Even if they've been feuding....

Pretty typical.....

Suddenly . . .

What, did she eat a bran muffin or something?

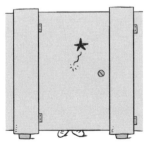

Not another stomach attack!

Stupid Mia.

It's all her fault.

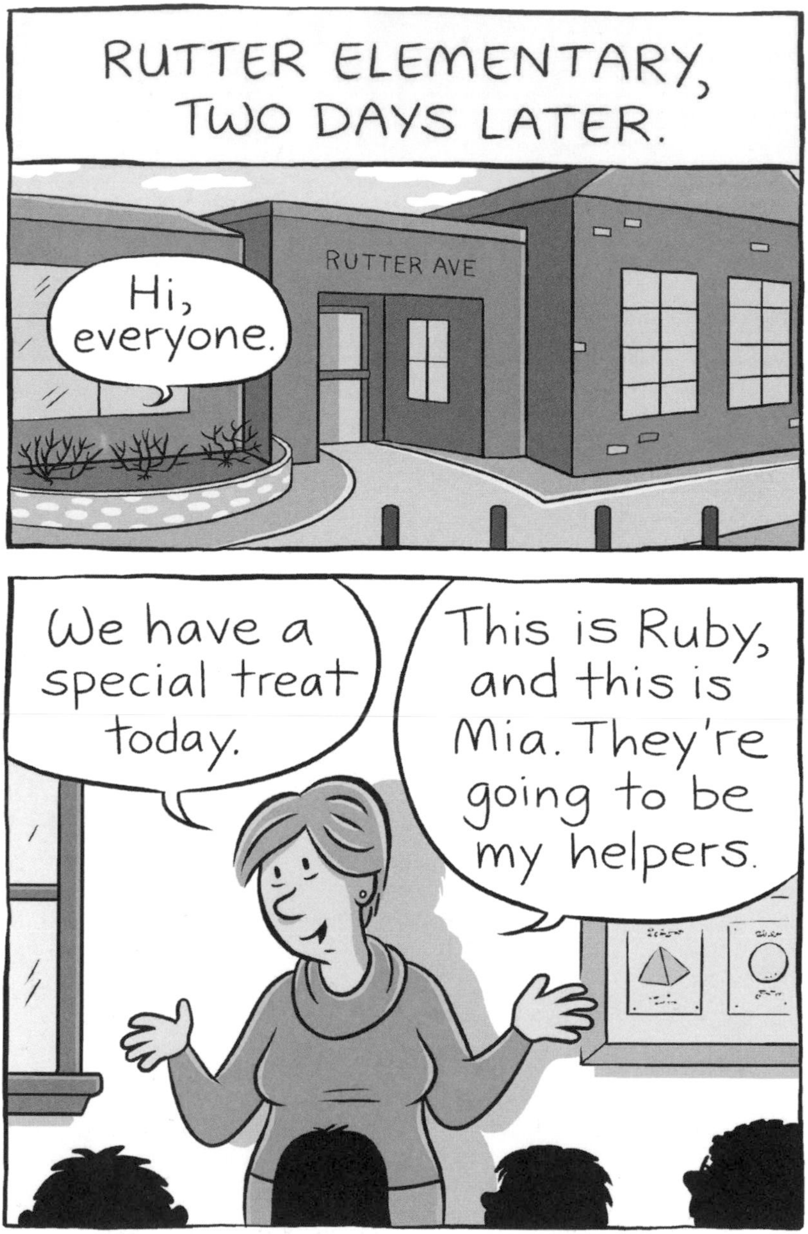
RUTTER ELEMENTARY, TWO DAYS LATER.
RUTTER AVE
Hi, everyone.
We have a special treat today.
This is Ruby, and this is Mia. They're going to be my helpers.

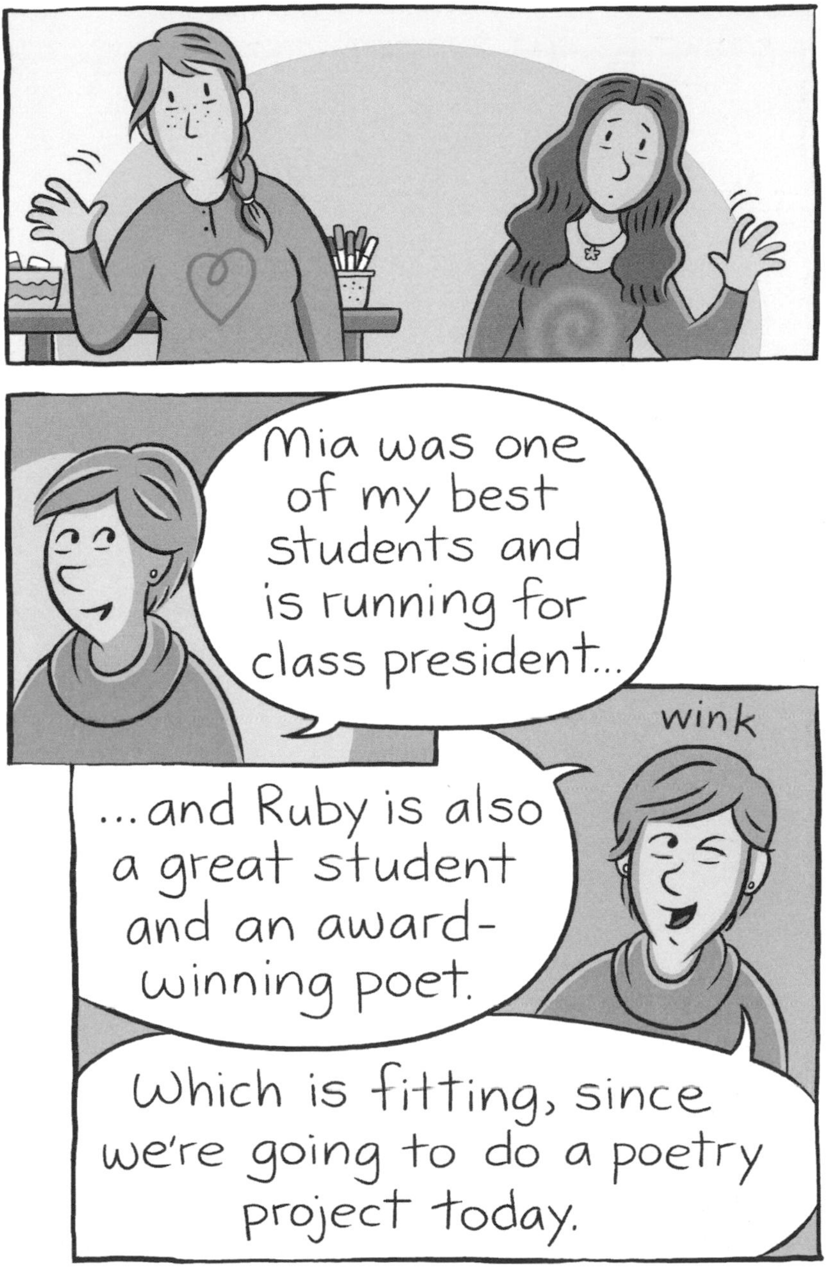
Mia was one of my best students and is running for class president...
wink
...and Ruby is also a great student and an award-winning poet.
Which is fitting, since we're going to do a poetry project today.

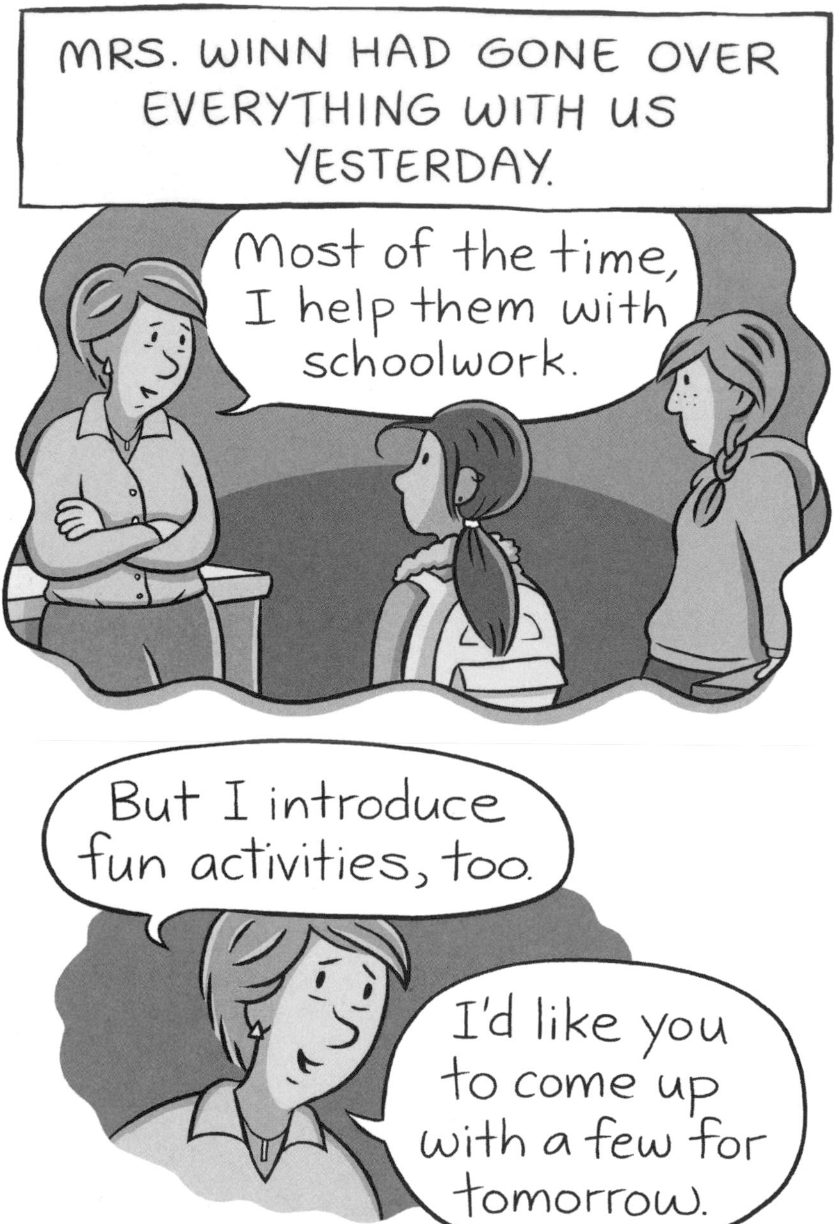
MRS. WINN HAD GONE OVER EVERYTHING WITH US YESTERDAY.
Most of the time, I help them with schoolwork.
But I introduce fun activities, too.
I'd like you to come up with a few for tomorrow.

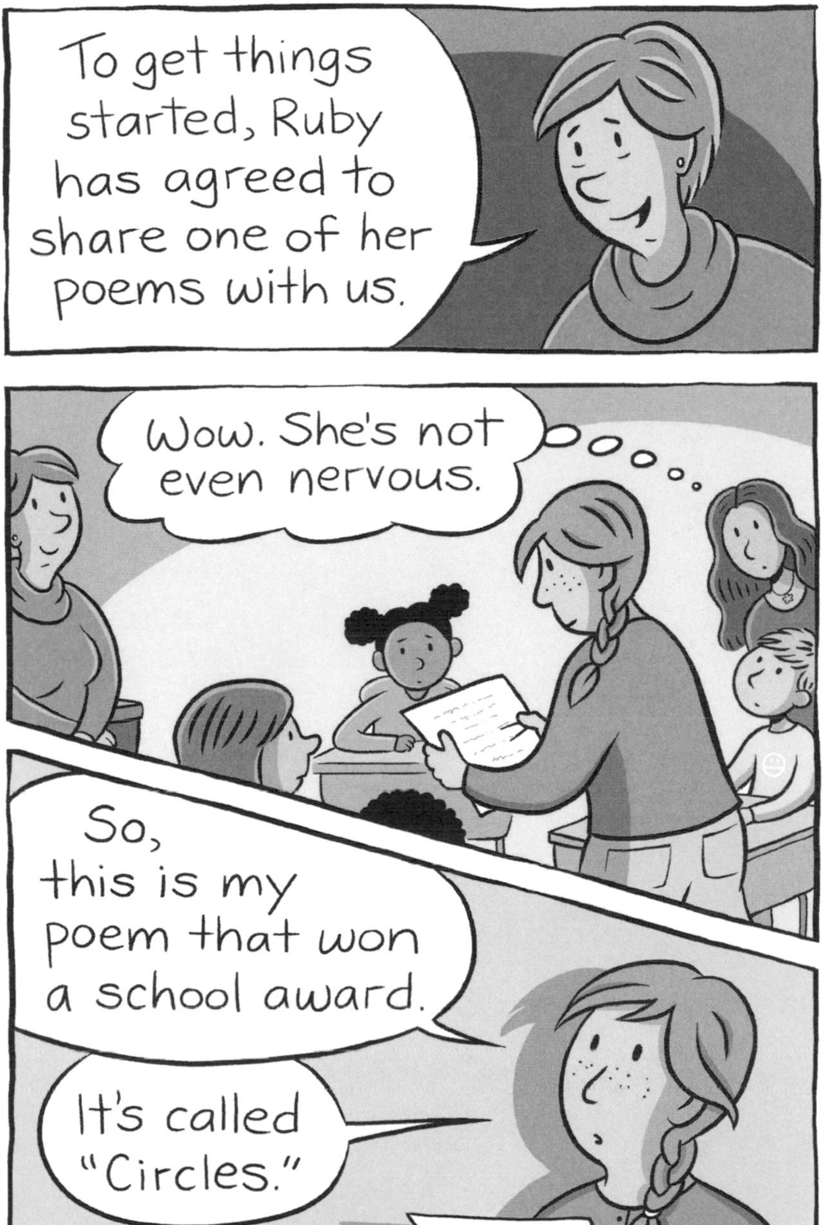
To get things started, Ruby has agreed to share one of her poems with us.
Wow. She's not even nervous.
So, this is my poem that won a school award.
It's called "Circles."

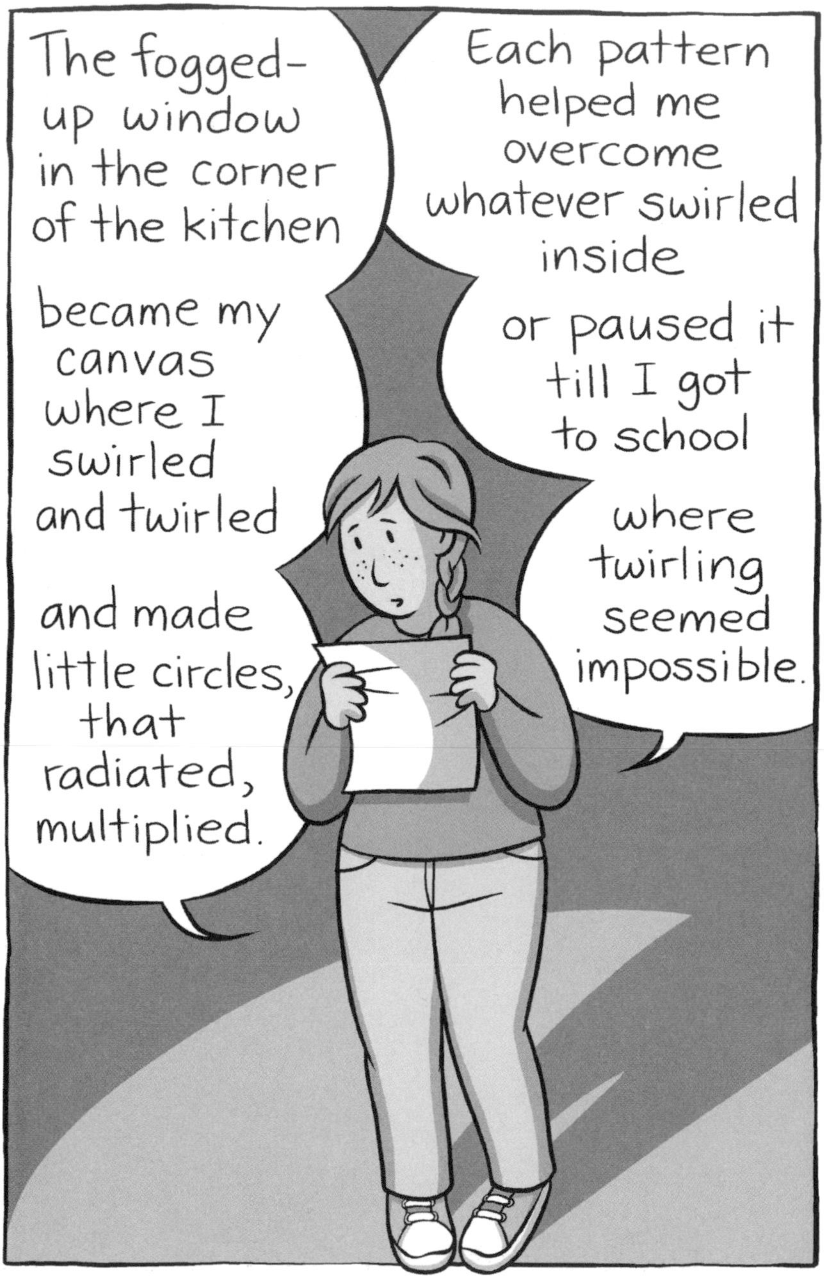
The fogged-up window in the corner of the kitchen
became my canvas where I swirled and twirled
and made little circles, that radiated, multiplied.
Each pattern helped me overcome whatever swirled inside
or paused it till I got to school
where twirling seemed impossible.

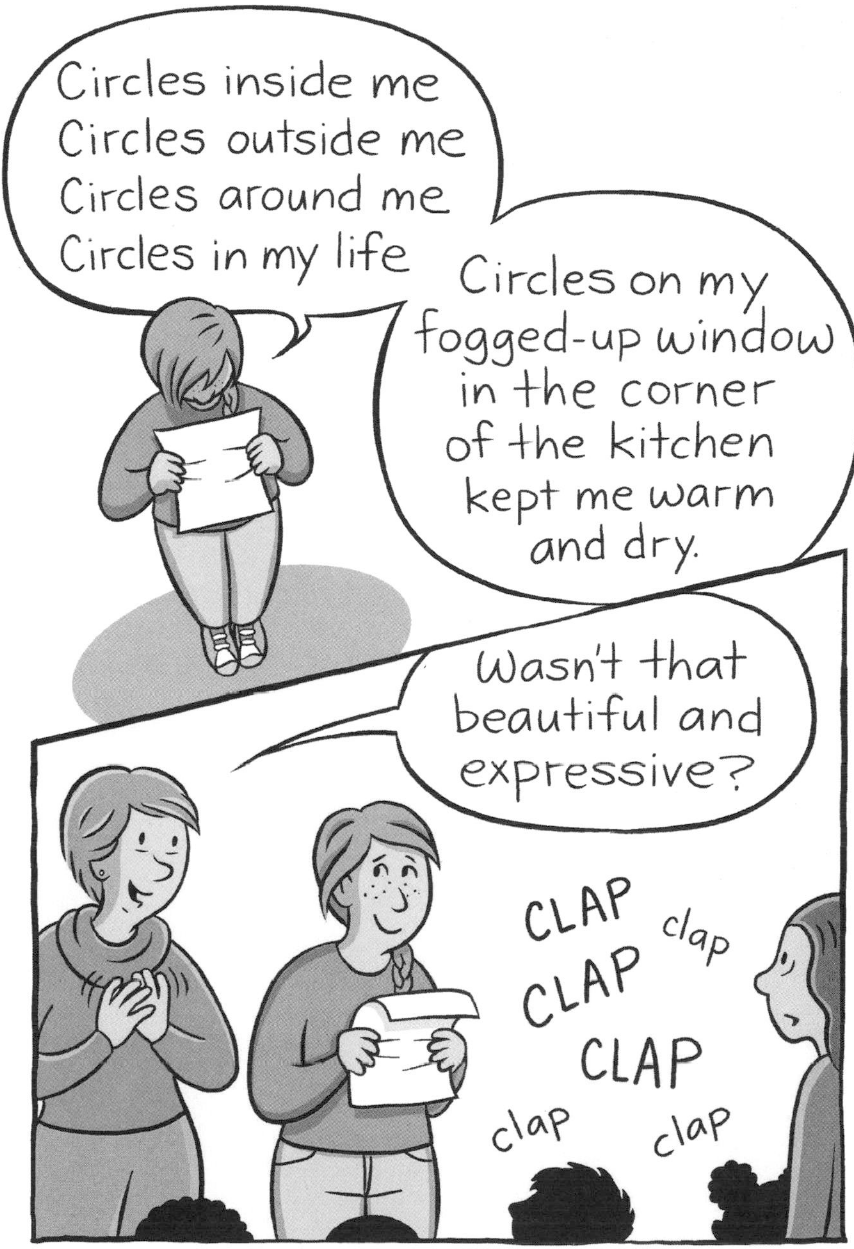
Circles inside me
Circles outside me
Circles around me
Circles in my life
Circles on my fogged-up window in the corner of the kitchen kept me warm and dry.
Wasn't that beautiful and expressive?
CLAP
clap
CLAP
CLAP
clap
clap

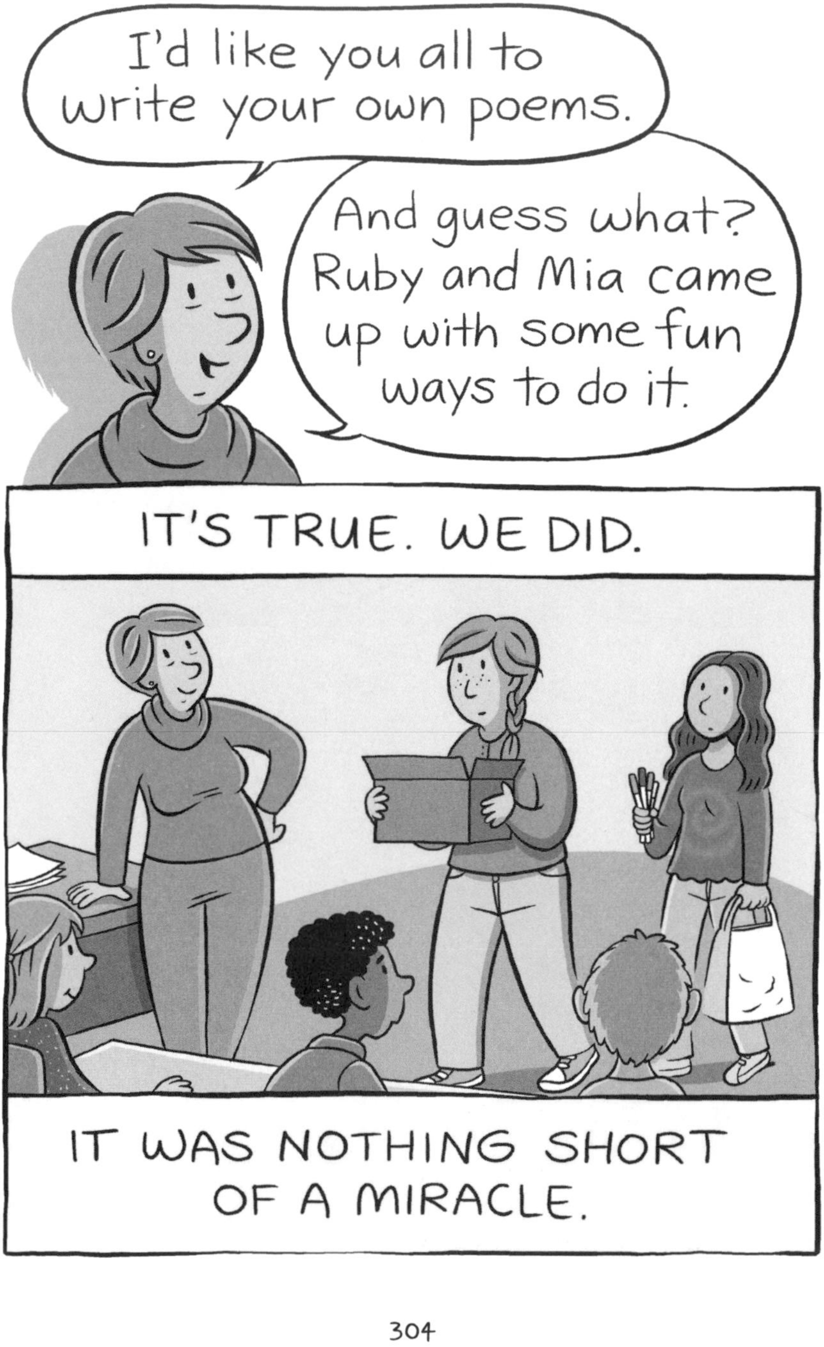
I'd like you all to write your own poems.
And guess what? Ruby and Mia came up with some fun ways to do it.
IT'S TRUE. WE DID.
IT WAS NOTHING SHORT OF A MIRACLE.

RUBY

Here's what happened yesterday after dinner:

We had to come up with two poetry projects for Mrs. Winn's after-school program. Which we didn't want to do . . .
 . . . together.

But we did. At first, it was weird.

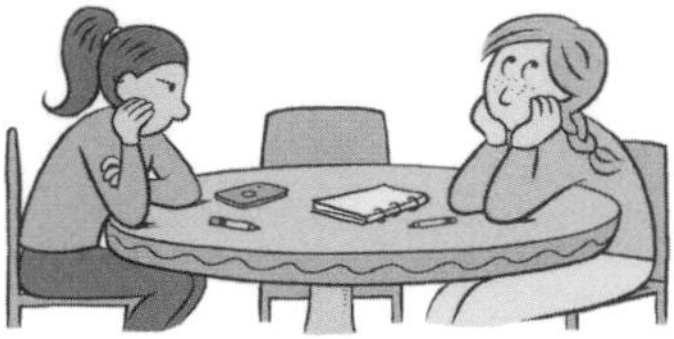

And awkward.

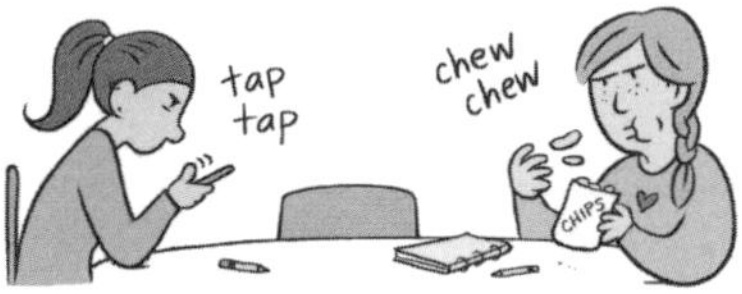

tap tap
chew chew
CHIPS

And kinda infuriating.

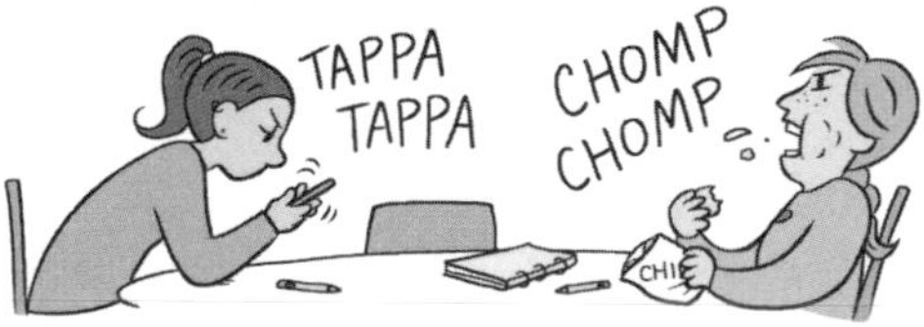

TAPPA TAPPA
CHOMP CHOMP

But then Mom walked in.

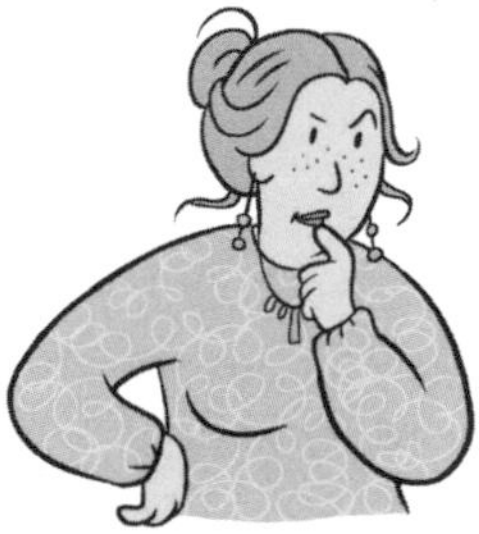

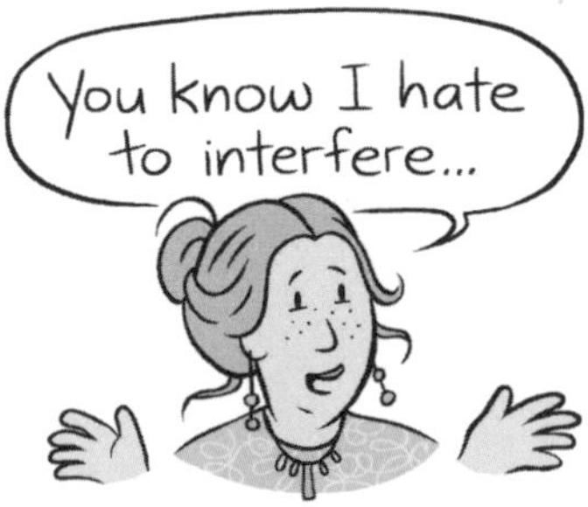

You know I hate to interfere...

I actually choked on a chip.

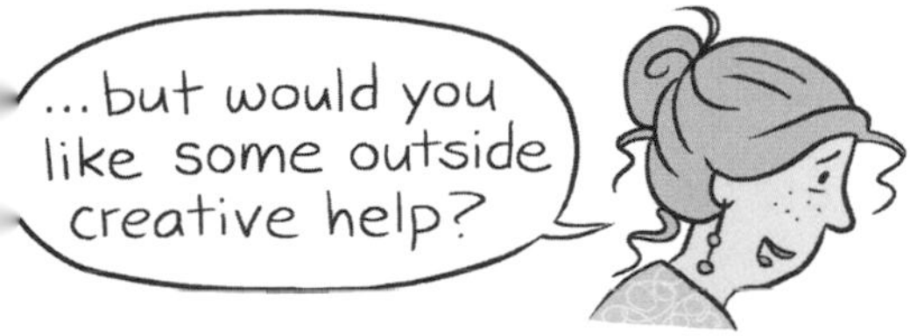
...but would you like some outside creative help?

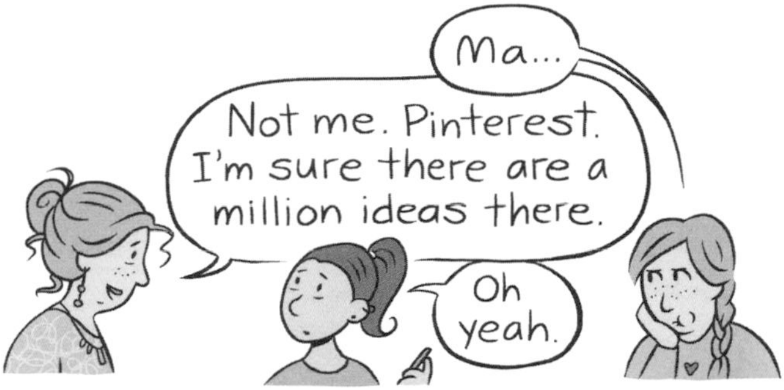
Ma...
Not me. Pinterest. I'm sure there are a million ideas there.
Oh yeah.

So we checked it out. Or Mia checked it out while I hung back at first. After a minute, I quietly tiptoed over, as if walking normally would make her explode or something. She didn't say anything, so I peeked over a shoulder.

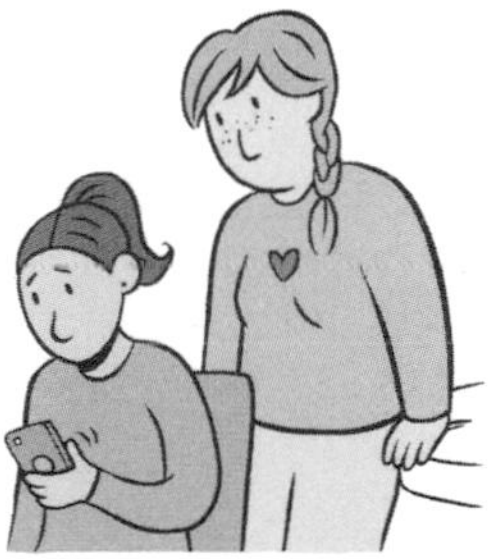

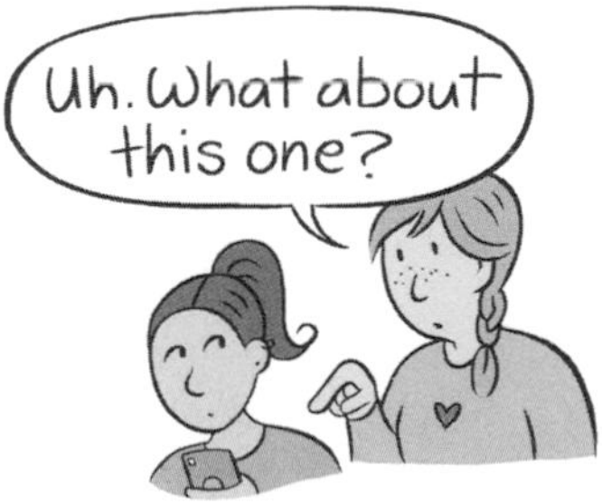
Uh. What about this one?

I was ready for her to tell me off. But instead, she looked closer.

That's... sorta cool, actually.

You think?

Yeah.

She didn't say anything for a couple seconds. Then:

We'll need Sharpies. And magazines.

Ms. Laurie has all that in the art room.

She was quiet for another moment. But not mad-quiet. Just thinking.

What if, instead of crossing everything out...

She told me her idea. I had to admit, it was pretty good. We talked about it without arguing. And then we scrolled more.

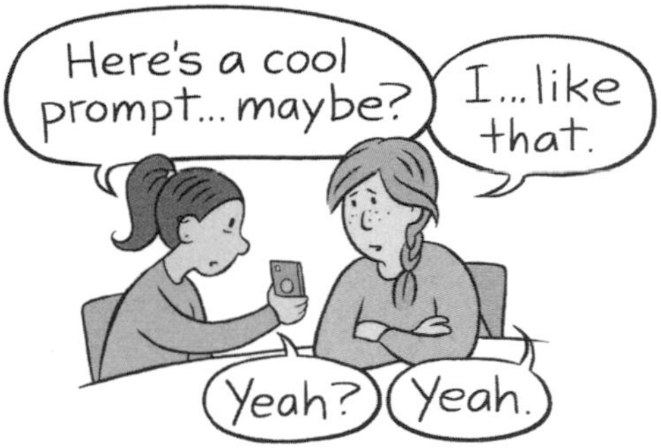
Here's a cool prompt... maybe?
I... like that.
Yeah?
Yeah.

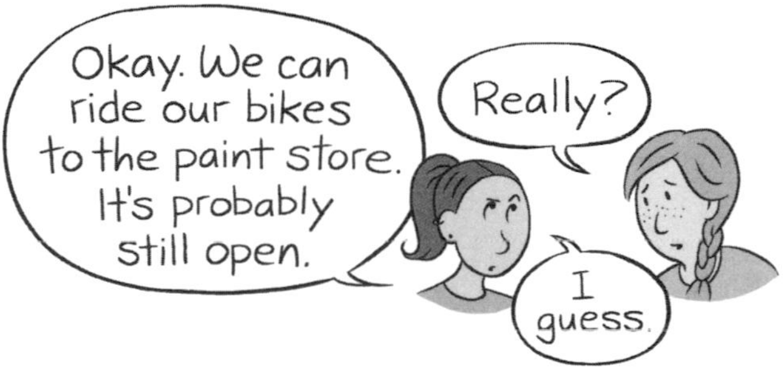
Okay. We can ride our bikes to the paint store. It's probably still open.
Really?
I guess.

And we did.

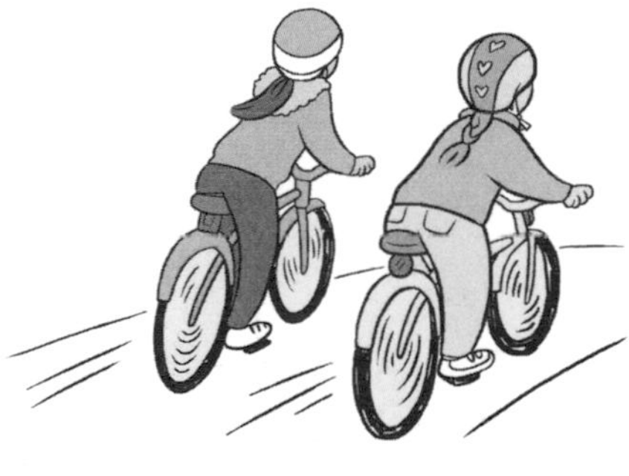

Somehow, we managed to spend two hours together, doing things, without ticking each other off. It almost seemed like old times.

And today . . .

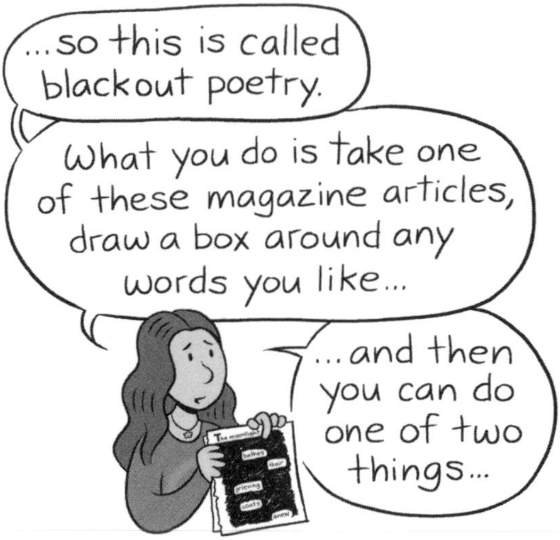
...so this is called blackout poetry.
What you do is take one of these magazine articles, draw a box around any words you like...
...and then you can do one of two things...

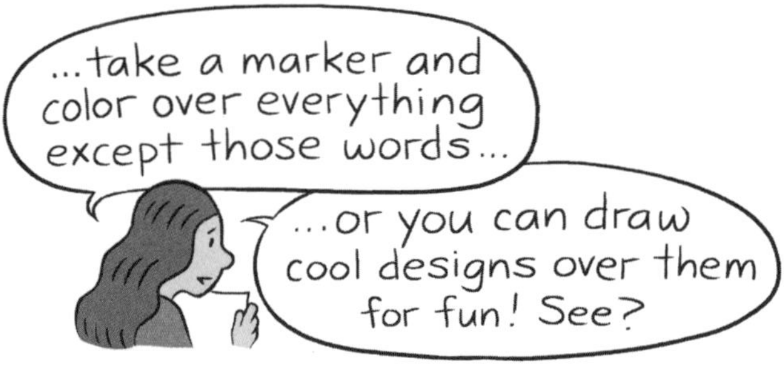
...take a marker and color over everything except those words...
...or you can draw cool designs over them for fun! See?

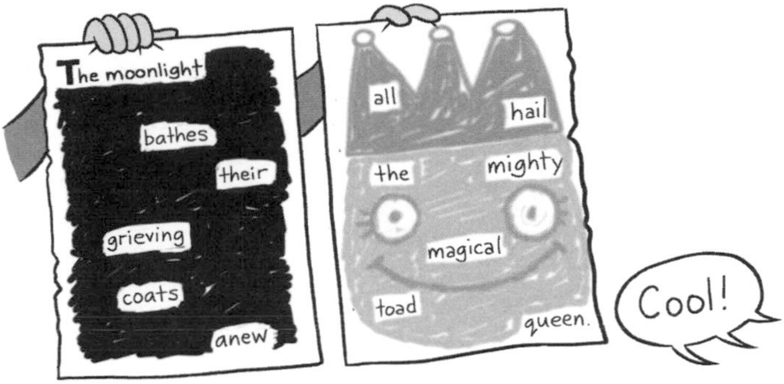
The moonlight
bathes
their
grieving
coats
anew
all
hail
the
mighty
magical
toad
queen.
Cool!

We get them started by passing out magazine pages, and their excitement grows. Sometimes I even catch myself smiling over something cute that a kid says. I notice two strange things:

1. I don't have that usual left-out feeling I have at school. These kids are easy to talk to. And their enthusiasm is catching.

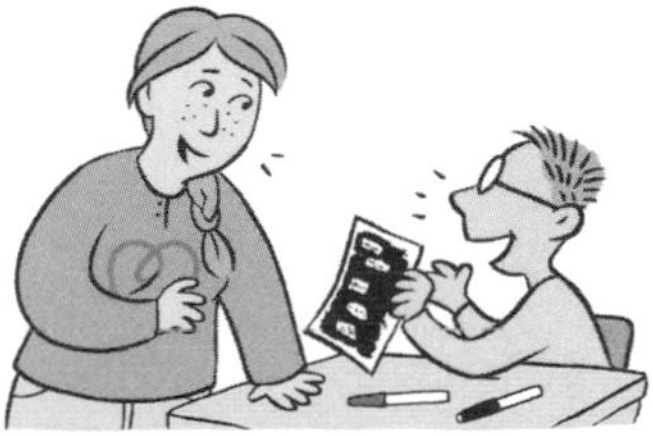

2. I start to forget why I'm here in the first place.

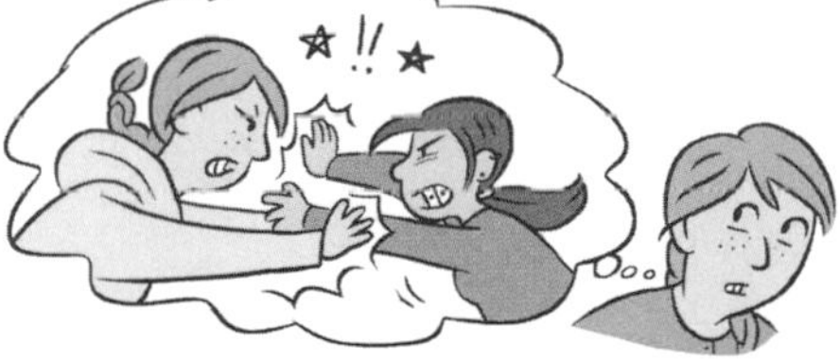

Oh yeah.

While the students work, Mia comes over.

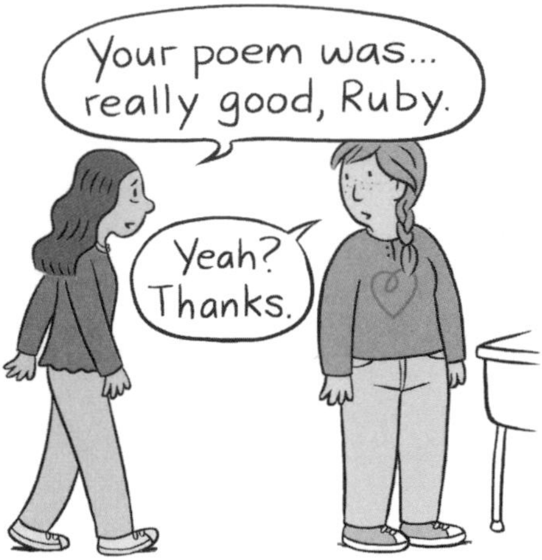
Your poem was... really good, Ruby.
Yeah? Thanks.

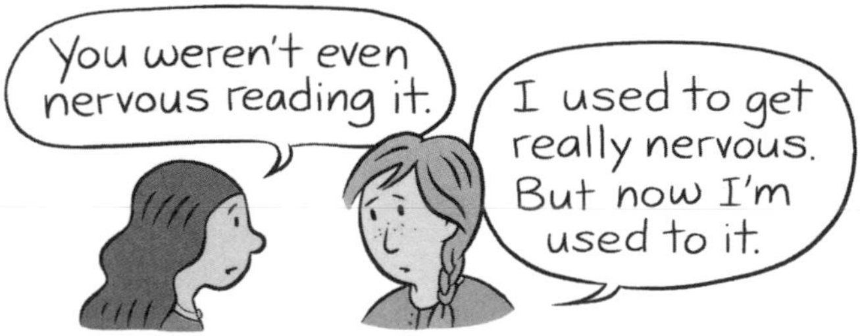
You weren't even nervous reading it.
I used to get really nervous. But now I'm used to it.

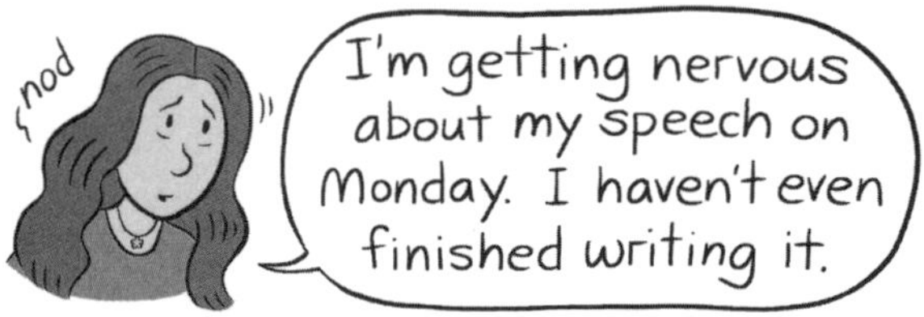
nod
I'm getting nervous about my speech on Monday. I haven't even finished writing it.

It's been a long time since she's confessed anything to me.
I can't believe I say this:

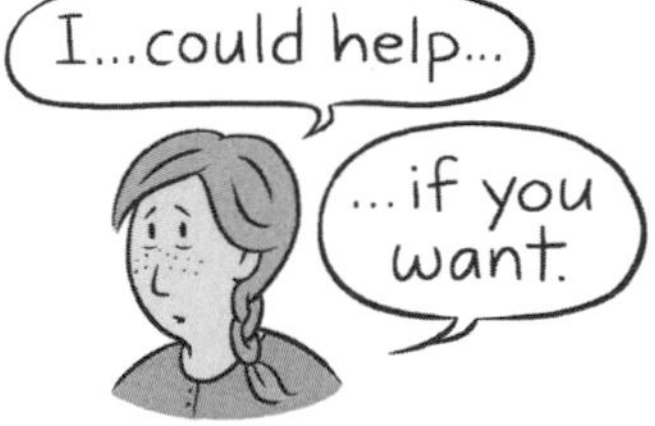
I...could help...
...if you want.

A small boy in glasses tugs on my shirt.

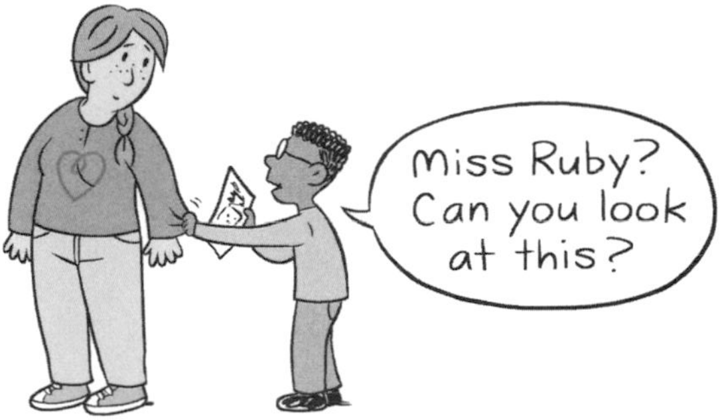
Miss Ruby? Can you look at this?

After I help him, we move on to the next project. Mia and I pass out paint chips—the kind that have five different gradating colors and artsy names.

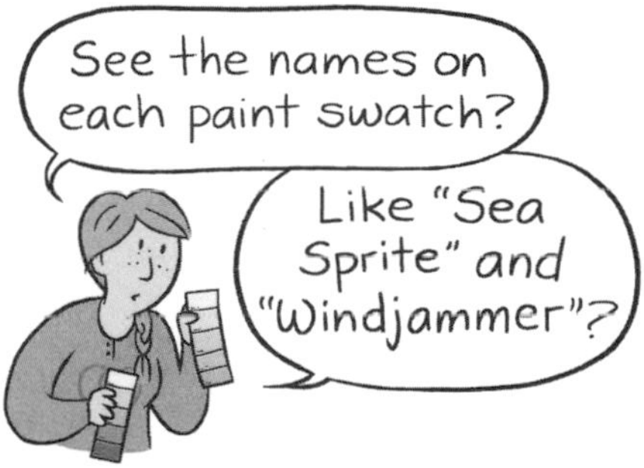
See the names on each paint swatch?
Like "Sea Sprite" and "Windjammer"?

Your job is to connect each word with other words.
You can use sentences or even just a single word. Put together, it'll form a cool poem.

Example:
The
SEA SPRITE
dove into the
TROPICAL POOL.
This
LITTLE POND,
a dazzling
COSTA RICA BLUE,
fooled the eye. She thought she was at sea. There, a
WINDJAMMER!
[windjammer: a merchant sailing ship]

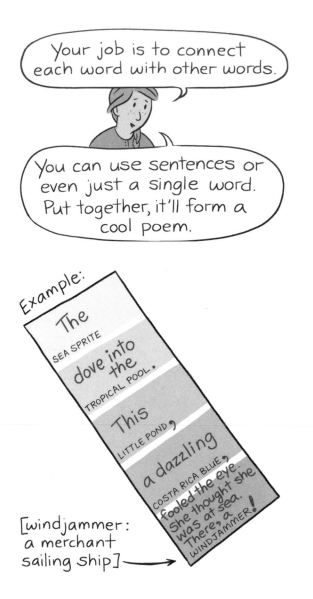

At first, there's arguing over who gets what colors. Luckily, Mia and I thought ahead and got duplicates.

As the kids work, Mrs. Winn walks over.

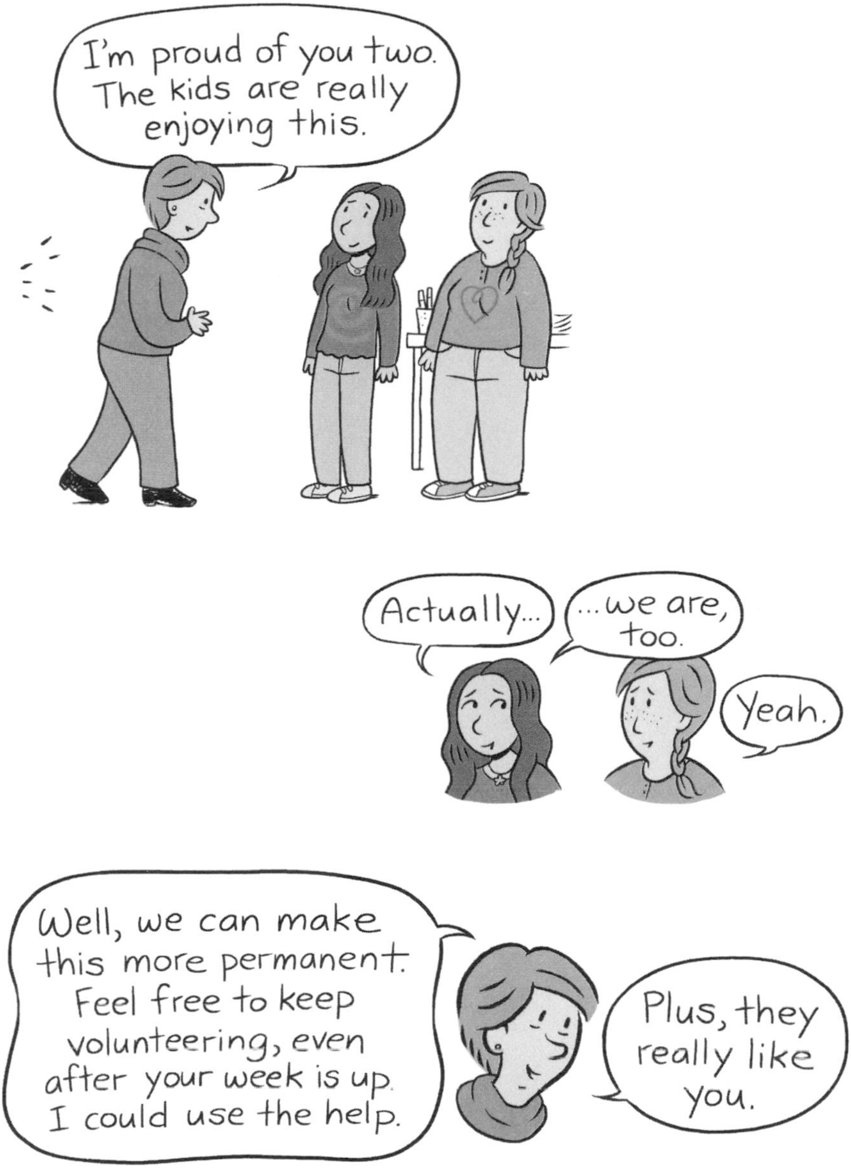
I'm proud of you two. The kids are really enjoying this.
Actually...
...we are, too.
Yeah.
Well, we can make this more permanent. Feel free to keep volunteering, even after your week is up. I could use the help.
Plus, they really like you.

As if on cue, a fourth grader named Lydia calls out.

Miss Ruby or Miss Mia? Can you help me?

Mia goes to her while I check on some other kids. What I love is, they don't look at me like I don't belong. They look at me with . . .

. . . well, respect.

The same way I look at Mrs. Winn.

It's then and there that I start thinking, maybe, just maybe . . .

. . . I might want to be a teacher, too.

Mia

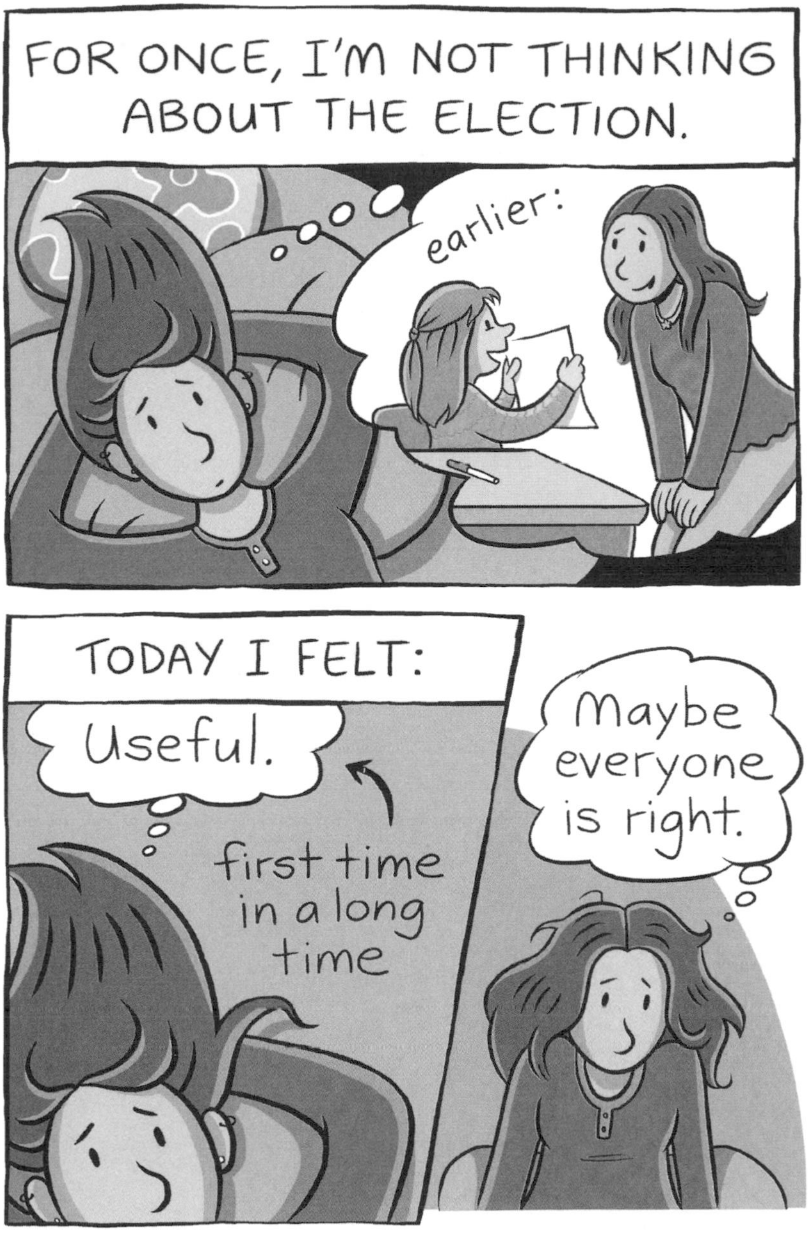
FOR ONCE, I'M NOT THINKING ABOUT THE ELECTION.
earlier:
TODAY I FELT:
Useful.
first time in a long time
Maybe everyone is right.

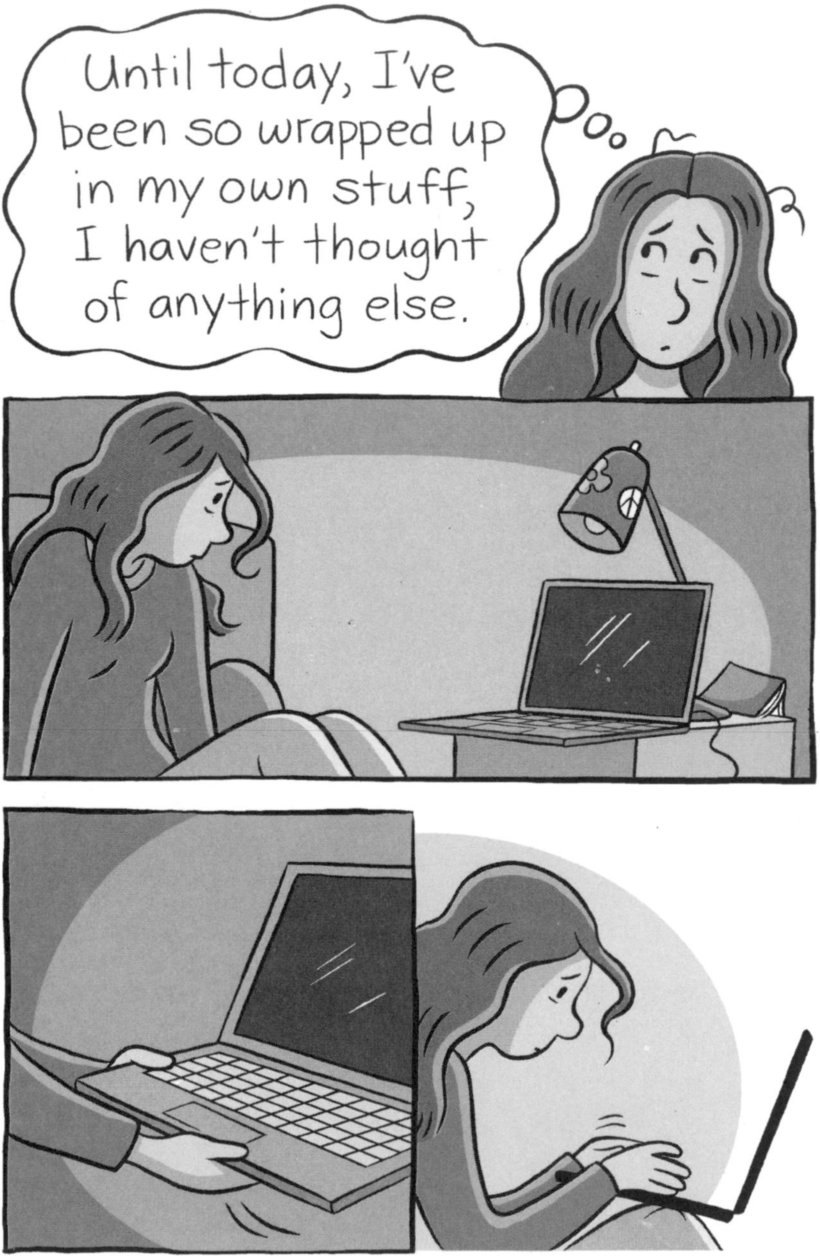
Until today, I've been so wrapped up in my own stuff, I haven't thought of anything else.

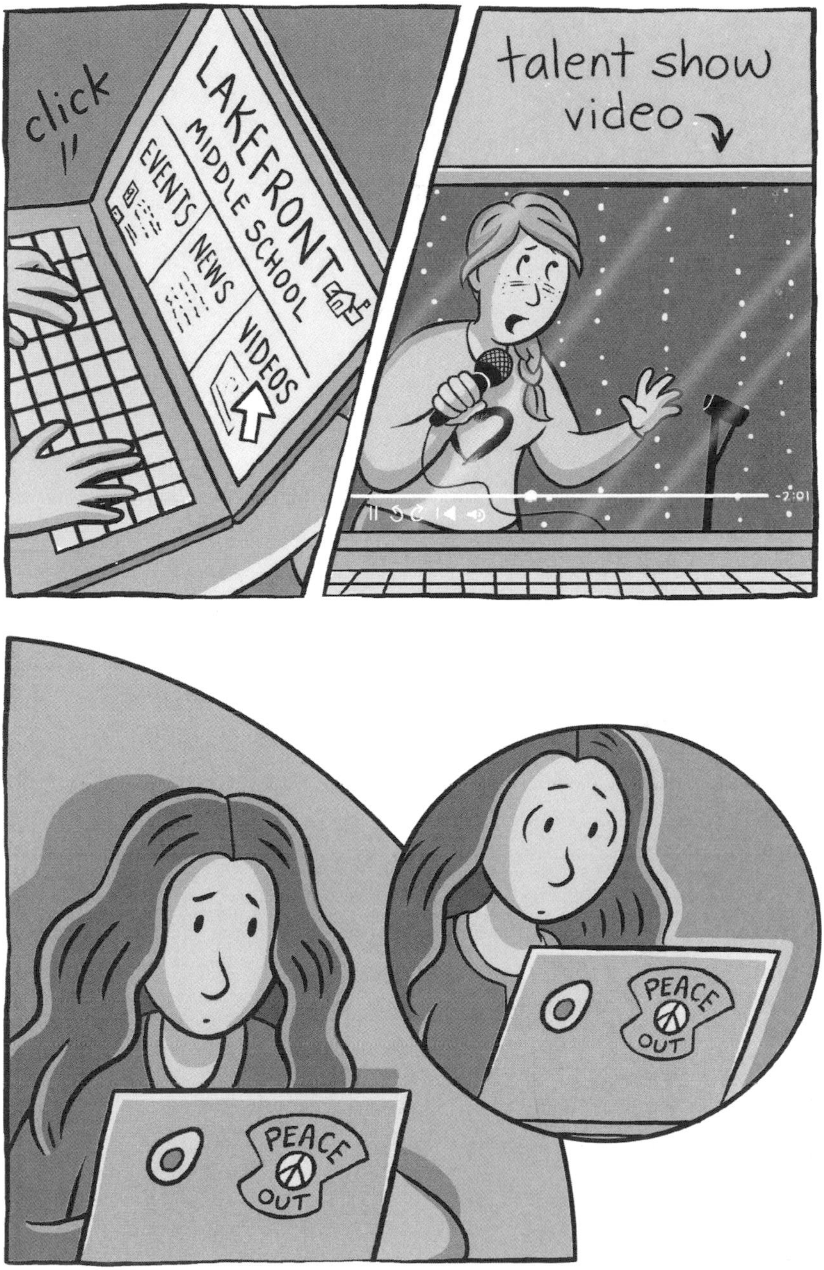
click
LAKEFRONT MIDDLE SCHOOL
EVENTS
NEWS
VIDEOS
talent show video
-2:01
PEACE OUT
PEACE OUT

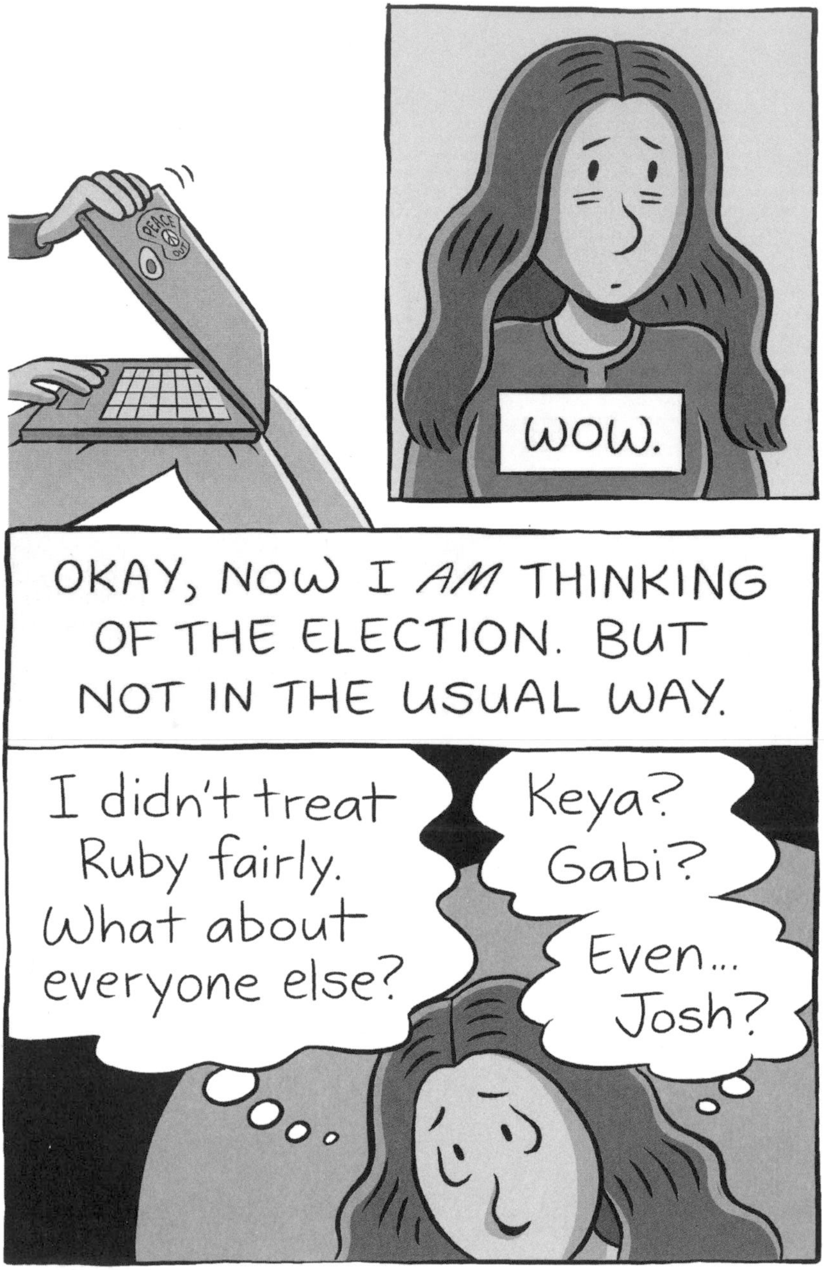
PEACE OUT
WOW.
OKAY, NOW I *AM* THINKING OF THE ELECTION. BUT NOT IN THE USUAL WAY.
I didn't treat Ruby fairly. What about everyone else?
Keya? Gabi?
Even... Josh?

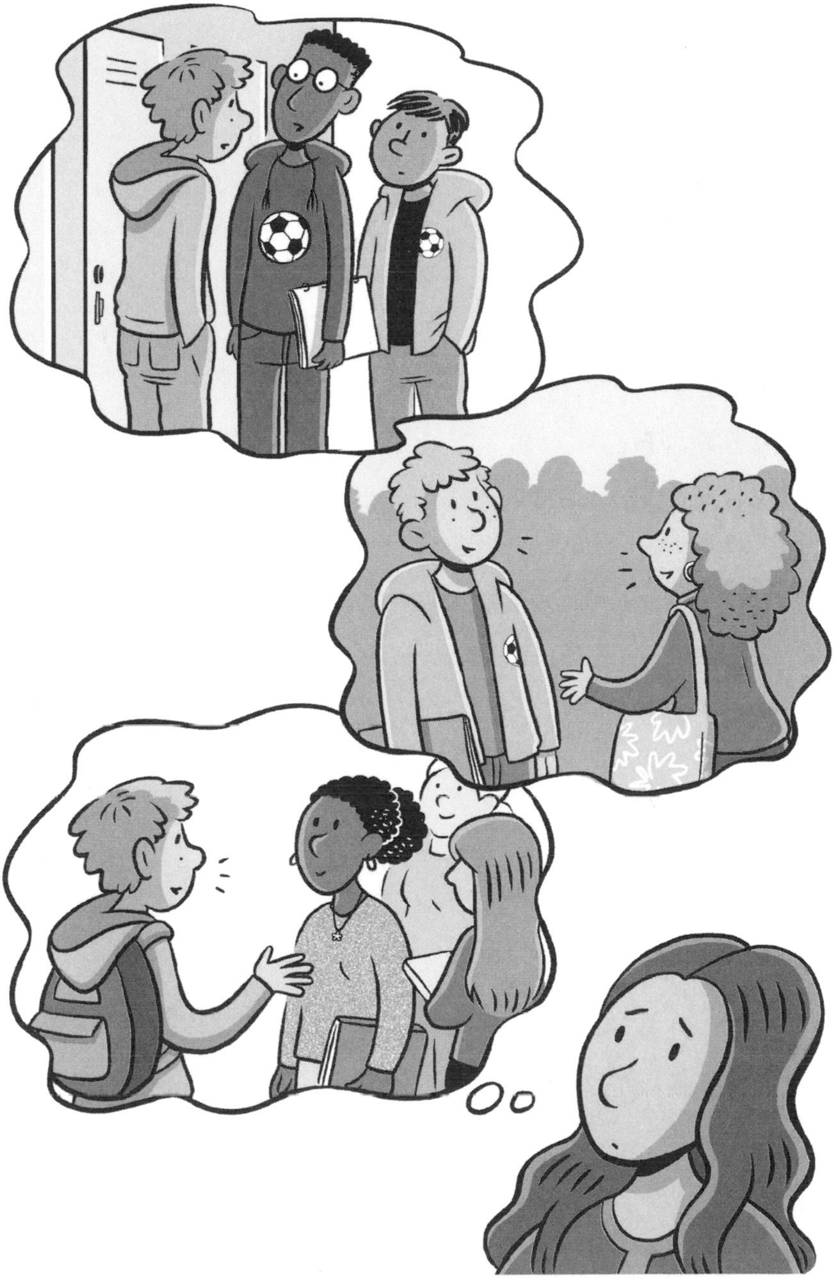

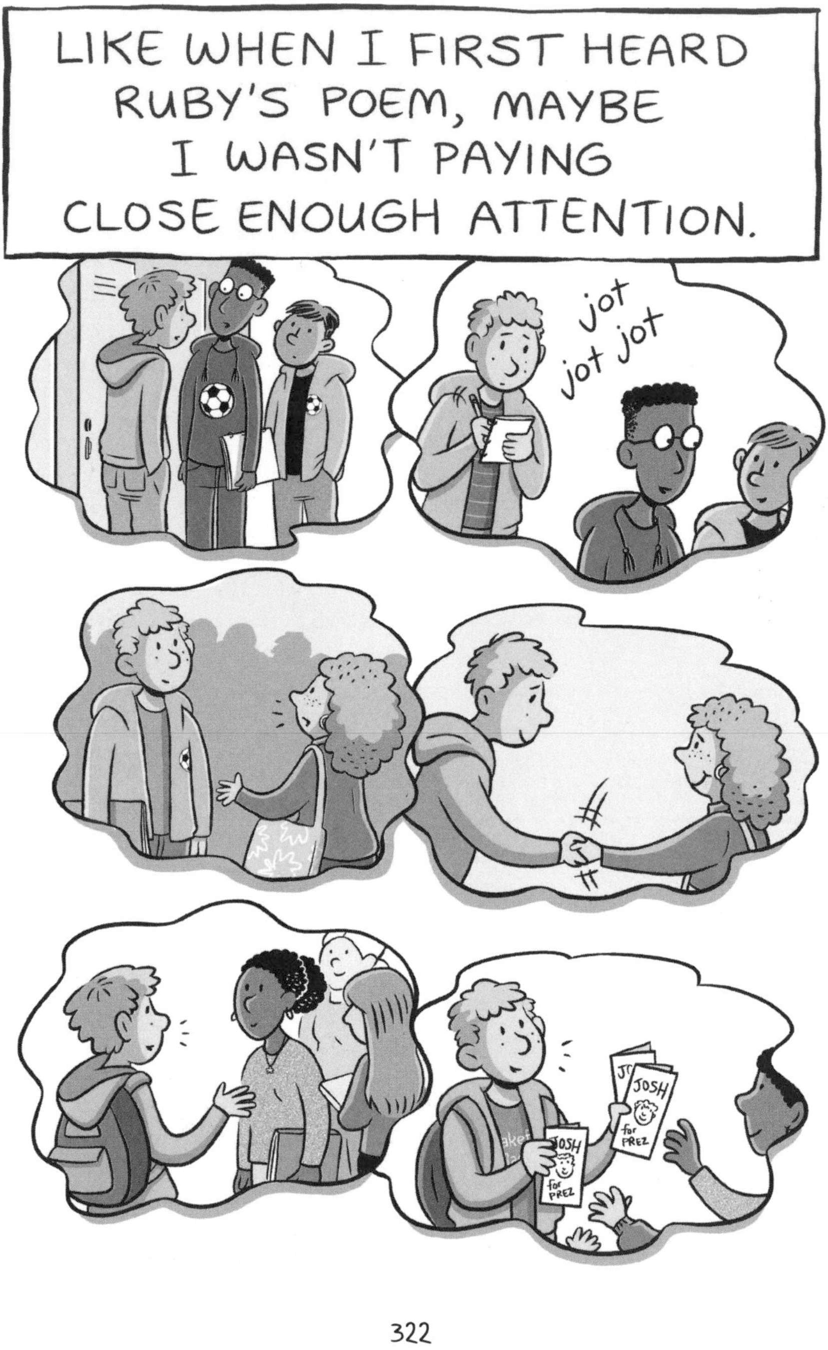
LIKE WHEN I FIRST HEARD RUBY'S POEM, MAYBE I WASN'T PAYING CLOSE ENOUGH ATTENTION.
jot jot jot
JOSH for PREZ
JOSH for PREZ
JOSH for PREZ

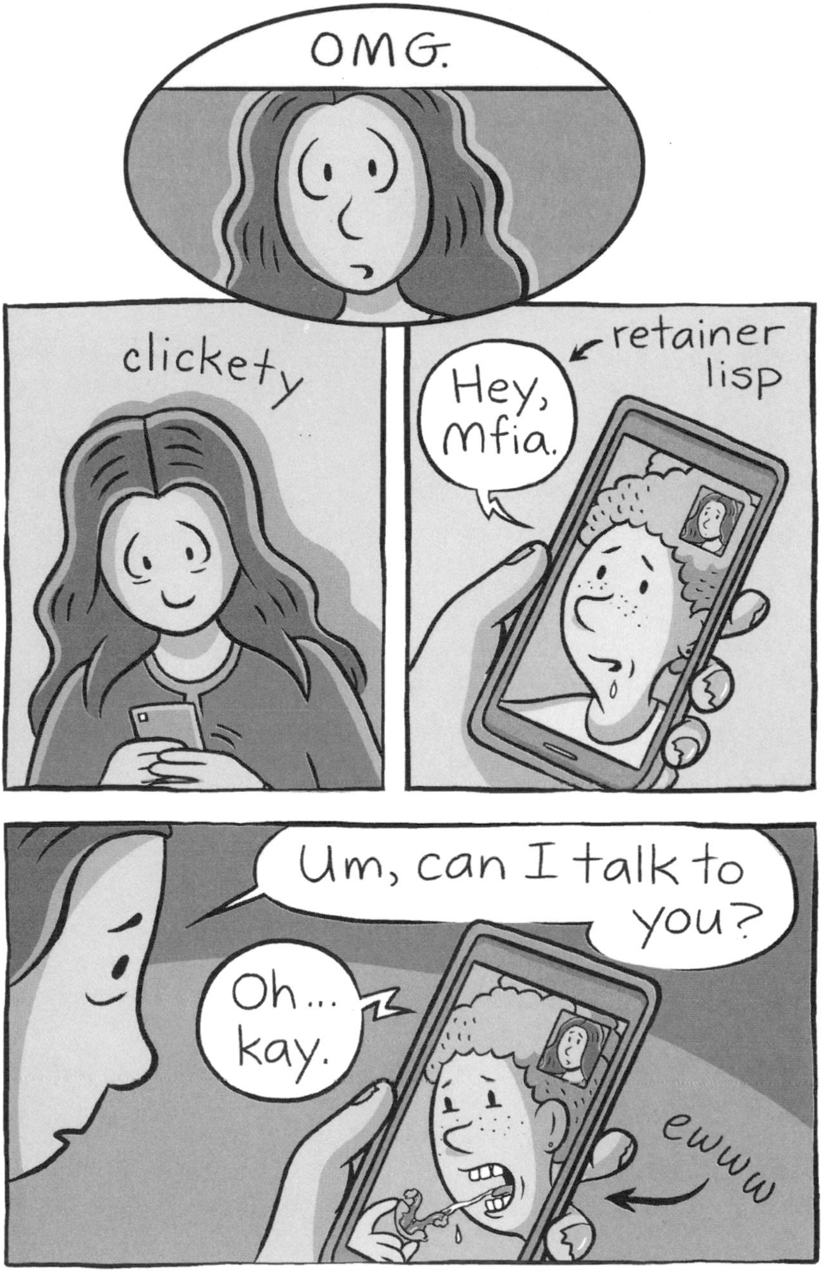
OMG.
clickety
Hey, Mfia.
retainer lisp
Um, can I talk to you?
Oh... kay.
ewww

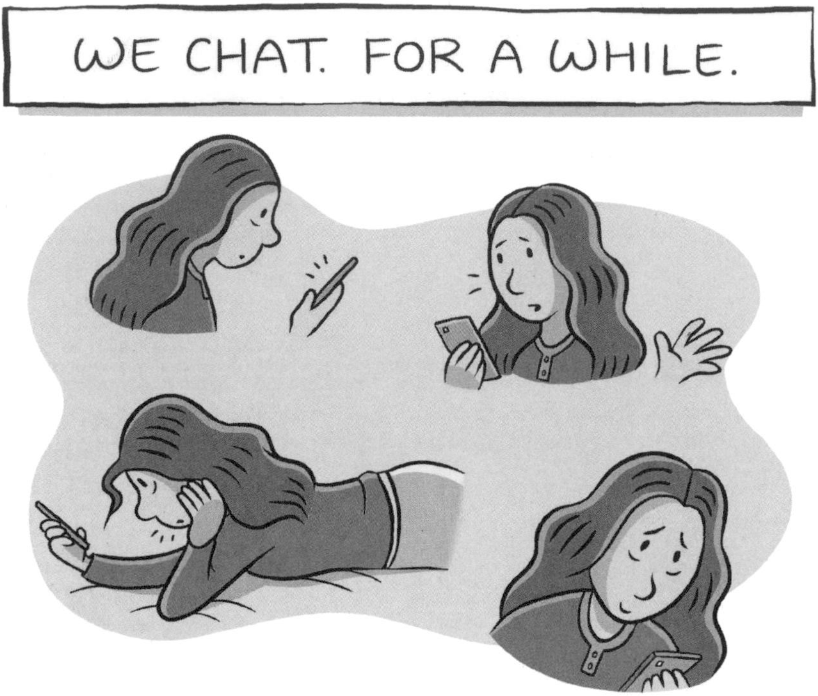
WE CHAT. FOR A WHILE.

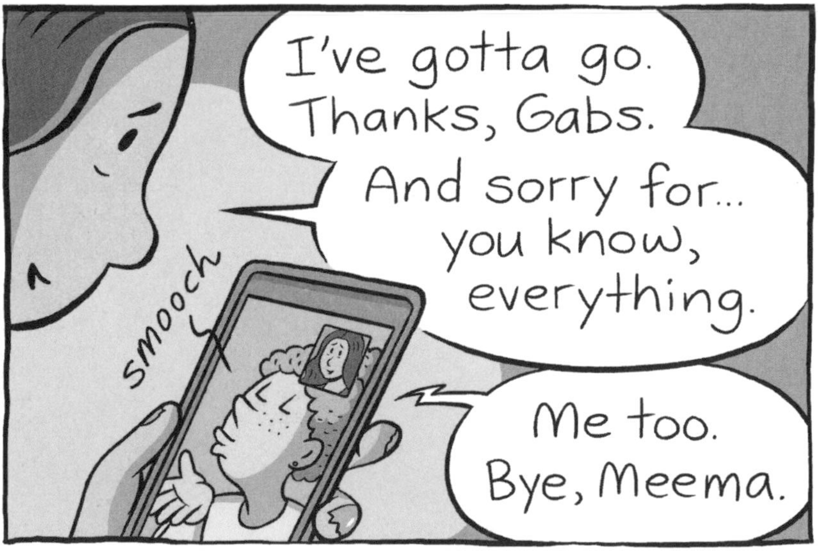
I've gotta go. Thanks, Gabs.
And sorry for... you know, everything.
smooch
Me too. Bye, Meema.

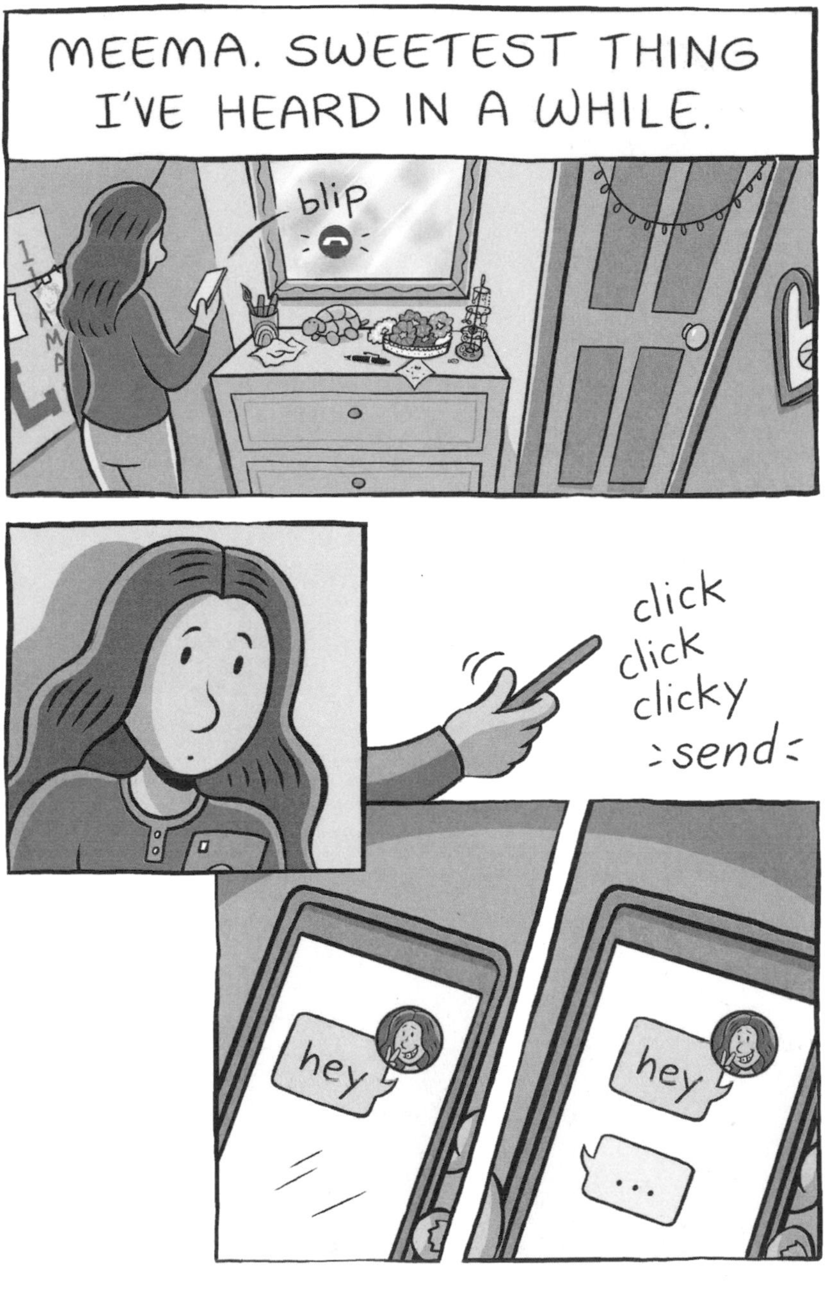
MEEMA. SWEETEST THING I'VE HEARD IN A WHILE.
blip
click
click
clicky
send
hey
hey
...

RUBY

I'm writing in my journal when I get the text.

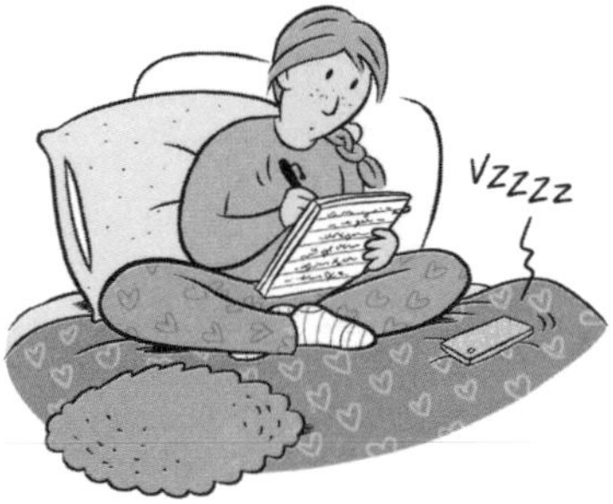
VZZZZ

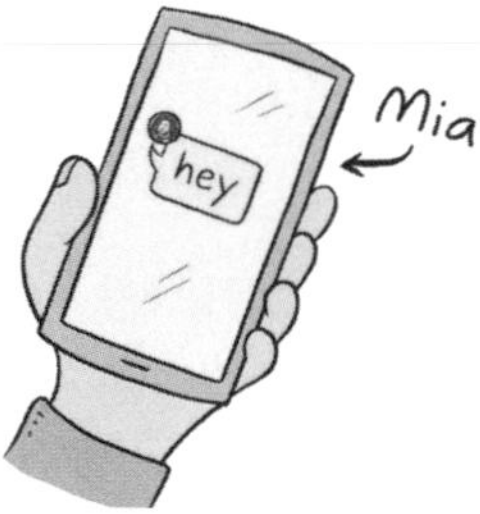
hey
Mia

Whoa.

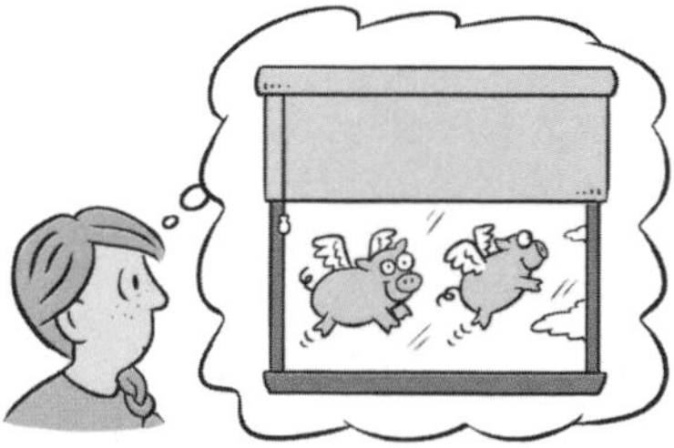

I stare at the screen for a long time.

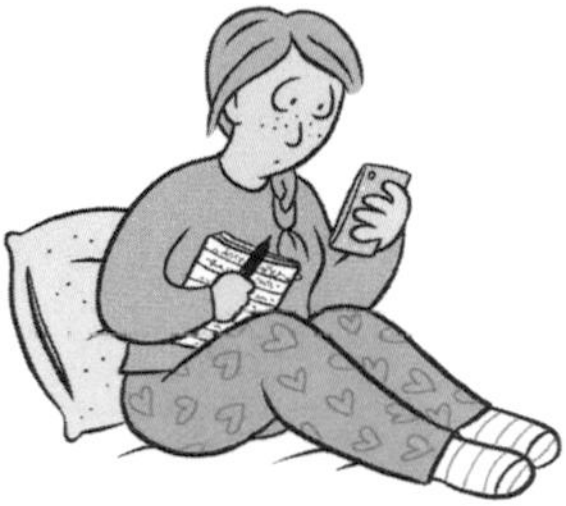

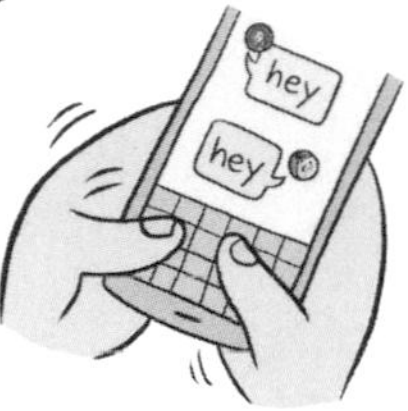
hey
hey

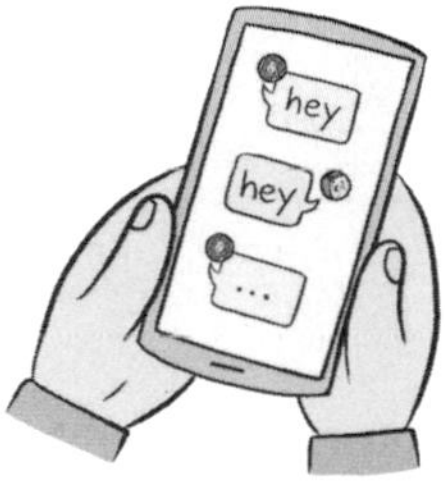
hey
hey
...

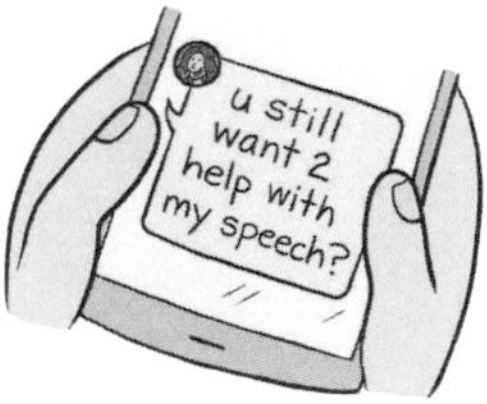
u still want 2 help with my speech?

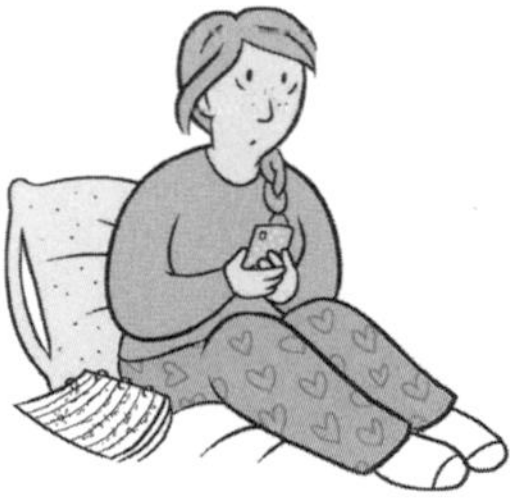

Do I?

Is she finally forgiving me for everything?

Am I forgiving **her**?

Typical Mia, making peace by asking for a favor.

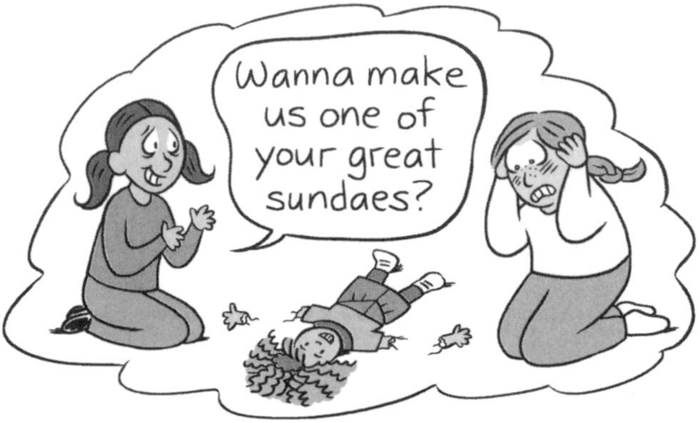
Wanna make us one of your great sundaes?

Still, she **is** reaching out.

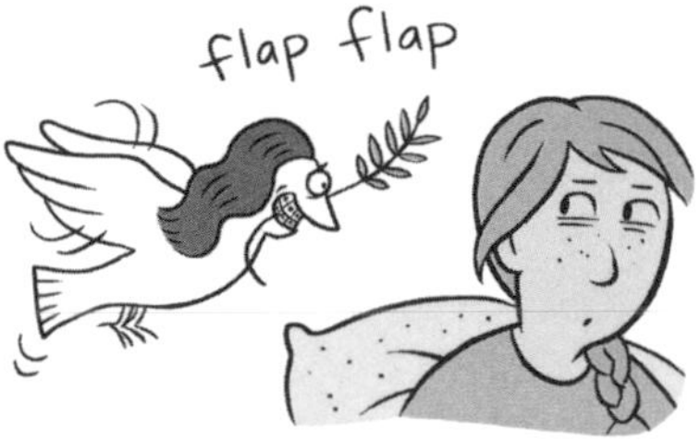
flap flap

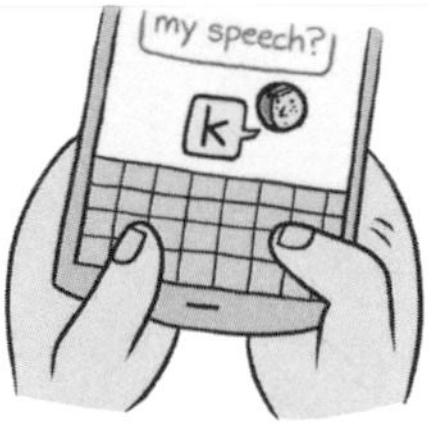
my speech?
k

Soon, I'm in her room. Hard to believe.

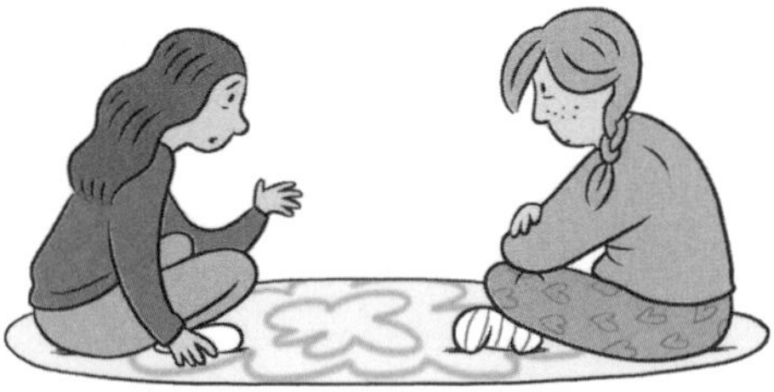

We don't get started right away. We talk. For a long time. I guess we need to "hash things out," as grown-ups say. Now I know where that expression comes from.

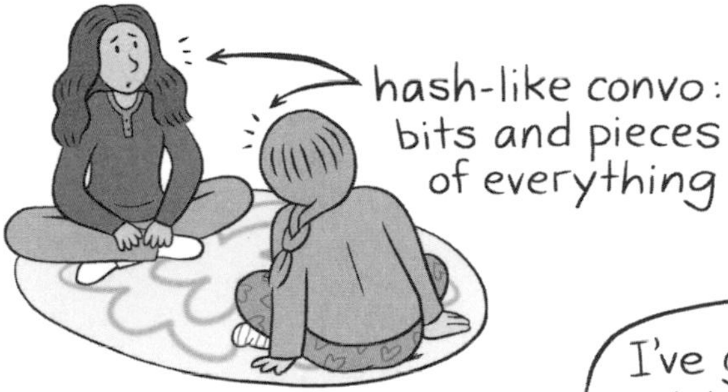
hash-like convo: bits and pieces of everything

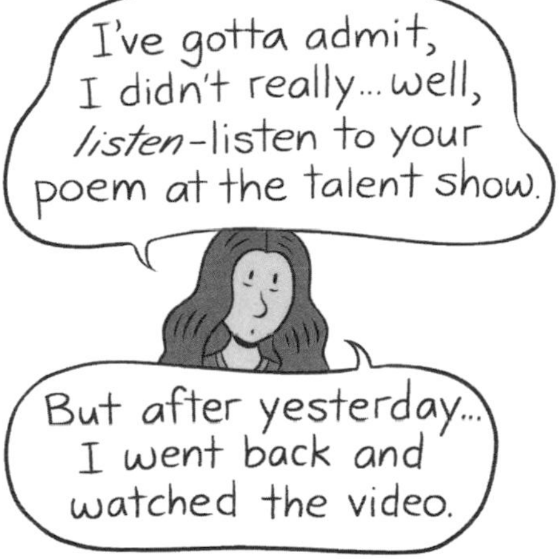
I've gotta admit, I didn't really... well, *listen*-listen to your poem at the talent show.
But after yesterday... I went back and watched the video.

She did?

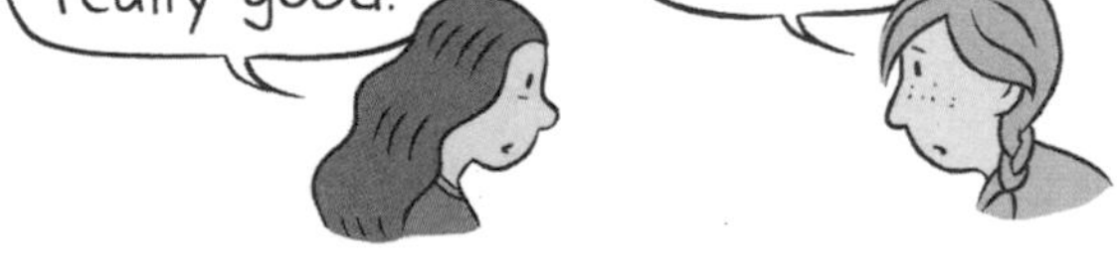
It was really, really good.
Thanks.

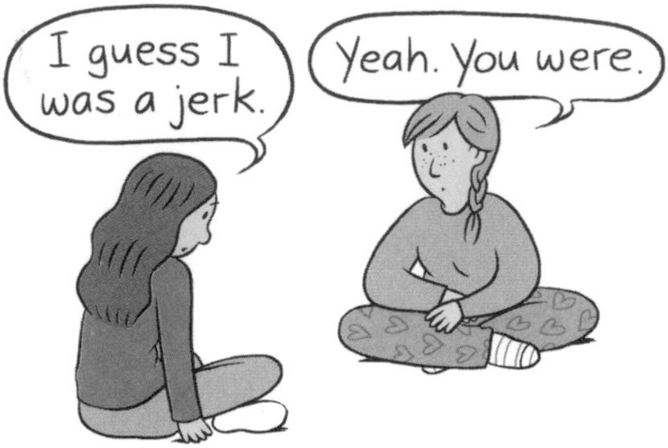
I guess I was a jerk.
Yeah. You were.

She looks at me and I half smile. She laughs a little.

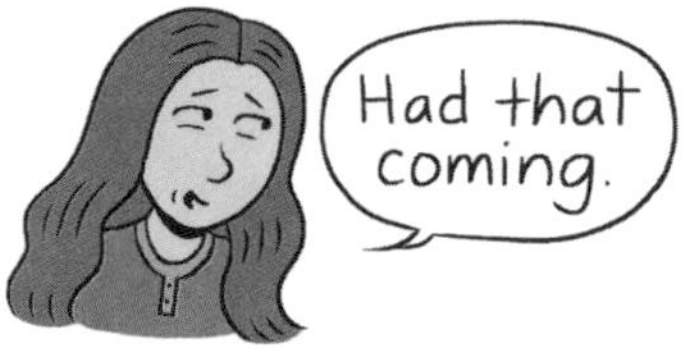
Had that coming.

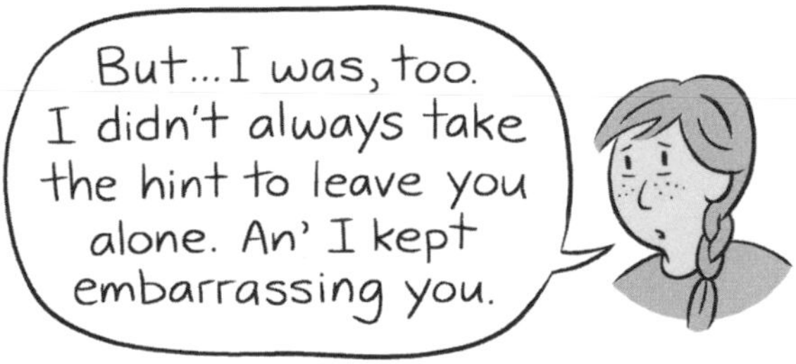
But... I was, too. I didn't always take the hint to leave you alone. An' I kept embarrassing you.

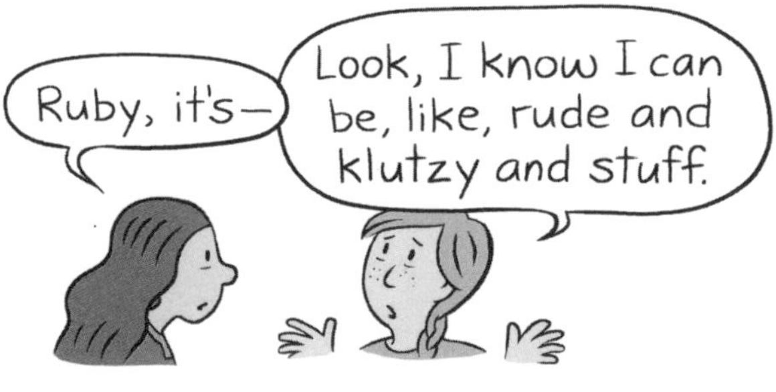
Ruby, it's—
Look, I know I can be, like, rude and klutzy and stuff.

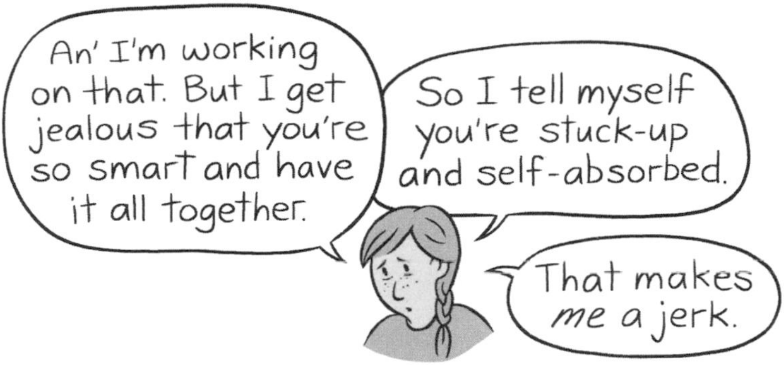
An' I'm working on that. But I get jealous that you're so smart and have it all together.
So I tell myself you're stuck-up and self-absorbed.
That makes *me* a jerk.

Mia thinks about this.

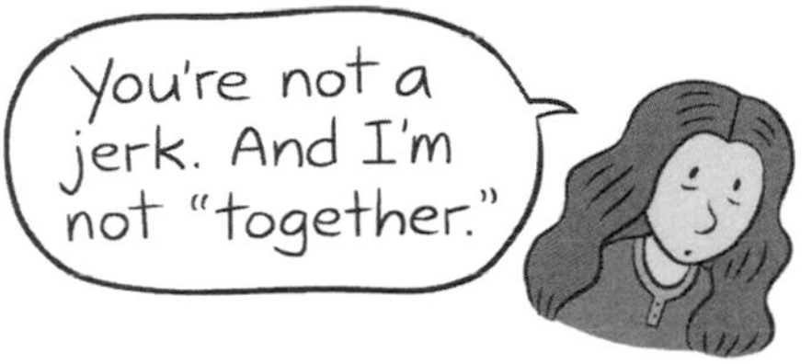
You're not a jerk. And I'm not "together."

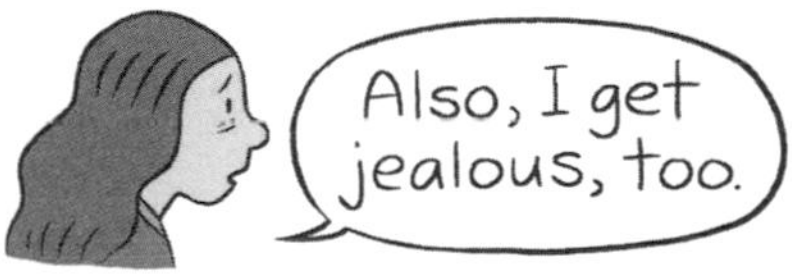
Also, I get jealous, too.

Say what?

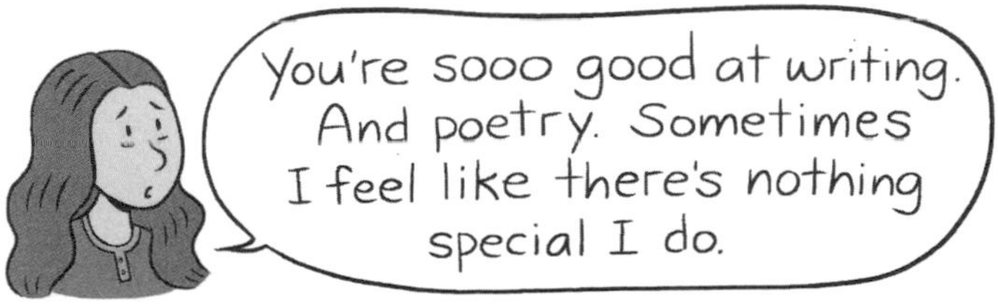
You're sooo good at writing. And poetry. Sometimes I feel like there's nothing special I do.

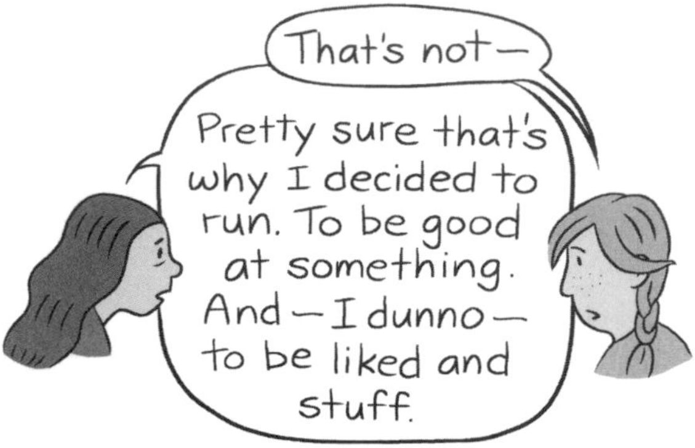
That's not—
Pretty sure that's why I decided to run. To be good at something. And—I dunno—to be liked and stuff.

A pause.

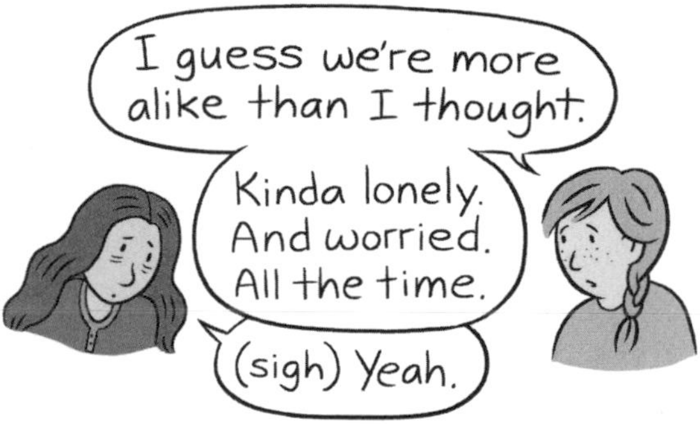
I guess we're more alike than I thought.
Kinda lonely. And worried. All the time.
(sigh) Yeah.

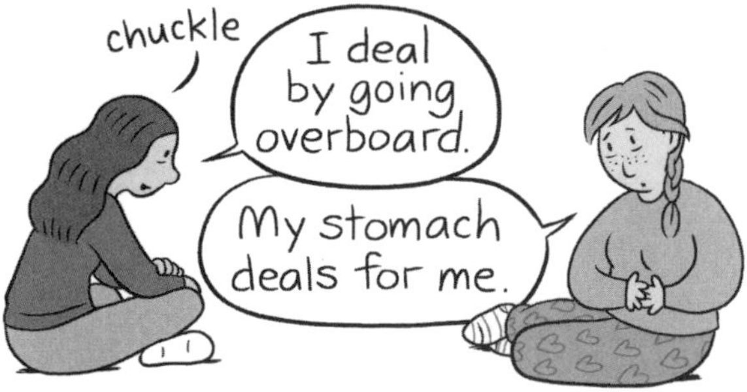
chuckle
I deal by going overboard.
My stomach deals for me.

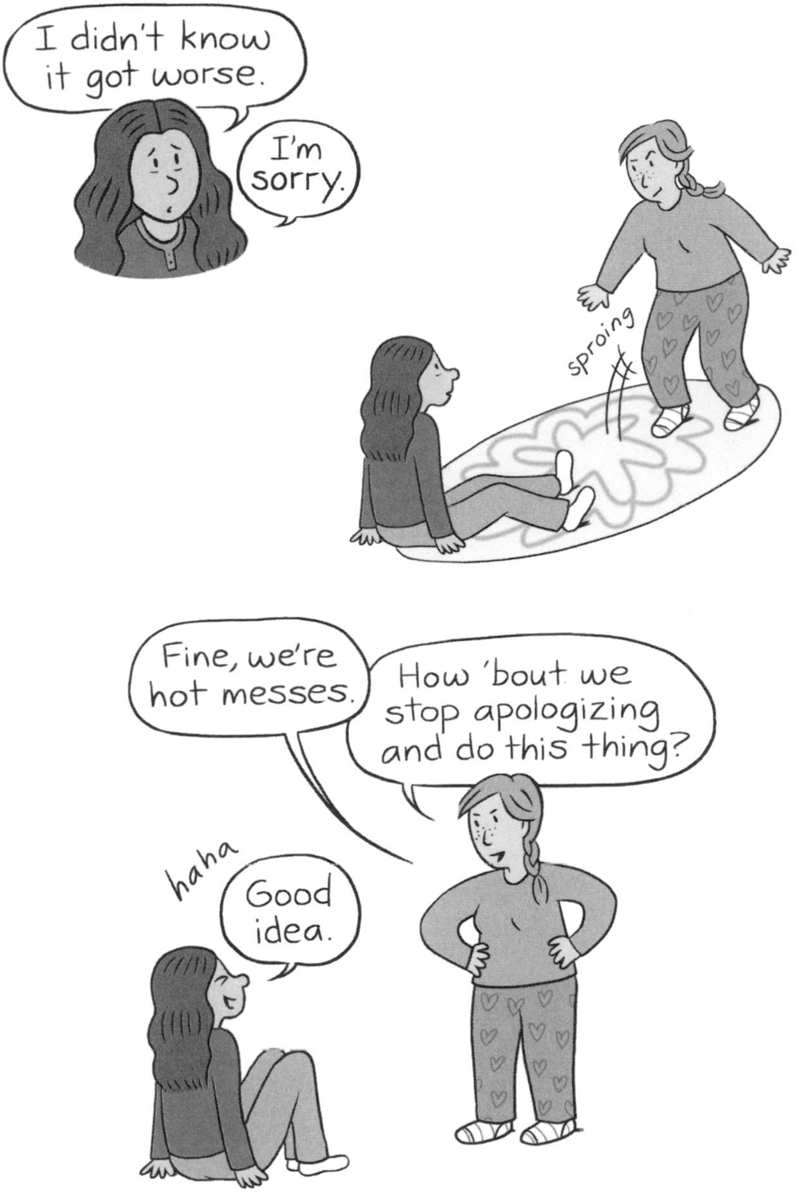
I didn't know it got worse.
I'm sorry.
sproing
Fine, we're hot messes.
How 'bout we stop apologizing and do this thing?
haha
Good idea.

I help her. When we're done, she reads it aloud to me.

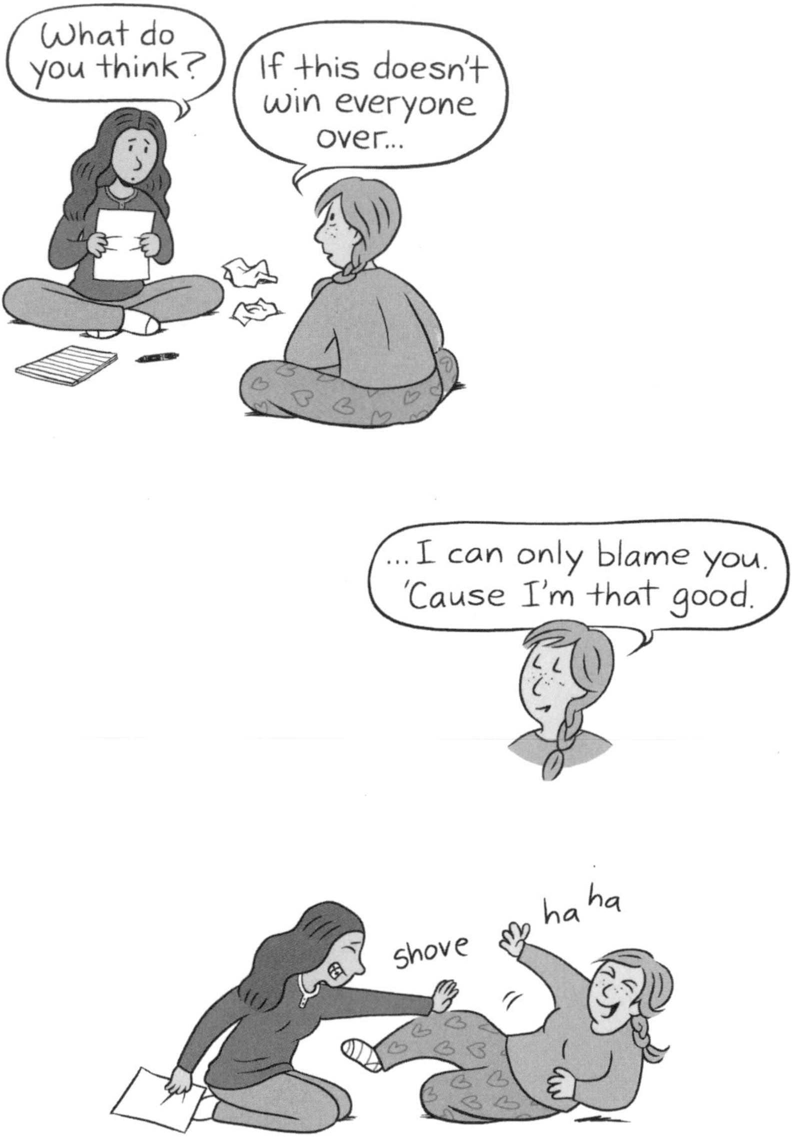
What do you think?
If this doesn't win everyone over...
...I can only blame you. 'Cause I'm that good.
shove
ha ha

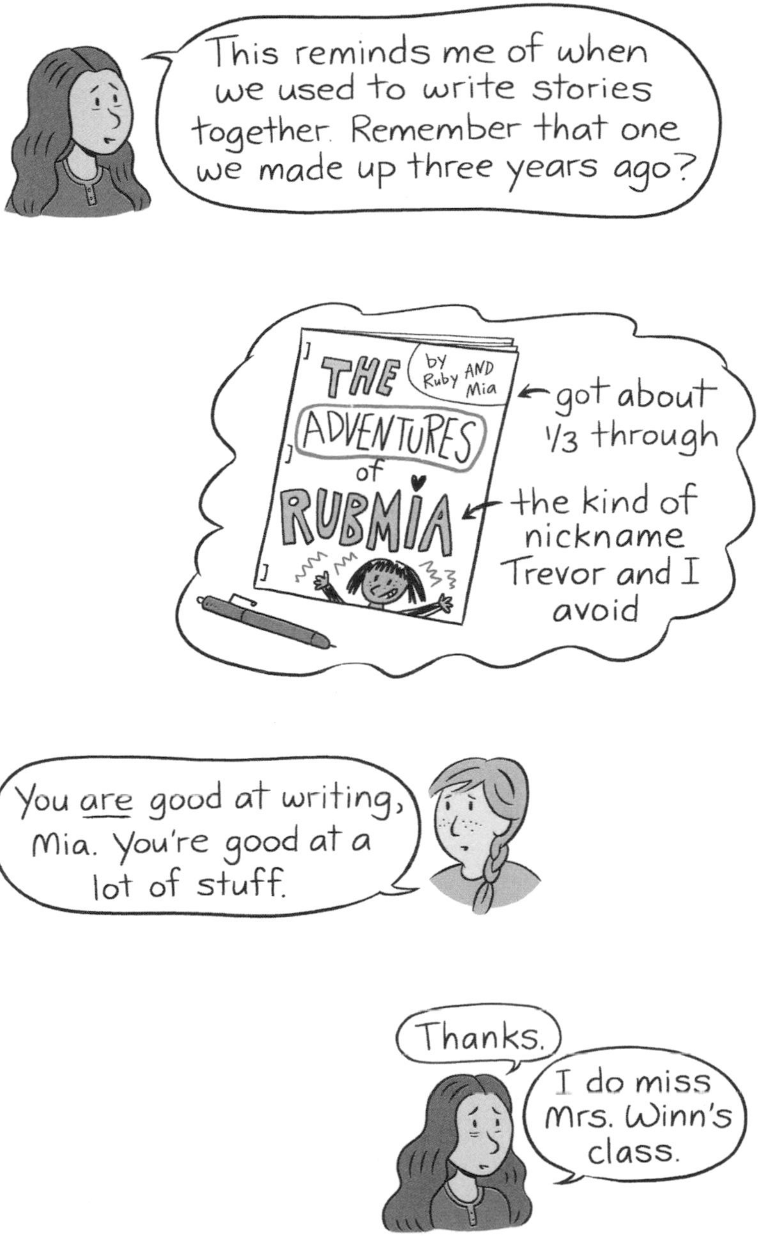
This reminds me of when we used to write stories together. Remember that one we made up three years ago?
THE ADVENTURES of RUBMIA
by Ruby AND Mia
got about 1/3 through
the kind of nickname Trevor and I avoid
You are good at writing, Mia. You're good at a lot of stuff.
Thanks.
I do miss Mrs. Winn's class.

She goes silent for a few seconds, remembering, probably. Then she looks up and smiles.

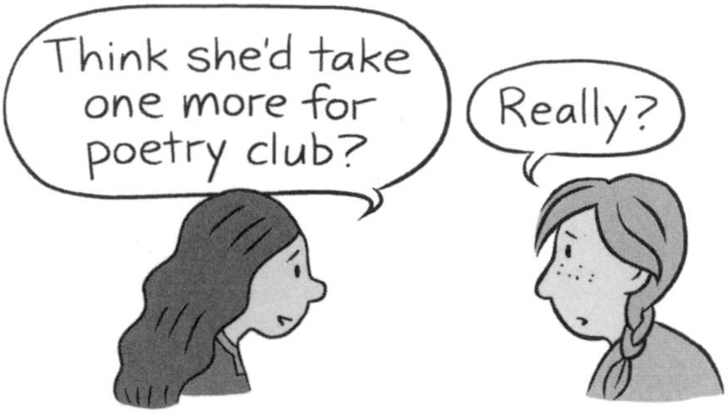
Think she'd take one more for poetry club?
Really?

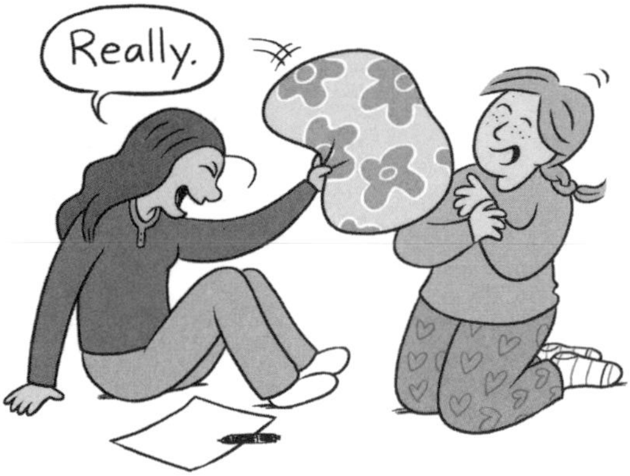
Really.

Mia

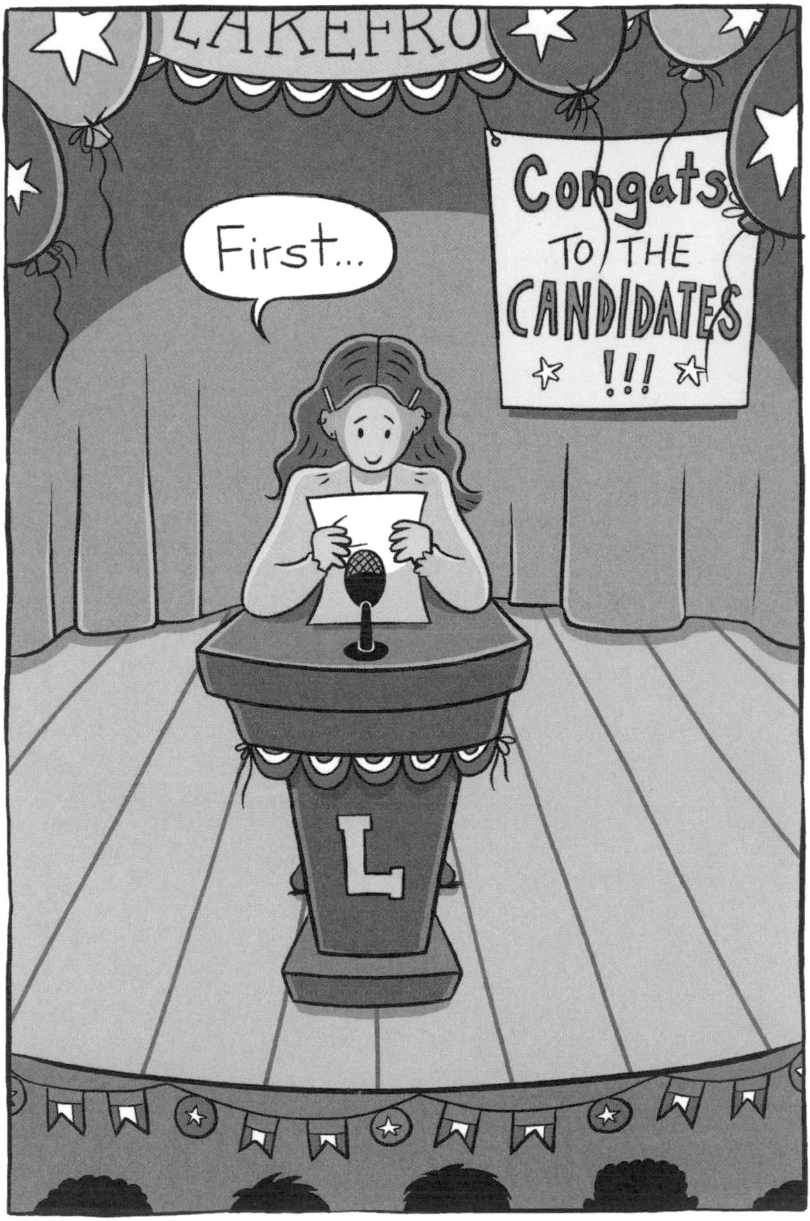
LAKEFRO
Congats TO THE CANDIDATES !!!
First...
L

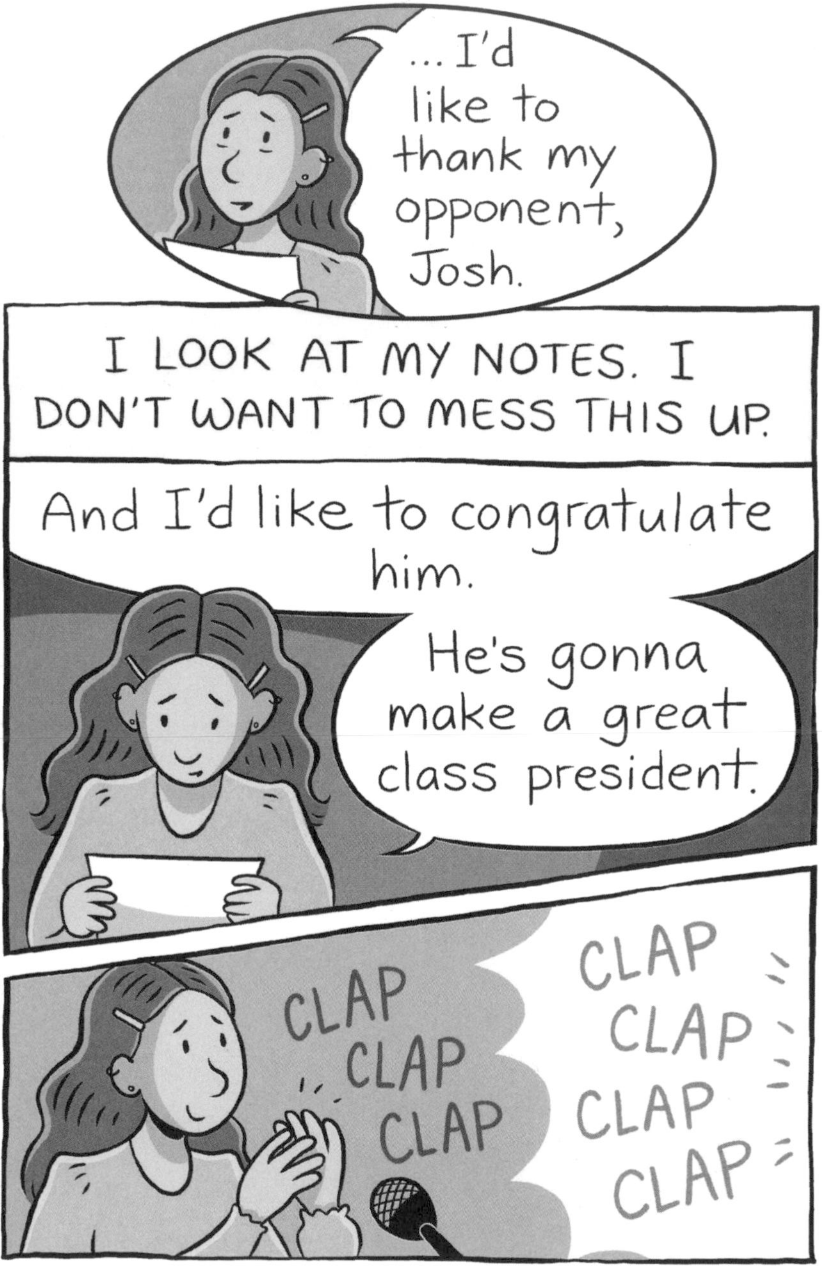
...I'd like to thank my opponent, Josh.
I LOOK AT MY NOTES. I DON'T WANT TO MESS THIS UP.
And I'd like to congratulate him.
He's gonna make a great class president.
CLAP CLAP CLAP
CLAP CLAP CLAP CLAP

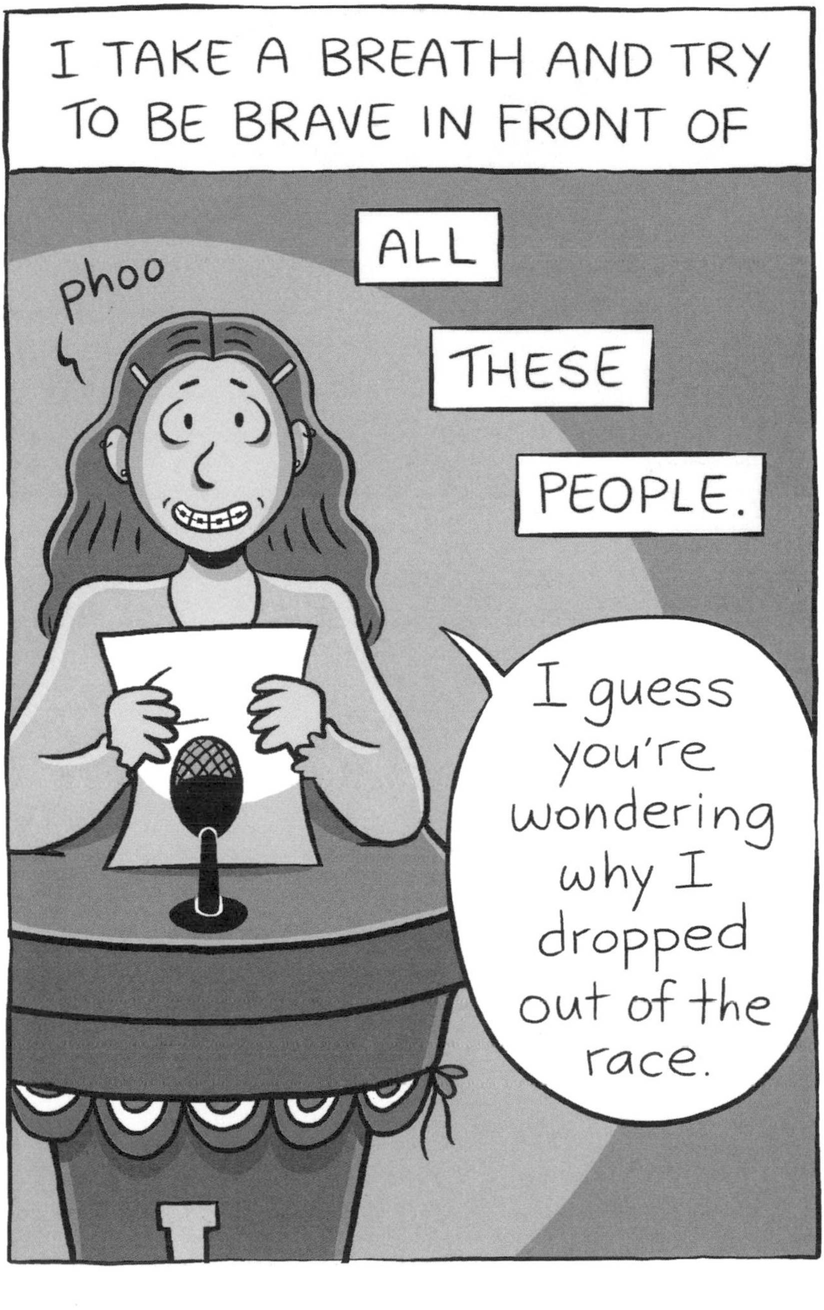
I TAKE A BREATH AND TRY TO BE BRAVE IN FRONT OF
phoo
ALL
THESE
PEOPLE.
I guess you're wondering why I dropped out of the race.

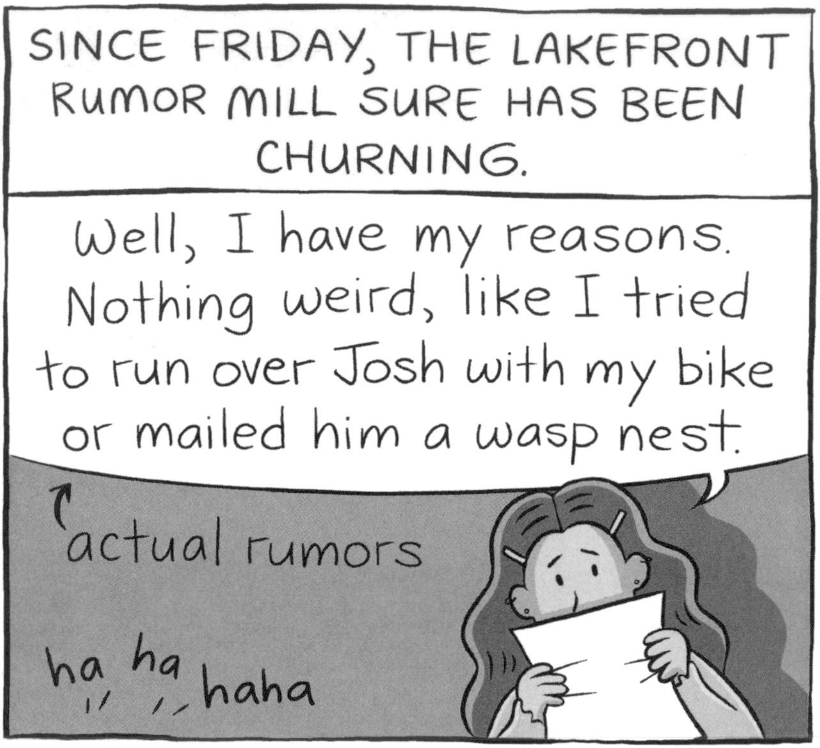
SINCE FRIDAY, THE LAKEFRONT RUMOR MILL SURE HAS BEEN CHURNING.
Well, I have my reasons. Nothing weird, like I tried to run over Josh with my bike or mailed him a wasp nest.
actual rumors
ha ha haha

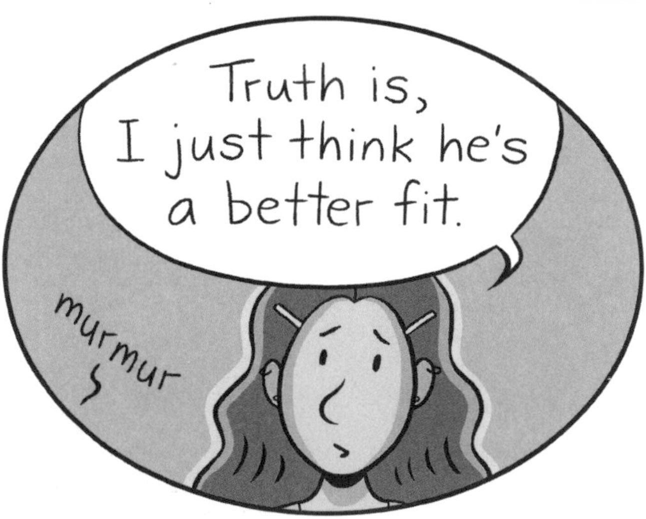
Truth is, I just think he's a better fit.
murmur

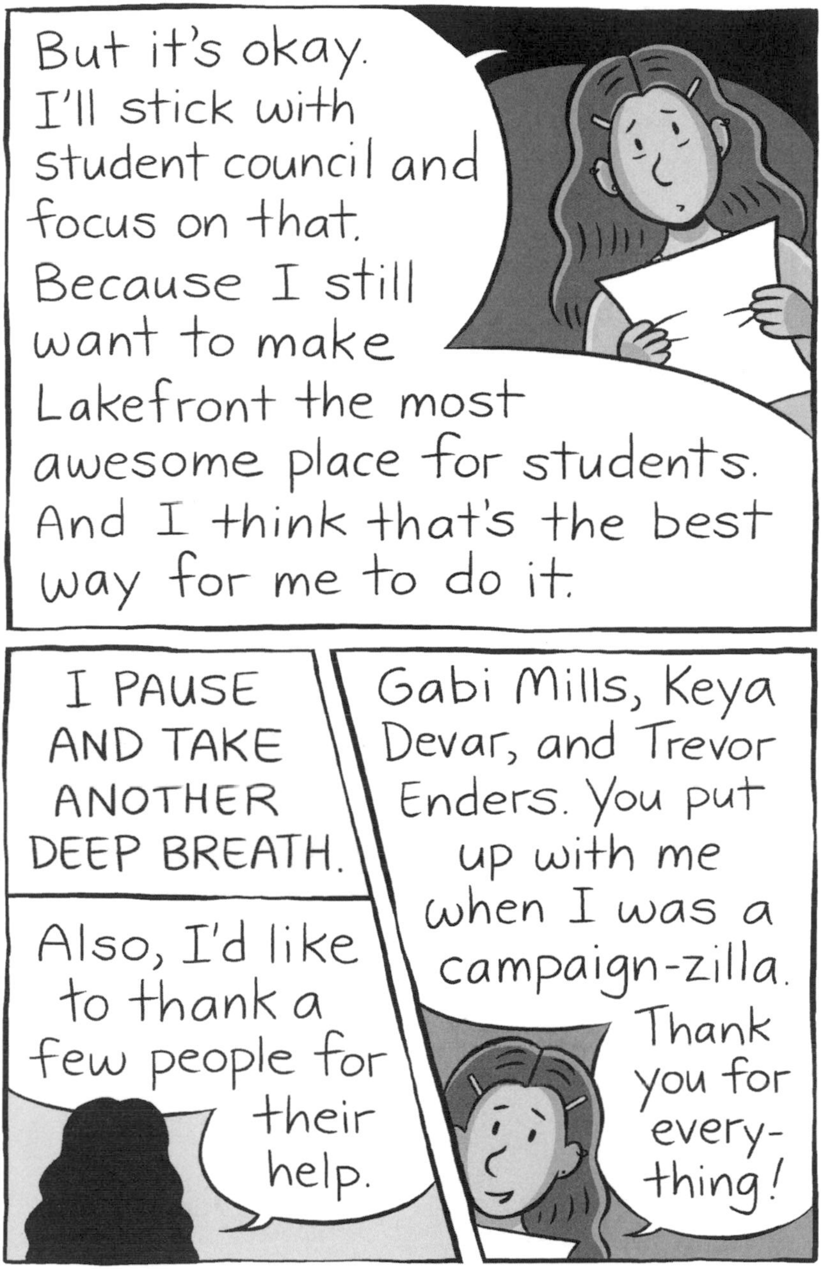
But it's okay. I'll stick with student council and focus on that. Because I still want to make Lakefront the most awesome place for students. And I think that's the best way for me to do it.
I PAUSE AND TAKE ANOTHER DEEP BREATH.
Also, I'd like to thank a few people for their help.
Gabi Mills, Keya Devar, and Trevor Enders. You put up with me when I was a campaign-zilla.
Thank you for every-thing!

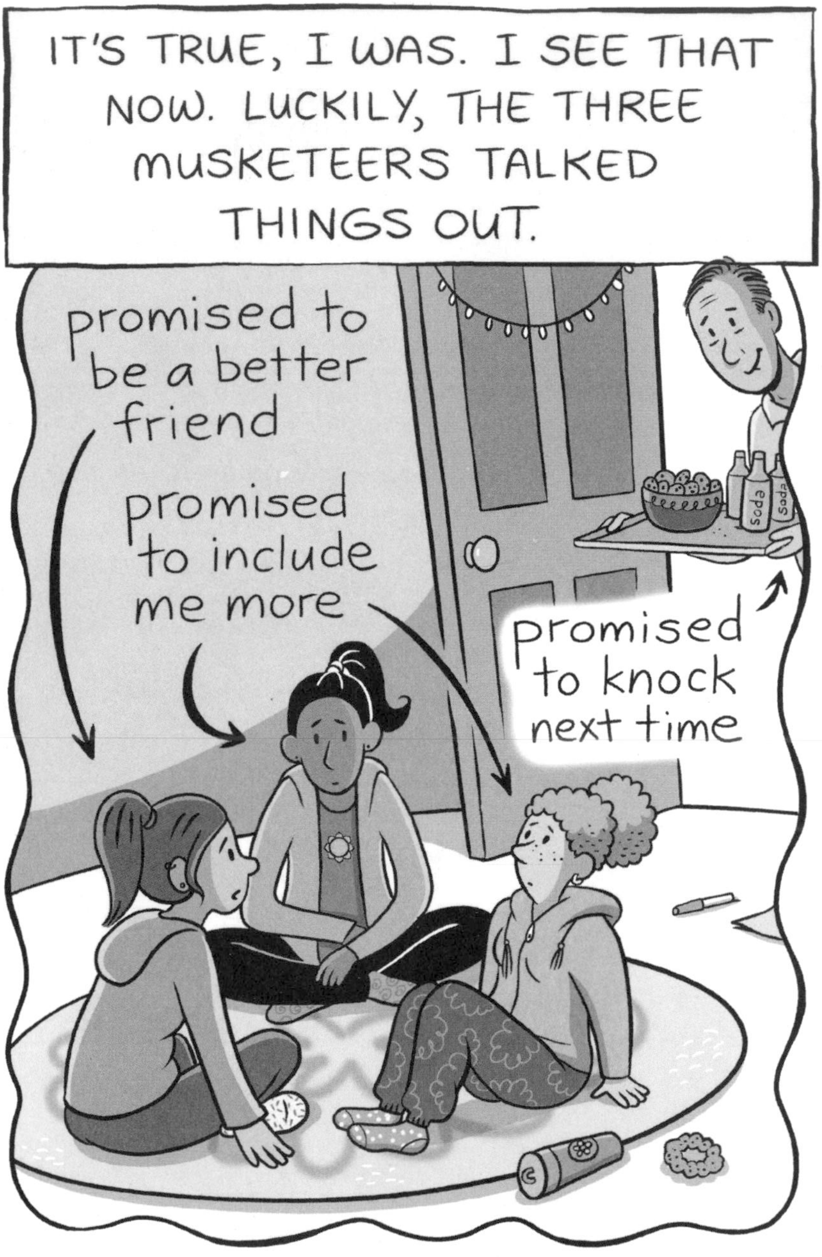
IT'S TRUE, I WAS. I SEE THAT NOW. LUCKILY, THE THREE MUSKETEERS TALKED THINGS OUT.
promised to be a better friend
promised to include me more
promised to knock next time
Soda
Soda

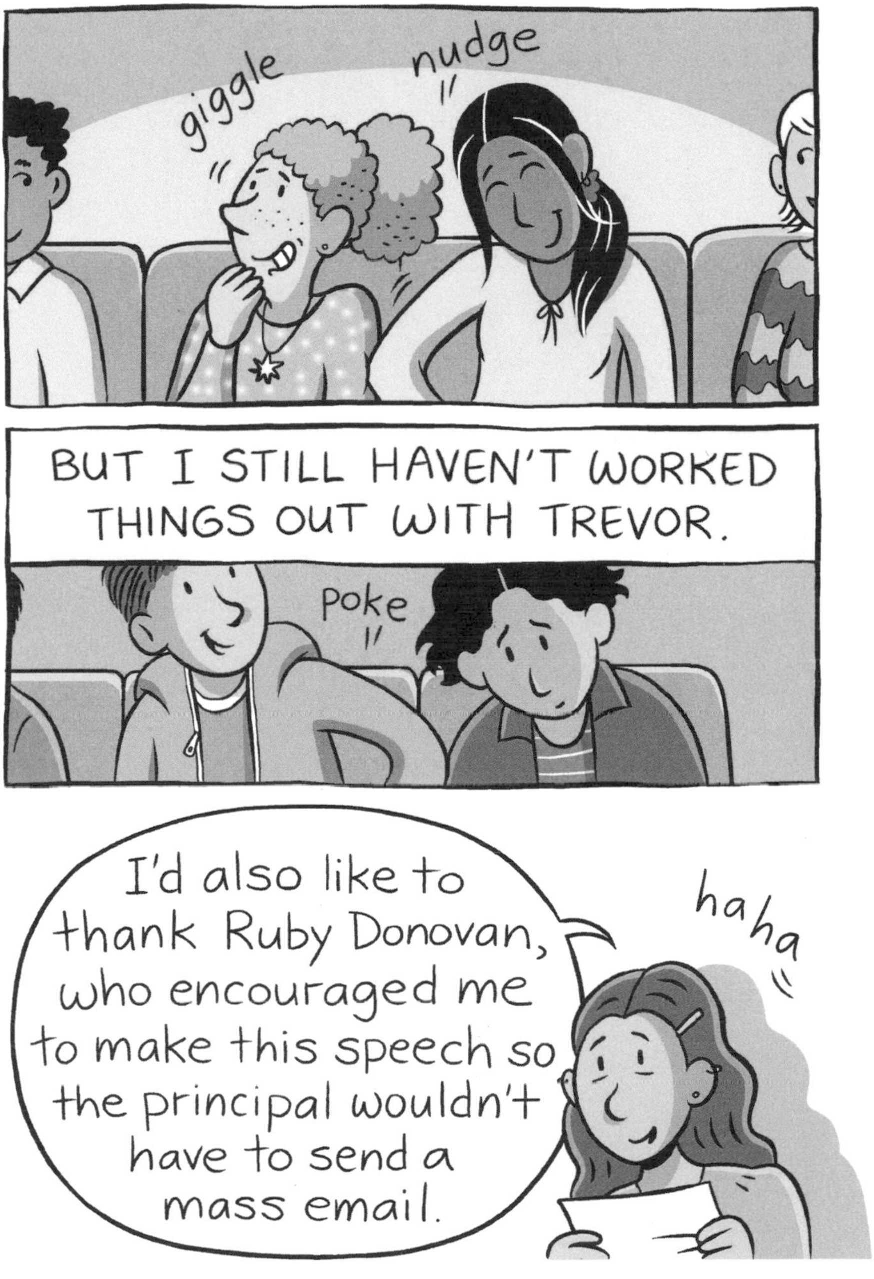
giggle
nudge
BUT I STILL HAVEN'T WORKED THINGS OUT WITH TREVOR.
poke
I'd also like to thank Ruby Donovan, who encouraged me to make this speech so the principal wouldn't have to send a mass email.
haha

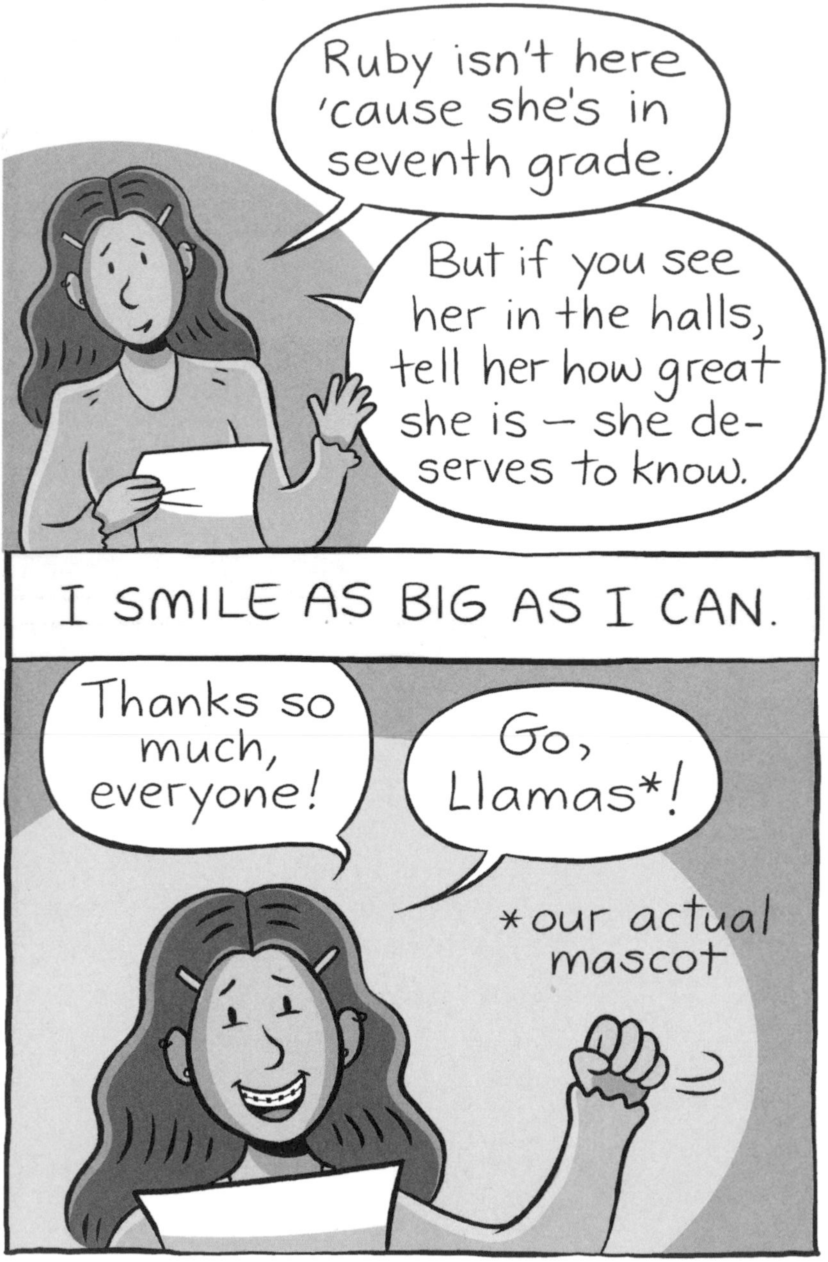
Ruby isn't here 'cause she's in seventh grade.
But if you see her in the halls, tell her how great she is — she de-serves to know.
I SMILE AS BIG AS I CAN.
Thanks so much, everyone!
Go, Llamas*!
*our actual mascot

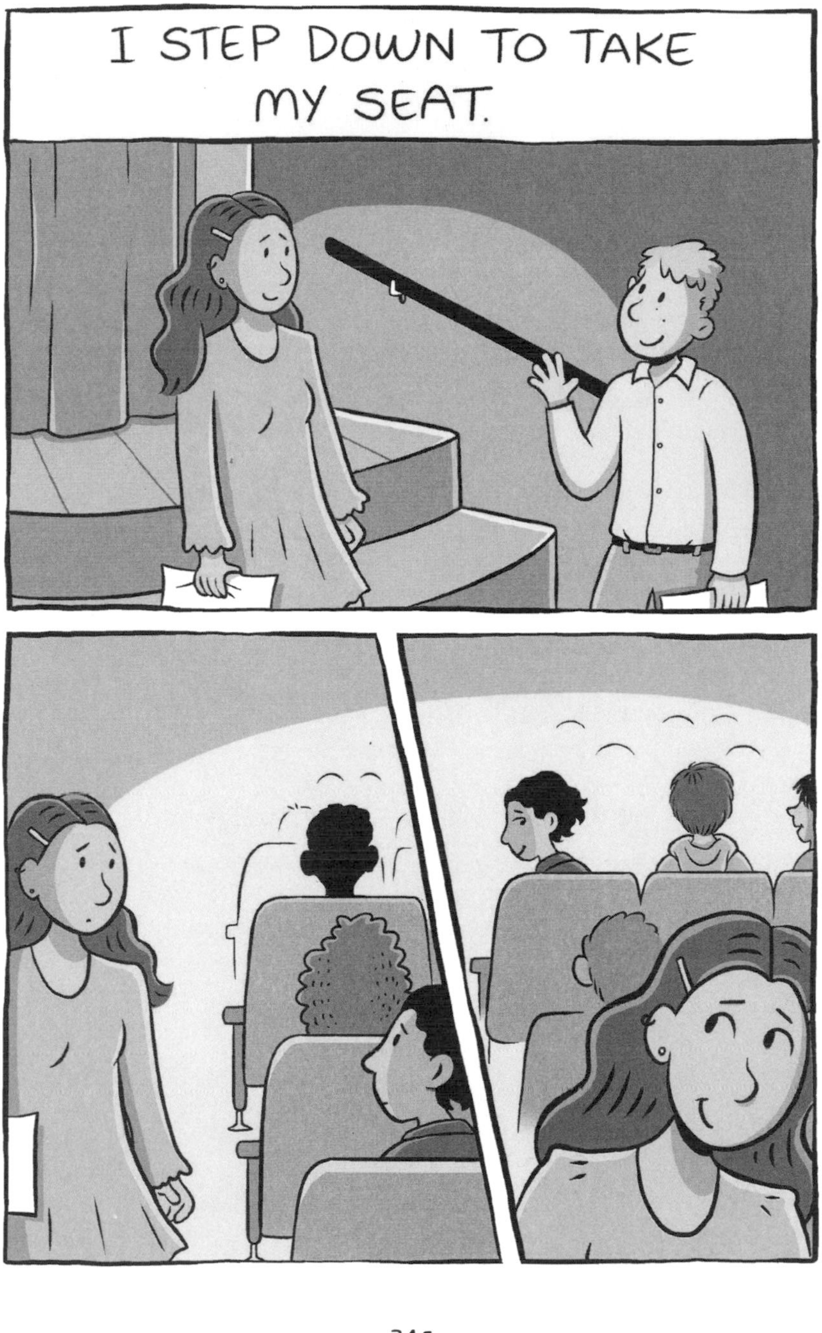
I STEP DOWN TO TAKE MY SEAT.

RUBY

Writing in my journal. Got a lot to say lately.

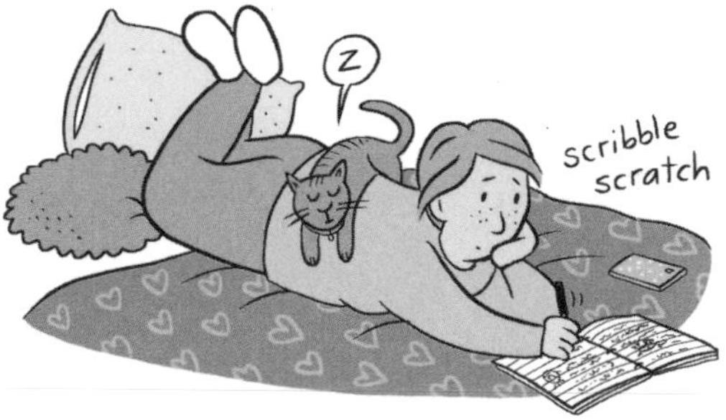
z
scribble
scratch

Good things this time. Well, mostly. Some iffy, too. Like Joe Lungo, who thinks spitballs are the best way to get the teacher's attention, even when I'm in the line of fire.

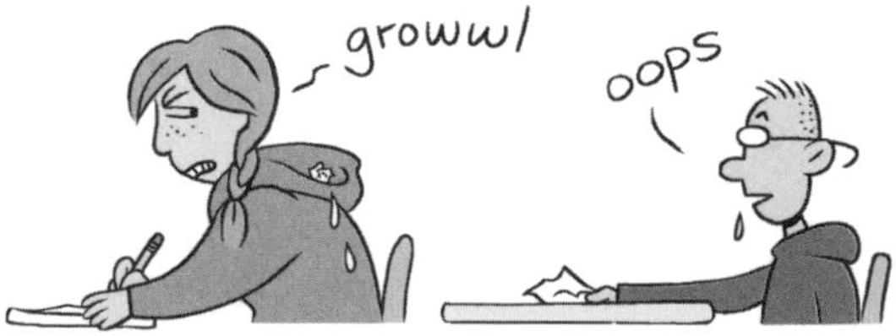
growwl
oops

Also, asparagus, which is what Mom served on top of a perfectly good pile of spaghetti tonight. What gives?

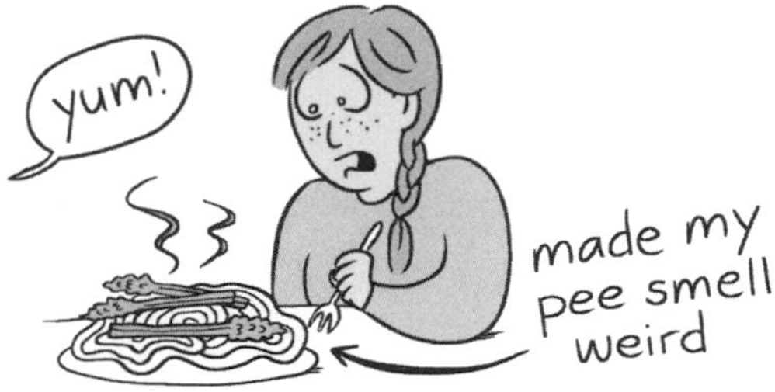
yum!
made my pee smell weird

Speaking of food (and pee), I went back to the doctor to get my nervous stomach checked. This time, the doctor sent me to my very first . . .

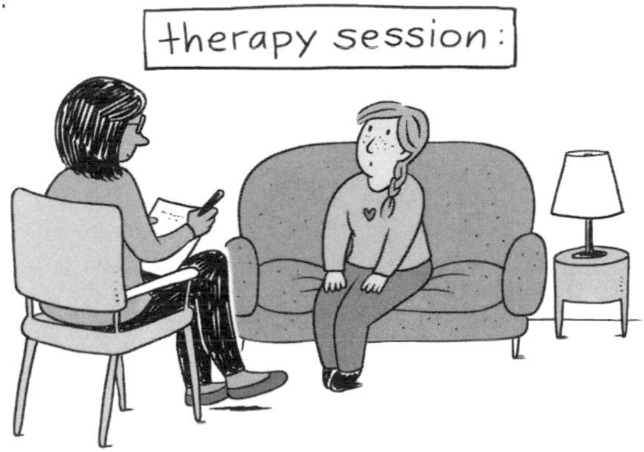
therapy session:

She gave me a mental "tool kit" of tricks to start helping me with anxiety. Like meditating, breathing, and my favorite . . .

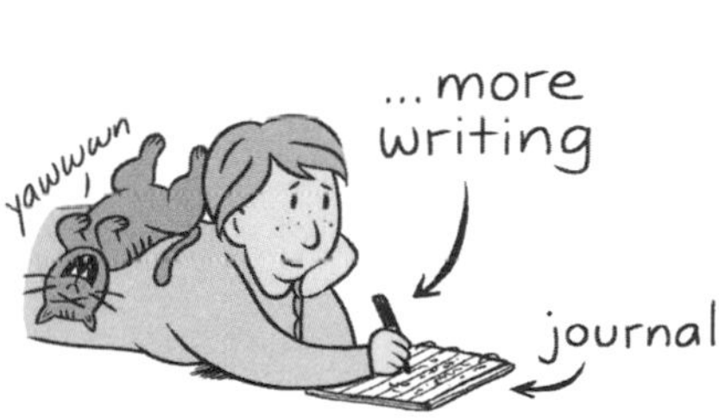
yawwwn
. . . more writing
journal

I had only one session, but I guess I'm meeting again with her in a few weeks. She seemed okay. Well, more than okay. She seemed to get me.

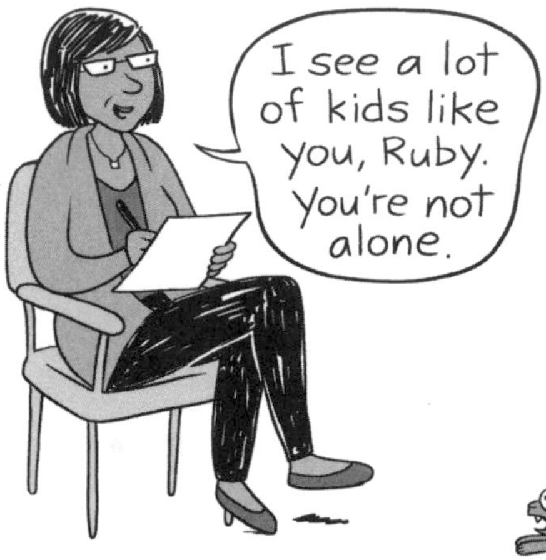
I see a lot of kids like you, Ruby. You're not alone.

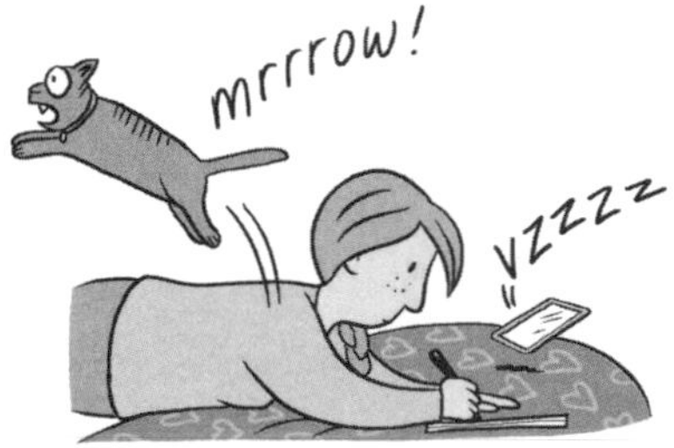
mrrrow!
VZZZZ

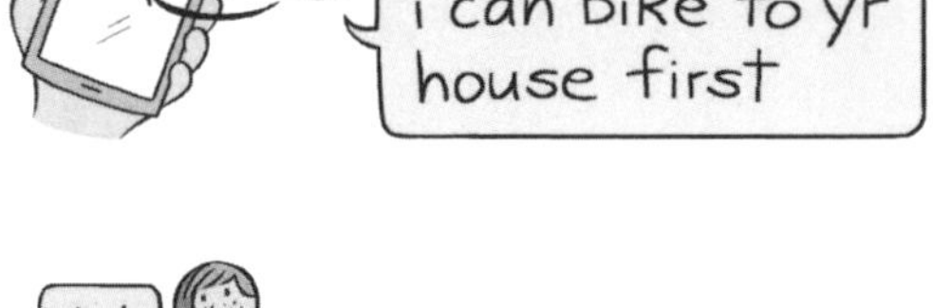
Leah
taystees tmw? i can bike to yr house first

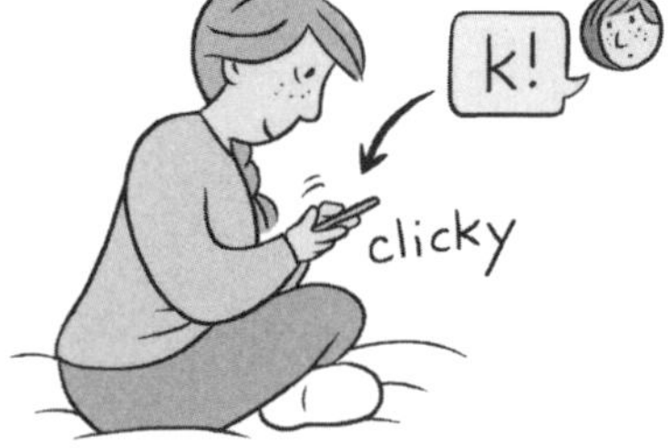
k!
clicky

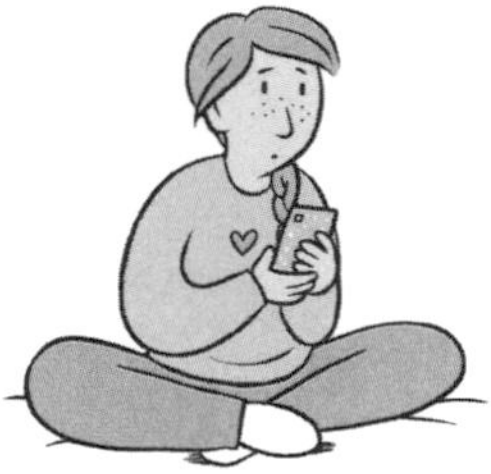

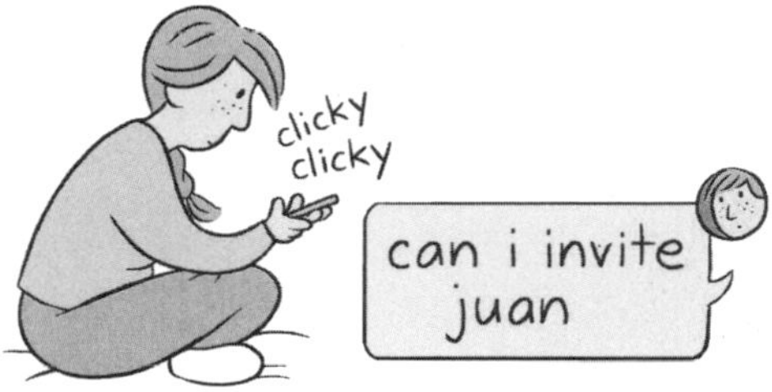
clicky
clicky
can i invite juan

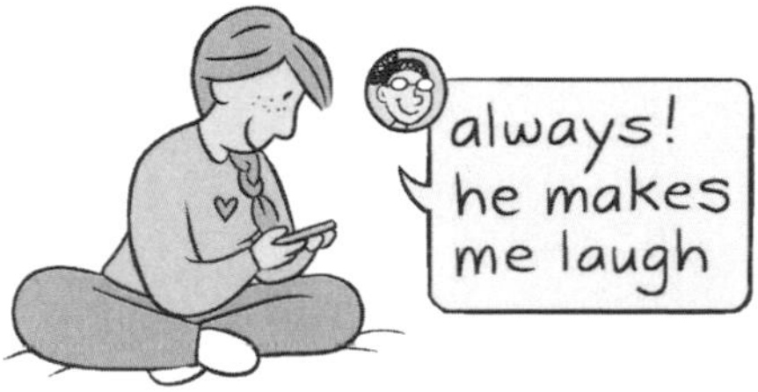
always! he makes me laugh

I text Juan and invite him to Taystee's. He texts back, telling me he wrote a poem about Taystee's. I believe it. Juan can make a poem about anything.

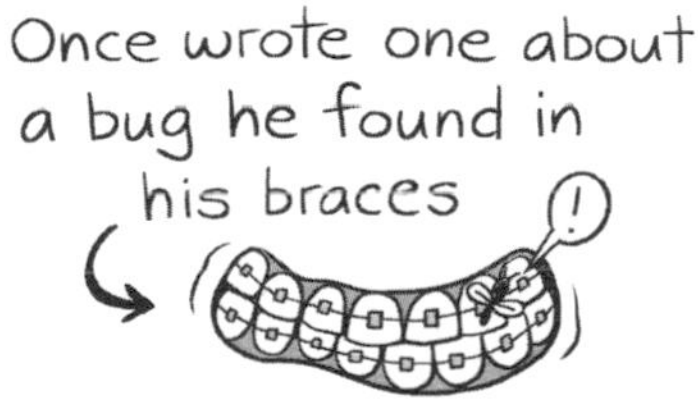
Once wrote one about a bug he found in his braces
!

My phone dings again. I'm still not used to it. I'm used to the quiet.

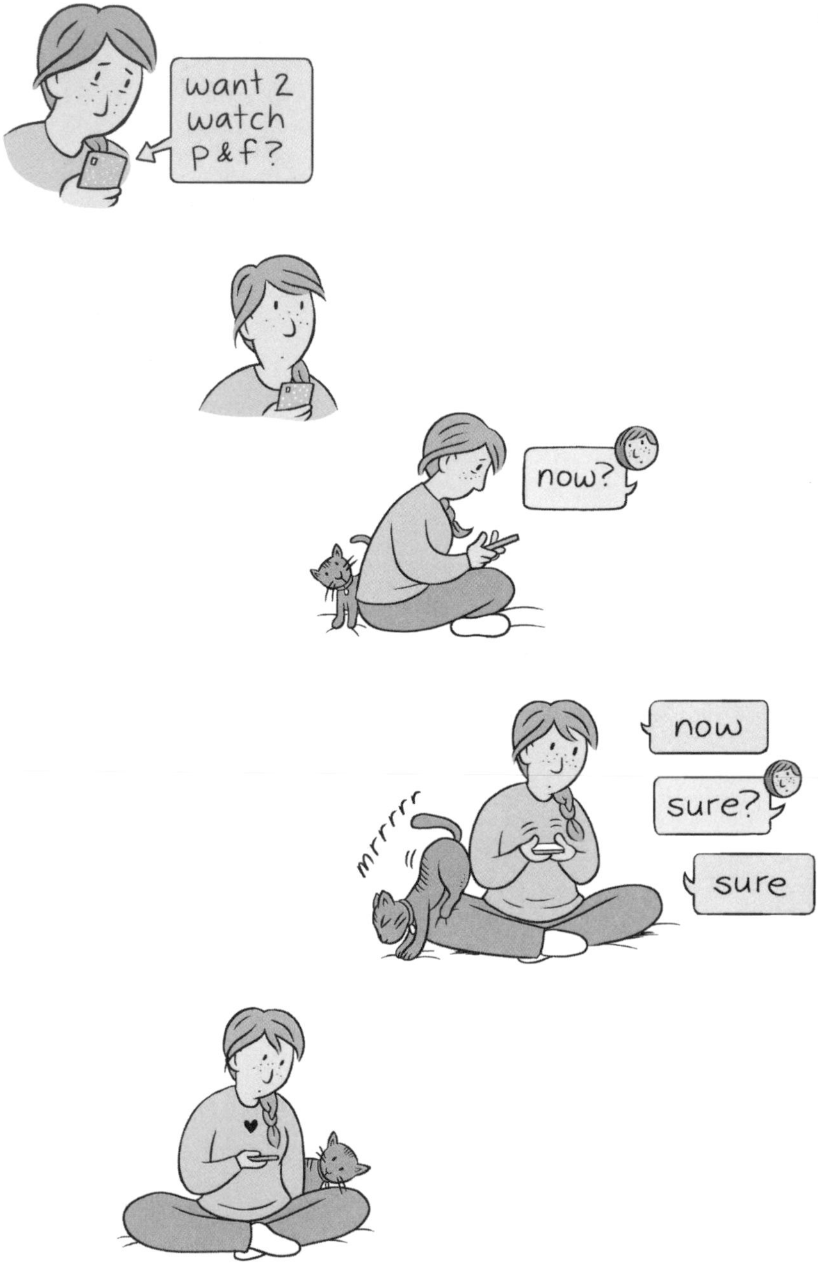
want 2 watch p&f?
now?
now
sure?
sure
mrrrrr

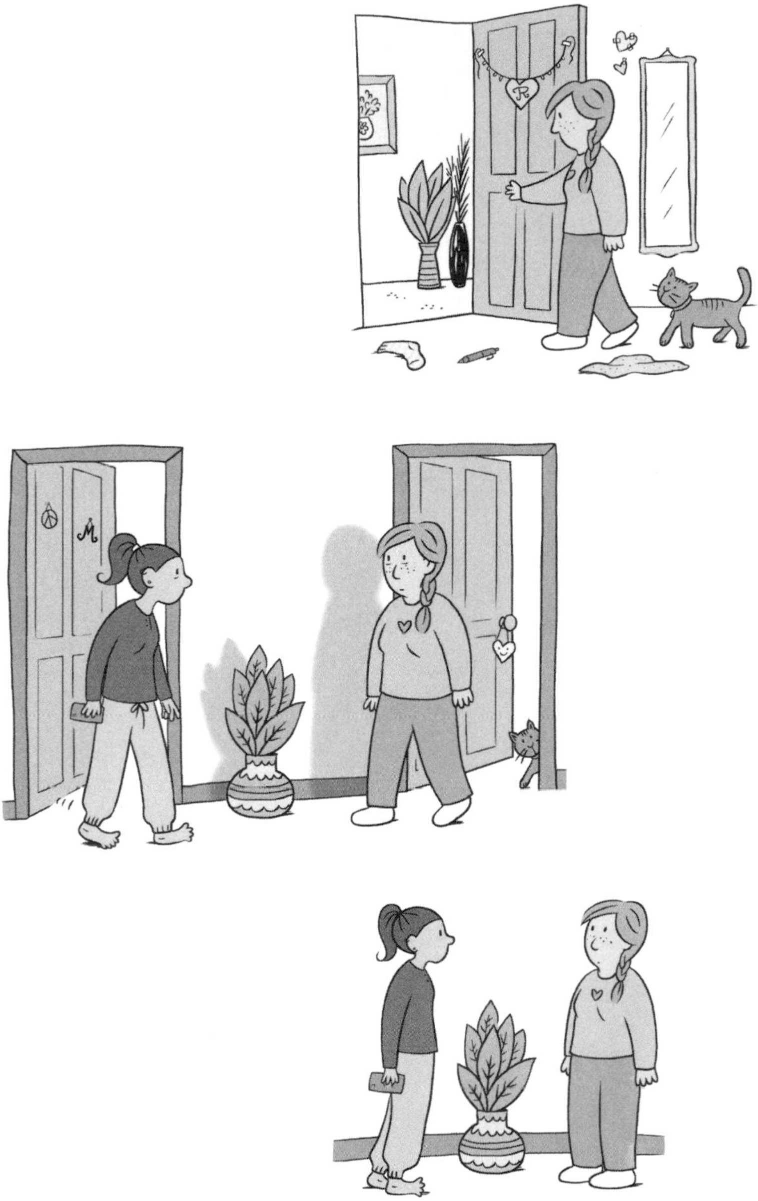

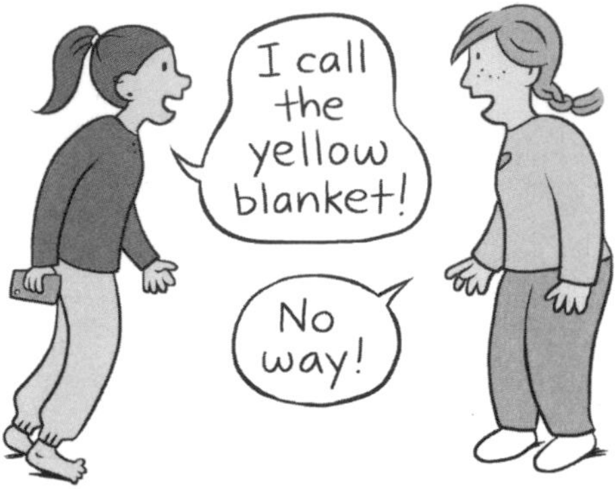
I call the yellow blanket!
No way!

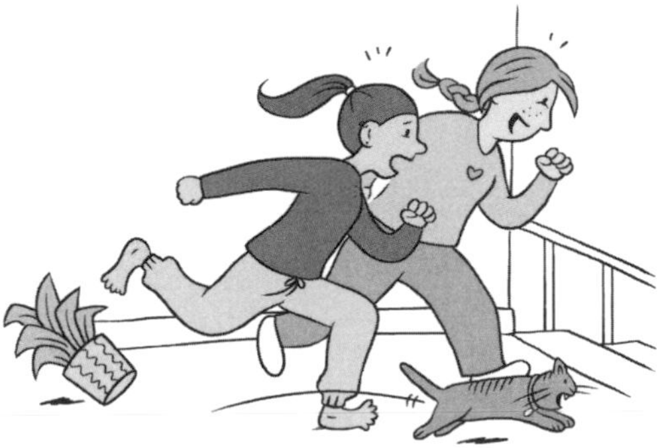

Half an hour later:

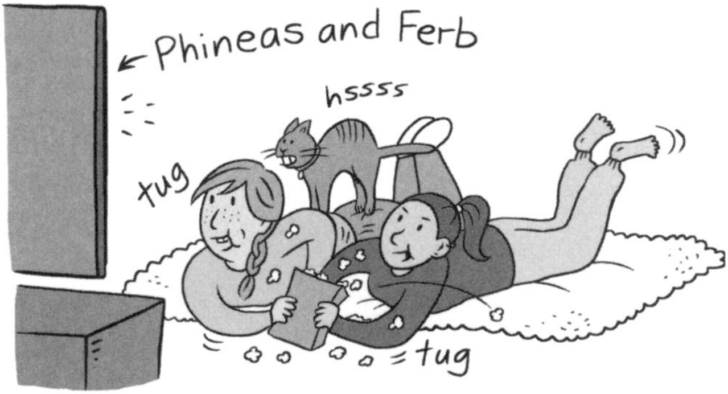
Phineas and Ferb
hssss
tug
tug

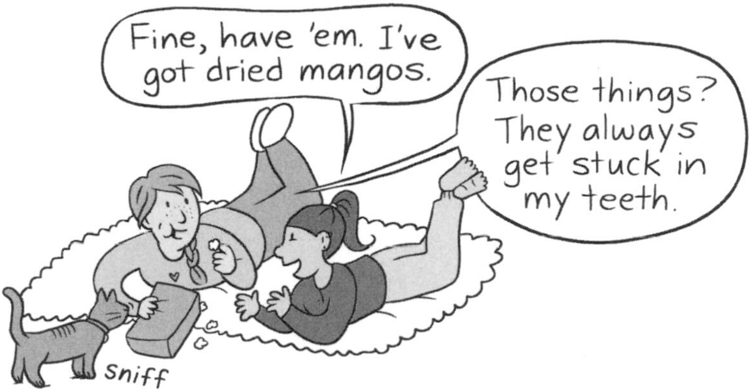
Fine, have 'em. I've got dried mangos.
Those things? They always get stuck in my teeth.
sniff

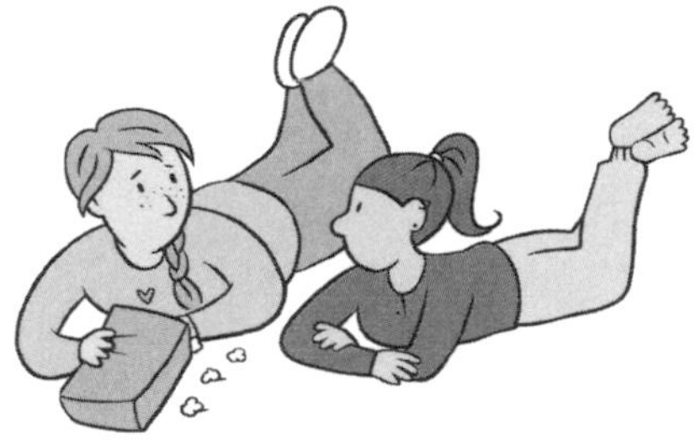

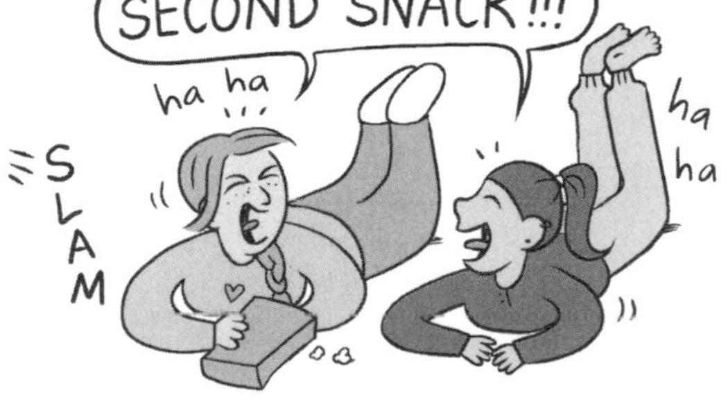
SECOND SNACK!!!
ha ha
ha ha
SLAM

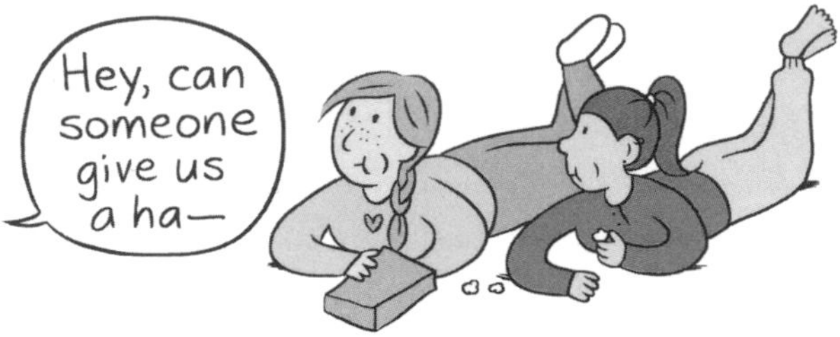
Hey, can someone give us a ha—

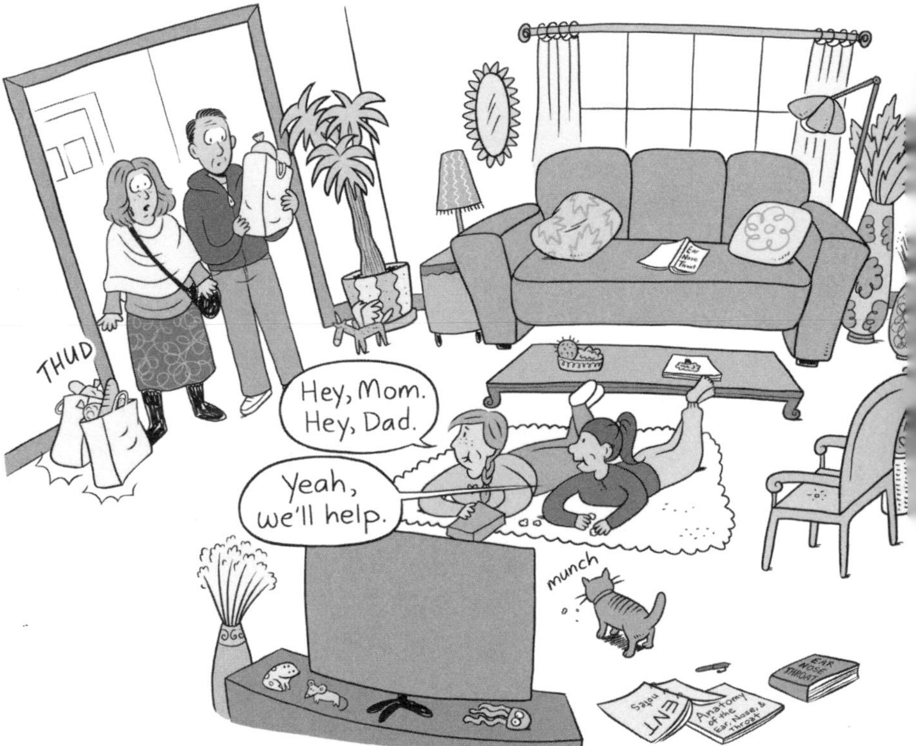
THUD
Hey, Mom. Hey, Dad.
Yeah, we'll help.
munch
Ear Nose Throat
ENT notes
Anatomy of the Ear, Nose, & Throat
EAR NOSE THROAT

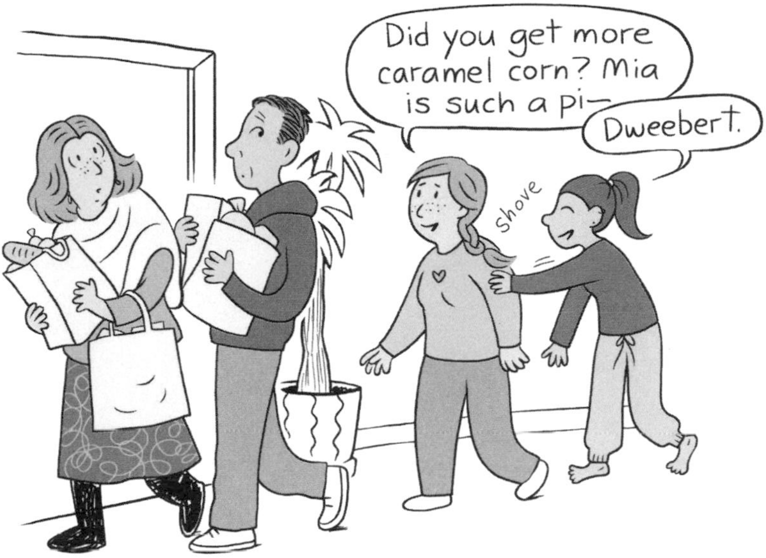
Did you get more caramel corn? Mia is such a pi—
Dweebert.
shove

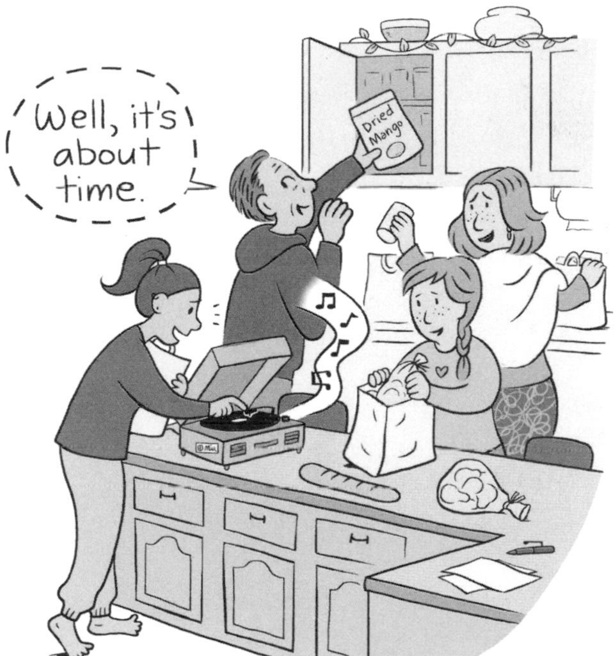
Well, it's about time.
Dried Mango

EPILOGUE: Mia

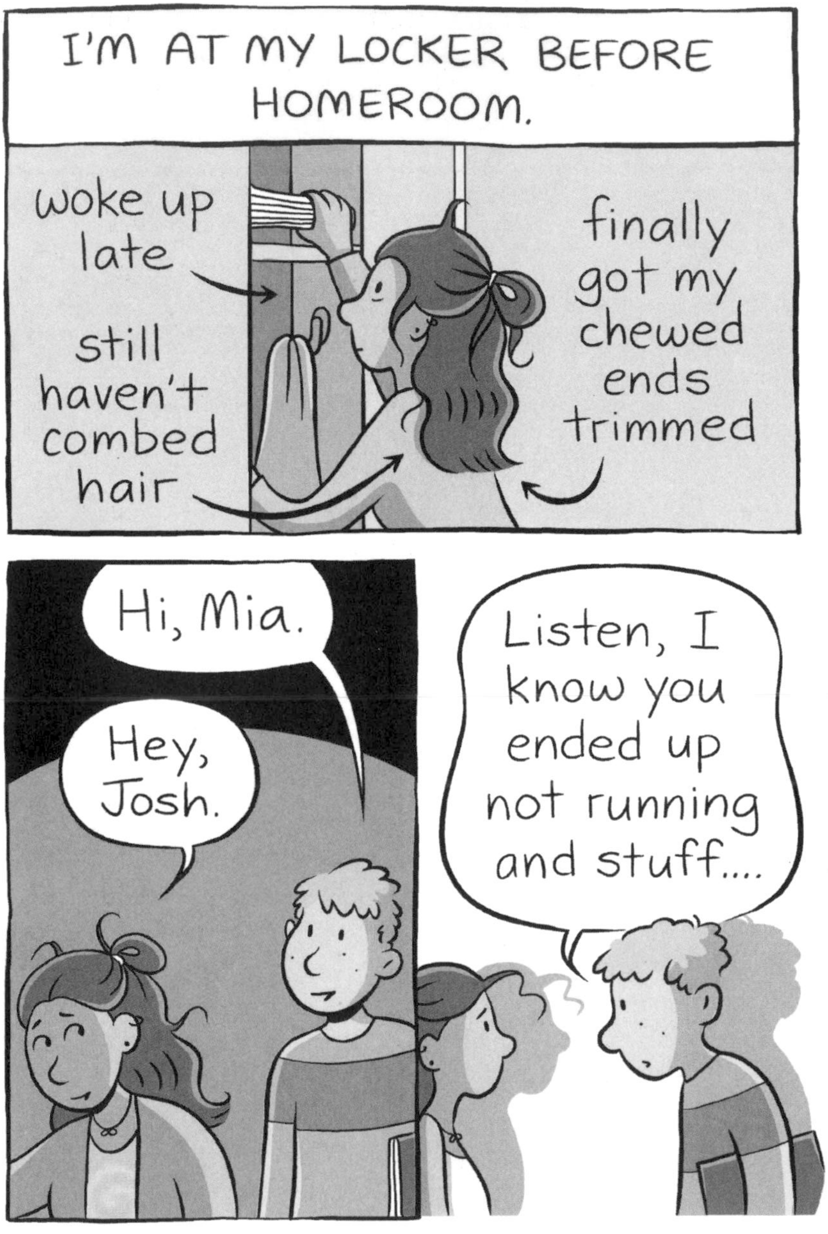
I'M AT MY LOCKER BEFORE HOMEROOM.
woke up late
still haven't combed hair
finally got my chewed ends trimmed
Hi, Mia.
Hey, Josh.
Listen, I know you ended up not running and stuff....

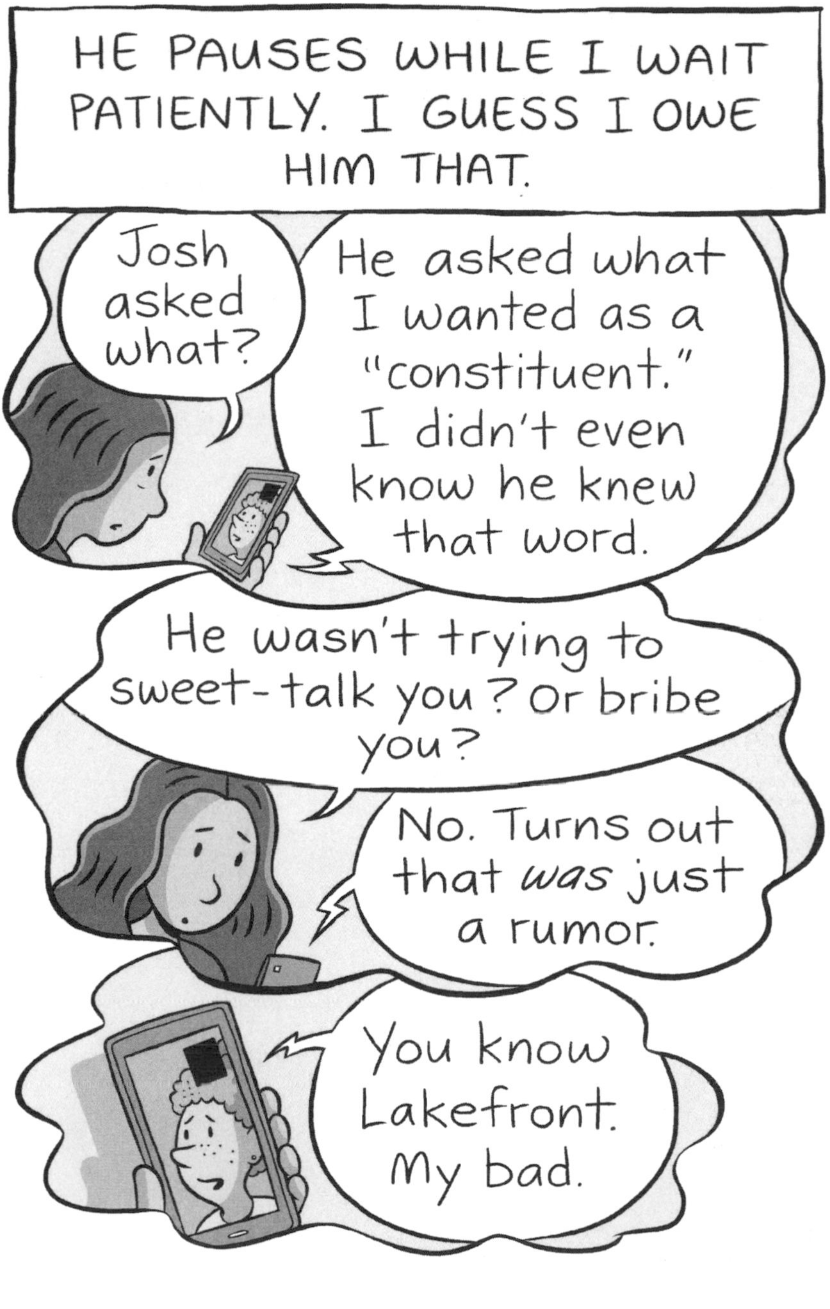
HE PAUSES WHILE I WAIT PATIENTLY. I GUESS I OWE HIM THAT.
Josh asked what?
He asked what I wanted as a "constituent." I didn't even know he knew that word.
He wasn't trying to sweet-talk you? Or bribe you?
No. Turns out that *was* just a rumor.
You know Lakefront. My bad.

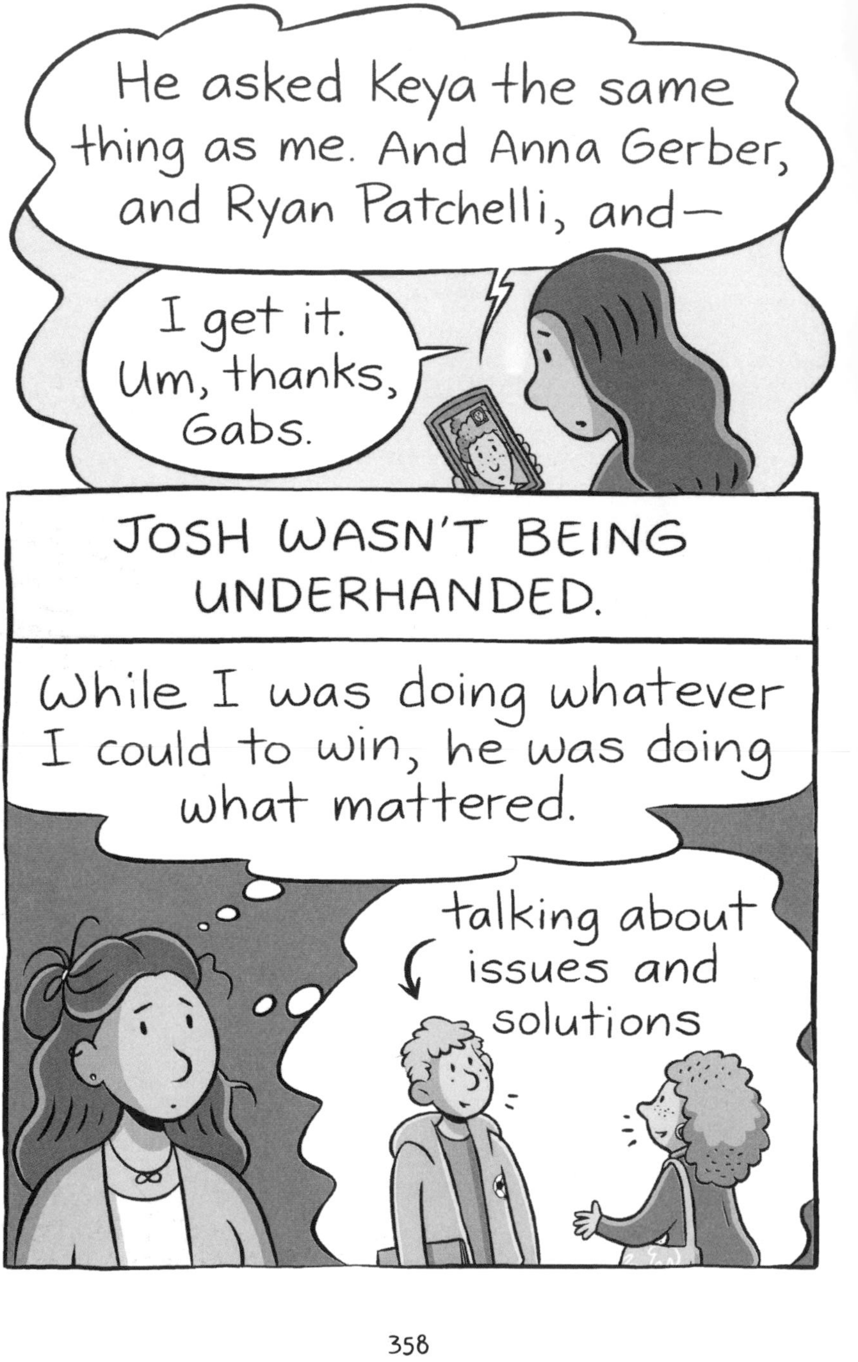
He asked Keya the same thing as me. And Anna Gerber, and Ryan Patchelli, and—
I get it. Um, thanks, Gabs.
JOSH WASN'T BEING UNDERHANDED.
While I was doing whatever I could to win, he was doing what mattered.
talking about issues and solutions

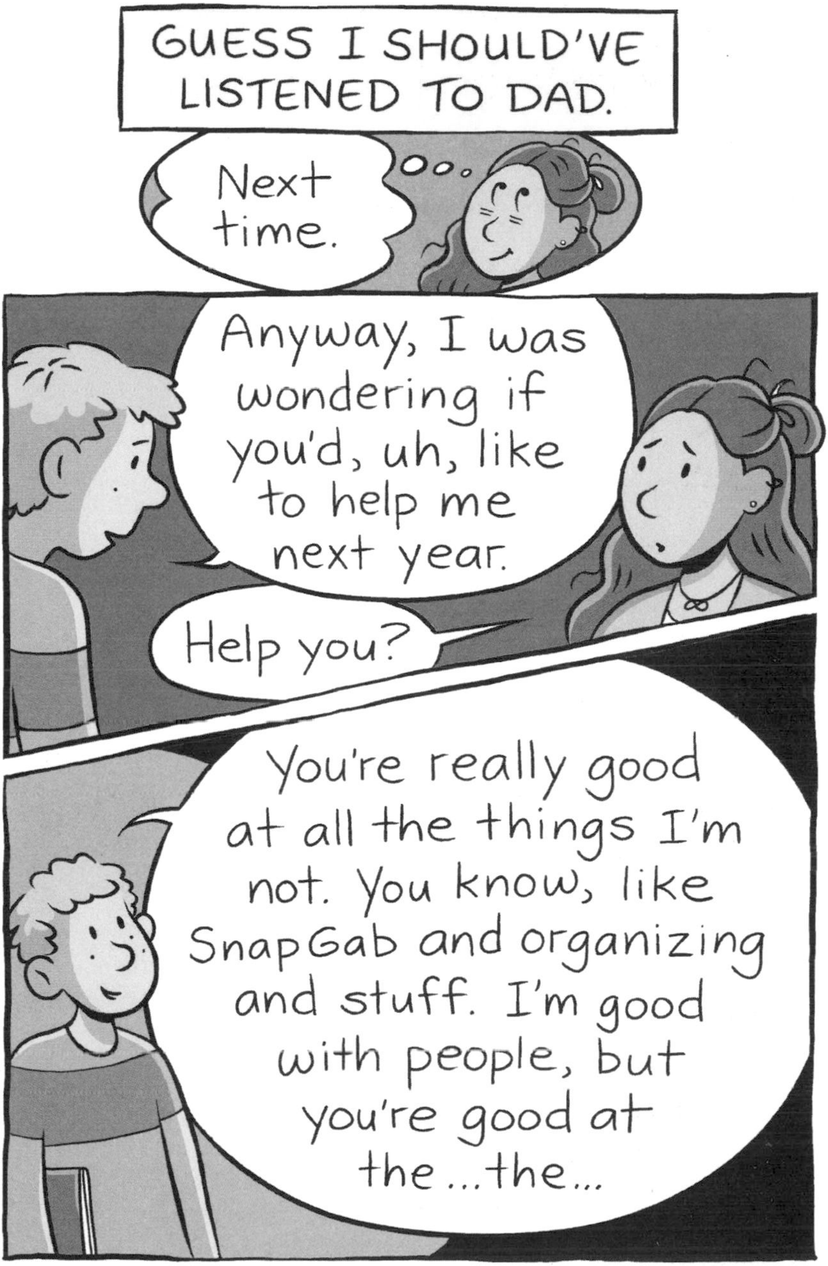
GUESS I SHOULD'VE LISTENED TO DAD.
Next time.
Anyway, I was wondering if you'd, uh, like to help me next year.
Help you?
You're really good at all the things I'm not. You know, like SnapGab and organizing and stuff. I'm good with people, but you're good at the...the...

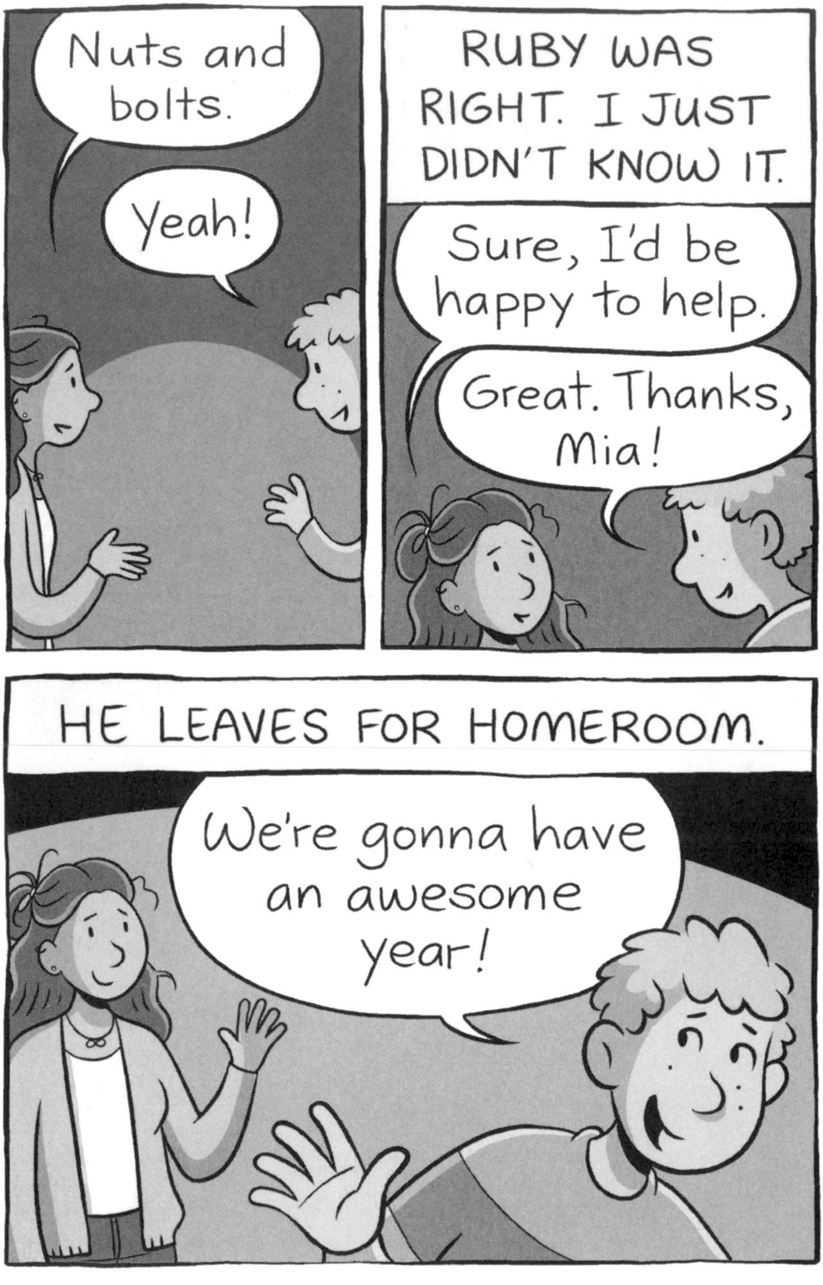
Nuts and bolts.
Yeah!
RUBY WAS RIGHT. I JUST DIDN'T KNOW IT.
Sure, I'd be happy to help.
Great. Thanks, Mia!
HE LEAVES FOR HOMEROOM.
We're gonna have an awesome year!

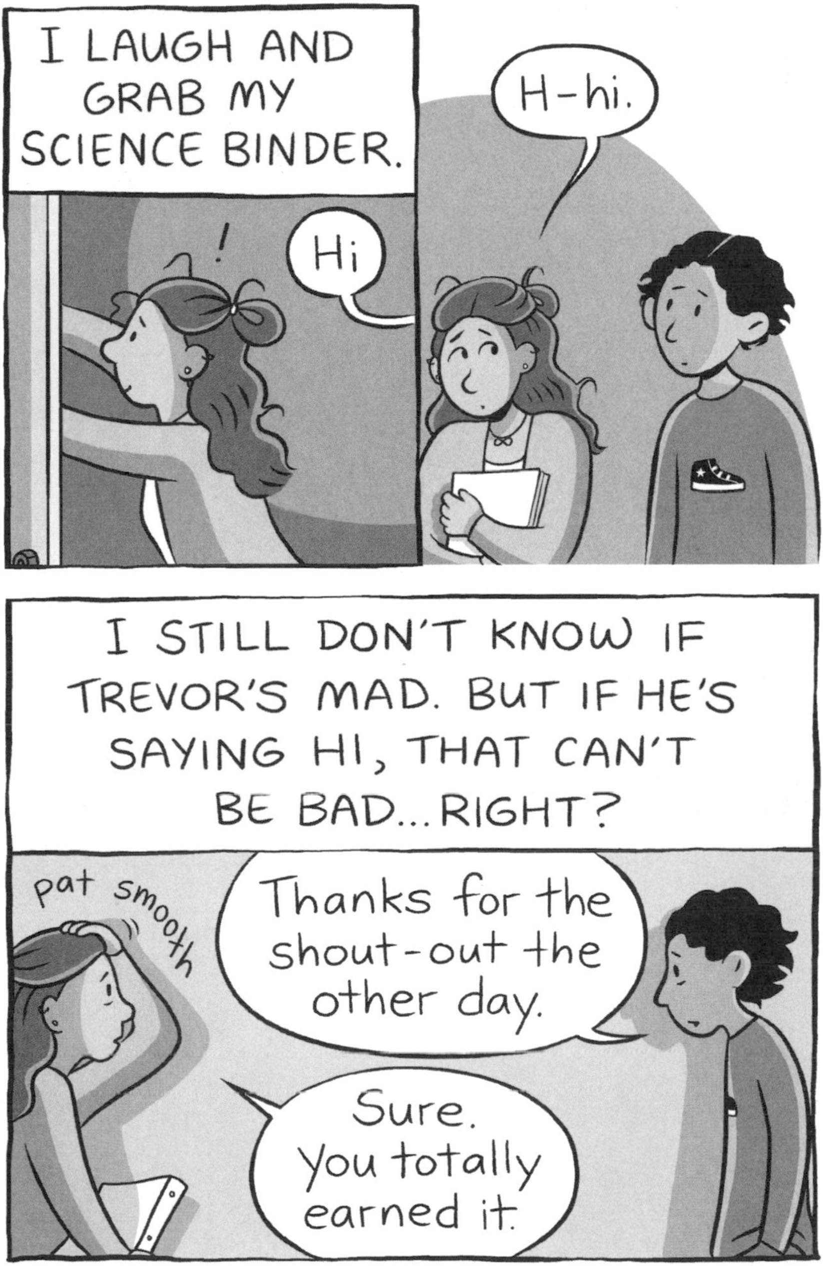
I LAUGH AND GRAB MY SCIENCE BINDER.
!
Hi
H-hi.
I STILL DON'T KNOW IF TREVOR'S MAD. BUT IF HE'S SAYING HI, THAT CAN'T BE BAD...RIGHT?
pat smooth
Thanks for the shout-out the other day.
Sure. You totally earned it.

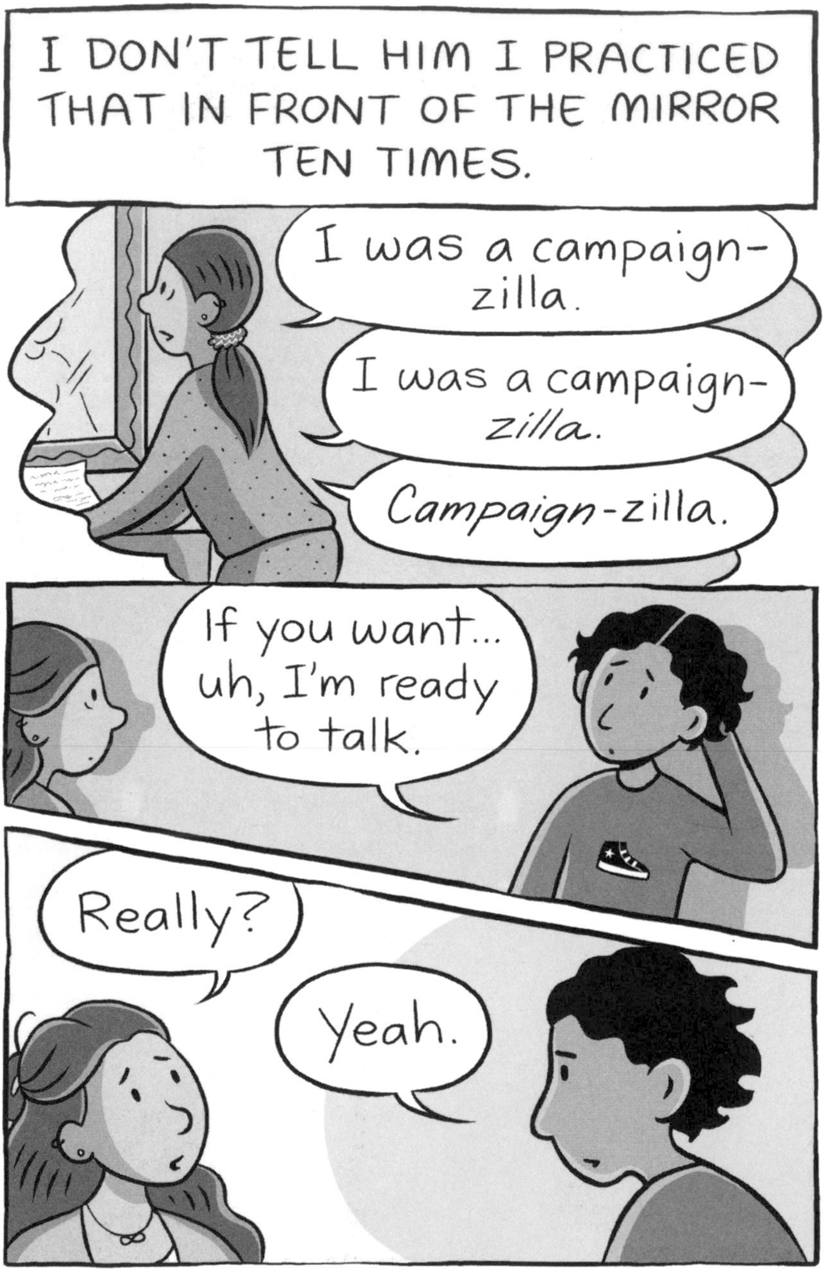
I DON'T TELL HIM I PRACTICED THAT IN FRONT OF THE MIRROR TEN TIMES.
I was a campaign-zilla.
I was a campaign-zilla.
Campaign-zilla.
If you want... uh, I'm ready to talk.
Really?
Yeah.

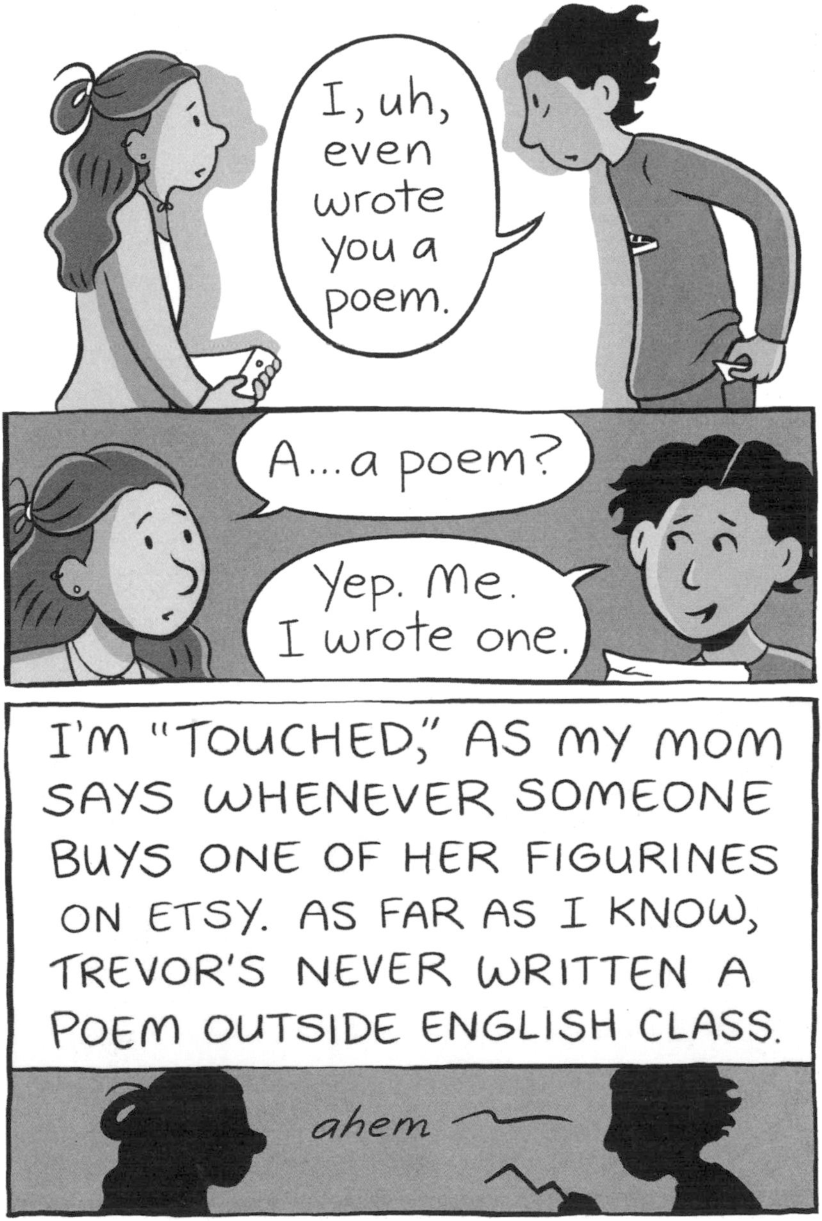
I, uh, even wrote you a poem.
A...a poem?
Yep. Me. I wrote one.
I'M "TOUCHED," AS MY MOM SAYS WHENEVER SOMEONE BUYS ONE OF HER FIGURINES ON ETSY. AS FAR AS I KNOW, TREVOR'S NEVER WRITTEN A POEM OUTSIDE ENGLISH CLASS.
ahem

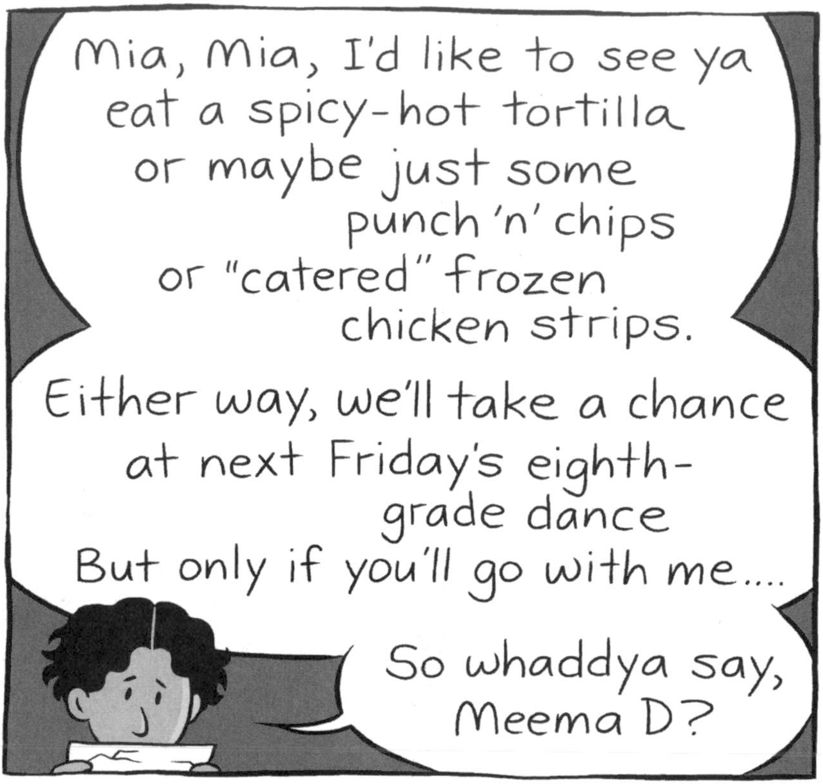
Mia, Mia, I'd like to see ya
eat a spicy-hot tortilla
or maybe just some
punch 'n' chips
or "catered" frozen
chicken strips.
Either way, we'll take a chance
at next Friday's eighth-
grade dance
But only if you'll go with me....
So whaddya say,
Meema D?

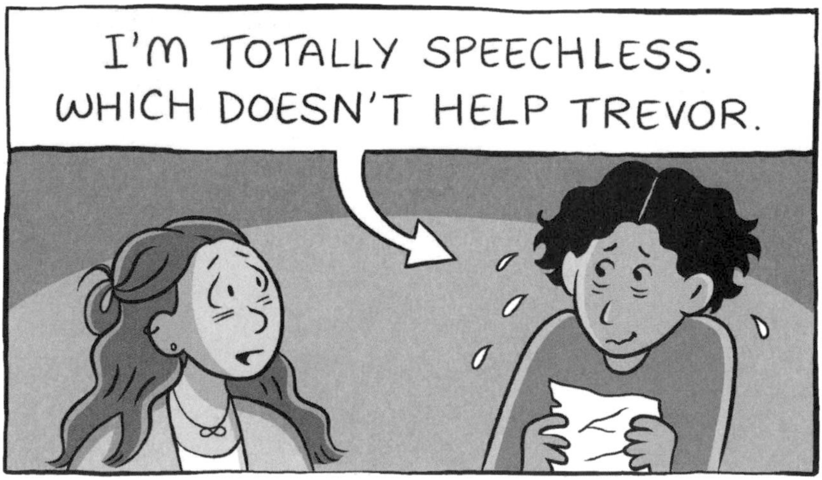
I'M TOTALLY SPEECHLESS.
WHICH DOESN'T HELP TREVOR.

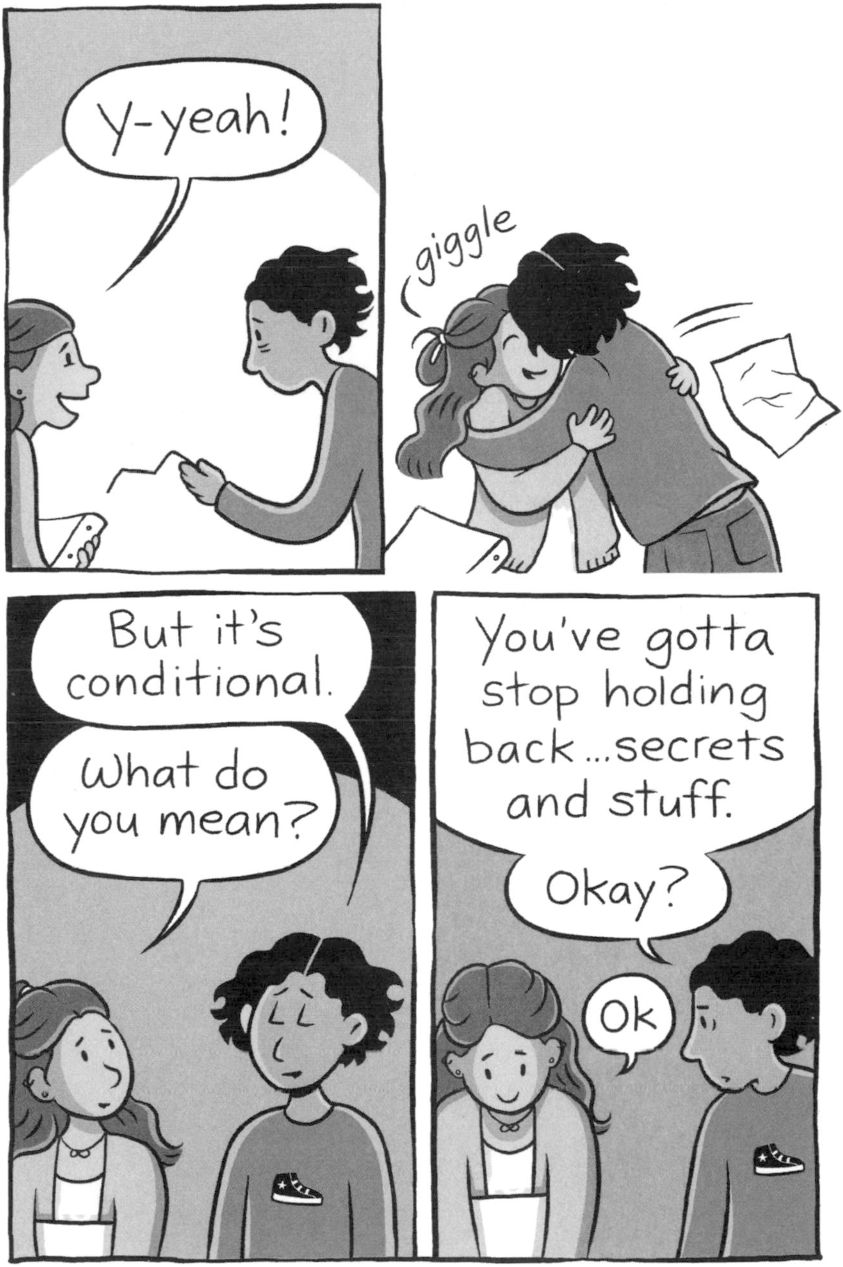
Y-yeah!
giggle
But it's conditional.
What do you mean?
You've gotta stop holding back...secrets and stuff.
Okay?
Ok

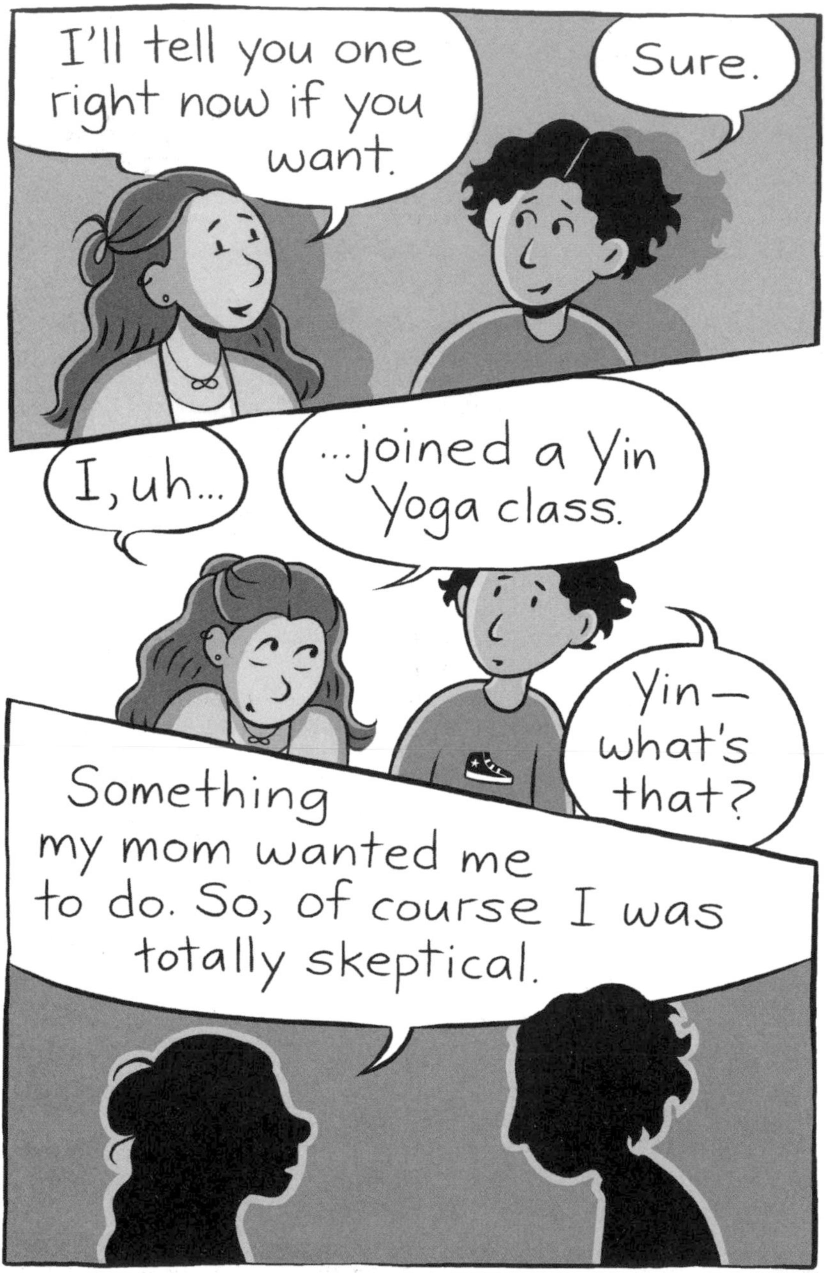
I'll tell you one right now if you want.
Sure.
I, uh...
...joined a Yin Yoga class.
Yin— what's that?
Something my mom wanted me to do. So, of course I was totally skeptical.

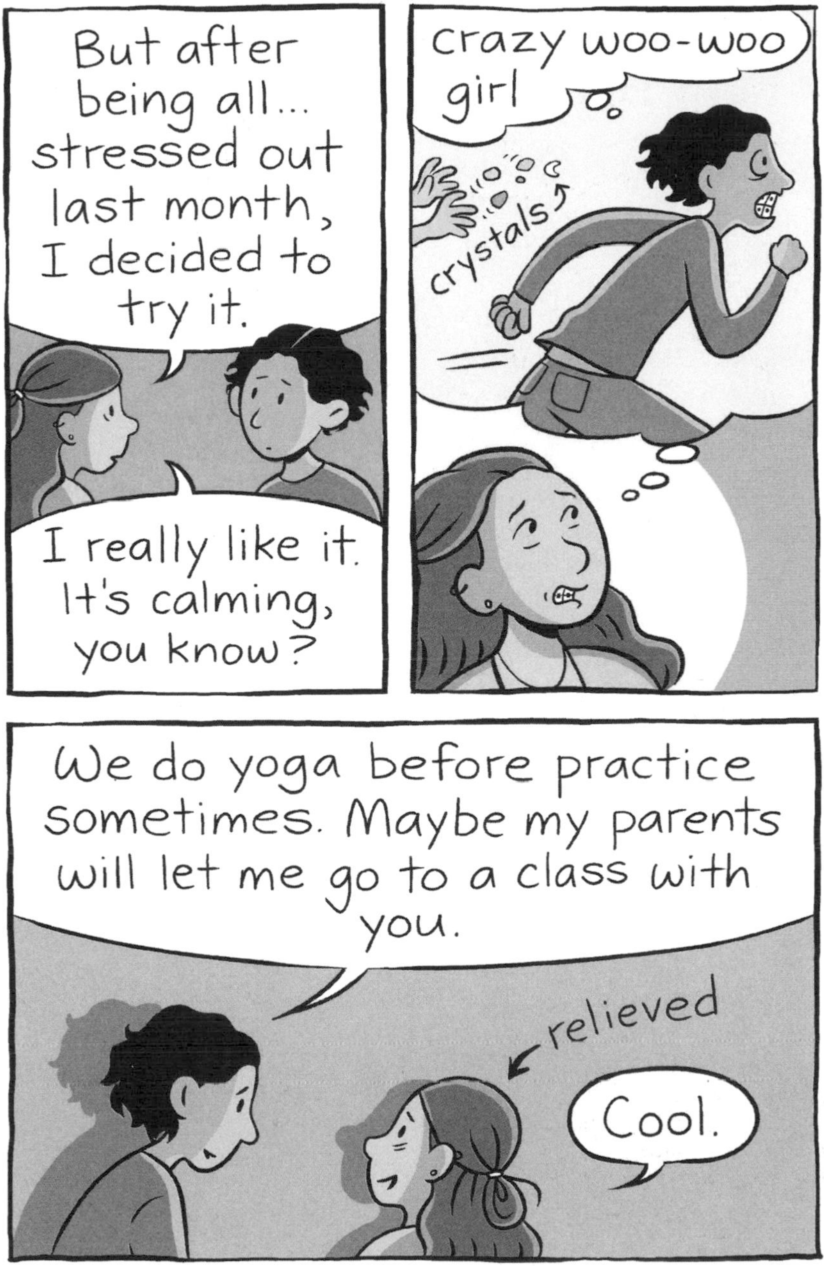
But after being all... stressed out last month, I decided to try it.
I really like it. It's calming, you know?
crazy woo-woo girl
crystals
We do yoga before practice sometimes. Maybe my parents will let me go to a class with you.
relieved
Cool.

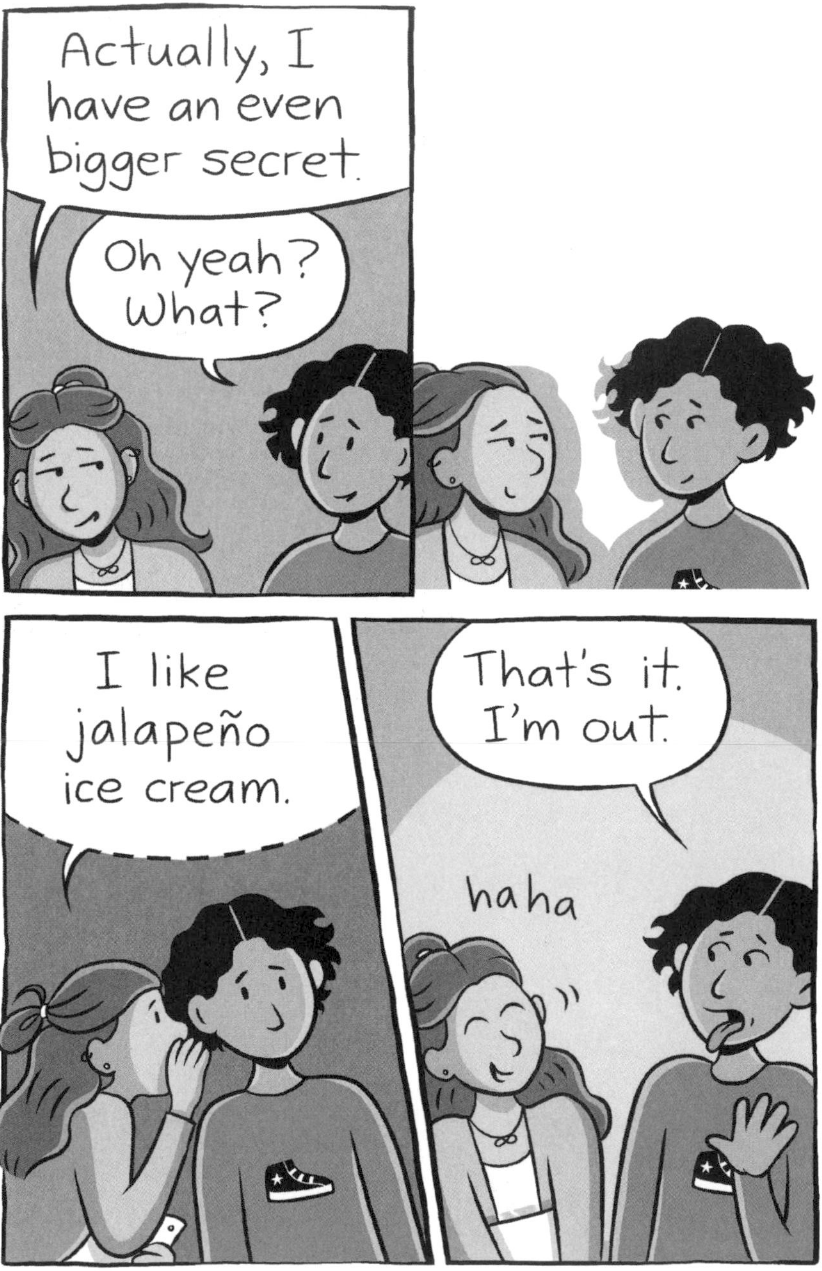
Actually, I have an even bigger secret.
Oh yeah? What?
I like jalapeño ice cream.
That's it. I'm out.
haha

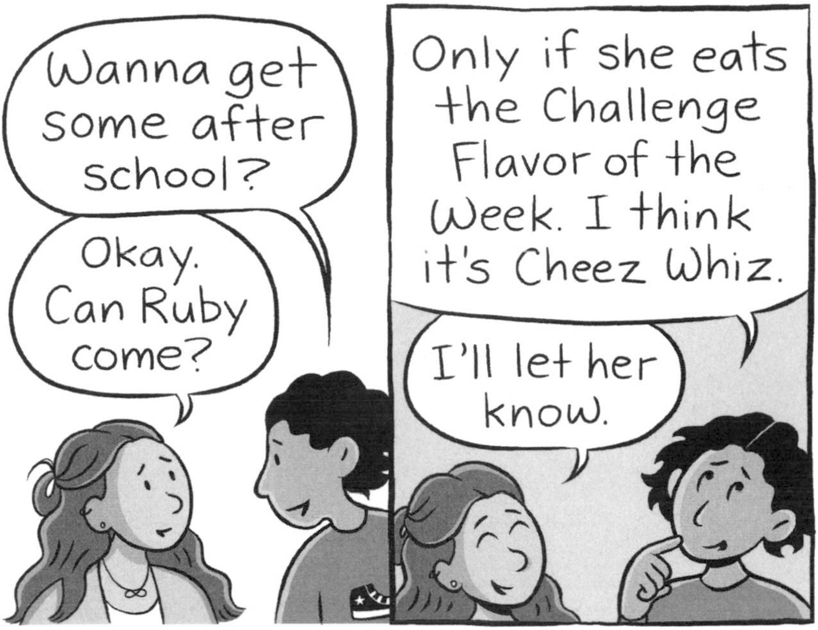
Wanna get some after school?
Okay. Can Ruby come?
Only if she eats the Challenge Flavor of the Week. I think it's Cheez Whiz.
I'll let her know.

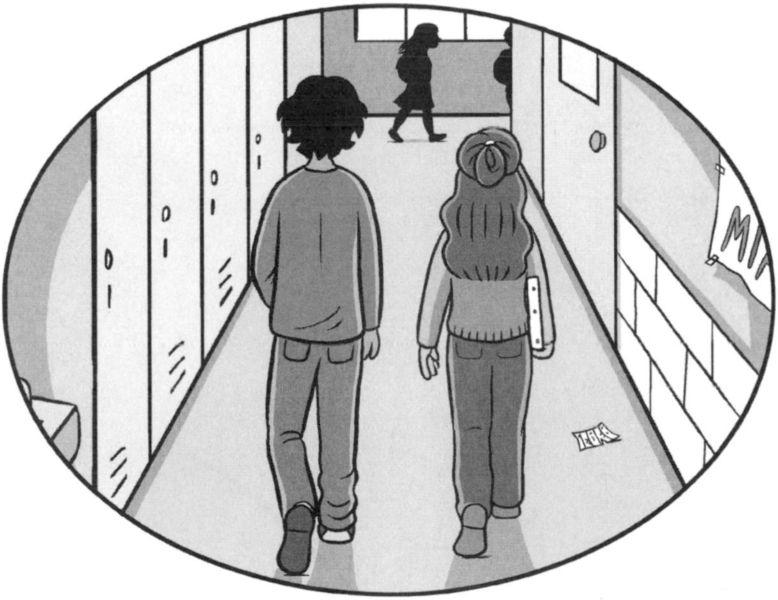

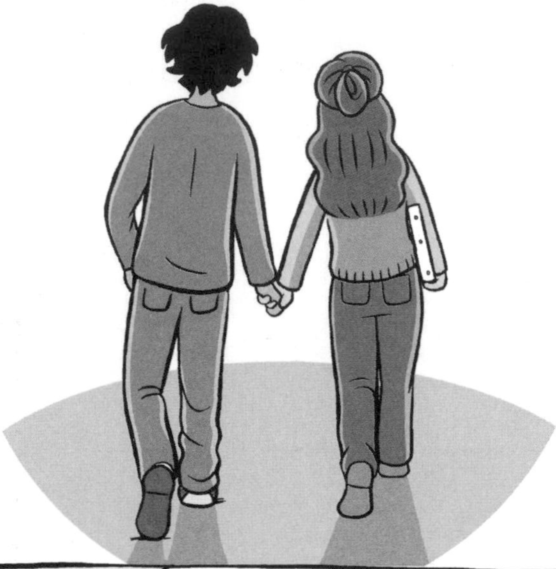

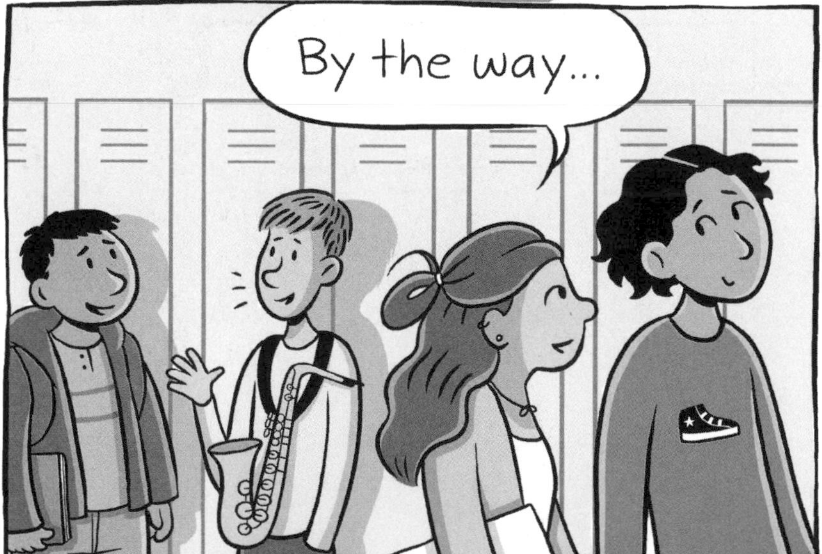
By the way...

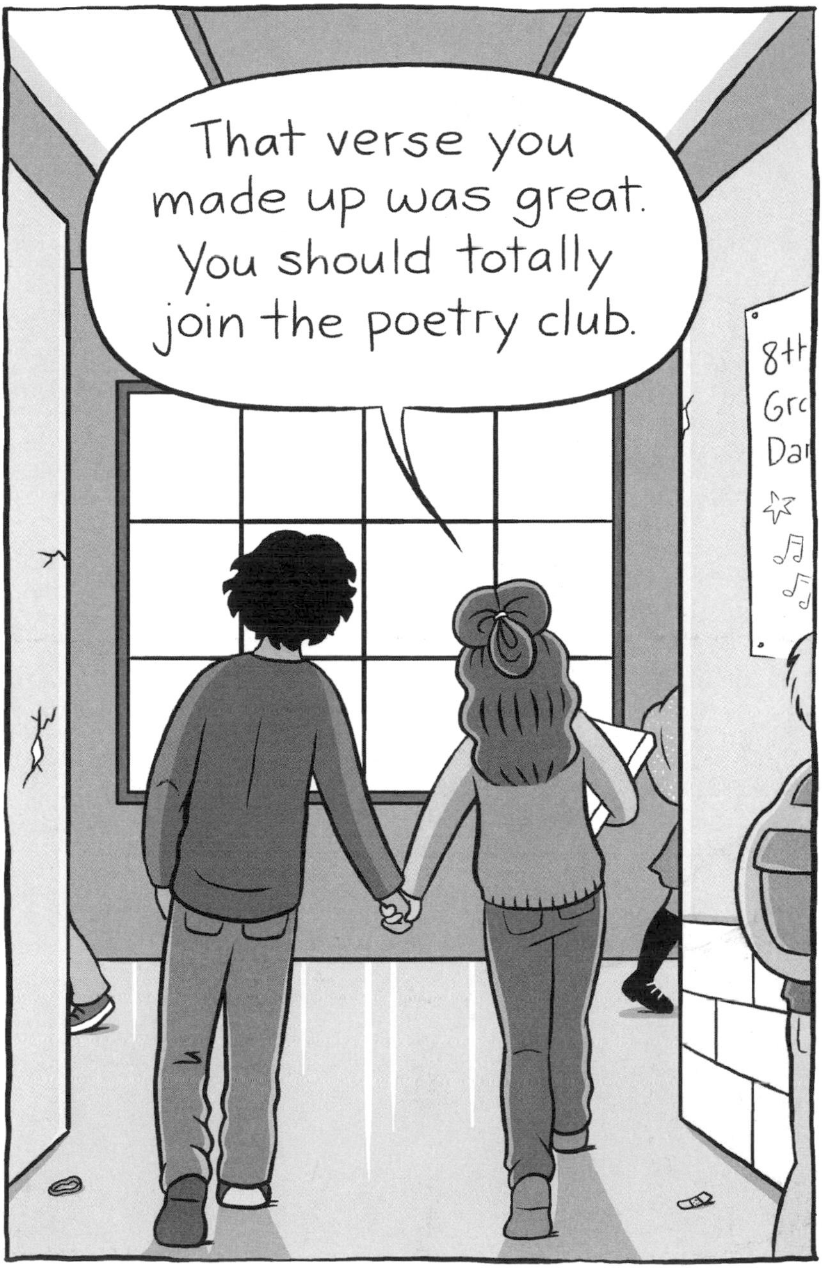
That verse you made up was great. You should totally join the poetry club.
8th
Gr
Da

OUTTAKES

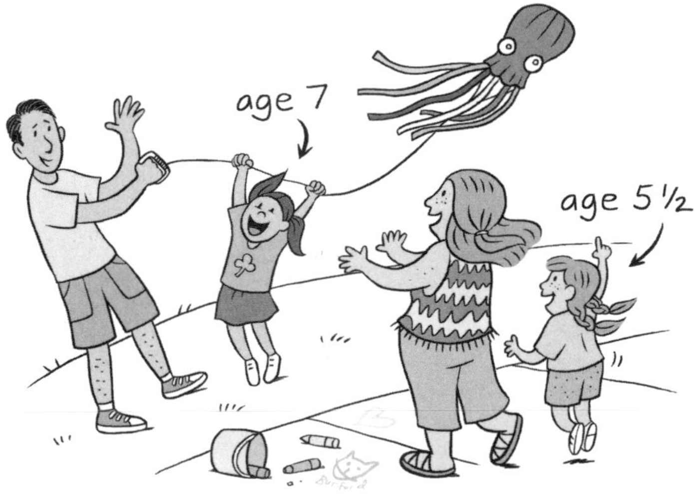
age 7
age 5 1/2

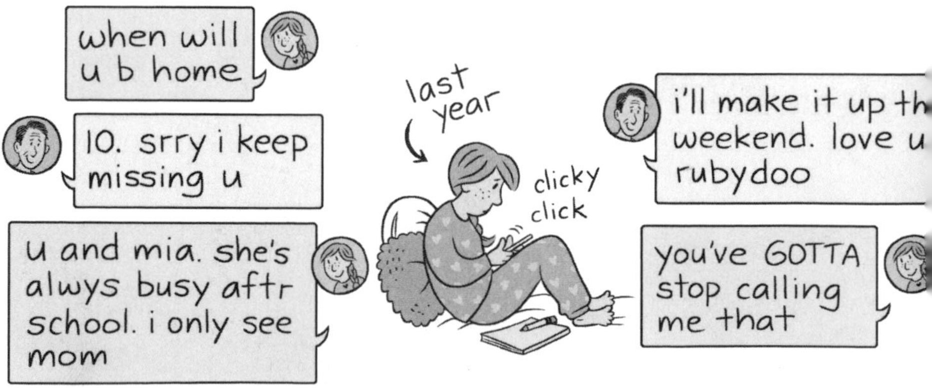
when will u b home
10. srry i keep missing u
u and mia. she's alwys busy aftr school. i only see mom
last year
clicky click
i'll make it up th
weekend. love u rubydoo
you've GOTTA stop calling me that

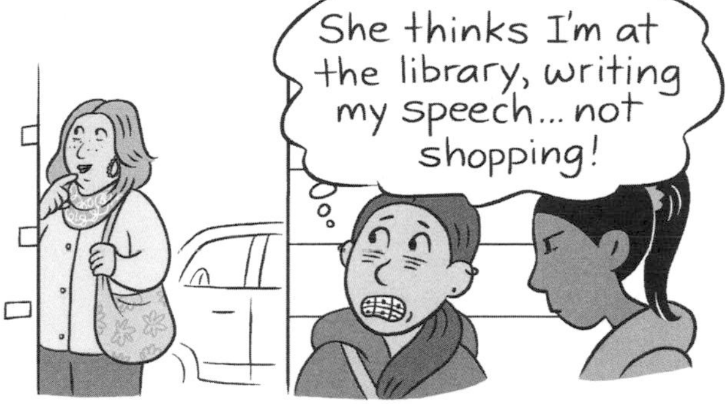
She thinks I'm at the library, writing my speech... not shopping!

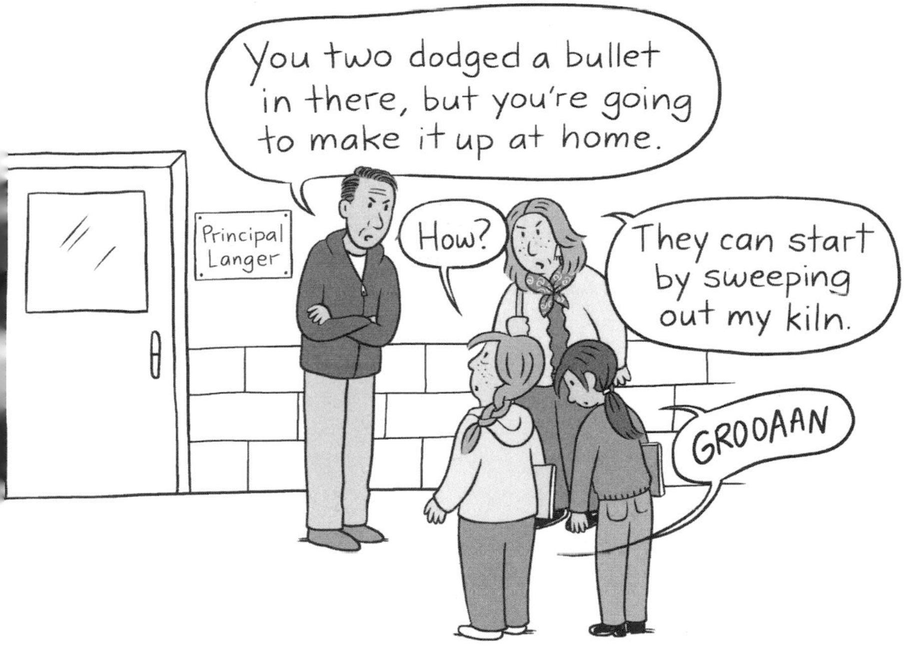
You two dodged a bullet in there, but you're going to make it up at home.
Principal Langer
How?
They can start by sweeping out my kiln.
GROOAAN

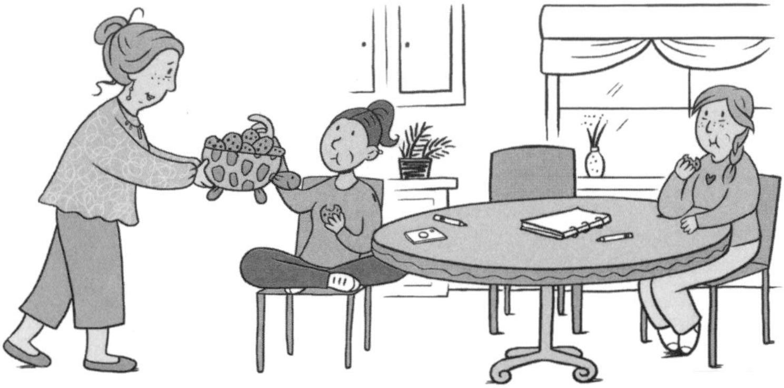

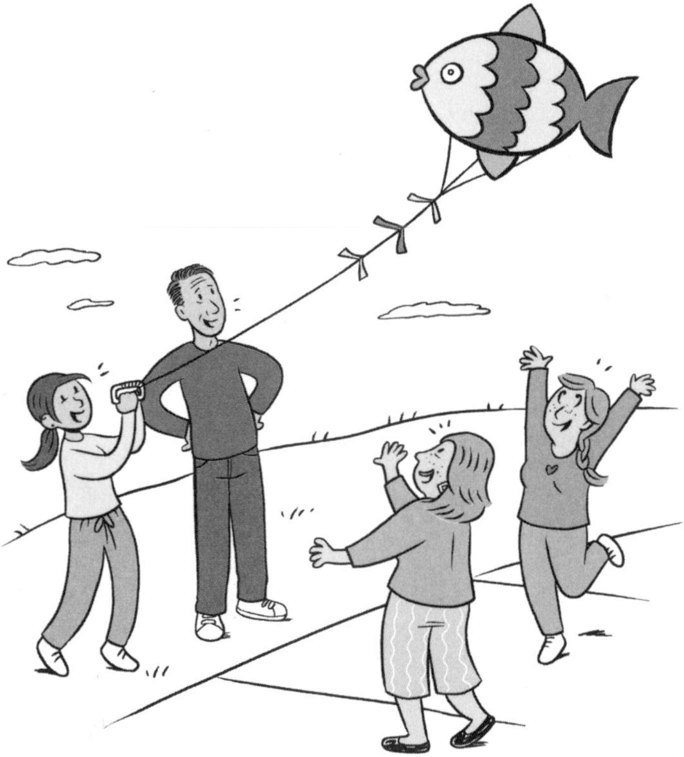

ACKNOWLEDGMENTS

One of the things I love about this series is the opportunity to switch up the main characters. Sure, it's a challenge to create new personalities, but as I write, the personalities sometimes create themselves. Such was the case with Ruby.

Like Jaime, Maya, and Tyler, Ruby (aka Baked Bean Girl) was a background character who I thought deserved her own story (something many readers requested as well). It was a good choice—she was a joy to write for. Creating Mia was more of a challenge, but once she was fleshed out, everything clicked. In fact, I see so much of Mia in myself, it's a little—okay, very—frightening. (Type A, anyone?)

REMARKABLY RUBY couldn't have been brought to life without the following people:

Donna Bray, my wonderful editor who never steers me wrong. You are the best.

Ditto for Dan Lazar, my incredible agent who also never steers me wrong and is also the best.

Laura Mock, Amy Ryan, Mitch Thorpe, Vaishali Nayak, and the rest of the talented, tireless team at HarperCollins. You all rock—especially during these challenging times.

My incredibly patient husband, Mike, and kids, Mollie and Nikki, who held the house together while I was on deadline. No small feat.

All my friends and relatives, who keep buying my books and enjoying them—or at least telling me they do.

My dog, Rosie, who gives me soothing cuddles and gets me out of the house. Even if I don't know it at the time, I need it.

And, of course, all my readers, who keep me creating and loving it. You are my greatest motivators. Thank you!

Pandemic pup, all grown up
and rocking it on Halloween